AMAZING GRAPES

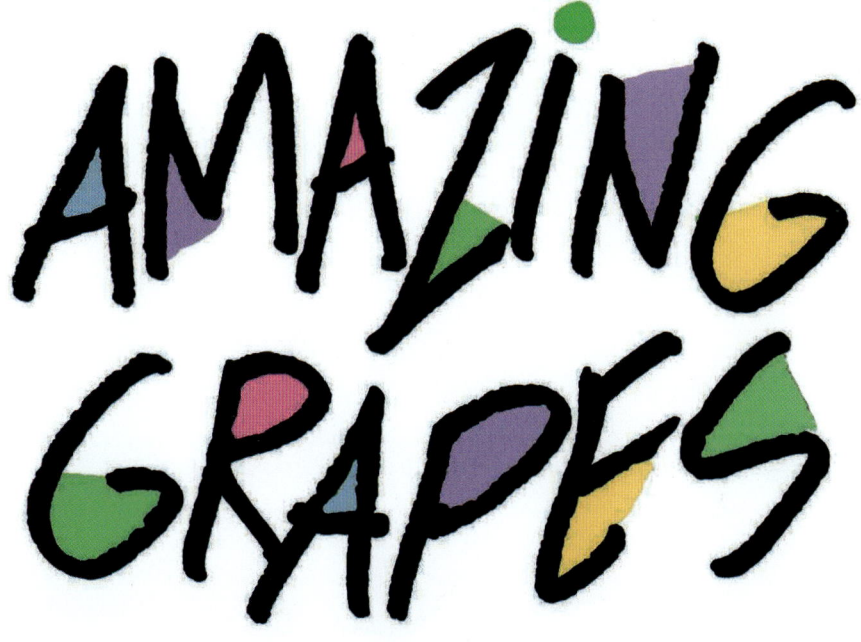

AMAZING GRAPES
AND THE LOST DIMENSION

JULES FEIFFER

MICHAEL DI CAPUA BOOKS
HARPER COLLINS PUBLISHERS

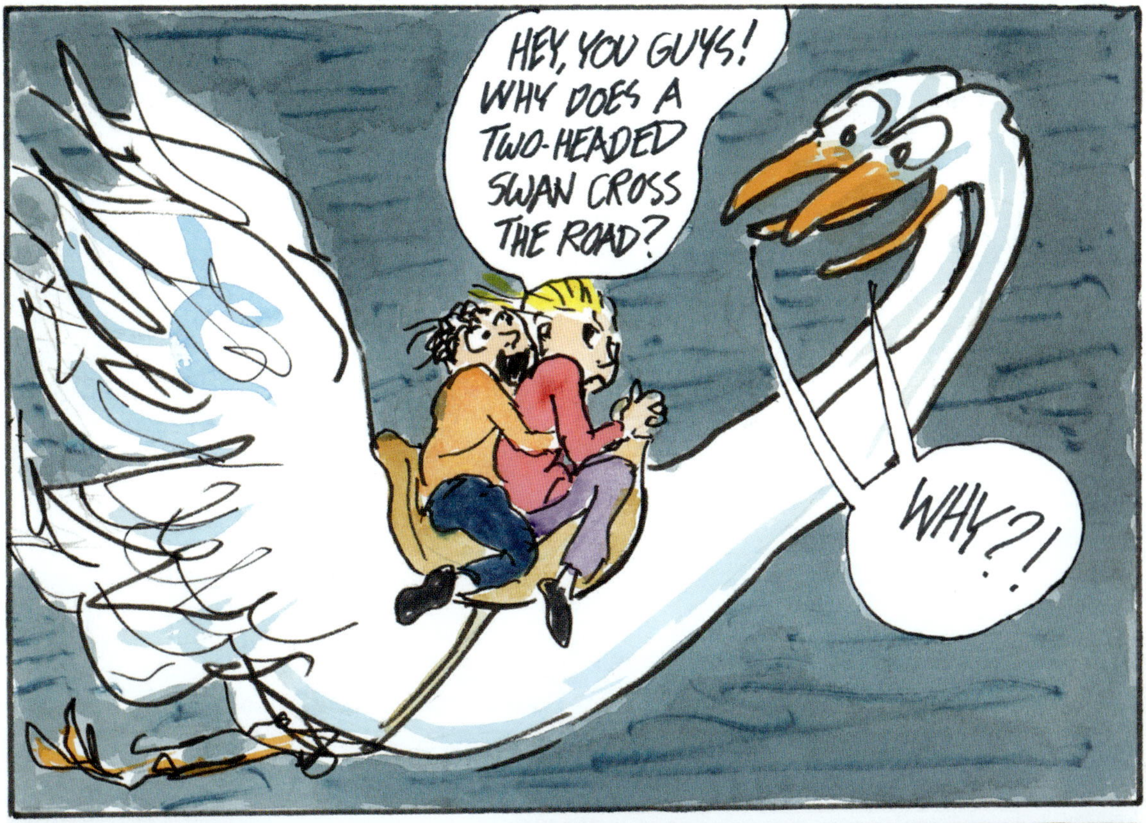
HEY, YOU GUYS! WHY DOES A TWO-HEADED SWAN CROSS THE ROAD?
WHY?!

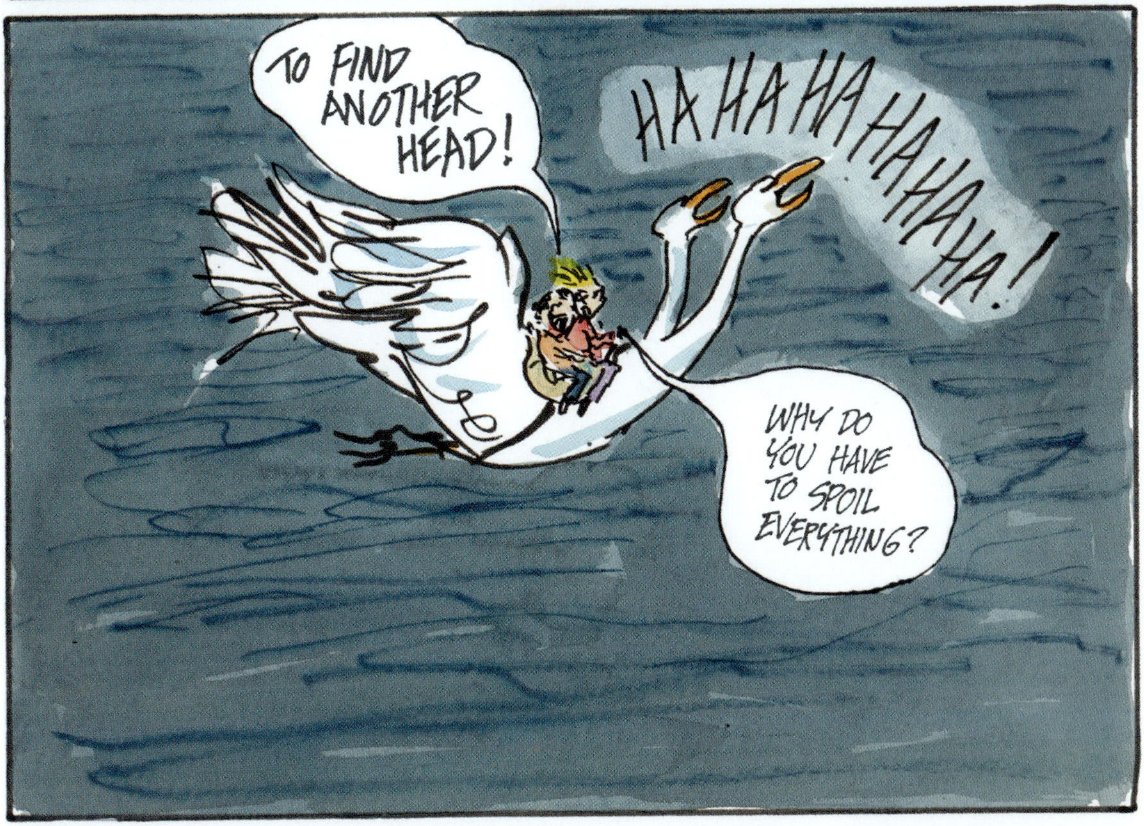
TO FIND ANOTHER HEAD!
HA HA HA HA HA HA HA!
WHY DO YOU HAVE TO SPOIL EVERYTHING?

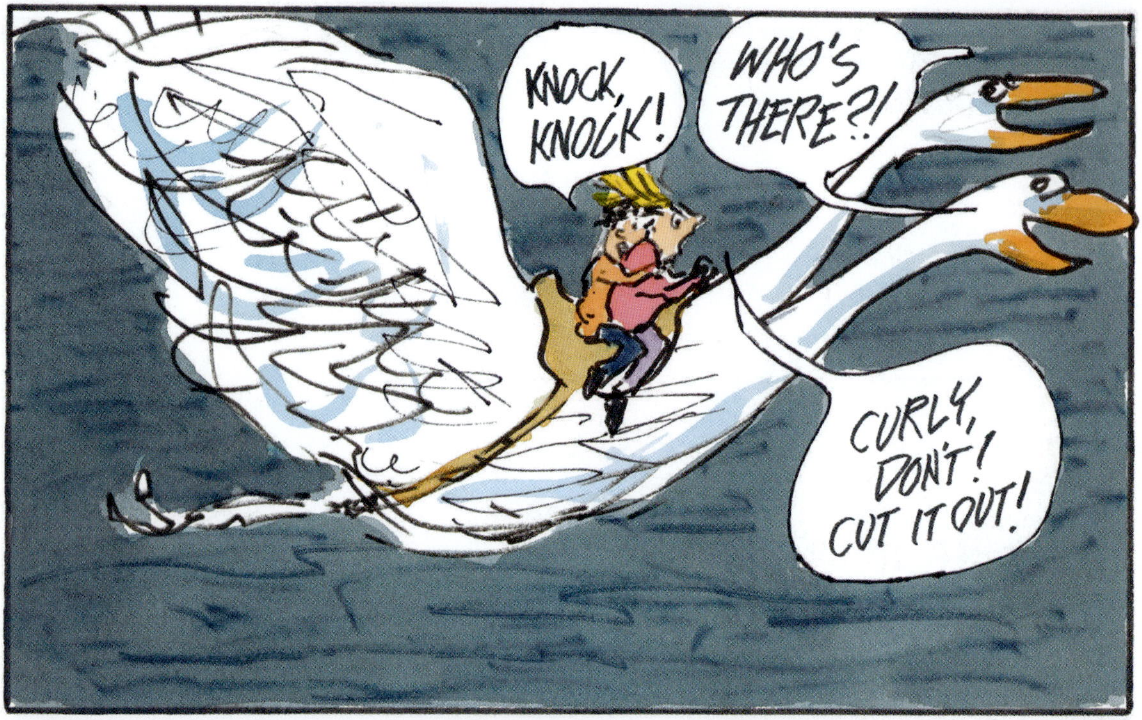
KNOCK, KNOCK!
WHO'S THERE?!
CURLY, DON'T! CUT IT OUT!

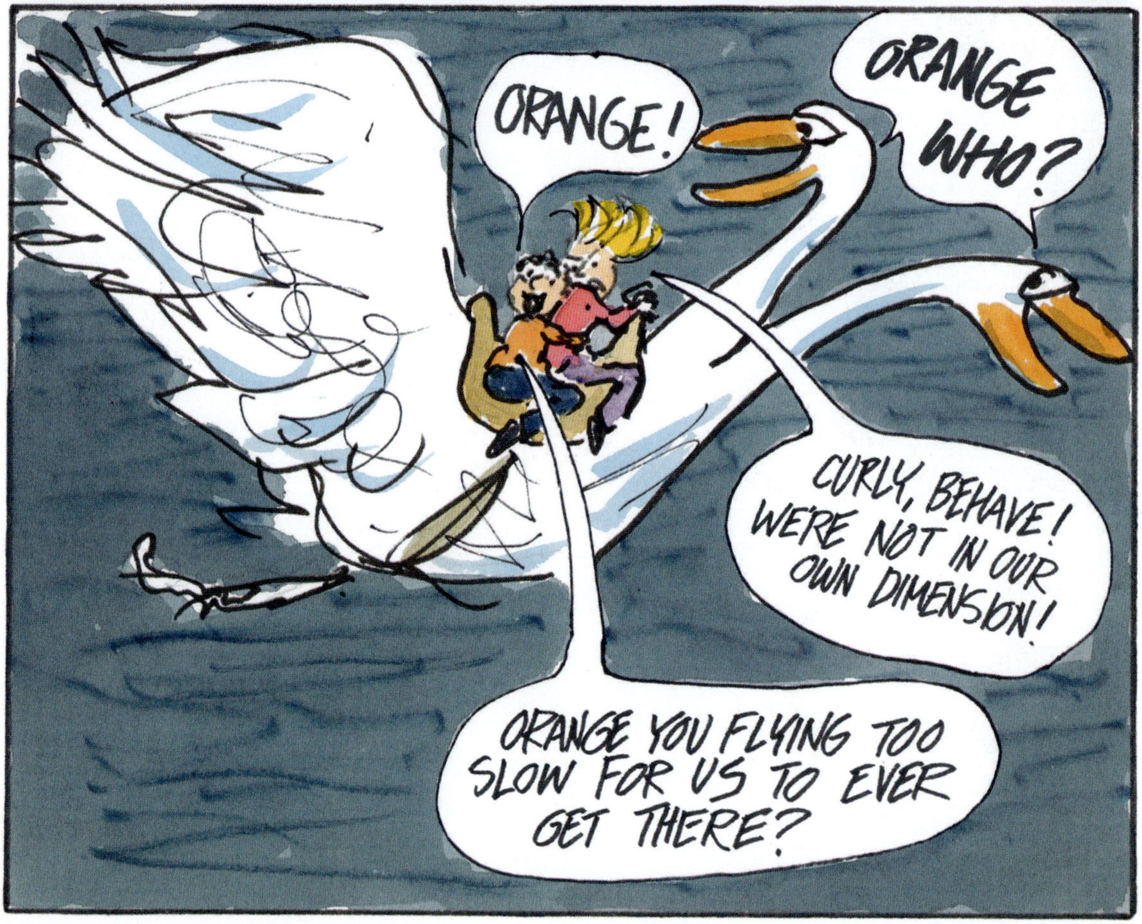
ORANGE!
ORANGE WHO?
CURLY, BEHAVE! WE'RE NOT IN OUR OWN DIMENSION!
ORANGE YOU FLYING TOO SLOW FOR US TO EVER GET THERE?

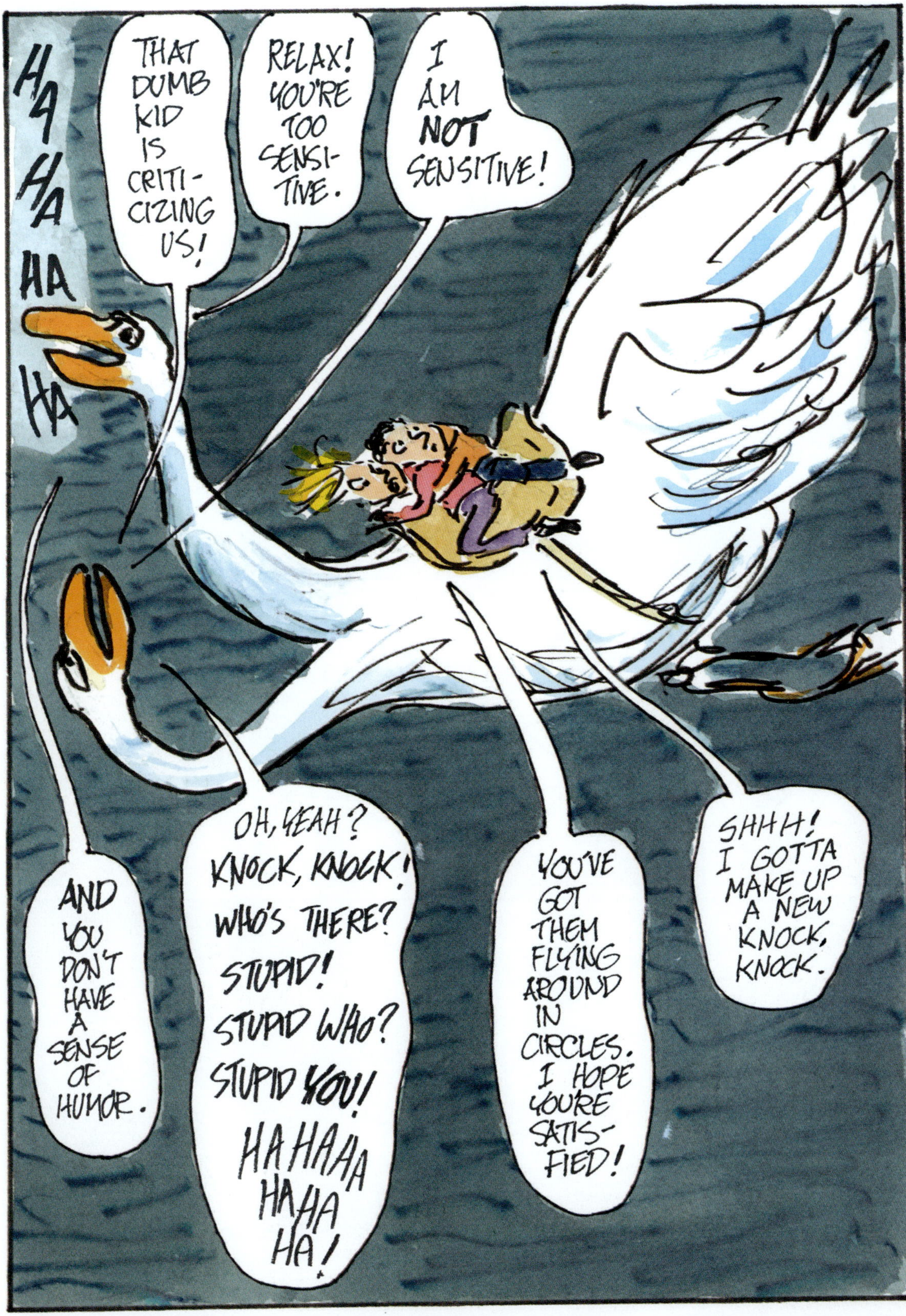
HA HA HA HA HA
THAT DUMB KID IS CRITI-CIZING US!
RELAX! YOU'RE TOO SENSI-TIVE.
I AM **NOT** SENSITIVE!
AND YOU DON'T HAVE A SENSE OF HUMOR.
OH, YEAH? KNOCK, KNOCK! WHO'S THERE? STUPID! STUPID WHO? STUPID **YOU**! HA HA HAA HA HA HA!
YOU'VE GOT THEM FLYING AROUND IN CIRCLES. I HOPE YOU'RE SATIS-FIED!
SHHH! I GOTTA MAKE UP A NEW KNOCK, KNOCK.

CHAPTER 6 • MEANYOPOLIS

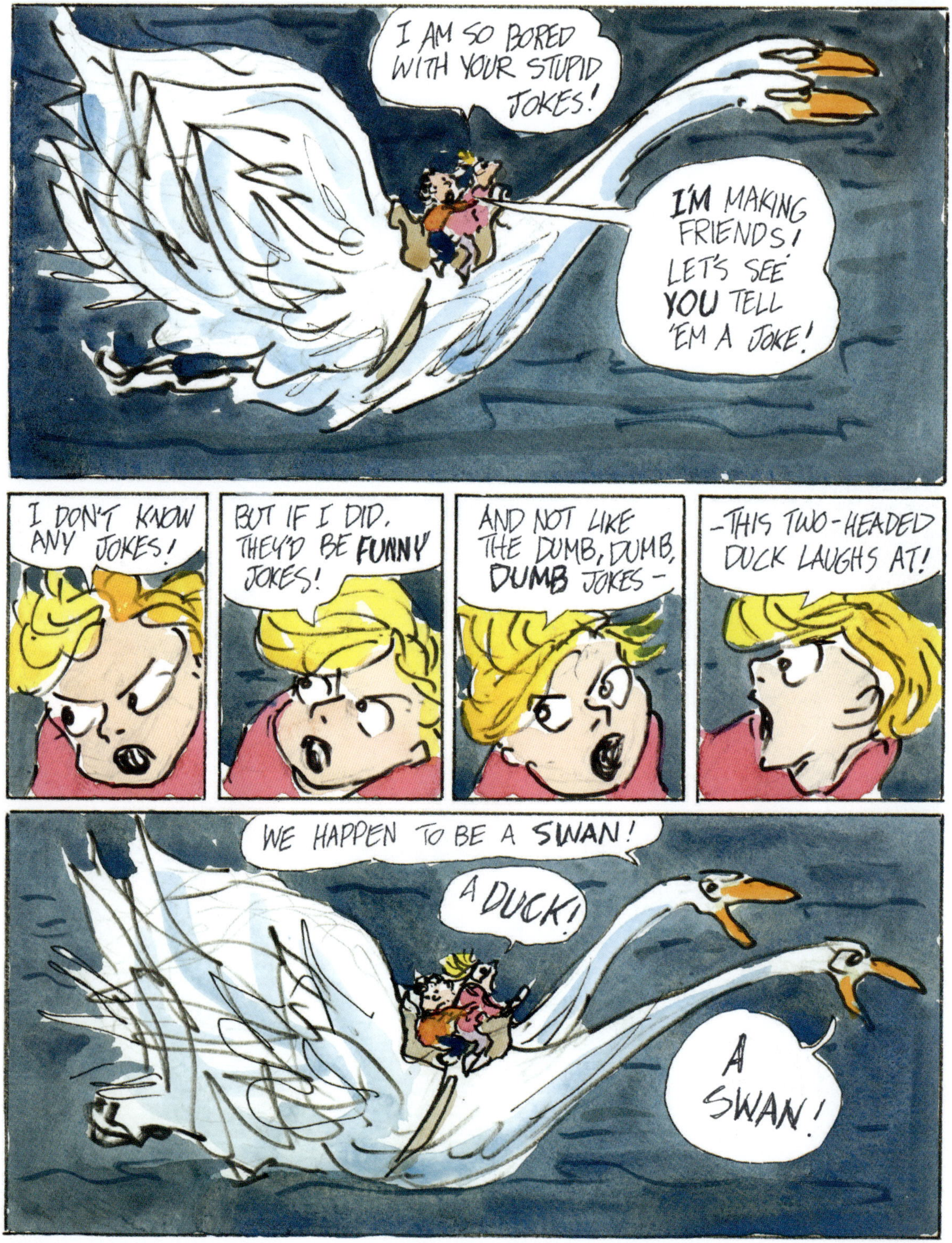

I AM SO BORED WITH YOUR STUPID JOKES!
I'M MAKING FRIENDS! LET'S SEE YOU TELL 'EM A JOKE!
I DON'T KNOW ANY JOKES!
BUT IF I DID, THEY'D BE FUNNY JOKES!
AND NOT LIKE THE DUMB, DUMB, DUMB JOKES -
- THIS TWO-HEADED DUCK LAUGHS AT!
WE HAPPEN TO BE A SWAN!
A DUCK!
A SWAN!

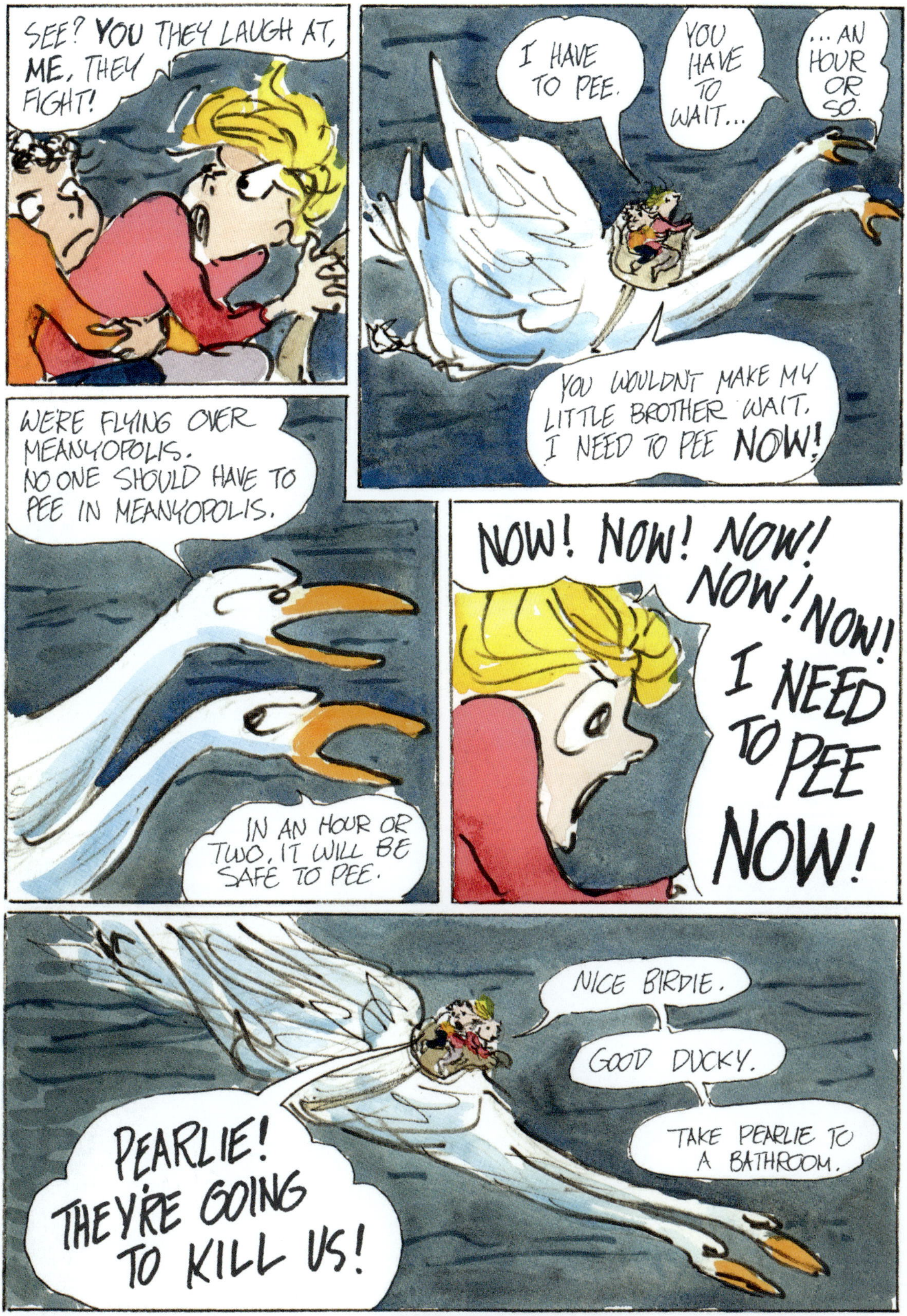
SEE? YOU THEY LAUGH AT, ME, THEY FIGHT!
I HAVE TO PEE.
YOU HAVE TO WAIT...
...AN HOUR OR SO.
YOU WOULDN'T MAKE MY LITTLE BROTHER WAIT. I NEED TO PEE NOW!
WE'RE FLYING OVER MEANYOPOLIS. NO ONE SHOULD HAVE TO PEE IN MEANYOPOLIS.
IN AN HOUR OR TWO, IT WILL BE SAFE TO PEE.
NOW! NOW! NOW! NOW! NOW! I NEED TO PEE NOW!
NICE BIRDIE.
GOOD DUCKY.
TAKE PEARLIE TO A BATHROOM.
PEARLIE! THEY'RE GOING TO KILL US!

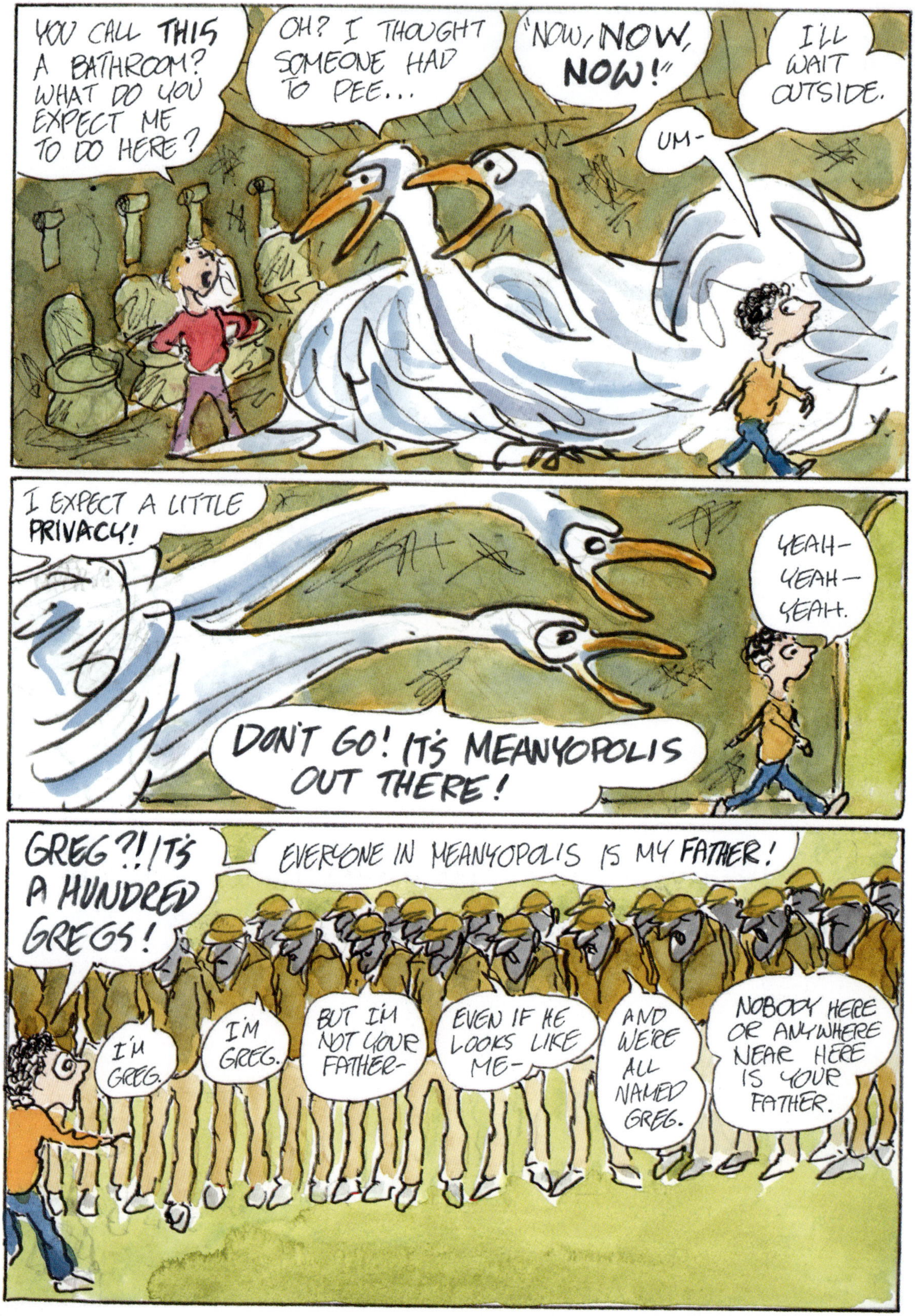
YOU CALL THIS A BATHROOM? WHAT DO YOU EXPECT ME TO DO HERE?
OH? I THOUGHT SOMEONE HAD TO PEE...
"NOW, NOW, NOW!"
UM-
I'LL WAIT OUTSIDE.
I EXPECT A LITTLE PRIVACY!
YEAH-YEAH-YEAH.
DON'T GO! IT'S MEANYOPOLIS OUT THERE!
GREG?!/IT'S A HUNDRED GREGS!
EVERYONE IN MEANYOPOLIS IS MY FATHER!
I'M GREG.
I'M GREG.
BUT I'M NOT YOUR FATHER-
EVEN IF HE LOOKS LIKE ME-
AND WE'RE ALL NAMED GREG.
NOBODY HERE OR ANYWHERE NEAR HERE IS YOUR FATHER.

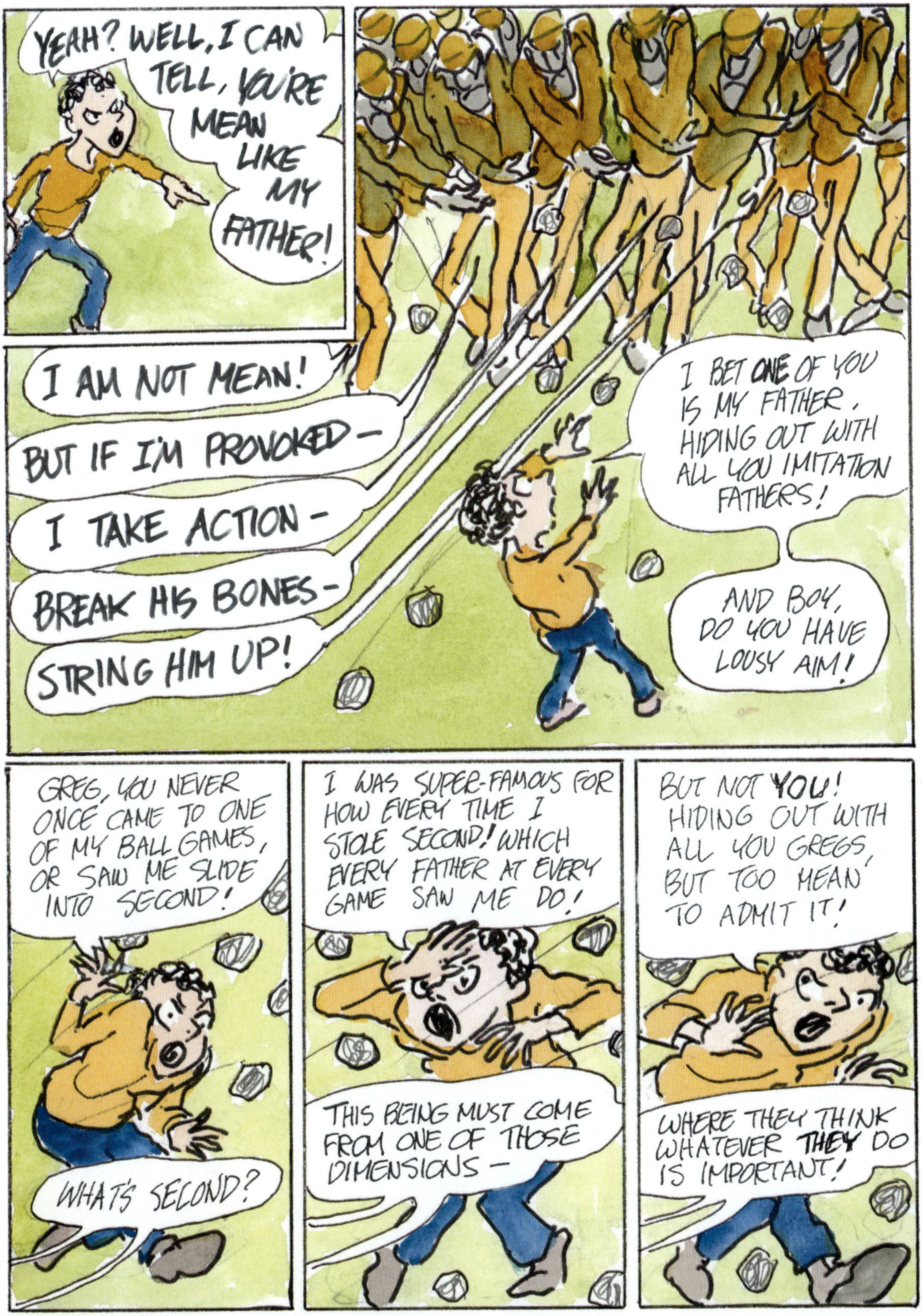
YEAH? WELL, I CAN TELL, YOU'RE MEAN LIKE MY FATHER!
I AM NOT MEAN!
BUT IF I'M PROVOKED—
I TAKE ACTION—
BREAK HIS BONES—
STRING HIM UP!
I BET ONE OF YOU IS MY FATHER, HIDING OUT WITH ALL YOU IMITATION FATHERS!
AND BOY, DO YOU HAVE LOUSY AIM!
GREG, YOU NEVER ONCE CAME TO ONE OF MY BALL GAMES, OR SAW ME SLIDE INTO SECOND!
WHAT'S SECOND?
I WAS SUPER-FAMOUS FOR HOW EVERY TIME I STOLE SECOND! WHICH EVERY FATHER AT EVERY GAME SAW ME DO!
THIS BEING MUST COME FROM ONE OF THOSE DIMENSIONS—
BUT NOT YOU! HIDING OUT WITH ALL YOU GREGS, BUT TOO MEAN TO ADMIT IT!
WHERE THEY THINK WHATEVER THEY DO IS IMPORTANT!

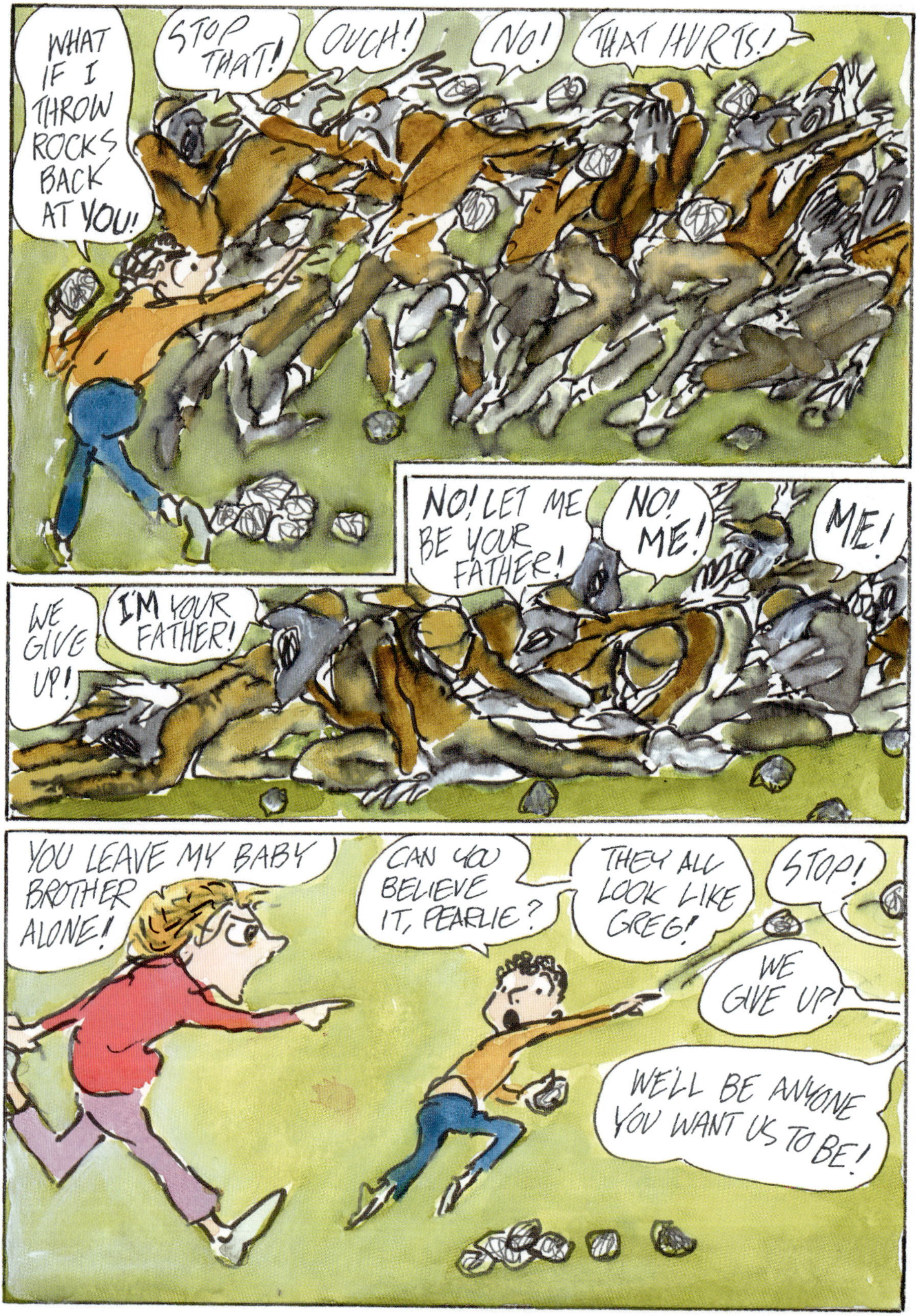
WHAT IF I THROW ROCKS BACK AT YOU!
STOP THAT!
OUCH!
NO!
THAT HURTS!
NO! LET ME BE YOUR FATHER!
NO! ME!
ME!
WE GIVE UP!
I'M YOUR FATHER!
YOU LEAVE MY BABY BROTHER ALONE!
CAN YOU BELIEVE IT, PEARLIE?
THEY ALL LOOK LIKE GREG!
STOP!
WE GIVE UP!
WE'LL BE ANYONE YOU WANT US TO BE!

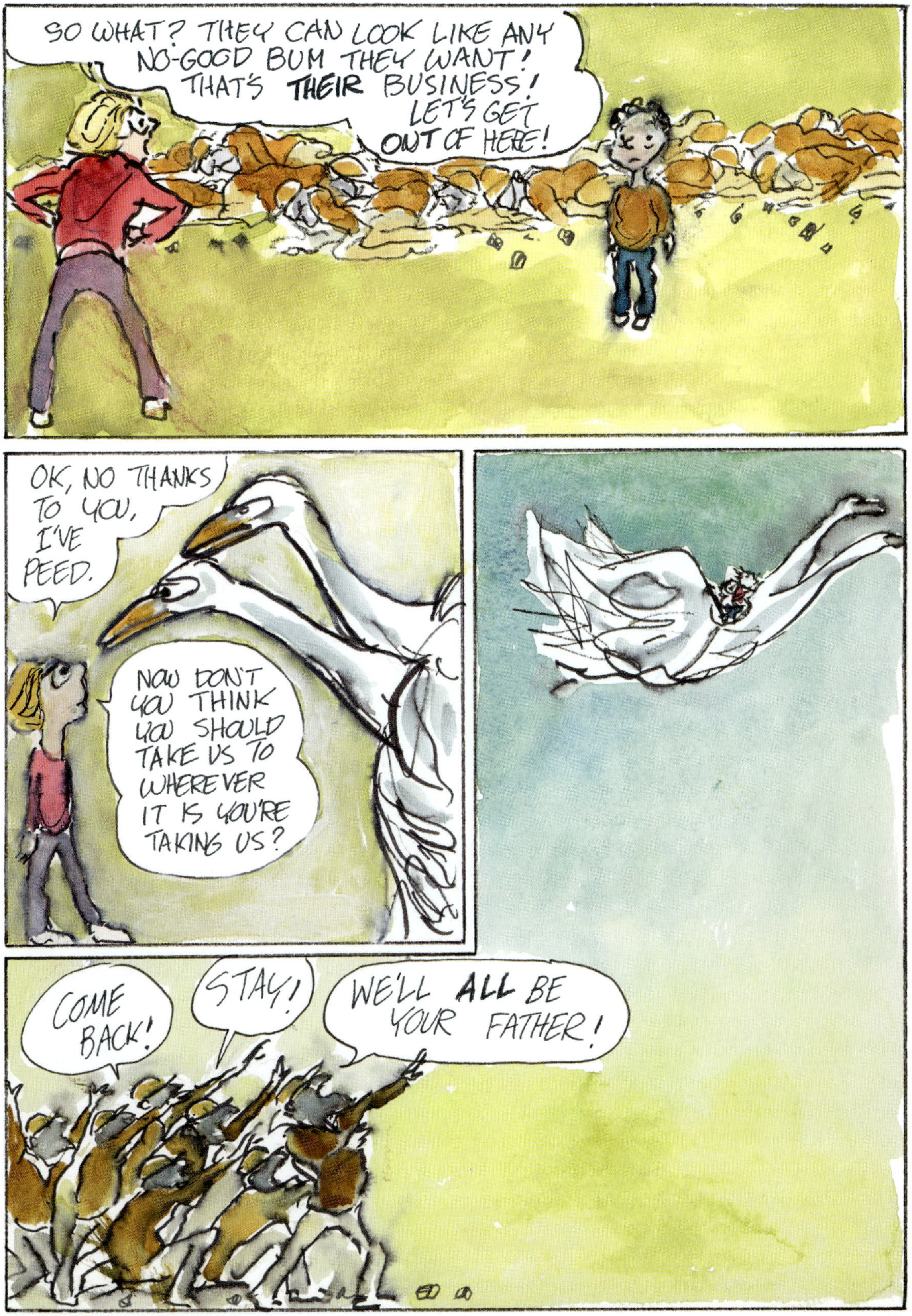
SO WHAT? THEY CAN LOOK LIKE ANY NO-GOOD BUM THEY WANT! THAT'S **THEIR** BUSINESS! LET'S GET **OUT** OF HERE!
OK, NO THANKS TO YOU, I'VE PEED.
NOW DON'T YOU THINK YOU SHOULD TAKE US TO WHEREVER IT IS YOU'RE TAKING US?
COME BACK!
STAY!
WE'LL **ALL** BE YOUR FATHER!

CHAPTER 7 • FUN AND GAMES

Flying over forests and gullies and mountains and deserts, Curly tells one joke after another, as the two-headed swan laughs its heads off!

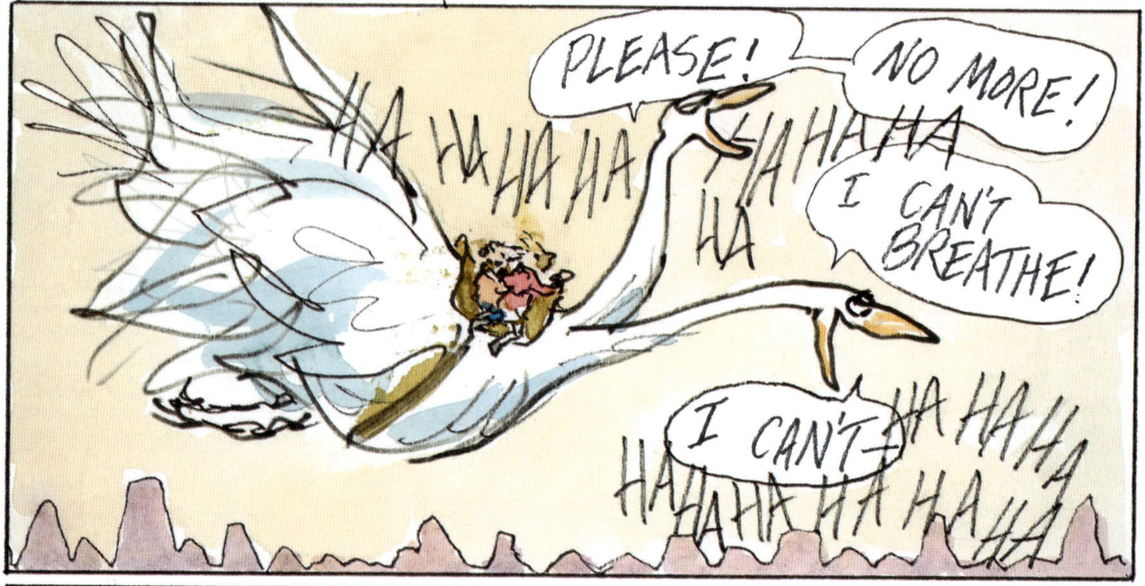
PLEASE!
NO MORE!
HA HA HA HA HA
HAHAHA HA
I CAN'T BREATHE!
I CAN'T—
HA HA HA HA HA HA HA HA HA HA HA

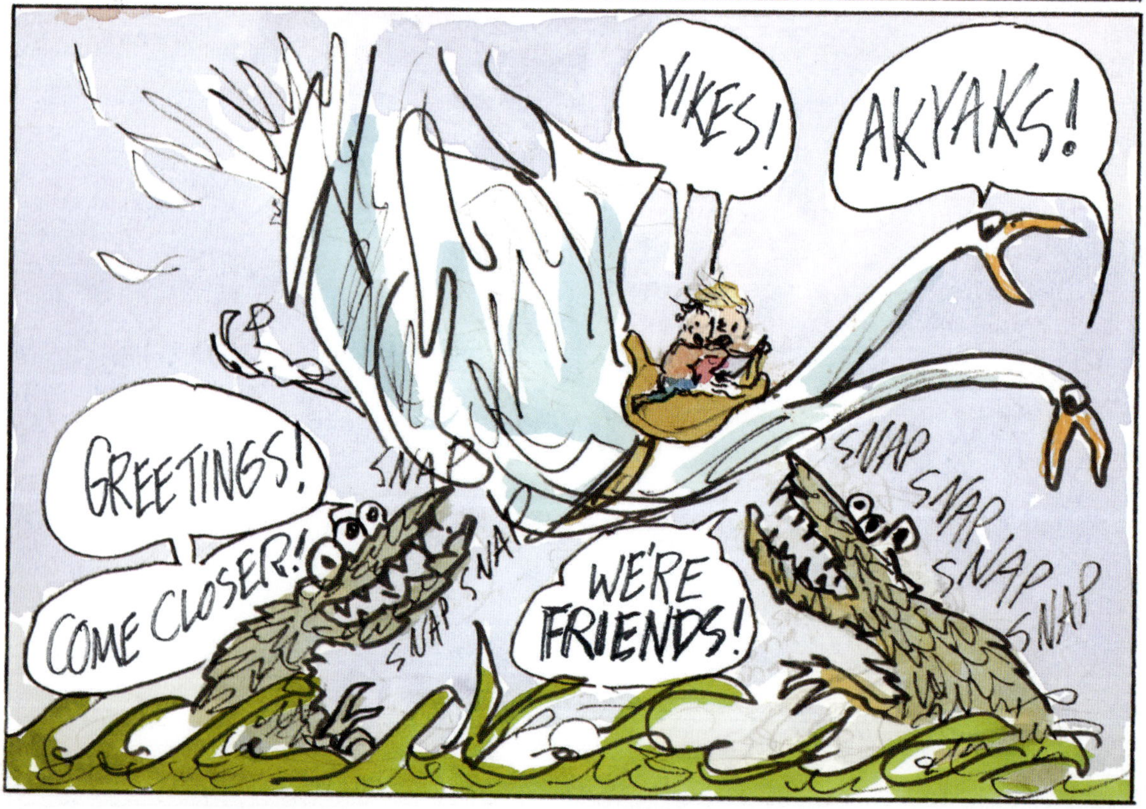
YIKES!
AKYAKS!
GREETINGS!
COME CLOSER!
WE'RE FRIENDS!
SNAP
SNAP
SNAP
SNAP SNAP SNAP SNAP SNAP

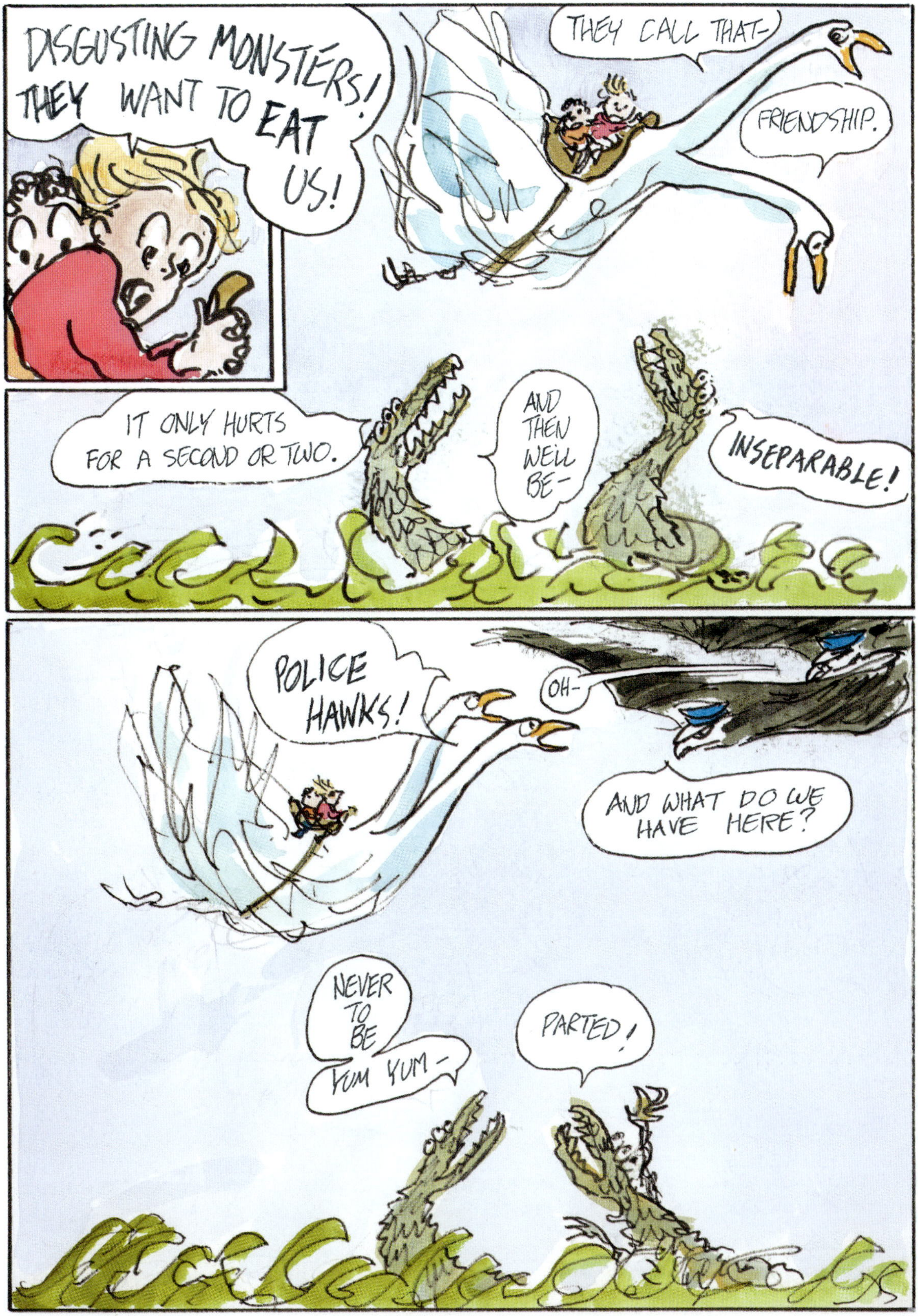
DISGUSTING MONSTERS! THEY WANT TO EAT US!
THEY CALL THAT-
FRIENDSHIP.
IT ONLY HURTS FOR A SECOND OR TWO.
AND THEN WE'LL BE-
INSEPARABLE!
POLICE HAWKS!
OH-
AND WHAT DO WE HAVE HERE?
NEVER TO BE
YUM YUM-
PARTED!

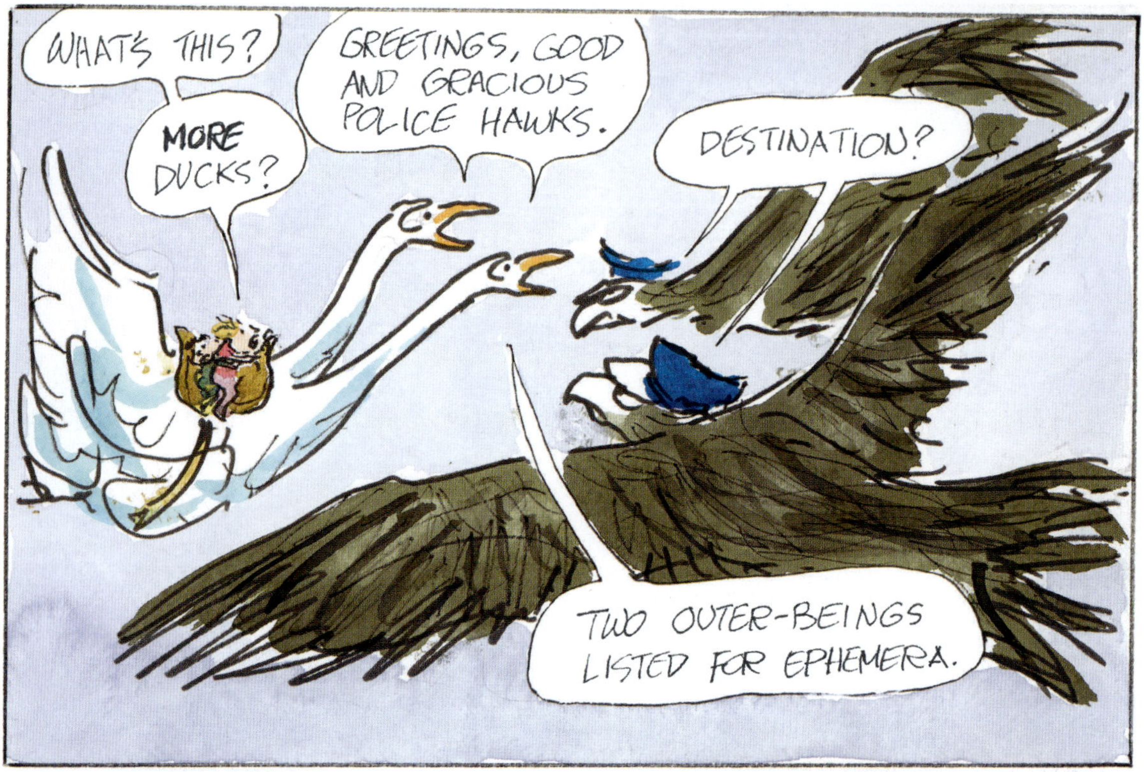
WHAT'S THIS?
MORE DUCKS?
GREETINGS, GOOD AND GRACIOUS POLICE HAWKS.
DESTINATION?
TWO OUTER-BEINGS LISTED FOR EPHEMERA.

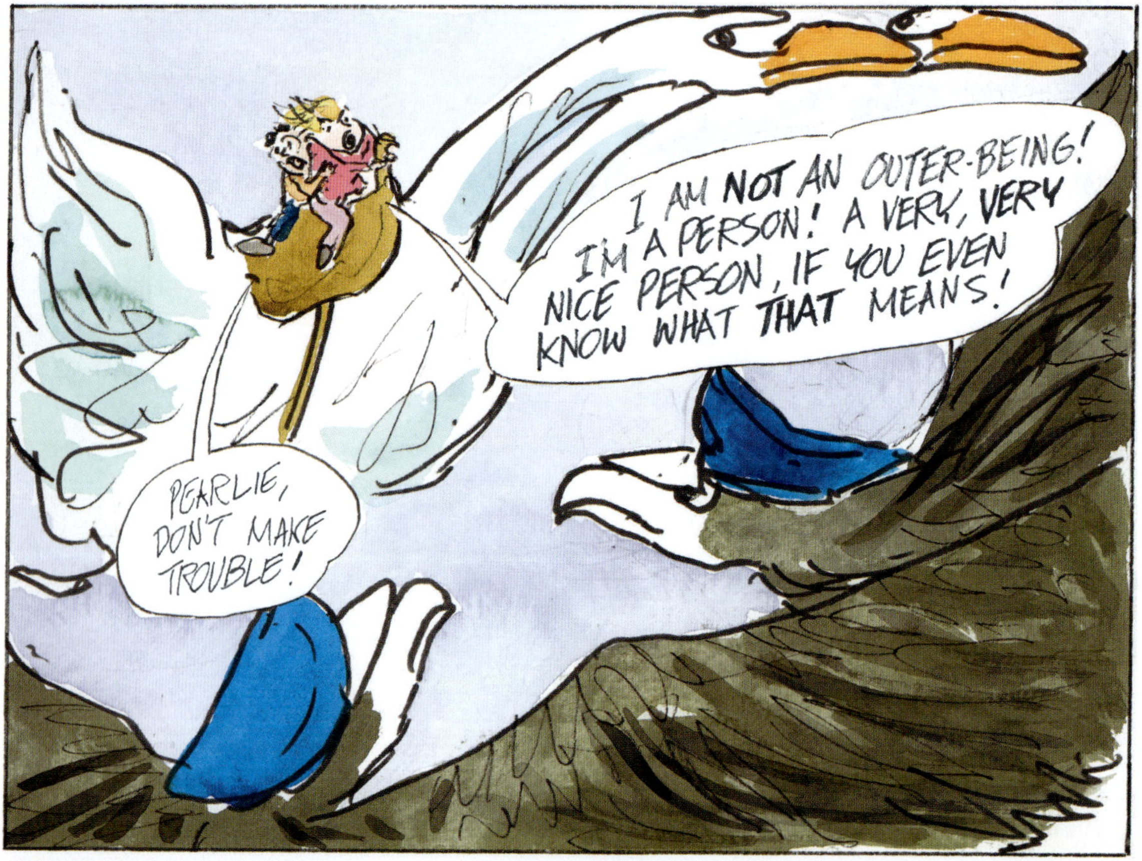
I AM NOT AN OUTER-BEING! I'M A PERSON! A VERY, VERY NICE PERSON, IF YOU EVEN KNOW WHAT THAT MEANS!
PEARLIE, DON'T MAKE TROUBLE!

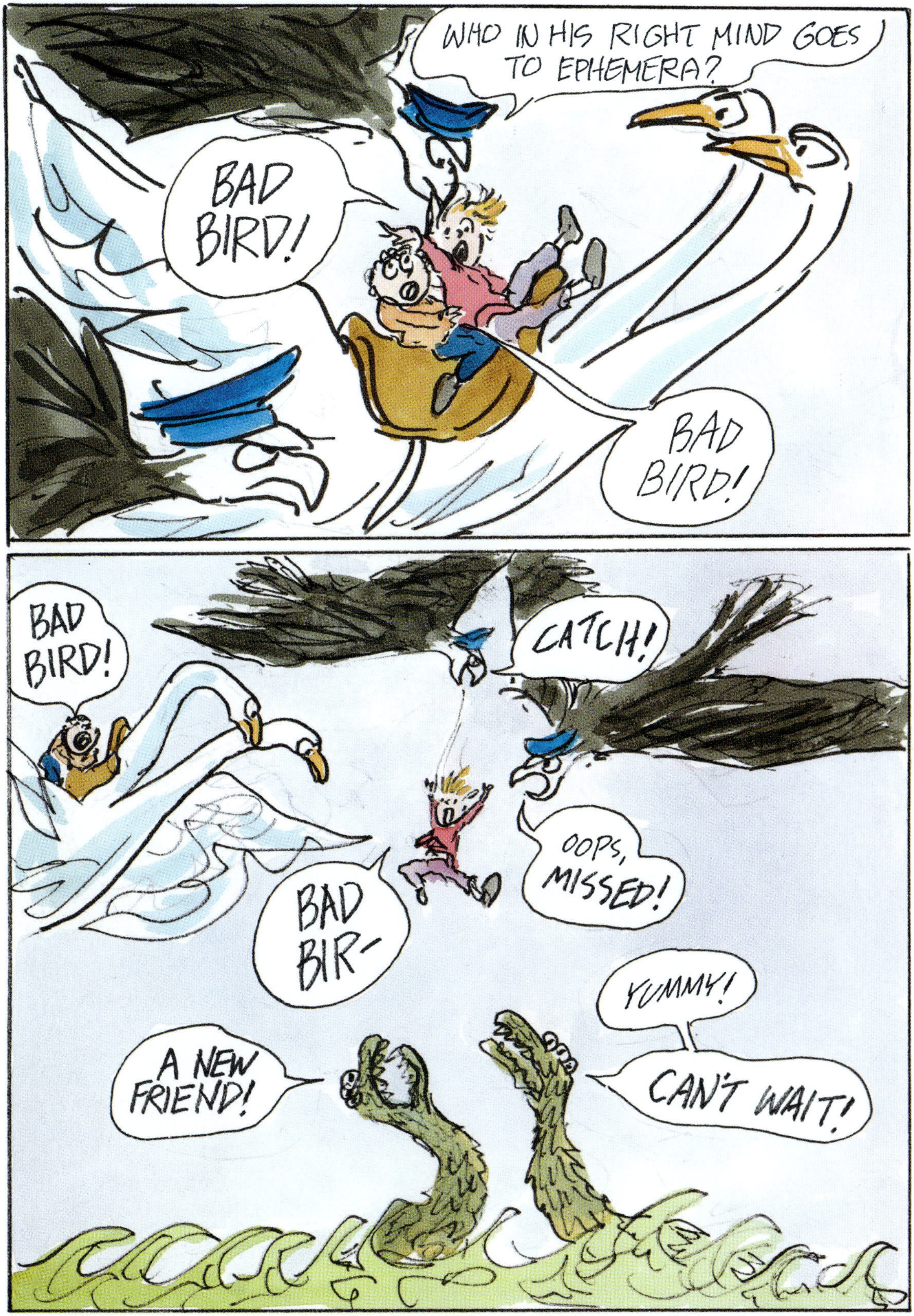
WHO IN HIS RIGHT MIND GOES TO EPHEMERA?
BAD BIRD!
BAD BIRD!
BAD BIRD!
CATCH!
OOPS, MISSED!
BAD BIR-
YUMMY!
A NEW FRIEND!
CAN'T WAIT!

CHAPTER 8 • DROPPED YA, GOTCHA

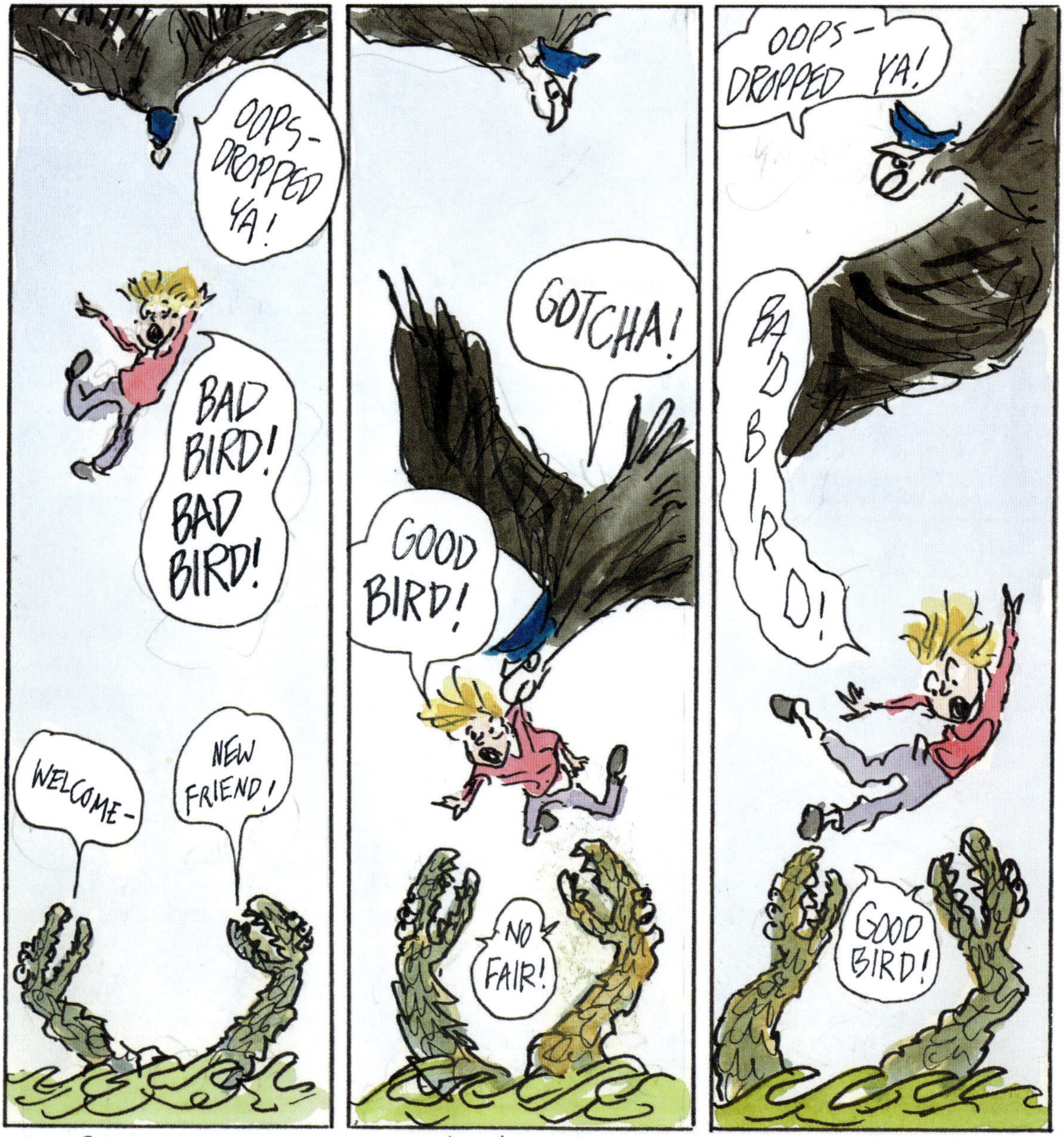
OOPS-DROPPED YA!
BAD BIRD! BAD BIRD!
WELCOME-
NEW FRIEND!
GOTCHA!
GOOD BIRD!
NO FAIR!
OOPS-DROPPED YA!
BAD BIRD!
GOOD BIRD!

The Police Hawks are having the best time playing a game of "Dropped Ya, Gotcha." The rules of the game are as follows: One Police Hawk lets go of Pearlie, and a second or two before she falls into the jaws of the akyaks, the other Police Hawk swoops in for a last-second "Gotcha!" Back and forth they go. Who knows how many hours? Or days? Certain-death drops, followed by last-second saves.

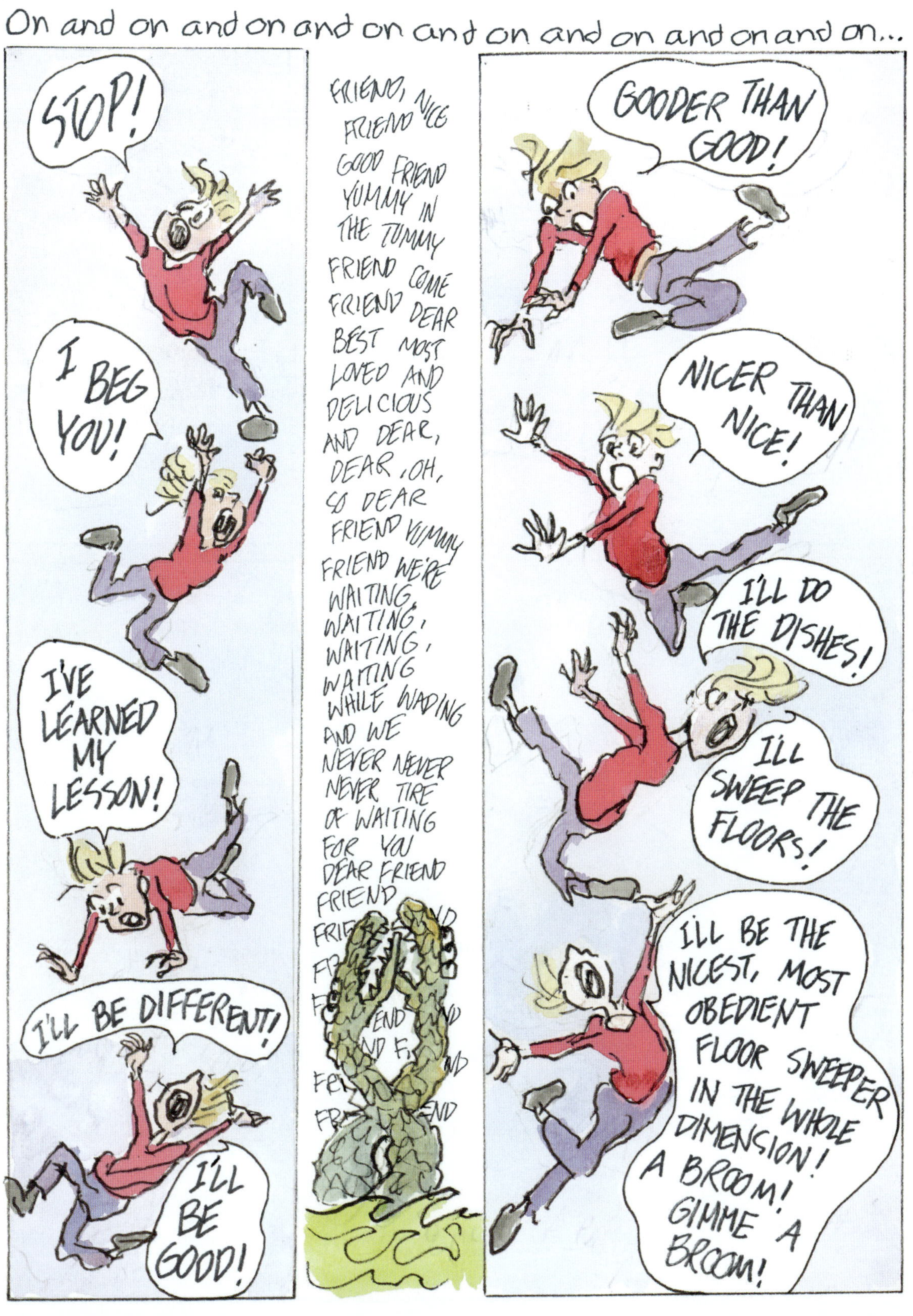
On and on and on and on and on and on and on and on and on...
STOP!
I BEG YOU!
I'VE LEARNED MY LESSON!
I'LL BE DIFFERENT!
I'LL BE GOOD!
FRIEND, NICE FRIEND NICE GOOD FRIEND YUMMY IN THE TUMMY FRIEND COME FRIEND DEAR BEST MOST LOVED AND DELICIOUS AND DEAR, DEAR, OH, SO DEAR FRIEND YUMMY FRIEND WE'RE WAITING, WAITING, WAITING, WAITING WHILE WADING AND WE NEVER NEVER NEVER TIRE OF WAITING FOR YOU DEAR FRIEND FRIEND
GOODER THAN GOOD!
NICER THAN NICE!
I'LL DO THE DISHES!
I'LL SWEEP THE FLOORS!
I'LL BE THE NICEST, MOST OBEDIENT FLOOR SWEEPER IN THE WHOLE DIMENSION! A BROOM! GIMME A BROOM!

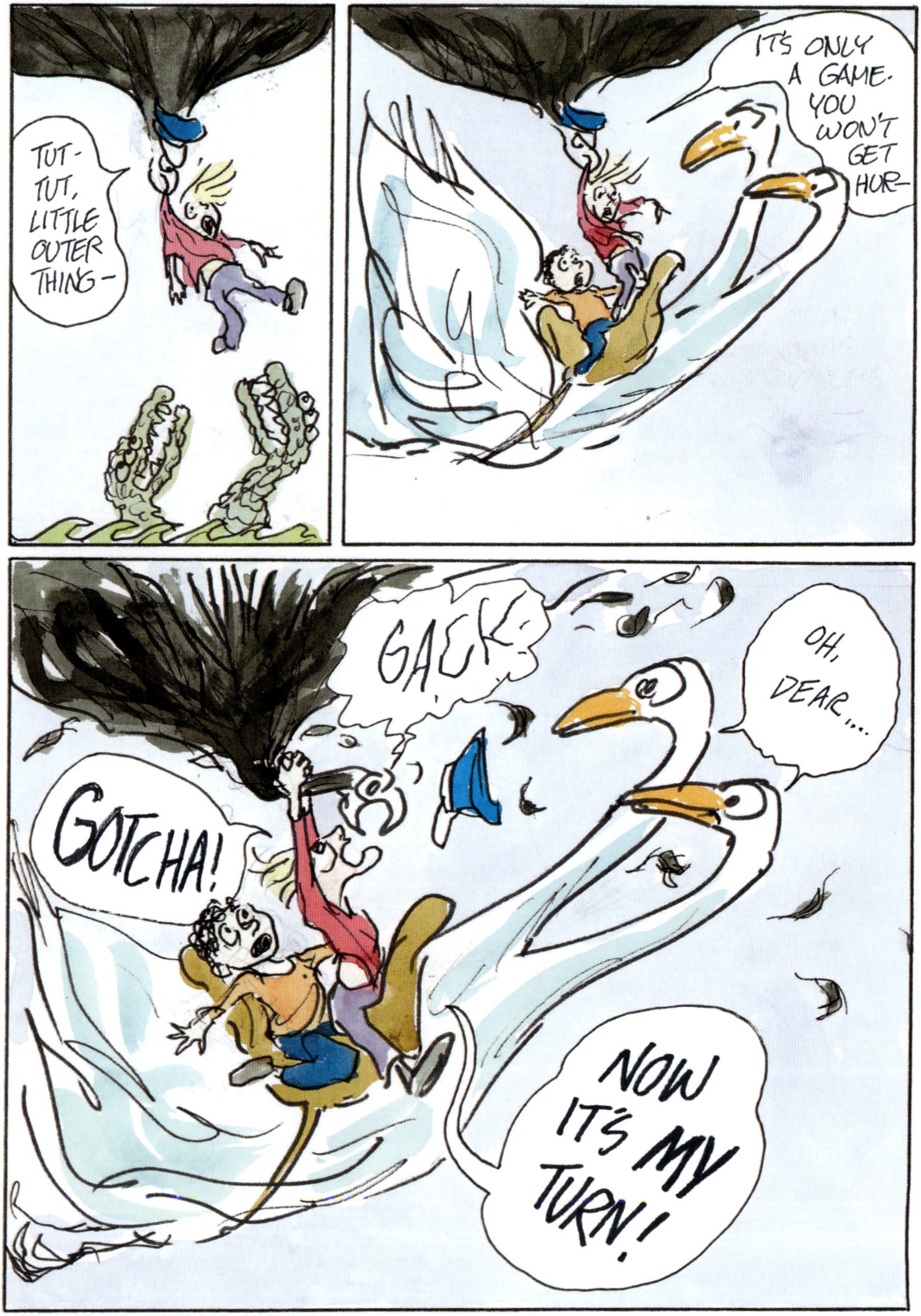
TUT-TUT, LITTLE OUTER THING-
IT'S ONLY A GAME. YOU WON'T GET HUR-
GACK!
OH, DEAR....
GOTCHA!
NOW IT'S MY TURN!

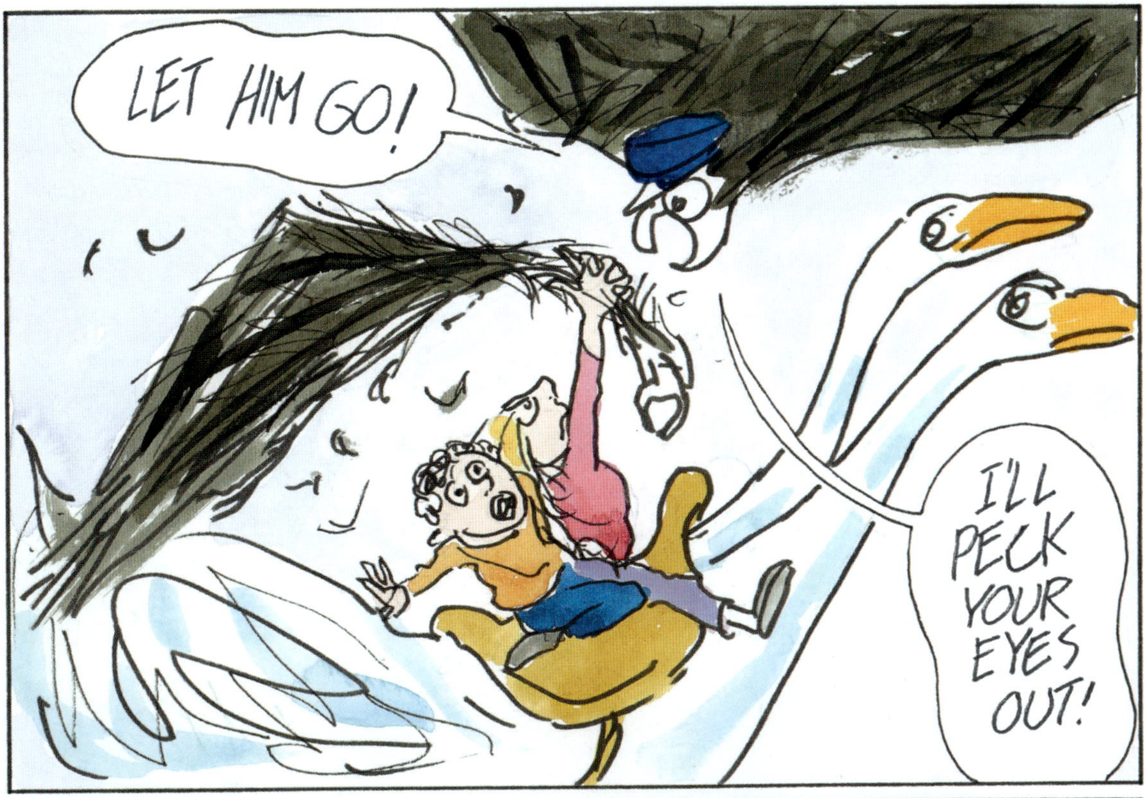
LET HIM GO!
I'LL PECK YOUR EYES OUT!

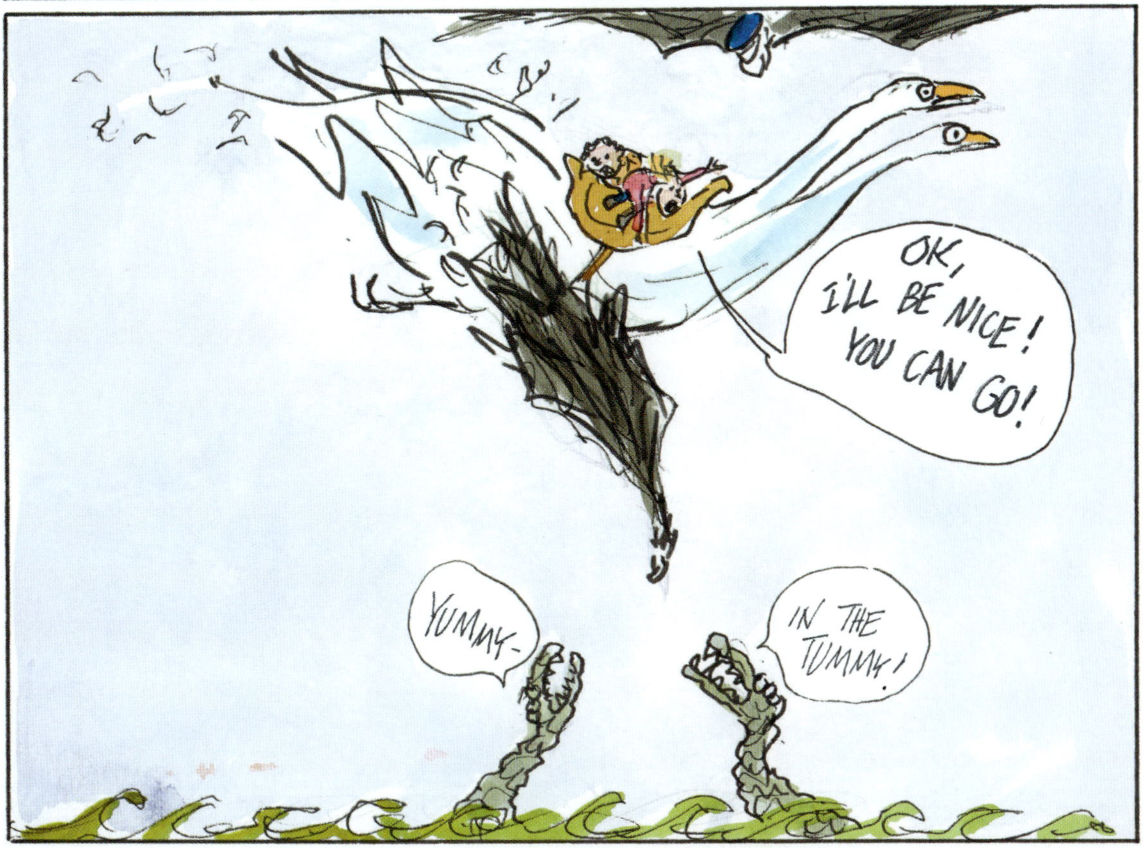
OK, I'LL BE NICE! YOU CAN GO!
YUMMY-
IN THE TUMMY!

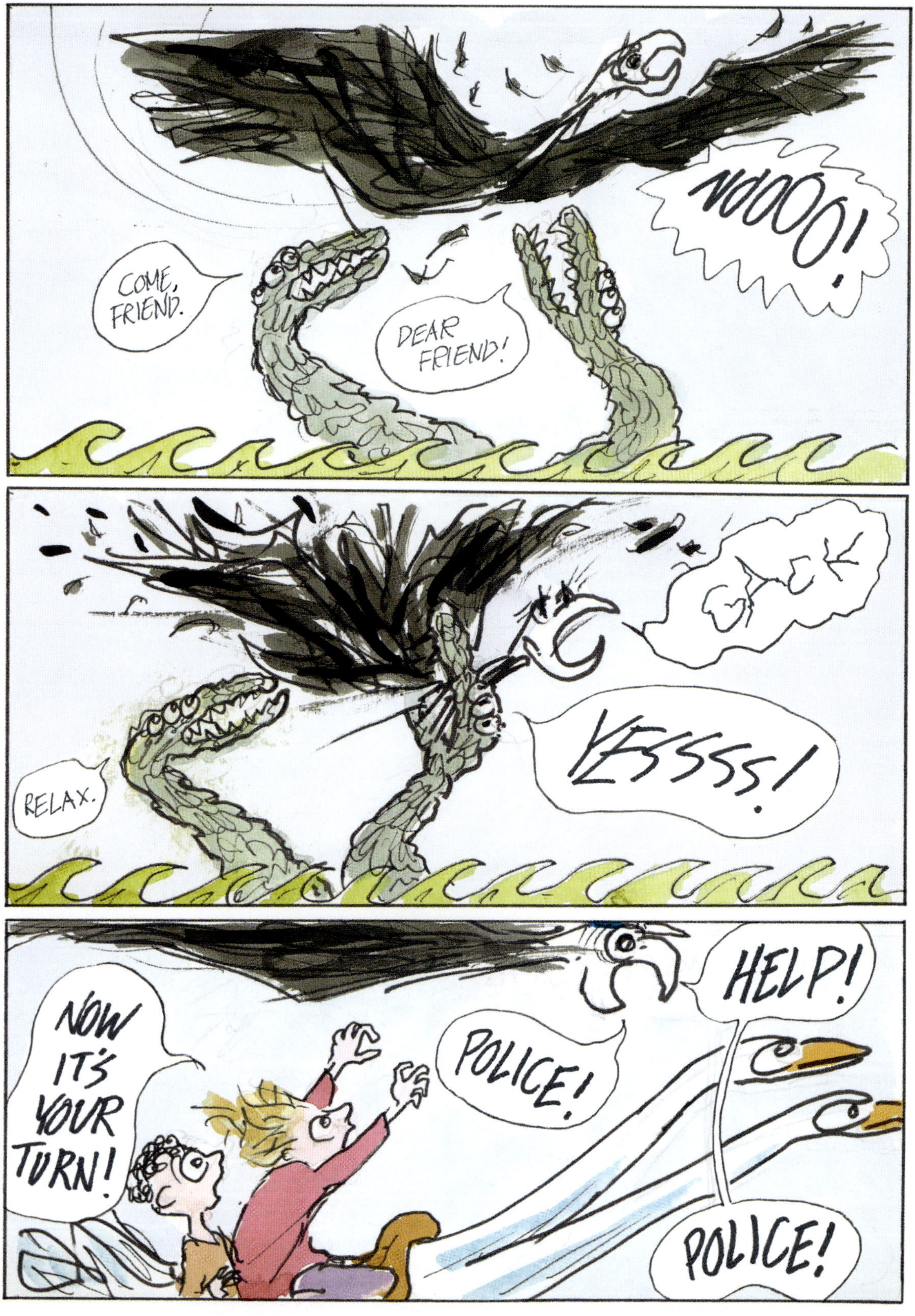
NOOOO!
COME, FRIEND.
DEAR FRIEND!
CRACK
YESSSS!
RELAX.
HELP!
POLICE!
NOW IT'S YOUR TURN!
POLICE!

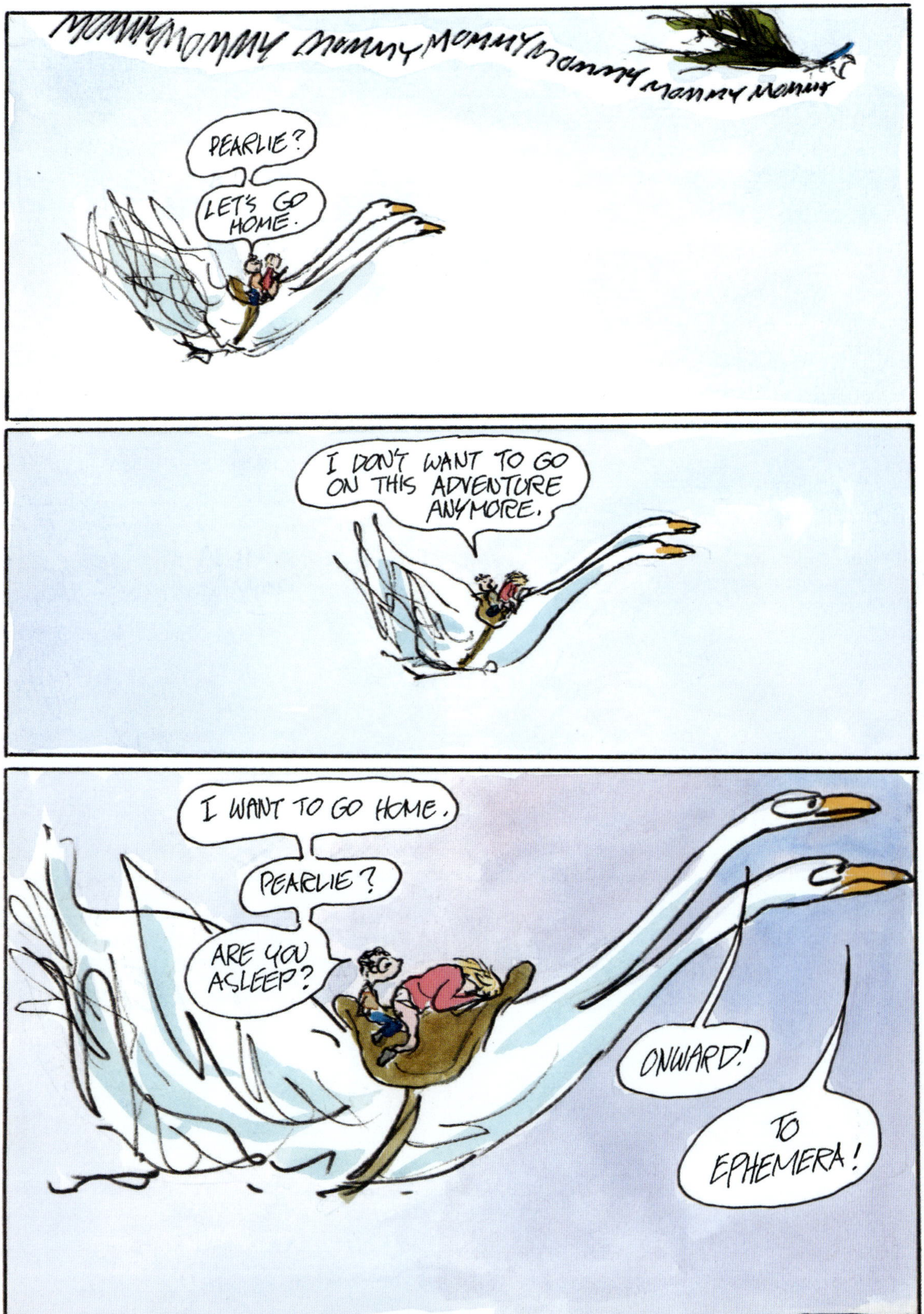
MOMMY MOMMY MOMMY MOMMY MOMMY MOMMY MOMMY MOMMY
PEARLIE?
LET'S GO HOME.
I DON'T WANT TO GO ON THIS ADVENTURE ANYMORE.
I WANT TO GO HOME.
PEARLIE?
ARE YOU ASLEEP?
ONWARD!
TO EPHEMERA!

CHAPTER 9 • THE EMERGENCY FEATHER

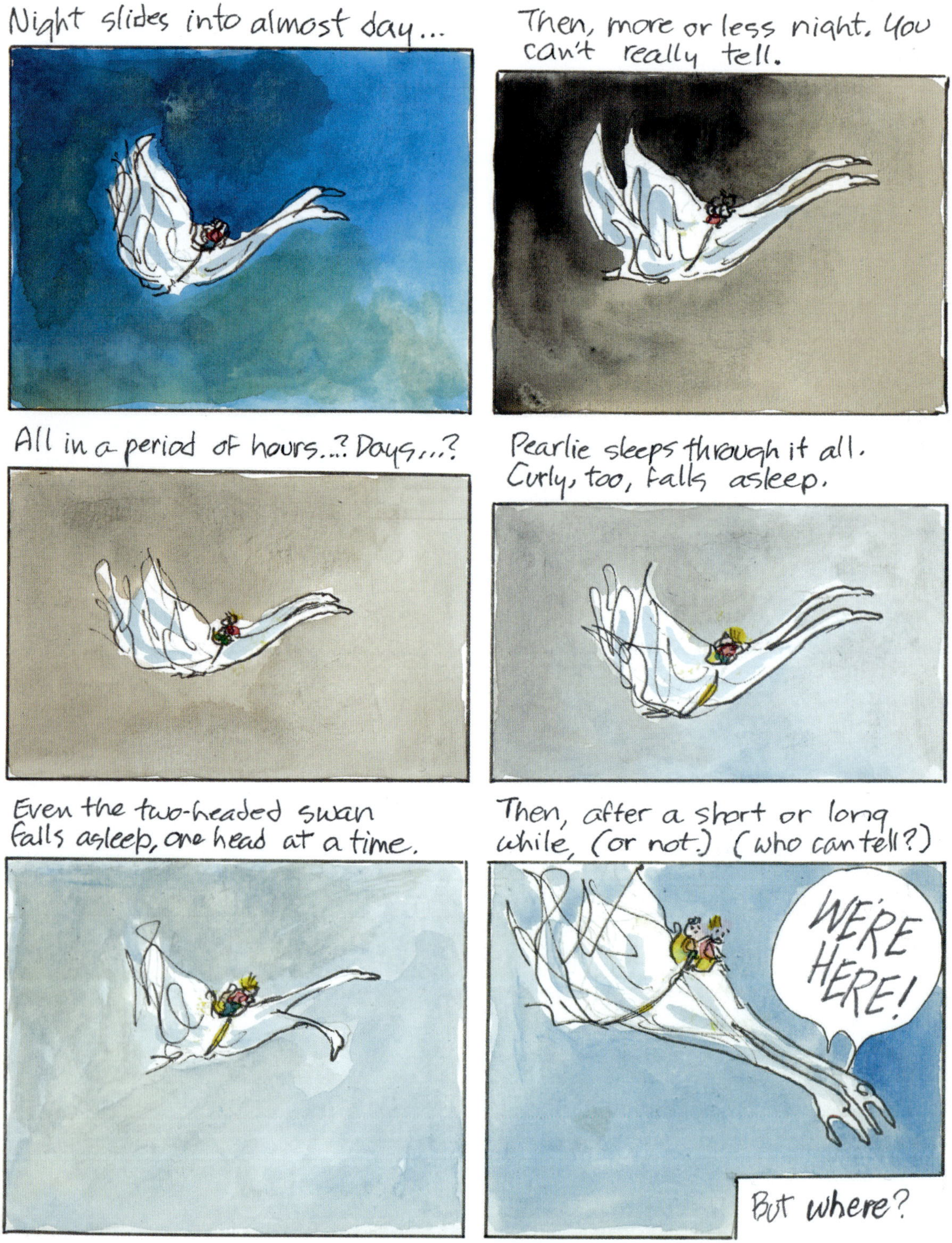
Night slides into almost day...
Then, more or less night. You can't really tell.
All in a period of hours...? Days...?
Pearlie sleeps through it all. Curly, too, falls asleep.
Even the two-headed swan falls asleep, one head at a time.
Then, after a short or long while, (or not.) (who can tell?)
WE'RE HERE!
But where?

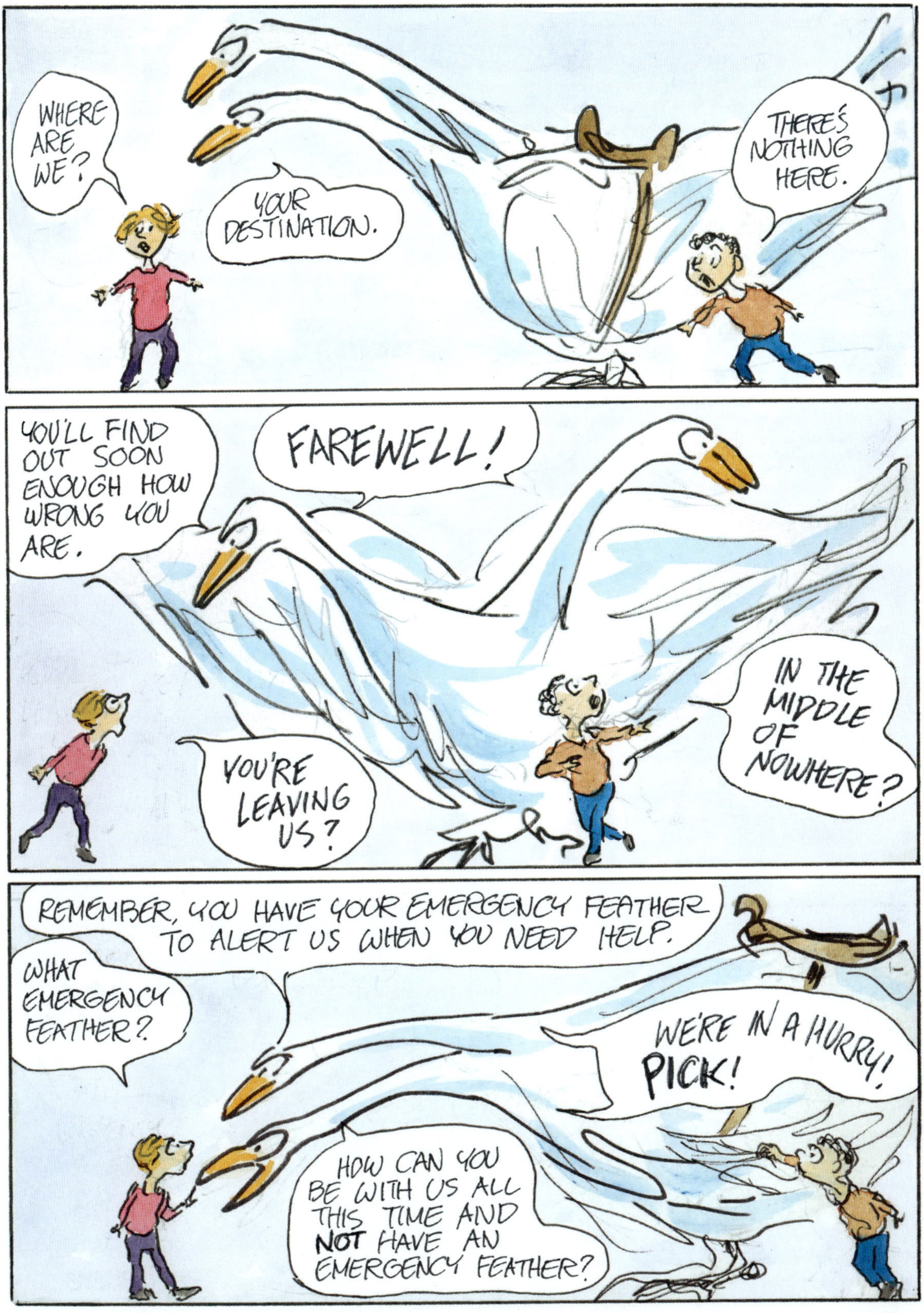
WHERE ARE WE?
YOUR DESTINATION.
THERE'S NOTHING HERE.
YOU'LL FIND OUT SOON ENOUGH HOW WRONG YOU ARE.
FAREWELL!
IN THE MIDDLE OF NOWHERE?
YOU'RE LEAVING US?
REMEMBER, YOU HAVE YOUR EMERGENCY FEATHER TO ALERT US WHEN YOU NEED HELP.
WHAT EMERGENCY FEATHER?
WE'RE IN A HURRY! PICK!
HOW CAN YOU BE WITH US ALL THIS TIME AND NOT HAVE AN EMERGENCY FEATHER?

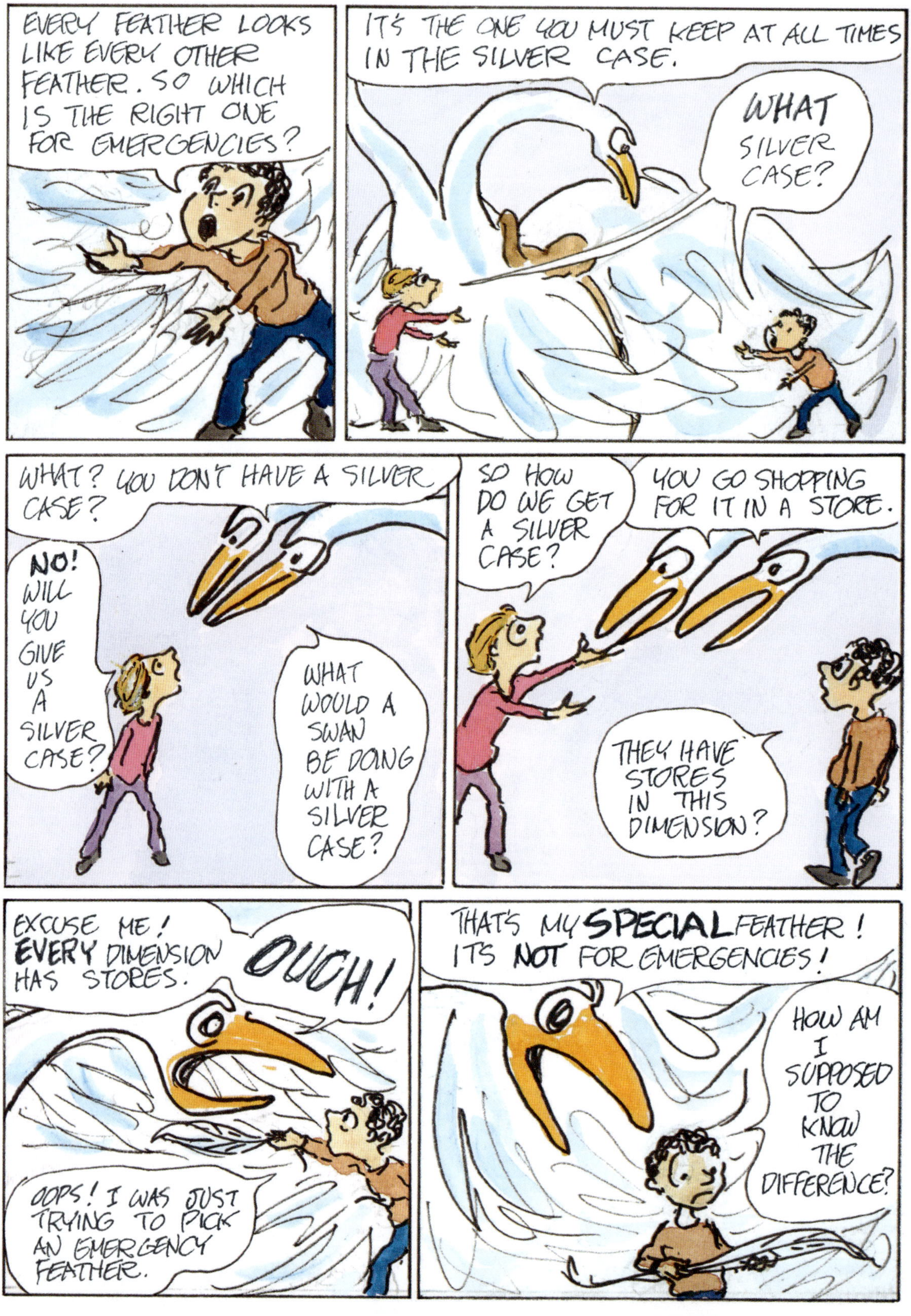
EVERY FEATHER LOOKS LIKE EVERY OTHER FEATHER. SO WHICH IS THE RIGHT ONE FOR EMERGENCIES?
IT'S THE ONE YOU MUST KEEP AT ALL TIMES IN THE SILVER CASE.
WHAT SILVER CASE?
WHAT? YOU DON'T HAVE A SILVER CASE?
NO! WILL YOU GIVE US A SILVER CASE?
WHAT WOULD A SWAN BE DOING WITH A SILVER CASE?
SO HOW DO WE GET A SILVER CASE?
YOU GO SHOPPING FOR IT IN A STORE.
THEY HAVE STORES IN THIS DIMENSION?
EXCUSE ME! EVERY DIMENSION HAS STORES.
OUCH!
OOPS! I WAS JUST TRYING TO PICK AN EMERGENCY FEATHER.
THAT'S MY SPECIAL FEATHER! IT'S NOT FOR EMERGENCIES!
HOW AM I SUPPOSED TO KNOW THE DIFFERENCE?

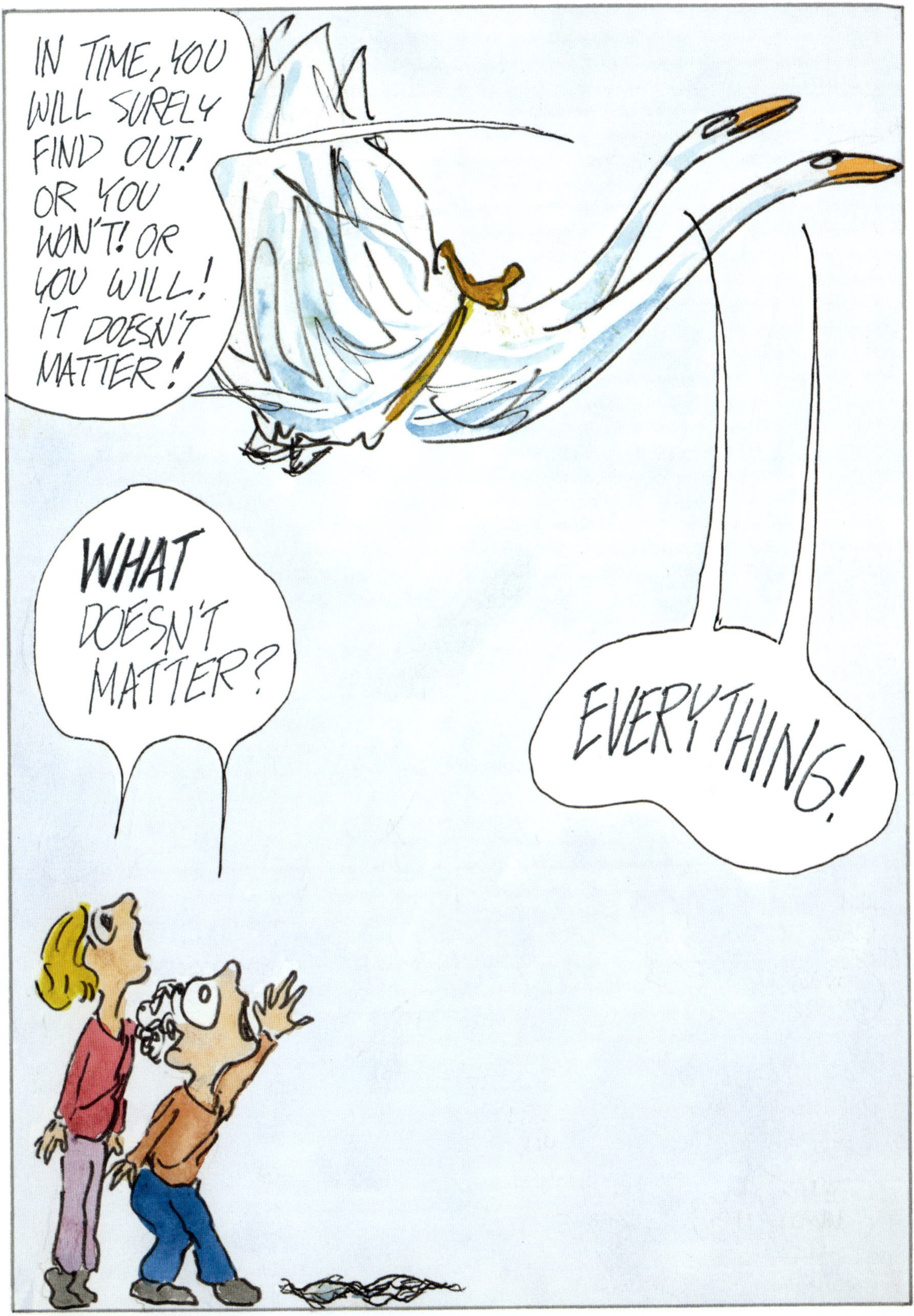
IN TIME, YOU WILL SURELY FIND OUT! OR YOU WON'T! OR YOU WILL! IT DOESN'T MATTER!
WHAT DOESN'T MATTER?
EVERYTHING!

CHAPTER 10 • I'M SORRY

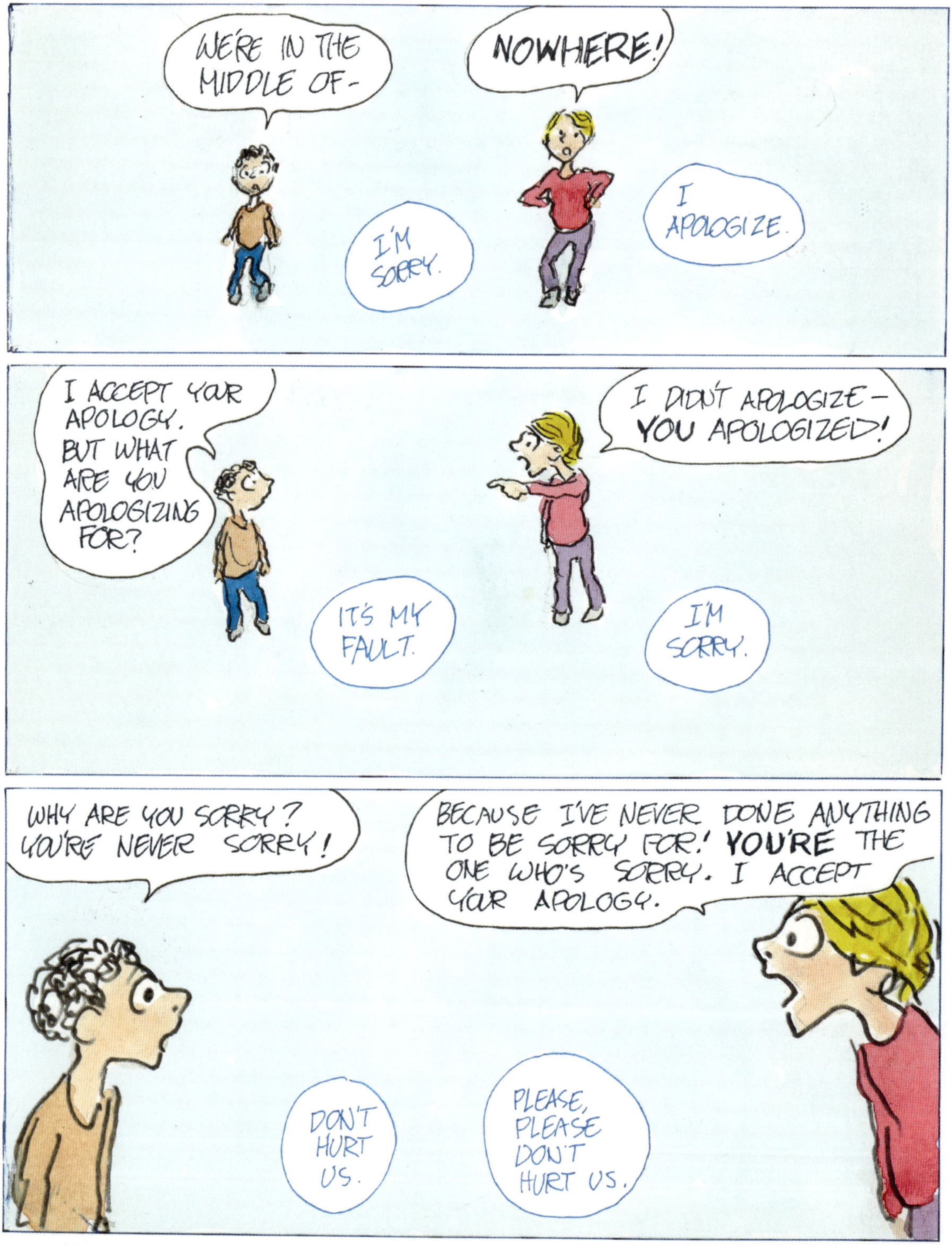
WE'RE IN THE MIDDLE OF-
NOWHERE!
I'M SORRY.
I APOLOGIZE.
I ACCEPT YOUR APOLOGY. BUT WHAT ARE YOU APOLOGIZING FOR?
I DIDN'T APOLOGIZE- YOU APOLOGIZED!
IT'S MY FAULT.
I'M SORRY.
WHY ARE YOU SORRY? YOU'RE NEVER SORRY!
BECAUSE I'VE NEVER DONE ANYTHING TO BE SORRY FOR! YOU'RE THE ONE WHO'S SORRY. I ACCEPT YOUR APOLOGY.
DON'T HURT US.
PLEASE, PLEASE DON'T HURT US.

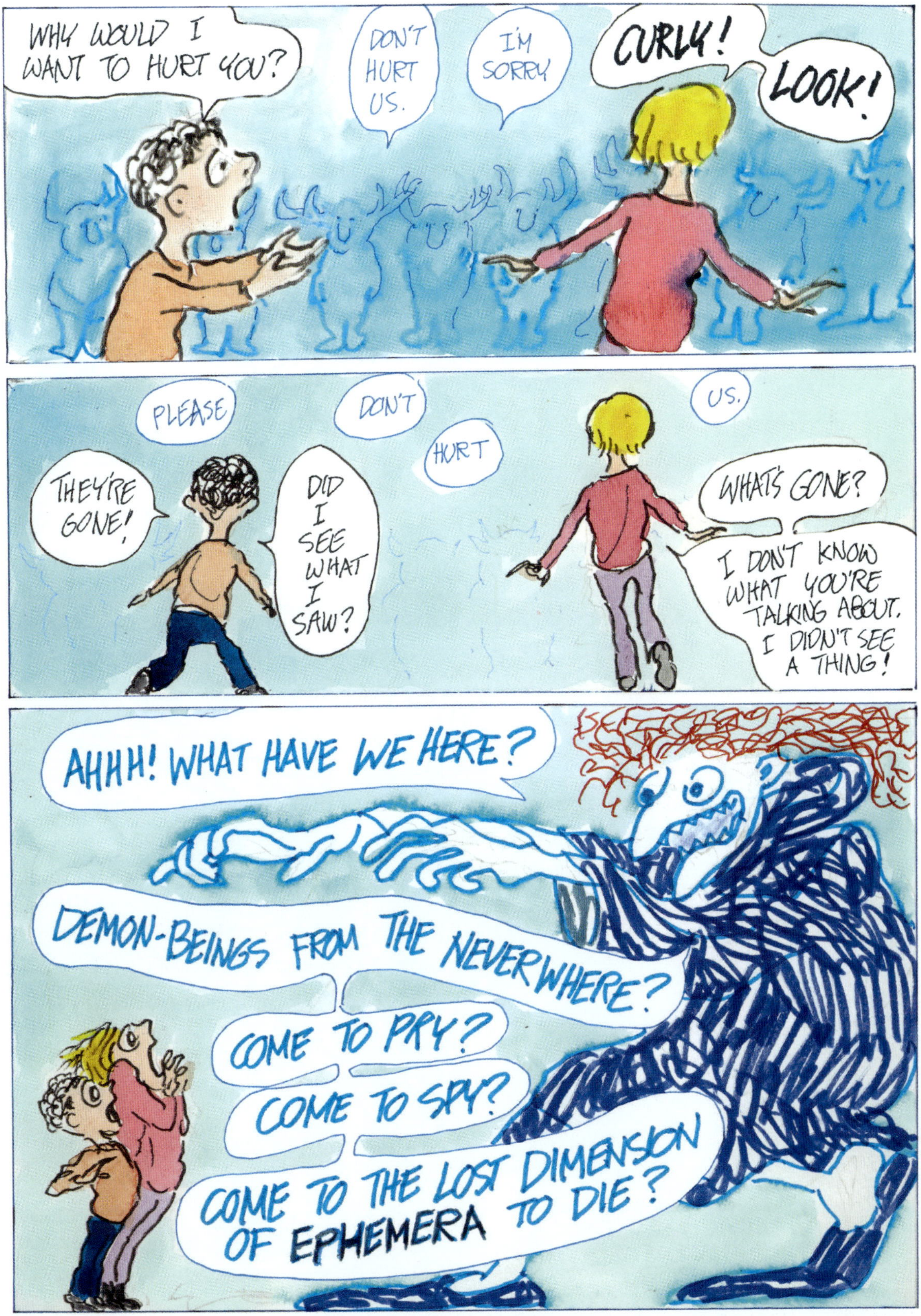

WHY WOULD I WANT TO HURT YOU?
DON'T HURT US.
I'M SORRY
CURLY!
LOOK!
PLEASE
DON'T
HURT
US.
THEY'RE GONE!
DID I SEE WHAT I SAW?
WHAT'S GONE?
I DON'T KNOW WHAT YOU'RE TALKING ABOUT. I DIDN'T SEE A THING!
AHHH! WHAT HAVE WE HERE?
DEMON-BEINGS FROM THE NEVERWHERE?
COME TO PRY?
COME TO SPY?
COME TO THE LOST DIMENSION OF EPHEMERA TO DIE?

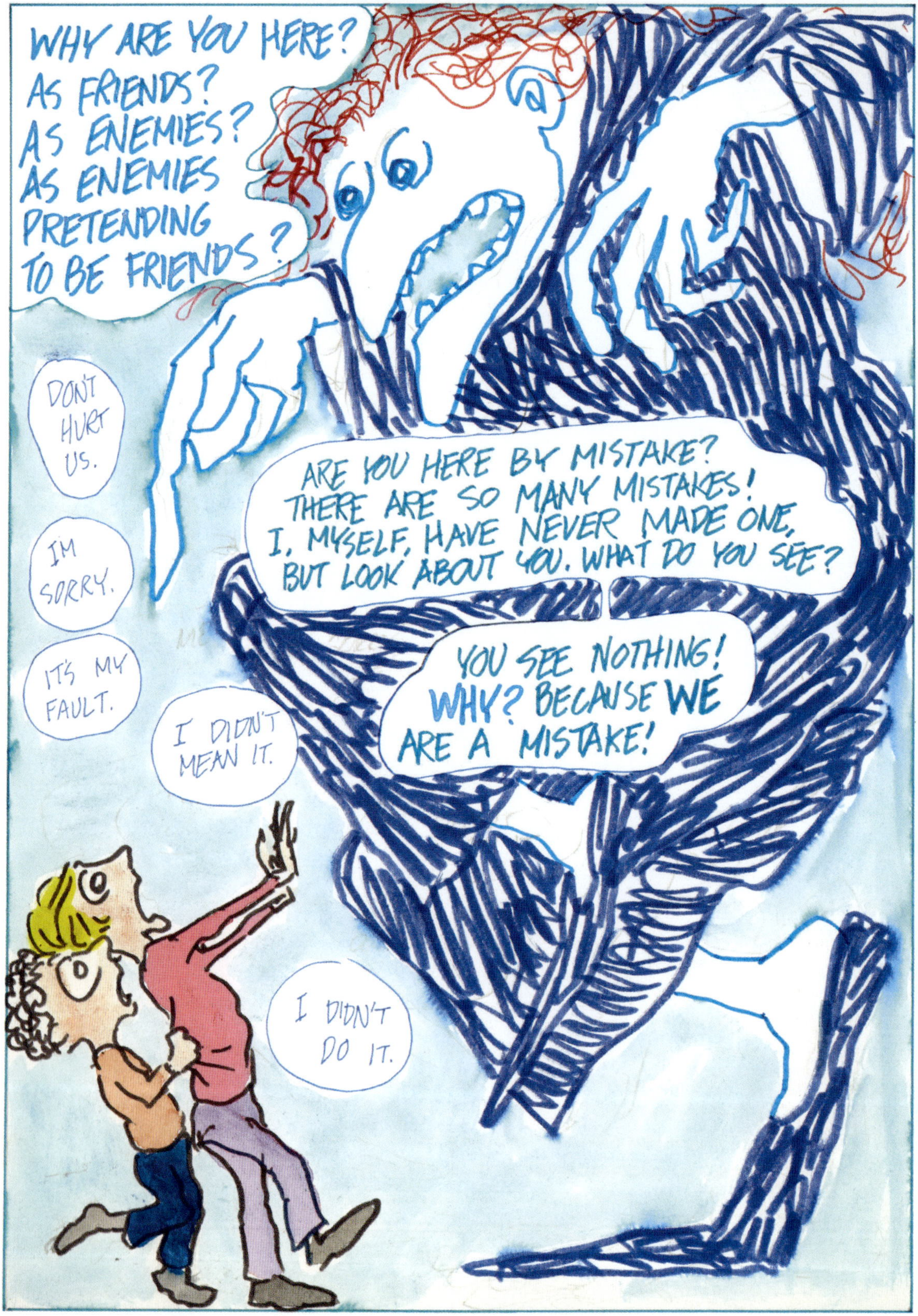
WHY ARE YOU HERE? AS FRIENDS? AS ENEMIES? AS ENEMIES PRETENDING TO BE FRIENDS?
DON'T HURT US.
I'M SORRY.
IT'S MY FAULT.
I DIDN'T MEAN IT.
I DIDN'T DO IT.
ARE YOU HERE BY MISTAKE? THERE ARE SO MANY MISTAKES! I, MYSELF, HAVE NEVER MADE ONE, BUT LOOK ABOUT YOU. WHAT DO YOU SEE?
YOU SEE NOTHING! WHY? BECAUSE WE ARE A MISTAKE!

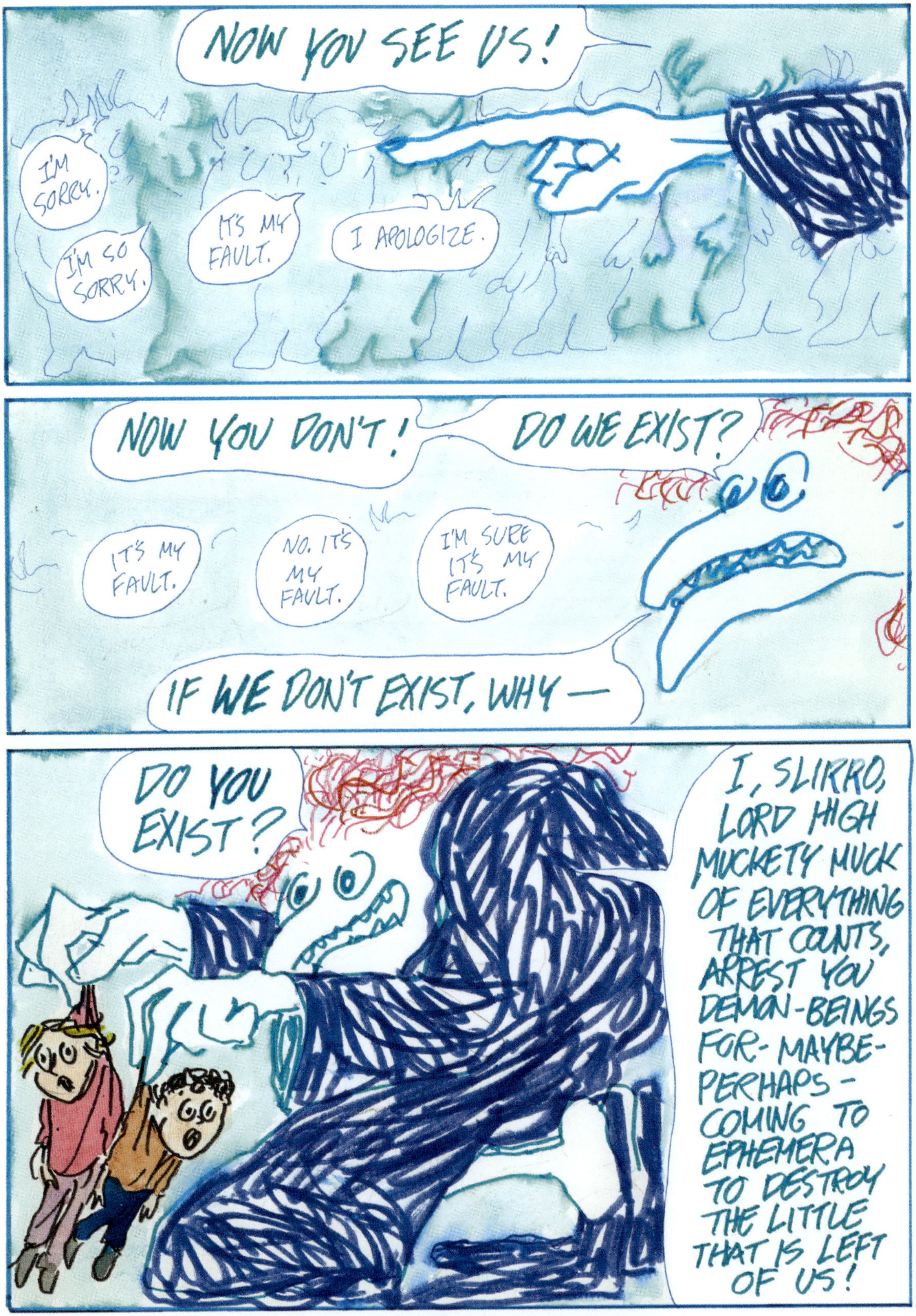
NOW YOU SEE US!
I'M SORRY.
I'M SO SORRY.
IT'S MY FAULT.
I APOLOGIZE.
NOW YOU DON'T!
DO WE EXIST?
IT'S MY FAULT.
NO. IT'S MY FAULT.
I'M SURE IT'S MY FAULT.
IF WE DON'T EXIST, WHY—
DO YOU EXIST?
I, SLIRRO, LORD HIGH MUCKETY MUCK OF EVERYTHING THAT COUNTS, ARREST YOU DEMON-BEINGS FOR-MAYBE-PERHAPS-COMING TO EPHEMERA TO DESTROY THE LITTLE THAT IS LEFT OF US!

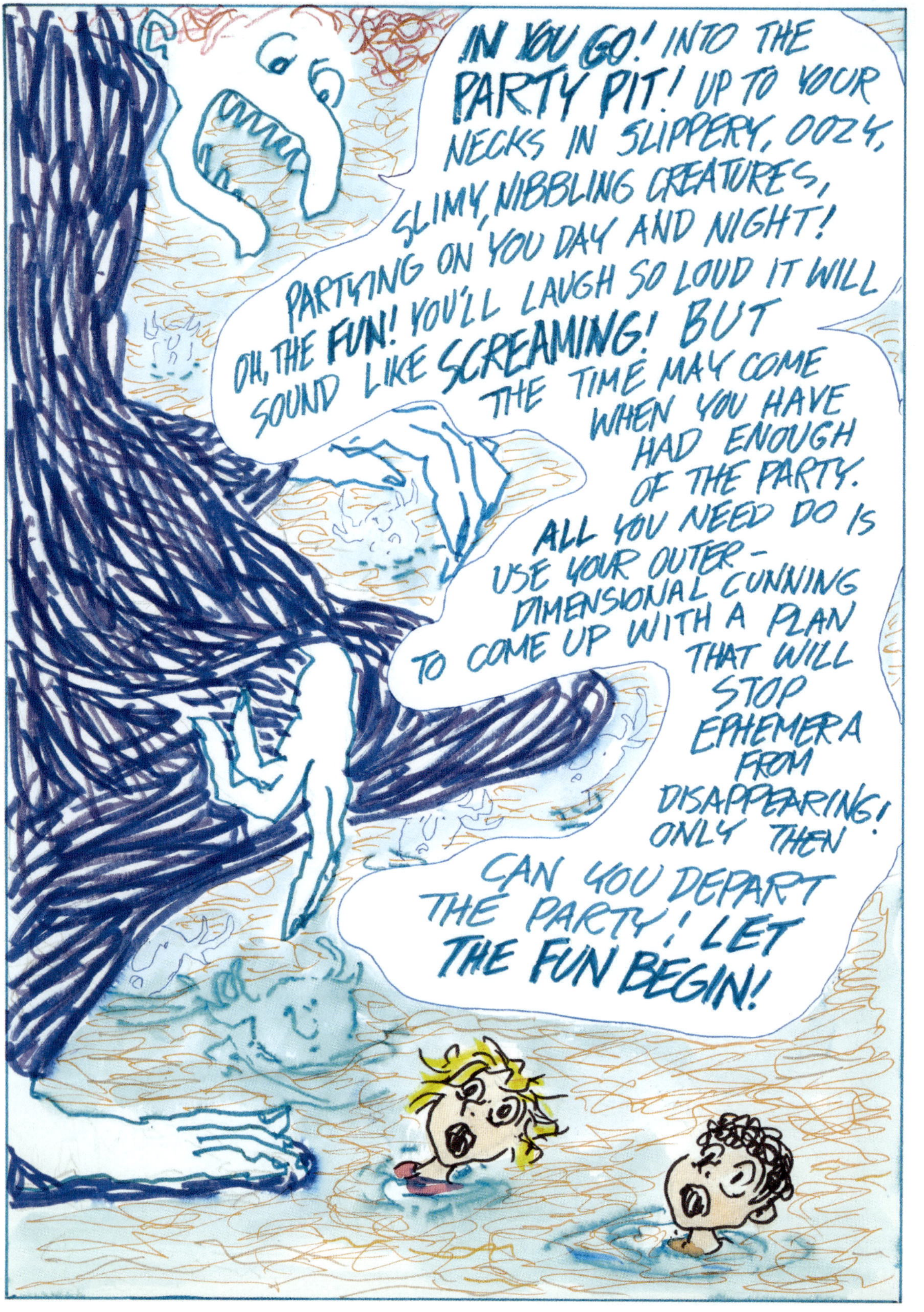
IN YOU GO! INTO THE PARTY PIT! UP TO YOUR NECKS IN SLIPPERY, OOZY, SLIMY, NIBBLING CREATURES, PARTYING ON YOU DAY AND NIGHT! OH, THE FUN! YOU'LL LAUGH SO LOUD IT WILL SOUND LIKE SCREAMING! BUT THE TIME MAY COME WHEN YOU HAVE HAD ENOUGH OF THE PARTY. ALL YOU NEED DO IS USE YOUR OUTER-DIMENSIONAL CUNNING TO COME UP WITH A PLAN THAT WILL STOP EPHEMERA FROM DISAPPEARING! ONLY THEN CAN YOU DEPART THE PARTY! LET THE FUN BEGIN!

CHAPTER 11 • BANKRUPT!?

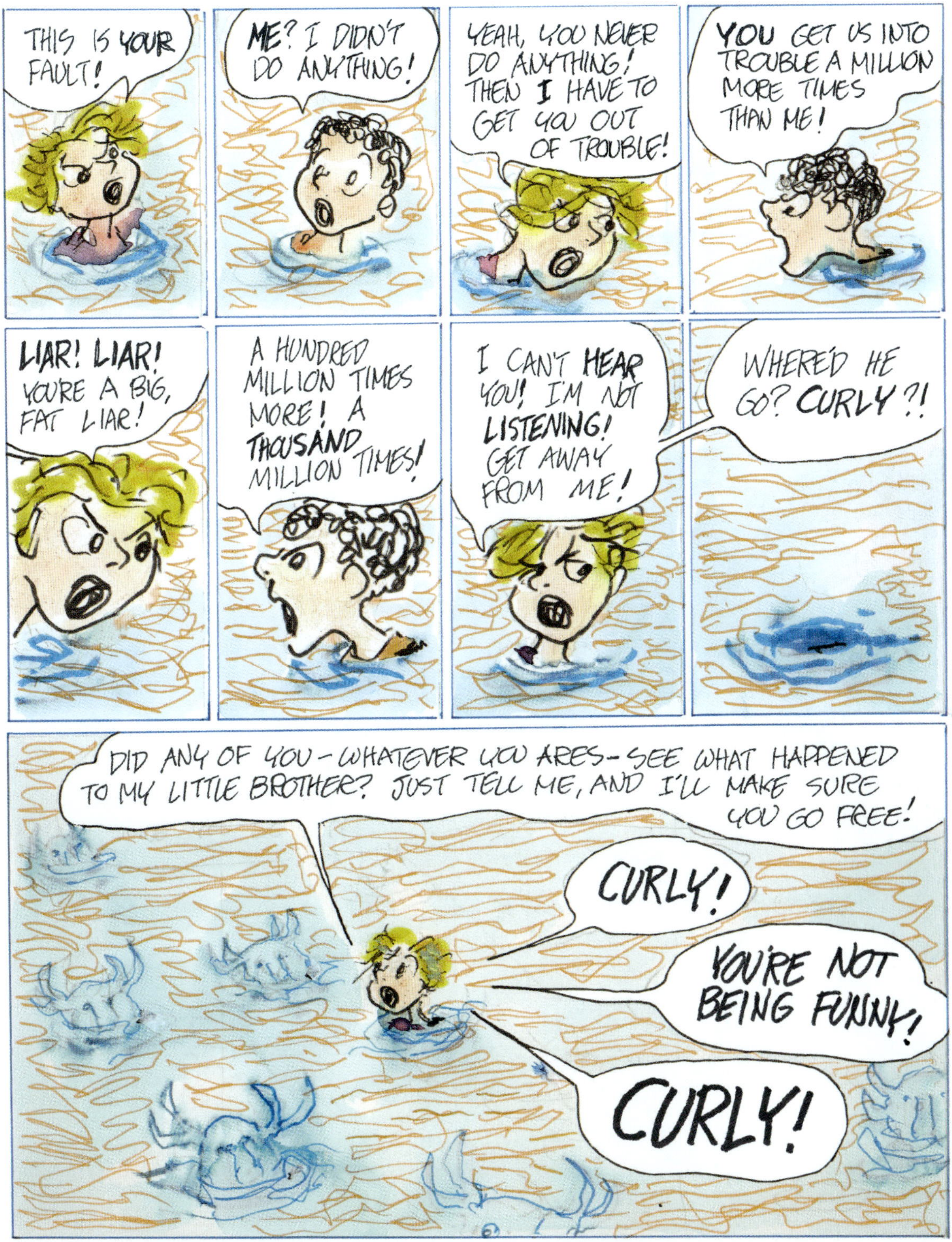
THIS IS **YOUR** FAULT!
ME? I DIDN'T DO ANYTHING!
YEAH, YOU NEVER DO ANYTHING! THEN **I** HAVE TO GET YOU OUT OF TROUBLE!
YOU GET US INTO TROUBLE A MILLION MORE TIMES THAN ME!
LIAR! LIAR! YOU'RE A BIG, FAT LIAR!
A HUNDRED MILLION TIMES MORE! A **THOUSAND** MILLION TIMES!
I CAN'T **HEAR** YOU! I'M NOT **LISTENING!** GET AWAY FROM ME!
WHERE'D HE GO? **CURLY**?!
DID ANY OF YOU—WHATEVER YOU ARES—SEE WHAT HAPPENED TO MY LITTLE BROTHER? JUST TELL ME, AND I'LL MAKE SURE YOU GO FREE!
CURLY!
YOU'RE NOT BEING FUNNY!
CURLY!

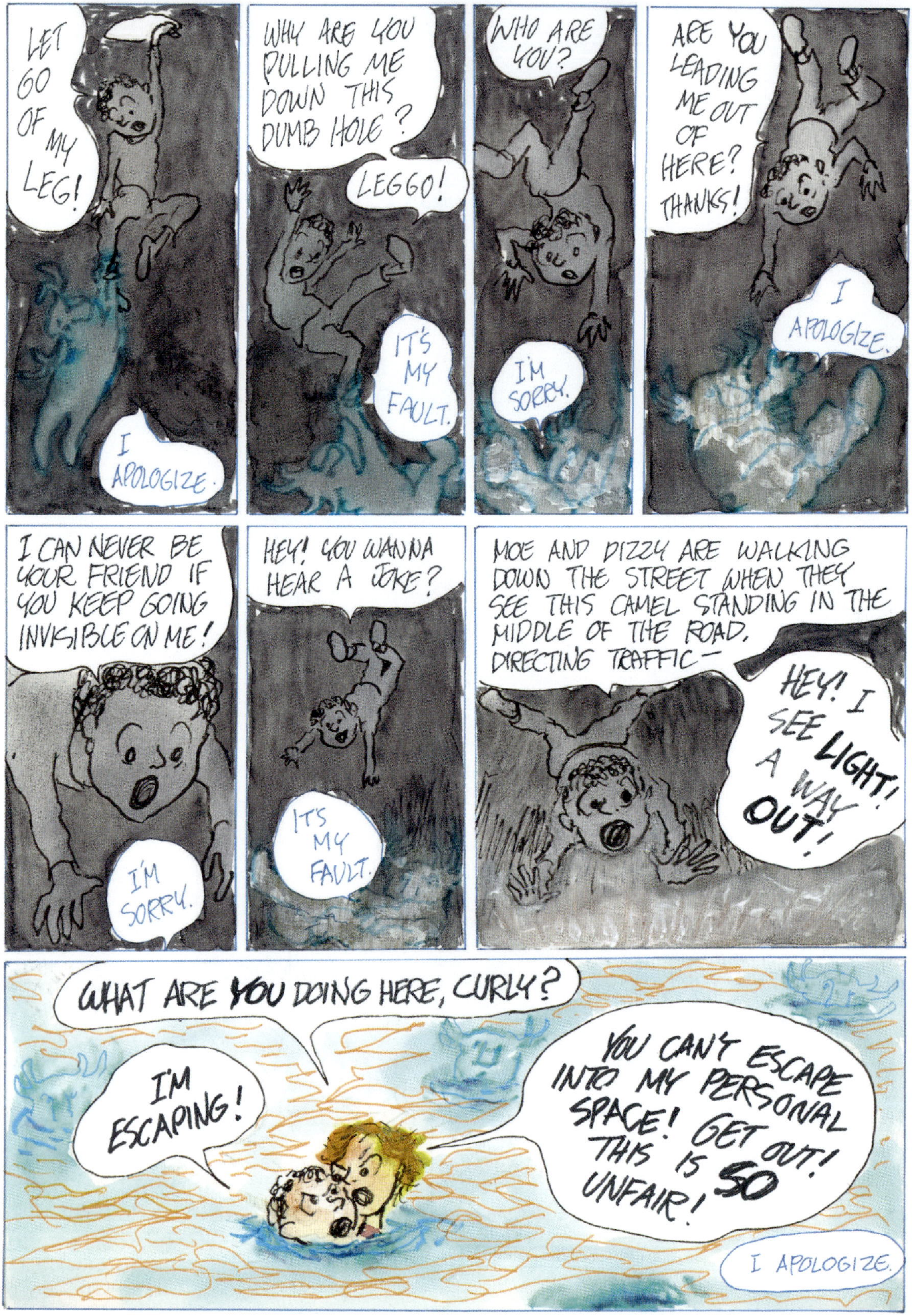
LET GO OF MY LEG!
I APOLOGIZE.
WHY ARE YOU PULLING ME DOWN THIS DUMB HOLE?
LEGGO!
IT'S MY FAULT.
WHO ARE YOU?
I'M SORRY.
ARE YOU LEADING ME OUT OF HERE? THANKS!
I APOLOGIZE.
I CAN NEVER BE YOUR FRIEND IF YOU KEEP GOING INVISIBLE ON ME!
I'M SORRY.
HEY! YOU WANNA HEAR A JOKE?
IT'S MY FAULT.
MOE AND DIZZY ARE WALKING DOWN THE STREET WHEN THEY SEE THIS CAMEL STANDING IN THE MIDDLE OF THE ROAD, DIRECTING TRAFFIC—
HEY! I SEE LIGHT! A WAY OUT!
WHAT ARE YOU DOING HERE, CURLY?
I'M ESCAPING!
YOU CAN'T ESCAPE INTO MY PERSONAL SPACE! GET OUT! THIS IS SO UNFAIR!
I APOLOGIZE.

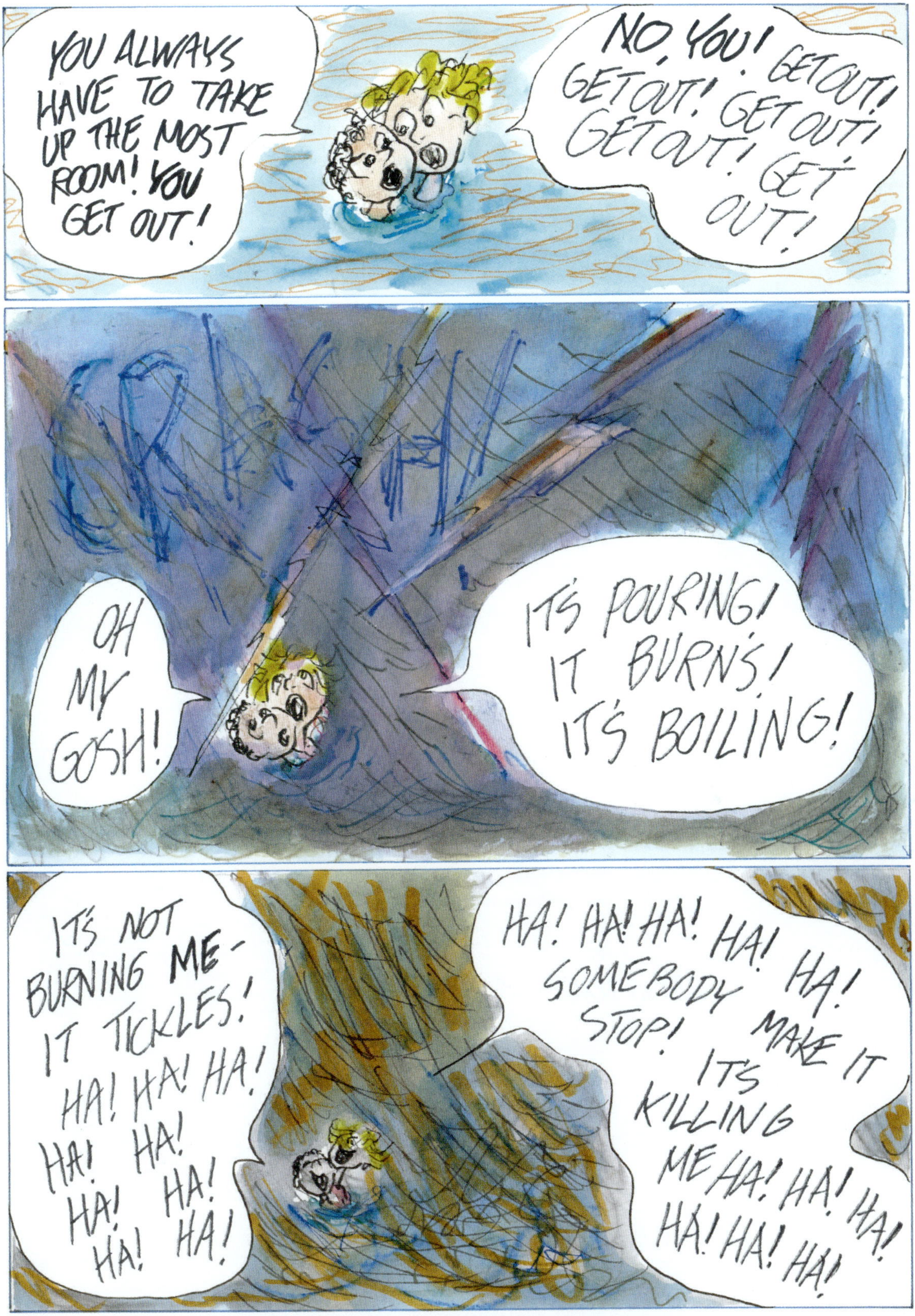
YOU ALWAYS HAVE TO TAKE UP THE MOST ROOM! YOU GET OUT!
NO, YOU! GET OUT! GET OUT! GET OUT! GET OUT! GET OUT!
CRASH!
OH MY GOSH!
IT'S POURING! IT BURNS! IT'S BOILING!
IT'S NOT BURNING ME- IT TICKLES! HA! HA! HA! HA! HA! HA! HA! HA! HA!
HA! HA! HA! HA! HA! SOMEBODY STOP! MAKE IT IT'S KILLING ME HA! HA! HA! HA! HA! HA! HA!

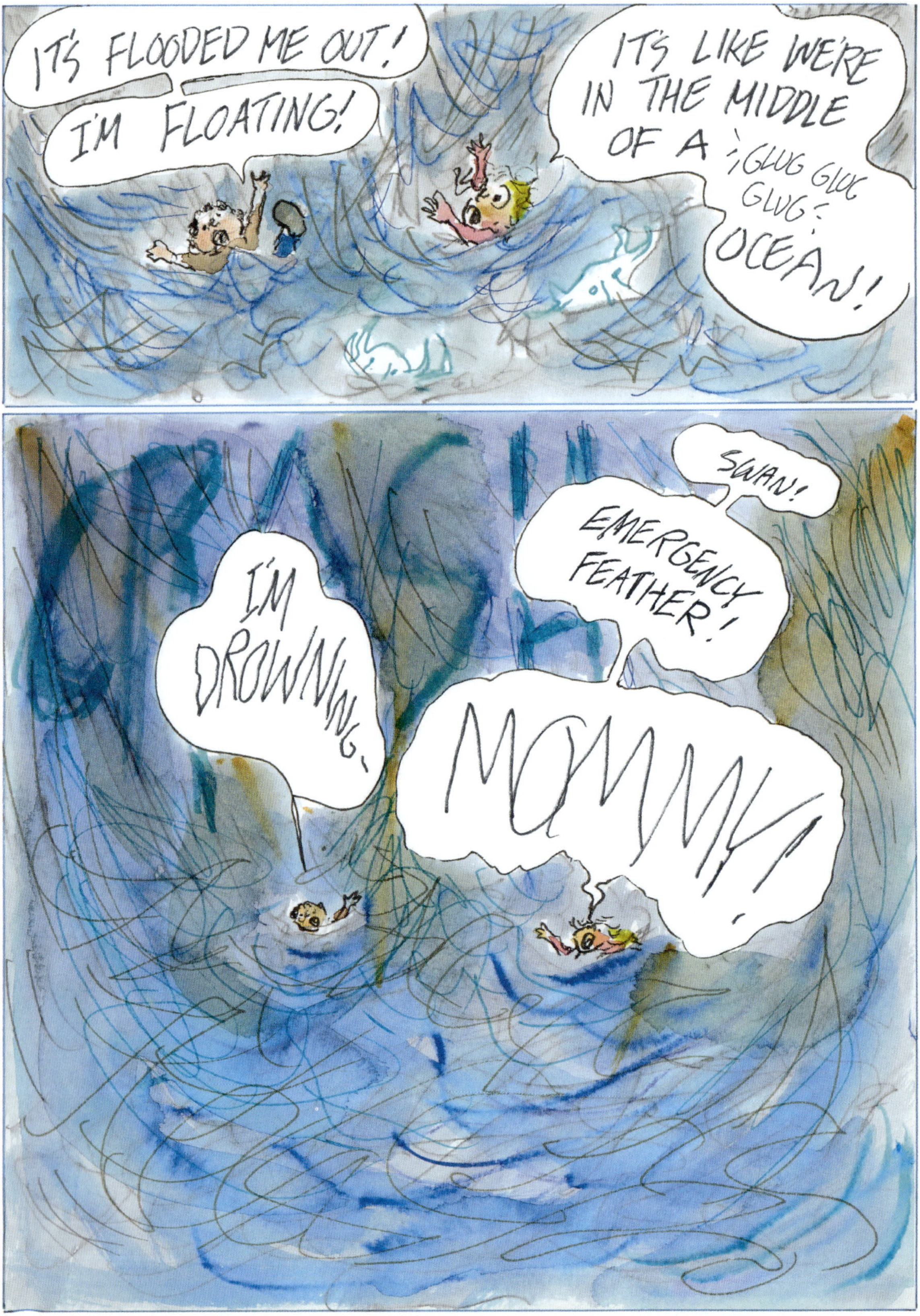
IT'S FLOODED ME OUT!
I'M FLOATING!
IT'S LIKE WE'RE IN THE MIDDLE OF A ¡GLUG GLUG GLUG! OCEAN!
I'M DROWNING.
MOMMY!
EMERGENCY FEATHER!
SWAN!

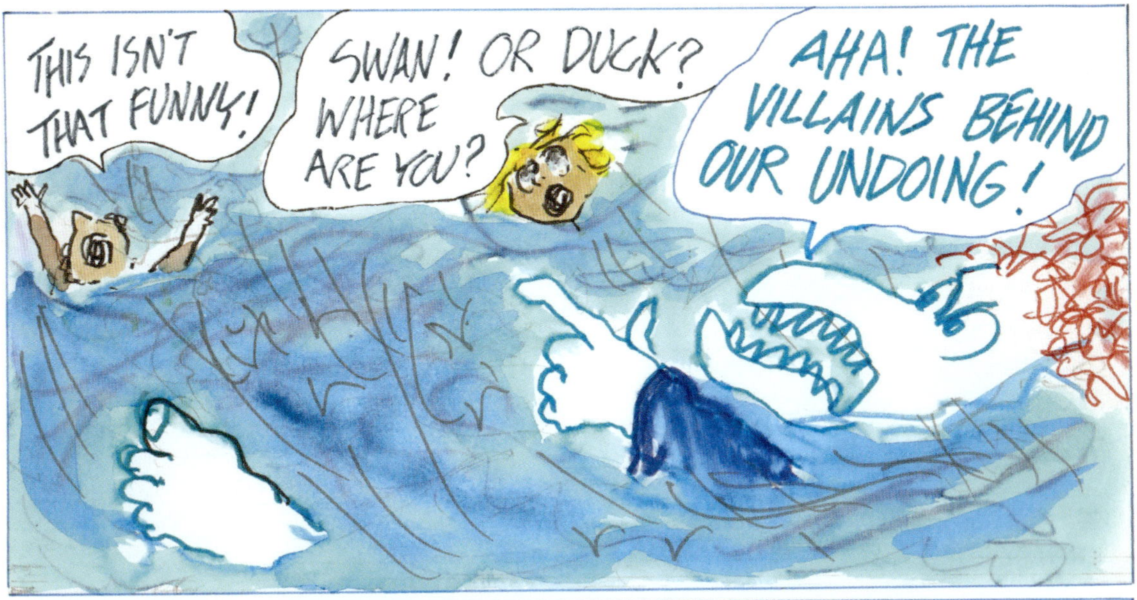
THIS ISN'T THAT FUNNY!
SWAN! OR DUCK? WHERE ARE YOU?
AHA! THE VILLAINS BEHIND OUR UNDOING!

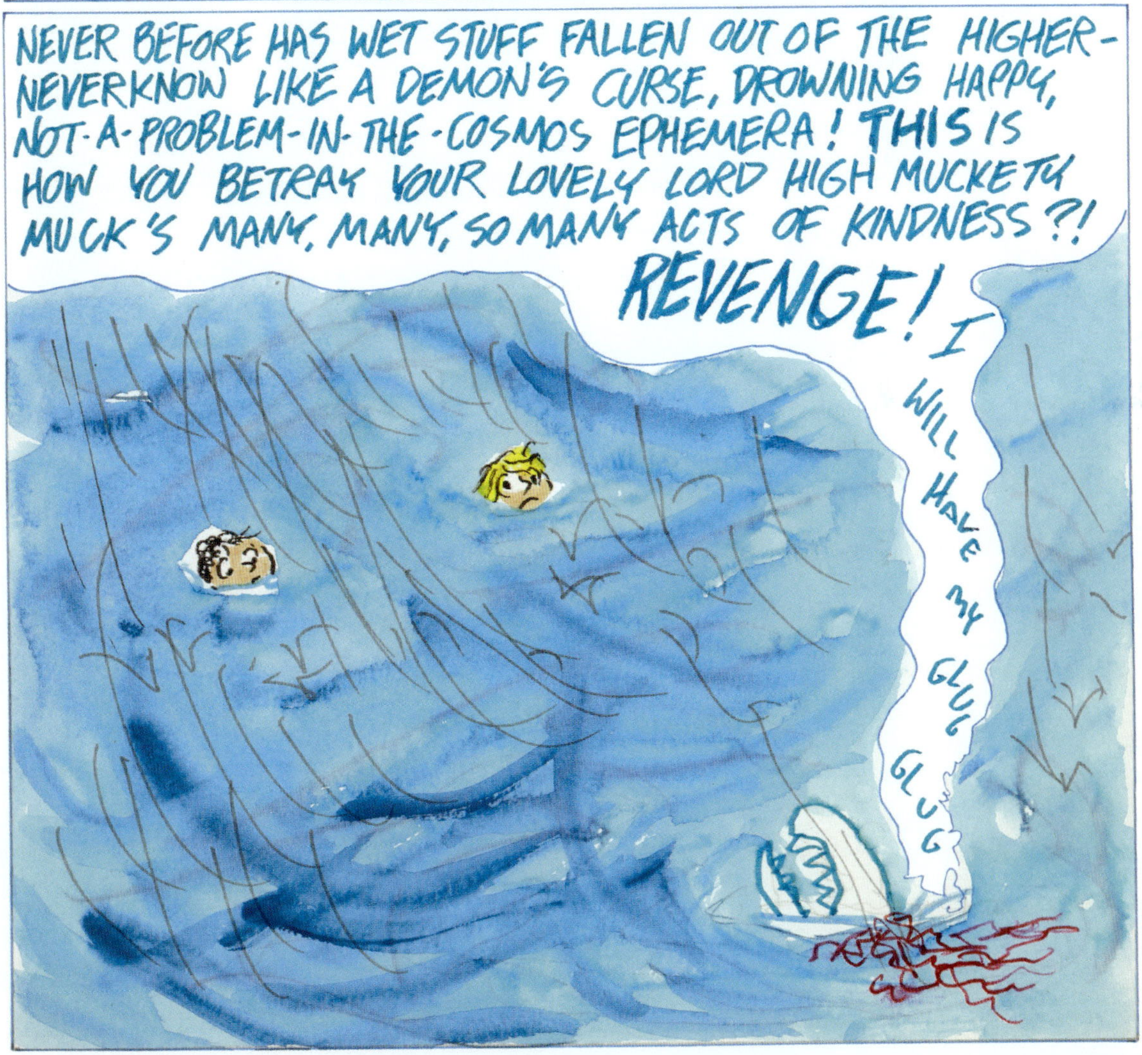
NEVER BEFORE HAS WET STUFF FALLEN OUT OF THE HIGHER-NEVERKNOW LIKE A DEMON'S CURSE, DROWNING HAPPY, NOT-A-PROBLEM-IN-THE-COSMOS EPHEMERA! THIS IS HOW YOU BETRAY YOUR LOVELY LORD HIGH MUCKETY MUCK'S MANY, MANY, SO MANY ACTS OF KINDNESS?!
REVENGE!
I WILL HAVE MY GLUG GLUG GLUG

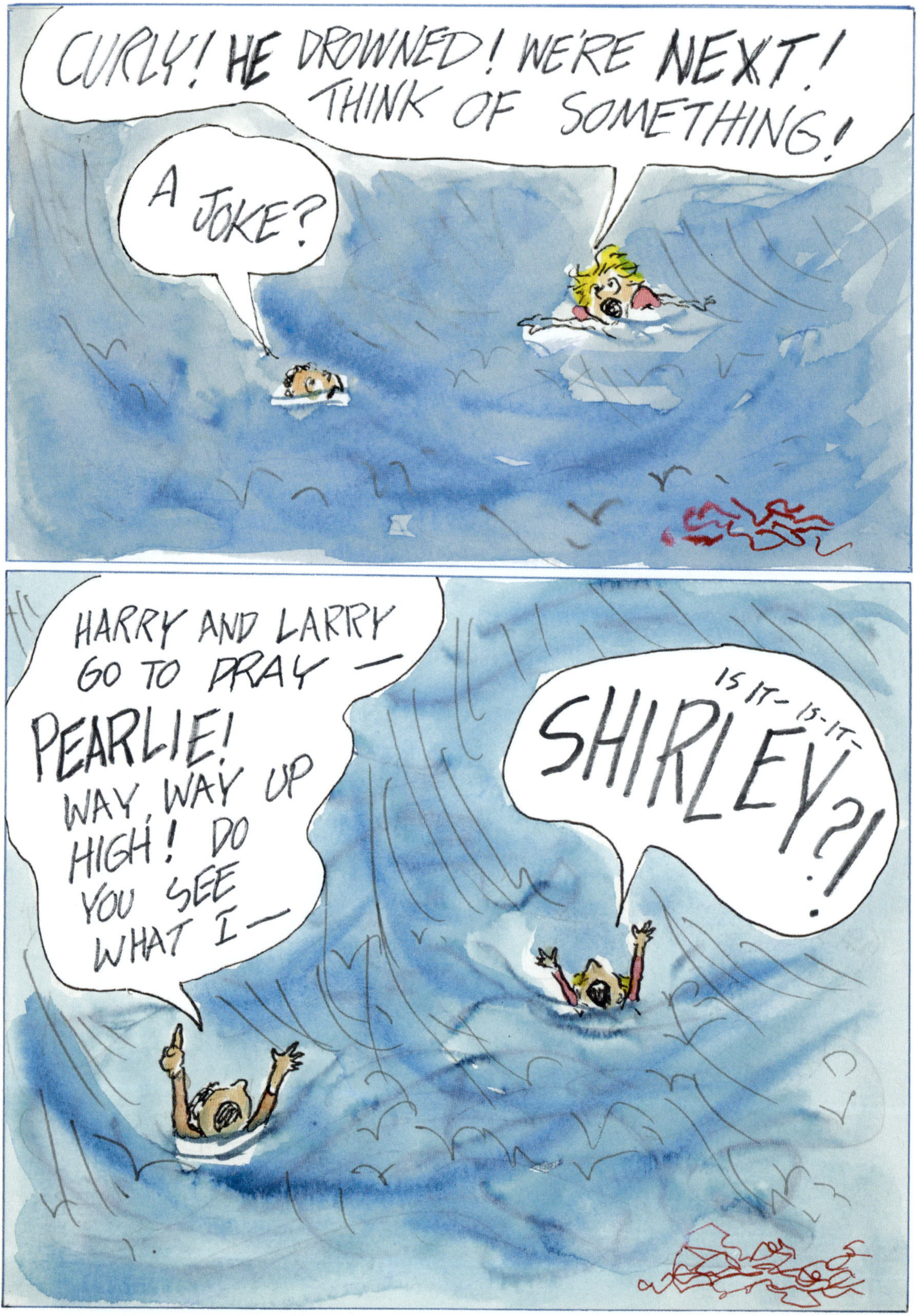
CURLY! HE DROWNED! WE'RE NEXT! THINK OF SOMETHING!
A JOKE?
HARRY AND LARRY GO TO PRAY — PEARLIE! WAY, WAY UP HIGH! DO YOU SEE WHAT I—
IS IT— IS IT— SHIRLEY?!

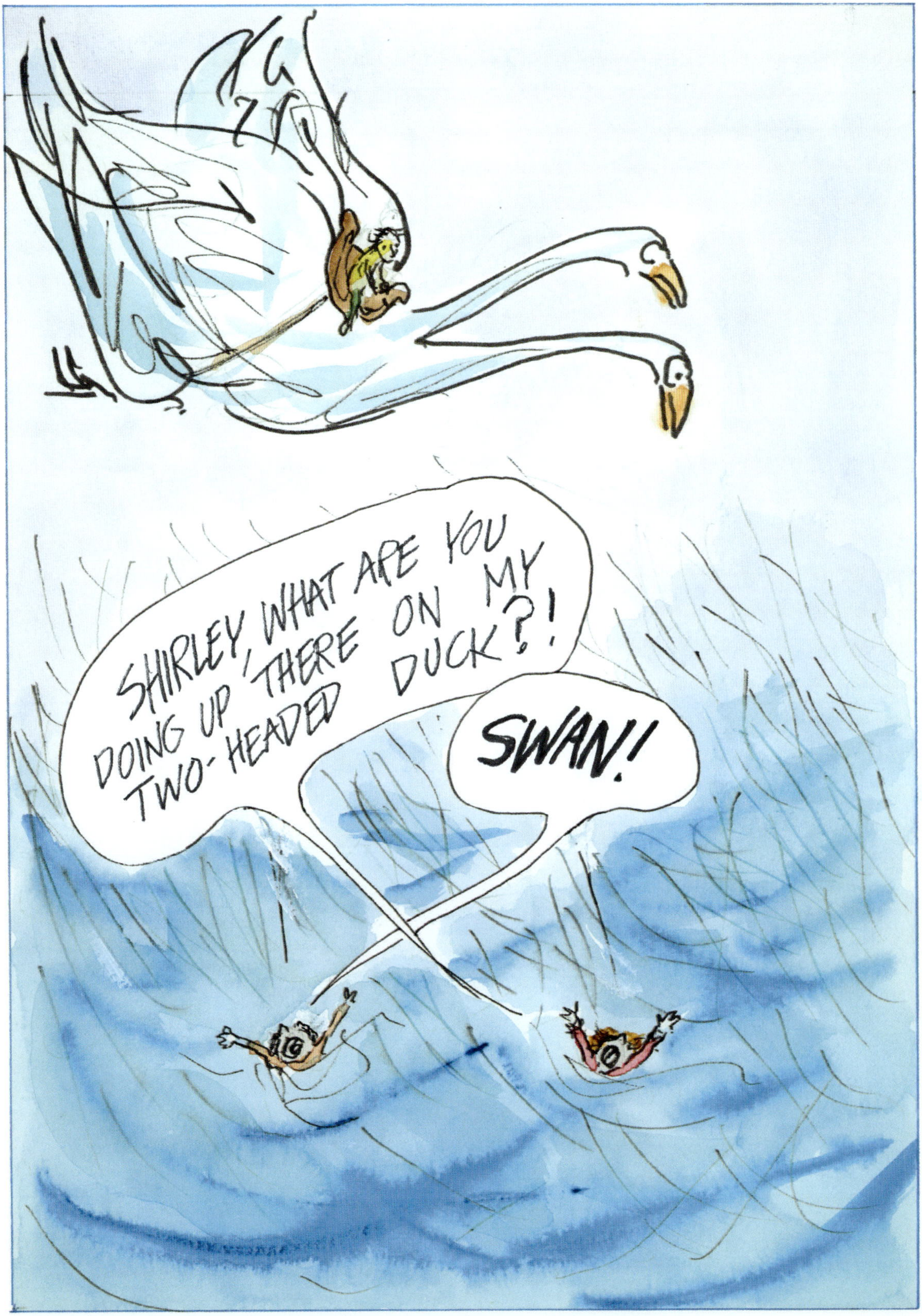
SHIRLEY, WHAT ARE YOU DOING UP THERE ON MY TWO-HEADED DUCK?!
SWAN!

CHAPTER 12 • AMAZING GRAPES

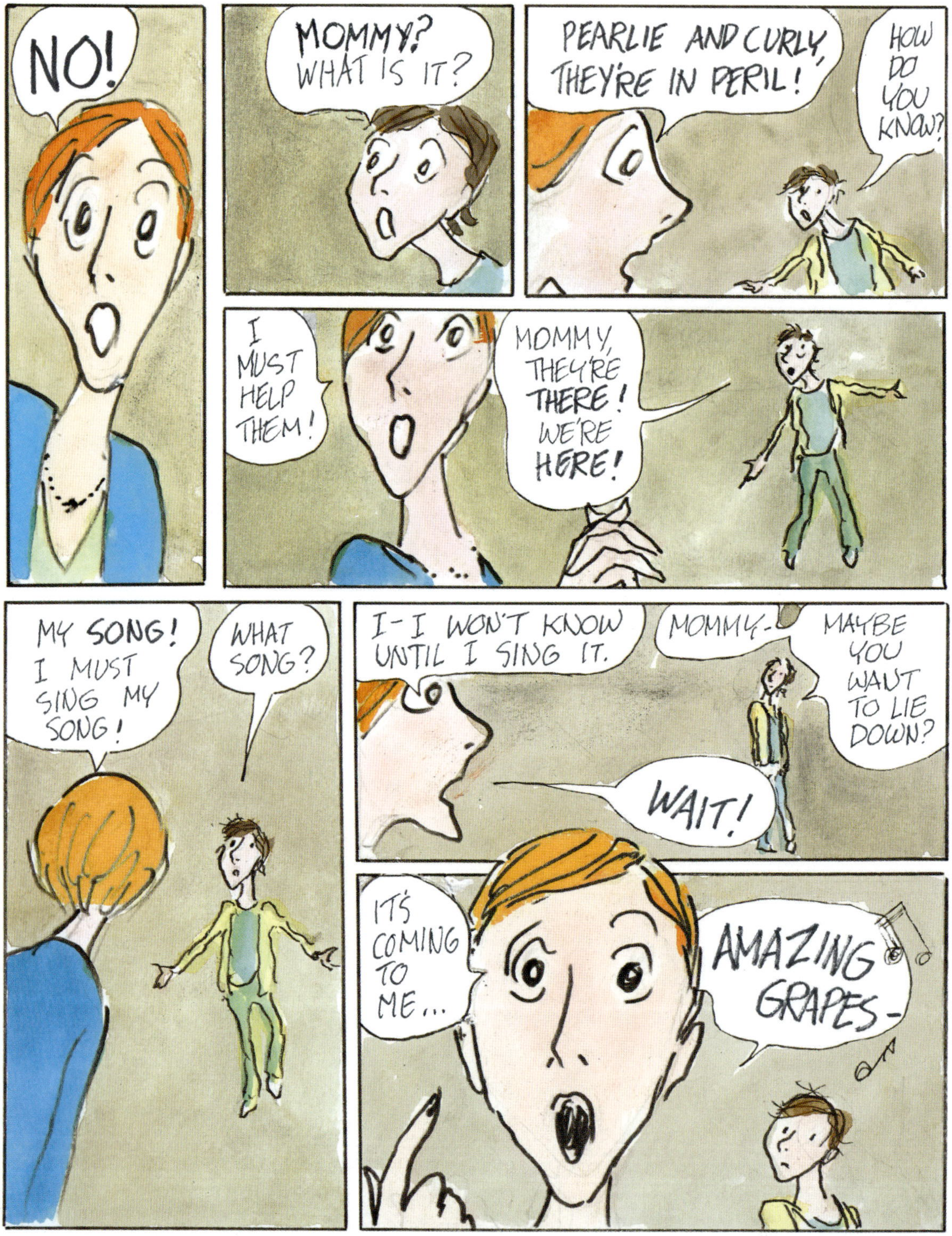

NO!
MOMMY? WHAT IS IT?
PEARLIE AND CURLY, THEY'RE IN PERIL!
HOW DO YOU KNOW?
I MUST HELP THEM!
MOMMY, THEY'RE THERE! WE'RE HERE!
MY SONG! I MUST SING MY SONG!
WHAT SONG?
I-I WON'T KNOW UNTIL I SING IT.
MOMMY-
MAYBE YOU WANT TO LIE DOWN?
WAIT!
IT'S COMING TO ME...
AMAZING GRAPES-

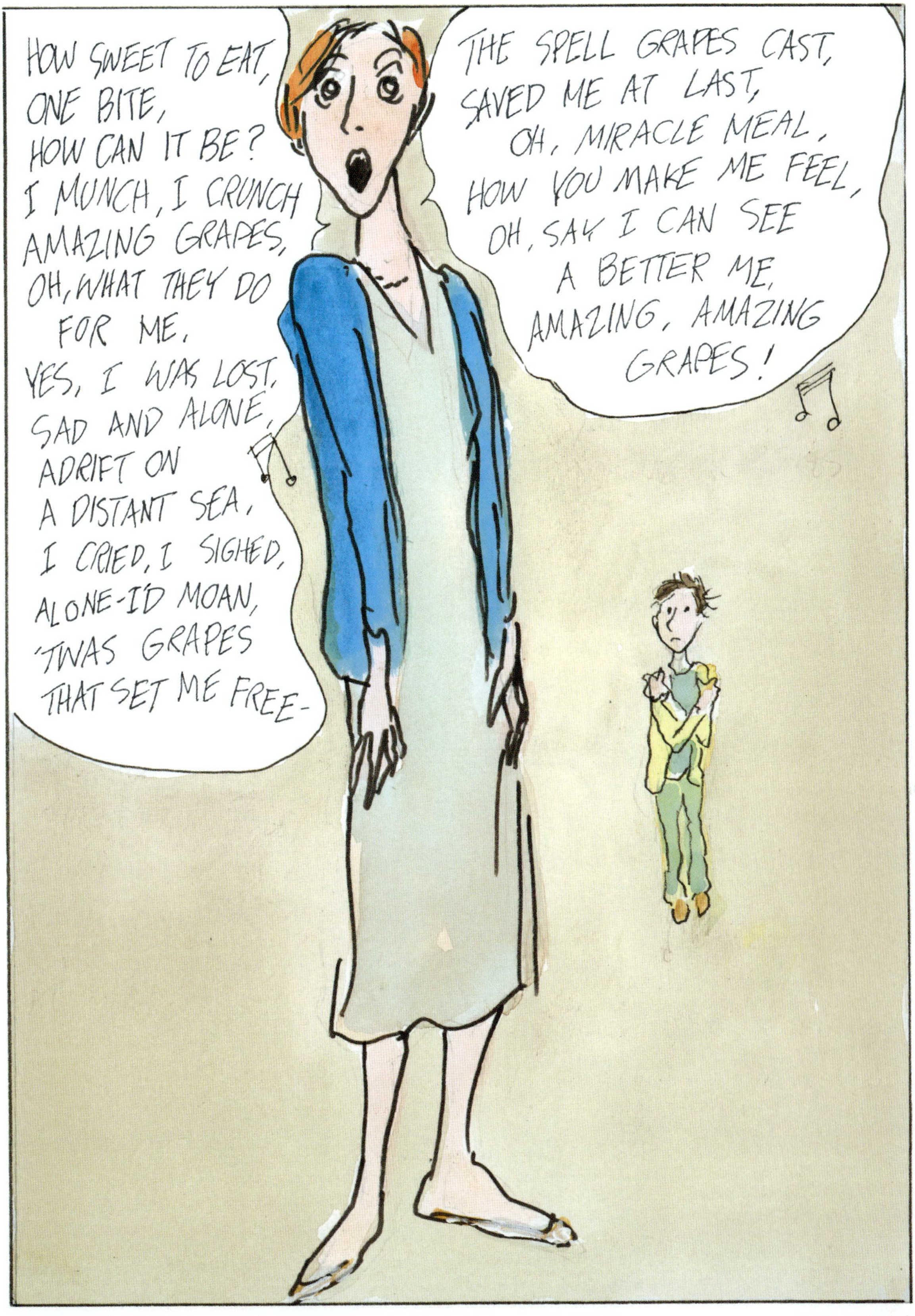
HOW SWEET TO EAT, ONE BITE, HOW CAN IT BE? I MUNCH, I CRUNCH AMAZING GRAPES, OH, WHAT THEY DO FOR ME. YES, I WAS LOST, SAD AND ALONE, ADRIFT ON A DISTANT SEA, I CRIED, I SIGHED, ALONE-I'D MOAN, 'TWAS GRAPES THAT SET ME FREE-
THE SPELL GRAPES CAST, SAVED ME AT LAST, OH, MIRACLE MEAL, HOW YOU MAKE ME FEEL, OH, SAY I CAN SEE A BETTER ME, AMAZING, AMAZING GRAPES!

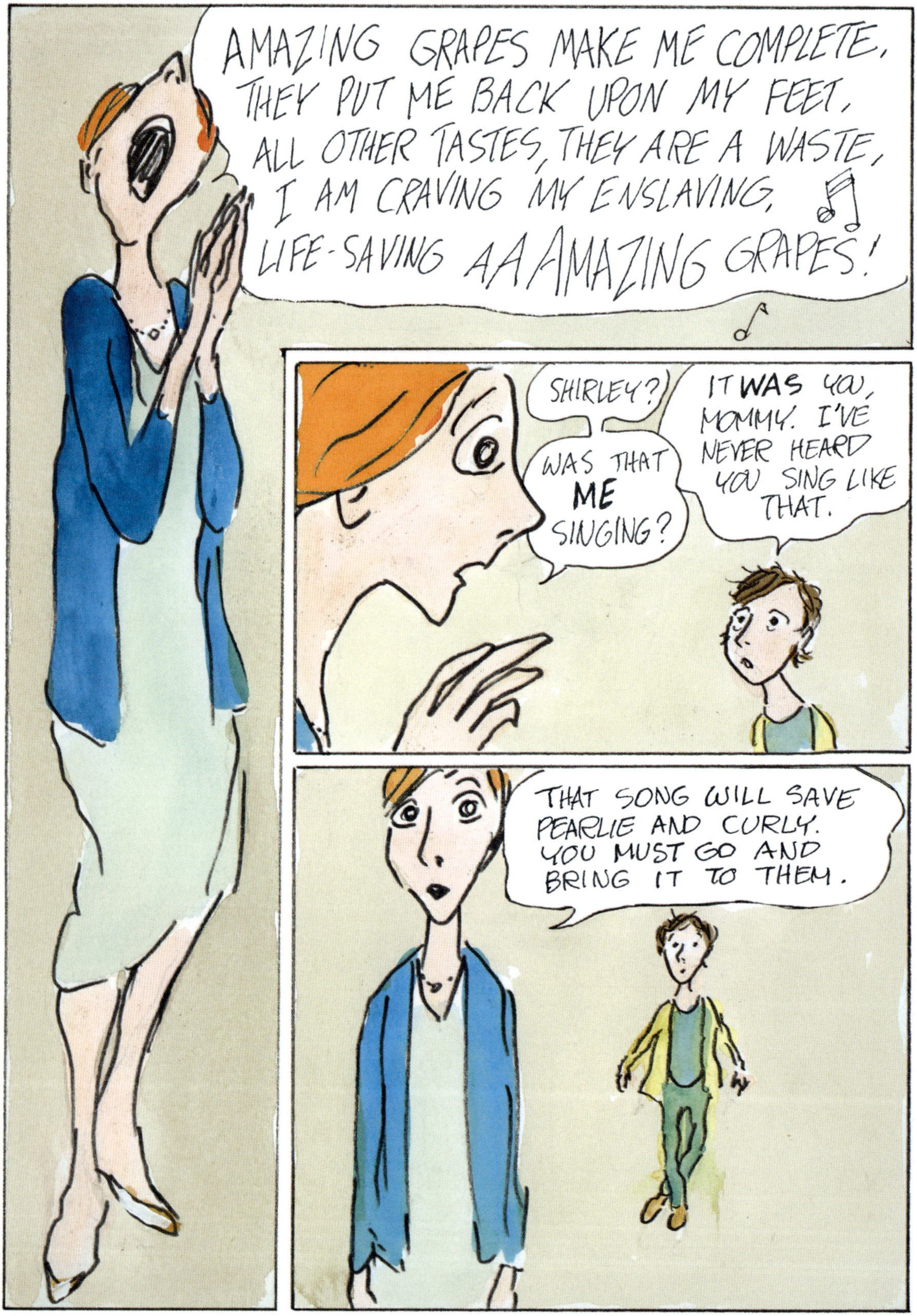
AMAZING GRAPES MAKE ME COMPLETE, THEY PUT ME BACK UPON MY FEET, ALL OTHER TASTES, THEY ARE A WASTE, I AM CRAVING MY ENSLAVING, LIFE-SAVING AAAMAZING GRAPES!
SHIRLEY?
WAS THAT ME SINGING?
IT WAS YOU, MOMMY. I'VE NEVER HEARD YOU SING LIKE THAT.
THAT SONG WILL SAVE PEARLIE AND CURLY. YOU MUST GO AND BRING IT TO THEM.

CHAPTER 13 • THE RESENTFUL RESCUE

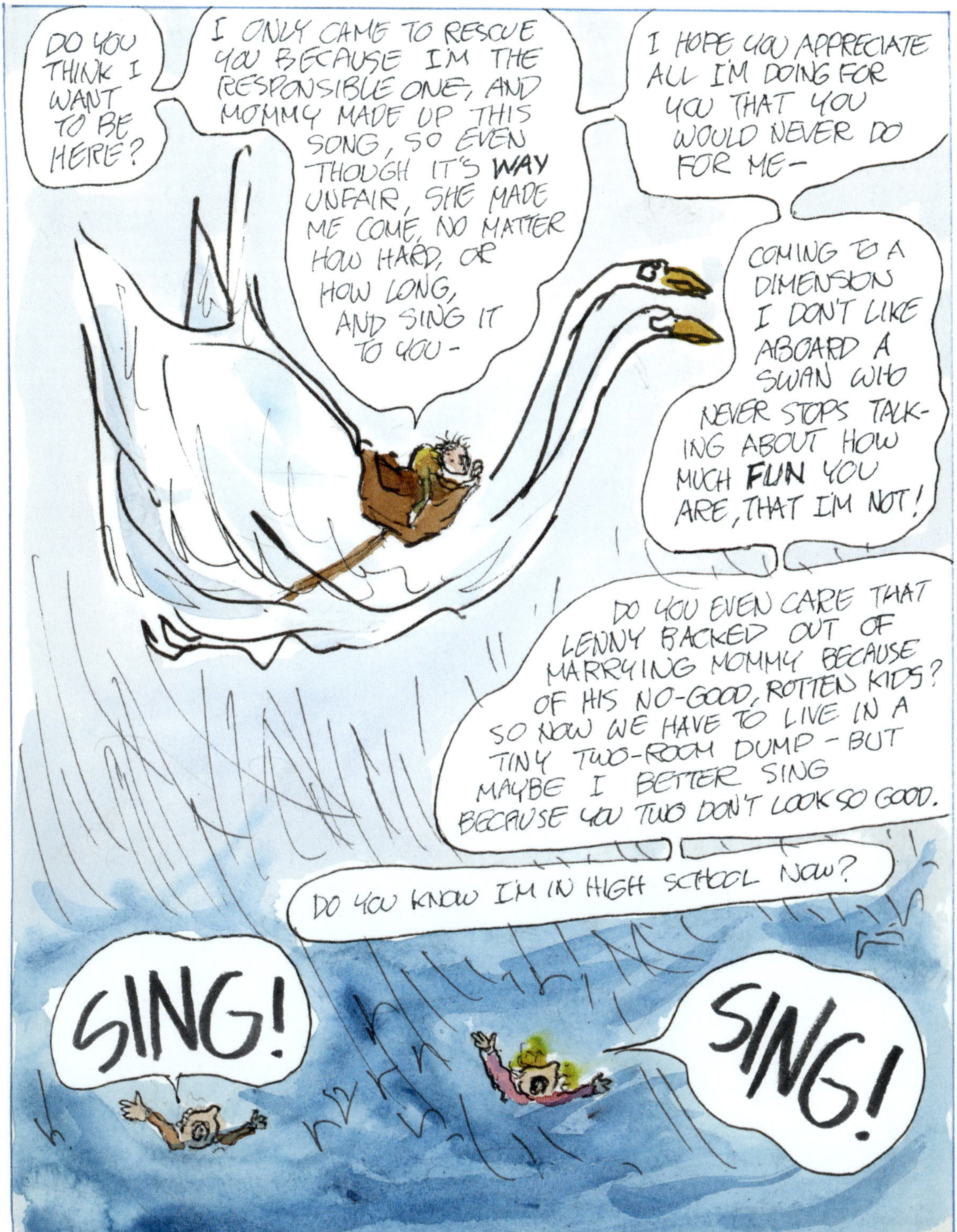

DO YOU THINK I WANT TO BE HERE?
I ONLY CAME TO RESCUE YOU BECAUSE I'M THE RESPONSIBLE ONE, AND MOMMY MADE UP THIS SONG, SO EVEN THOUGH IT'S **WAY** UNFAIR, SHE MADE ME COME, NO MATTER HOW HARD, OR HOW LONG, AND SING IT TO YOU-
I HOPE YOU APPRECIATE ALL I'M DOING FOR YOU THAT YOU WOULD NEVER DO FOR ME-
COMING TO A DIMENSION I DON'T LIKE ABOARD A SWAN WHO NEVER STOPS TALKING ABOUT HOW MUCH **FUN** YOU ARE, THAT I'M NOT!
DO YOU EVEN CARE THAT LENNY BACKED OUT OF MARRYING MOMMY BECAUSE OF HIS NO-GOOD, ROTTEN KIDS? SO NOW WE HAVE TO LIVE IN A TINY TWO-ROOM DUMP - BUT MAYBE I BETTER SING BECAUSE YOU TWO DON'T LOOK SO GOOD.
DO YOU KNOW I'M IN HIGH SCHOOL NOW?
SING!
SING!

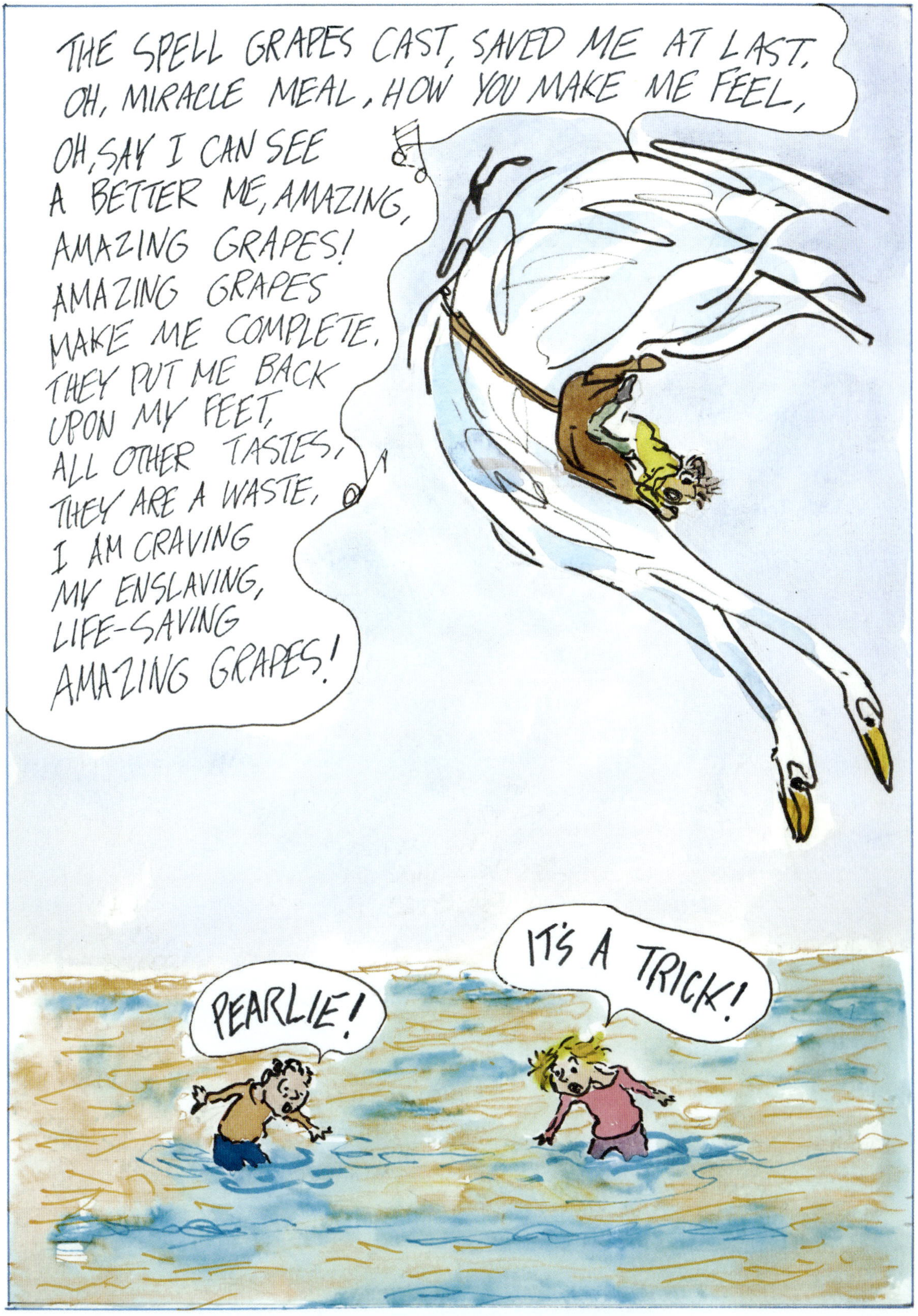
THE SPELL GRAPES CAST, SAVED ME AT LAST, OH, MIRACLE MEAL, HOW YOU MAKE ME FEEL, OH, SAY I CAN SEE A BETTER ME, AMAZING, AMAZING GRAPES! AMAZING GRAPES MAKE ME COMPLETE. THEY PUT ME BACK UPON MY FEET, ALL OTHER TASTES, THEY ARE A WASTE, I AM CRAVING MY ENSLAVING, LIFE-SAVING AMAZING GRAPES!
PEARLIE!
IT'S A TRICK!

CHAPTER 14 • GOODBYE HELLO

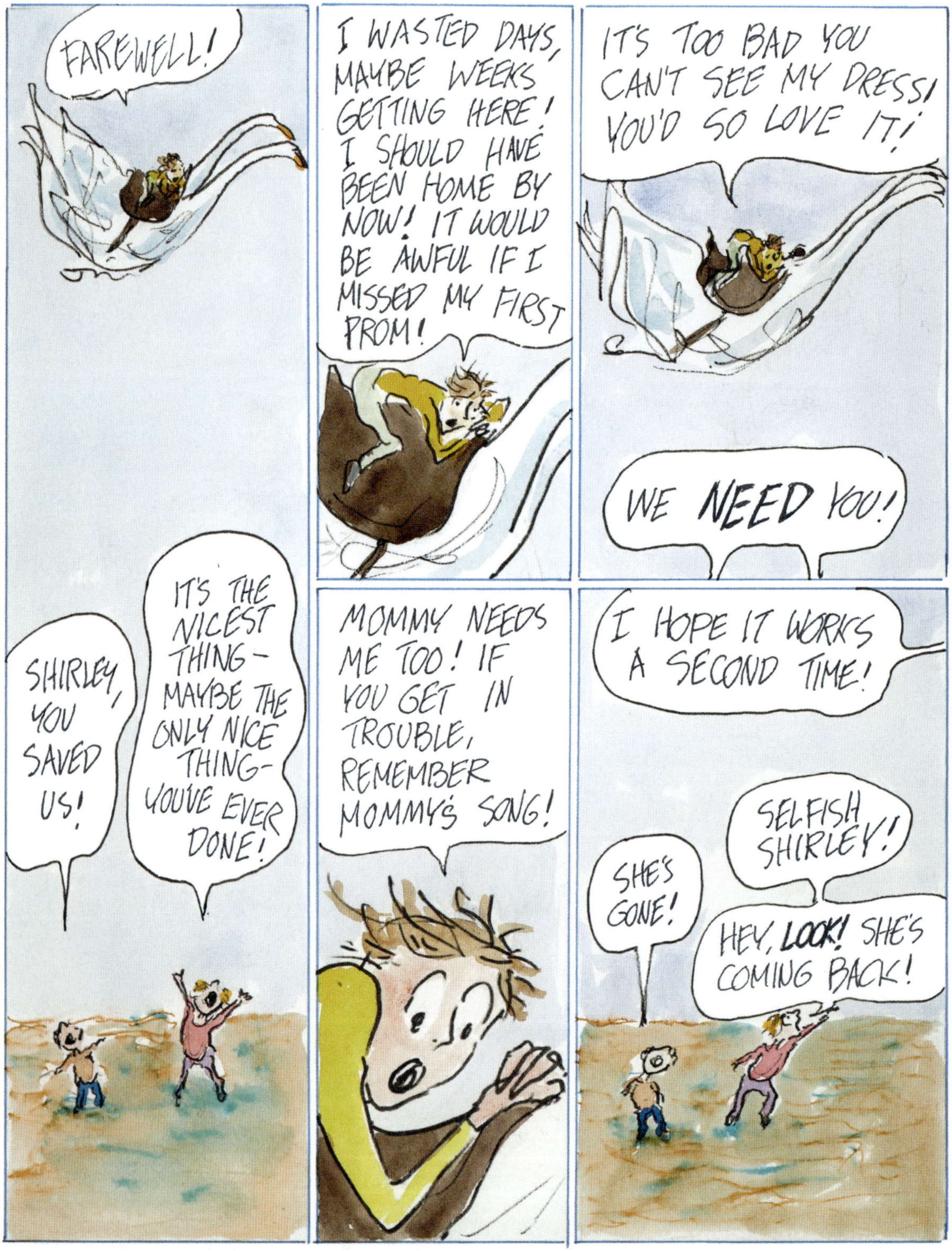
FAREWELL!
SHIRLEY, YOU SAVED US!
IT'S THE NICEST THING— MAYBE THE ONLY NICE THING— YOU'VE EVER DONE!
I WASTED DAYS, MAYBE WEEKS GETTING HERE! I SHOULD HAVE BEEN HOME BY NOW! IT WOULD BE AWFUL IF I MISSED MY FIRST PROM!
IT'S TOO BAD YOU CAN'T SEE MY DRESS! YOU'D SO LOVE IT!
WE NEED YOU!
MOMMY NEEDS ME TOO! IF YOU GET IN TROUBLE, REMEMBER MOMMY'S SONG!
I HOPE IT WORKS A SECOND TIME!
SHE'S GONE!
SELFISH SHIRLEY!
HEY, LOOK! SHE'S COMING BACK!

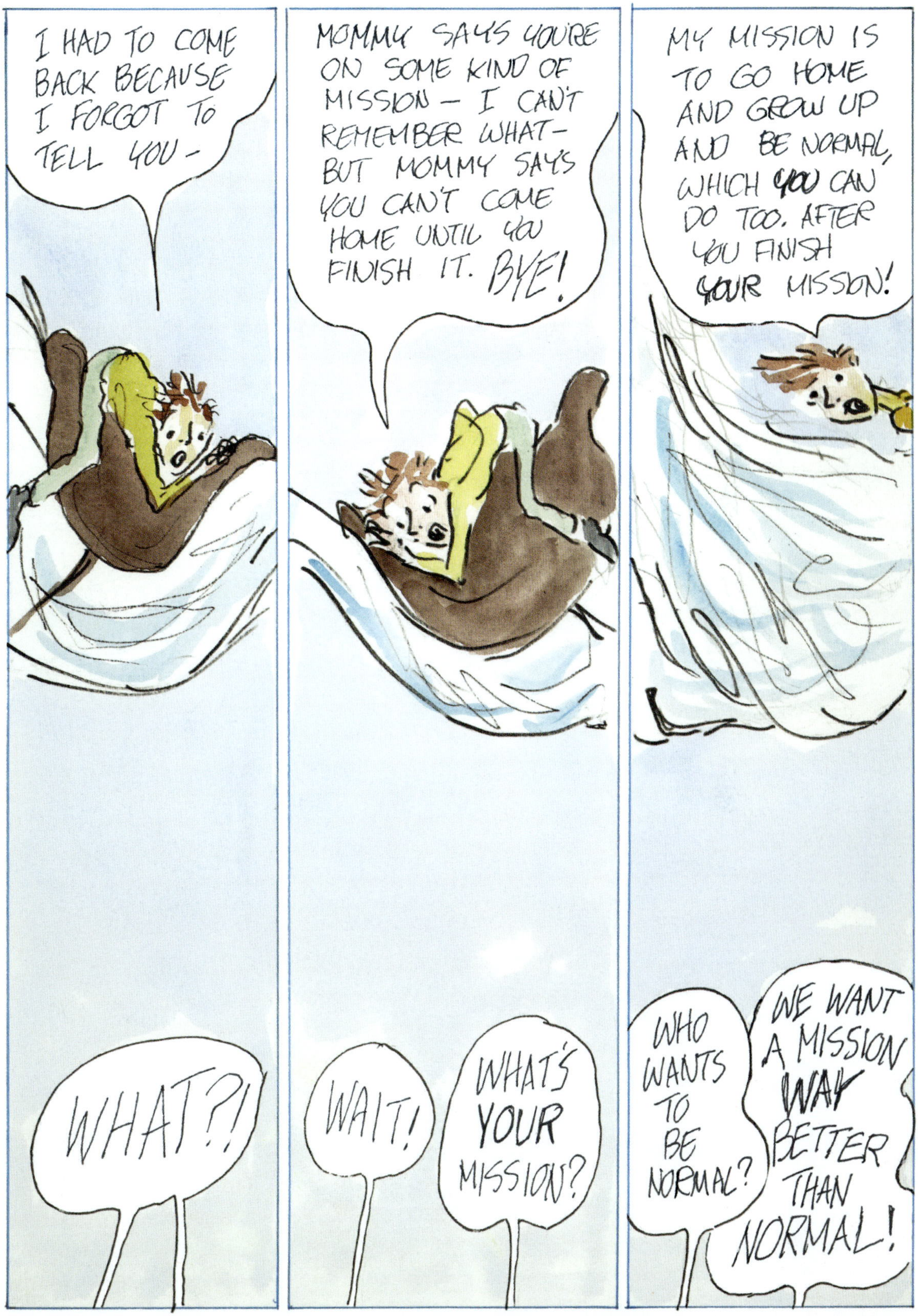
I HAD TO COME BACK BECAUSE I FORGOT TO TELL YOU-
WHAT?!
MOMMY SAYS YOU'RE ON SOME KIND OF MISSION – I CAN'T REMEMBER WHAT- BUT MOMMY SAYS YOU CAN'T COME HOME UNTIL YOU FINISH IT. BYE!
WAIT!
WHAT'S YOUR MISSION?
MY MISSION IS TO GO HOME AND GROW UP AND BE NORMAL, WHICH YOU CAN DO TOO. AFTER YOU FINISH YOUR MISSION!
WHO WANTS TO BE NORMAL?
WE WANT A MISSION WAY BETTER THAN NORMAL!

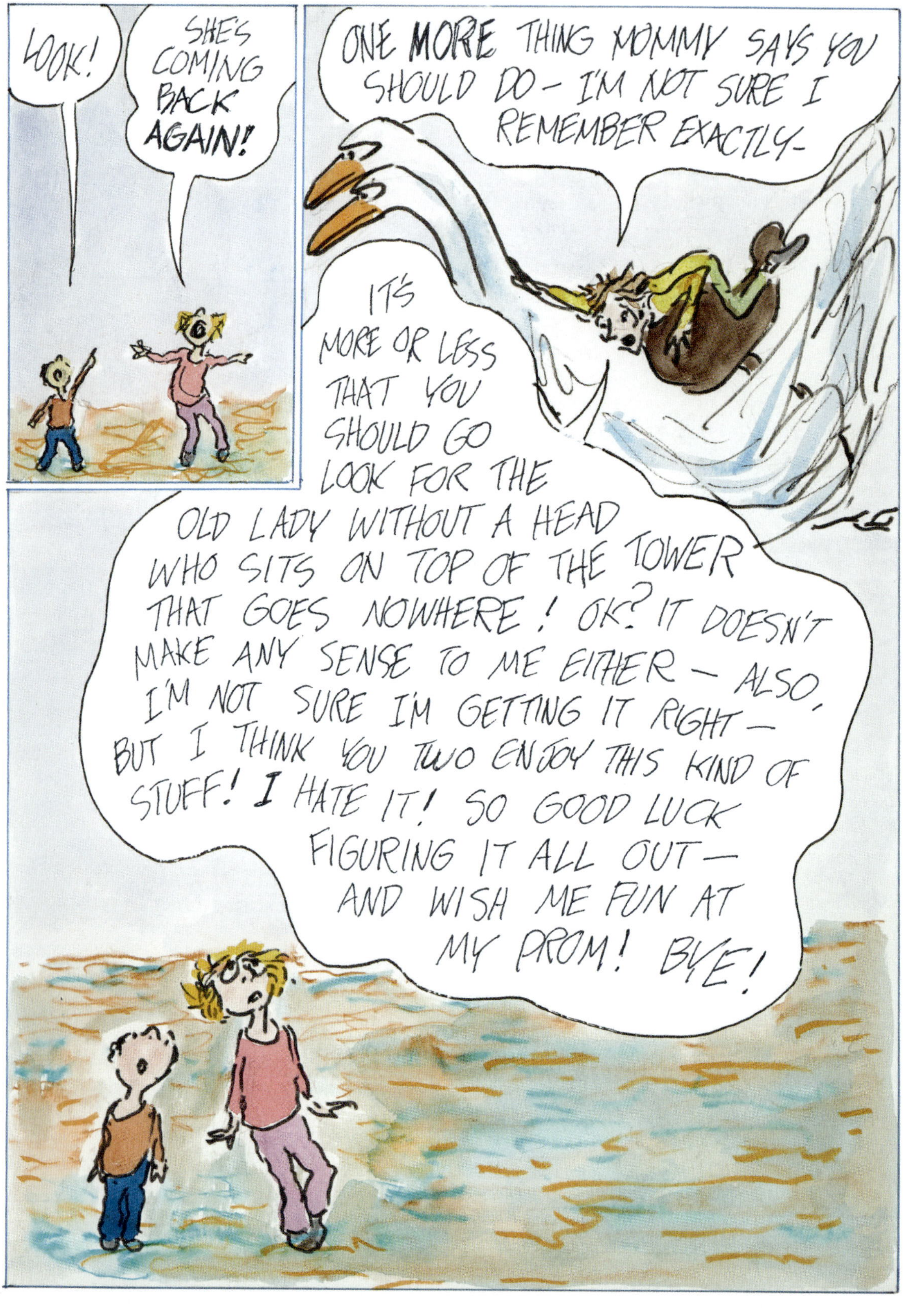
LOOK!
SHE'S COMING BACK AGAIN!
ONE MORE THING MOMMY SAYS YOU SHOULD DO— I'M NOT SURE I REMEMBER EXACTLY—
IT'S MORE OR LESS THAT YOU SHOULD GO LOOK FOR THE OLD LADY WITHOUT A HEAD WHO SITS ON TOP OF THE TOWER THAT GOES NOWHERE! OK? IT DOESN'T MAKE ANY SENSE TO ME EITHER— ALSO, I'M NOT SURE I'M GETTING IT RIGHT— BUT I THINK YOU TWO ENJOY THIS KIND OF STUFF! I HATE IT! SO GOOD LUCK FIGURING IT ALL OUT— AND WISH ME FUN AT MY PROM! BYE!

CHAPTER 15 • MA-MA, DA-DA!

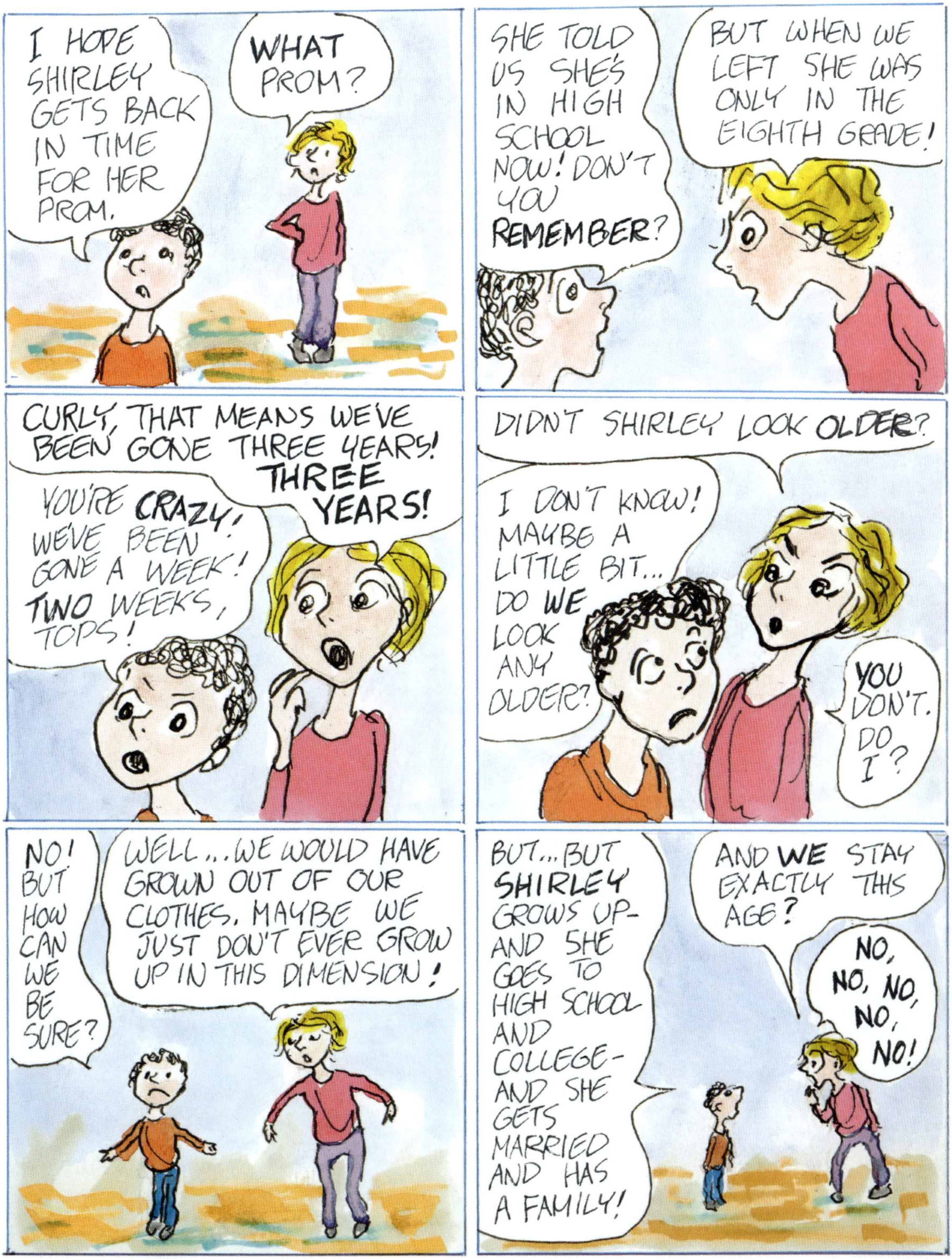

I HOPE SHIRLEY GETS BACK IN TIME FOR HER PROM.
WHAT PROM?
SHE TOLD US SHE'S IN HIGH SCHOOL NOW! DON'T YOU REMEMBER?
BUT WHEN WE LEFT SHE WAS ONLY IN THE EIGHTH GRADE!
CURLY, THAT MEANS WE'VE BEEN GONE THREE YEARS! THREE YEARS!
YOU'RE CRAZY! WE'VE BEEN GONE A WEEK! TWO WEEKS, TOPS!
DIDN'T SHIRLEY LOOK OLDER?
I DON'T KNOW! MAYBE A LITTLE BIT... DO WE LOOK ANY OLDER?
YOU DON'T. DO I?
NO! BUT HOW CAN WE BE SURE?
WELL... WE WOULD HAVE GROWN OUT OF OUR CLOTHES. MAYBE WE JUST DON'T EVER GROW UP IN THIS DIMENSION!
BUT... BUT SHIRLEY GROWS UP-AND SHE GOES TO HIGH SCHOOL AND COLLEGE-AND SHE GETS MARRIED AND HAS A FAMILY!
AND WE STAY EXACTLY THIS AGE?
NO, NO, NO, NO, NO!

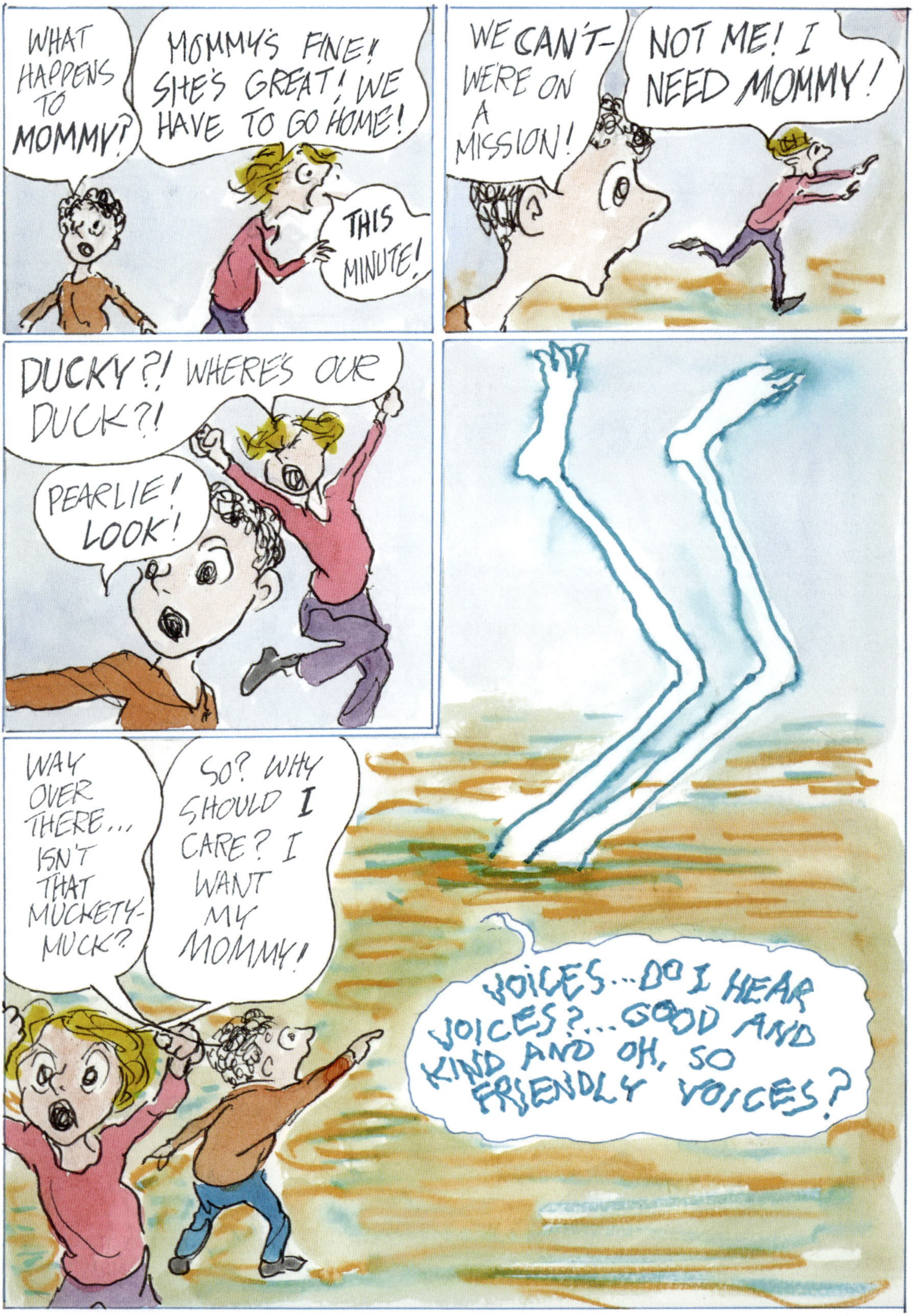
WHAT HAPPENS TO MOMMY?
MOMMY'S FINE! SHE'S GREAT! WE HAVE TO GO HOME!
THIS MINUTE!
WE CAN'T- WE'RE ON A MISSION!
NOT ME! I NEED MOMMY!
DUCKY?! WHERE'S OUR DUCK?!
PEARLIE! LOOK!
WAY OVER THERE... ISN'T THAT MUCKETY-MUCK?
SO? WHY SHOULD I CARE? I WANT MY MOMMY!
VOICES...DO I HEAR VOICES?...GOOD AND KIND AND OH, SO FRIENDLY VOICES?

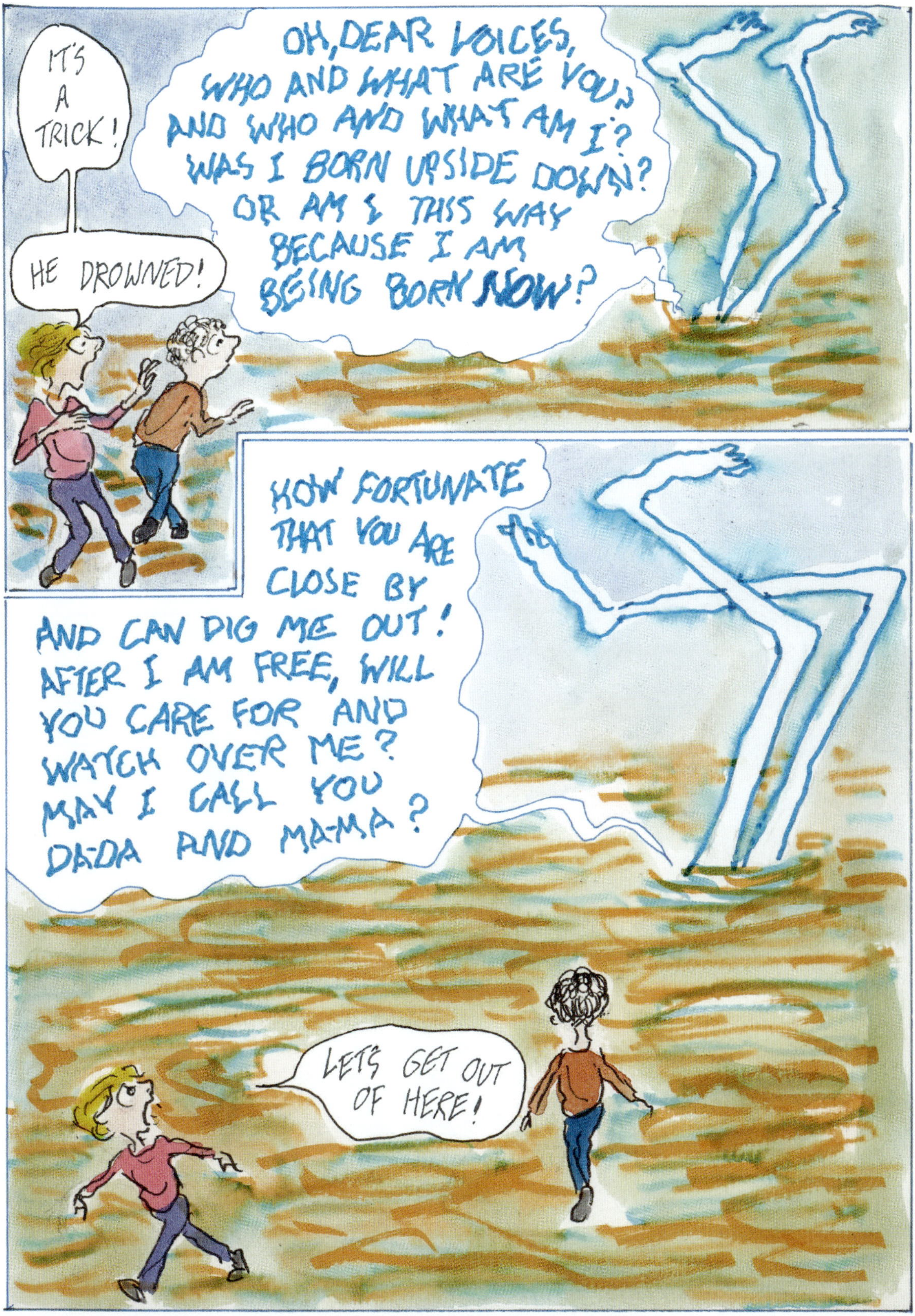
IT'S A TRICK!
HE DROWNED!
OH, DEAR VOICES, WHO AND WHAT ARE YOU? AND WHO AND WHAT AM I? WAS I BORN UPSIDE DOWN? OR AM I THIS WAY BECAUSE I AM BEING BORN NOW?
HOW FORTUNATE THAT YOU ARE CLOSE BY AND CAN DIG ME OUT! AFTER I AM FREE, WILL YOU CARE FOR AND WATCH OVER ME? MAY I CALL YOU DA-DA AND MA-MA?
LETS GET OUT OF HERE!

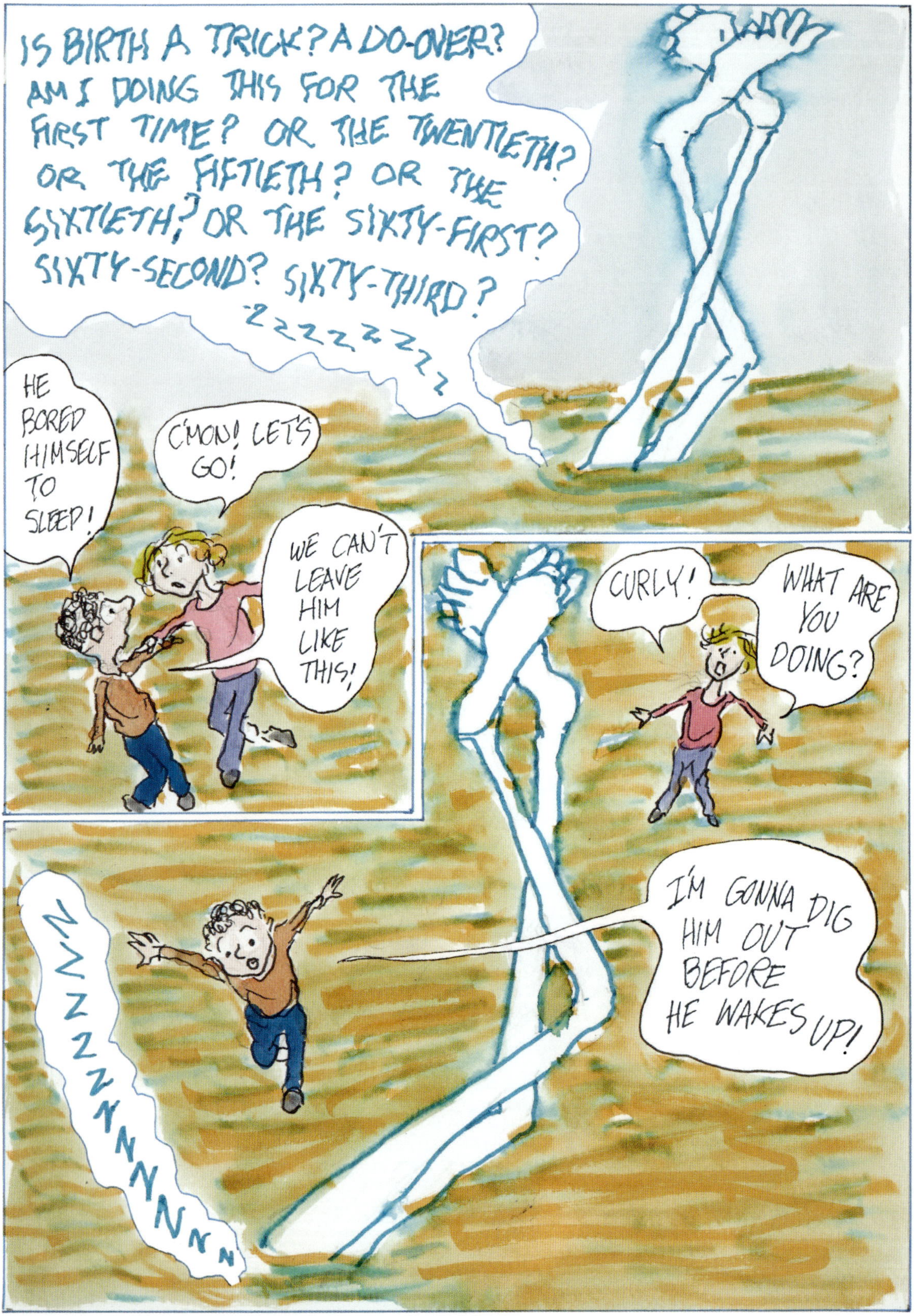
IS BIRTH A TRICK? A DO-OVER? AM I DOING THIS FOR THE FIRST TIME? OR THE TWENTIETH? OR THE FIFTIETH? OR THE SIXTIETH? OR THE SIXTY-FIRST? SIXTY-SECOND? SIXTY-THIRD?
ZZZZZZZZZZ
HE BORED HIMSELF TO SLEEP!
C'MON! LET'S GO!
WE CAN'T LEAVE HIM LIKE THIS!
CURLY!
WHAT ARE YOU DOING?
I'M GONNA DIG HIM OUT BEFORE HE WAKES UP!
ZZZZZNNNNNNNN

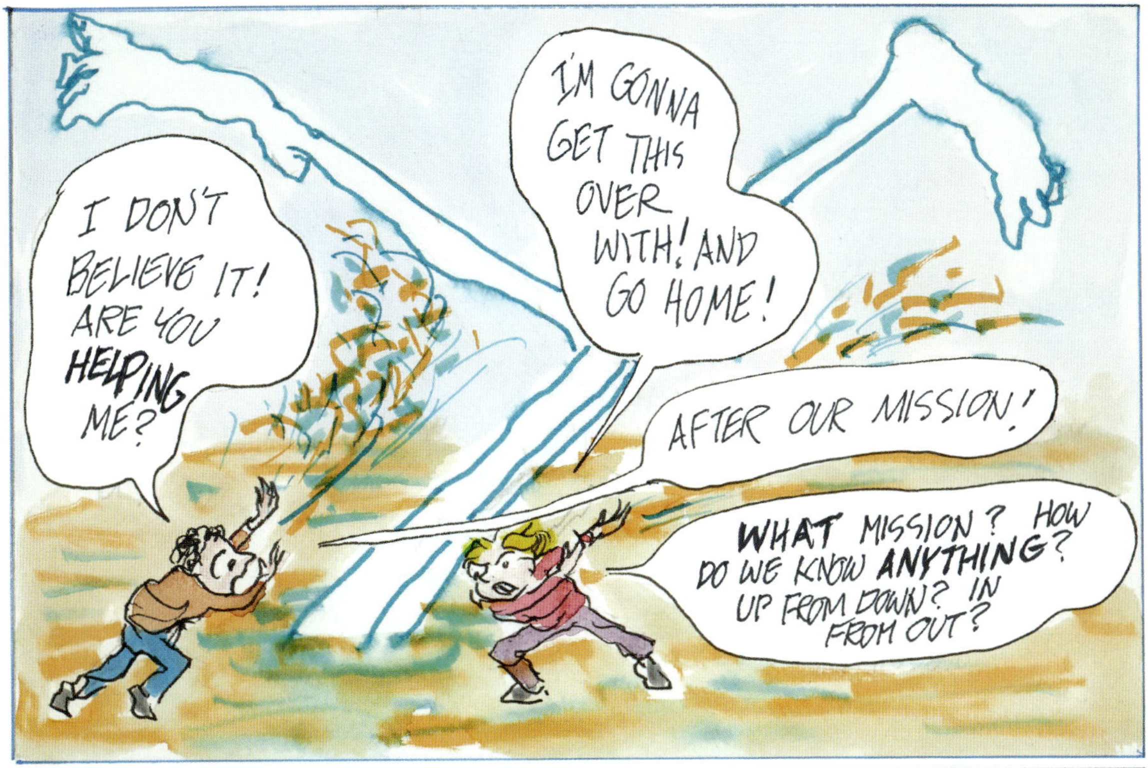
I DON'T BELIEVE IT! ARE YOU **HELPING** ME?
I'M GONNA GET THIS OVER WITH! AND GO HOME!
AFTER OUR MISSION!
WHAT MISSION? HOW DO WE KNOW **ANYTHING**? UP FROM DOWN? IN FROM OUT?

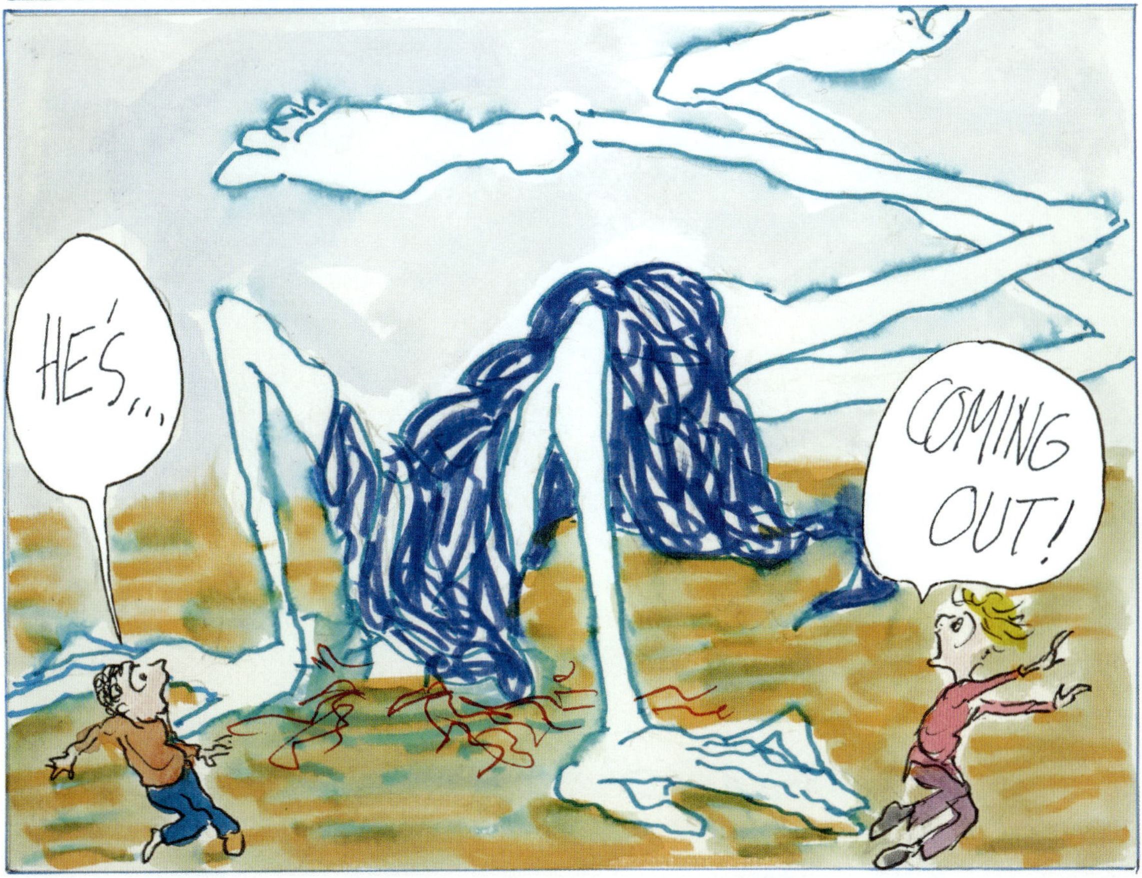
HE'S...
COMING OUT!

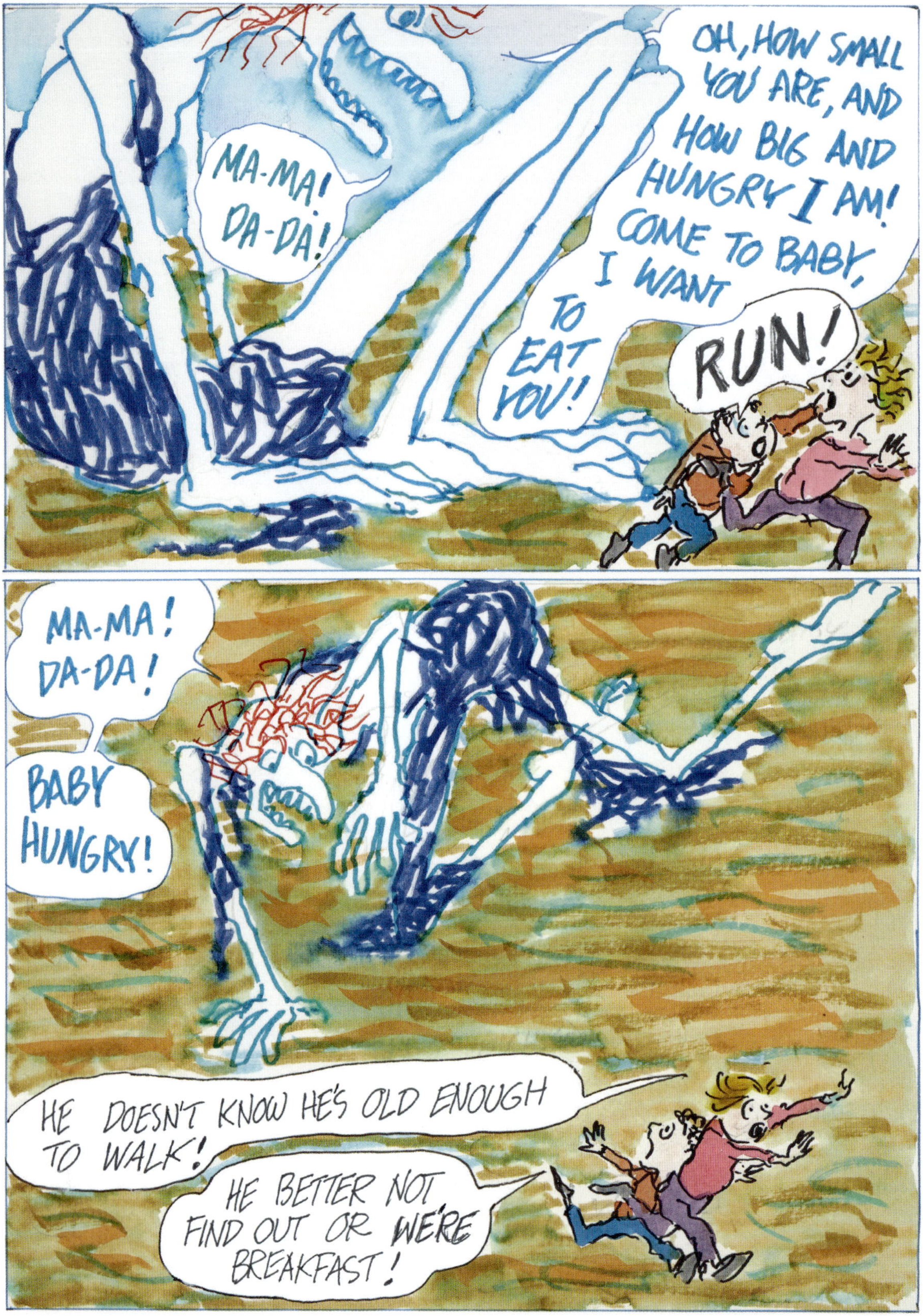
MA-MA! DA-DA!
OH, HOW SMALL YOU ARE, AND HOW BIG AND HUNGRY I AM! COME TO BABY. I WANT TO EAT YOU!
RUN!
MA-MA! DA-DA!
BABY HUNGRY!
HE DOESN'T KNOW HE'S OLD ENOUGH TO WALK!
HE BETTER NOT FIND OUT OR WE'RE BREAKFAST!

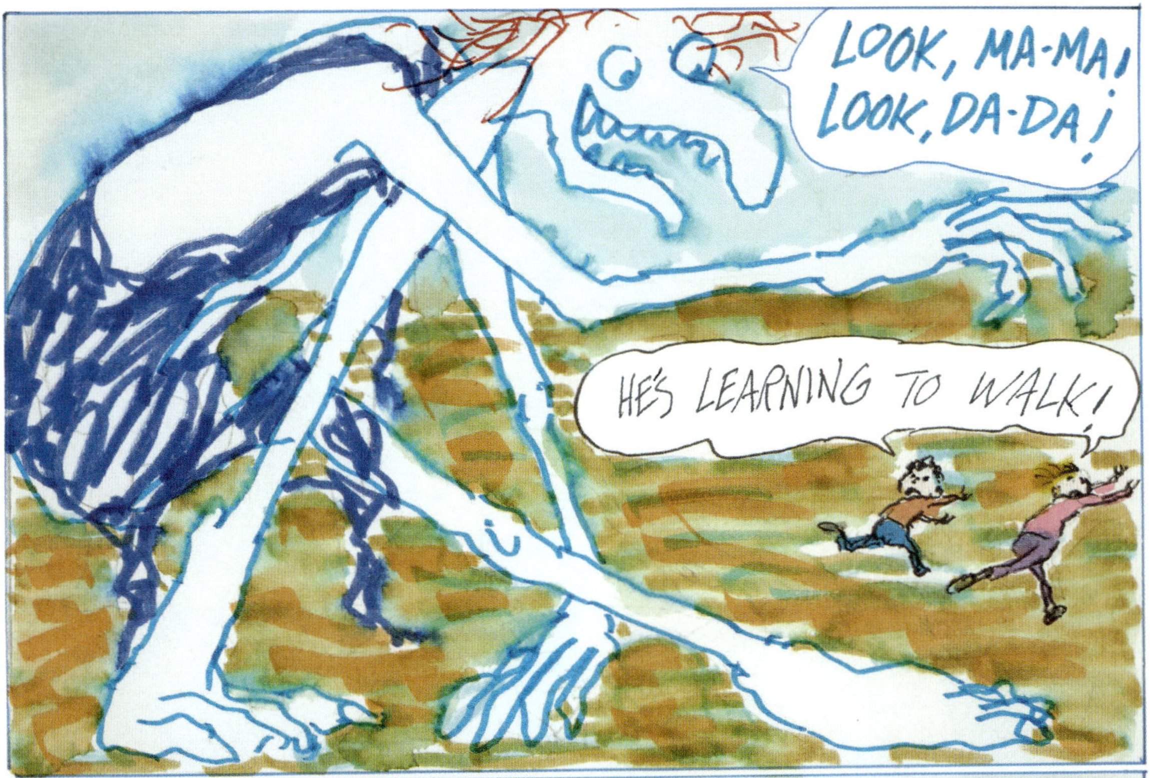
LOOK, MA-MA! LOOK, DA-DA!
HE'S LEARNING TO WALK!

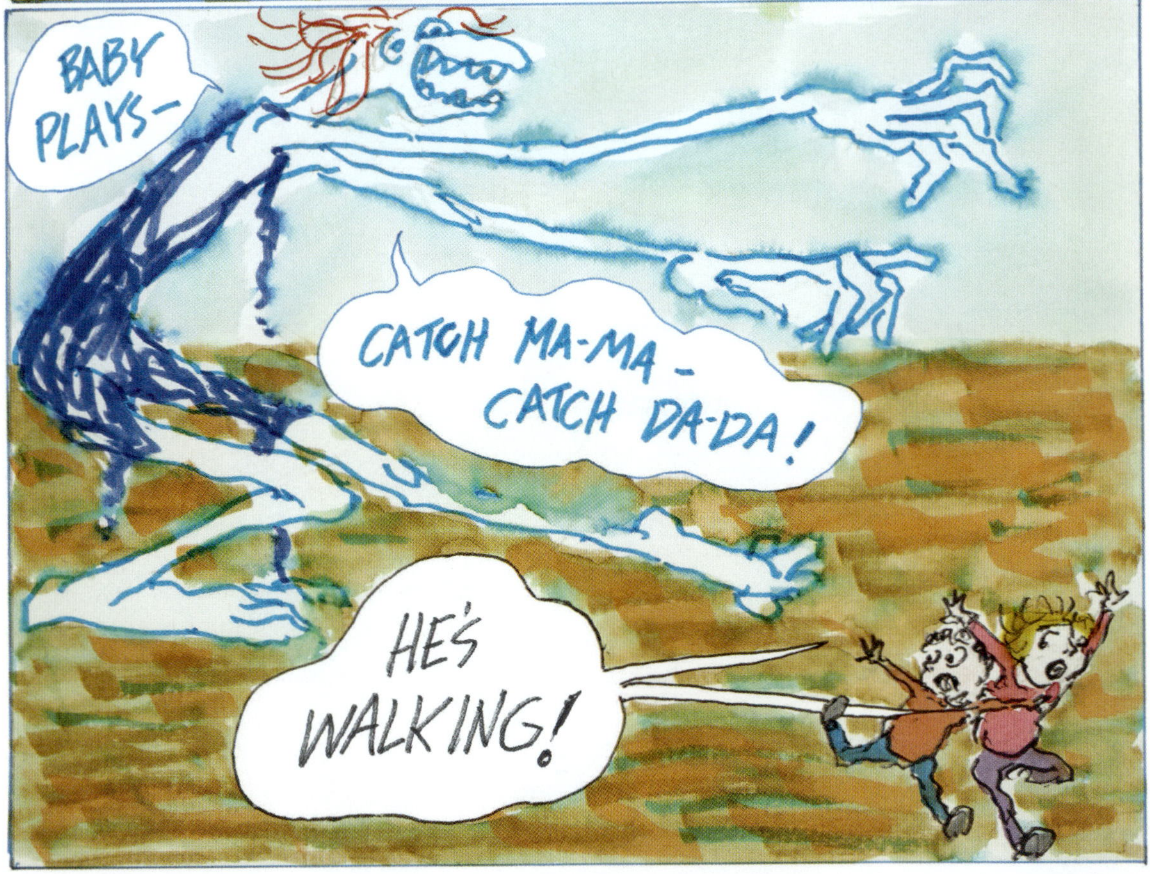
BABY PLAYS-
CATCH MA-MA-CATCH DA-DA!
HE'S WALKING!

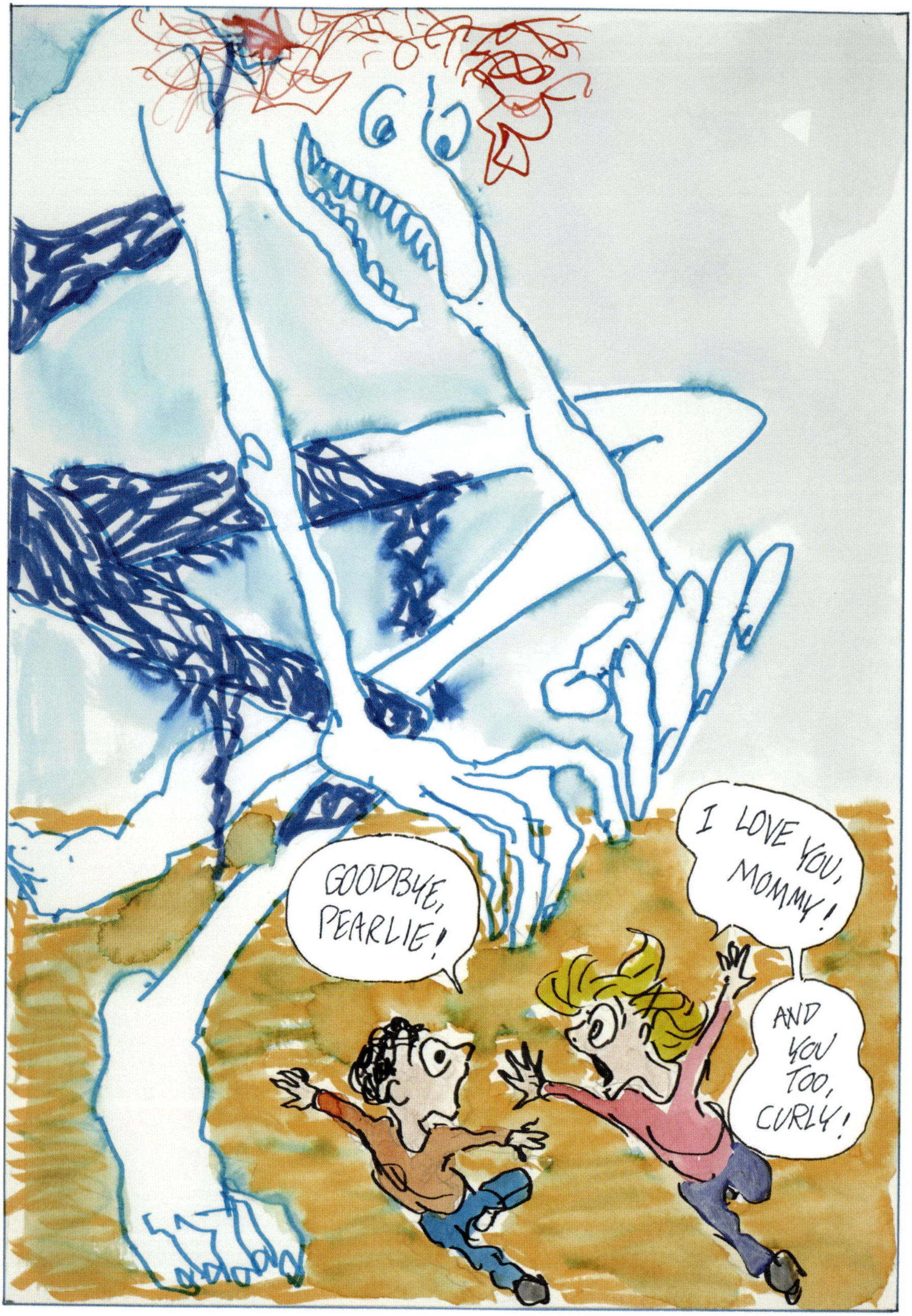
GOODBYE, PEARLIE!
I LOVE YOU, MOMMY!
AND YOU TOO, CURLY!

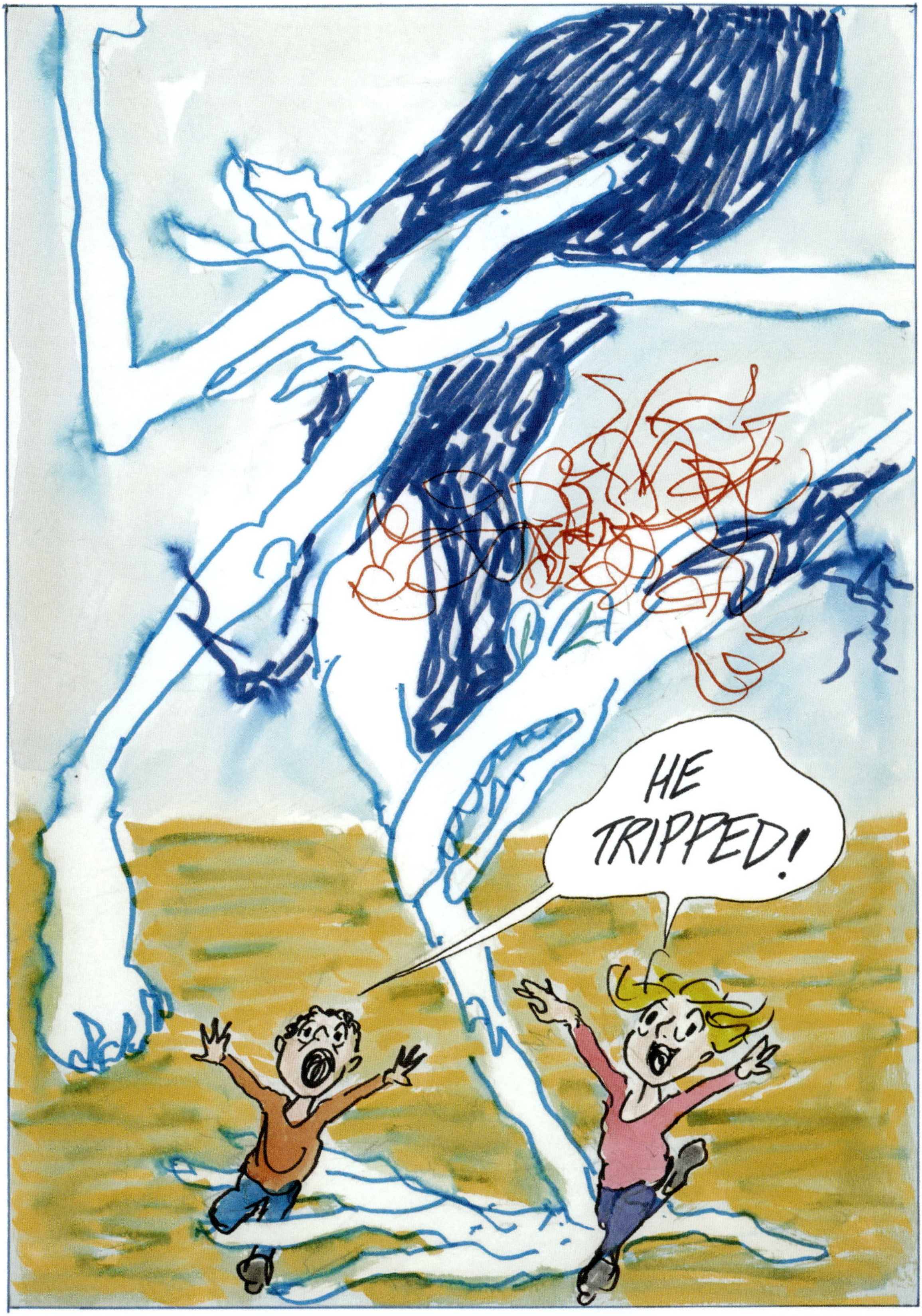
HE TRIPPED!

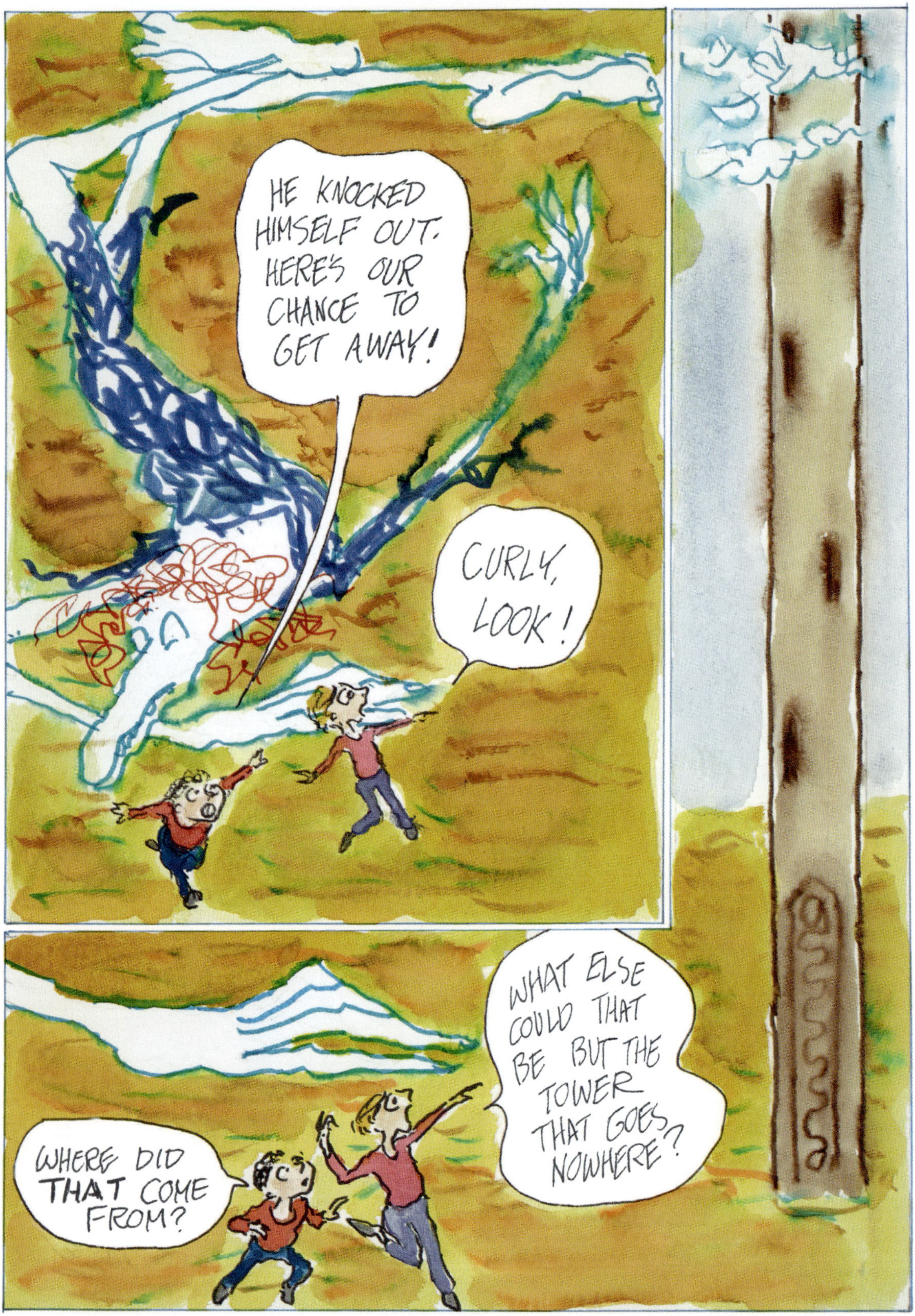
HE KNOCKED HIMSELF OUT. HERE'S OUR CHANCE TO GET AWAY!
CURLY, LOOK!
WHAT ELSE COULD THAT BE BUT THE TOWER THAT GOES NOWHERE?
WHERE DID **THAT** COME FROM?

CHAPTER 16 • WHICH TOWER?

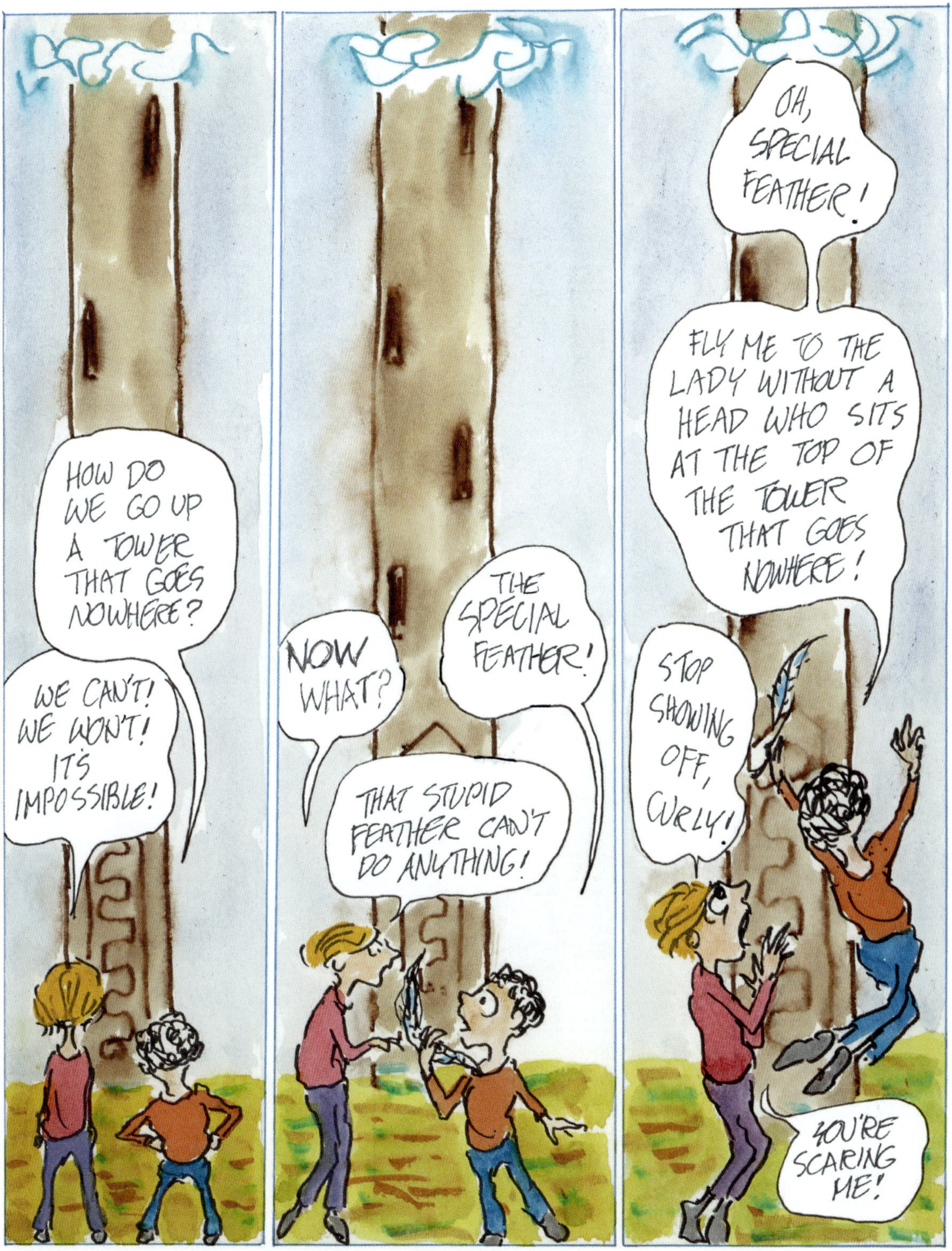

HOW DO WE GO UP A TOWER THAT GOES NOWHERE?
WE CAN'T! WE WON'T! IT'S IMPOSSIBLE!
NOW WHAT?
THE SPECIAL FEATHER!
THAT STUPID FEATHER CAN'T DO ANYTHING!
OH, SPECIAL FEATHER!
FLY ME TO THE LADY WITHOUT A HEAD WHO SITS AT THE TOP OF THE TOWER THAT GOES NOWHERE!
STOP SHOWING OFF, CURLY!
YOU'RE SCARING ME!

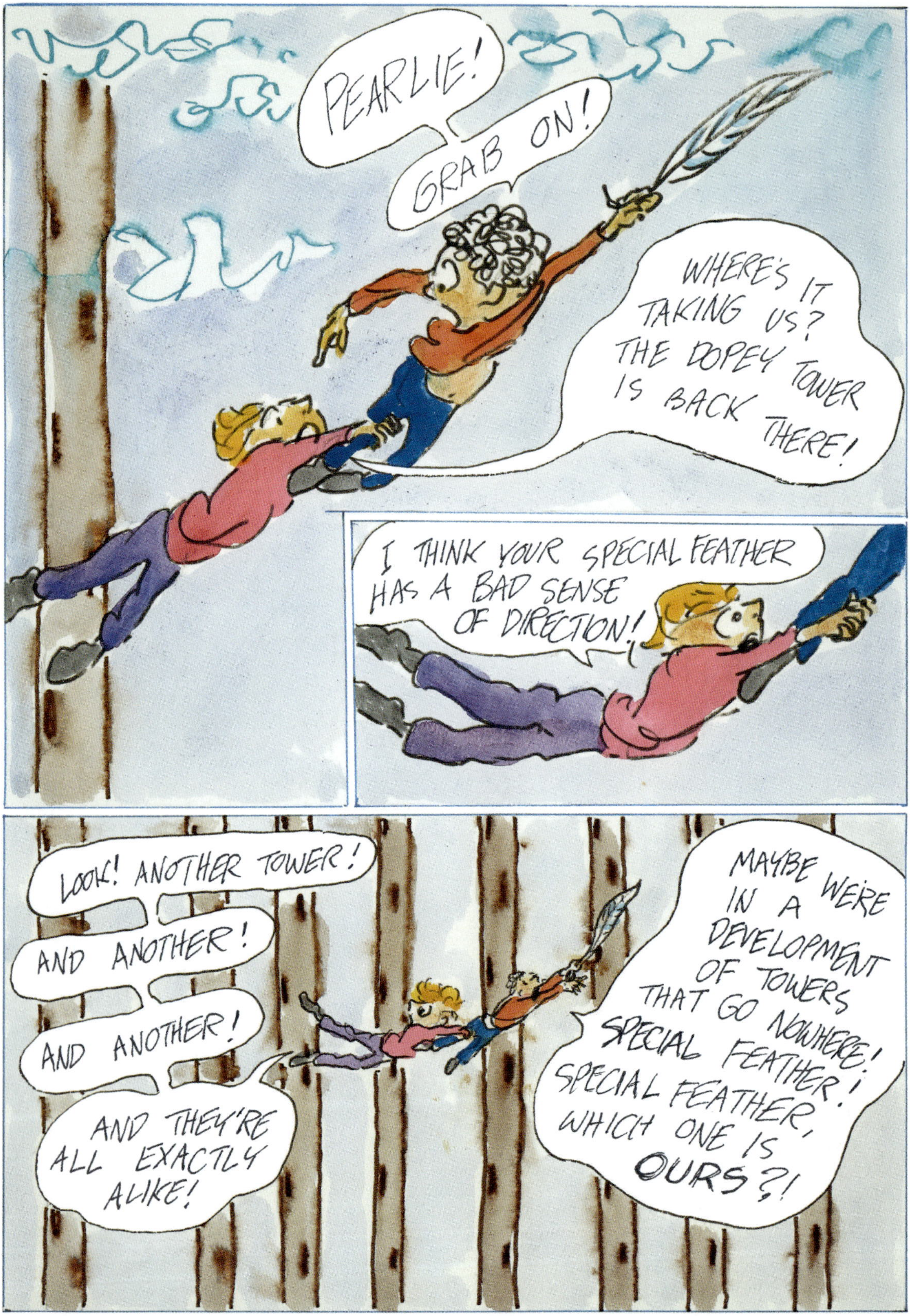
PEARLIE!
GRAB ON!
WHERE'S IT TAKING US? THE DOPEY TOWER IS BACK THERE!
I THINK YOUR SPECIAL FEATHER HAS A BAD SENSE OF DIRECTION!
LOOK! ANOTHER TOWER!
AND ANOTHER!
AND ANOTHER!
AND THEY'RE ALL EXACTLY ALIKE!
MAYBE WE'RE IN A DEVELOPMENT OF TOWERS THAT GO NOWHERE! SPECIAL FEATHER! SPECIAL FEATHER, WHICH ONE IS OURS?!

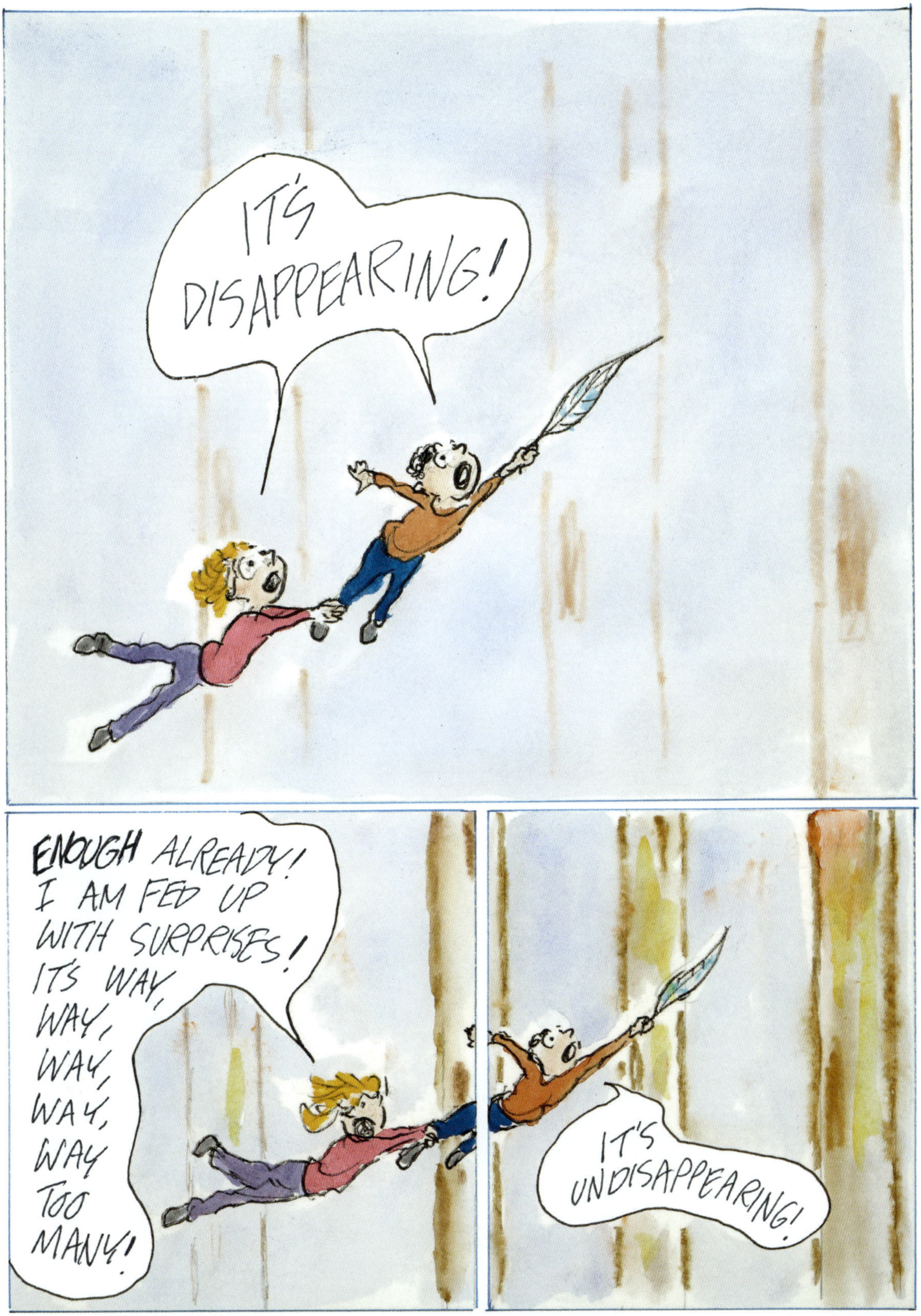
IT'S DISAPPEARING!
ENOUGH ALREADY! I AM FED UP WITH SURPRISES! IT'S WAY, WAY, WAY, WAY, WAY TOO MANY!
IT'S UNDISAPPEARING!

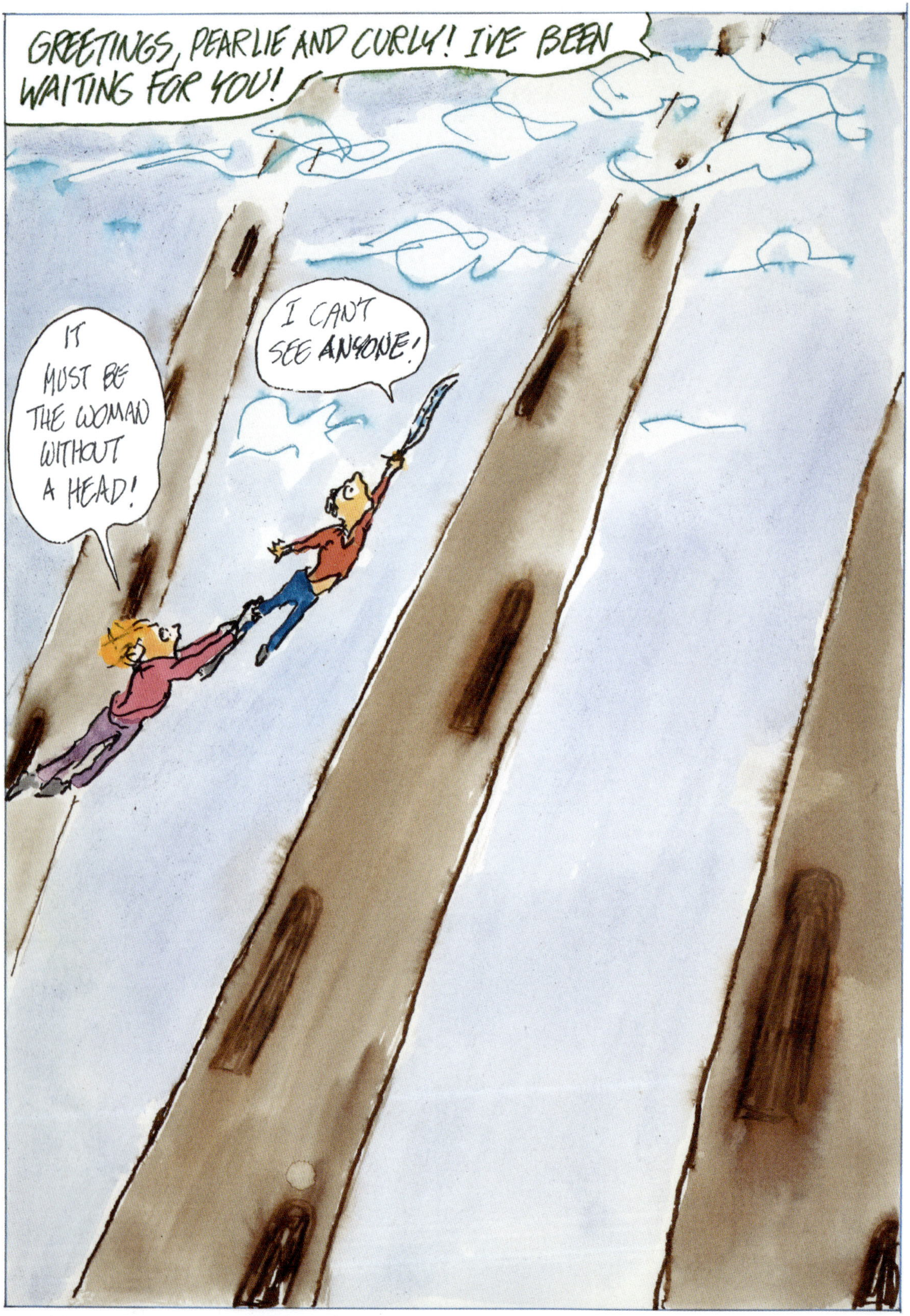
GREETINGS, PEARLIE AND CURLY! I'VE BEEN WAITING FOR YOU!
IT MUST BE THE WOMAN WITHOUT A HEAD!
I CAN'T SEE ANYONE!

CHAPTER 17 • HEADLESS

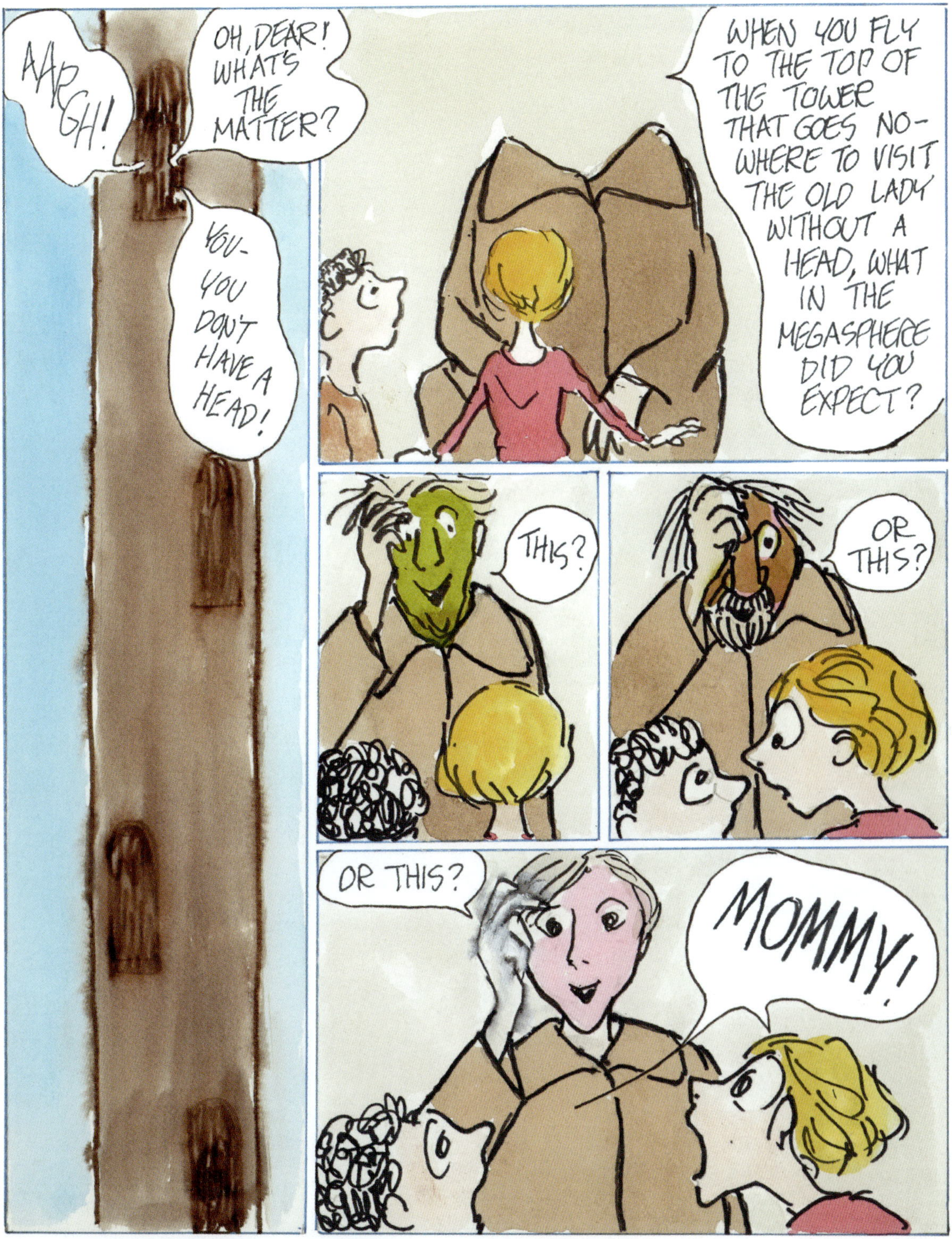
AARGH!
OH, DEAR! WHAT'S THE MATTER?
YOU- YOU DON'T HAVE A HEAD!
WHEN YOU FLY TO THE TOP OF THE TOWER THAT GOES NO-WHERE TO VISIT THE OLD LADY WITHOUT A HEAD, WHAT IN THE MEGASPHERE DID YOU EXPECT?
THIS?
OR THIS?
OR THIS?
MOMMY!

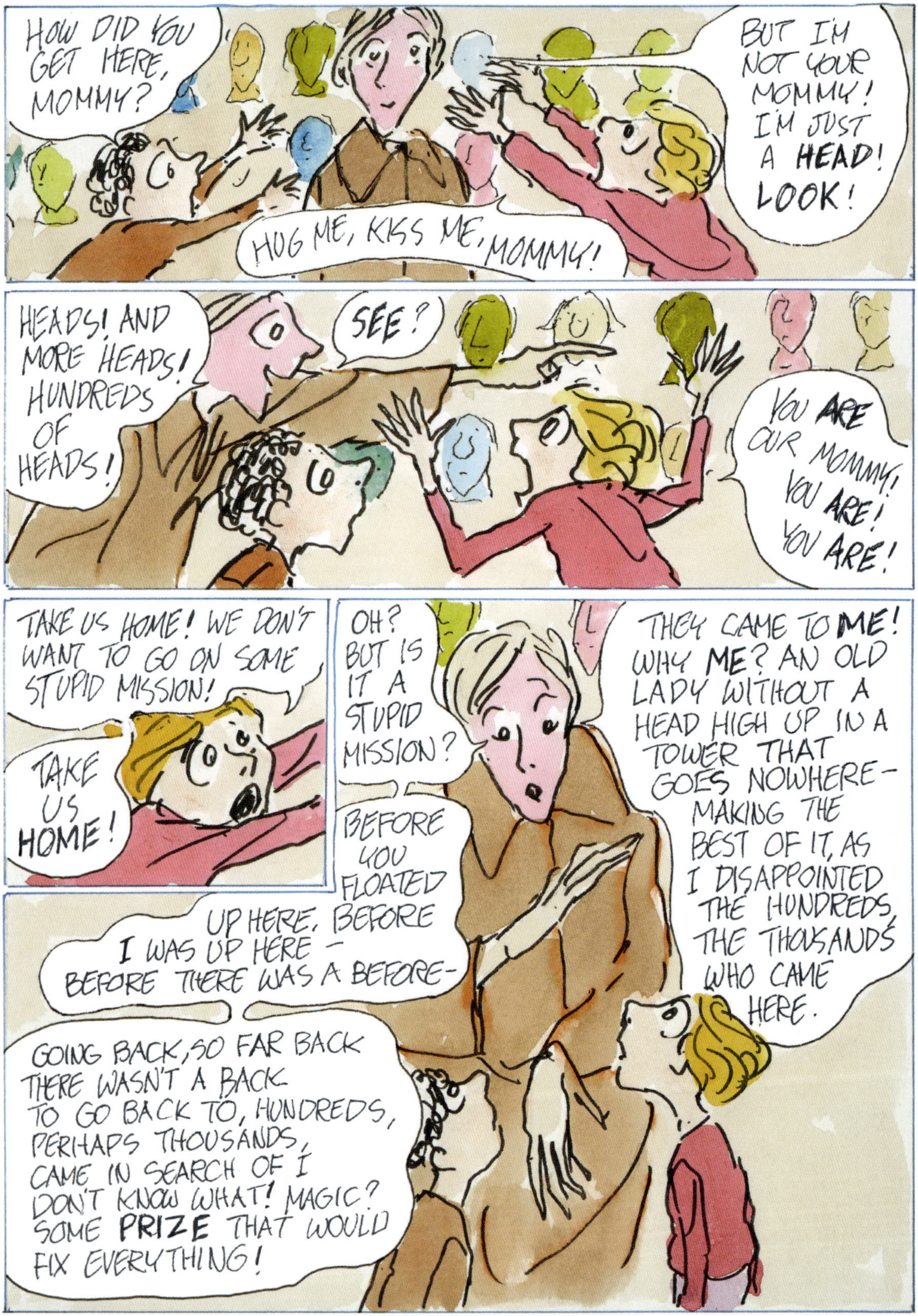
HOW DID YOU GET HERE, MOMMY?
BUT I'M NOT YOUR MOMMY! I'M JUST A **HEAD**! **LOOK**!
HUG ME, KISS ME, MOMMY!
HEADS! AND MORE HEADS! HUNDREDS OF HEADS!
SEE?
YOU **ARE** OUR MOMMY! YOU **ARE**! YOU **ARE**!
TAKE US **HOME**! WE DON'T WANT TO GO ON SOME STUPID MISSION!
TAKE US **HOME**!
OH? BUT IS IT A STUPID MISSION?
THEY CAME TO **ME**! WHY **ME**? AN OLD LADY WITHOUT A HEAD HIGH UP IN A TOWER THAT GOES NOWHERE - MAKING THE BEST OF IT, AS I DISAPPOINTED THE HUNDREDS, THE THOUSANDS WHO CAME HERE.
BEFORE YOU FLOATED UP HERE. BEFORE I WAS UP HERE - BEFORE THERE WAS A BEFORE-
GOING BACK, SO FAR BACK THERE WASN'T A BACK TO GO BACK TO, HUNDREDS, PERHAPS THOUSANDS, CAME IN SEARCH OF I DON'T KNOW WHAT! MAGIC? SOME **PRIZE** THAT WOULD FIX EVERYTHING!

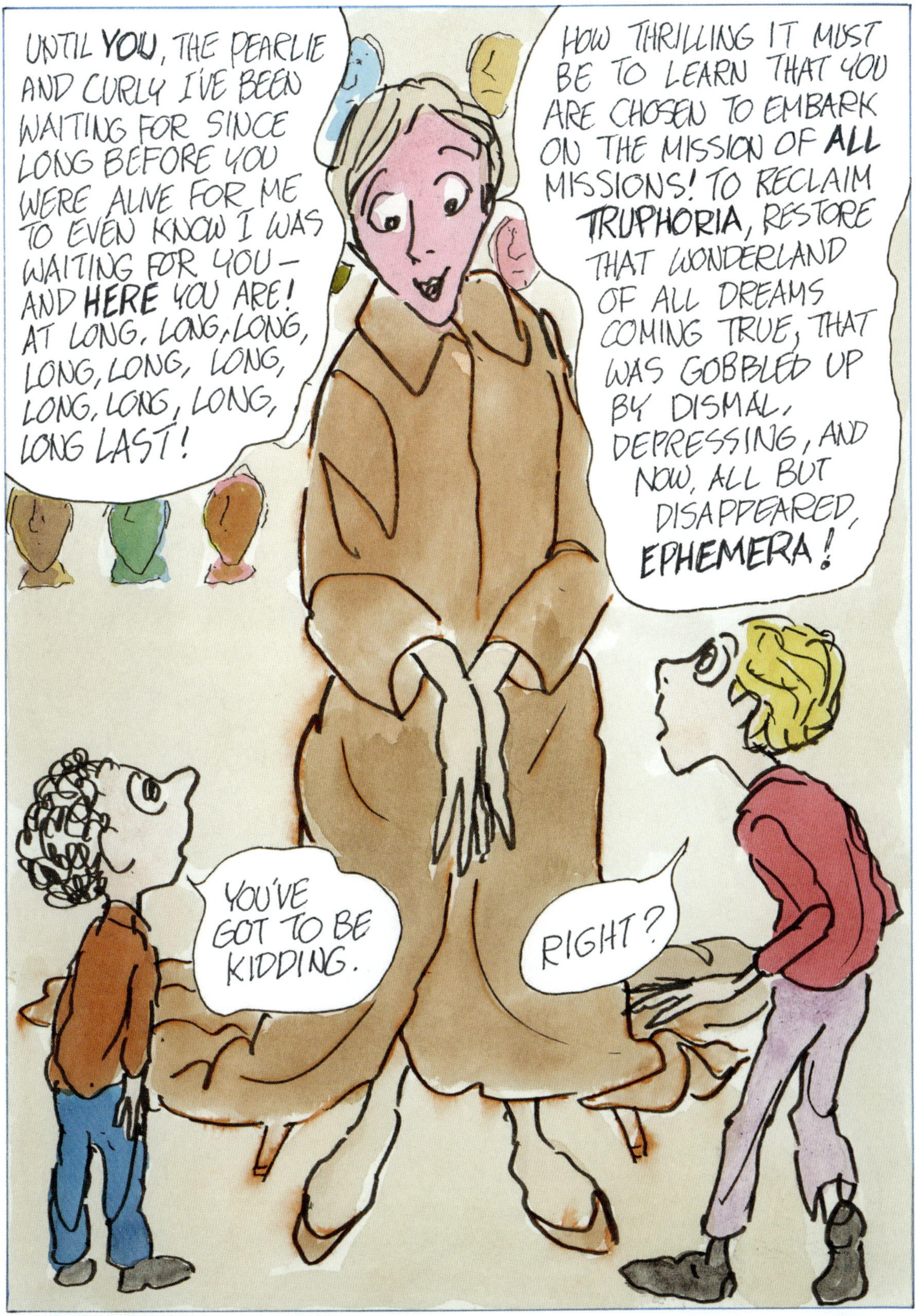
UNTIL YOU, THE PEARLIE AND CURLY I'VE BEEN WAITING FOR SINCE LONG BEFORE YOU WERE ALIVE FOR ME TO EVEN KNOW I WAS WAITING FOR YOU— AND HERE YOU ARE! AT LONG, LONG, LONG, LONG, LONG, LONG, LONG, LONG, LONG, LONG LAST!
HOW THRILLING IT MUST BE TO LEARN THAT YOU ARE CHOSEN TO EMBARK ON THE MISSION OF ALL MISSIONS! TO RECLAIM TRUPHORIA, RESTORE THAT WONDERLAND OF ALL DREAMS COMING TRUE, THAT WAS GOBBLED UP BY DISMAL, DEPRESSING, AND NOW, ALL BUT DISAPPEARED, EPHEMERA!
YOU'VE GOT TO BE KIDDING.
RIGHT?

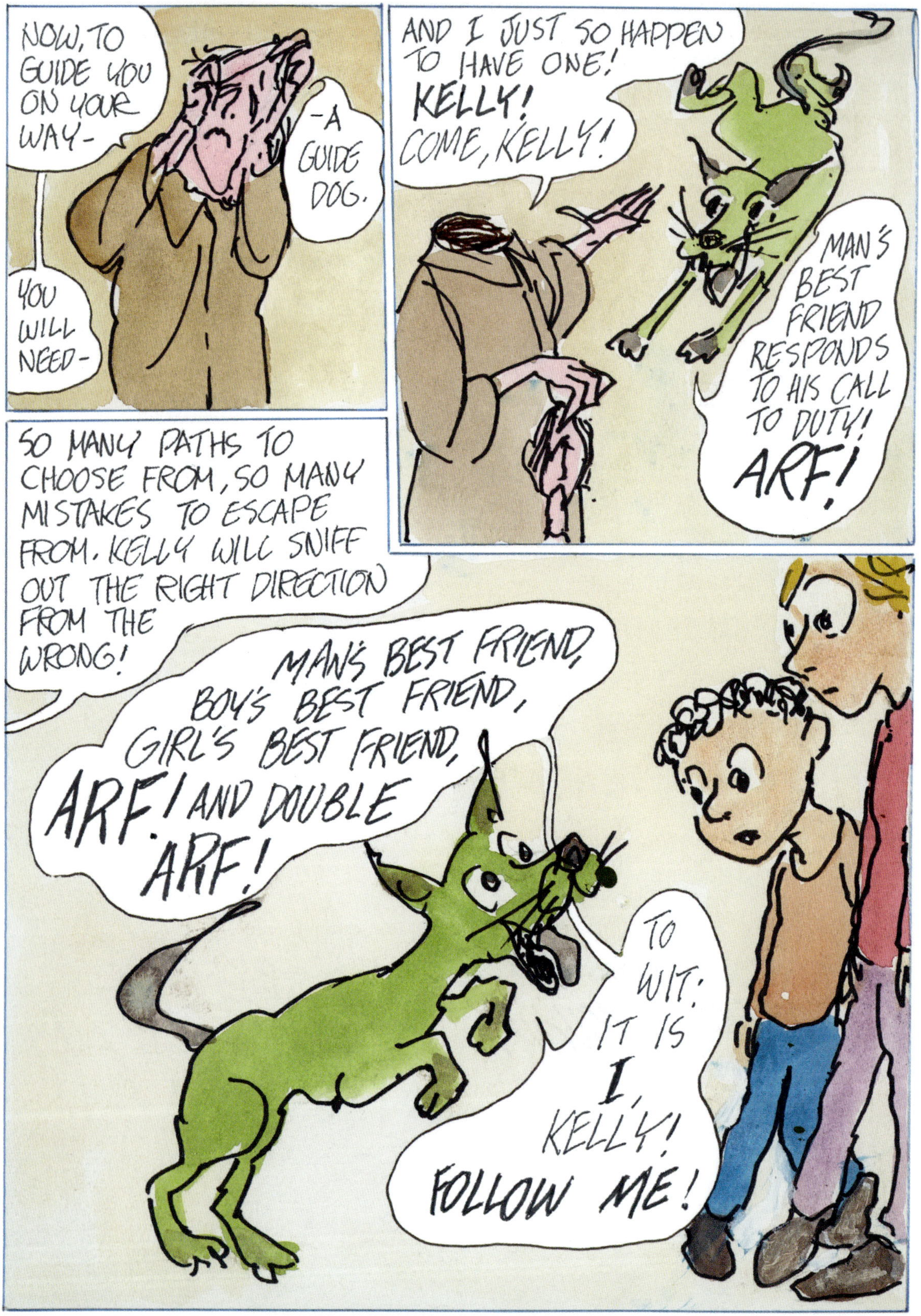
NOW, TO GUIDE YOU ON YOUR WAY-
YOU WILL NEED-
-A GUIDE DOG.
AND I JUST SO HAPPEN TO HAVE ONE! KELLY! COME, KELLY!
MAN'S BEST FRIEND RESPONDS TO HIS CALL TO DUTY! ARF!
SO MANY PATHS TO CHOOSE FROM, SO MANY MISTAKES TO ESCAPE FROM. KELLY WILL SNIFF OUT THE RIGHT DIRECTION FROM THE WRONG!
MAN'S BEST FRIEND, BOY'S BEST FRIEND, GIRL'S BEST FRIEND, ARF! AND DOUBLE ARF!
TO WIT: IT IS I, KELLY! FOLLOW ME!

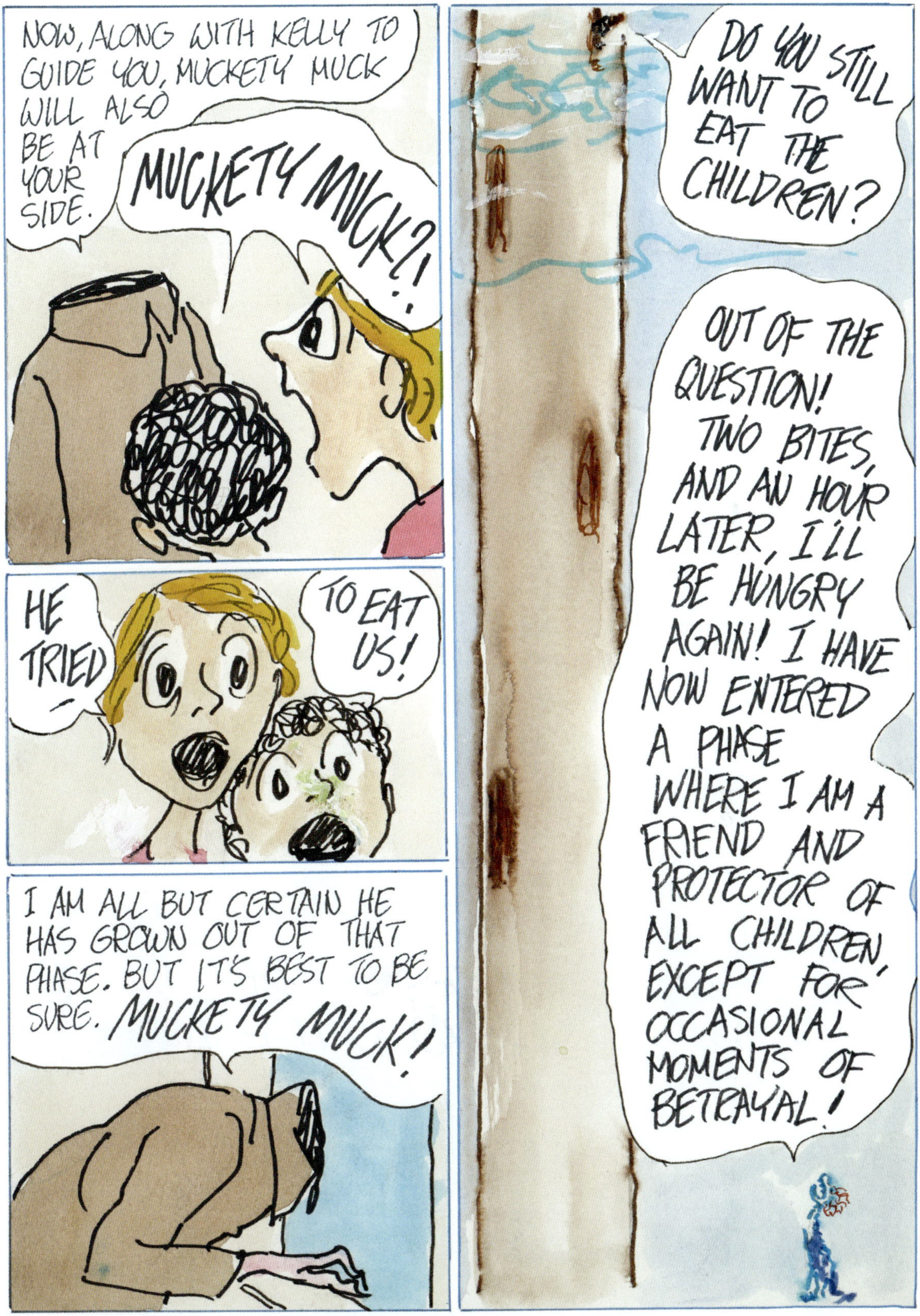
NOW, ALONG WITH KELLY TO GUIDE YOU, MUCKETY MUCK WILL ALSO BE AT YOUR SIDE.
MUCKETY MUCK?!
HE TRIED -
TO EAT US!
I AM ALL BUT CERTAIN HE HAS GROWN OUT OF THAT PHASE. BUT IT'S BEST TO BE SURE. MUCKETY MUCK!
DO YOU STILL WANT TO EAT THE CHILDREN?
OUT OF THE QUESTION! TWO BITES, AND AN HOUR LATER, I'LL BE HUNGRY AGAIN! I HAVE NOW ENTERED A PHASE WHERE I AM A FRIEND AND PROTECTOR OF ALL CHILDREN, EXCEPT FOR OCCASIONAL MOMENTS OF BETRAYAL!

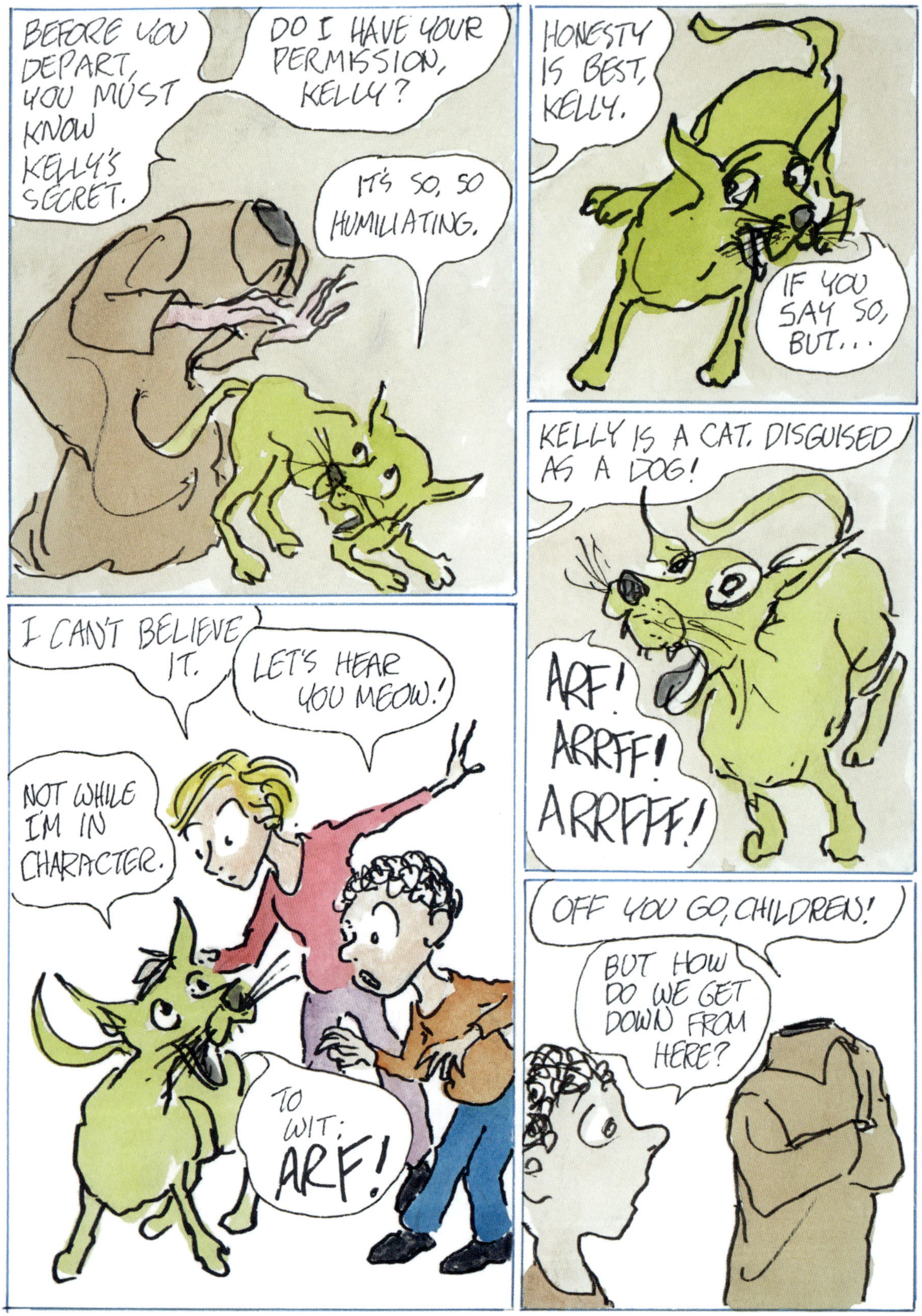
BEFORE YOU DEPART, YOU MUST KNOW KELLY'S SECRET.
DO I HAVE YOUR PERMISSION, KELLY?
IT'S SO, SO HUMILIATING.
HONESTY IS BEST, KELLY.
IF YOU SAY SO, BUT...
KELLY IS A CAT. DISGUISED AS A DOG!
ARF! ARRFF! ARRFFF!
I CAN'T BELIEVE IT.
LET'S HEAR YOU MEOW!
NOT WHILE I'M IN CHARACTER.
TO WIT: ARF!
OFF YOU GO, CHILDREN!
BUT HOW DO WE GET DOWN FROM HERE?

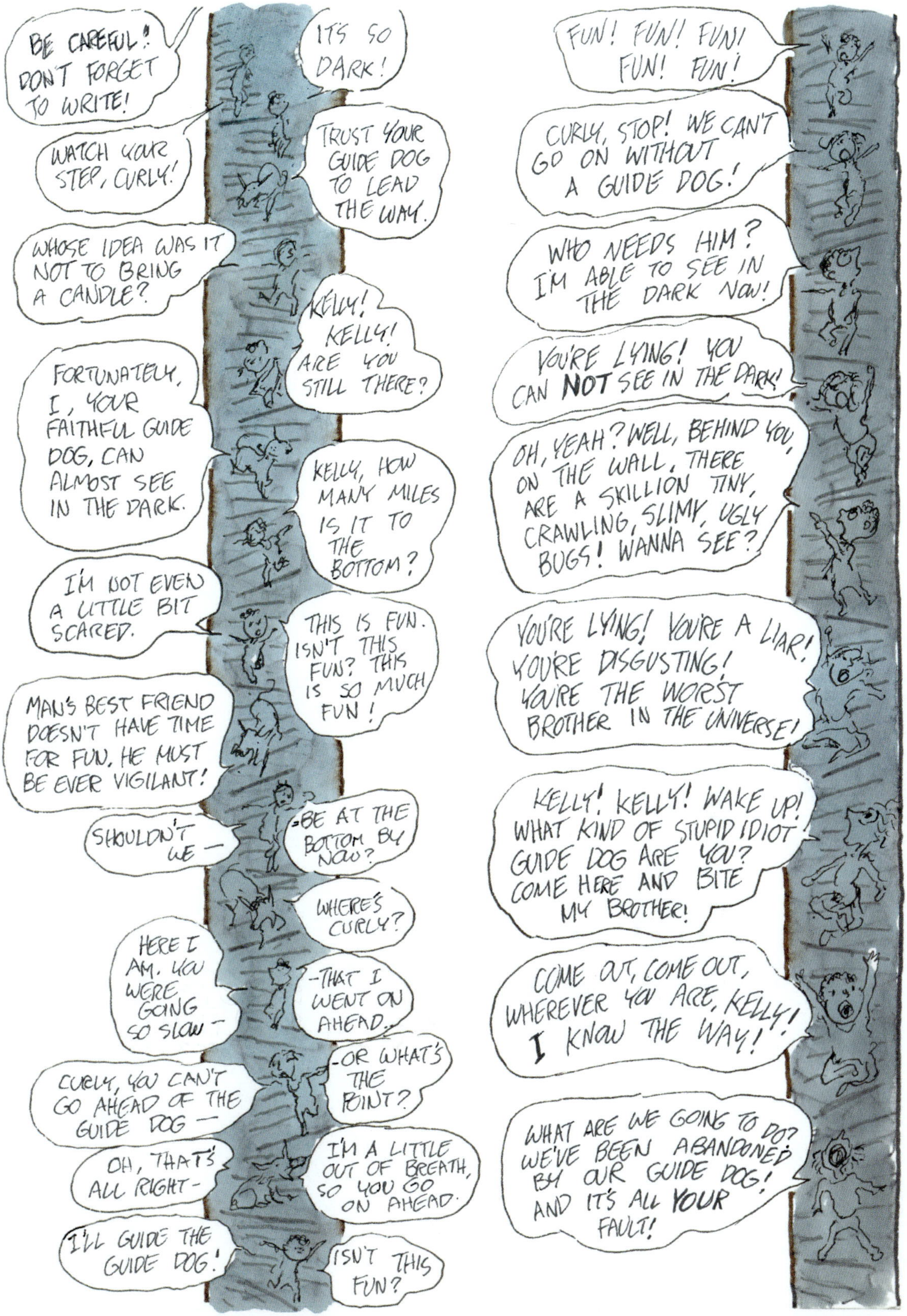
BE CAREFUL! DON'T FORGET TO WRITE!
IT'S SO DARK!
WATCH YOUR STEP, CURLY!
TRUST YOUR GUIDE DOG TO LEAD THE WAY.
WHOSE IDEA WAS IT NOT TO BRING A CANDLE?
KELLY! KELLY! ARE YOU STILL THERE?
FORTUNATELY, I, YOUR FAITHFUL GUIDE DOG, CAN ALMOST SEE IN THE DARK.
KELLY, HOW MANY MILES IS IT TO THE BOTTOM?
I'M NOT EVEN A LITTLE BIT SCARED.
THIS IS FUN. ISN'T THIS FUN? THIS IS SO MUCH FUN!
MAN'S BEST FRIEND DOESN'T HAVE TIME FOR FUN. HE MUST BE EVER VIGILANT!
SHOULDN'T WE —
—BE AT THE BOTTOM BY NOW?
WHERE'S CURLY?
HERE I AM. YOU WERE GOING SO SLOW —
—THAT I WENT ON AHEAD.
CURLY, YOU CAN'T GO AHEAD OF THE GUIDE DOG —
—OR WHAT'S THE POINT?
OH, THAT'S ALL RIGHT—
I'M A LITTLE OUT OF BREATH, SO YOU GO ON AHEAD.
I'LL GUIDE THE GUIDE DOG!
ISN'T THIS FUN?
FUN! FUN! FUN! FUN! FUN!
CURLY, STOP! WE CAN'T GO ON WITHOUT A GUIDE DOG!
WHO NEEDS HIM? I'M ABLE TO SEE IN THE DARK NOW!
YOU'RE LYING! YOU CAN **NOT** SEE IN THE DARK!
OH, YEAH? WELL, BEHIND YOU, ON THE WALL, THERE ARE A SKILLION TINY, CRAWLING, SLIMY, UGLY BUGS! WANNA SEE?
YOU'RE LYING! YOU'RE A LIAR! YOU'RE DISGUSTING! YOU'RE THE WORST BROTHER IN THE UNIVERSE!
KELLY! KELLY! WAKE UP! WHAT KIND OF STUPID IDIOT GUIDE DOG ARE YOU? COME HERE AND BITE MY BROTHER!
COME OUT, COME OUT, WHEREVER YOU ARE, KELLY! **I** KNOW THE WAY!
WHAT ARE WE GOING TO DO? WE'VE BEEN ABANDONED BY OUR GUIDE DOG! AND IT'S ALL **YOUR** FAULT!

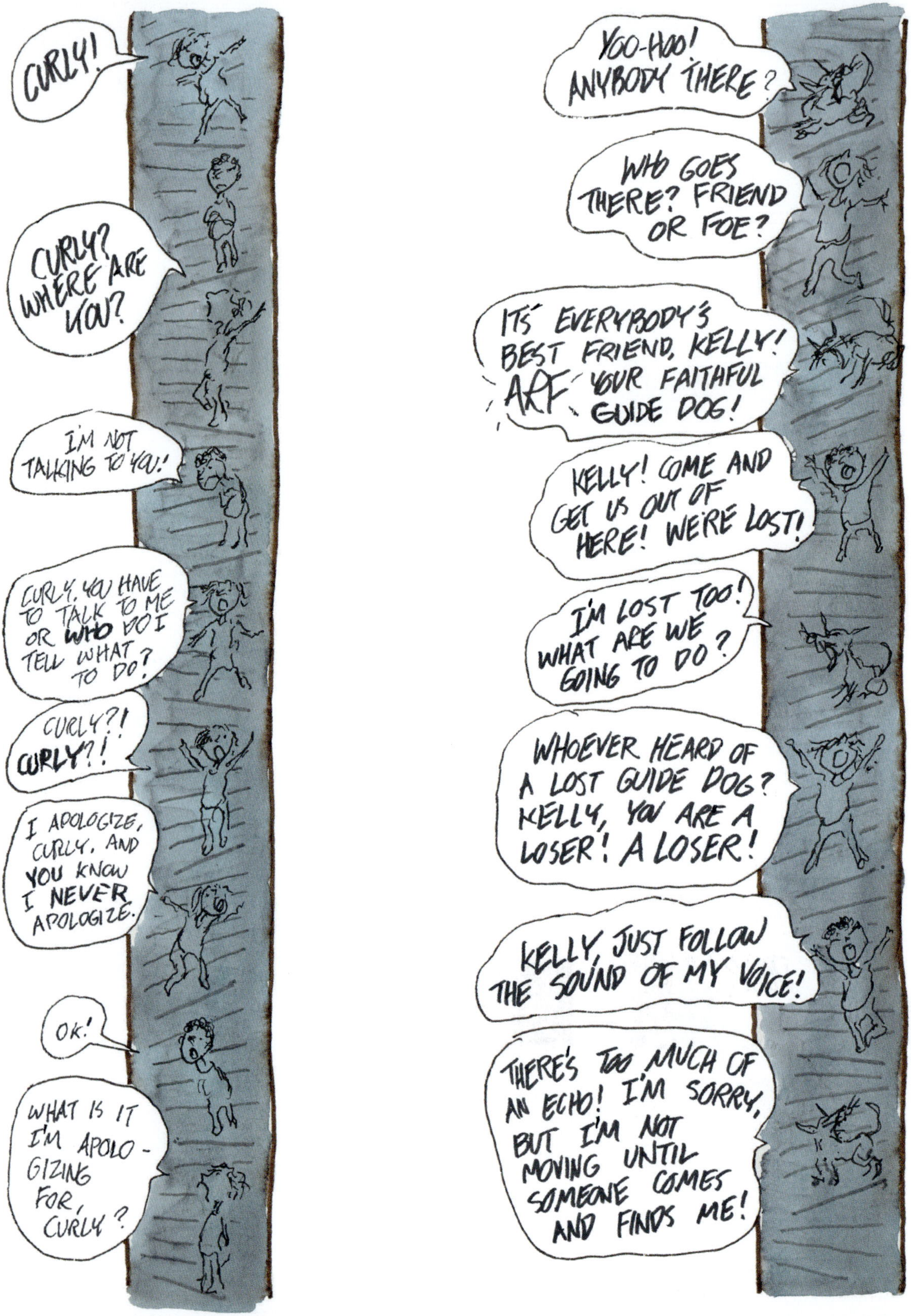
CURLY!
CURLY? WHERE ARE YOU?
I'M NOT TALKING TO YOU!
CURLY, YOU HAVE TO TALK TO ME OR **WHO** DO I TELL WHAT TO DO?
CURLY?! **CURLY**?!
I APOLOGIZE, CURLY. AND YOU KNOW I **NEVER** APOLOGIZE.
OK!
WHAT IS IT I'M APOLO-GIZING FOR, CURLY?
YOO-HOO! ANYBODY THERE?
WHO GOES THERE? FRIEND OR FOE?
IT'S EVERYBODY'S BEST FRIEND, KELLY! ARF YOUR FAITHFUL GUIDE DOG!
KELLY! COME AND GET US OUT OF HERE! WE'RE LOST!
I'M LOST TOO! WHAT ARE WE GOING TO DO?
WHOEVER HEARD OF A LOST GUIDE DOG? KELLY, YOU ARE A LOSER! A LOSER!
KELLY, JUST FOLLOW THE SOUND OF MY VOICE!
THERE'S TOO MUCH OF AN ECHO! I'M SORRY, BUT I'M NOT MOVING UNTIL SOMEONE COMES AND FINDS ME!

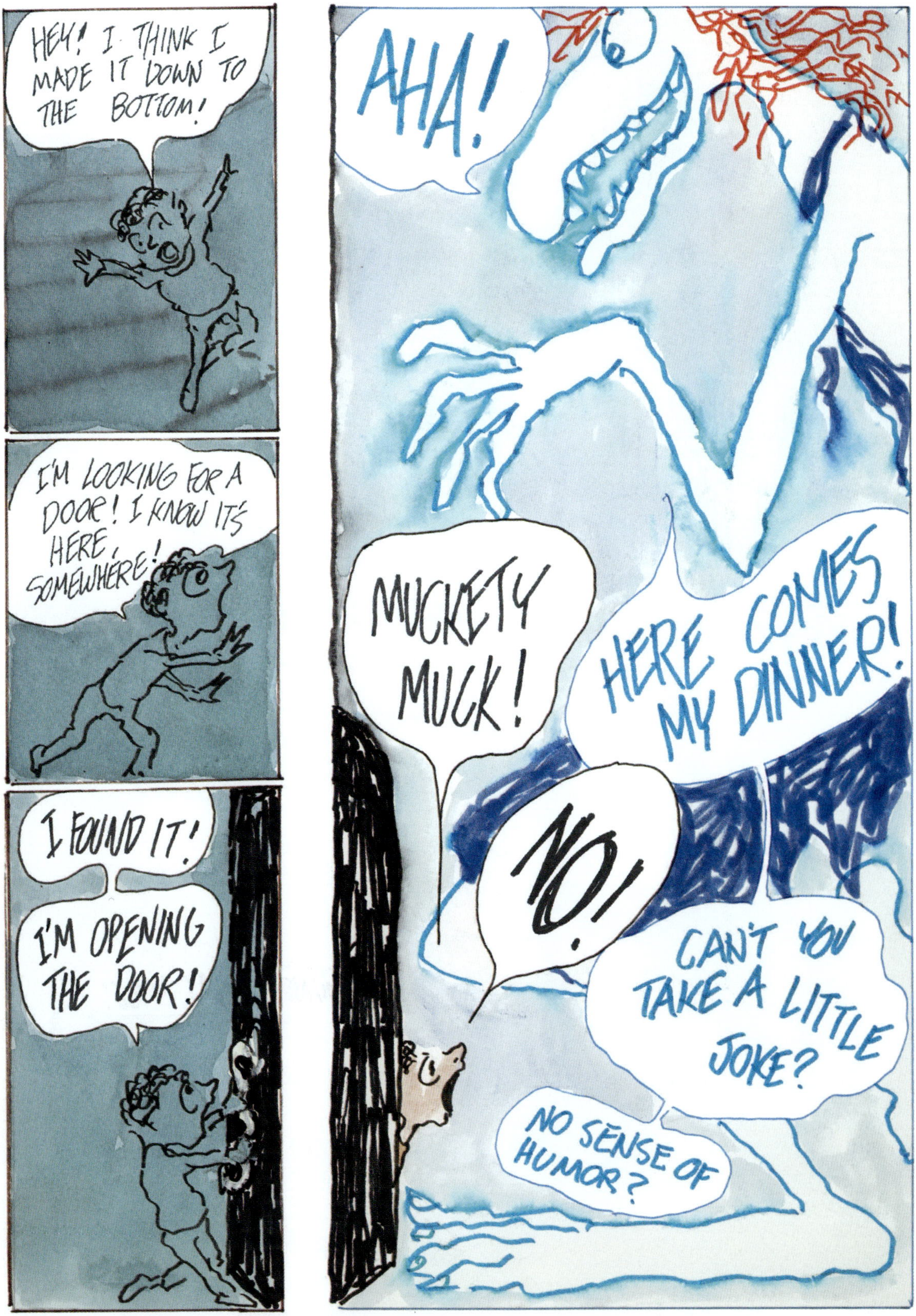
HEY! I THINK I MADE IT DOWN TO THE BOTTOM!
I'M LOOKING FOR A DOOR! I KNOW IT'S HERE, SOMEWHERE!
I FOUND IT!
I'M OPENING THE DOOR!
AHA!
HERE COMES MY DINNER!
MUCKETY MUCK!
NO!
CAN'T YOU TAKE A LITTLE JOKE?
NO SENSE OF HUMOR?

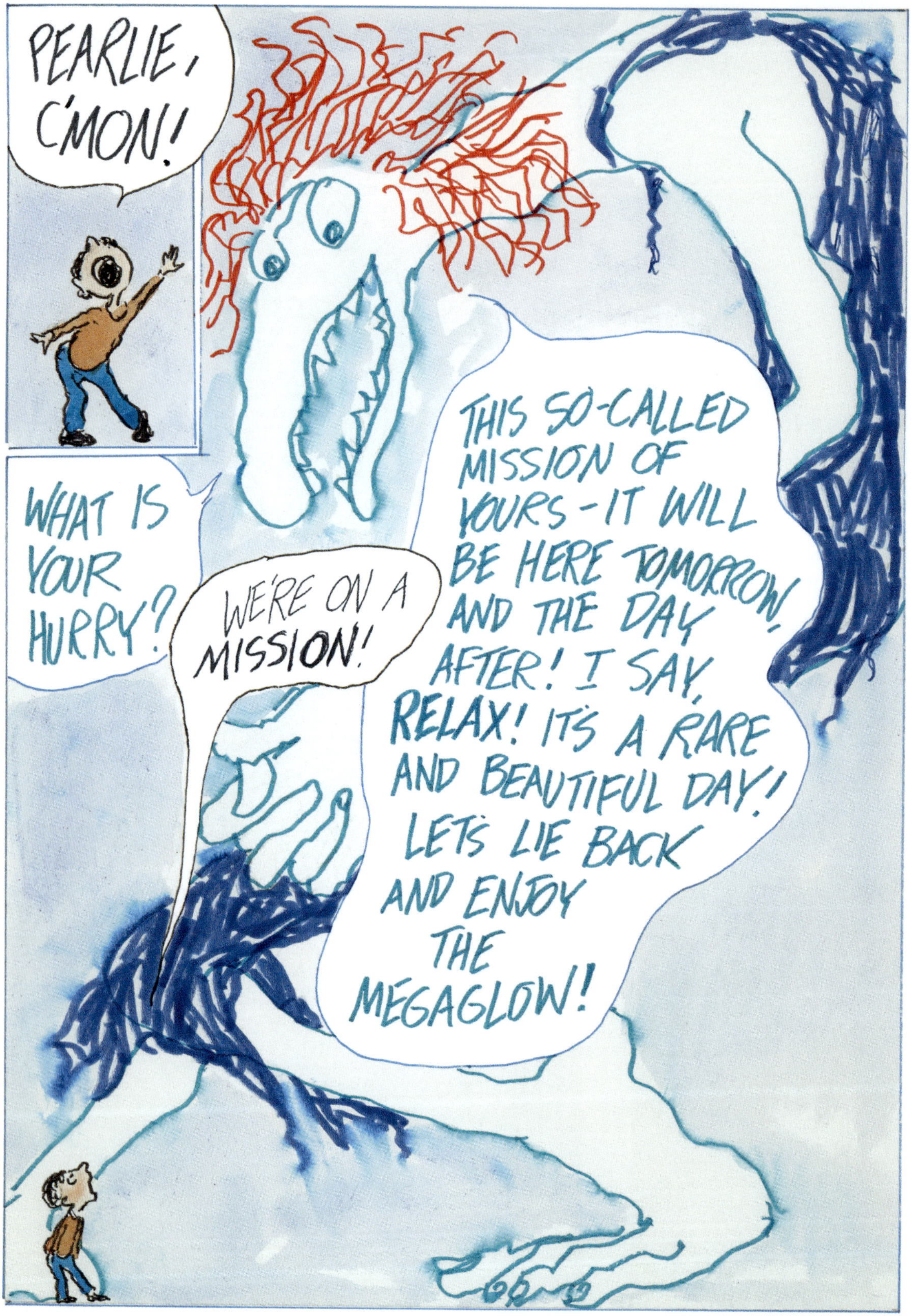
PEARLIE, C'MON!
WHAT IS YOUR HURRY?
WE'RE ON A MISSION!
THIS SO-CALLED MISSION OF YOURS - IT WILL BE HERE TOMORROW, AND THE DAY AFTER! I SAY, RELAX! IT'S A RARE AND BEAUTIFUL DAY! LET'S LIE BACK AND ENJOY THE MEGAGLOW!

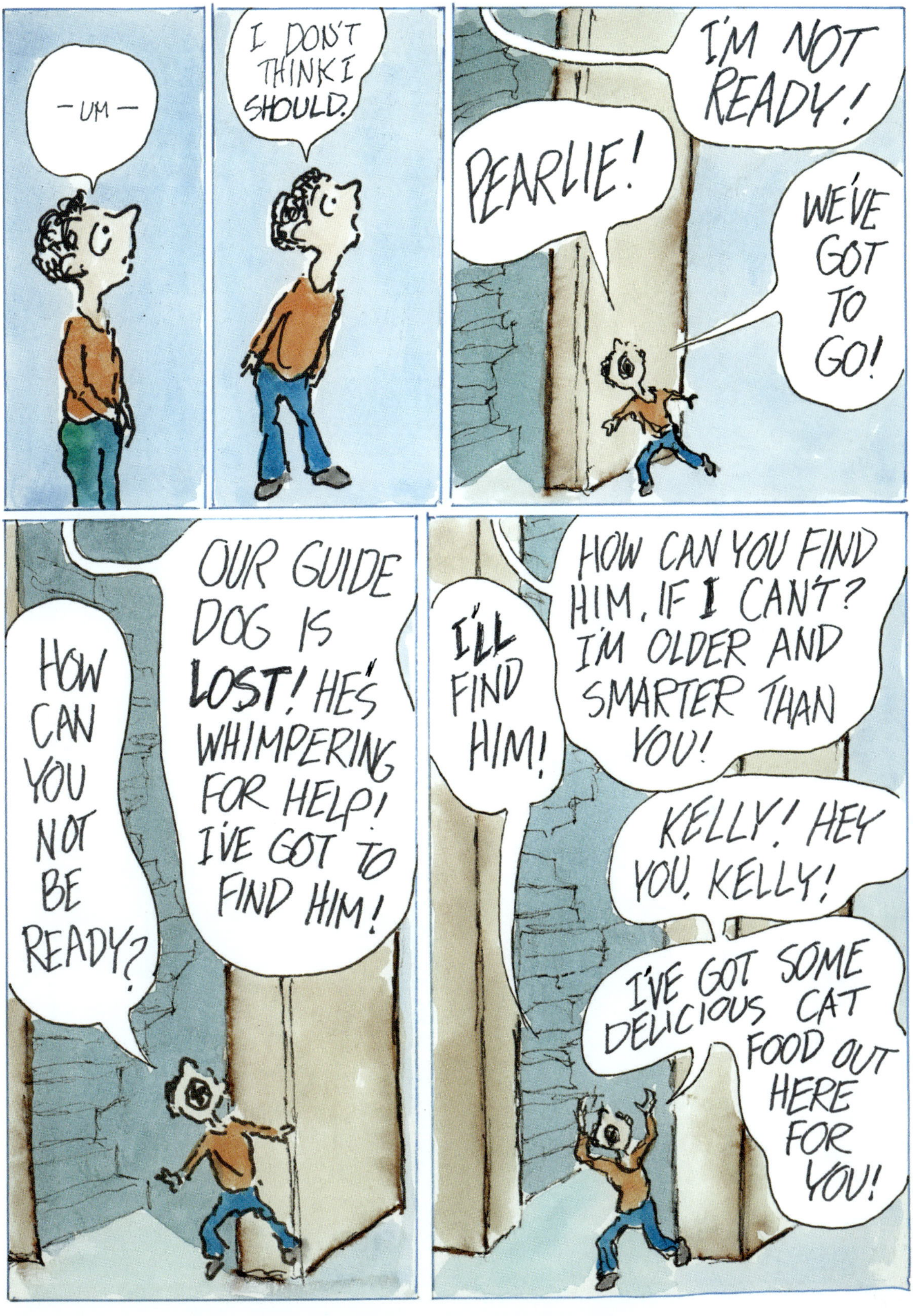
—UM—
I DON'T THINK I SHOULD.
I'M NOT READY!
PEARLIE!
WE'VE GOT TO GO!
OUR GUIDE DOG IS LOST! HE'S WHIMPERING FOR HELP! I'VE GOT TO FIND HIM!
HOW CAN YOU NOT BE READY?
HOW CAN YOU FIND HIM, IF I CAN'T? I'M OLDER AND SMARTER THAN YOU!
I'LL FIND HIM!
KELLY! HEY YOU, KELLY!
I'VE GOT SOME DELICIOUS CAT FOOD OUT HERE FOR YOU!

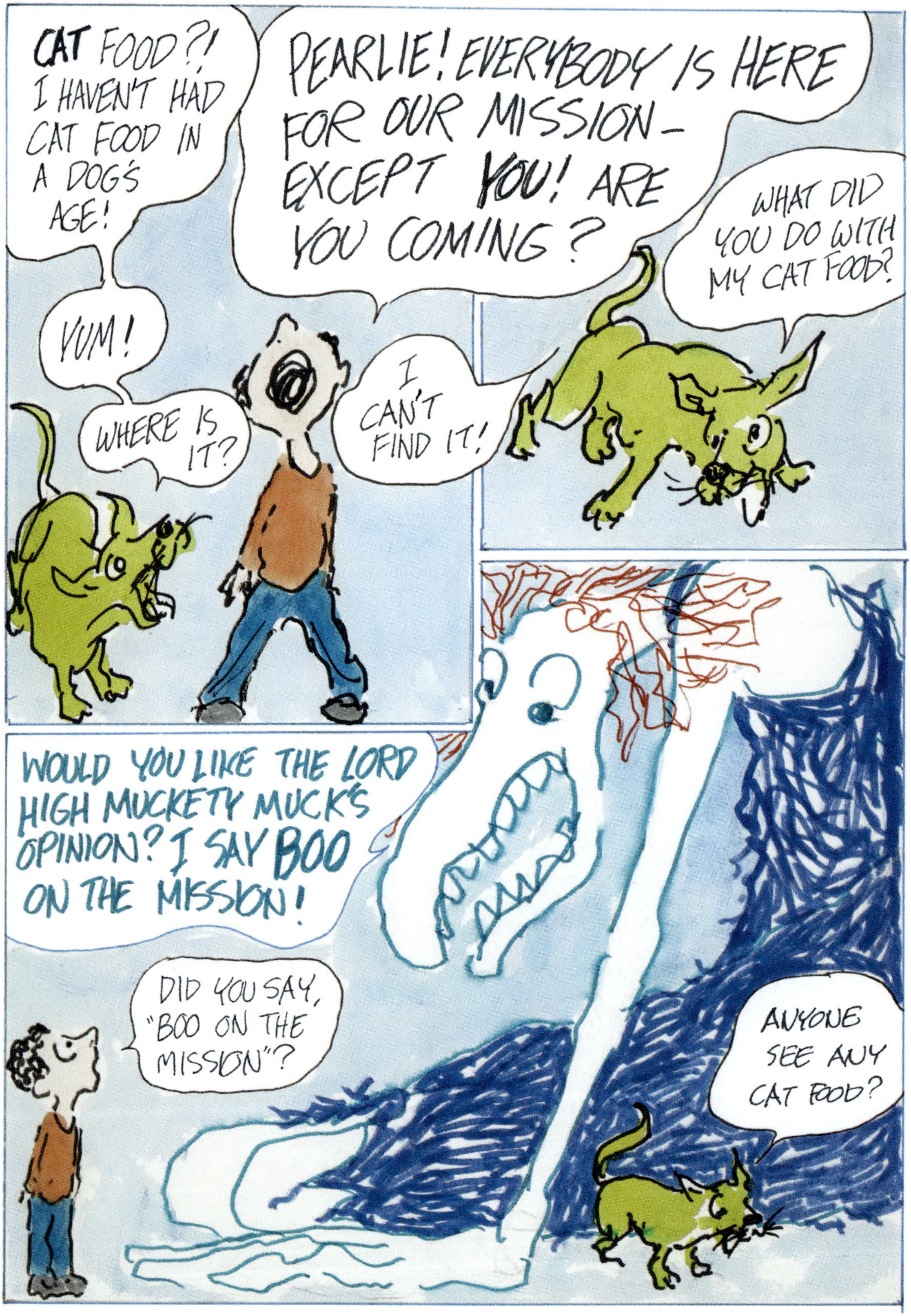
CAT FOOD?! I HAVEN'T HAD CAT FOOD IN A DOG'S AGE!
YUM!
WHERE IS IT?
PEARLIE! EVERYBODY IS HERE FOR OUR MISSION - EXCEPT YOU! ARE YOU COMING?
I CAN'T FIND IT!
WHAT DID YOU DO WITH MY CAT FOOD?
WOULD YOU LIKE THE LORD HIGH MUCKETY MUCK'S OPINION? I SAY BOO ON THE MISSION!
DID YOU SAY, "BOO ON THE MISSION"?
ANYONE SEE ANY CAT FOOD?

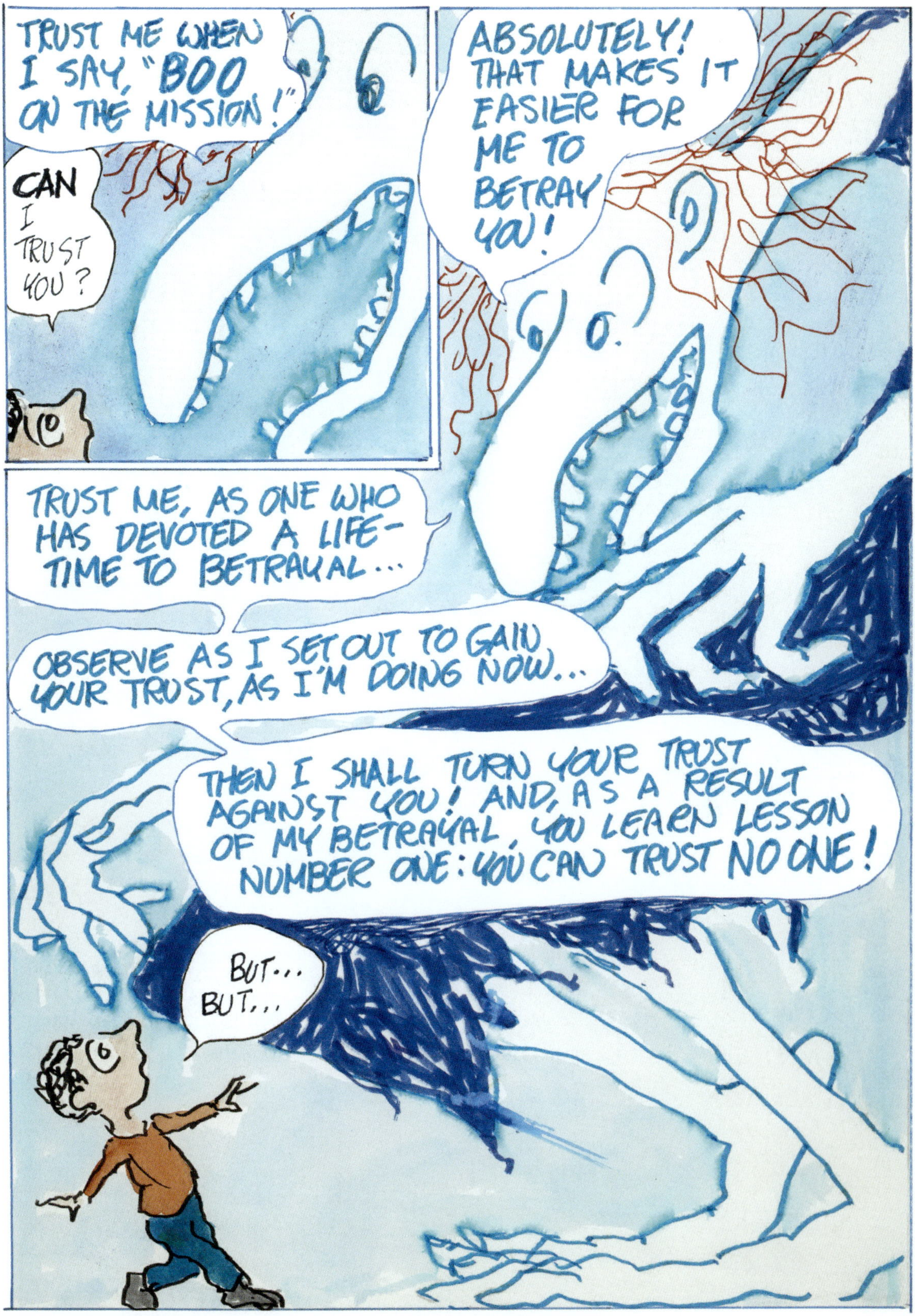
TRUST ME WHEN I SAY, "BOO ON THE MISSION!"
CAN I TRUST YOU?
ABSOLUTELY! THAT MAKES IT EASIER FOR ME TO BETRAY YOU!
TRUST ME, AS ONE WHO HAS DEVOTED A LIFE-TIME TO BETRAYAL...
OBSERVE AS I SET OUT TO GAIN YOUR TRUST, AS I'M DOING NOW...
THEN I SHALL TURN YOUR TRUST AGAINST YOU! AND, AS A RESULT OF MY BETRAYAL, YOU LEARN LESSON NUMBER ONE: YOU CAN TRUST NO ONE!
BUT... BUT...

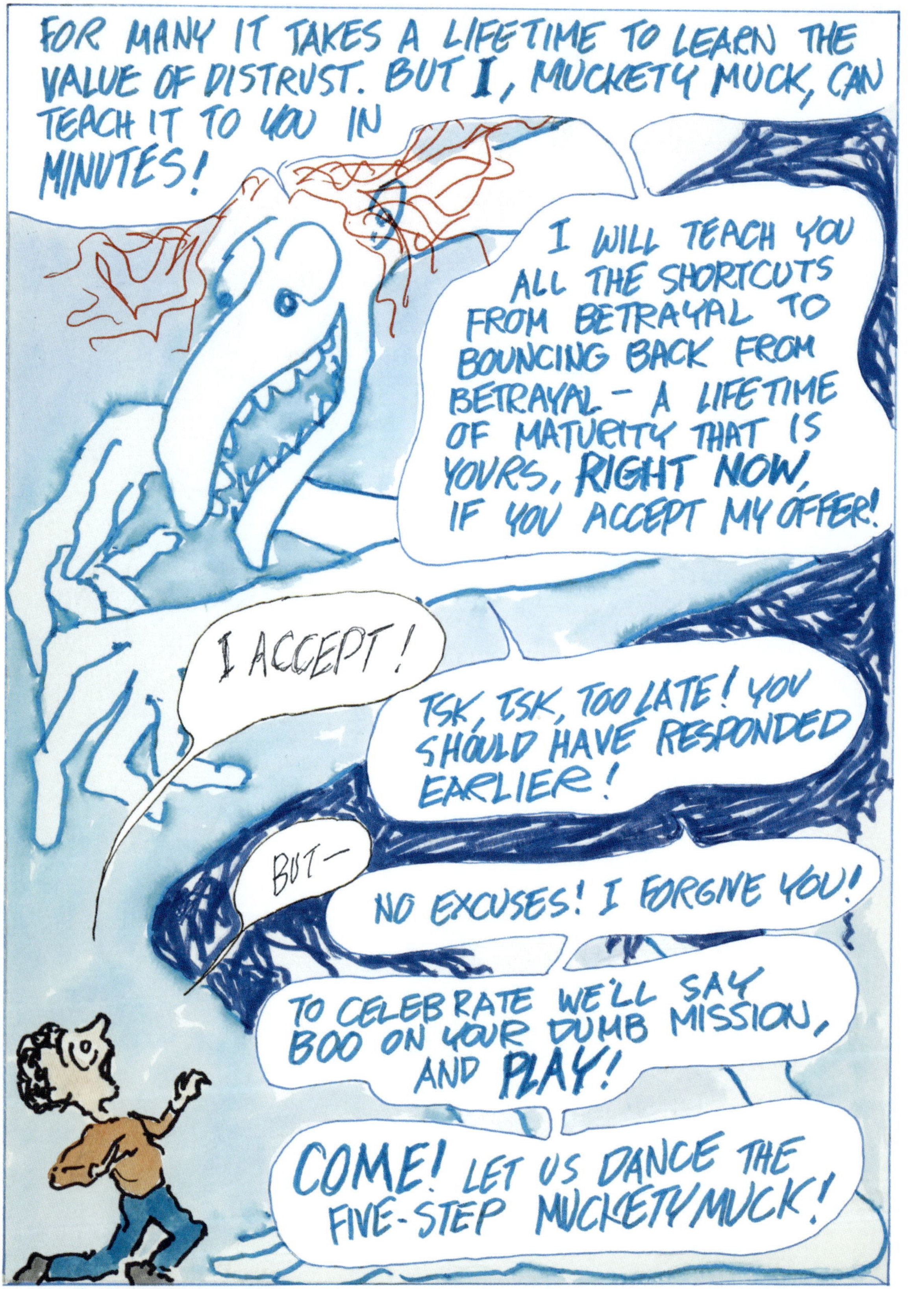
FOR MANY IT TAKES A LIFETIME TO LEARN THE VALUE OF DISTRUST. BUT I, MUCKETY MUCK, CAN TEACH IT TO YOU IN MINUTES!
I WILL TEACH YOU ALL THE SHORTCUTS FROM BETRAYAL TO BOUNCING BACK FROM BETRAYAL— A LIFETIME OF MATURITY THAT IS YOURS, RIGHT NOW, IF YOU ACCEPT MY OFFER!
I ACCEPT!
TSK, TSK, TOO LATE! YOU SHOULD HAVE RESPONDED EARLIER!
BUT—
NO EXCUSES! I FORGIVE YOU!
TO CELEBRATE WE'LL SAY BOO ON YOUR DUMB MISSION, AND PLAY!
COME! LET US DANCE THE FIVE-STEP MUCKETY MUCK!

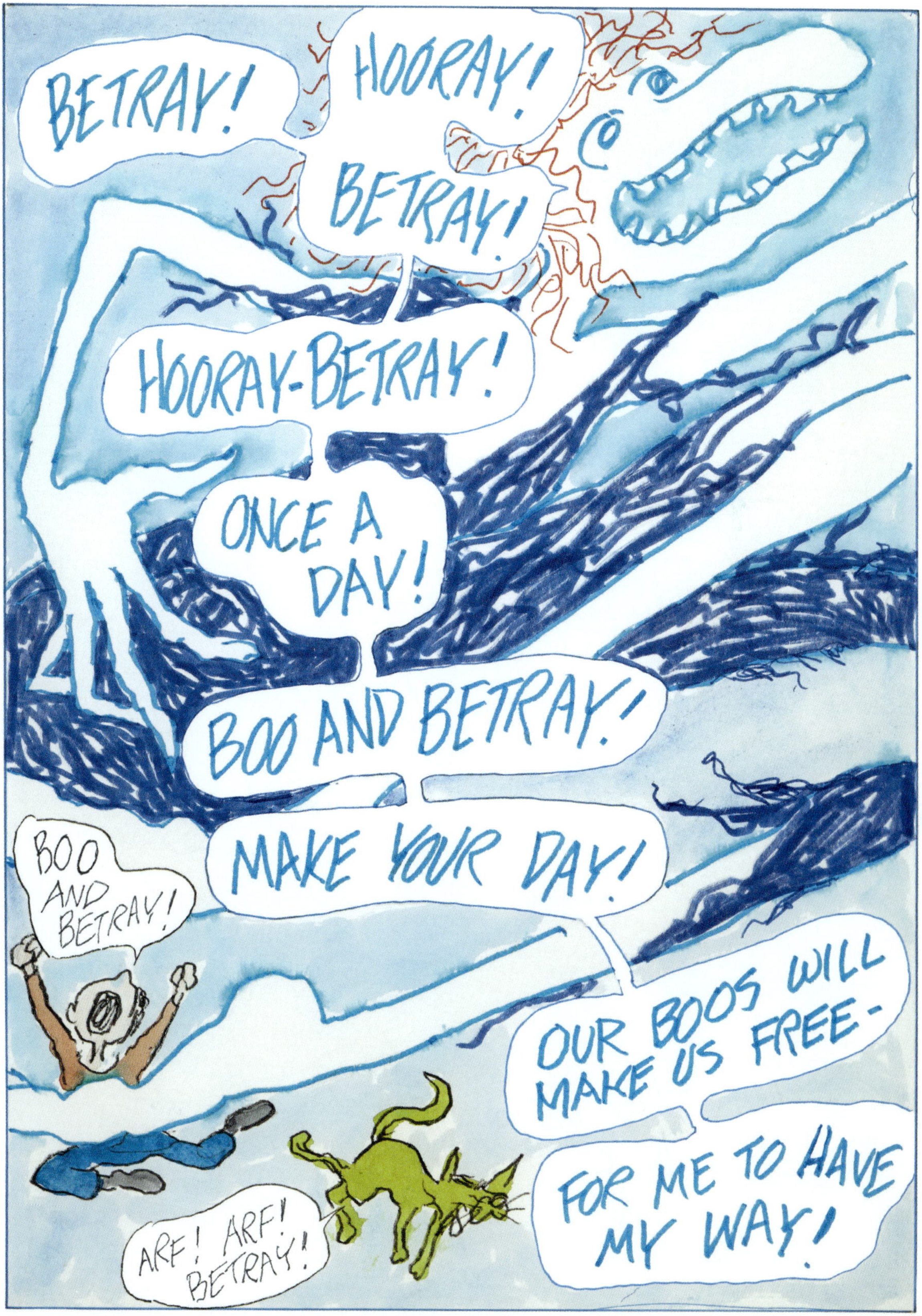
BETRAY!
HOORAY!
BETRAY!
HOORAY-BETRAY!
ONCE A DAY!
BOO AND BETRAY!
MAKE YOUR DAY!
BOO AND BETRAY!
OUR BOOS WILL MAKE US FREE-
FOR ME TO HAVE MY WAY!
ARF! ARF! BETRAY!

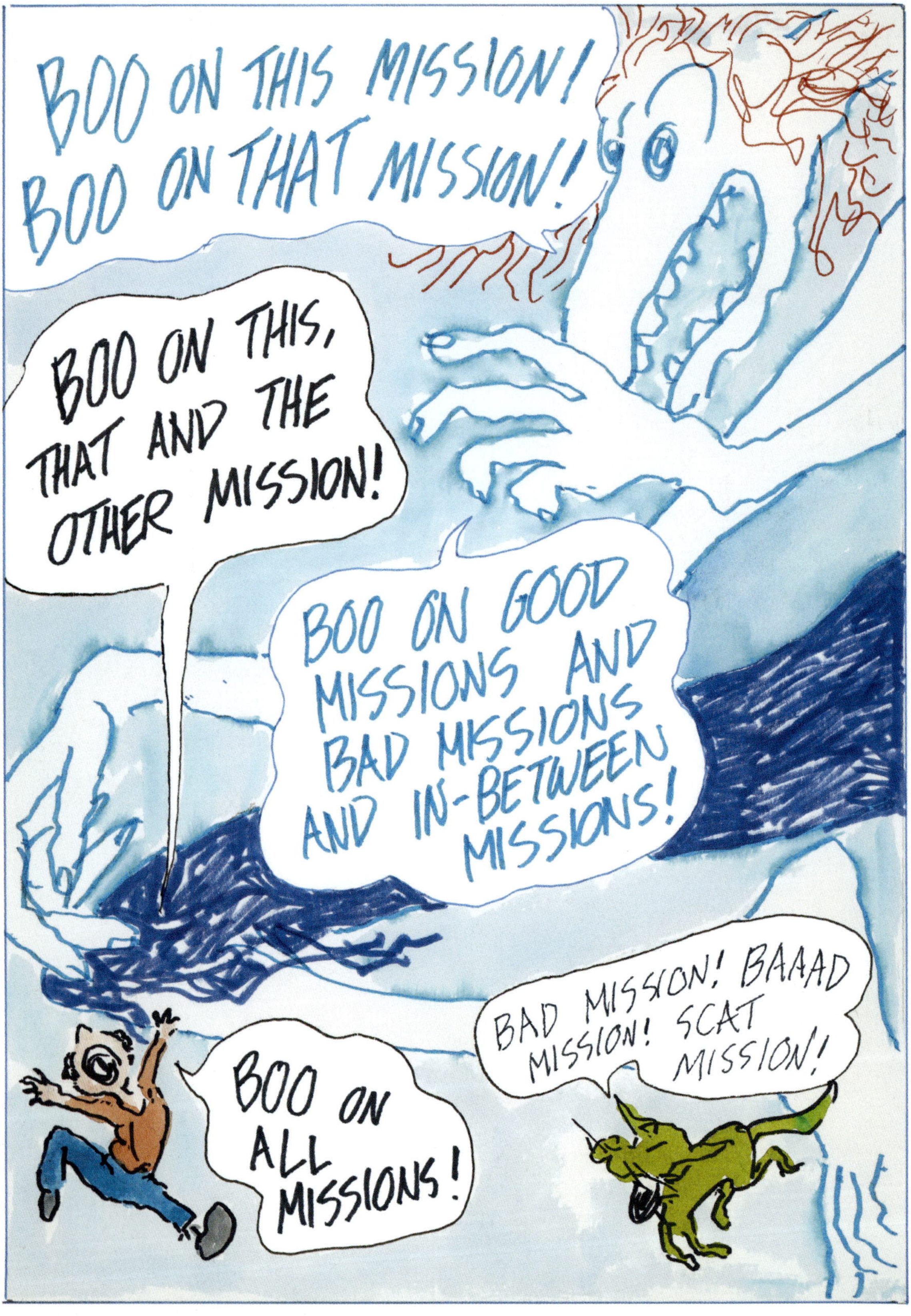
BOO ON THIS MISSION! BOO ON THAT MISSION!
BOO ON THIS, THAT AND THE OTHER MISSION!
BOO ON GOOD MISSIONS AND BAD MISSIONS AND IN-BETWEEN MISSIONS!
BOO ON ALL MISSIONS!
BAD MISSION! BAAAD MISSION! SCAT MISSION!

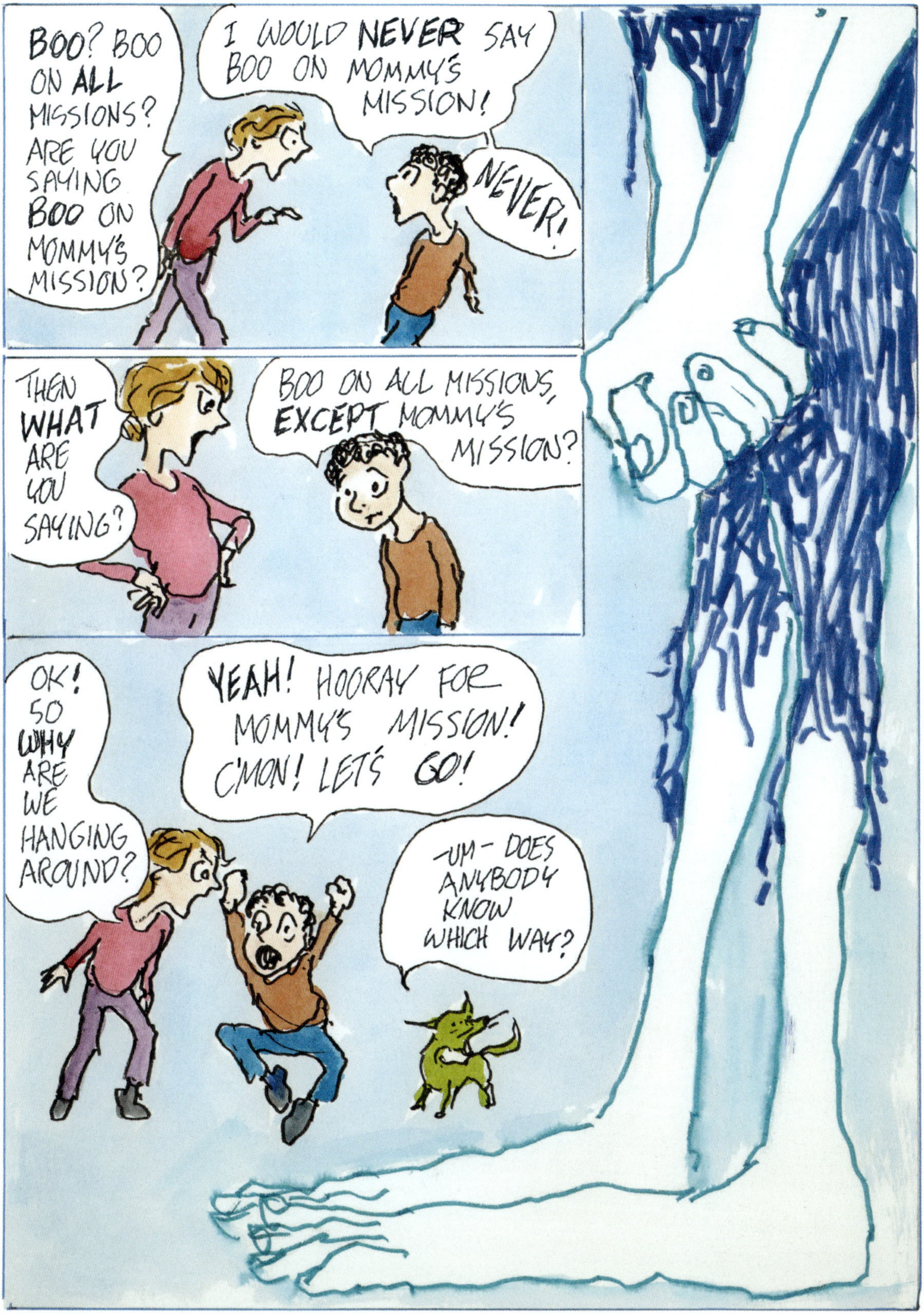
BOO? BOO ON ALL MISSIONS? ARE YOU SAYING BOO ON MOMMY'S MISSION?
I WOULD NEVER SAY BOO ON MOMMY'S MISSION!
NEVER!
THEN WHAT ARE YOU SAYING?
BOO ON ALL MISSIONS, EXCEPT MOMMY'S MISSION?
OK! SO WHY ARE WE HANGING AROUND?
YEAH! HOORAY FOR MOMMY'S MISSION! C'MON! LET'S GO!
-UM- DOES ANYBODY KNOW WHICH WAY?

CHAPTER 18 • THIS WAY →

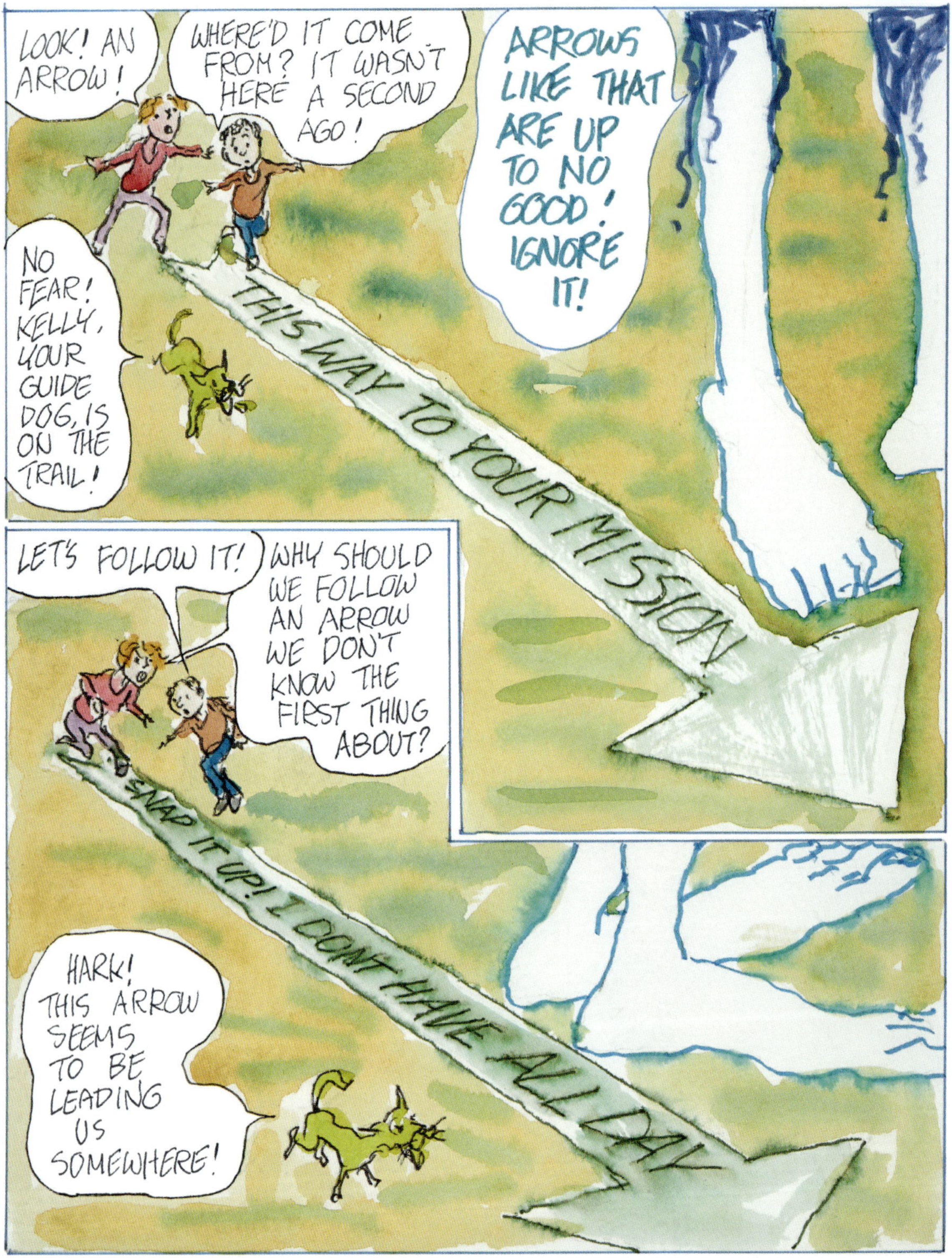

LOOK! AN ARROW!
WHERE'D IT COME FROM? IT WASN'T HERE A SECOND AGO!
ARROWS LIKE THAT ARE UP TO NO GOOD! IGNORE IT!
NO FEAR! KELLY, YOUR GUIDE DOG, IS ON THE TRAIL!
THIS WAY TO YOUR MISSION
LET'S FOLLOW IT!
WHY SHOULD WE FOLLOW AN ARROW WE DON'T KNOW THE FIRST THING ABOUT?
SNAP IT UP! I DON'T HAVE ALL DAY
HARK! THIS ARROW SEEMS TO BE LEADING US SOMEWHERE!

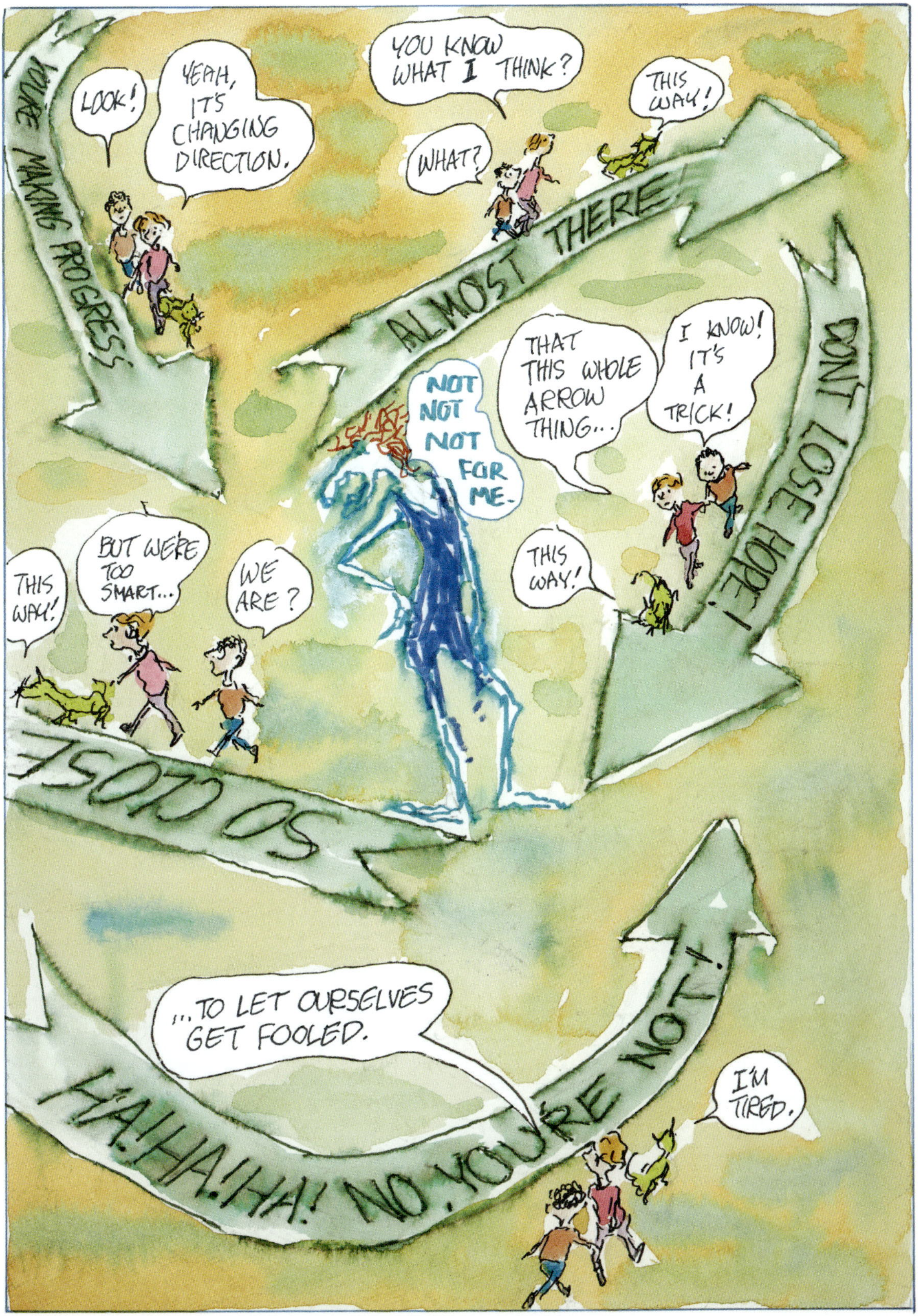
YOU'RE MAKING PROGRESS!
LOOK!
YEAH, IT'S CHANGING DIRECTION.
YOU KNOW WHAT I THINK?
WHAT?
THIS WAY!
ALMOST THERE
DON'T LOSE HOPE!
NOT NOT NOT FOR ME.
THAT THIS WHOLE ARROW THING...
I KNOW! IT'S A TRICK!
THIS WAY!
BUT WE'RE TOO SMART...
WE ARE?
THIS WAY!
SO CLOSE
...TO LET OURSELVES GET FOOLED.
HA! HA! HA! HA! NO, YOU'RE NOT!
I'M TIRED.

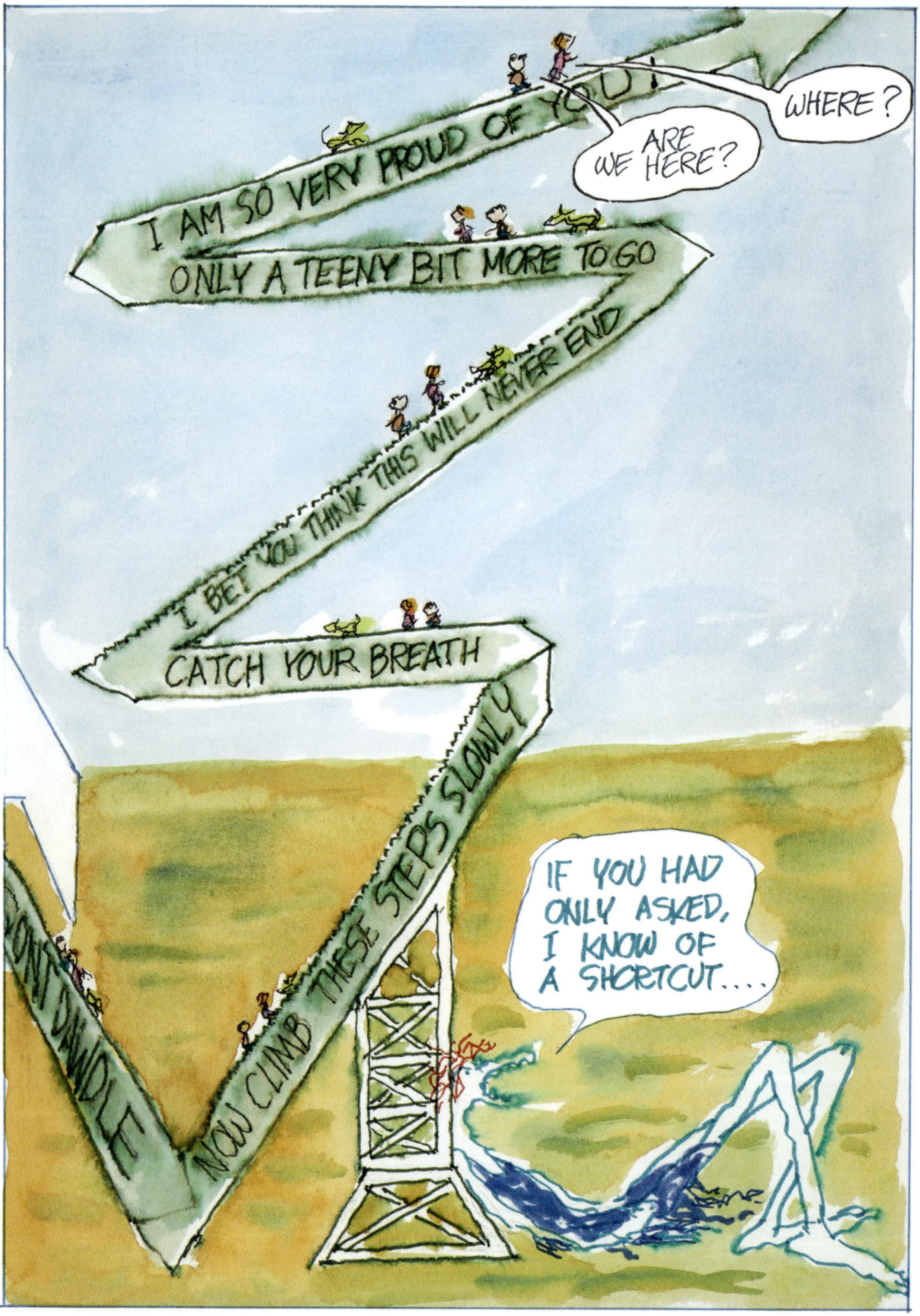
DONT DAWDLE
NOW CLIMB THESE STEPS SLOWLY
CATCH YOUR BREATH
I BET YOU THINK THIS WILL NEVER END
ONLY A TEENY BIT MORE TO GO
I AM SO VERY PROUD OF YOU!
ARE WE HERE?
WHERE?
IF YOU HAD ONLY ASKED, I KNOW OF A SHORTCUT....

CHAPTER 19 • LOOKING FOR TRUPHORIA

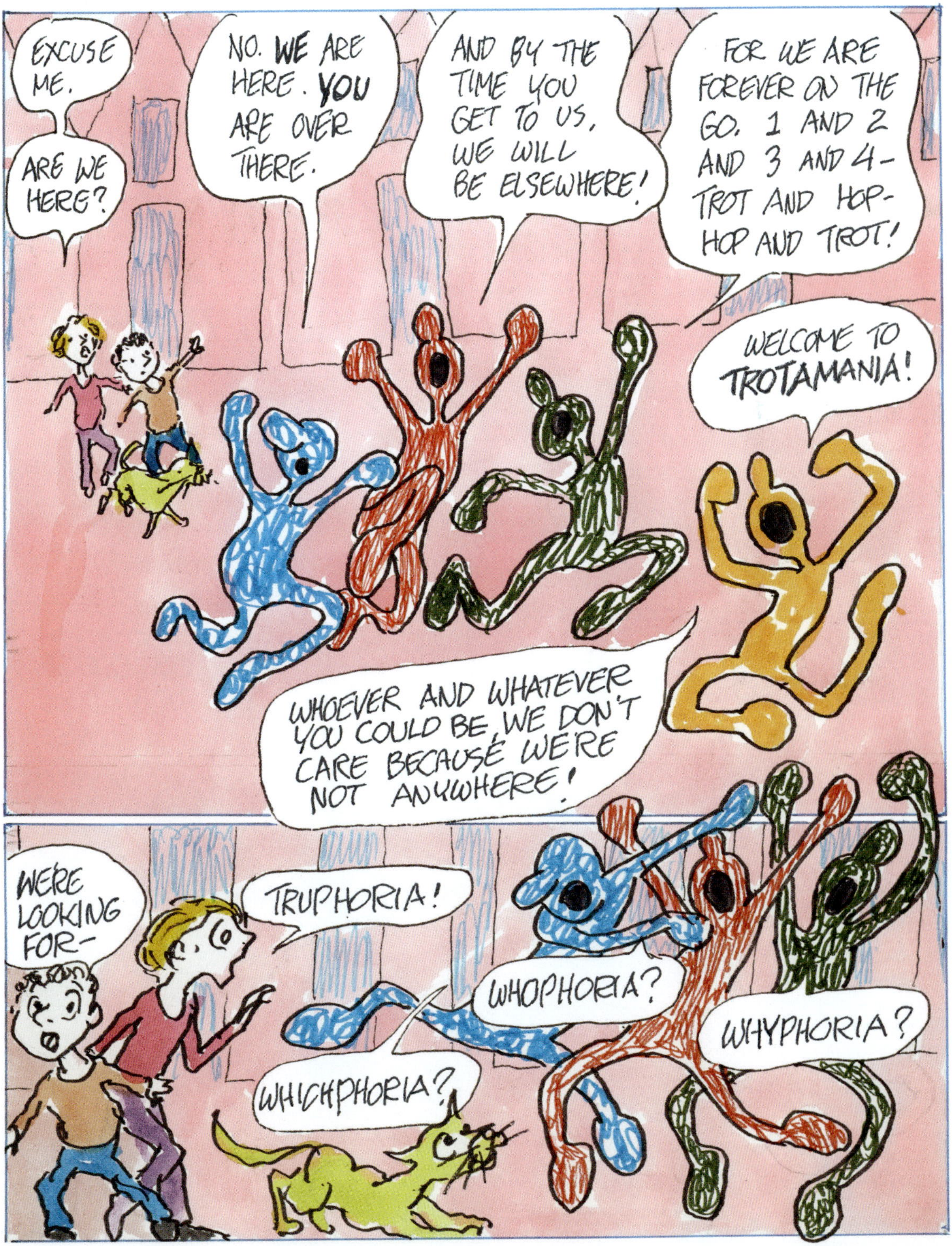
EXCUSE ME.
ARE WE HERE?
NO. WE ARE HERE. YOU ARE OVER THERE.
AND BY THE TIME YOU GET TO US, WE WILL BE ELSEWHERE!
FOR WE ARE FOREVER ON THE GO. 1 AND 2 AND 3 AND 4- TROT AND HOP- HOP AND TROT!
WELCOME TO TROTAMANIA!
WHOEVER AND WHATEVER YOU COULD BE, WE DON'T CARE BECAUSE WE'RE NOT ANYWHERE!
WE'RE LOOKING FOR-
TRUPHORIA!
WHOPHORIA?
WHYPHORIA?
WHICHPHORIA?

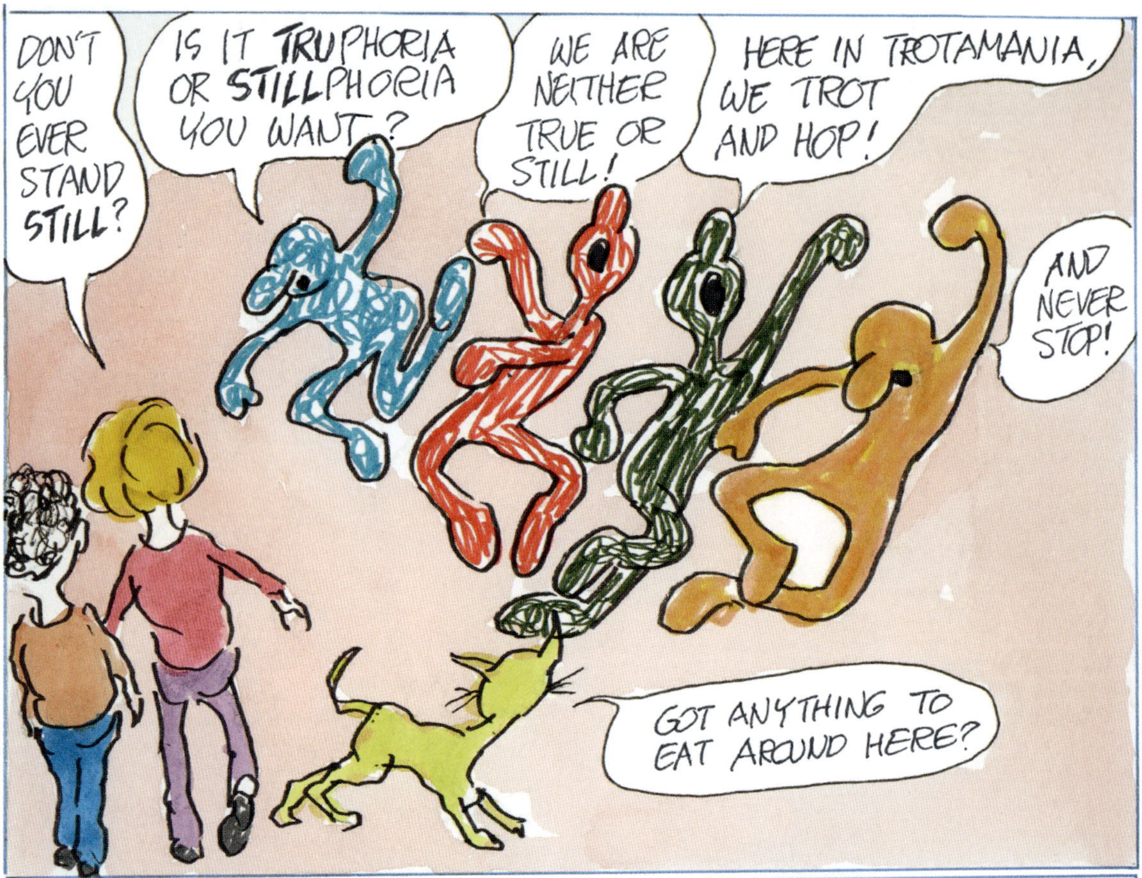
DON'T YOU EVER STAND STILL?
IS IT TRUPHORIA OR STILLPHORIA YOU WANT?
WE ARE NEITHER TRUE OR STILL!
HERE IN TROTAMANIA, WE TROT AND HOP!
AND NEVER STOP!
GOT ANYTHING TO EAT AROUND HERE?

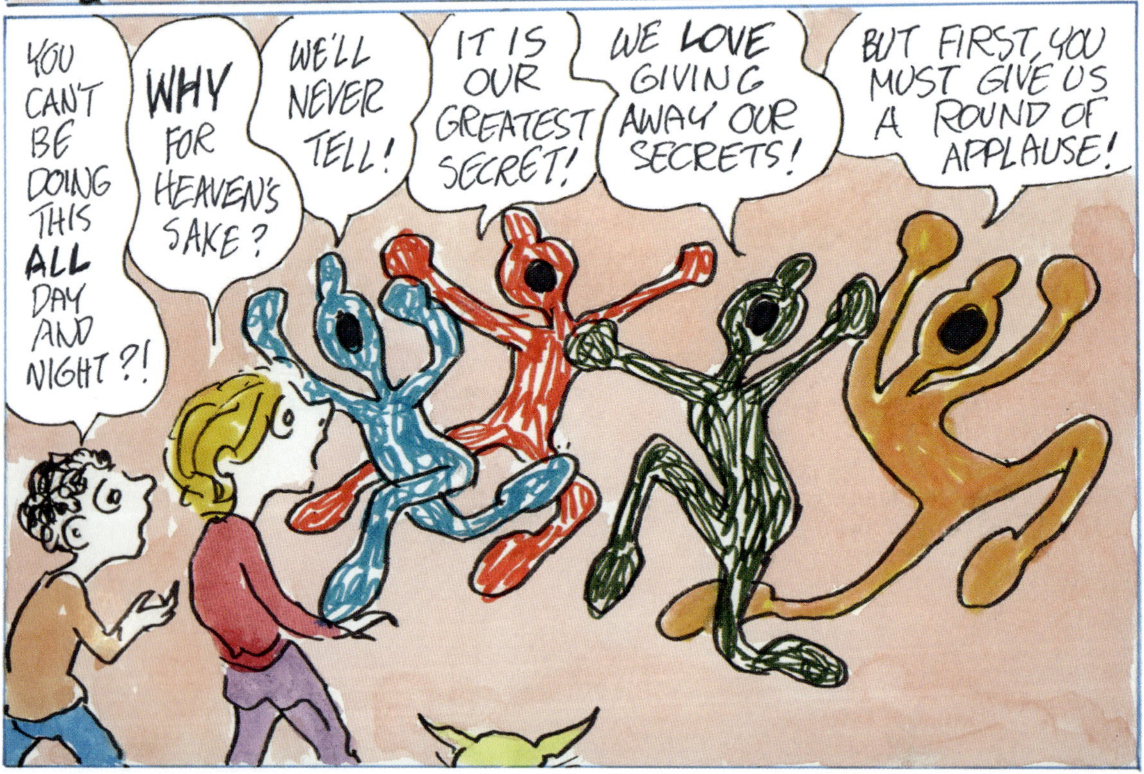
YOU CAN'T BE DOING THIS ALL DAY AND NIGHT?!
WHY FOR HEAVEN'S SAKE?
WE'LL NEVER TELL!
IT IS OUR GREATEST SECRET!
WE LOVE GIVING AWAY OUR SECRETS!
BUT FIRST, YOU MUST GIVE US A ROUND OF APPLAUSE!

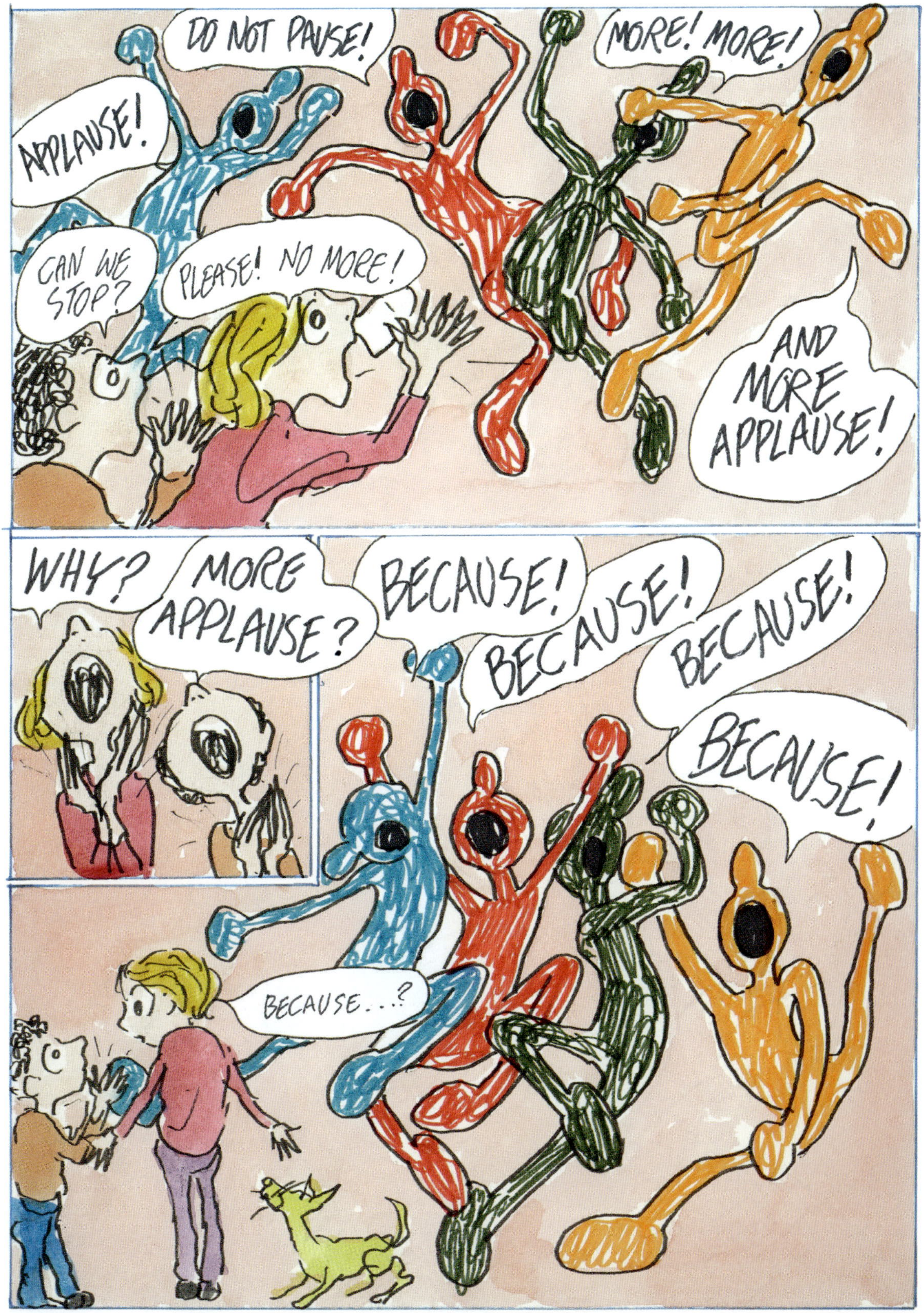
DO NOT PAUSE!
APPLAUSE!
MORE! MORE!
CAN WE STOP?
PLEASE! NO MORE!
AND MORE APPLAUSE!
WHY?
MORE APPLAUSE?
BECAUSE!
BECAUSE!
BECAUSE!
BECAUSE!
BECAUSE...?

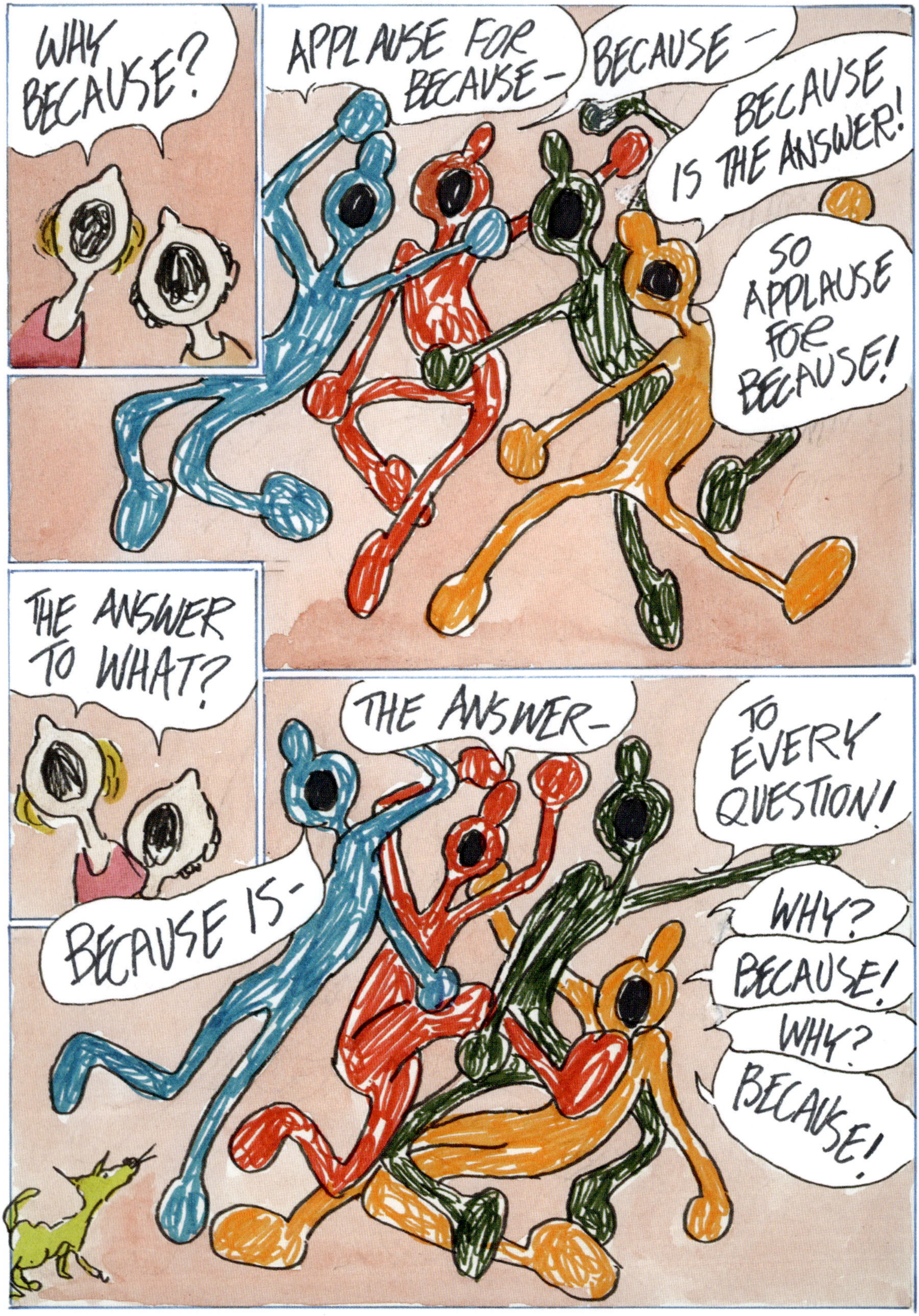
WHY BECAUSE?
APPLAUSE FOR BECAUSE—
BECAUSE—
BECAUSE IS THE ANSWER!
SO APPLAUSE FOR BECAUSE!
THE ANSWER TO WHAT?
BECAUSE IS—
THE ANSWER—
TO EVERY QUESTION!
WHY?
BECAUSE!
WHY?
BECAUSE!

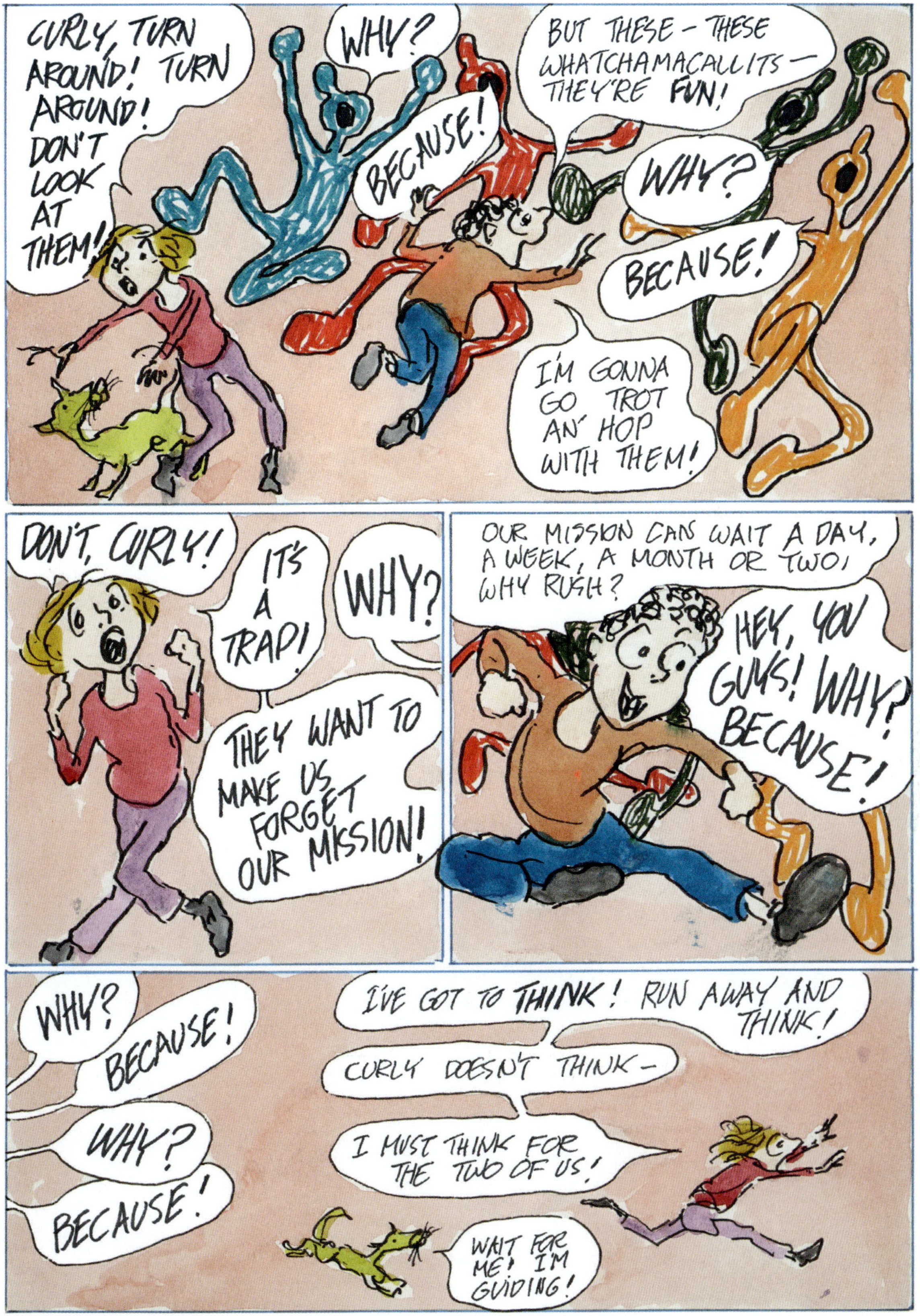
CURLY, TURN AROUND! TURN AROUND! DON'T LOOK AT THEM!
WHY?
BECAUSE!
BUT THESE - THESE WHATCHAMACALLITS - THEY'RE FUN!
WHY?
BECAUSE!
I'M GONNA GO TROT AN' HOP WITH THEM!
DON'T, CURLY!
IT'S A TRAP!
WHY?
THEY WANT TO MAKE US FORGET OUR MISSION!
OUR MISSION CAN WAIT A DAY, A WEEK, A MONTH OR TWO! WHY RUSH?
HEY, YOU GUYS! WHY? BECAUSE!
WHY?
BECAUSE!
WHY?
BECAUSE!
I'VE GOT TO THINK! RUN AWAY AND THINK!
CURLY DOESN'T THINK -
I MUST THINK FOR THE TWO OF US!
WAIT FOR ME! I'M GUIDING!

CHAPTER 20 • WHERE'S CURLY?

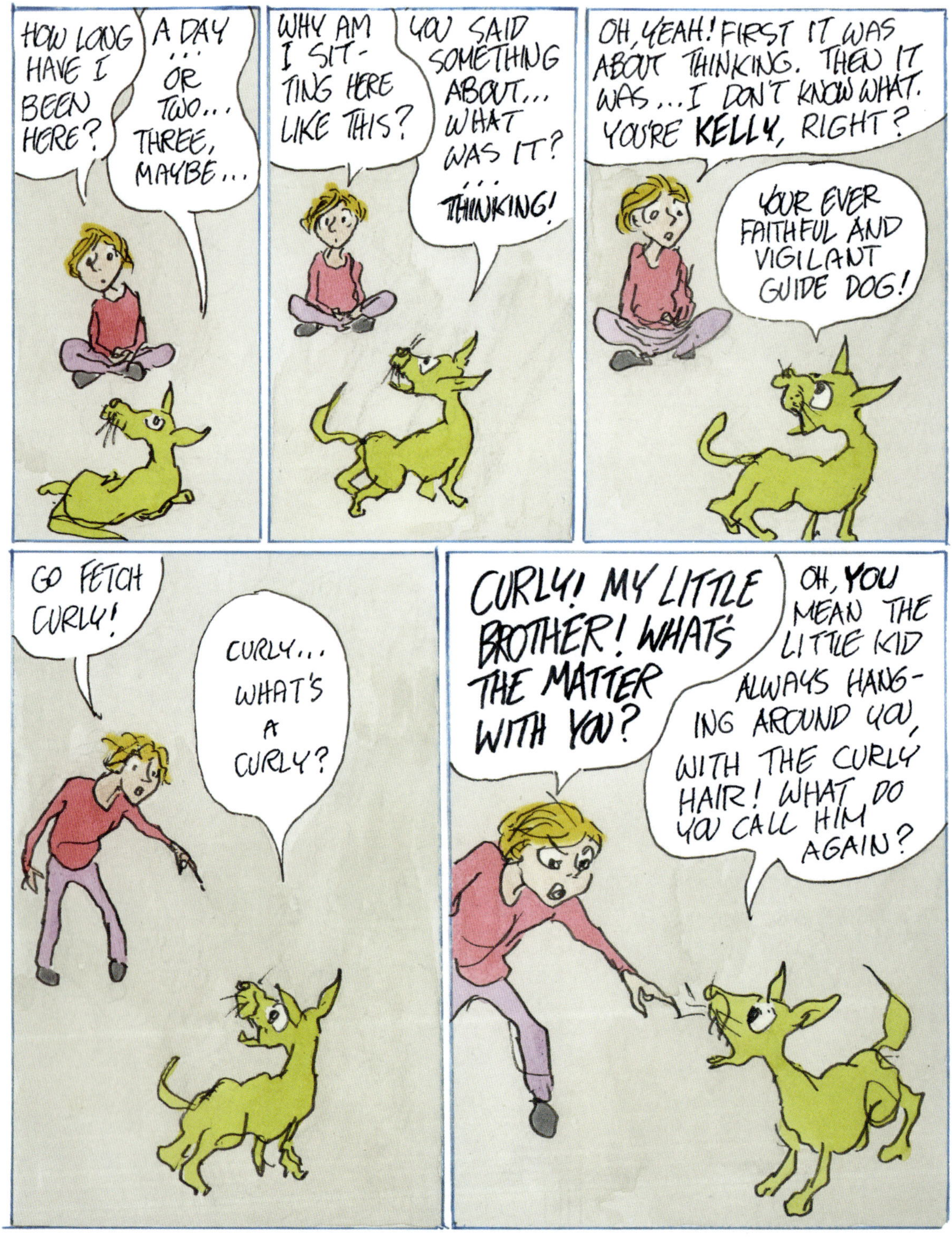
HOW LONG HAVE I BEEN HERE?
A DAY ... OR TWO... THREE, MAYBE...
WHY AM I SIT-TING HERE LIKE THIS?
YOU SAID SOMETHING ABOUT... WHAT WAS IT? ... THINKING!
OH, YEAH! FIRST IT WAS ABOUT THINKING. THEN IT WAS... I DON'T KNOW WHAT. YOU'RE KELLY, RIGHT?
YOUR EVER FAITHFUL AND VIGILANT GUIDE DOG!
GO FETCH CURLY!
CURLY... WHAT'S A CURLY?
CURLY! MY LITTLE BROTHER! WHAT'S THE MATTER WITH YOU?
OH, YOU MEAN THE LITTLE KID ALWAYS HANG-ING AROUND YOU, WITH THE CURLY HAIR! WHAT DO YOU CALL HIM AGAIN?

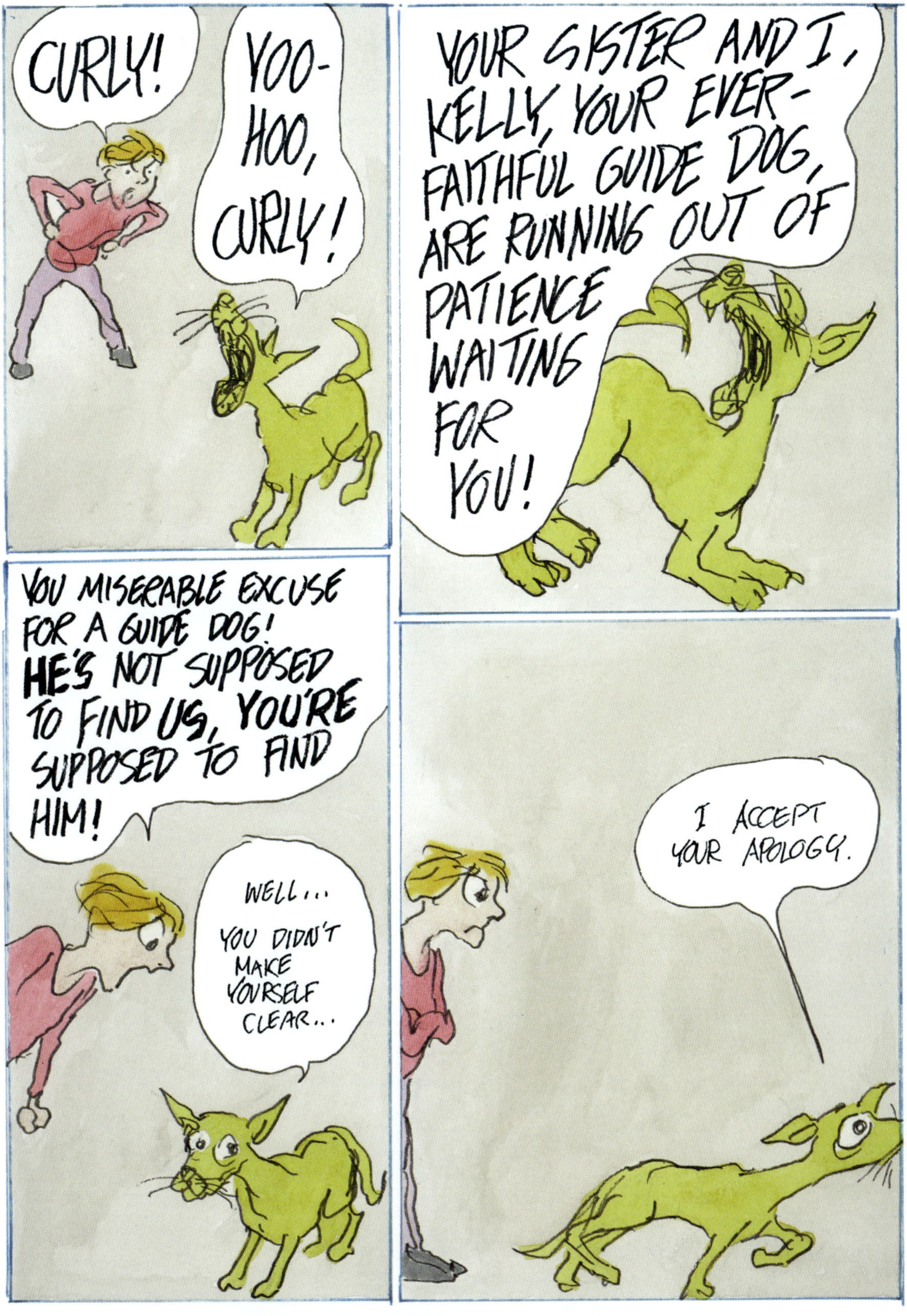
CURLY!
YOO-HOO, CURLY!
YOUR SISTER AND I, KELLY, YOUR EVER-FAITHFUL GUIDE DOG, ARE RUNNING OUT OF PATIENCE WAITING FOR YOU!
YOU MISERABLE EXCUSE FOR A GUIDE DOG! HE'S NOT SUPPOSED TO FIND US, YOU'RE SUPPOSED TO FIND HIM!
WELL... YOU DIDN'T MAKE YOURSELF CLEAR...
I ACCEPT YOUR APOLOGY.

CHAPTER 21 • WHERE'S KELLY?

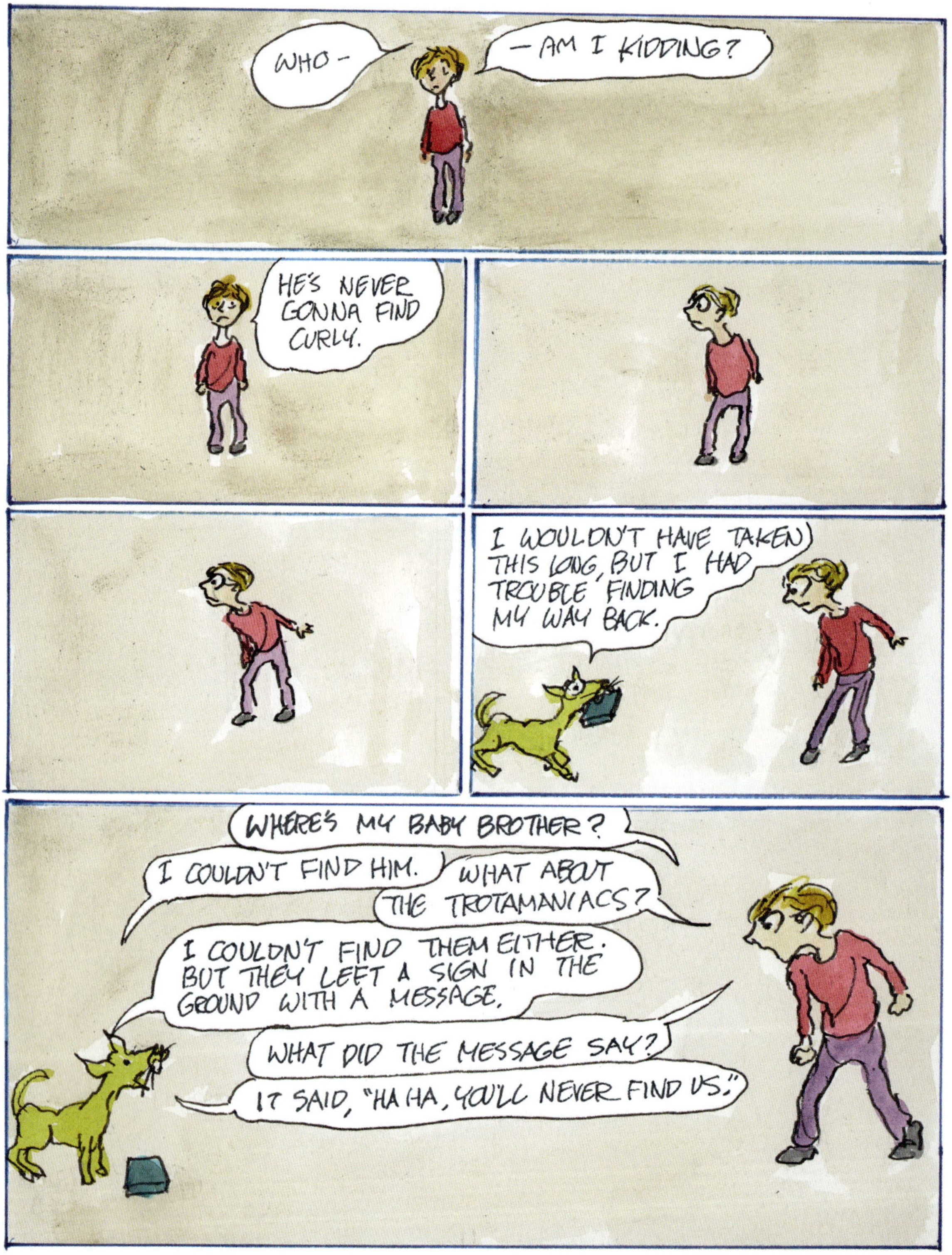
WHO-
-AM I KIDDING?
HE'S NEVER GONNA FIND CURLY.
I WOULDN'T HAVE TAKEN THIS LONG, BUT I HAD TROUBLE FINDING MY WAY BACK.
WHERE'S MY BABY BROTHER?
I COULDN'T FIND HIM.
WHAT ABOUT THE TROTAMANIACS?
I COULDN'T FIND THEM EITHER. BUT THEY LEFT A SIGN IN THE GROUND WITH A MESSAGE.
WHAT DID THE MESSAGE SAY?
IT SAID, "HA HA, YOU'LL NEVER FIND US."

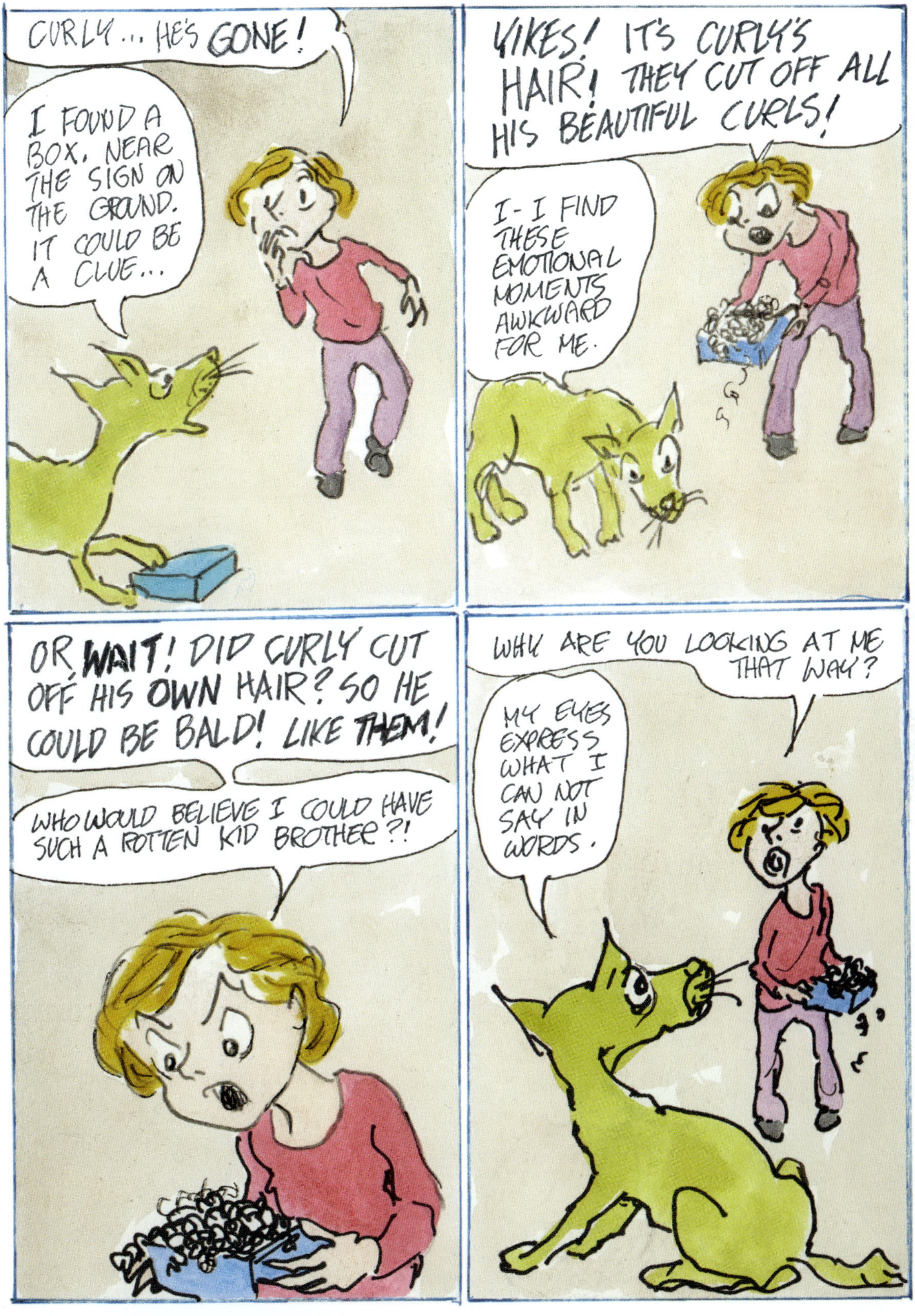
CURLY... HE'S GONE!
I FOUND A BOX, NEAR THE SIGN ON THE GROUND. IT COULD BE A CLUE...
YIKES! IT'S CURLY'S HAIR! THEY CUT OFF ALL HIS BEAUTIFUL CURLS!
I- I FIND THESE EMOTIONAL MOMENTS AWKWARD FOR ME.
OR WAIT! DID CURLY CUT OFF HIS OWN HAIR? SO HE COULD BE BALD! LIKE THEM!
WHO WOULD BELIEVE I COULD HAVE SUCH A ROTTEN KID BROTHER?!
WHY ARE YOU LOOKING AT ME THAT WAY?
MY EYES EXPRESS WHAT I CAN NOT SAY IN WORDS.

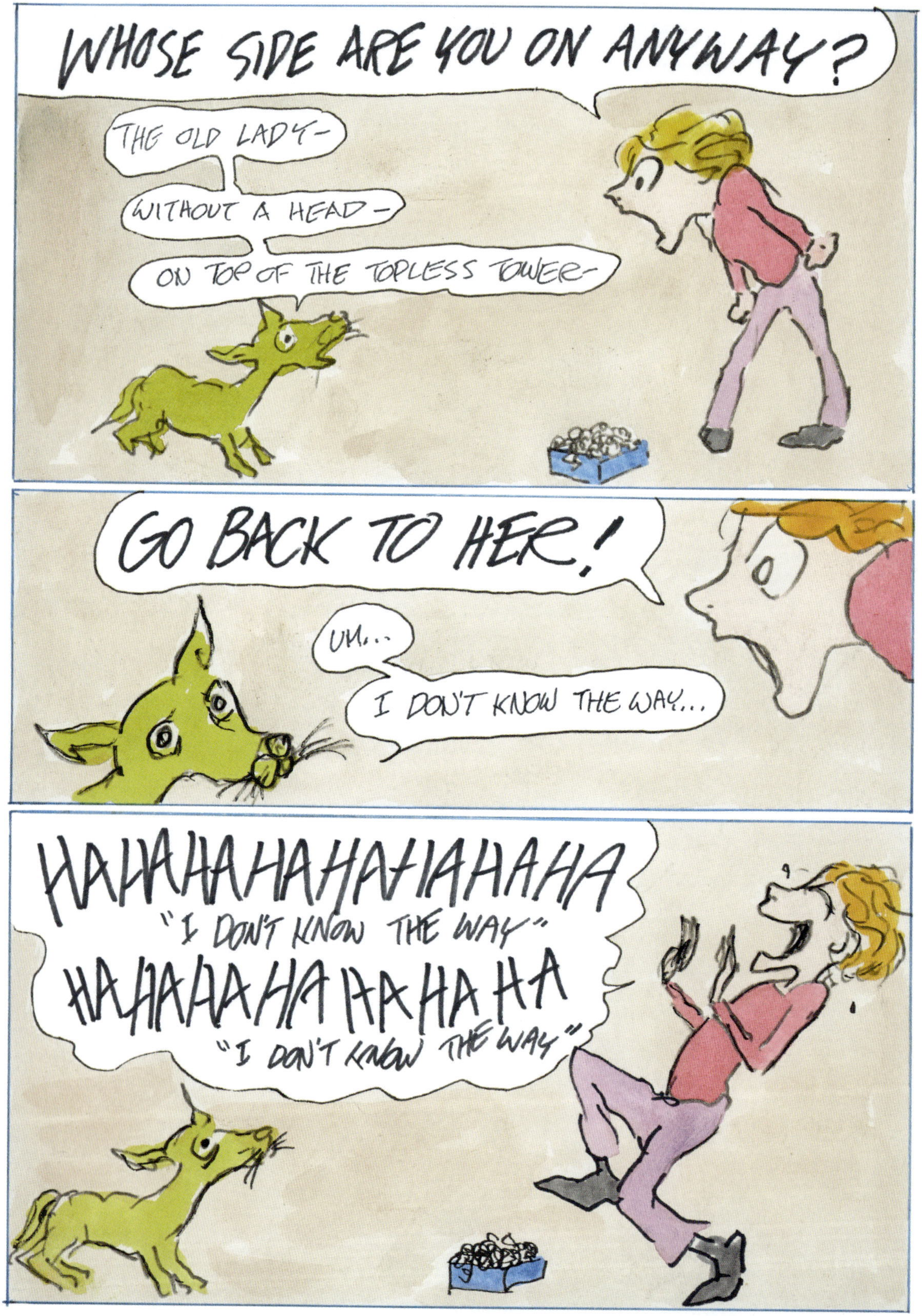
WHOSE SIDE ARE YOU ON ANYWAY?
THE OLD LADY-
WITHOUT A HEAD-
ON TOP OF THE TOPLESS TOWER-
GO BACK TO HER!
UM...
I DON'T KNOW THE WAY...
HAHAHAHAHAHAHAHA
"I DON'T KNOW THE WAY"
HAHAHAHA HA HA HA
"I DON'T KNOW THE WAY"

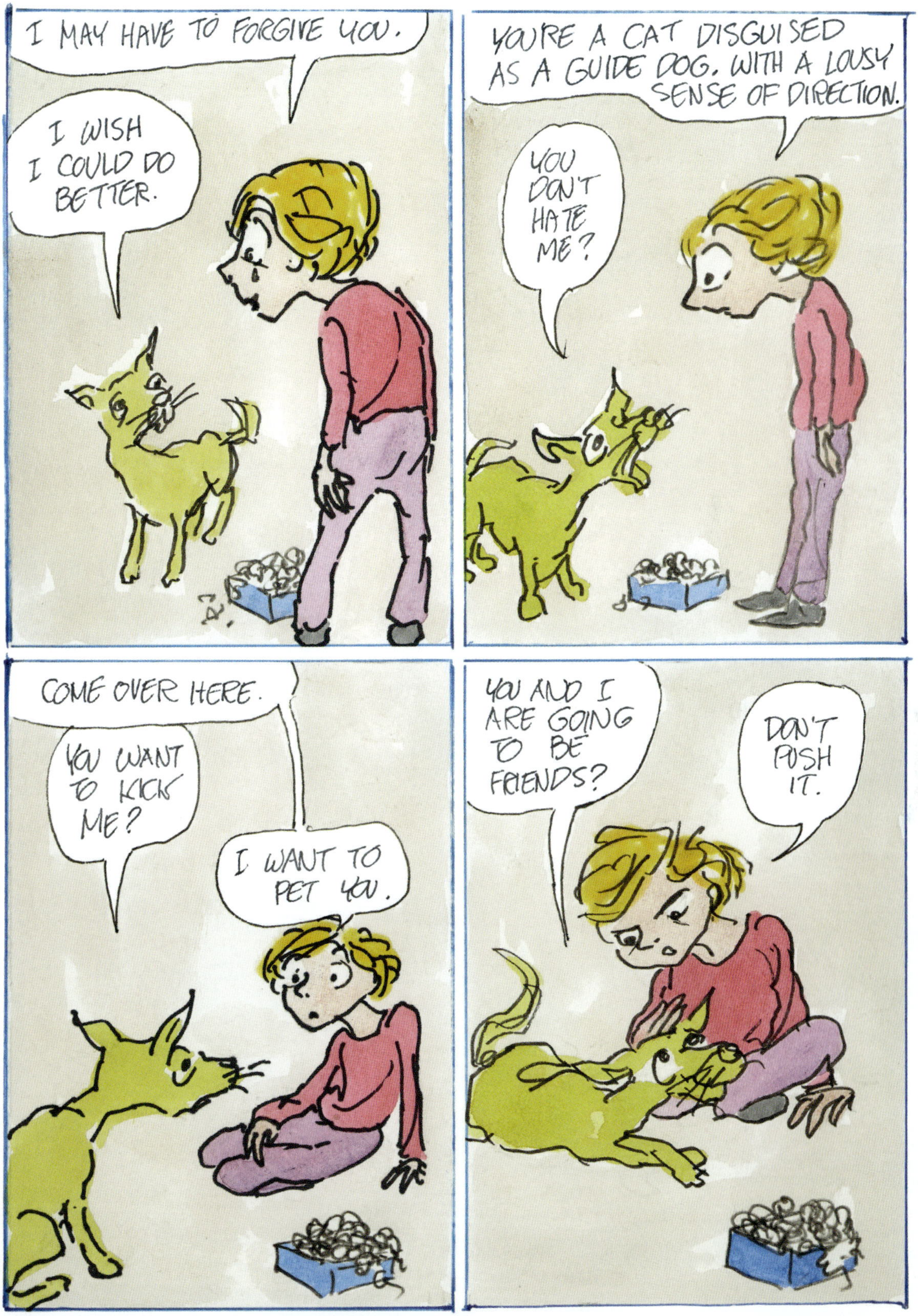
I MAY HAVE TO FORGIVE YOU.
I WISH I COULD DO BETTER.
YOU'RE A CAT DISGUISED AS A GUIDE DOG. WITH A LOUSY SENSE OF DIRECTION.
YOU DON'T HATE ME?
COME OVER HERE.
YOU WANT TO KICK ME?
I WANT TO PET YOU.
YOU AND I ARE GOING TO BE FRIENDS?
DON'T PUSH IT.

CHAPTER 22 • BALDY???

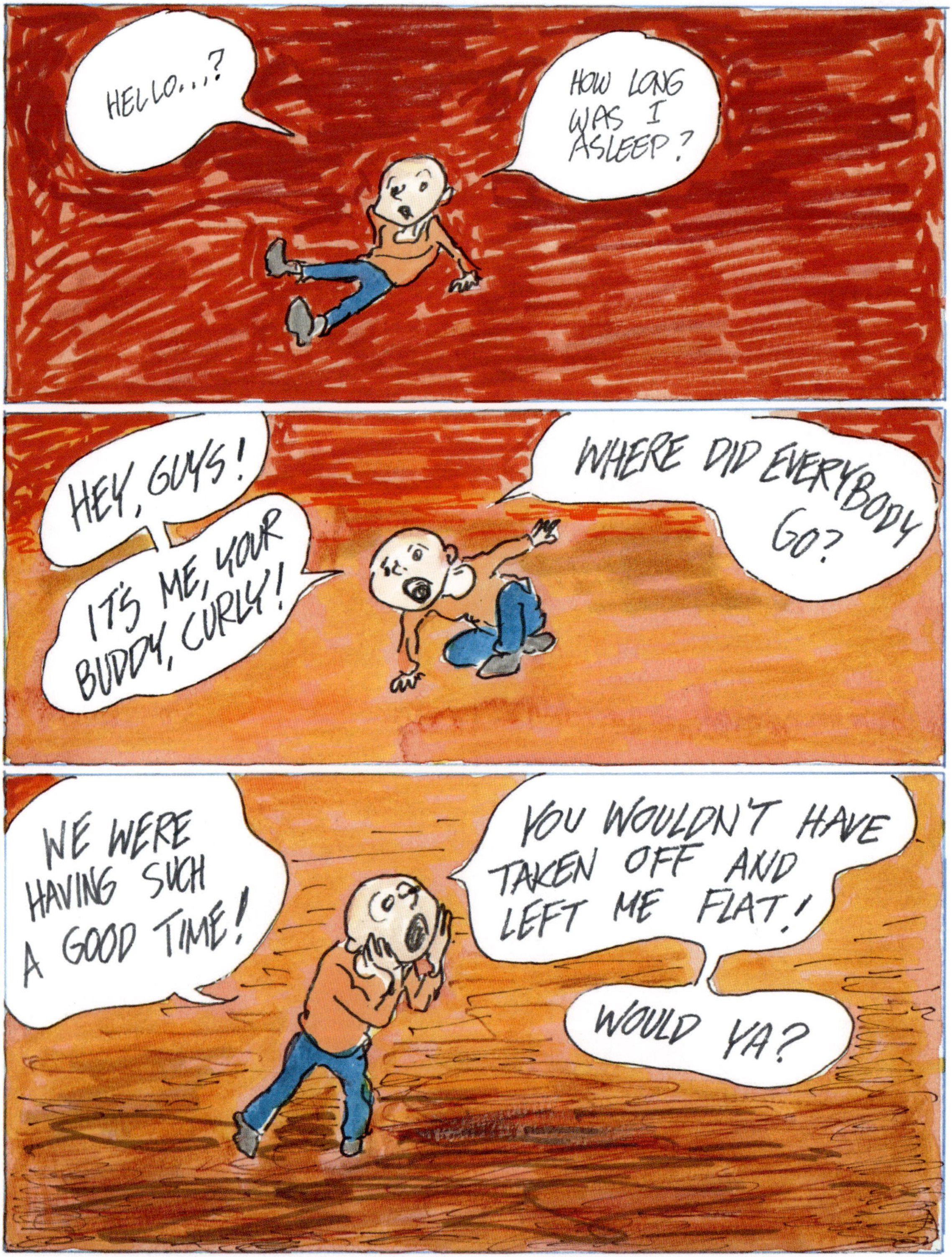
HELLO...?
HOW LONG WAS I ASLEEP?
HEY, GUYS!
IT'S ME, YOUR BUDDY, CURLY!
WHERE DID EVERYBODY GO?
WE WERE HAVING SUCH A GOOD TIME!
YOU WOULDN'T HAVE TAKEN OFF AND LEFT ME FLAT!
WOULD YA?

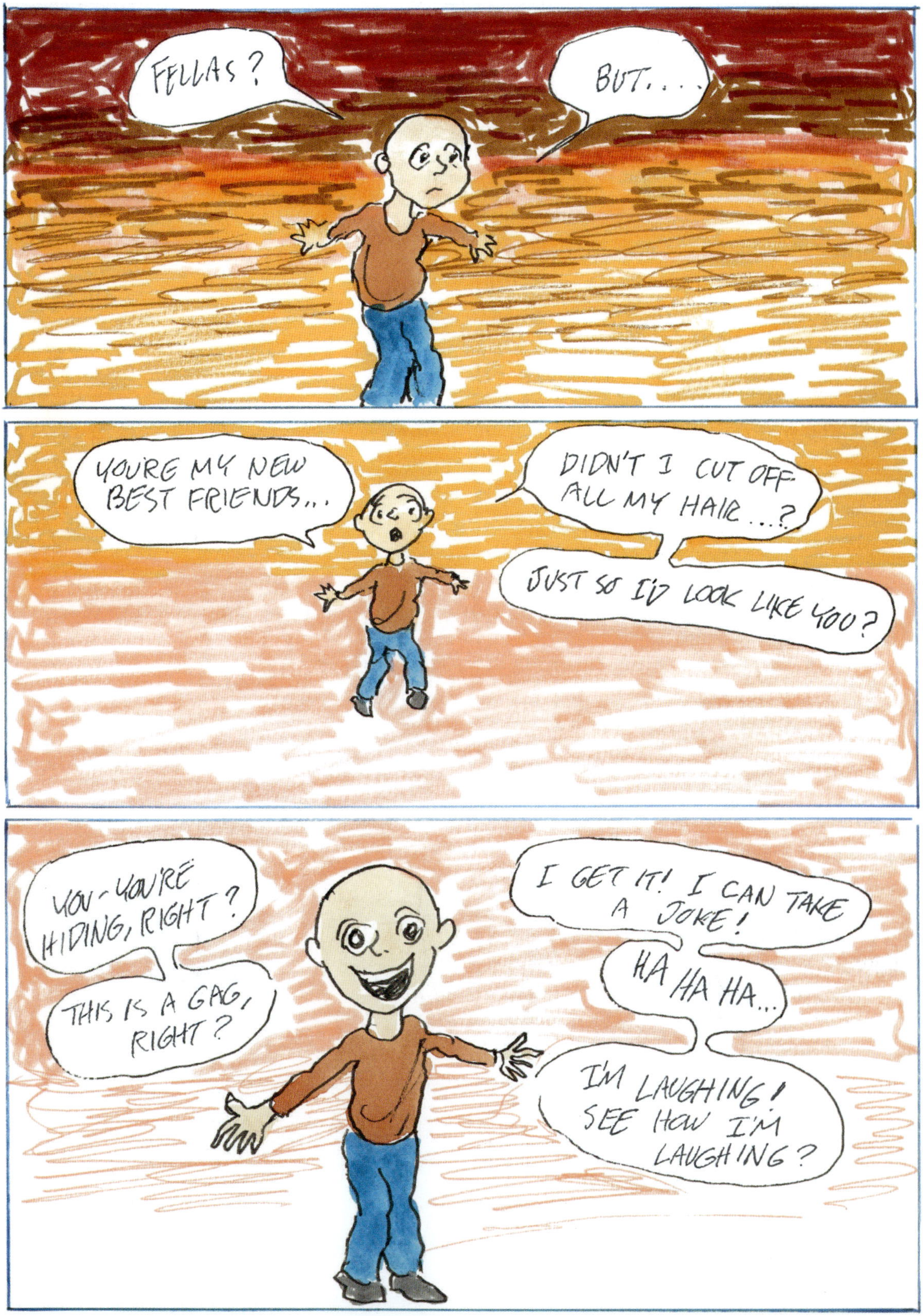
FELLAS?
BUT....
YOU'RE MY NEW BEST FRIENDS...
DIDN'T I CUT OFF ALL MY HAIR...?
JUST SO I'D LOOK LIKE YOU?
YOU-YOU'RE HIDING, RIGHT?
THIS IS A GAG, RIGHT?
I GET IT! I CAN TAKE A JOKE!
HA HA HA...
I'M LAUGHING! SEE HOW I'M LAUGHING?

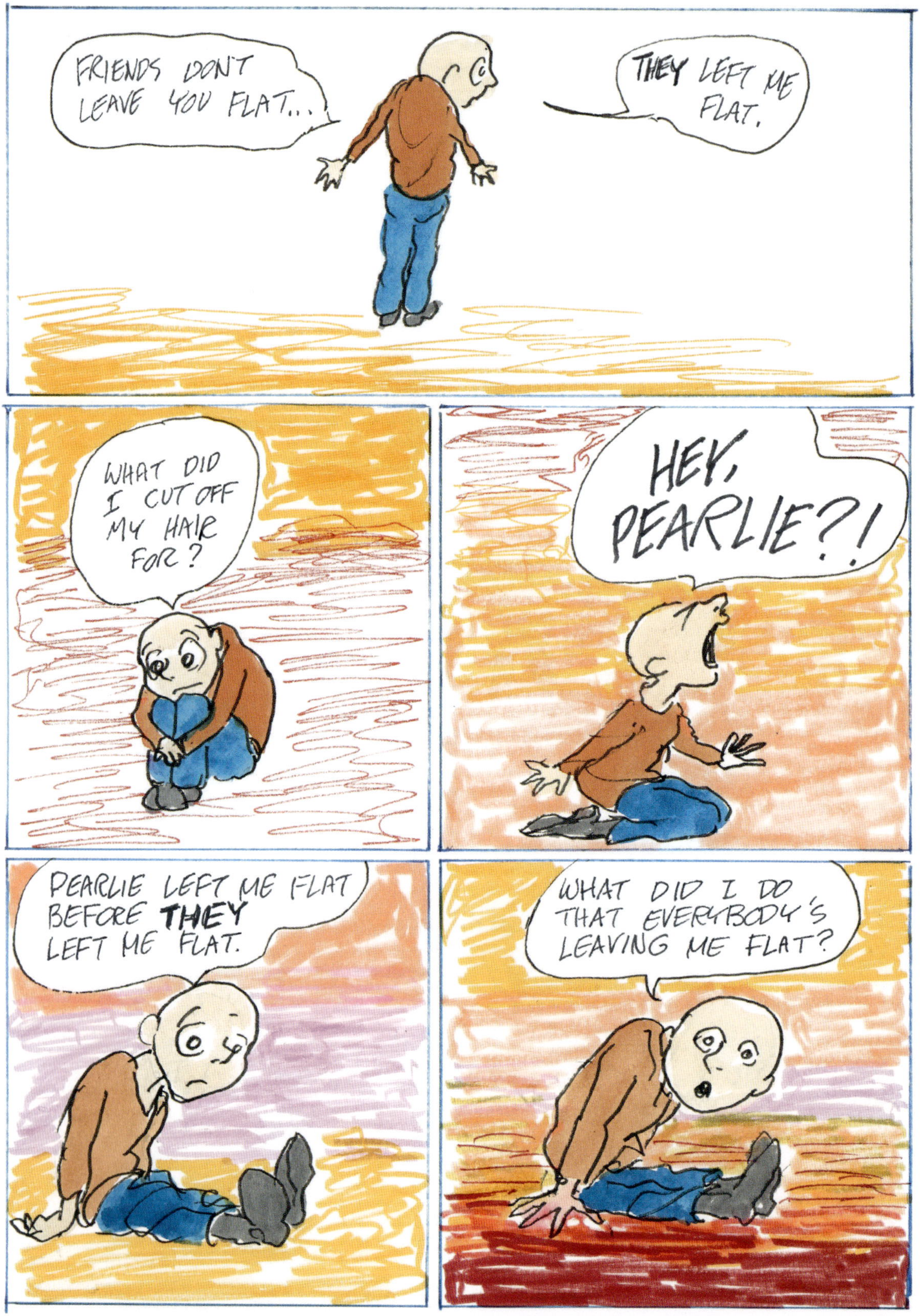
FRIENDS DON'T LEAVE YOU FLAT...
THEY LEFT ME FLAT.
WHAT DID I CUT OFF MY HAIR FOR?
HEY, PEARLIE?!
PEARLIE LEFT ME FLAT BEFORE THEY LEFT ME FLAT.
WHAT DID I DO THAT EVERYBODY'S LEAVING ME FLAT?

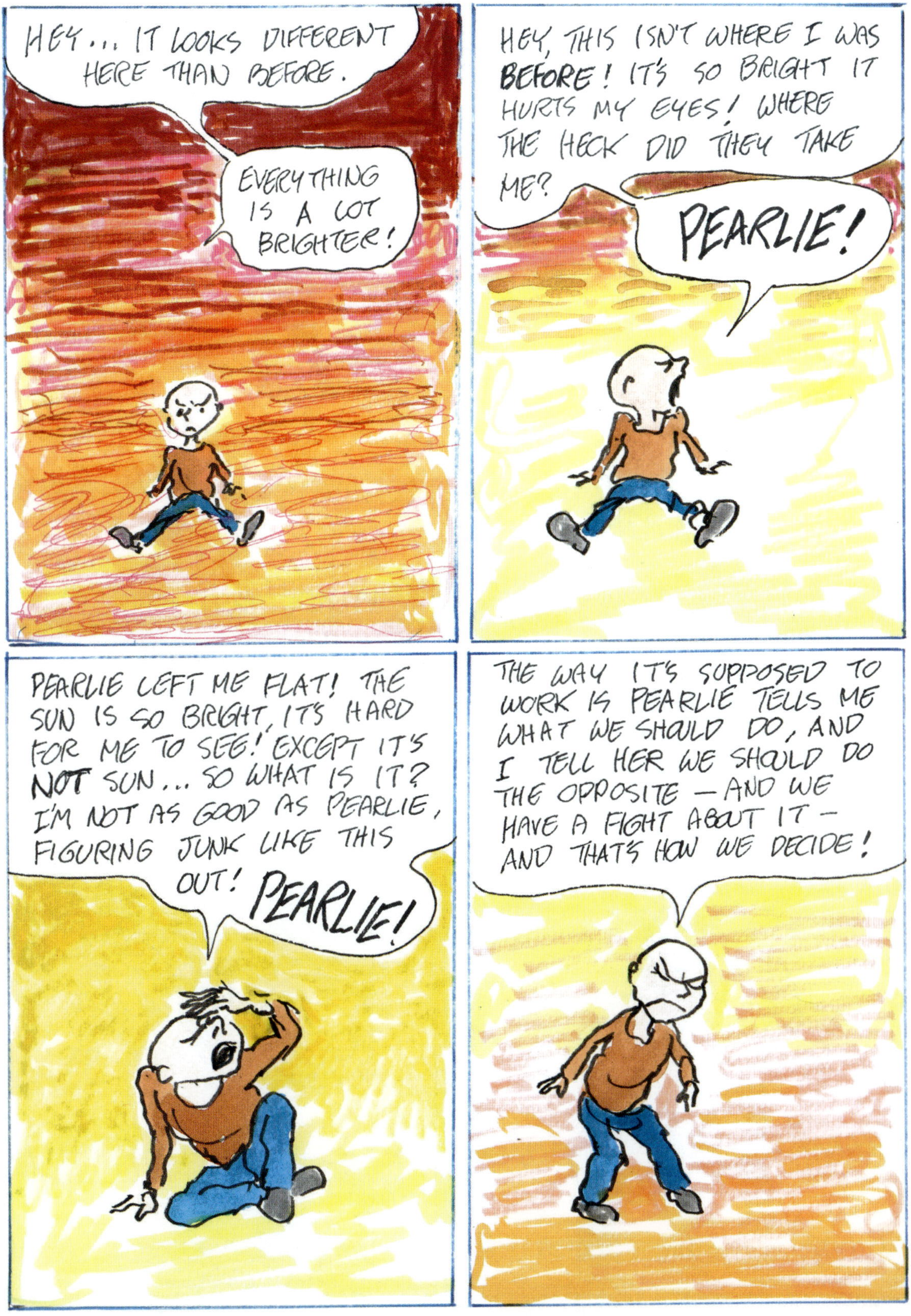
HEY... IT LOOKS DIFFERENT HERE THAN BEFORE.
EVERYTHING IS A LOT BRIGHTER!
HEY, THIS ISN'T WHERE I WAS **BEFORE**! IT'S SO BRIGHT IT HURTS MY EYES! WHERE THE HECK DID THEY TAKE ME?
PEARLIE!
PEARLIE LEFT ME FLAT! THE SUN IS SO BRIGHT, IT'S HARD FOR ME TO SEE! EXCEPT IT'S **NOT** SUN... SO WHAT IS IT? I'M NOT AS GOOD AS PEARLIE, FIGURING JUNK LIKE THIS OUT!
PEARLIE!
THE WAY IT'S SUPPOSED TO WORK IS PEARLIE TELLS ME WHAT WE SHOULD DO, AND I TELL HER WE SHOULD DO THE OPPOSITE — AND WE HAVE A FIGHT ABOUT IT — AND THAT'S HOW WE DECIDE!

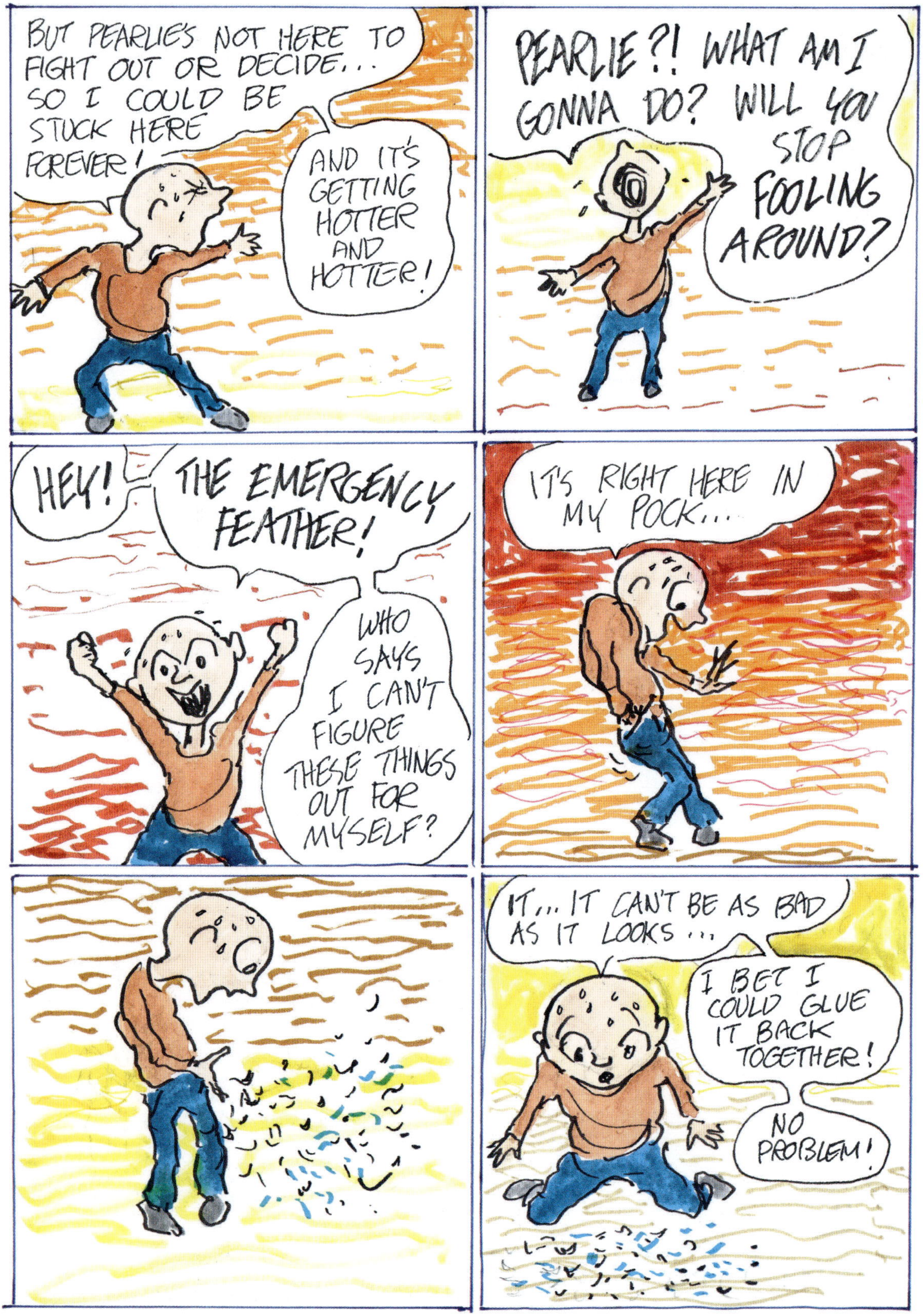
BUT PEARLIE'S NOT HERE TO FIGHT OUT OR DECIDE... SO I COULD BE STUCK HERE FOREVER!
AND IT'S GETTING HOTTER AND HOTTER!
PEARLIE?! WHAT AM I GONNA DO? WILL YOU STOP FOOLING AROUND?
HEY!
THE EMERGENCY FEATHER!
WHO SAYS I CAN'T FIGURE THESE THINGS OUT FOR MYSELF?
IT'S RIGHT HERE IN MY POCK...
IT... IT CAN'T BE AS BAD AS IT LOOKS...
I BET I COULD GLUE IT BACK TOGETHER!
NO PROBLEM!

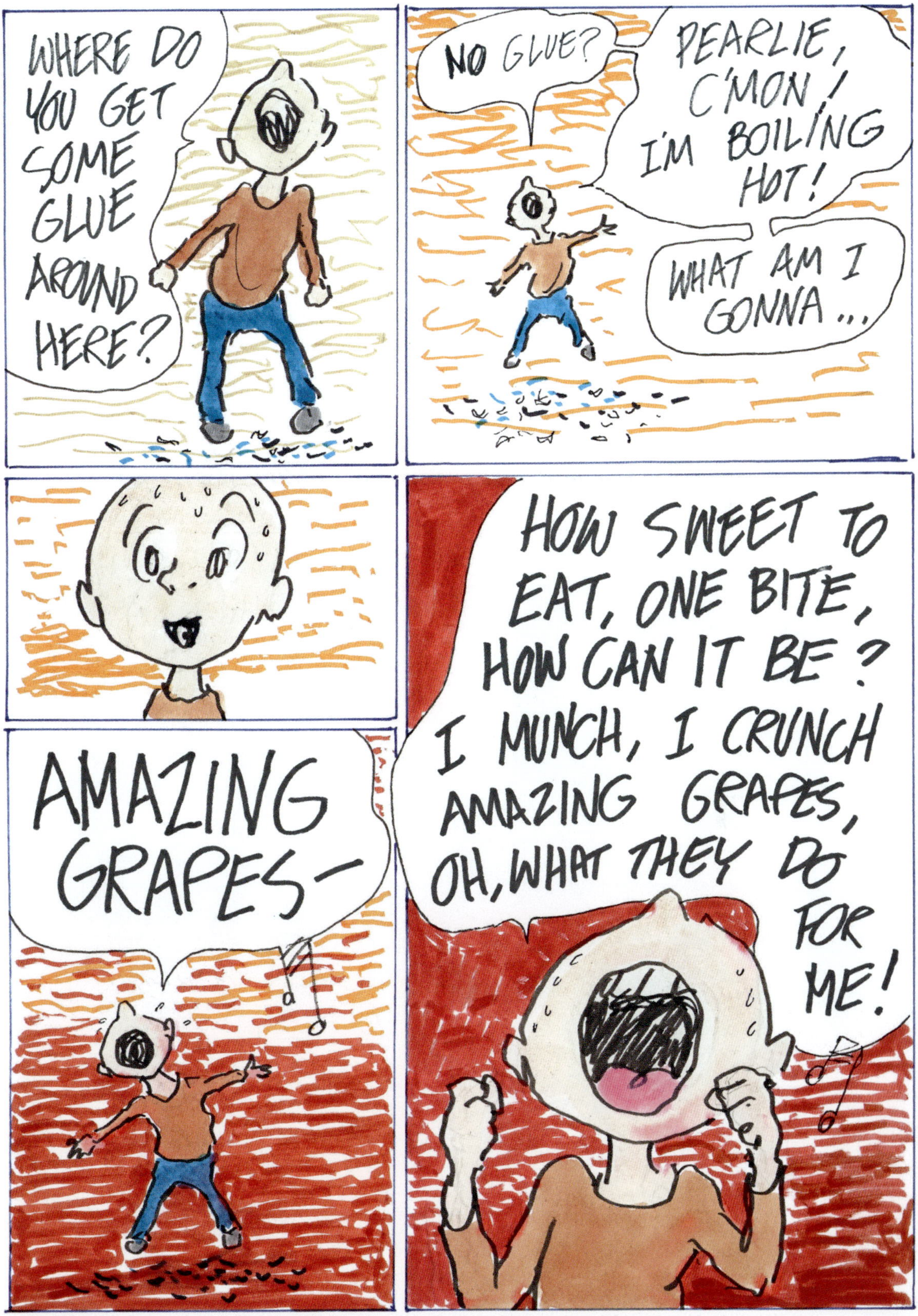
WHERE DO YOU GET SOME GLUE AROUND HERE?
NO GLUE?
PEARLIE, C'MON! I'M BOILING HOT!
WHAT AM I GONNA...
AMAZING GRAPES—
HOW SWEET TO EAT, ONE BITE, HOW CAN IT BE? I MUNCH, I CRUNCH AMAZING GRAPES, OH, WHAT THEY DO FOR ME!

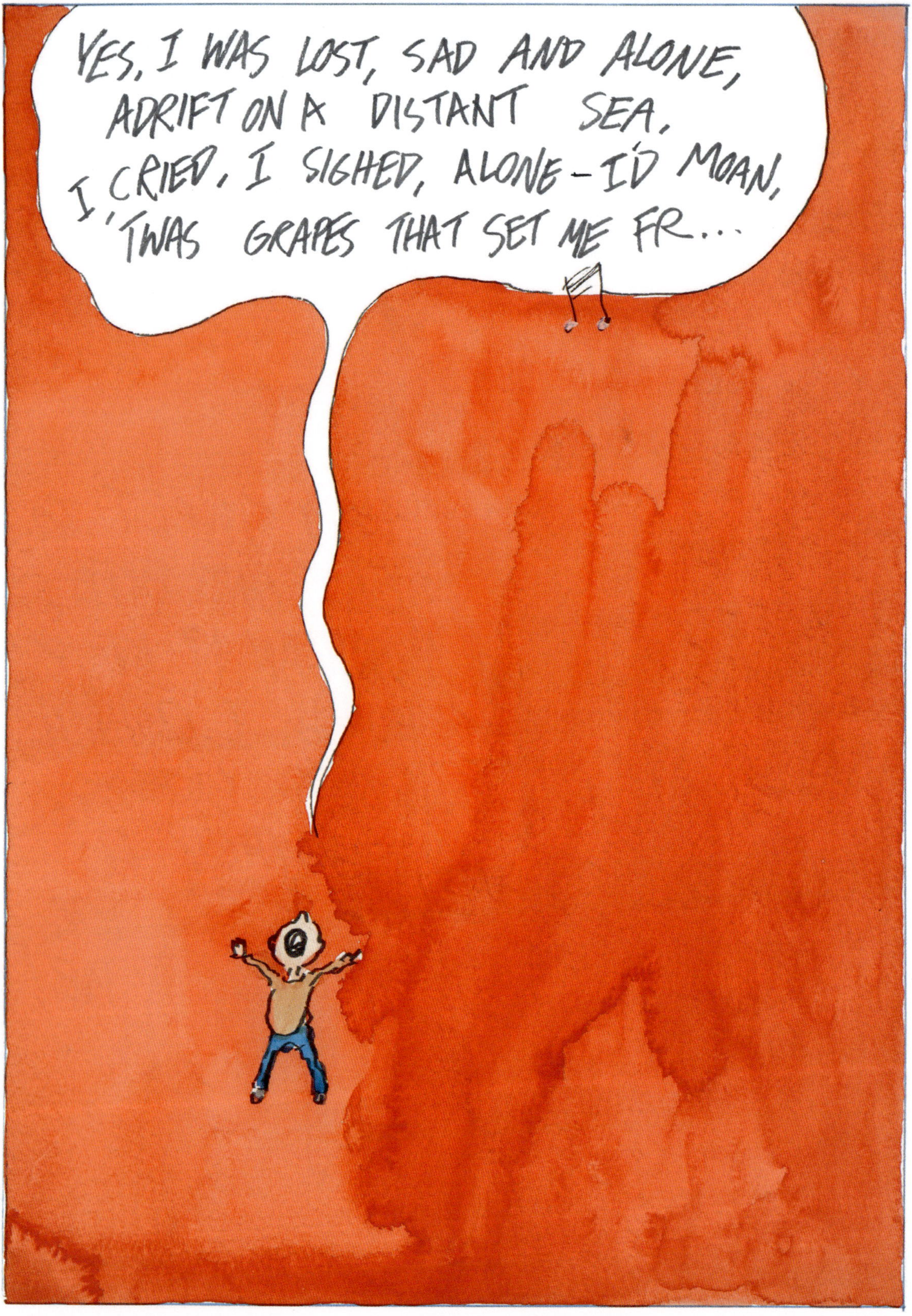
YES, I WAS LOST, SAD AND ALONE,
ADRIFT ON A DISTANT SEA.
I CRIED, I SIGHED, ALONE–I'D MOAN,
'TWAS GRAPES THAT SET ME FR...

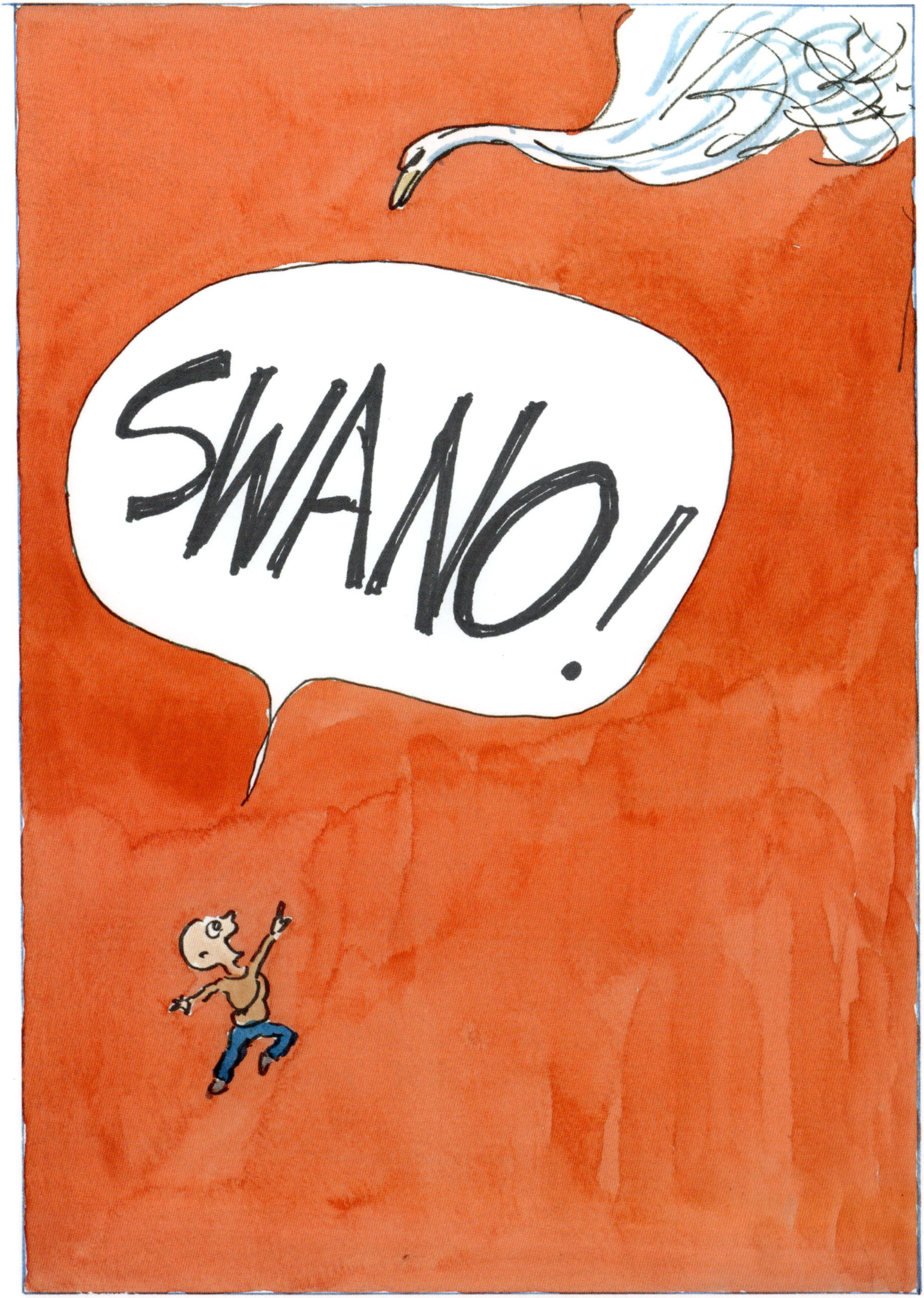
SWANO!

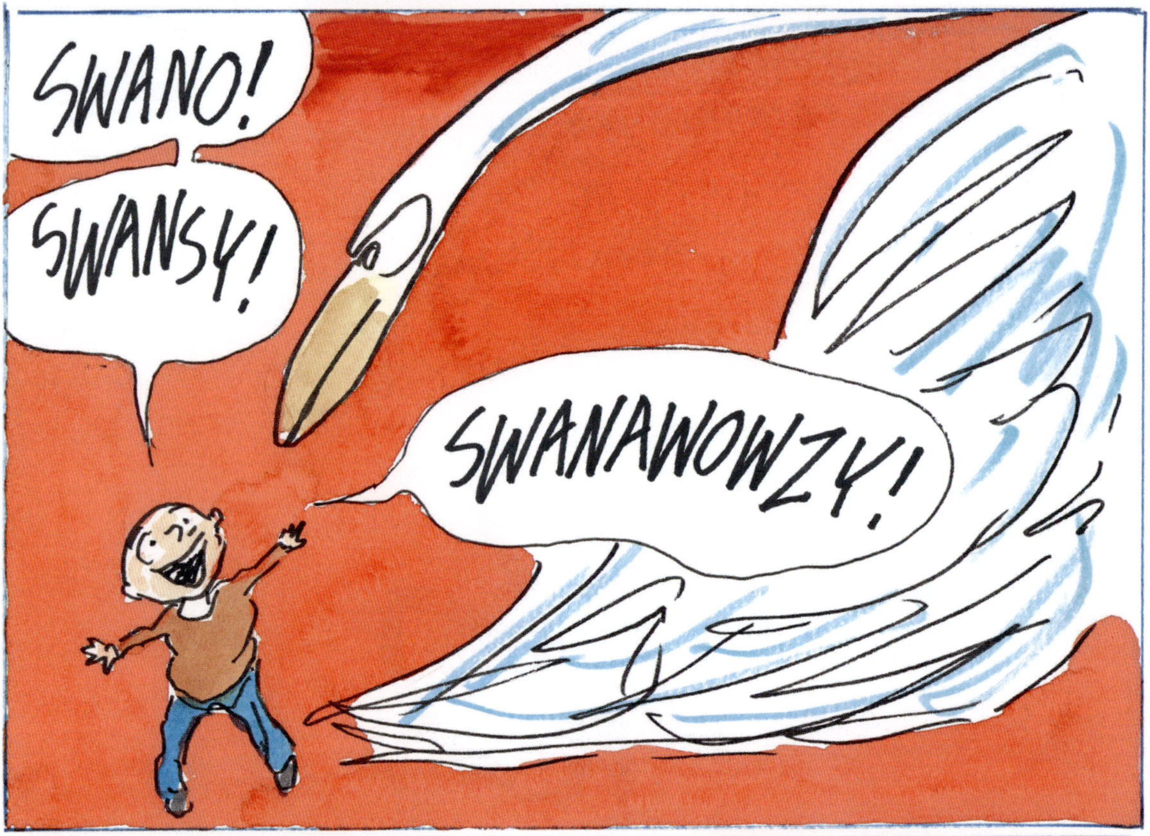
SWANO!
SWANSY!
SWANAWOWZY!

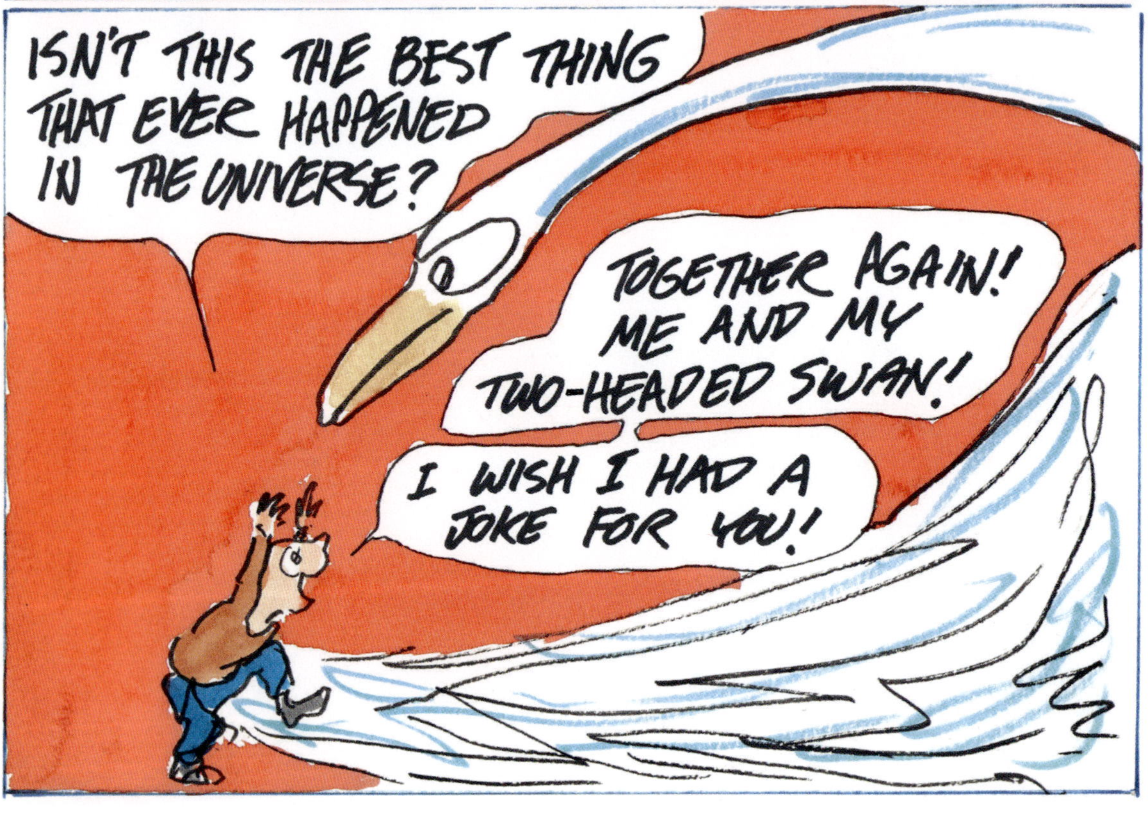
ISN'T THIS THE BEST THING THAT EVER HAPPENED IN THE UNIVERSE?
TOGETHER AGAIN! ME AND MY TWO-HEADED SWAN!
I WISH I HAD A JOKE FOR YOU!

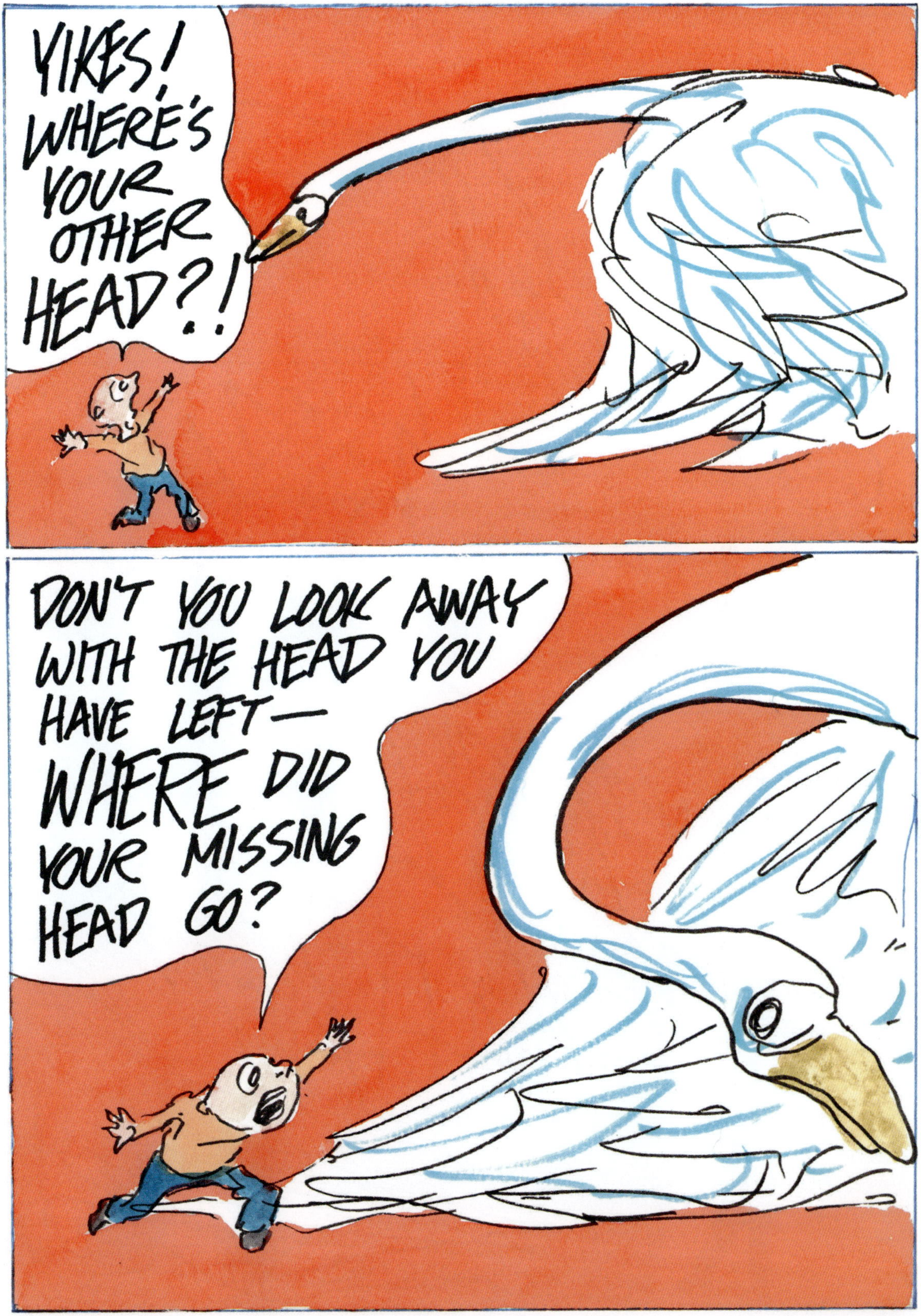
YIKES! WHERE'S YOUR OTHER HEAD?!
DON'T YOU LOOK AWAY WITH THE HEAD YOU HAVE LEFT— WHERE DID YOUR MISSING HEAD GO?

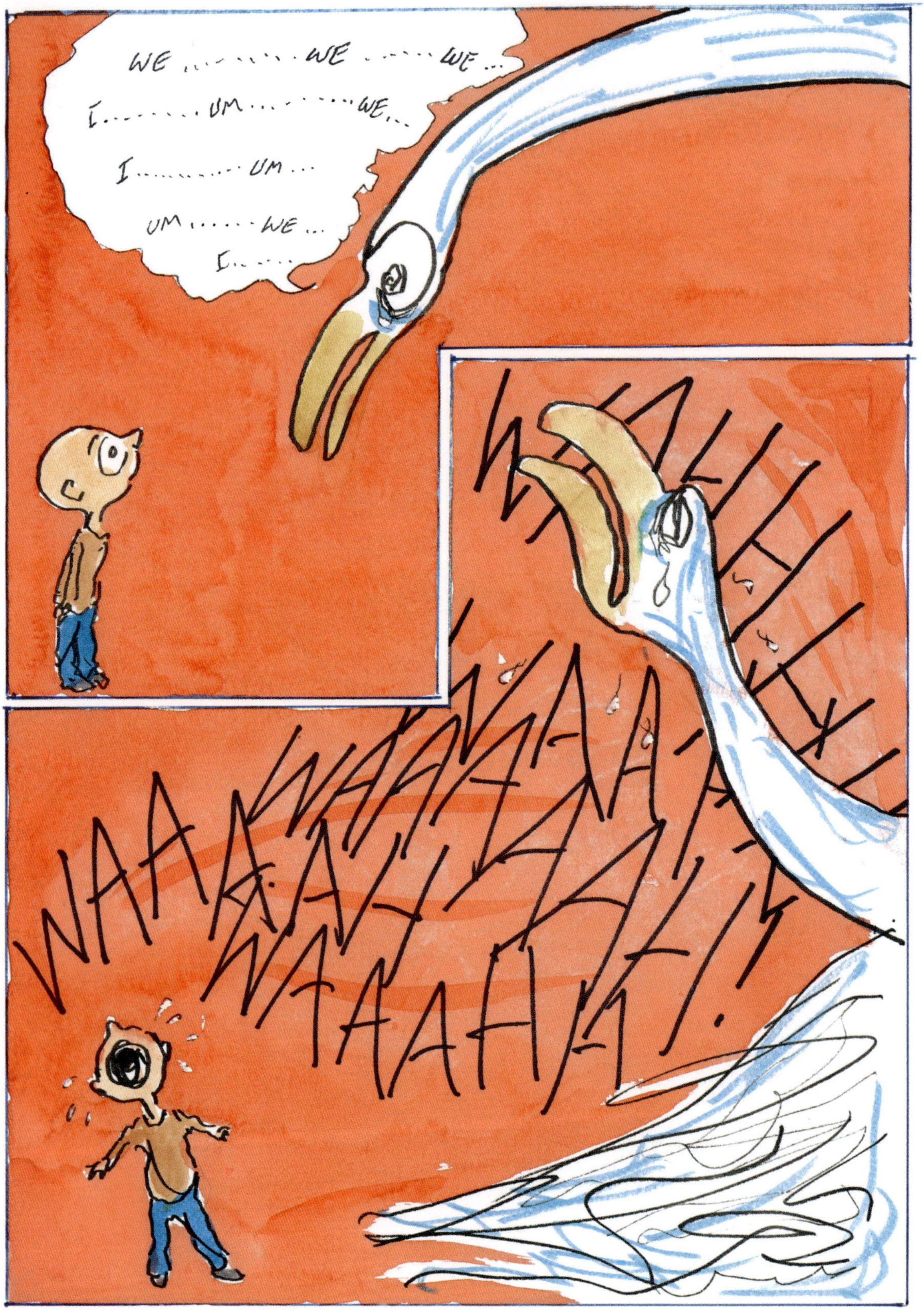
WE .... WE .... WE ...
I......... UM .... WE...
I............ UM ...
UM ...... WE ...
I......
WAAAAHHHHH
WAAAAAAAAAAAH!
WAAAAH!

CHAPTER 23 • DISAPPEARING

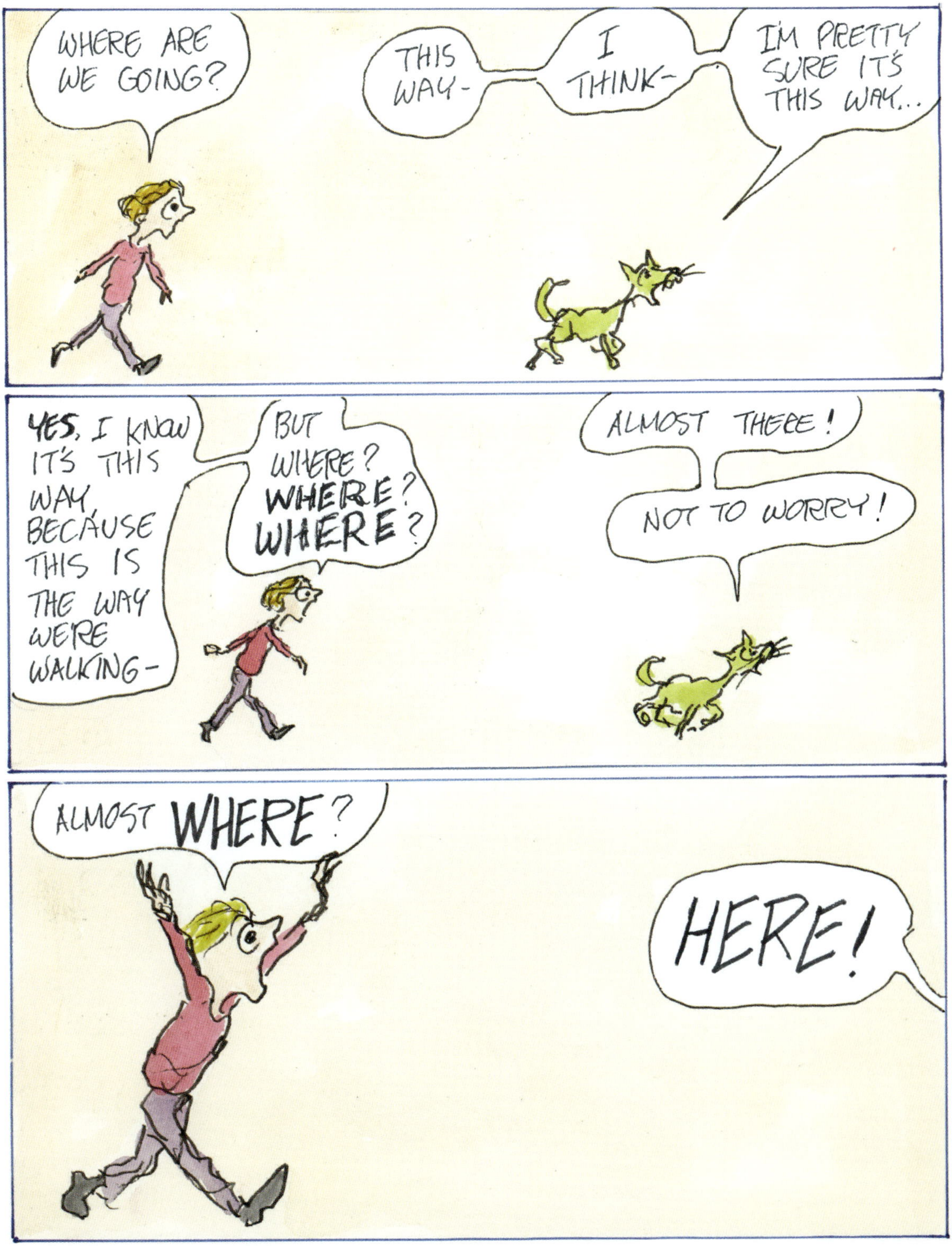

WHERE ARE WE GOING?
THIS WAY-
I THINK-
I'M PRETTY SURE IT'S THIS WAY...
YES, I KNOW IT'S THIS WAY, BECAUSE THIS IS THE WAY WE'RE WALKING-
BUT WHERE? WHERE? WHERE?
ALMOST THERE!
NOT TO WORRY!
ALMOST WHERE?
HERE!

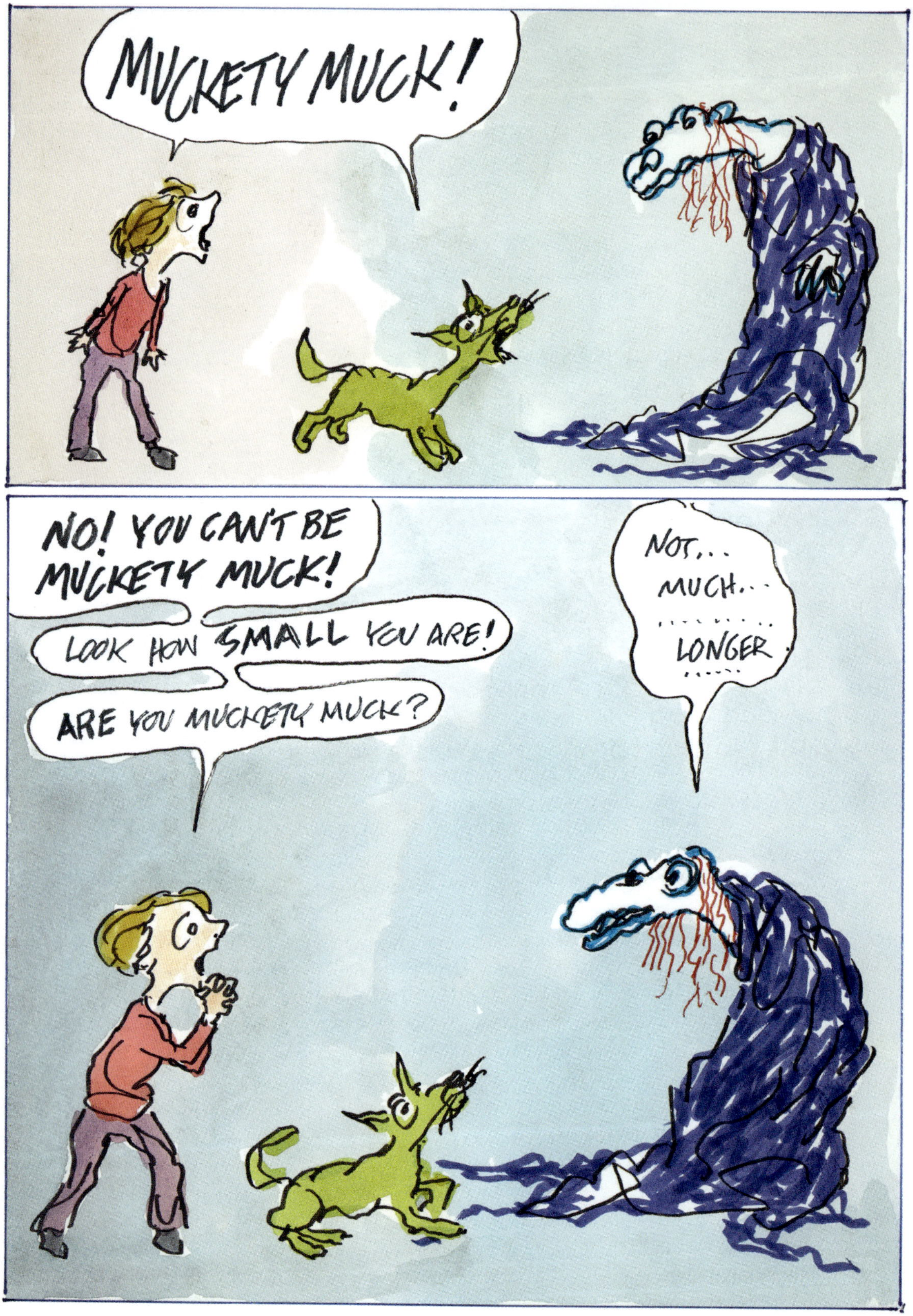
MUCKETY MUCK!
NO! YOU CAN'T BE MUCKETY MUCK!
LOOK HOW SMALL YOU ARE!
ARE YOU MUCKETY MUCK?
NOT... MUCH... .... LONGER

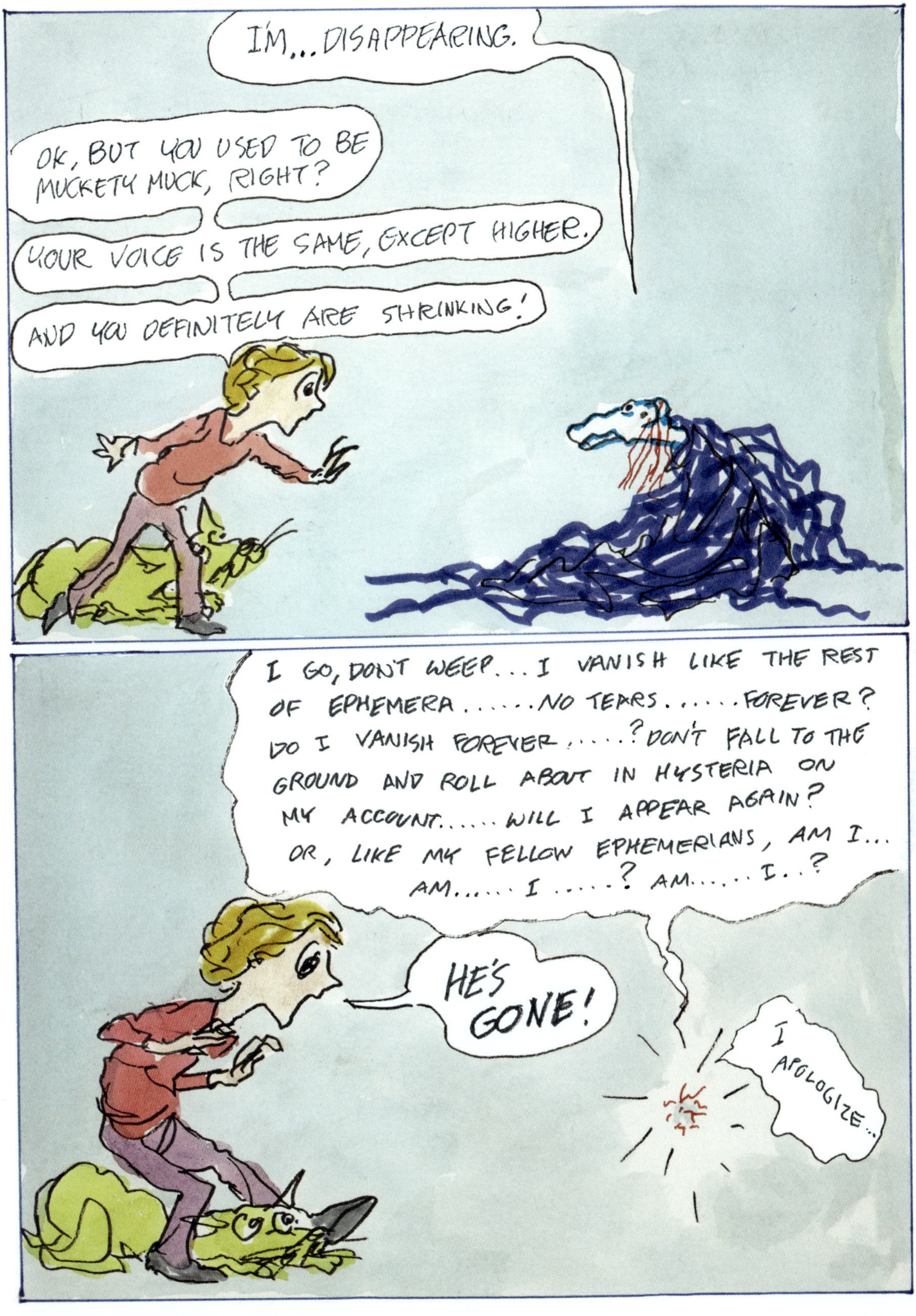
I'M...DISAPPEARING.
OK, BUT YOU USED TO BE MUCKETY MUCK, RIGHT?
YOUR VOICE IS THE SAME, EXCEPT HIGHER.
AND YOU DEFINITELY ARE SHRINKING!
I GO, DON'T WEEP... I VANISH LIKE THE REST OF EPHEMERA......NO TEARS......FOREVER? DO I VANISH FOREVER.....? DON'T FALL TO THE GROUND AND ROLL ABOUT IN HYSTERIA ON MY ACCOUNT......WILL I APPEAR AGAIN? OR, LIKE MY FELLOW EPHEMERIANS, AM I... AM......I.....? AM......I..?
HE'S GONE!
I APOLOGIZE...

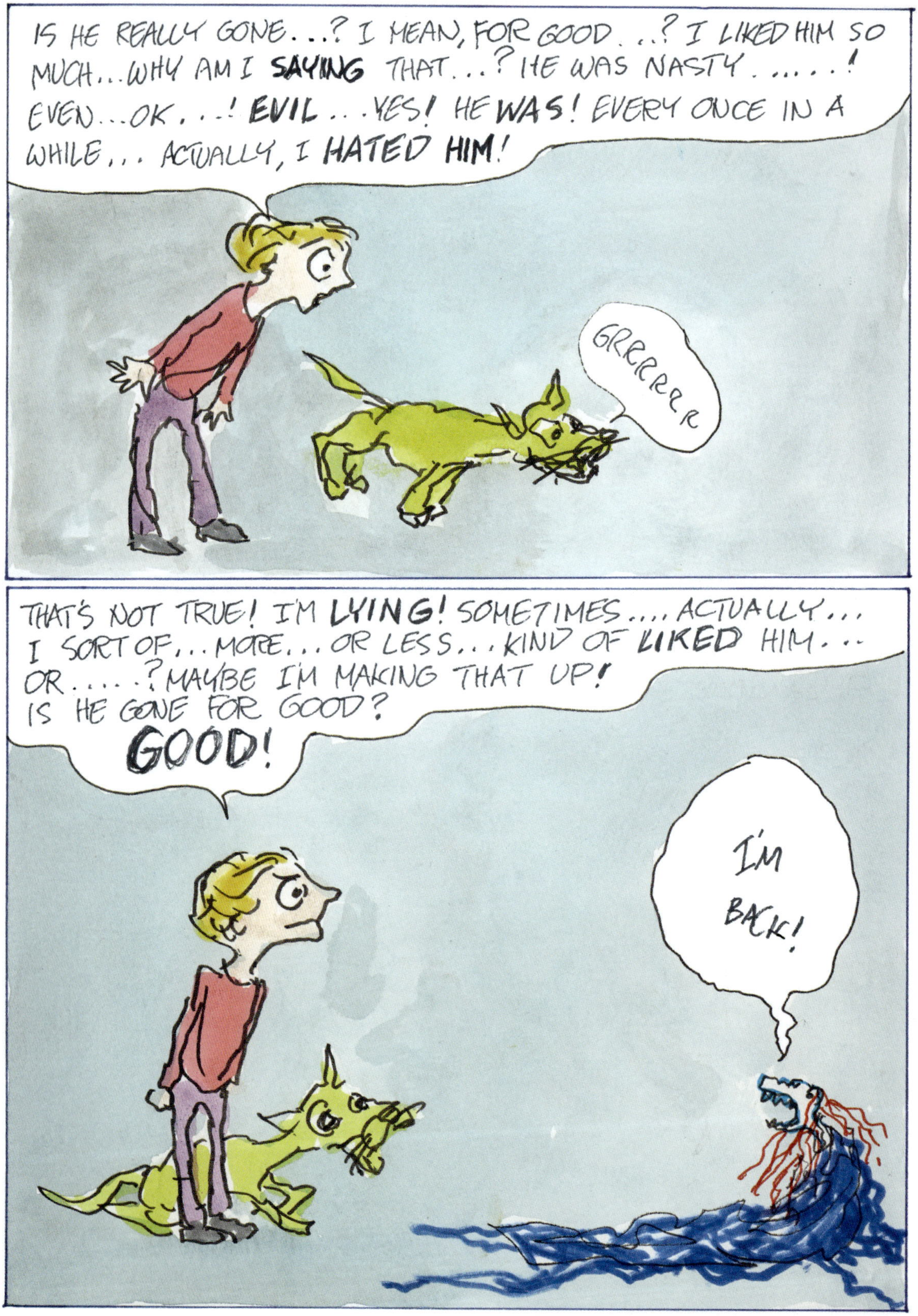
IS HE REALLY GONE...? I MEAN, FOR GOOD...? I LIKED HIM SO MUCH...WHY AM I **SAYING** THAT...? HE WAS NASTY......! EVEN...OK...! **EVIL**...YES! HE **WAS**! EVERY ONCE IN A WHILE... ACTUALLY, I **HATED HIM**!
GRRRRRRR
THAT'S NOT TRUE! I'M **LYING**! SOMETIMES.... ACTUALLY... I SORT OF...MORE...OR LESS...KIND OF **LIKED** HIM... OR.....? MAYBE I'M MAKING THAT UP! IS HE GONE FOR GOOD? **GOOD!**
I'M BACK!

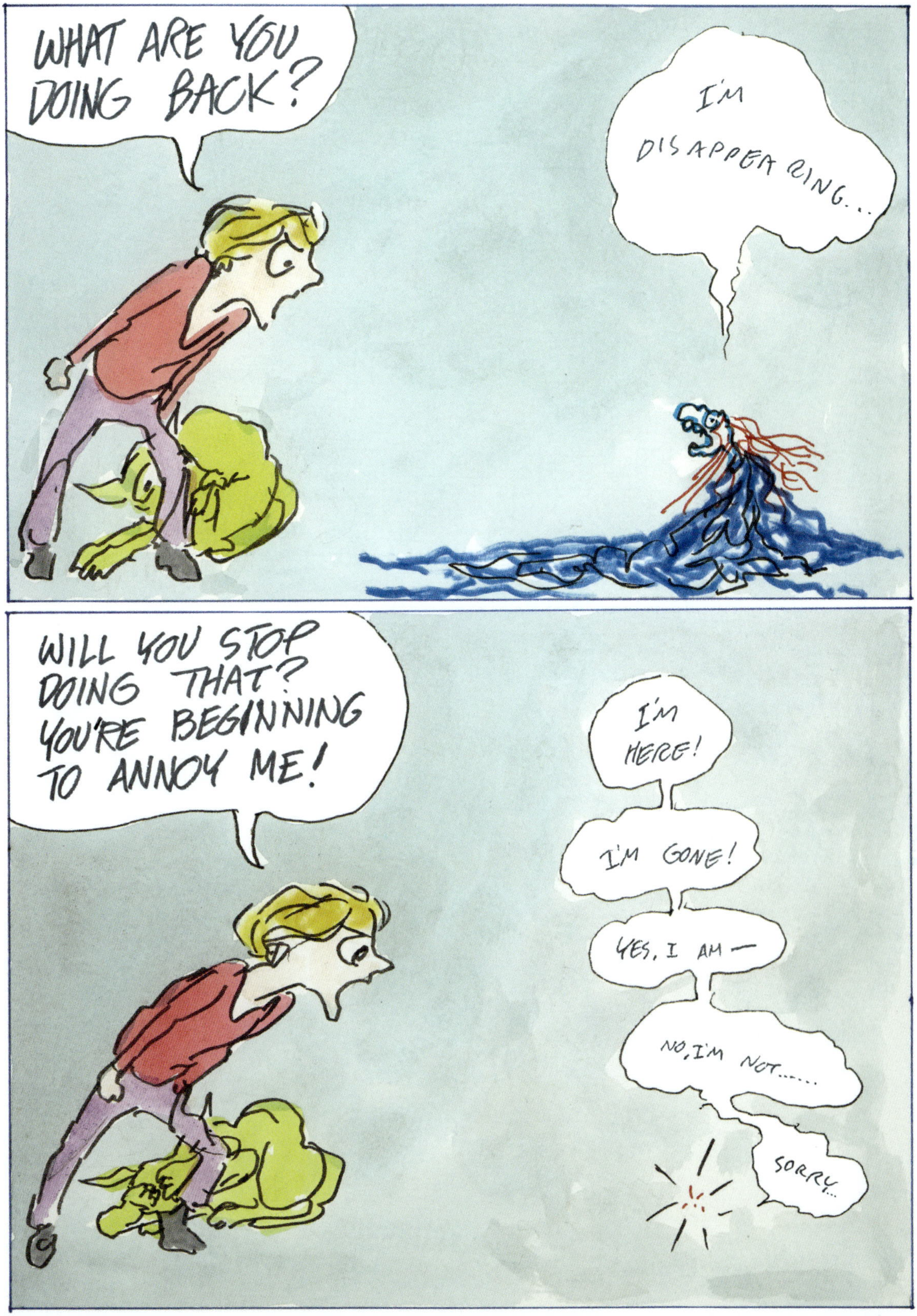
WHAT ARE YOU DOING BACK?
I'M DISAPPEARING...
WILL YOU STOP DOING THAT? YOU'RE BEGINNING TO ANNOY ME!
I'M HERE!
I'M GONE!
YES, I AM—
NO, I'M NOT......
SORRY...

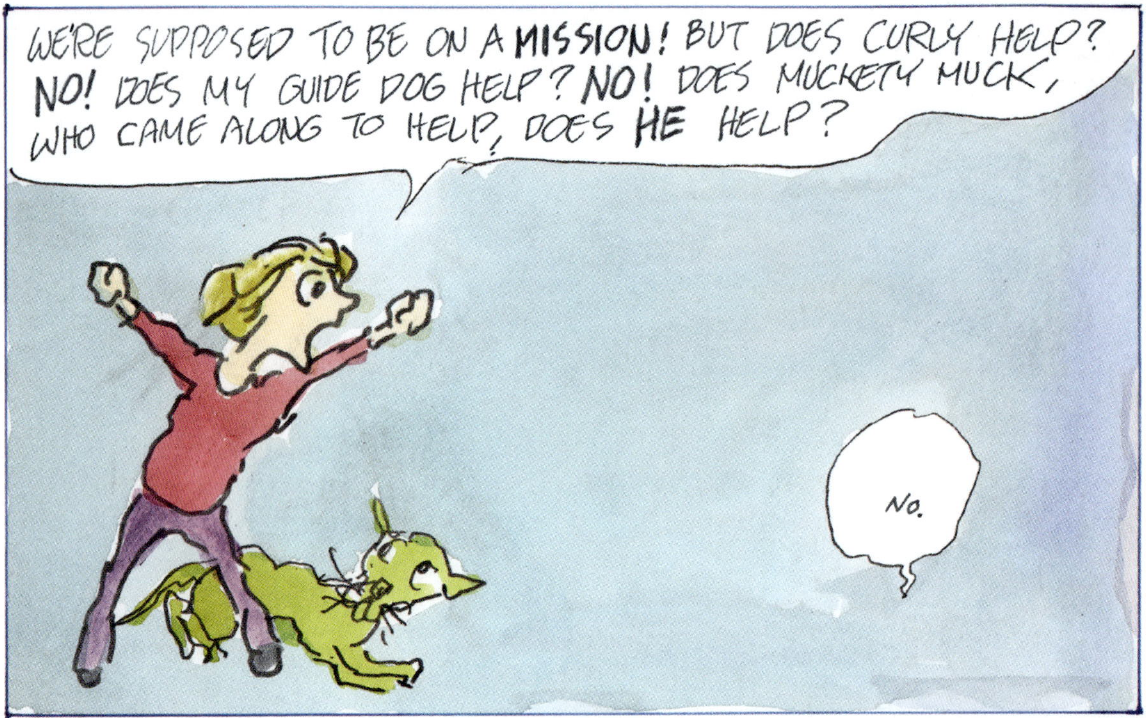
WE'RE SUPPOSED TO BE ON A **MISSION**! BUT DOES CURLY HELP? **NO!** DOES MY GUIDE DOG HELP? **NO!** DOES MUCKETY MUCK, WHO CAME ALONG TO HELP, DOES **HE** HELP?
NO.

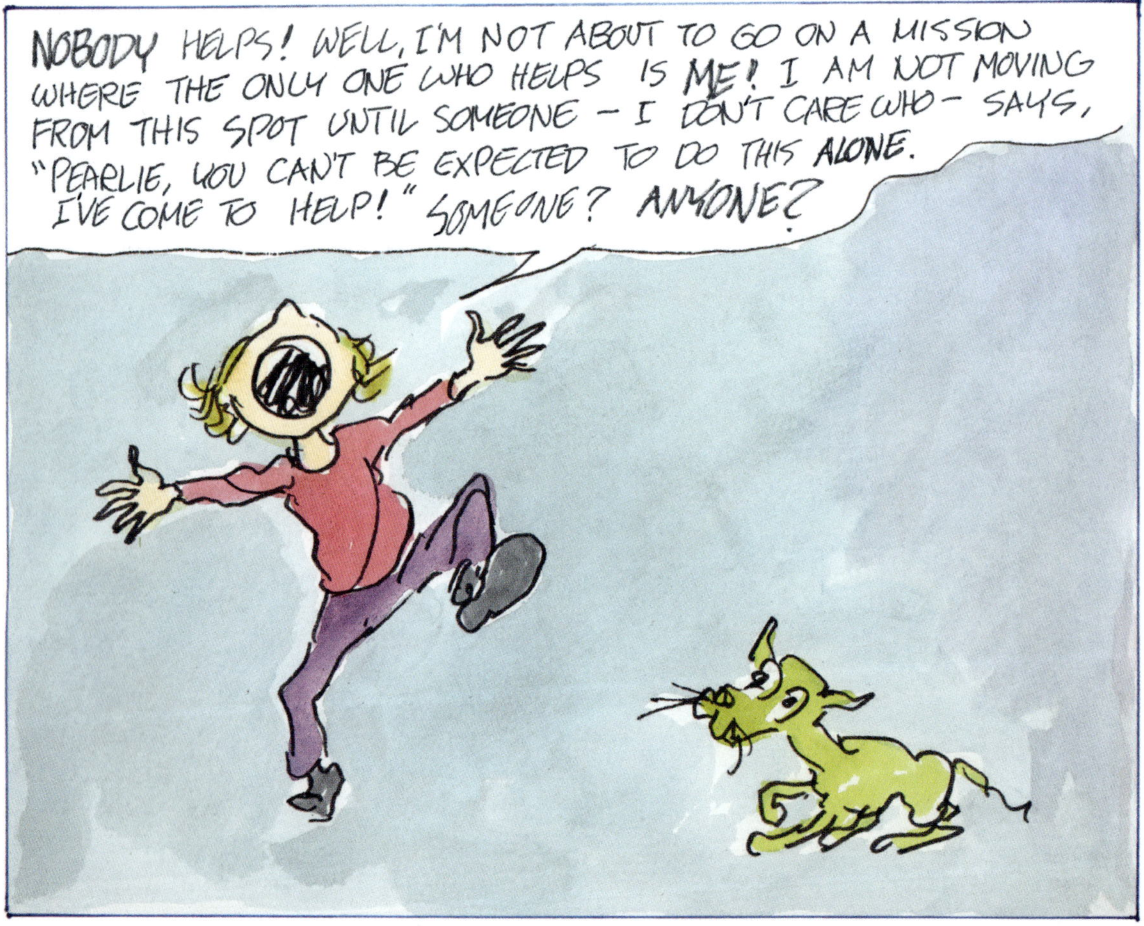
NOBODY HELPS! WELL, I'M NOT ABOUT TO GO ON A MISSION WHERE THE ONLY ONE WHO HELPS IS **ME**! I AM NOT MOVING FROM THIS SPOT UNTIL SOMEONE – I DON'T CARE WHO – SAYS, "PEARLIE, YOU CAN'T BE EXPECTED TO DO THIS **ALONE**. I'VE COME TO HELP!" SOMEONE? **ANYONE?**

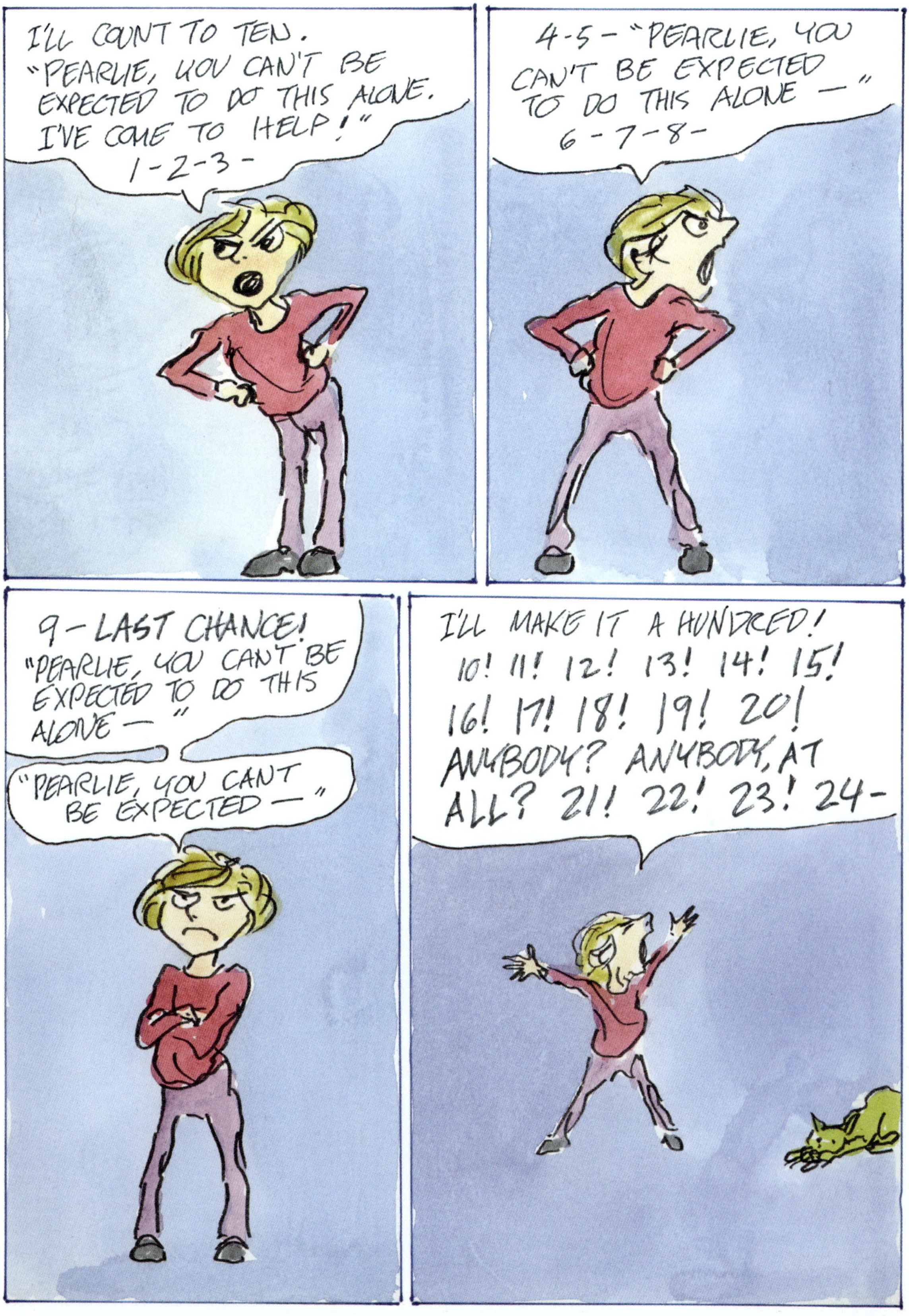

I'LL COUNT TO TEN. "PEARLIE, YOU CAN'T BE EXPECTED TO DO THIS ALONE. I'VE COME TO HELP!" 1-2-3-
4-5- "PEARLIE, YOU CAN'T BE EXPECTED TO DO THIS ALONE —" 6-7-8-
9 — LAST CHANCE! "PEARLIE, YOU CAN'T BE EXPECTED TO DO THIS ALONE — "
"PEARLIE, YOU CANT BE EXPECTED — "
I'LL MAKE IT A HUNDRED! 10! 11! 12! 13! 14! 15! 16! 17! 18! 19! 20! ANYBODY? ANYBODY, AT ALL? 21! 22! 23! 24-

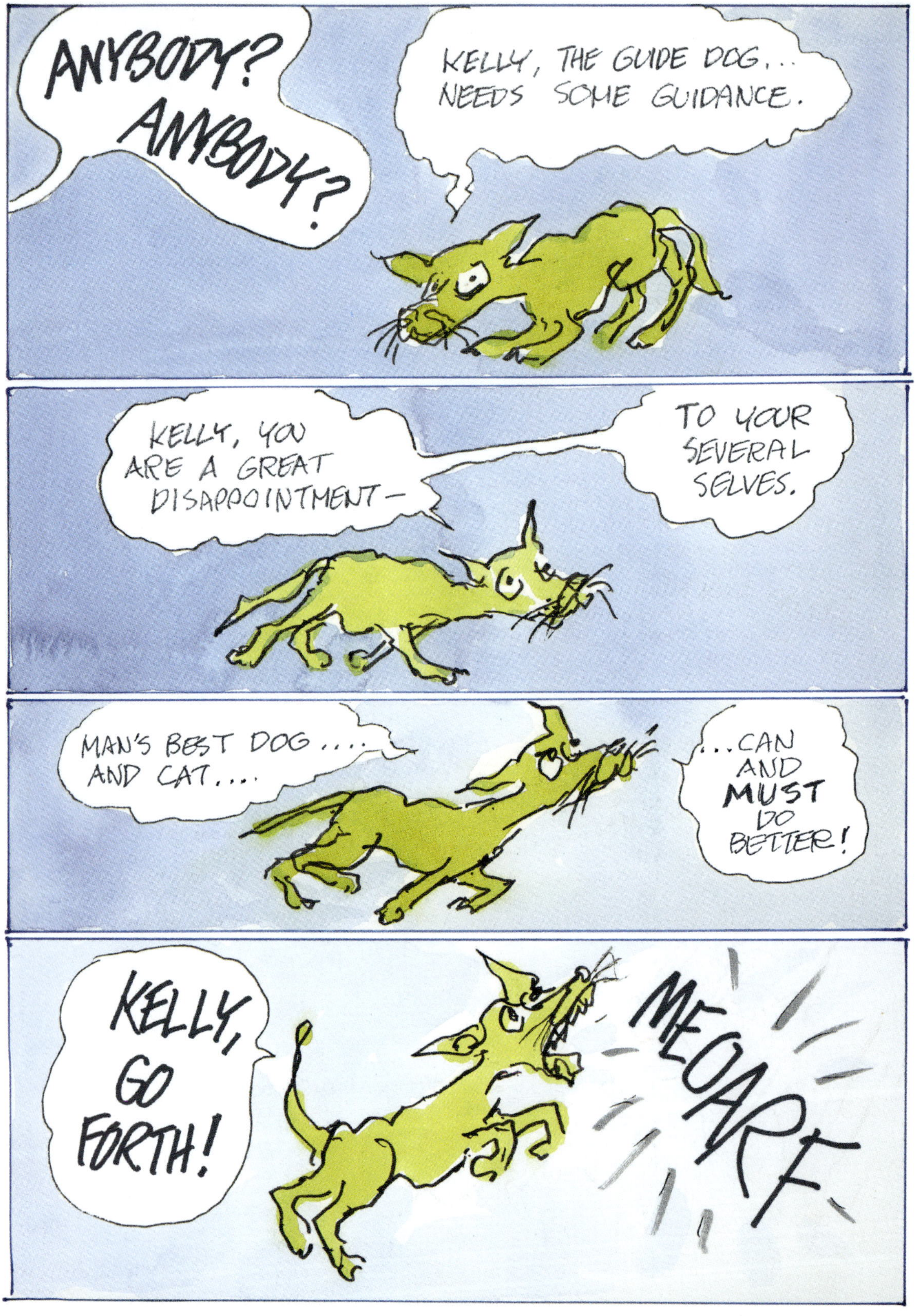

ANYBODY? ANYBODY? ANYBODY?
KELLY, THE GUIDE DOG... NEEDS SOME GUIDANCE.
KELLY, YOU ARE A GREAT DISAPPOINTMENT—
TO YOUR SEVERAL SELVES.
MAN'S BEST DOG.... AND CAT....
...CAN AND **MUST** DO BETTER!
KELLY, GO FORTH!
MEOARF

CHAPTER 24 • WHERE'S MOMMY?

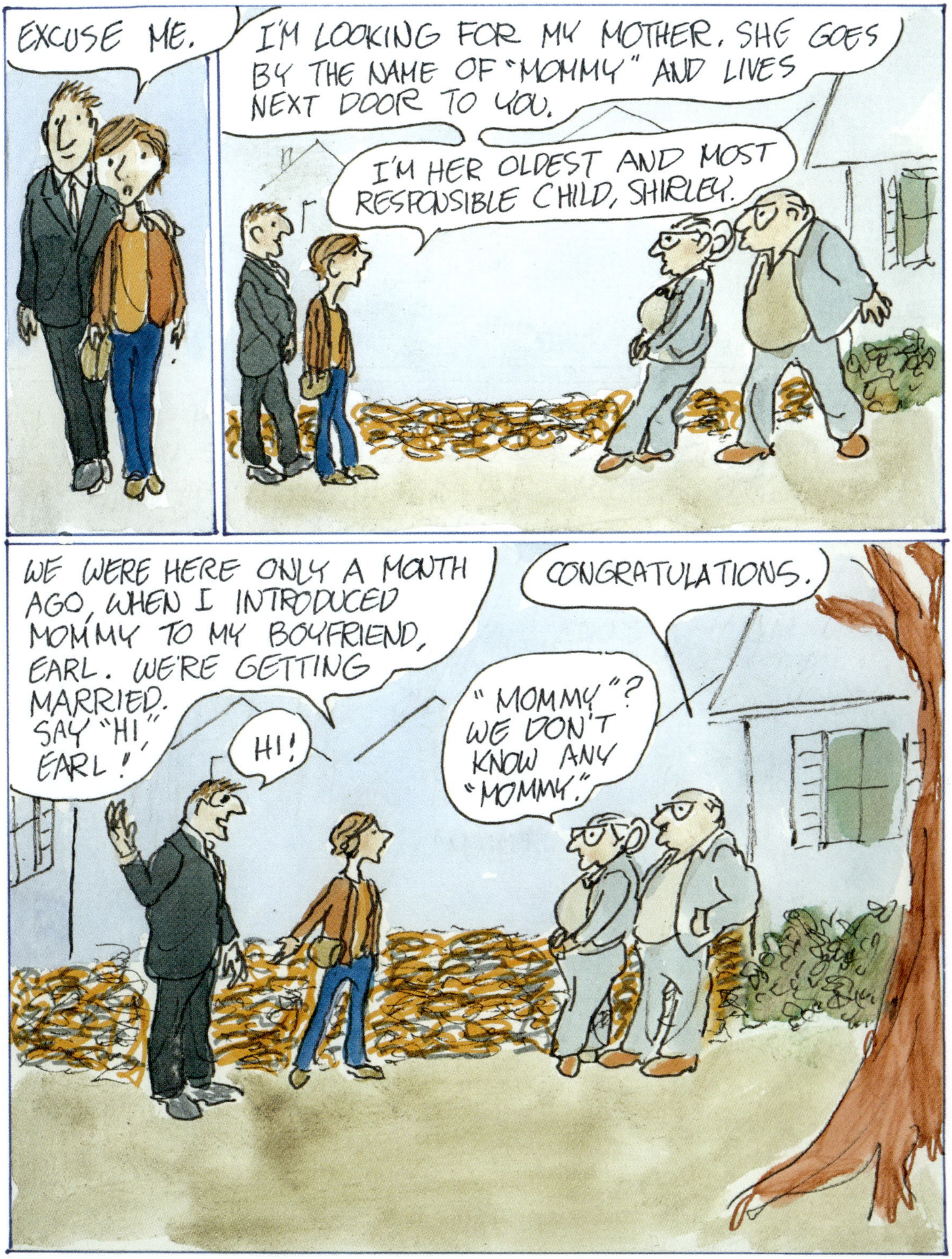
EXCUSE ME.
I'M LOOKING FOR MY MOTHER. SHE GOES BY THE NAME OF "MOMMY" AND LIVES NEXT DOOR TO YOU.
I'M HER OLDEST AND MOST RESPONSIBLE CHILD, SHIRLEY.
WE WERE HERE ONLY A MONTH AGO, WHEN I INTRODUCED MOMMY TO MY BOYFRIEND, EARL. WE'RE GETTING MARRIED. SAY "HI," EARL!
HI!
CONGRATULATIONS.
"MOMMY"? WE DON'T KNOW ANY "MOMMY."

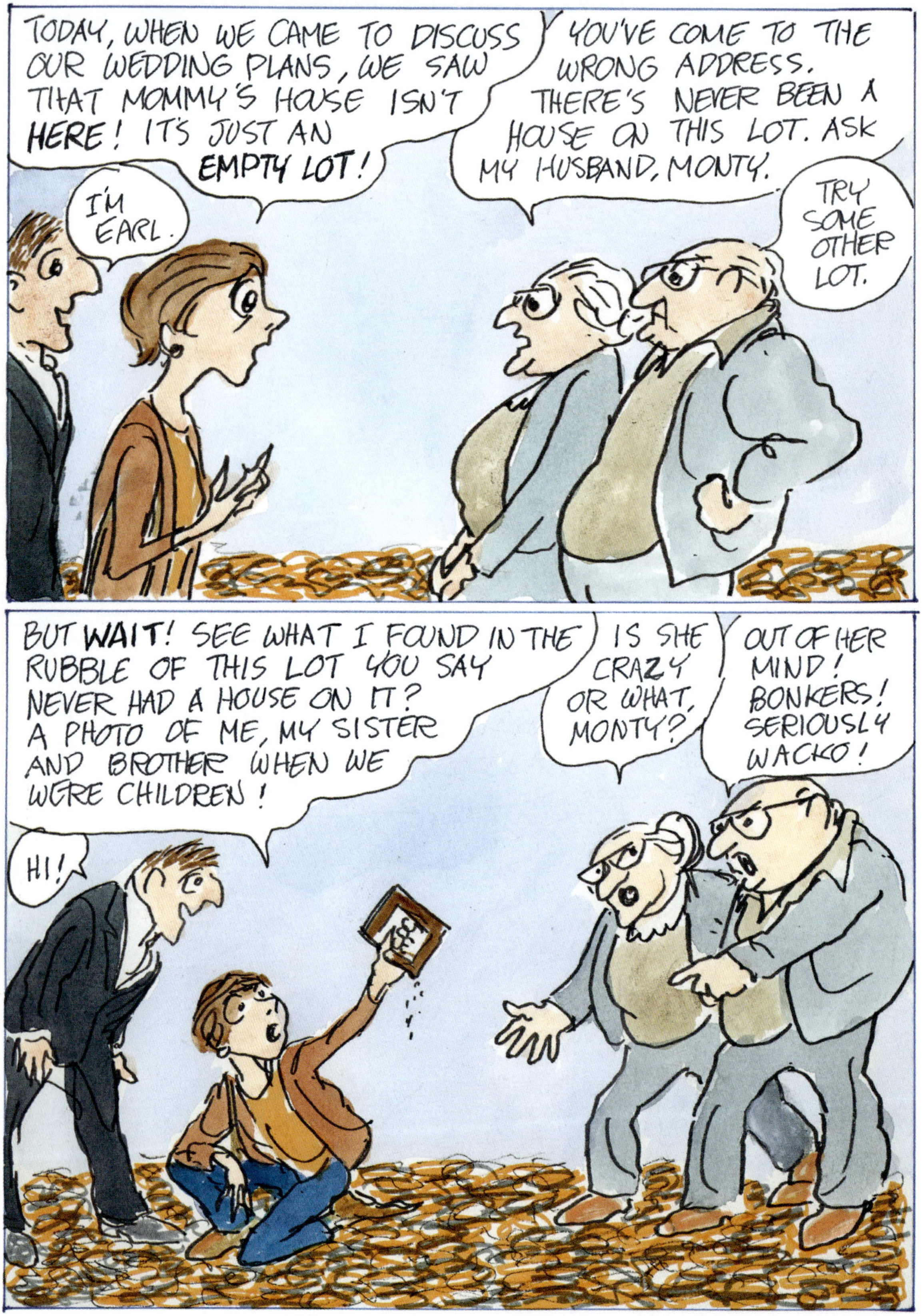
TODAY, WHEN WE CAME TO DISCUSS OUR WEDDING PLANS, WE SAW THAT MOMMY'S HOUSE ISN'T HERE! IT'S JUST AN EMPTY LOT!
I'M EARL.
YOU'VE COME TO THE WRONG ADDRESS. THERE'S NEVER BEEN A HOUSE ON THIS LOT. ASK MY HUSBAND, MONTY.
TRY SOME OTHER LOT.
BUT WAIT! SEE WHAT I FOUND IN THE RUBBLE OF THIS LOT YOU SAY NEVER HAD A HOUSE ON IT? A PHOTO OF ME, MY SISTER AND BROTHER WHEN WE WERE CHILDREN!
HI!
IS SHE CRAZY OR WHAT, MONTY?
OUT OF HER MIND! BONKERS! SERIOUSLY WACKO!

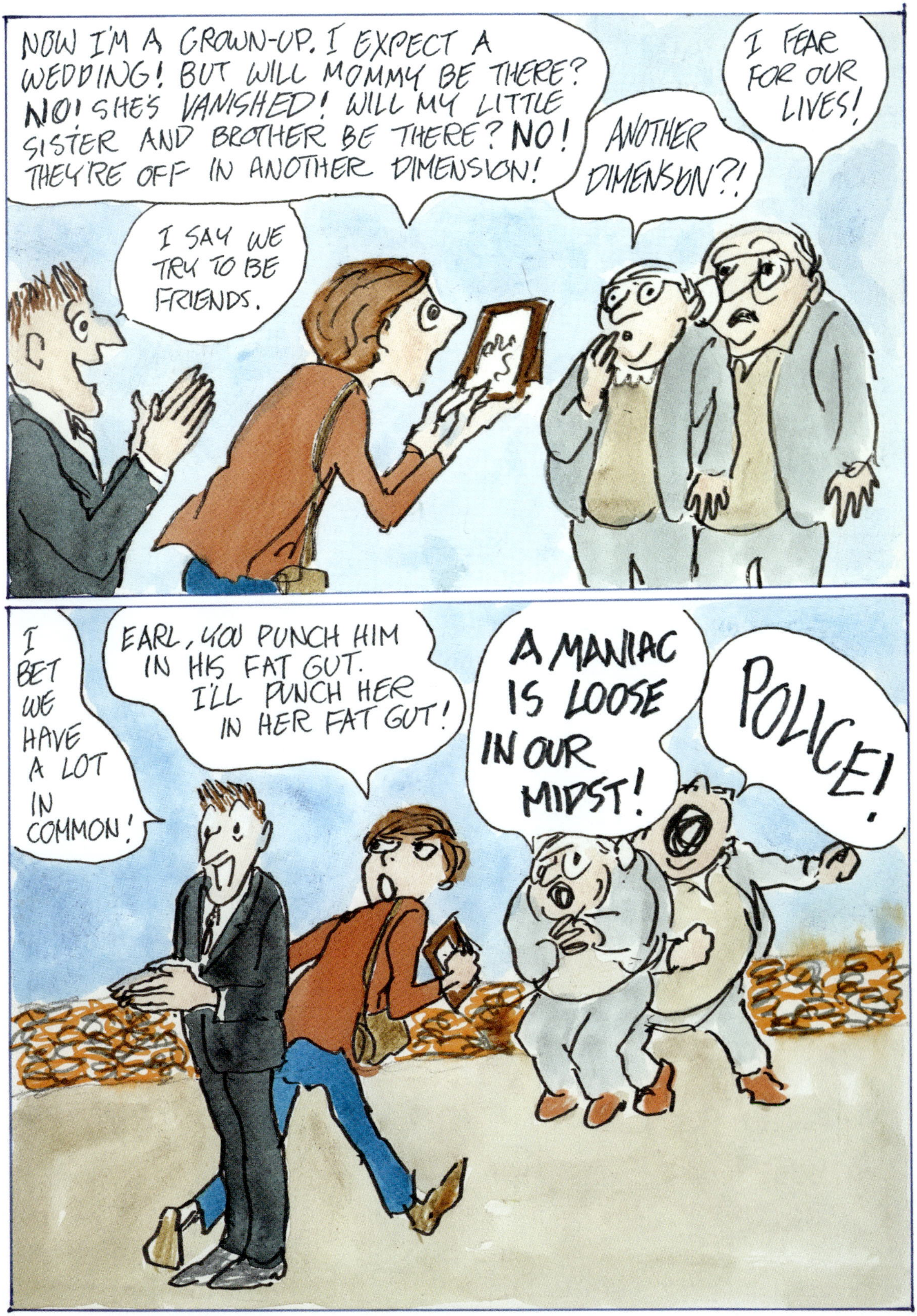
NOW I'M A GROWN-UP. I EXPECT A WEDDING! BUT WILL MOMMY BE THERE? NO! SHE'S VANISHED! WILL MY LITTLE SISTER AND BROTHER BE THERE? NO! THEY'RE OFF IN ANOTHER DIMENSION!
I SAY WE TRY TO BE FRIENDS.
ANOTHER DIMENSION?!
I FEAR FOR OUR LIVES!
I BET WE HAVE A LOT IN COMMON!
EARL, YOU PUNCH HIM IN HIS FAT GUT. I'LL PUNCH HER IN HER FAT GUT!
A MANIAC IS LOOSE IN OUR MIDST!
POLICE!

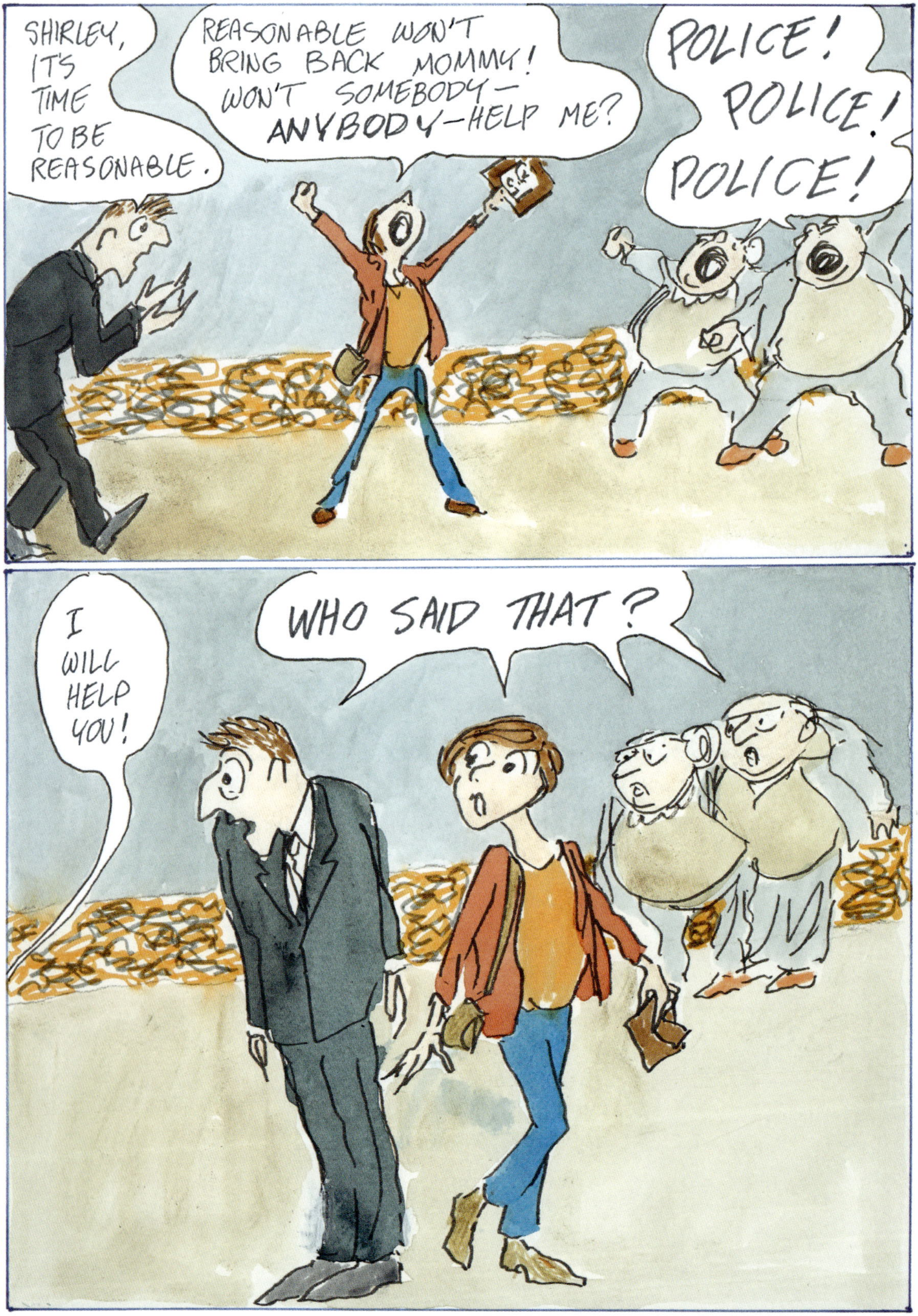
SHIRLEY, IT'S TIME TO BE REASONABLE.
REASONABLE WON'T BRING BACK MOMMY! WON'T SOMEBODY— ANYBODY—HELP ME?
POLICE! POLICE! POLICE!
I WILL HELP YOU!
WHO SAID THAT?

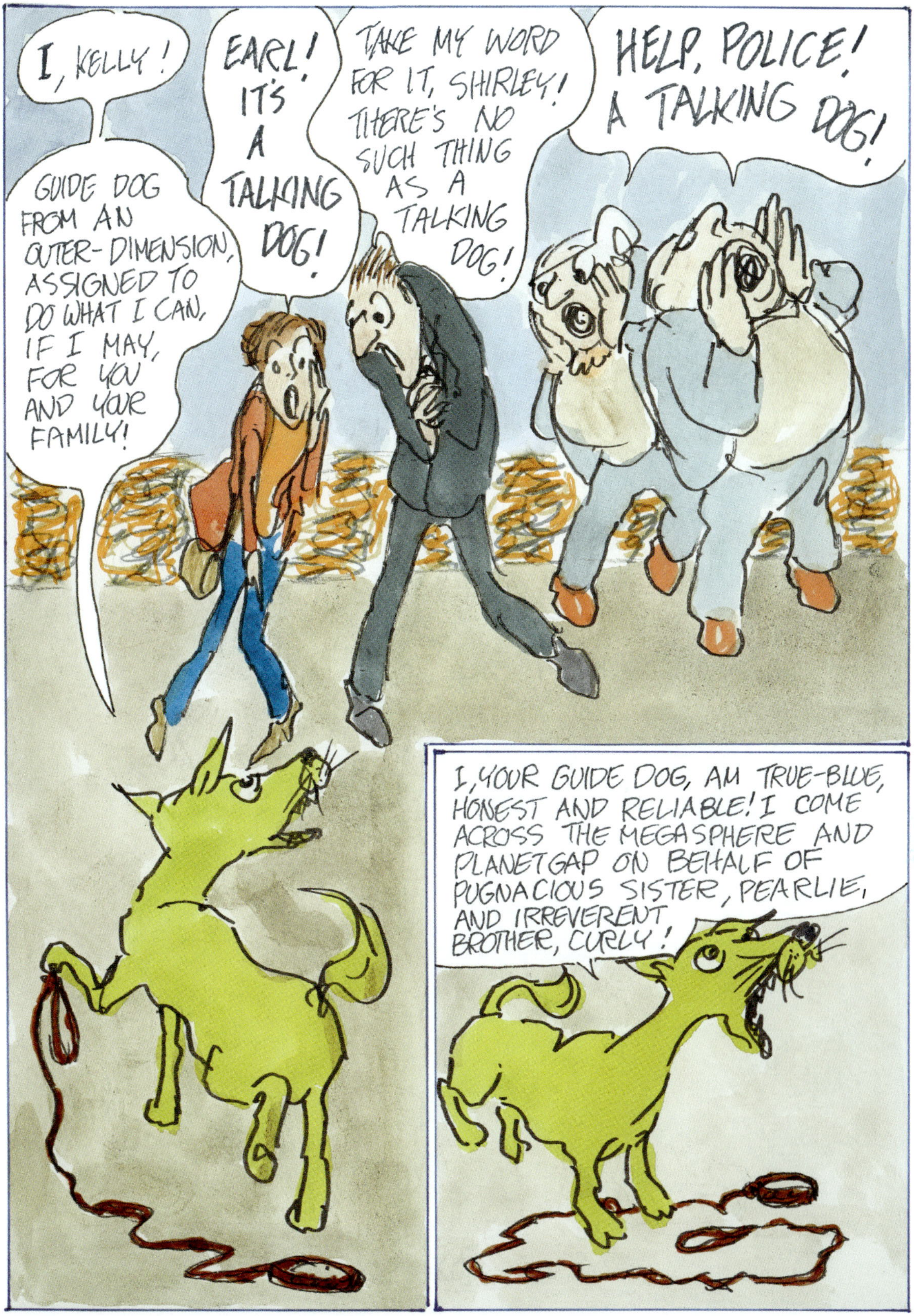
I, KELLY!
GUIDE DOG FROM AN OUTER-DIMENSION, ASSIGNED TO DO WHAT I CAN, IF I MAY, FOR YOU AND YOUR FAMILY!
EARL! IT'S A TALKING DOG!
TAKE MY WORD FOR IT, SHIRLEY! THERE'S NO SUCH THING AS A TALKING DOG!
HELP, POLICE! A TALKING DOG!
I, YOUR GUIDE DOG, AM TRUE-BLUE, HONEST AND RELIABLE! I COME ACROSS THE MEGASPHERE AND PLANETGAP ON BEHALF OF PUGNACIOUS SISTER, PEARLIE, AND IRREVERENT BROTHER, CURLY!

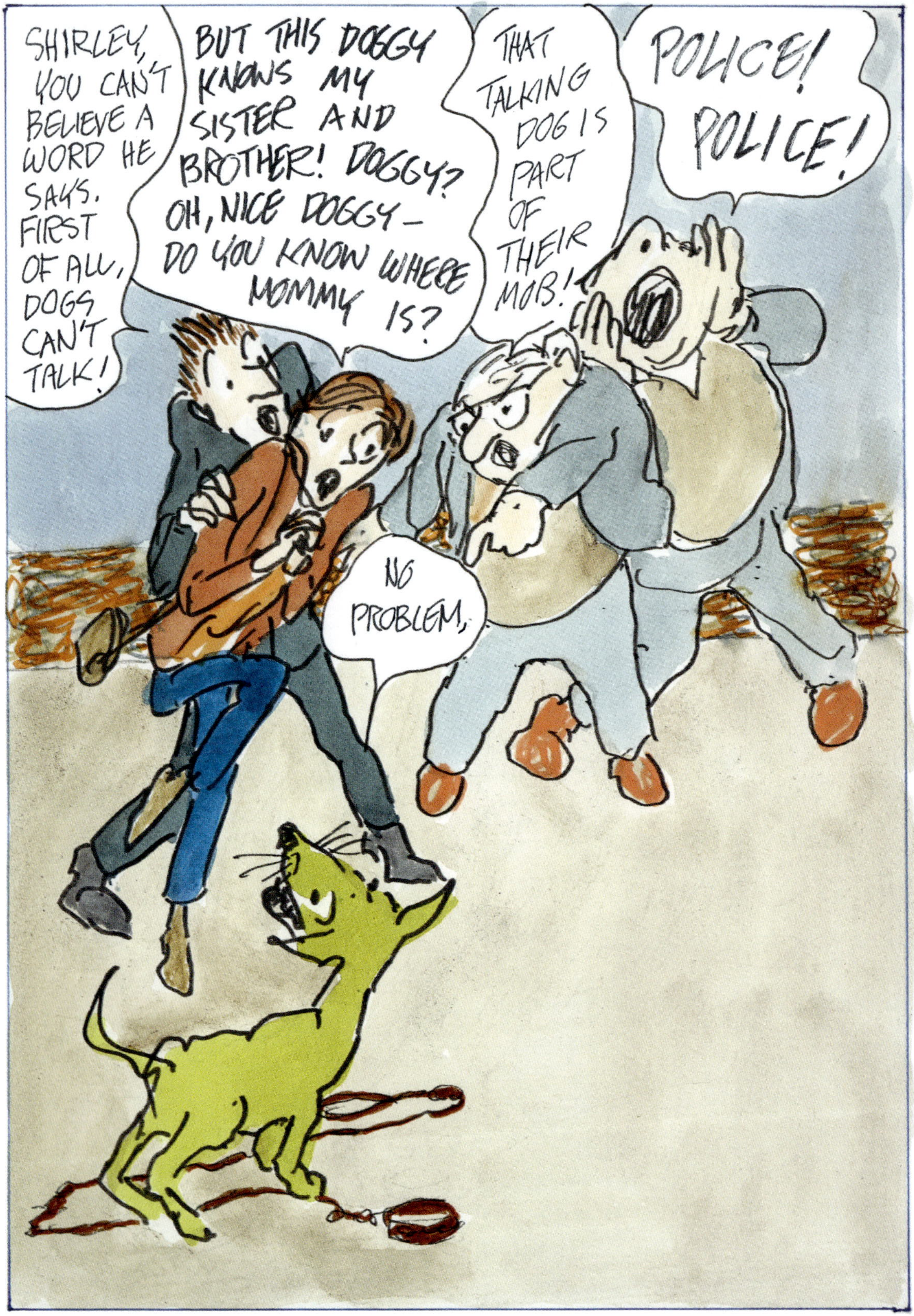
SHIRLEY, YOU CAN'T BELIEVE A WORD HE SAYS. FIRST OF ALL, DOGS CAN'T TALK!
BUT THIS DOGGY KNOWS MY SISTER AND BROTHER! DOGGY? OH, NICE DOGGY— DO YOU KNOW WHERE MOMMY IS?
THAT TALKING DOG IS PART OF THEIR MOB!
POLICE! POLICE!
NO PROBLEM,

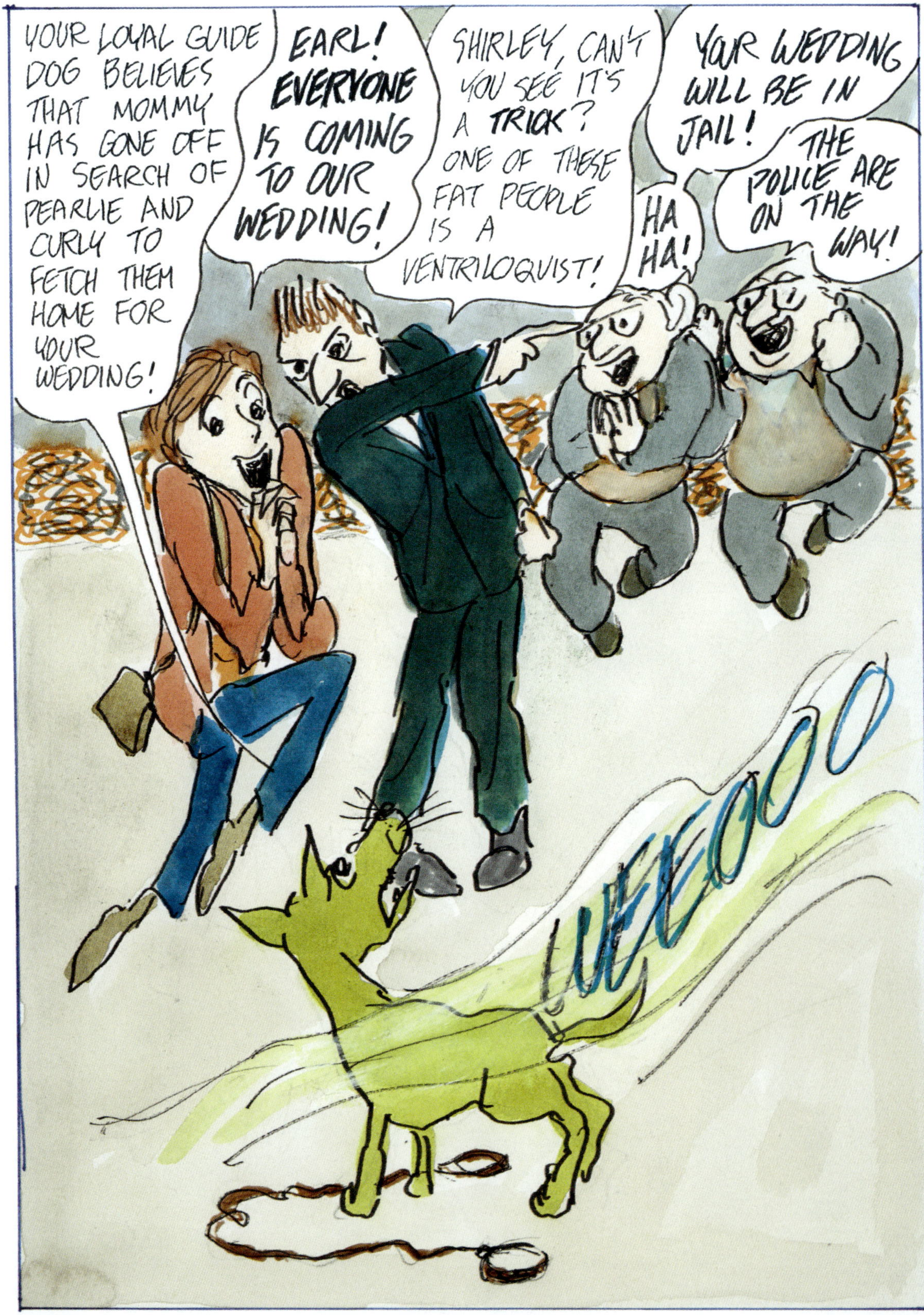
YOUR LOYAL GUIDE DOG BELIEVES THAT MOMMY HAS GONE OFF IN SEARCH OF PEARLIE AND CURLY TO FETCH THEM HOME FOR YOUR WEDDING!
EARL! EVERYONE IS COMING TO OUR WEDDING!
SHIRLEY, CAN'T YOU SEE IT'S A TRICK? ONE OF THESE FAT PEOPLE IS A VENTRILOQUIST!
YOUR WEDDING WILL BE IN JAIL!
HA HA!
THE POLICE ARE ON THE WAY!
UEEOOO

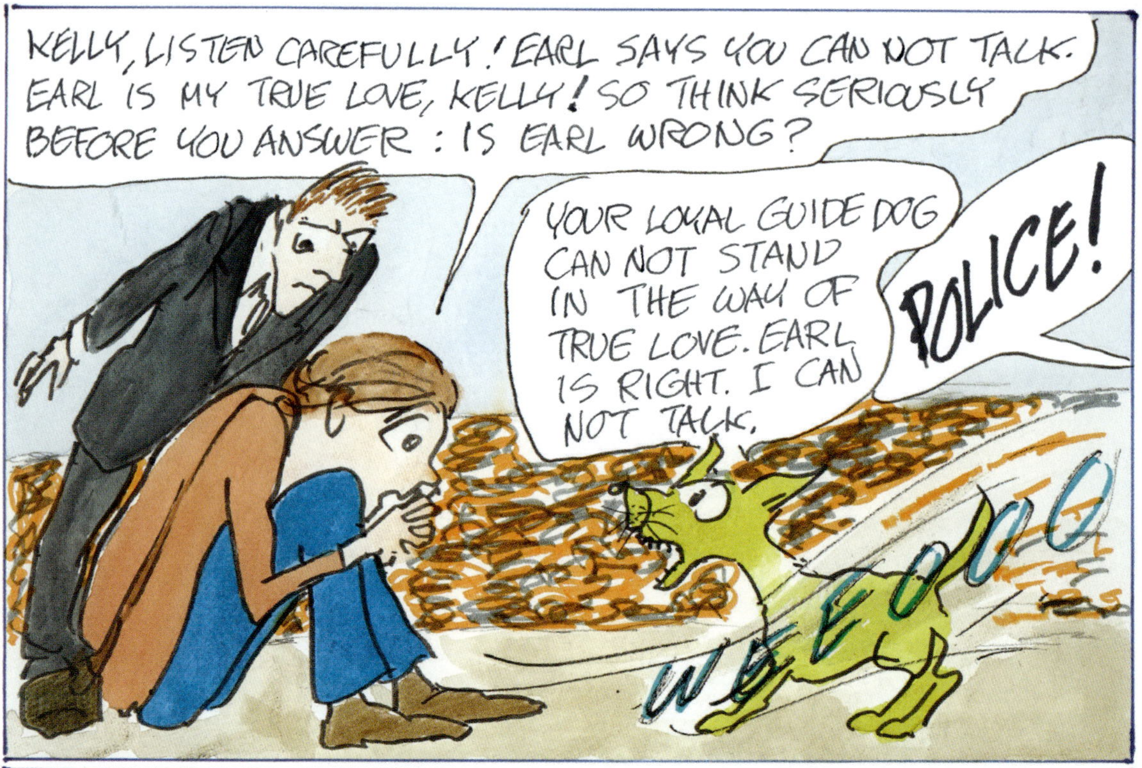
KELLY, LISTEN CAREFULLY! EARL SAYS YOU CAN NOT TALK. EARL IS MY TRUE LOVE, KELLY! SO THINK SERIOUSLY BEFORE YOU ANSWER: IS EARL WRONG?
YOUR LOYAL GUIDE DOG CAN NOT STAND IN THE WAY OF TRUE LOVE. EARL IS RIGHT. I CAN NOT TALK.
POLICE!
WEEEOOO

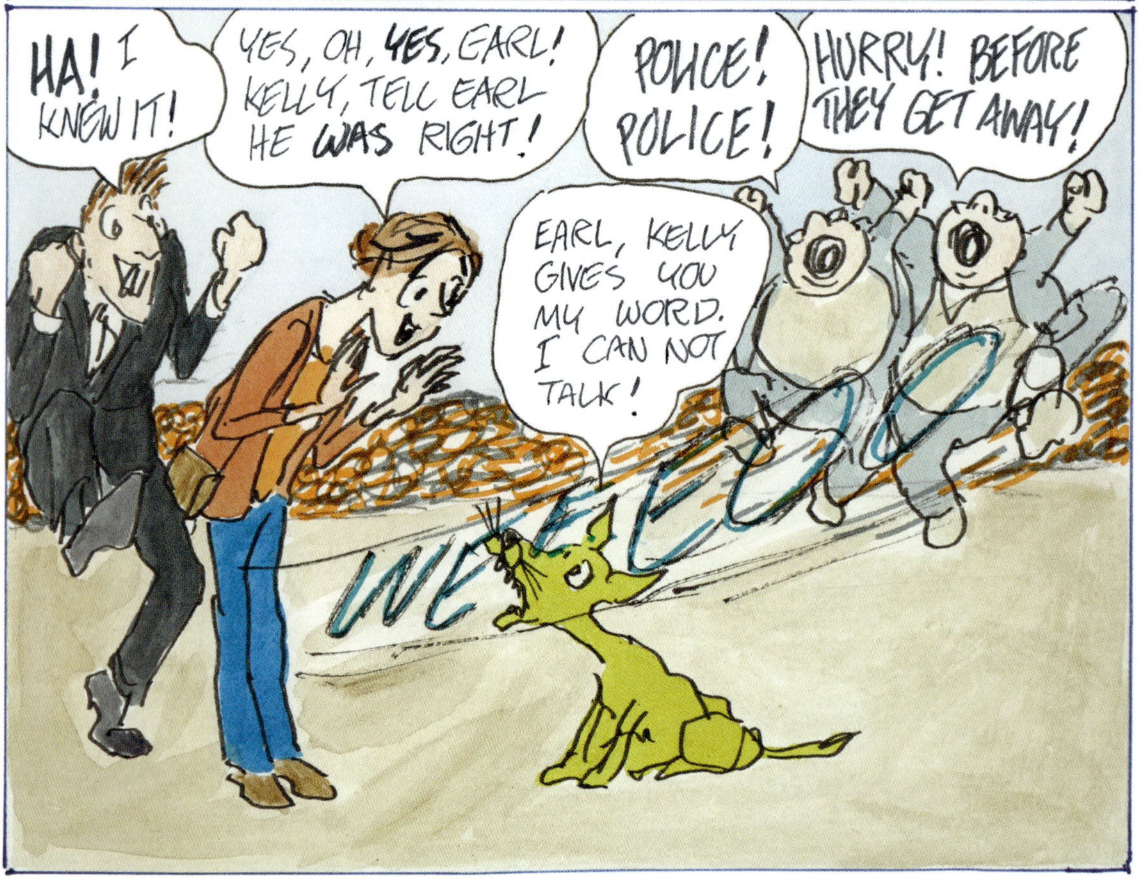
HA! I KNEW IT!
YES, OH, YES, EARL! KELLY, TELL EARL HE WAS RIGHT!
POLICE! POLICE!
HURRY! BEFORE THEY GET AWAY!
EARL, KELLY GIVES YOU MY WORD. I CAN NOT TALK!
WEEEOOO

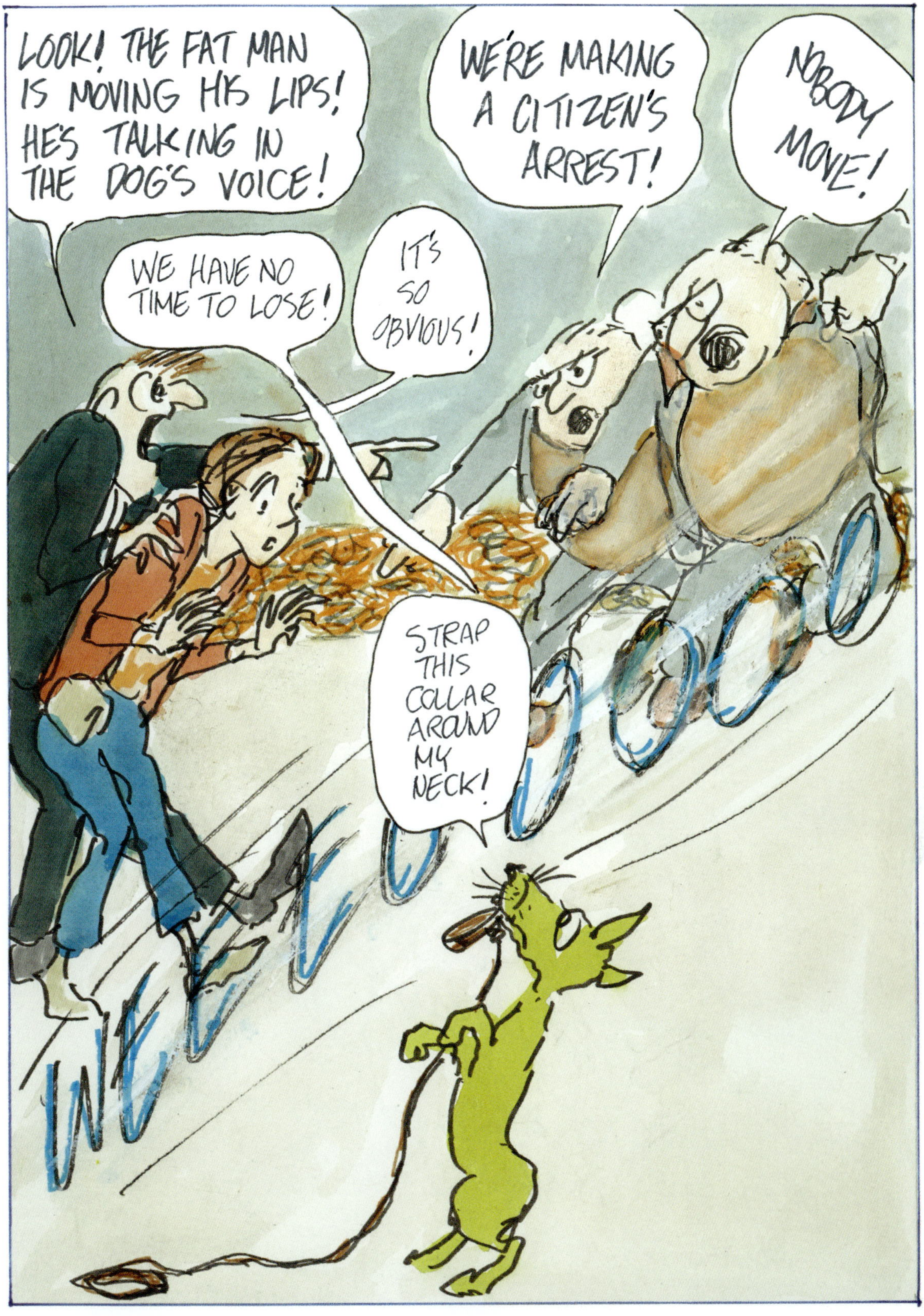
LOOK! THE FAT MAN IS MOVING HIS LIPS! HE'S TALKING IN THE DOG'S VOICE!
WE'RE MAKING A CITIZEN'S ARREST!
NOBODY MOVE!
WE HAVE NO TIME TO LOSE!
IT'S SO OBVIOUS!
STRAP THIS COLLAR AROUND MY NECK!

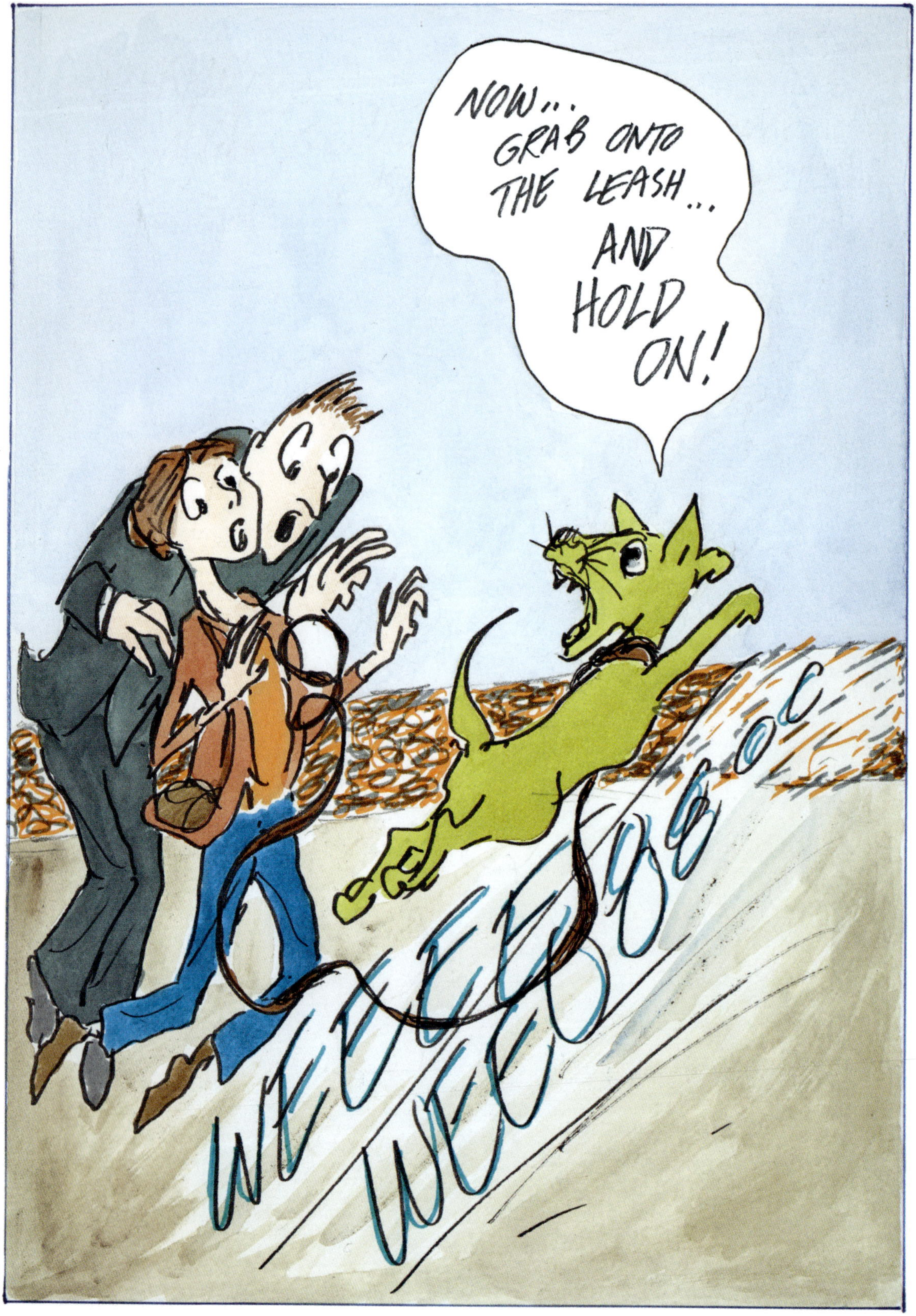
NOW... GRAB ONTO THE LEASH... AND HOLD ON!

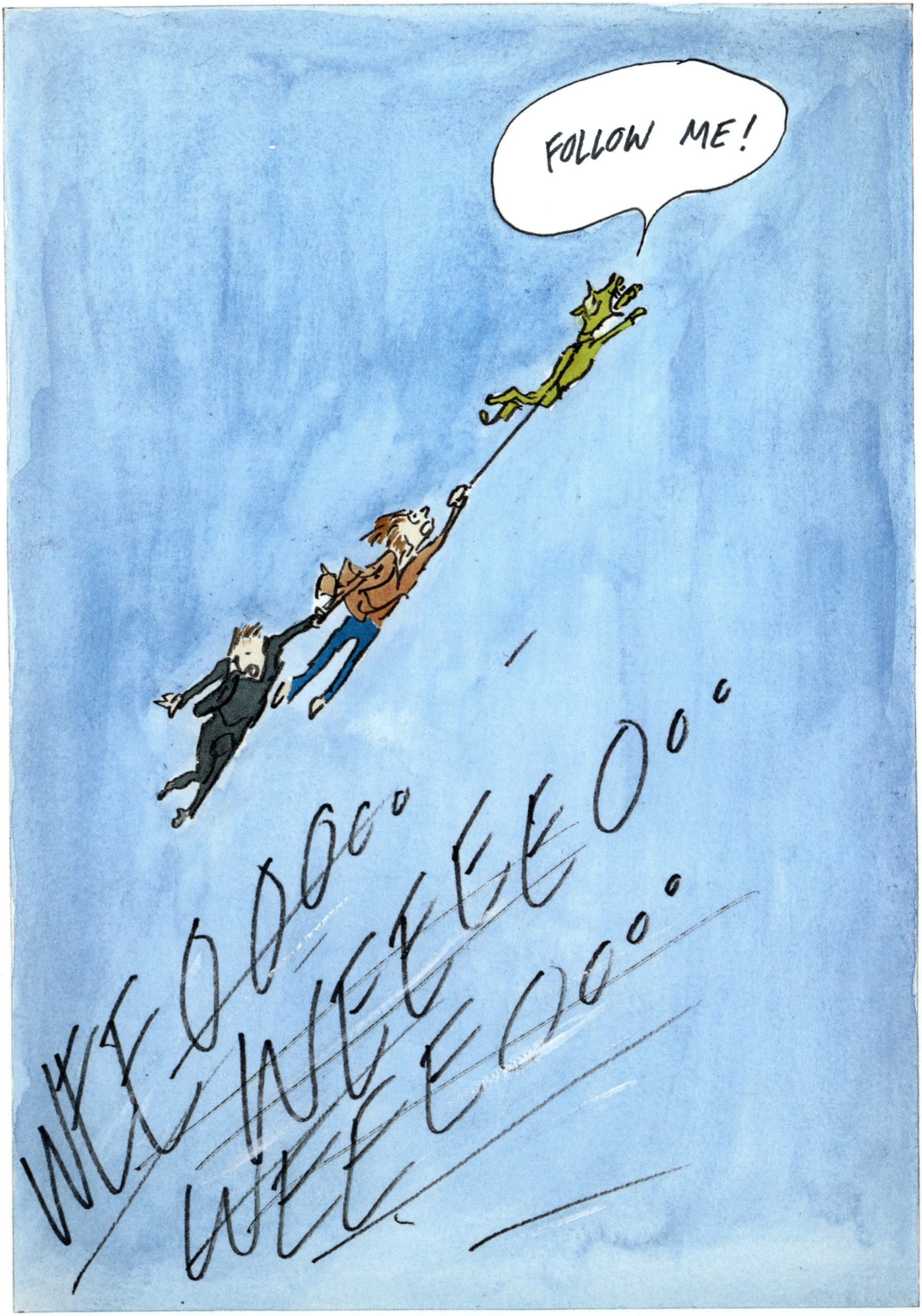
FOLLOW ME!

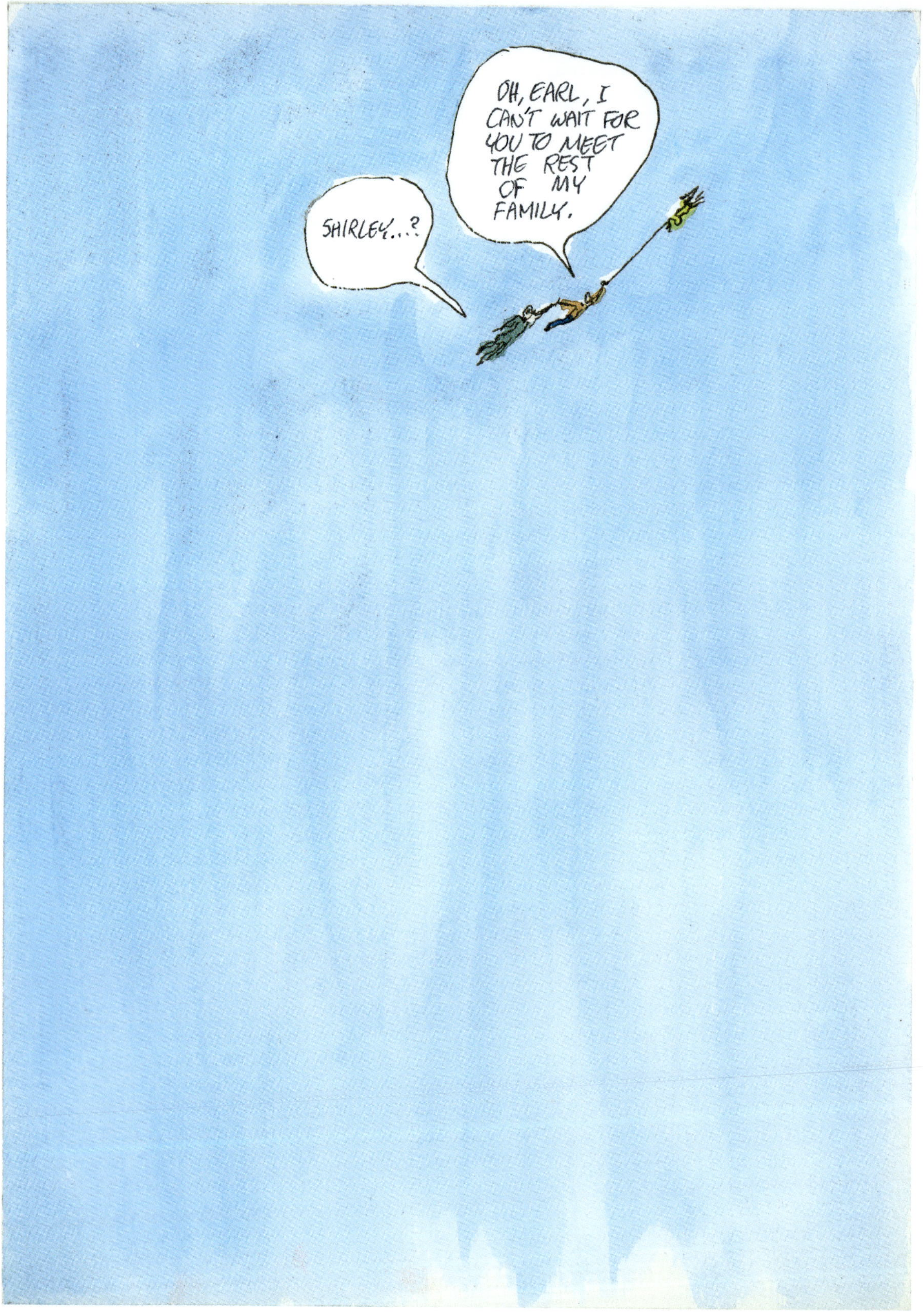
SHIRLEY...?
OH, EARL, I CAN'T WAIT FOR YOU TO MEET THE REST OF MY FAMILY.

CHAPTER 25 • MISSION HO!

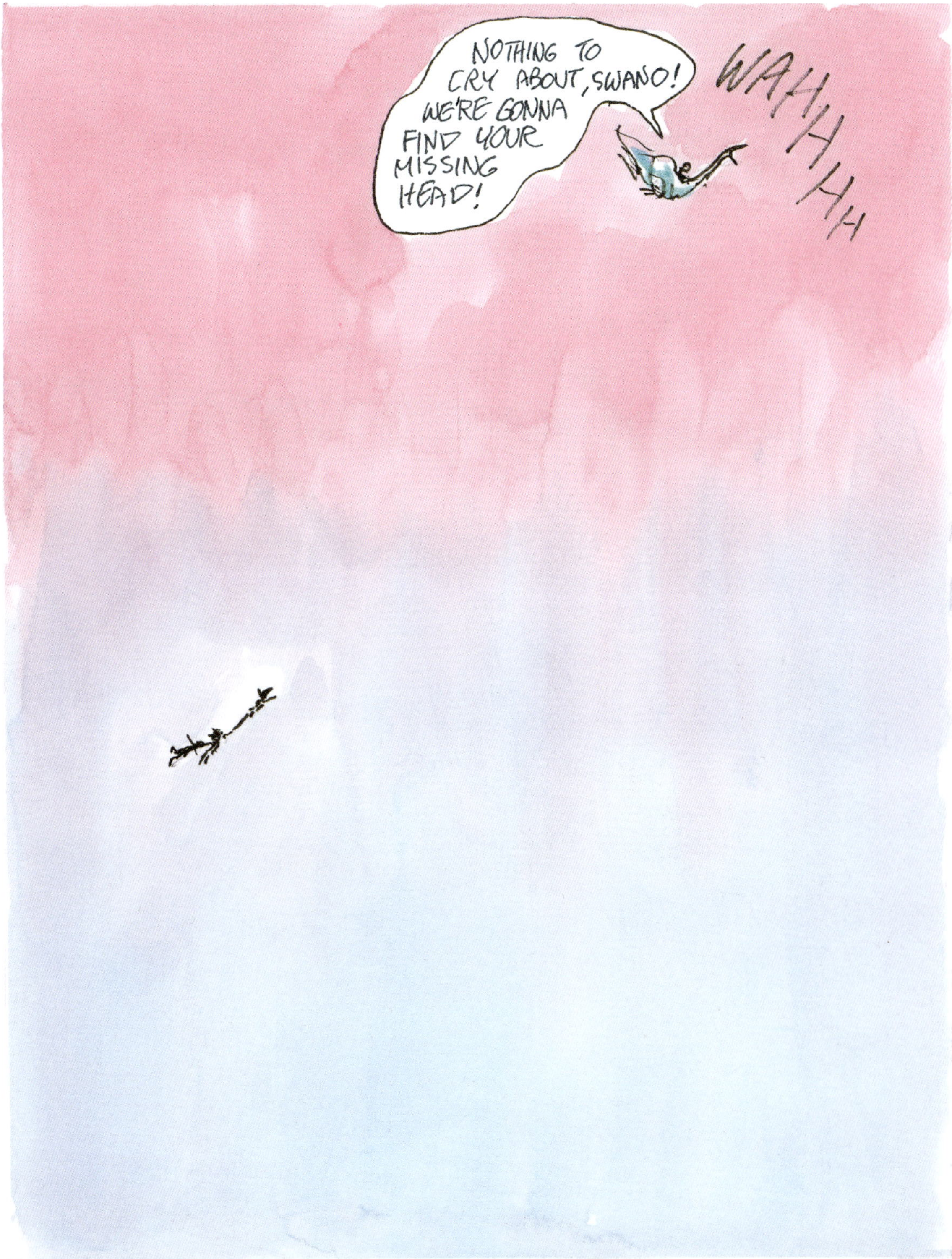
NOTHING TO CRY ABOUT, SWANO! WE'RE GONNA FIND YOUR MISSING HEAD!
WAHHHH

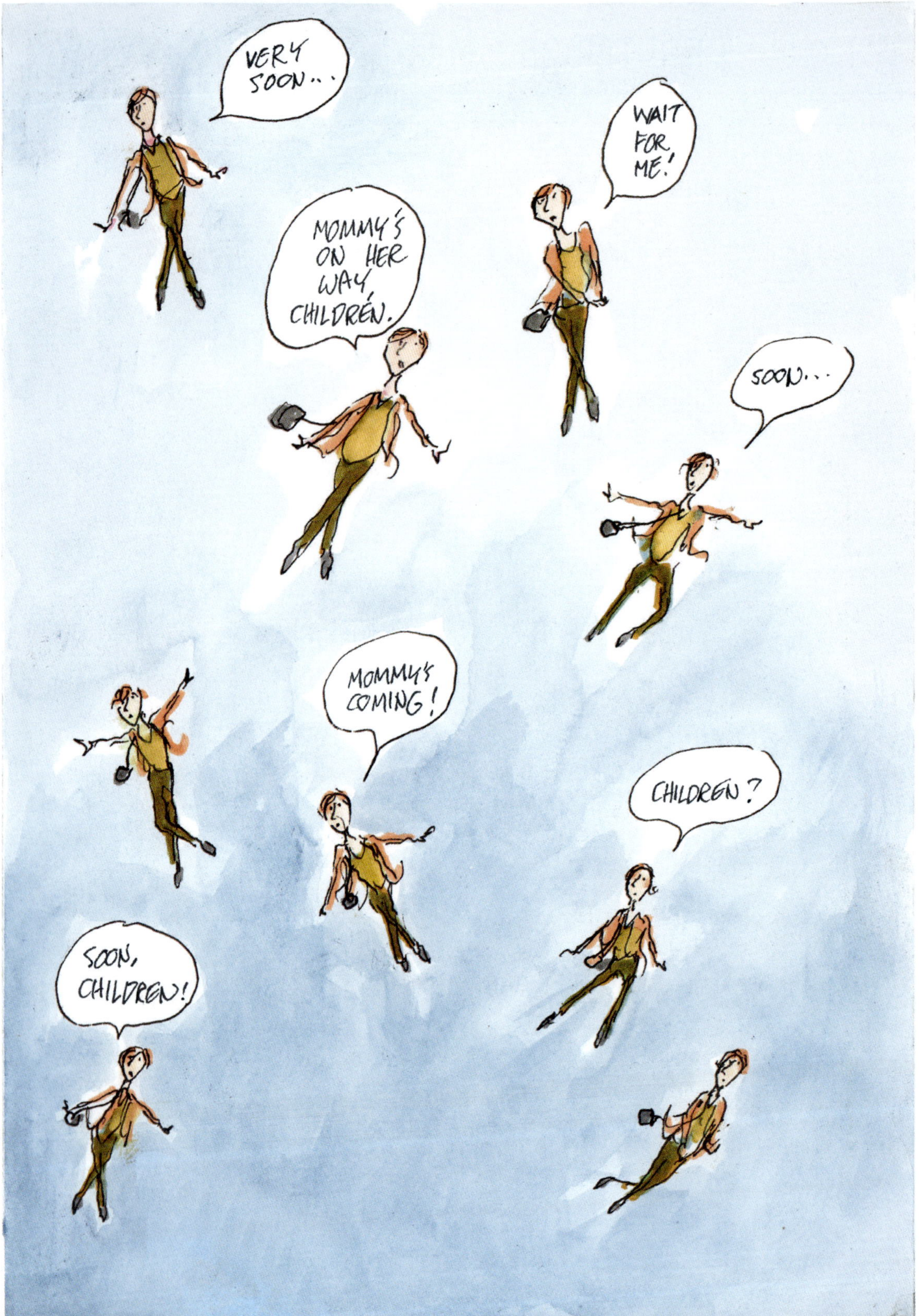
VERY SOON...
WAIT FOR ME!
MOMMY'S ON HER WAY, CHILDREN.
SOON...
MOMMY'S COMING!
CHILDREN?
SOON, CHILDREN!

CHAPTER 26 • THE ECHO

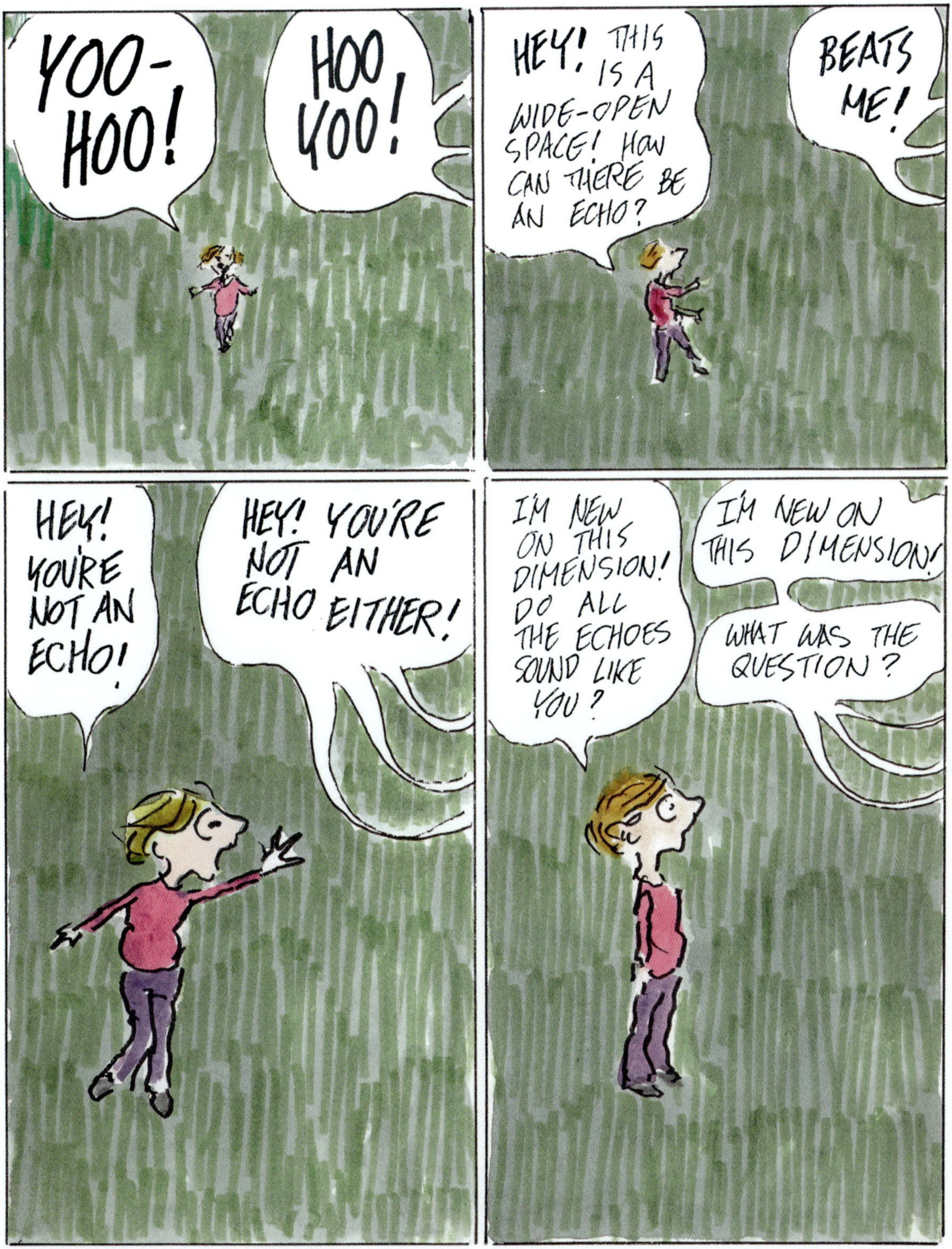
YOO-HOO!
HOO YOO!
HEY! THIS IS A WIDE-OPEN SPACE! HOW CAN THERE BE AN ECHO?
BEATS ME!
HEY! YOU'RE NOT AN ECHO!
HEY! YOU'RE NOT AN ECHO EITHER!
I'M NEW ON THIS DIMENSION! DO ALL THE ECHOES SOUND LIKE YOU?
I'M NEW ON THIS DIMENSION!
WHAT WAS THE QUESTION?

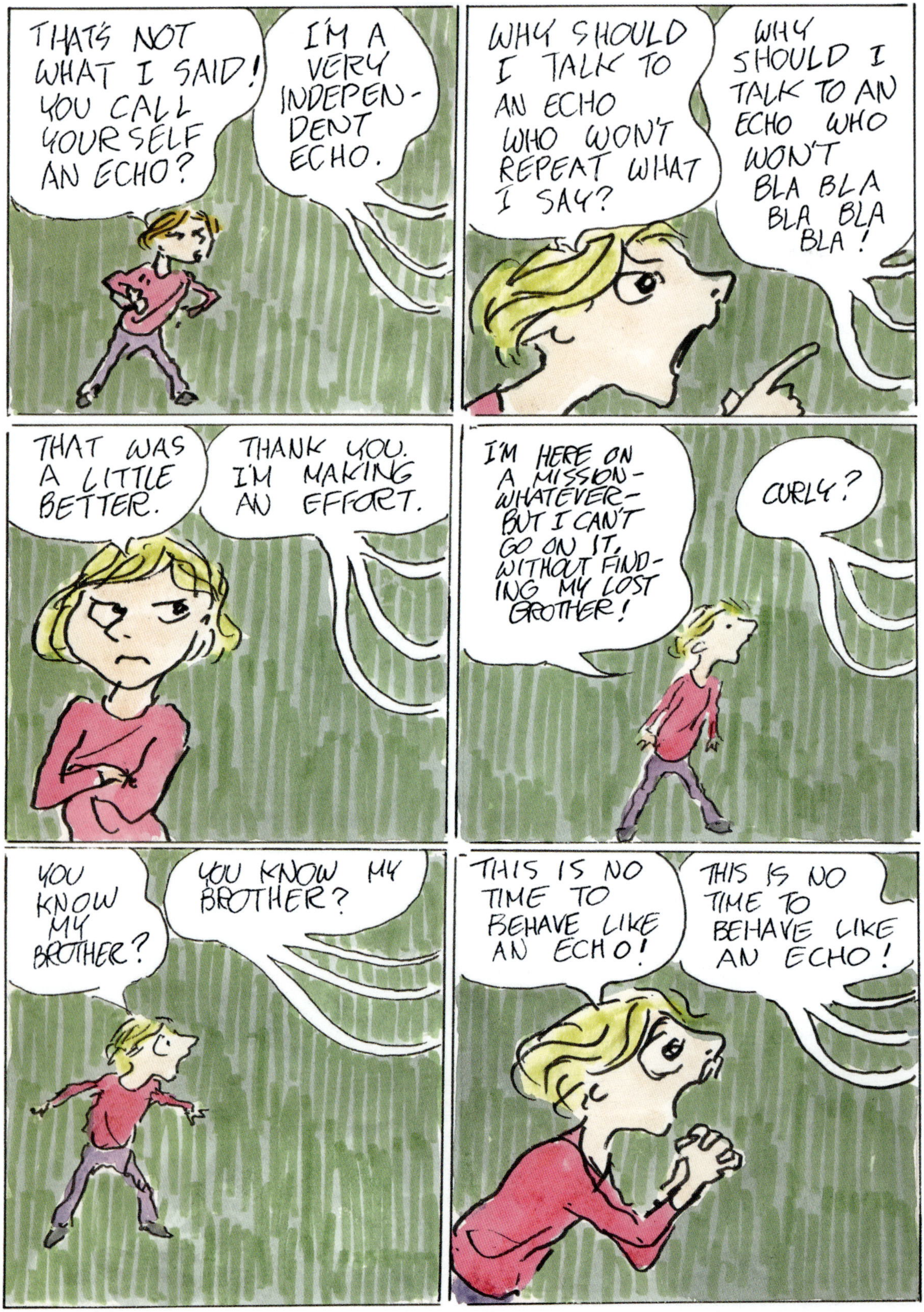
THAT'S NOT WHAT I SAID! YOU CALL YOURSELF AN ECHO?
I'M A VERY INDEPENDENT ECHO.
WHY SHOULD I TALK TO AN ECHO WHO WON'T REPEAT WHAT I SAY?
WHY SHOULD I TALK TO AN ECHO WHO WON'T BLA BLA BLA BLA BLA!
THAT WAS A LITTLE BETTER.
THANK YOU. I'M MAKING AN EFFORT.
I'M HERE ON A MISSION—WHATEVER—BUT I CAN'T GO ON IT, WITHOUT FINDING MY LOST BROTHER!
CURLY?
YOU KNOW MY BROTHER?
YOU KNOW MY BROTHER?
THIS IS NO TIME TO BEHAVE LIKE AN ECHO!
THIS IS NO TIME TO BEHAVE LIKE AN ECHO!

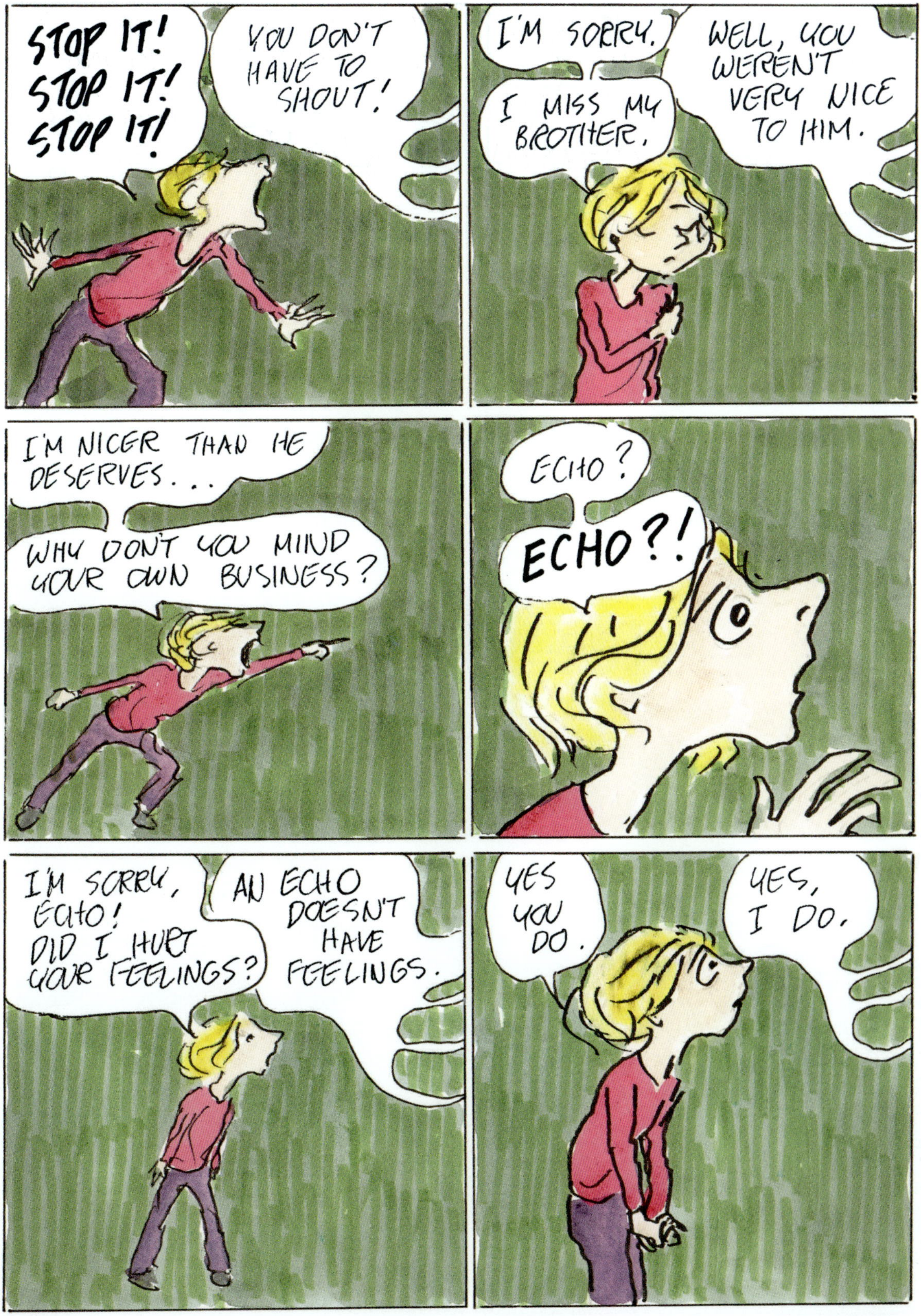
STOP IT! STOP IT! STOP IT!
YOU DON'T HAVE TO SHOUT!
I'M SORRY.
I MISS MY BROTHER.
WELL, YOU WEREN'T VERY NICE TO HIM.
I'M NICER THAN HE DESERVES...
WHY DON'T YOU MIND YOUR OWN BUSINESS?
ECHO?
ECHO?!
I'M SORRY, ECHO! DID I HURT YOUR FEELINGS?
AN ECHO DOESN'T HAVE FEELINGS.
YES YOU DO.
YES, I DO.

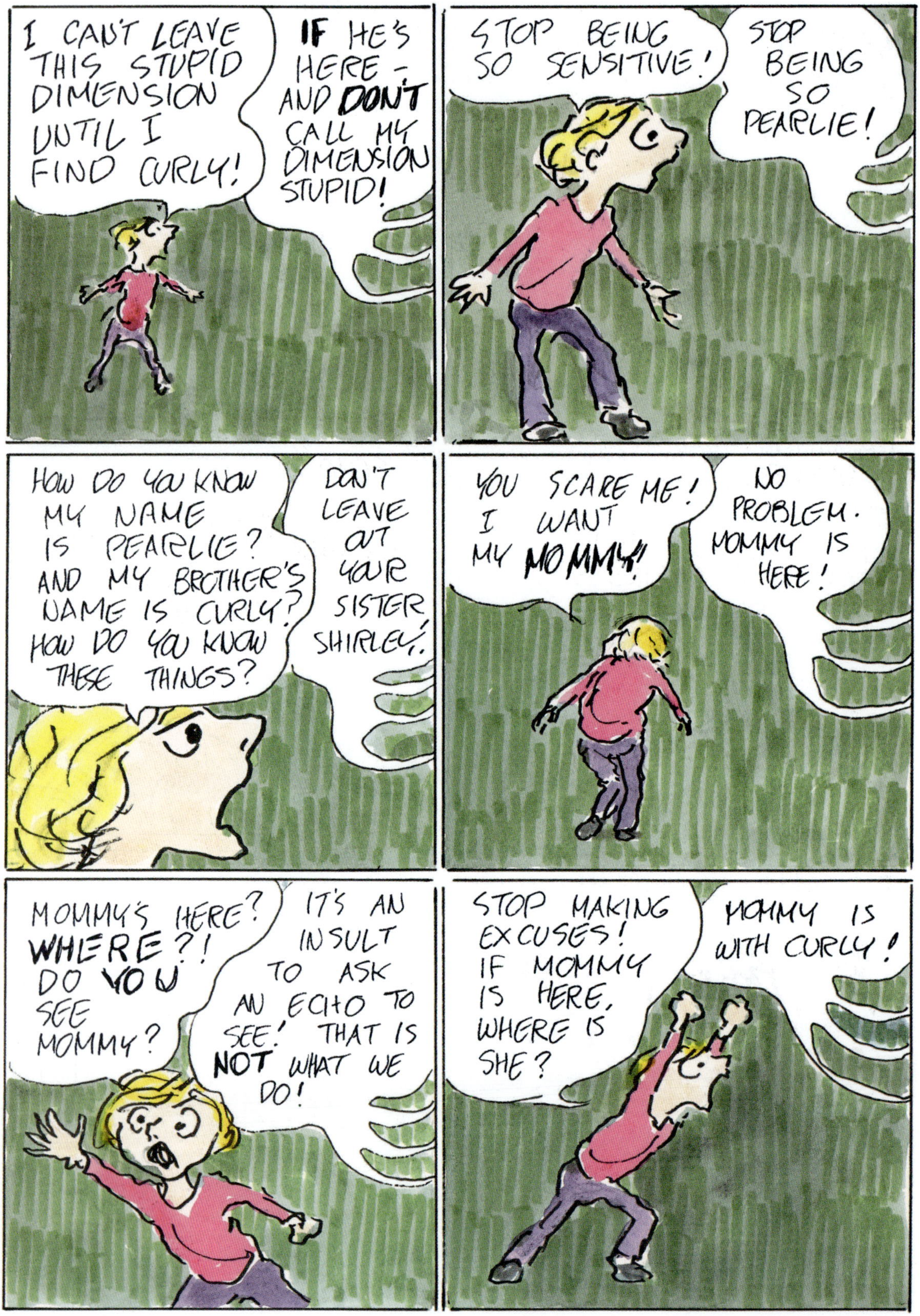
I CAN'T LEAVE THIS STUPID DIMENSION UNTIL I FIND CURLY!
IF HE'S HERE - AND DON'T CALL MY DIMENSION STUPID!
STOP BEING SO SENSITIVE!
STOP BEING SO PEARLIE!
HOW DO YOU KNOW MY NAME IS PEARLIE? AND MY BROTHER'S NAME IS CURLY? HOW DO YOU KNOW THESE THINGS?
DON'T LEAVE OUT YOUR SISTER SHIRLEY!
YOU SCARE ME! I WANT MY MOMMY!
NO PROBLEM. MOMMY IS HERE!
MOMMY'S HERE? WHERE?! DO YOU SEE MOMMY?
IT'S AN INSULT TO ASK AN ECHO TO SEE! THAT IS NOT WHAT WE DO!
STOP MAKING EXCUSES! IF MOMMY IS HERE, WHERE IS SHE?
MOMMY IS WITH CURLY!

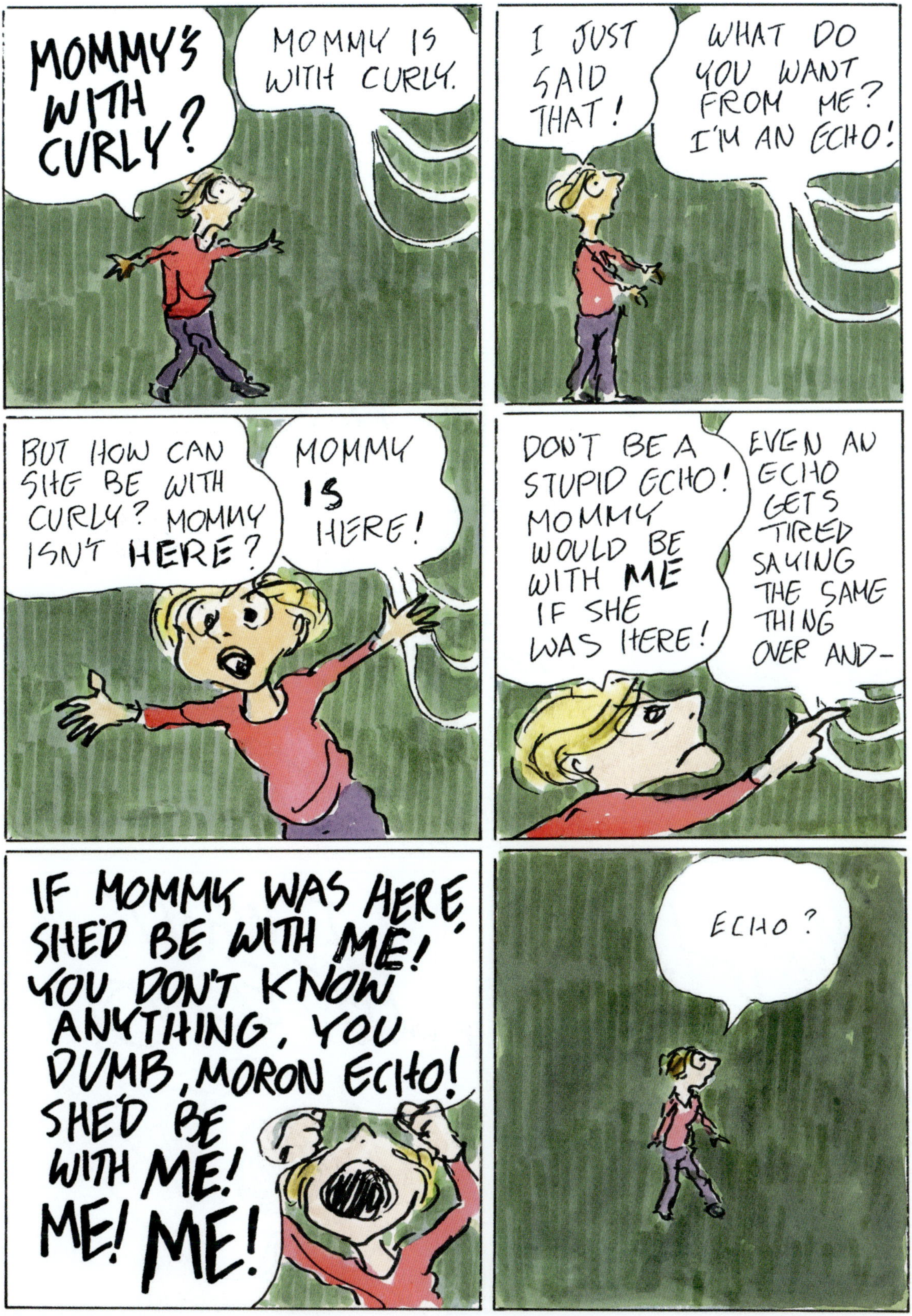
MOMMY'S WITH CURLY?
MOMMY IS WITH CURLY.
I JUST SAID THAT!
WHAT DO YOU WANT FROM ME? I'M AN ECHO!
BUT HOW CAN SHE BE WITH CURLY? MOMMY ISN'T HERE?
MOMMY IS HERE!
DON'T BE A STUPID ECHO! MOMMY WOULD BE WITH ME IF SHE WAS HERE!
EVEN AN ECHO GETS TIRED SAYING THE SAME THING OVER AND-
IF MOMMY WAS HERE, SHE'D BE WITH ME! YOU DON'T KNOW ANYTHING, YOU DUMB, MORON ECHO! SHE'D BE WITH ME! ME! ME!
ECHO?

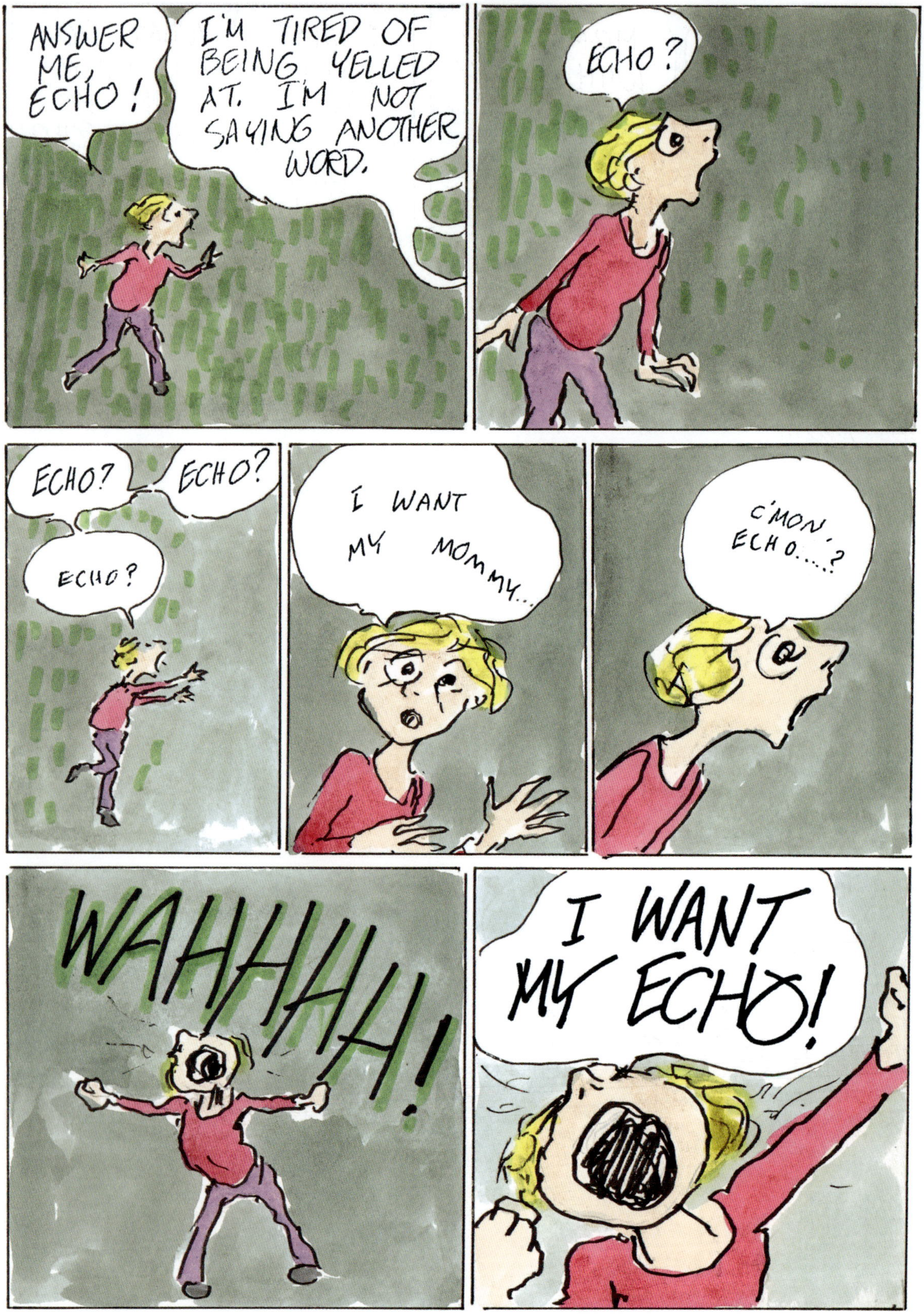
ANSWER ME, ECHO!
I'M TIRED OF BEING YELLED AT. I'M NOT SAYING ANOTHER WORD.
ECHO?
ECHO?
ECHO?
ECHO?
I WANT MY MOMMY...
C'MON ECHO....?
WAHHHH!
I WANT MY ECHO!

CHAPTER 27 • FLOATING MOMMY

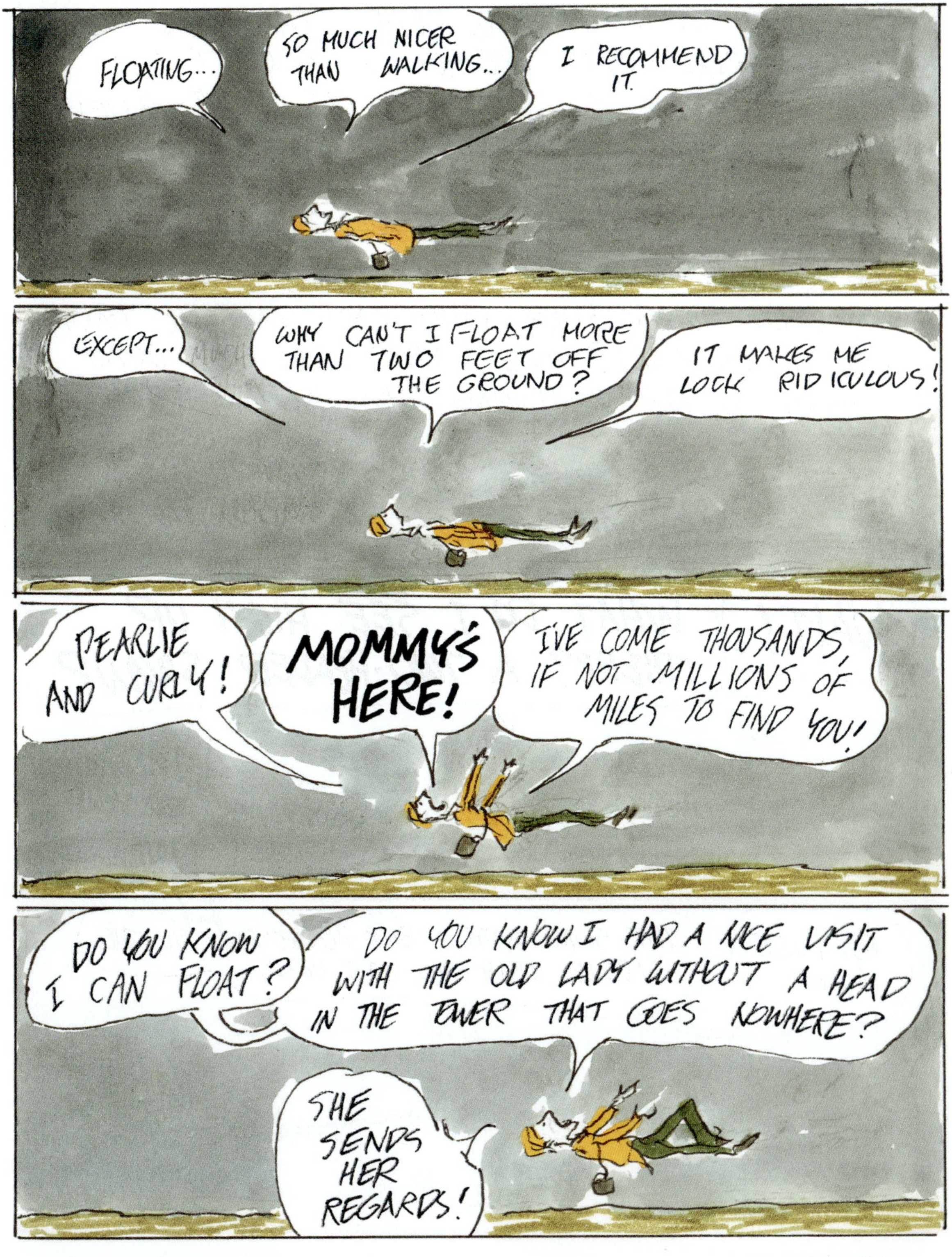

FLOATING...
SO MUCH NICER THAN WALKING...
I RECOMMEND IT.
EXCEPT...
WHY CAN'T I FLOAT MORE THAN TWO FEET OFF THE GROUND?
IT MAKES ME LOOK RIDICULOUS!
PEARLIE AND CURLY!
MOMMY'S HERE!
I'VE COME THOUSANDS, IF NOT MILLIONS OF MILES TO FIND YOU!
DO YOU KNOW I CAN FLOAT?
DO YOU KNOW I HAD A NICE VISIT WITH THE OLD LADY WITHOUT A HEAD IN THE TOWER THAT GOES NOWHERE?
SHE SENDS HER REGARDS!

Panel 1: She lent me this head that I'm wearing. It looks exactly like my real head, but when I wear THIS head over my real head, THIS head ages, and my real head doesn't. So even if I look old, don't believe it, because I'm NOT!

Panel 2: Are you alive, Pearlie and Curly? Please be alive! I've been to so many dimensions over so many years! Two years? Three? Five? We can't expect Shirley to keep postponing her wedding, just because I can't find you to bring you back!

Panel 3: WAIT! What do I see high up there? A TWO-HEADED SWAN?

Panel 4: No. False alarm... That swan with a bald-headed boy in the saddle only has one head.

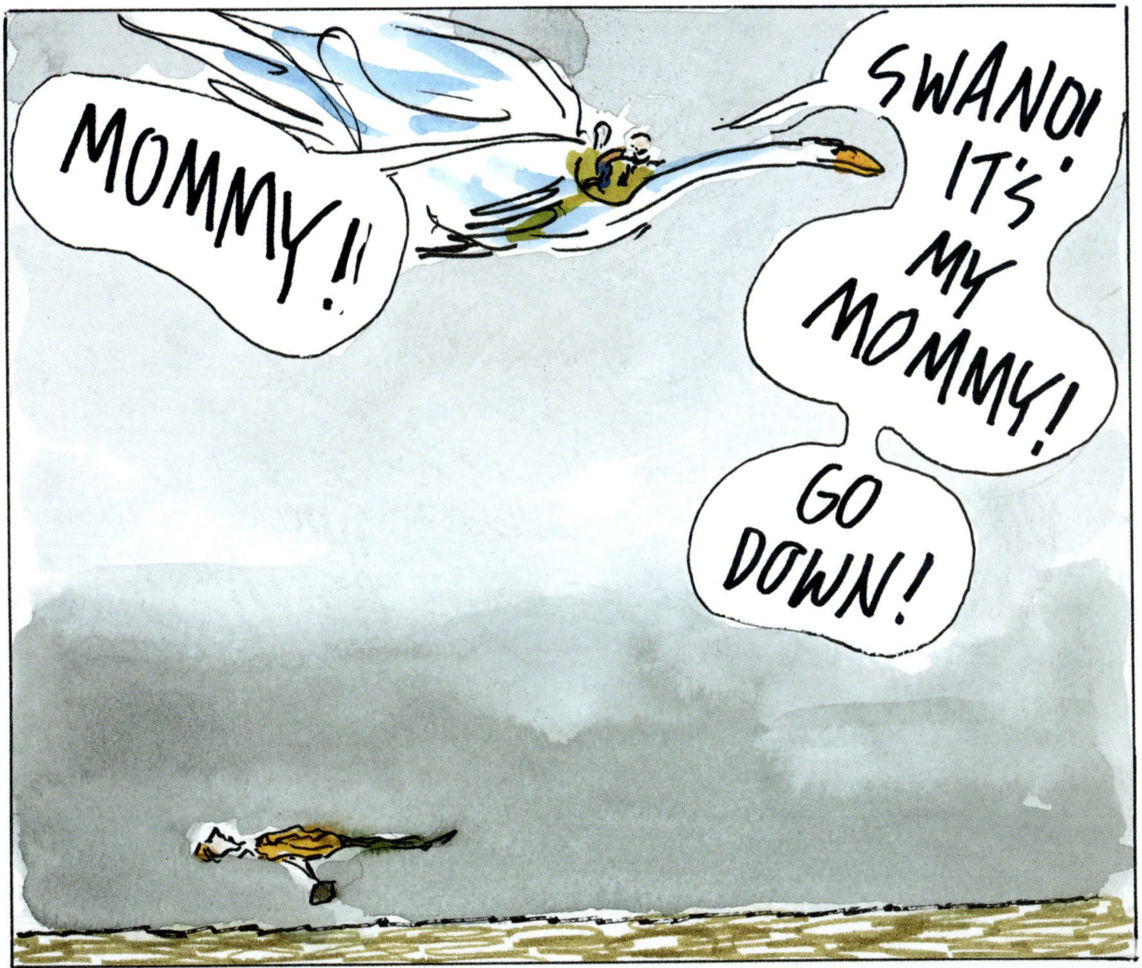
MOMMY!!
SWANO! IT'S MY MOMMY!
GO DOWN!

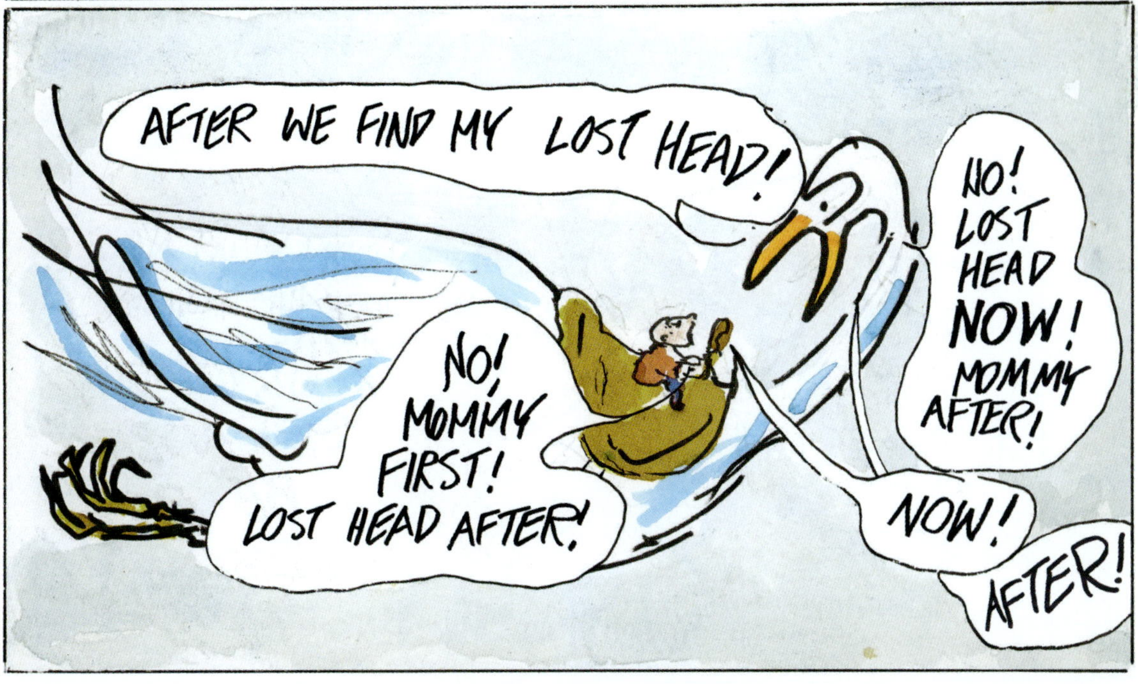
AFTER WE FIND MY LOST HEAD!
NO! LOST HEAD NOW! MOMMY AFTER!
NO! MOMMY FIRST! LOST HEAD AFTER!
NOW!
AFTER!

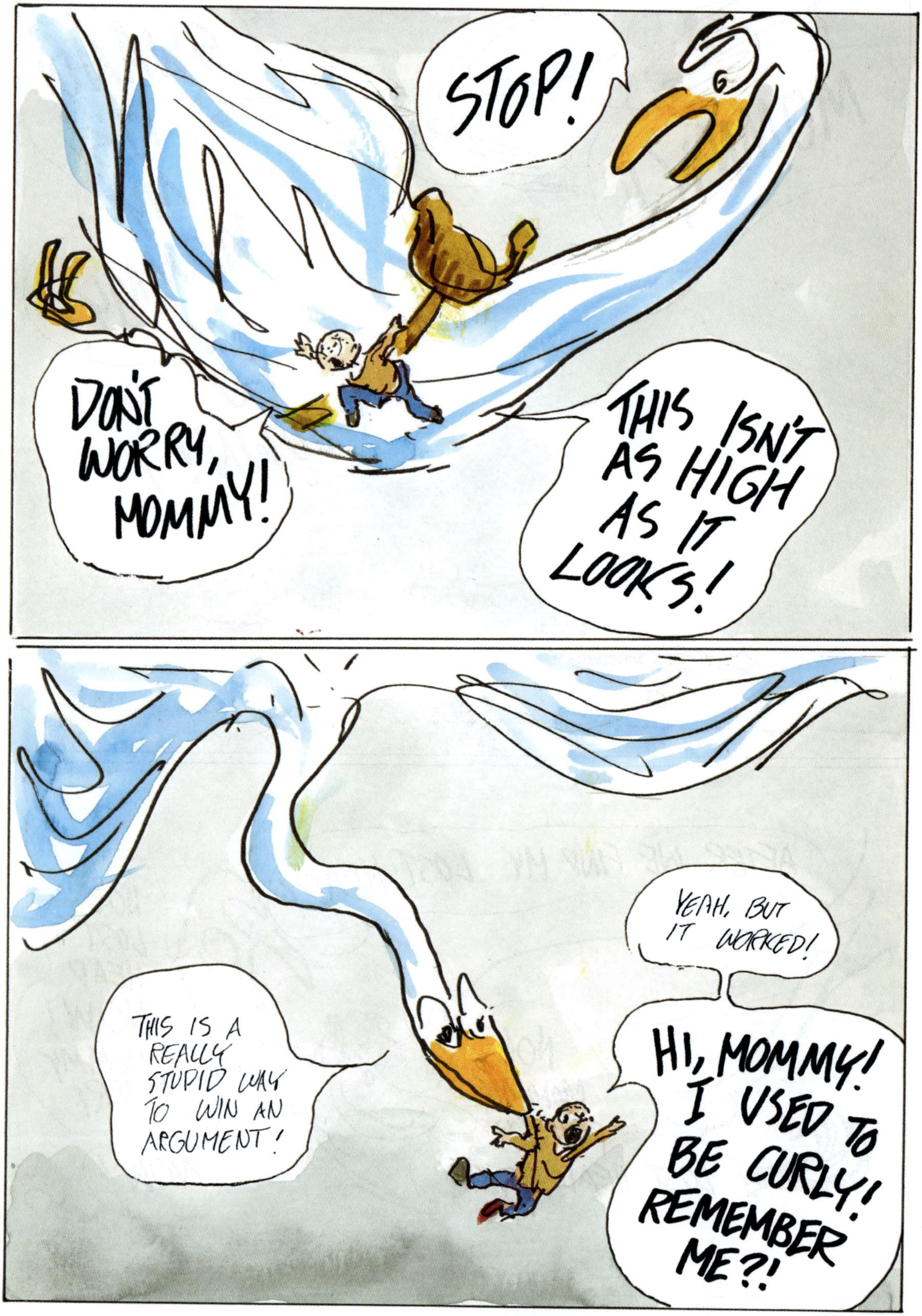
STOP!
DON'T WORRY, MOMMY!
THIS ISN'T AS HIGH AS IT LOOKS!
THIS IS A REALLY STUPID WAY TO WIN AN ARGUMENT!
YEAH, BUT IT WORKED!
HI, MOMMY! I USED TO BE CURLY! REMEMBER ME?!

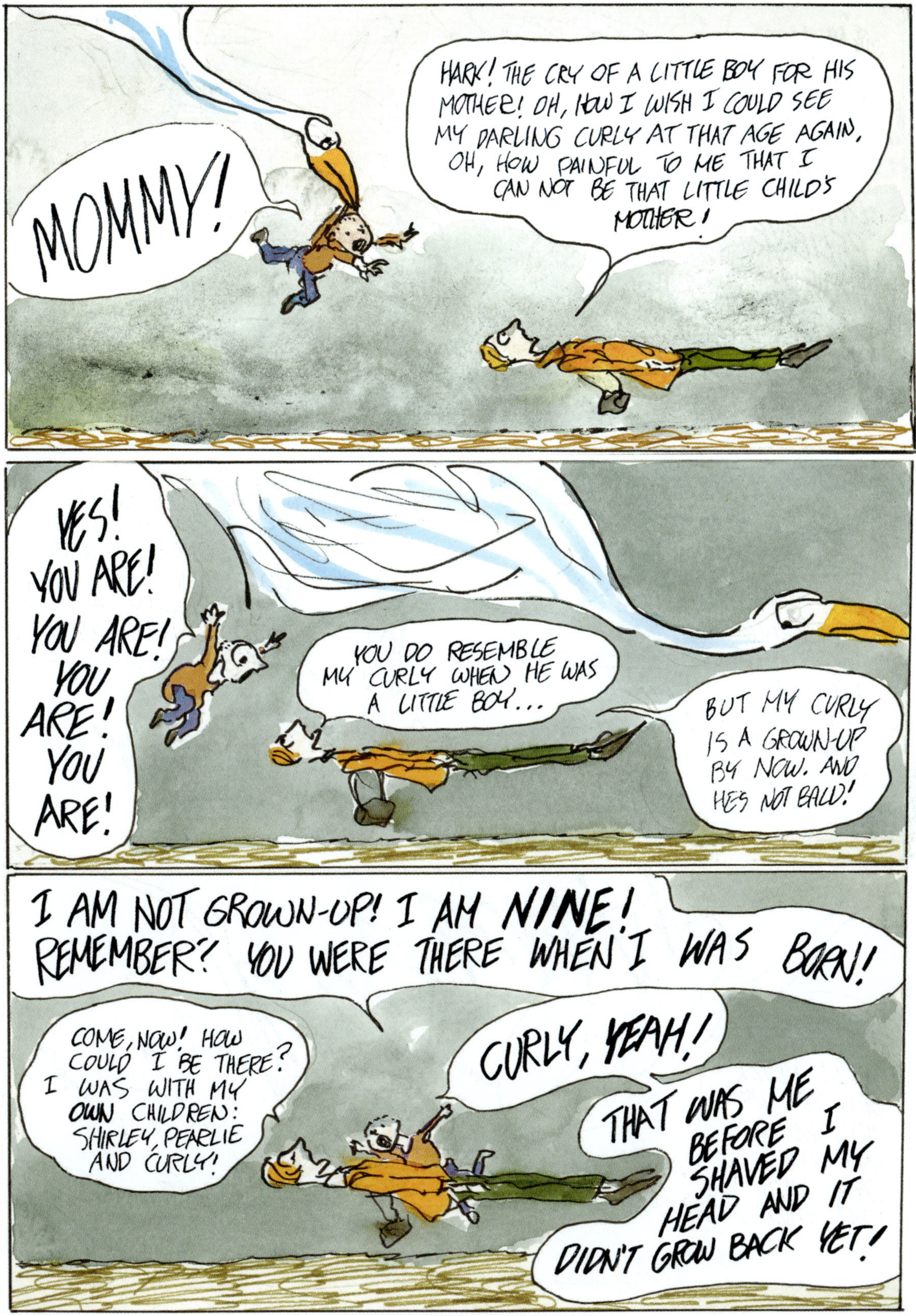
MOMMY!
HARK! THE CRY OF A LITTLE BOY FOR HIS MOTHER! OH, HOW I WISH I COULD SEE MY DARLING CURLY AT THAT AGE AGAIN. OH, HOW PAINFUL TO ME THAT I CAN NOT BE THAT LITTLE CHILD'S MOTHER!
YES! YOU ARE! YOU ARE! YOU ARE! YOU ARE!
YOU DO RESEMBLE MY CURLY WHEN HE WAS A LITTLE BOY...
BUT MY CURLY IS A GROWN-UP BY NOW. AND HE'S NOT BALD!
I AM NOT GROWN-UP! I AM NINE! REMEMBER? YOU WERE THERE WHEN I WAS BORN!
COME, NOW! HOW COULD I BE THERE? I WAS WITH MY OWN CHILDREN: SHIRLEY, PEARLIE AND CURLY!
CURLY, YEAH!
THAT WAS ME BEFORE I SHAVED MY HEAD AND IT DIDN'T GROW BACK YET!

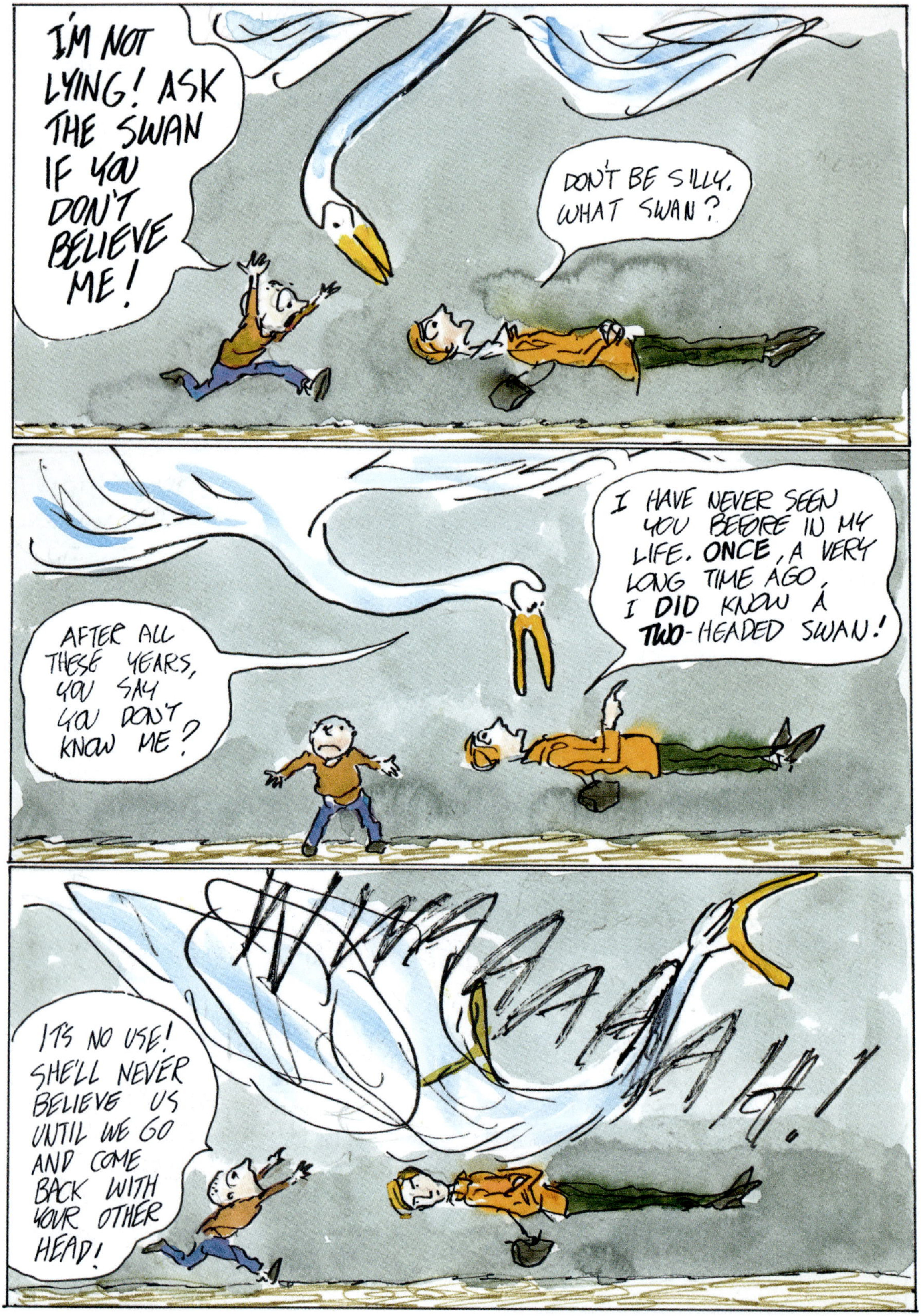
I'M NOT LYING! ASK THE SWAN IF YOU DON'T BELIEVE ME!
DON'T BE SILLY. WHAT SWAN?
I HAVE NEVER SEEN YOU BEFORE IN MY LIFE. ONCE, A VERY LONG TIME AGO, I DID KNOW A TWO-HEADED SWAN!
AFTER ALL THESE YEARS, YOU SAY YOU DON'T KNOW ME?
WAAAAAAH!
IT'S NO USE! SHE'LL NEVER BELIEVE US UNTIL WE GO AND COME BACK WITH YOUR OTHER HEAD!

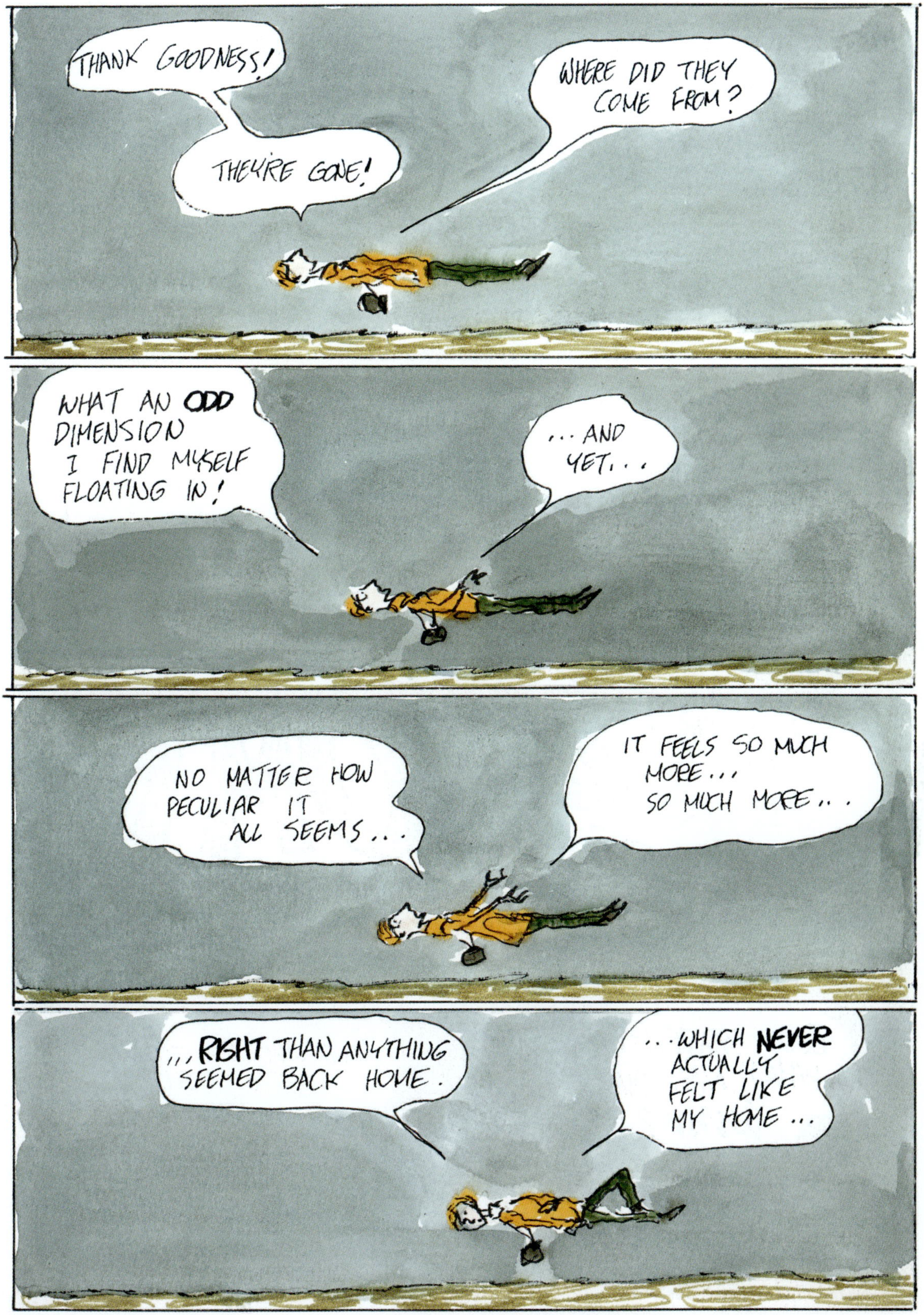
THANK GOODNESS!
THEY'RE GONE!
WHERE DID THEY COME FROM?
WHAT AN ODD DIMENSION I FIND MYSELF FLOATING IN!
...AND YET...
NO MATTER HOW PECULIAR IT ALL SEEMS...
IT FEELS SO MUCH MORE... SO MUCH MORE...
...RIGHT THAN ANYTHING SEEMED BACK HOME.
...WHICH NEVER ACTUALLY FELT LIKE MY HOME...

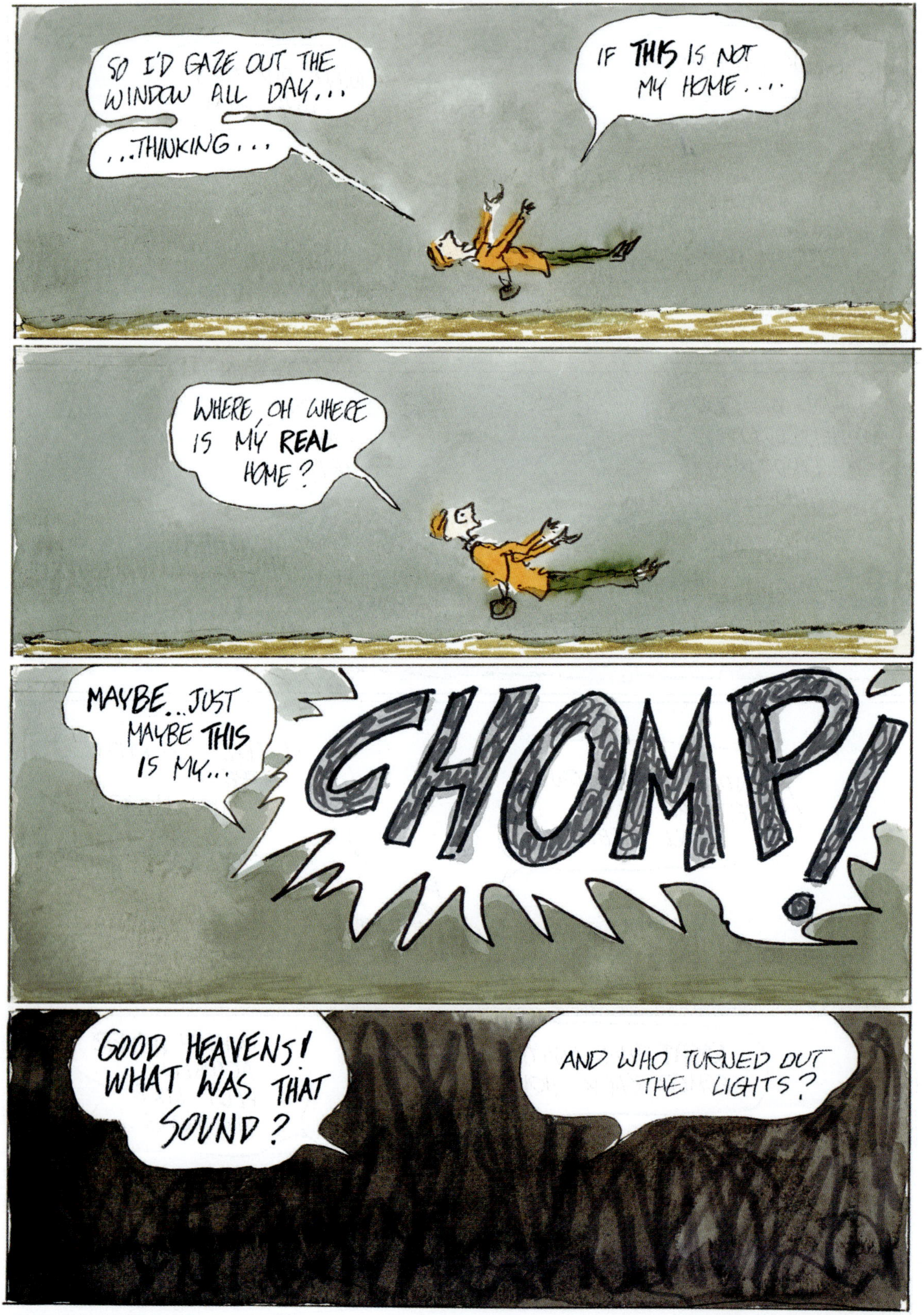
SO I'D GAZE OUT THE WINDOW ALL DAY...
...THINKING...
IF THIS IS NOT MY HOME....
WHERE, OH WHERE IS MY REAL HOME?
MAYBE...JUST MAYBE THIS IS MY...
CHOMP!
GOOD HEAVENS! WHAT WAS THAT SOUND?
AND WHO TURNED OUT THE LIGHTS?

CHAPTER 28 • NEW NAMES

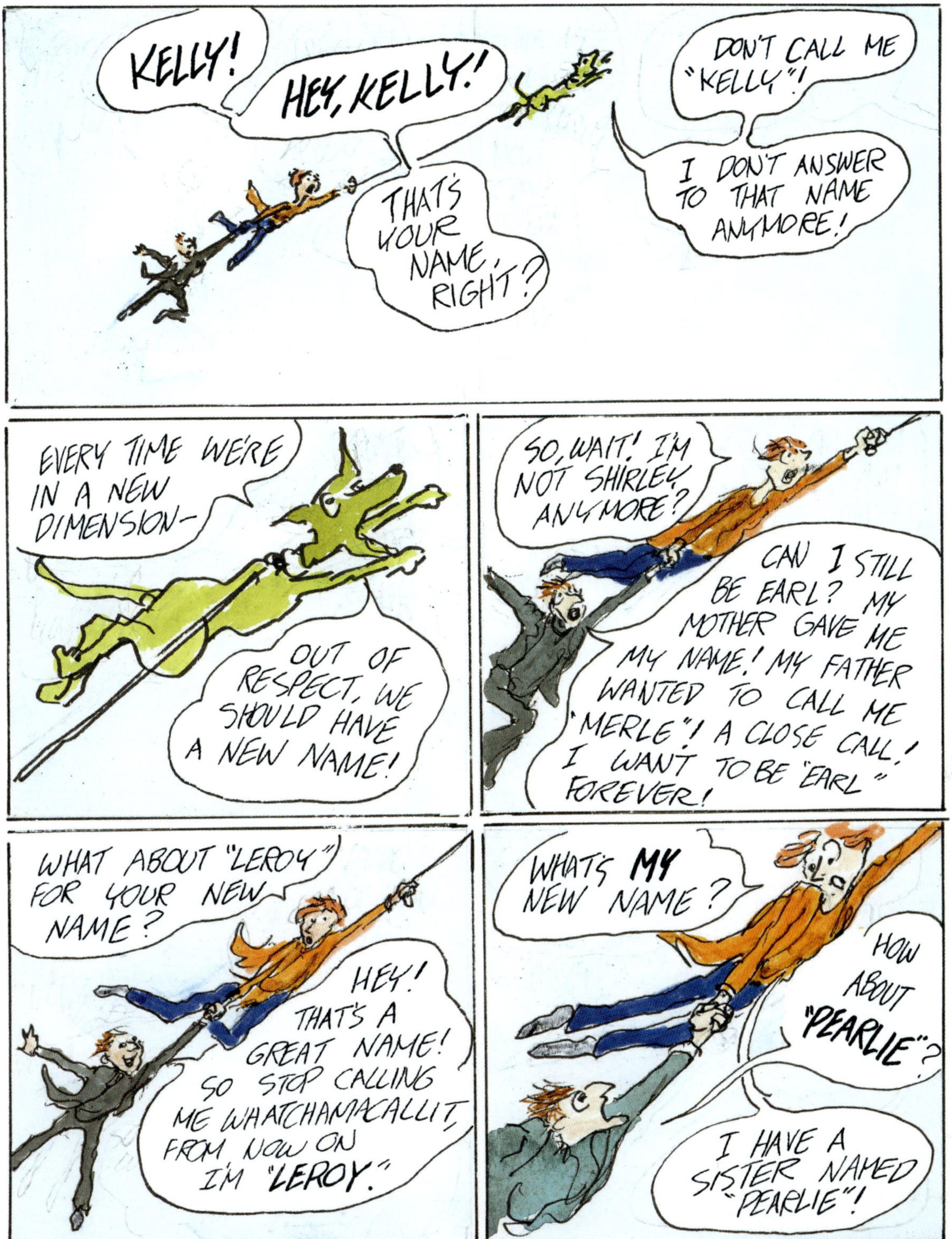
KELLY!
HEY, KELLY!
THAT'S YOUR NAME, RIGHT?
DON'T CALL ME "KELLY"!
I DON'T ANSWER TO THAT NAME ANYMORE!
EVERY TIME WE'RE IN A NEW DIMENSION-
OUT OF RESPECT, WE SHOULD HAVE A NEW NAME!
SO, WAIT! I'M NOT SHIRLEY ANYMORE?
CAN I STILL BE EARL? MY MOTHER GAVE ME MY NAME! MY FATHER WANTED TO CALL ME "MERLE"! A CLOSE CALL! I WANT TO BE "EARL" FOREVER!
WHAT ABOUT "LEROY" FOR YOUR NEW NAME?
HEY! THAT'S A GREAT NAME! SO STOP CALLING ME WHATCHAMACALLIT, FROM NOW ON I'M "LEROY."
WHAT'S MY NEW NAME?
HOW ABOUT "PEARLIE"?
I HAVE A SISTER NAMED "PEARLIE"!

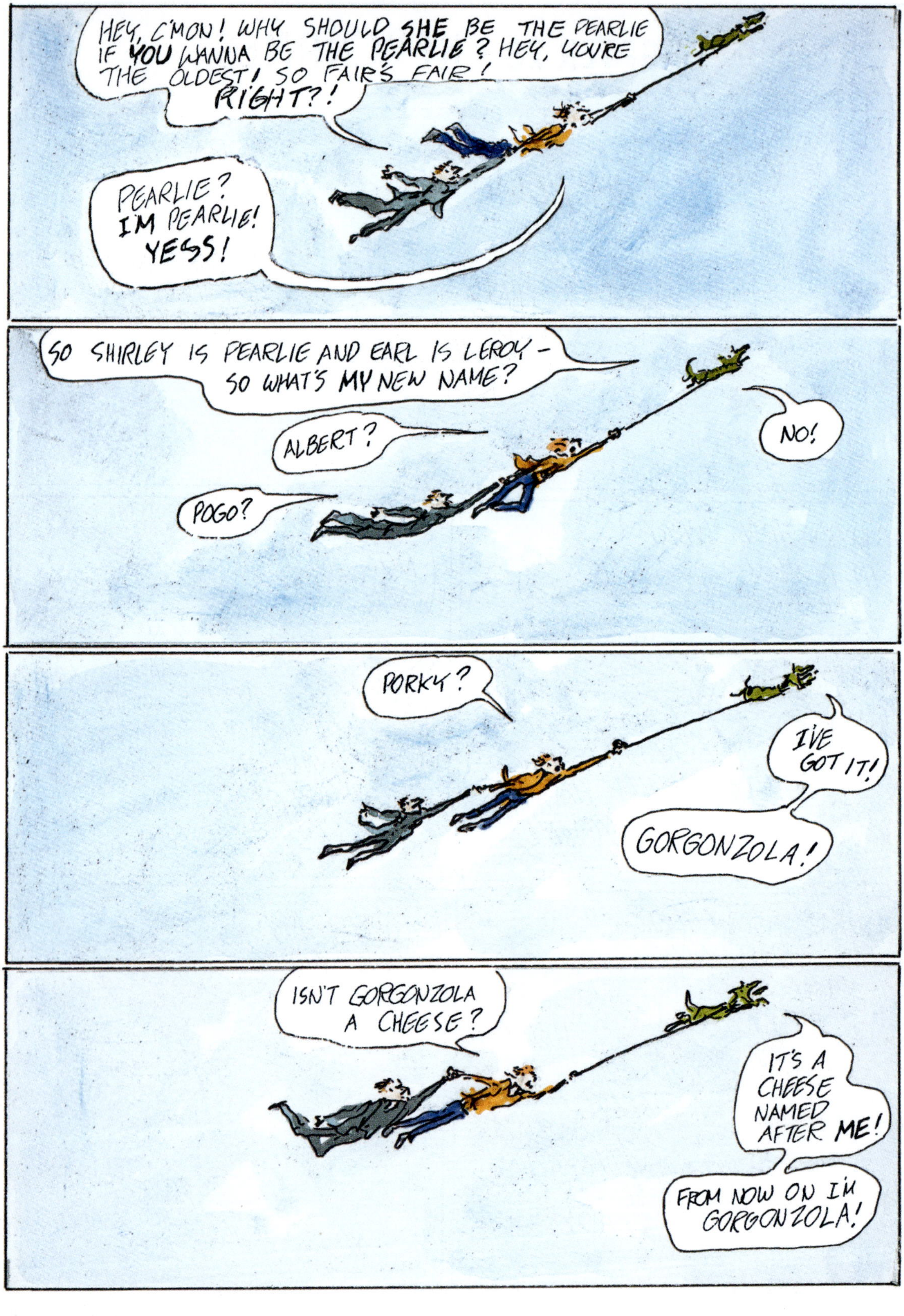
HEY, C'MON! WHY SHOULD SHE BE THE PEARLIE IF YOU WANNA BE THE PEARLIE? HEY, YOU'RE THE OLDEST! SO FAIR'S FAIR! RIGHT?!
PEARLIE? I'M PEARLIE! YESS!
SO SHIRLEY IS PEARLIE AND EARL IS LEROY - SO WHAT'S MY NEW NAME?
ALBERT?
NO!
POGO?
PORKY?
I'VE GOT IT!
GORGONZOLA!
ISN'T GORGONZOLA A CHEESE?
IT'S A CHEESE NAMED AFTER ME!
FROM NOW ON I'M GORGONZOLA!

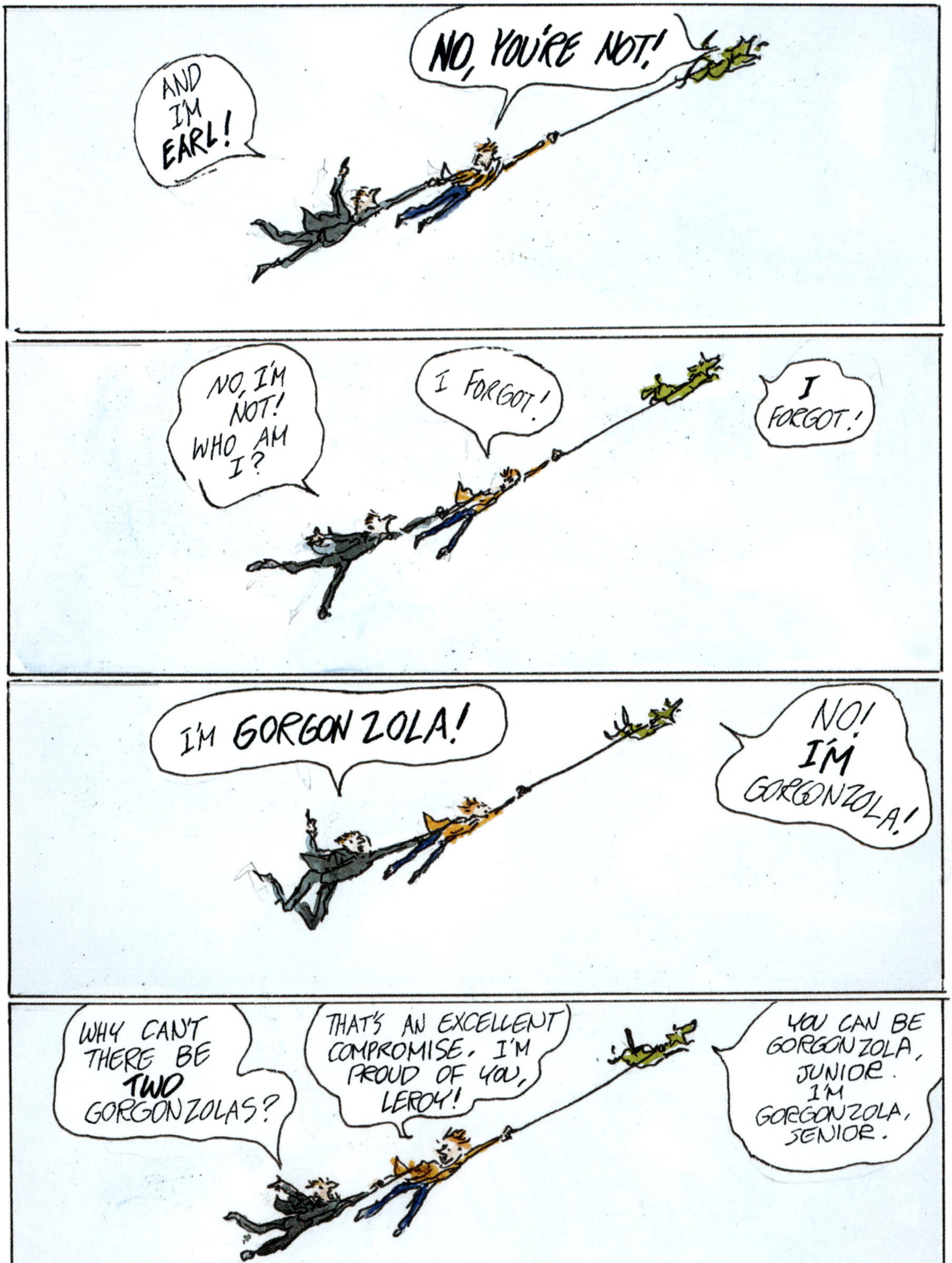
AND I'M EARL!
NO, YOU'RE NOT!
NO, I'M NOT! WHO AM I?
I FORGOT!
I FORGOT!
I'M GORGONZOLA!
NO! I'M GORGONZOLA!
WHY CAN'T THERE BE TWO GORGONZOLAS?
THAT'S AN EXCELLENT COMPROMISE, I'M PROUD OF YOU, LEROY!
YOU CAN BE GORGONZOLA, JUNIOR. I'M GORGONZOLA, SENIOR.

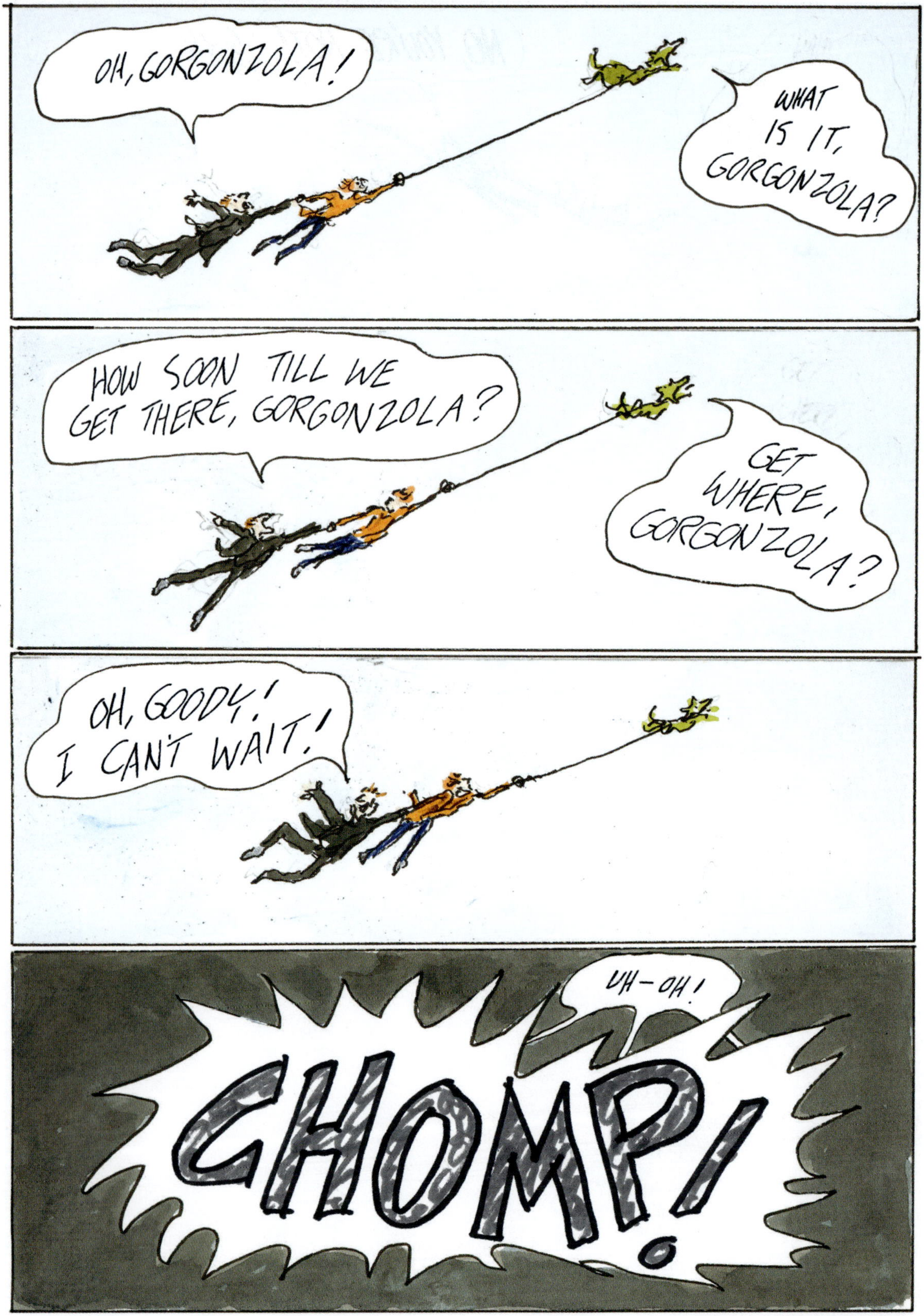
OH, GORGONZOLA!
WHAT IS IT, GORGONZOLA?
HOW SOON TILL WE GET THERE, GORGONZOLA?
GET WHERE, GORGONZOLA?
OH, GOODY! I CAN'T WAIT!
UH-OH!
CHOMP!

CHAPTER 29 • FEARTOPIA

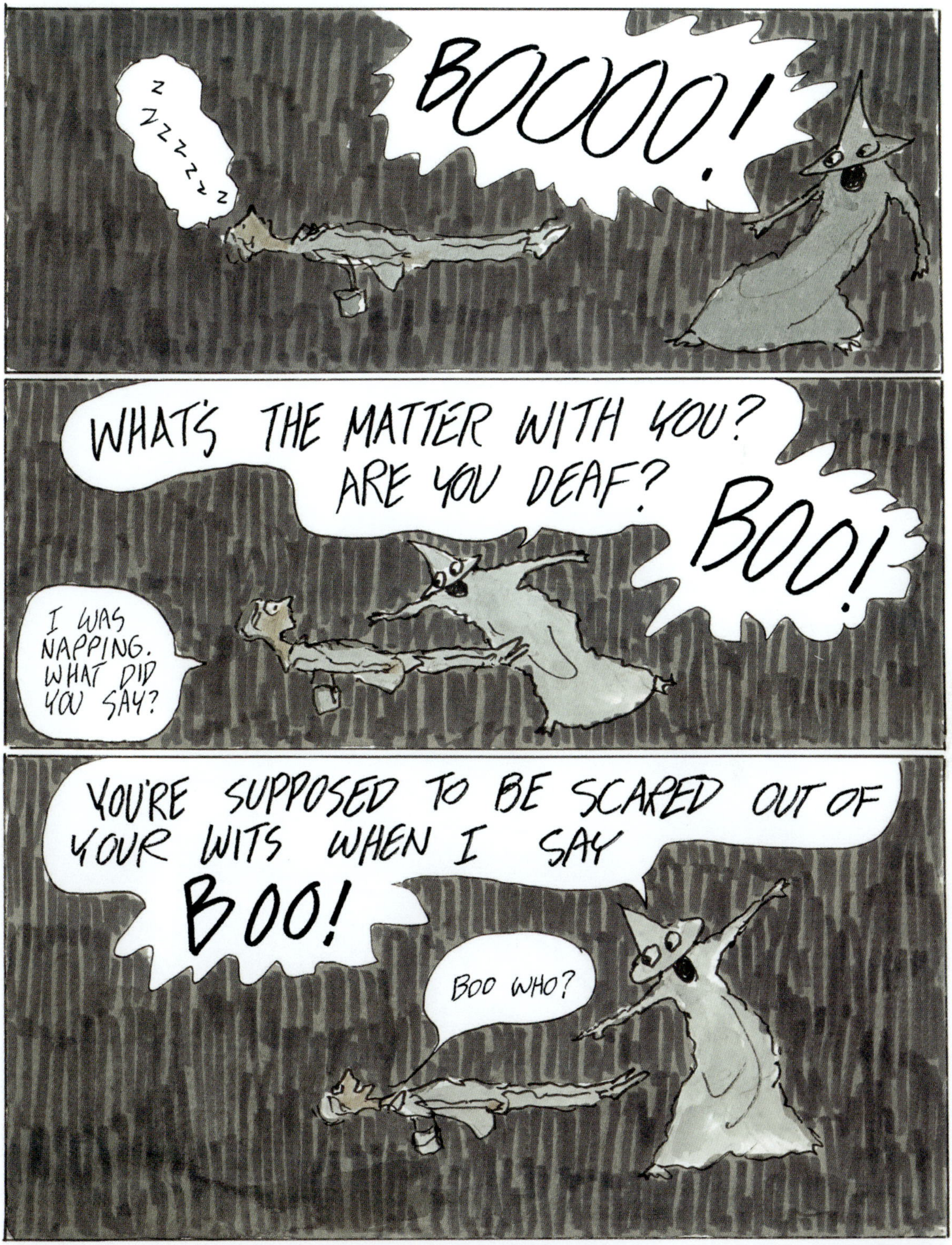

Z Z Z Z Z Z Z Z
BOOOOO!
WHAT'S THE MATTER WITH YOU? ARE YOU DEAF?
BOO!
I WAS NAPPING. WHAT DID YOU SAY?
YOU'RE SUPPOSED TO BE SCARED OUT OF YOUR WITS WHEN I SAY
BOO!
BOO WHO?

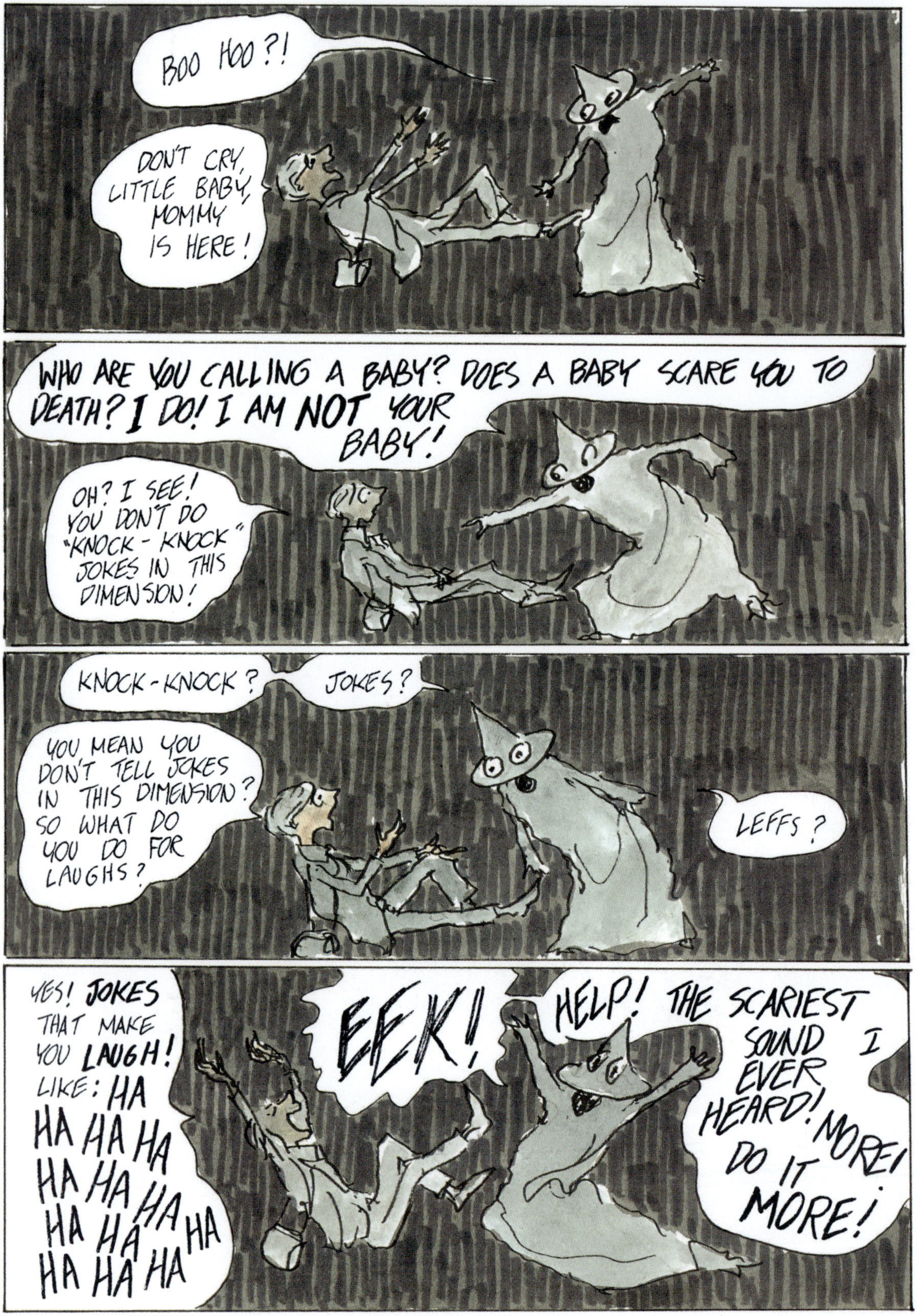
BOO HOO?!
DON'T CRY, LITTLE BABY, MOMMY IS HERE!
WHO ARE YOU CALLING A BABY? DOES A BABY SCARE YOU TO DEATH? I DO! I AM NOT YOUR BABY!
OH? I SEE! YOU DON'T DO "KNOCK-KNOCK" JOKES IN THIS DIMENSION!
KNOCK-KNOCK?
JOKES?
YOU MEAN YOU DON'T TELL JOKES IN THIS DIMENSION? SO WHAT DO YOU DO FOR LAUGHS?
LEFFS?
YES! JOKES THAT MAKE YOU LAUGH! LIKE: HA HA HA HA HA HA HA HA HA HA HA HA HA HA
EEK!
HELP! THE SCARIEST SOUND I EVER HEARD! MORE! DO IT MORE!

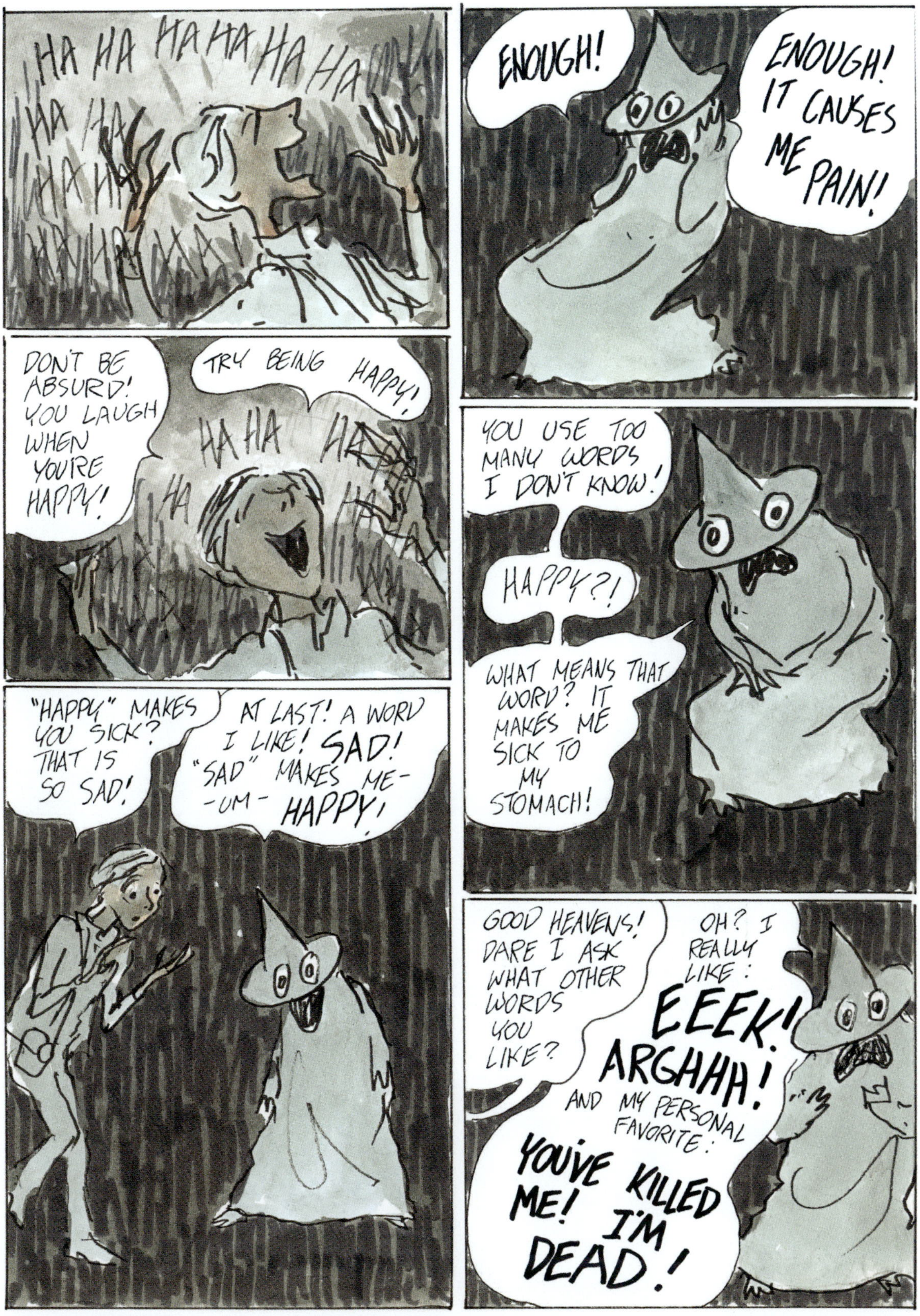
HA HA HA HA HA HA HA
HA HA HA HA HA HA
ENOUGH!
ENOUGH! IT CAUSES ME PAIN!
DON'T BE ABSURD! YOU LAUGH WHEN YOU'RE HAPPY!
TRY BEING HAPPY!
HA HA HA
YOU USE TOO MANY WORDS I DON'T KNOW!
HAPPY?!
WHAT MEANS THAT WORD? IT MAKES ME SICK TO MY STOMACH!
"HAPPY" MAKES YOU SICK? THAT IS SO SAD!
AT LAST! A WORD I LIKE! SAD! "SAD" MAKES ME -UM- HAPPY!
GOOD HEAVENS! DARE I ASK WHAT OTHER WORDS YOU LIKE?
OH? I REALLY LIKE: EEEK! ARGHHH! AND MY PERSONAL FAVORITE: YOU'VE KILLED ME! I'M DEAD!

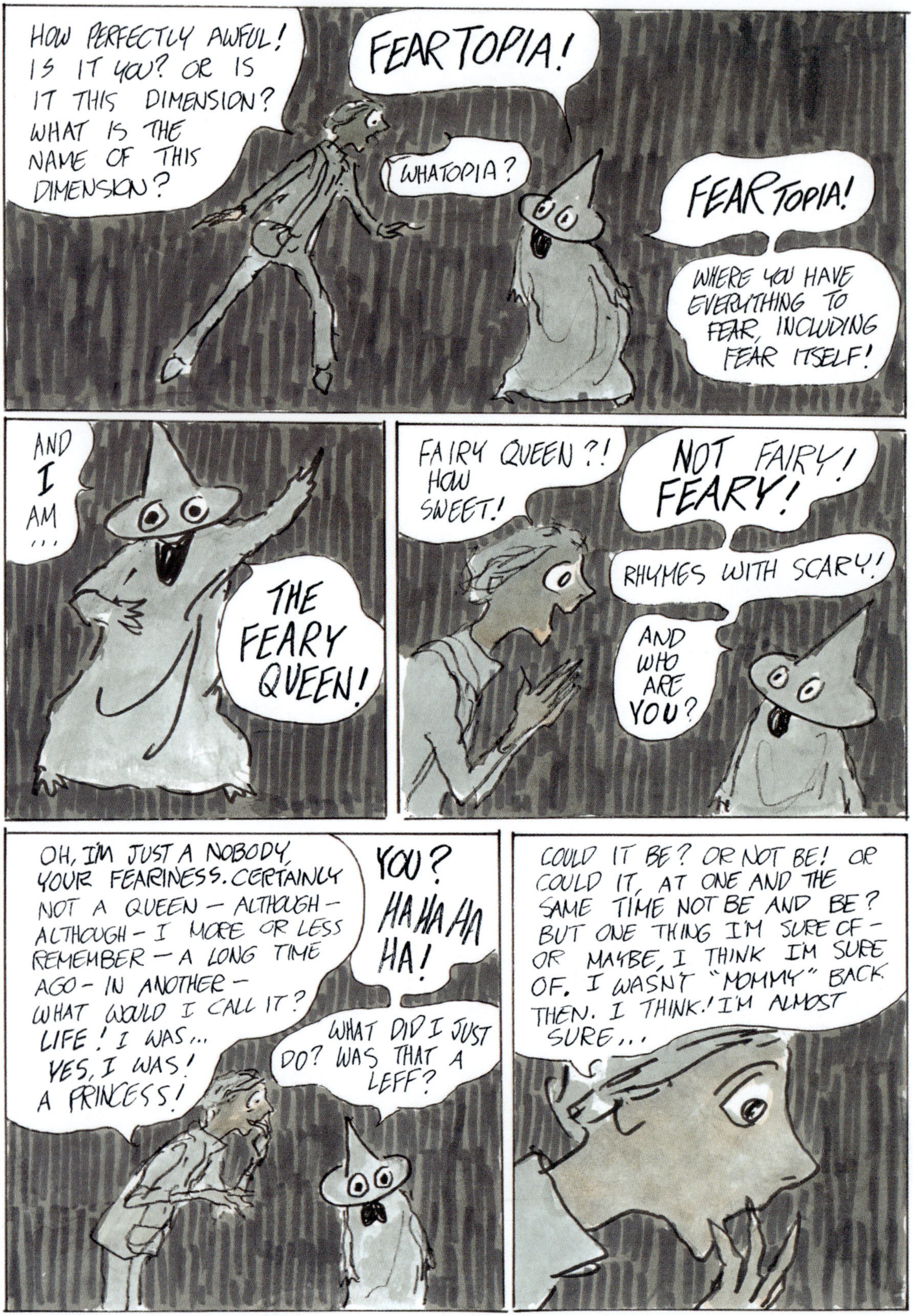
HOW PERFECTLY AWFUL! IS IT YOU? OR IS IT THIS DIMENSION? WHAT IS THE NAME OF THIS DIMENSION?
FEARTOPIA!
WHATOPIA?
FEARTOPIA!
WHERE YOU HAVE EVERYTHING TO FEAR, INCLUDING FEAR ITSELF!
AND I AM...
THE FEARY QUEEN!
FAIRY QUEEN?! HOW SWEET!
NOT FAIRY! FEARY!
RHYMES WITH SCARY!
AND WHO ARE YOU?
OH, I'M JUST A NOBODY, YOUR FEARINESS. CERTAINLY NOT A QUEEN — ALTHOUGH — ALTHOUGH — I MORE OR LESS REMEMBER — A LONG TIME AGO — IN ANOTHER — WHAT WOULD I CALL IT? LIFE! I WAS... YES, I WAS! A PRINCESS!
YOU? HA HA HA HA!
WHAT DID I JUST DO? WAS THAT A LEFF?
COULD IT BE? OR NOT BE! OR COULD IT, AT ONE AND THE SAME TIME NOT BE AND BE? BUT ONE THING I'M SURE OF — OR MAYBE, I THINK I'M SURE OF. I WASN'T "MOMMY" BACK THEN. I THINK! I'M ALMOST SURE...

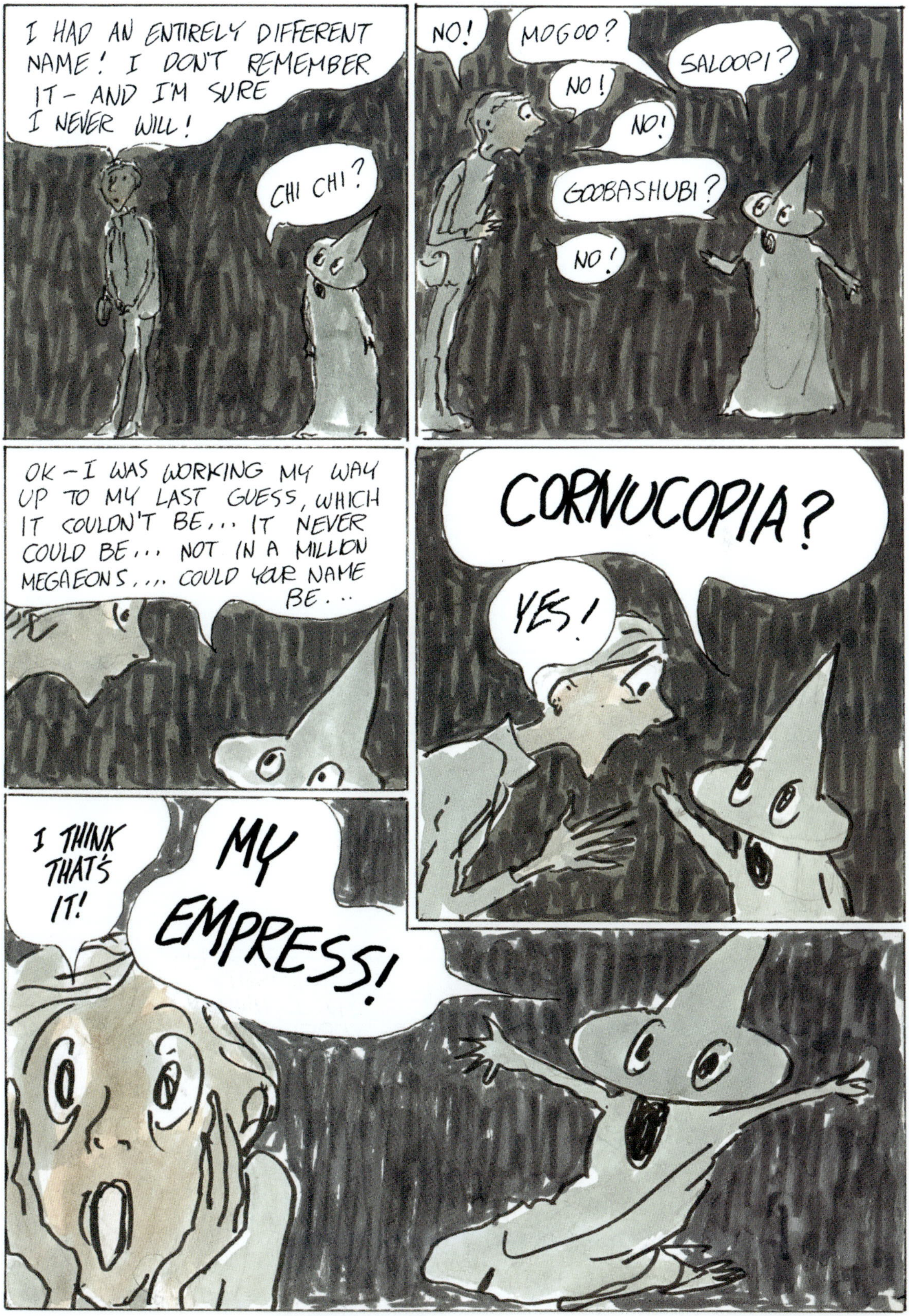
I HAD AN ENTIRELY DIFFERENT NAME! I DON'T REMEMBER IT- AND I'M SURE I NEVER WILL!
CHI CHI?
NO!
MOGOO?
NO!
SALOOPI?
NO!
GOOBASHUBI?
NO!
OK - I WAS WORKING MY WAY UP TO MY LAST GUESS, WHICH IT COULDN'T BE... IT NEVER COULD BE... NOT IN A MILLION MEGAEONS.... COULD YOUR NAME BE...
CORNUCOPIA?
YES!
I THINK THAT'S IT!
MY EMPRESS!

CHAPTER 30 • NOBODY CARES

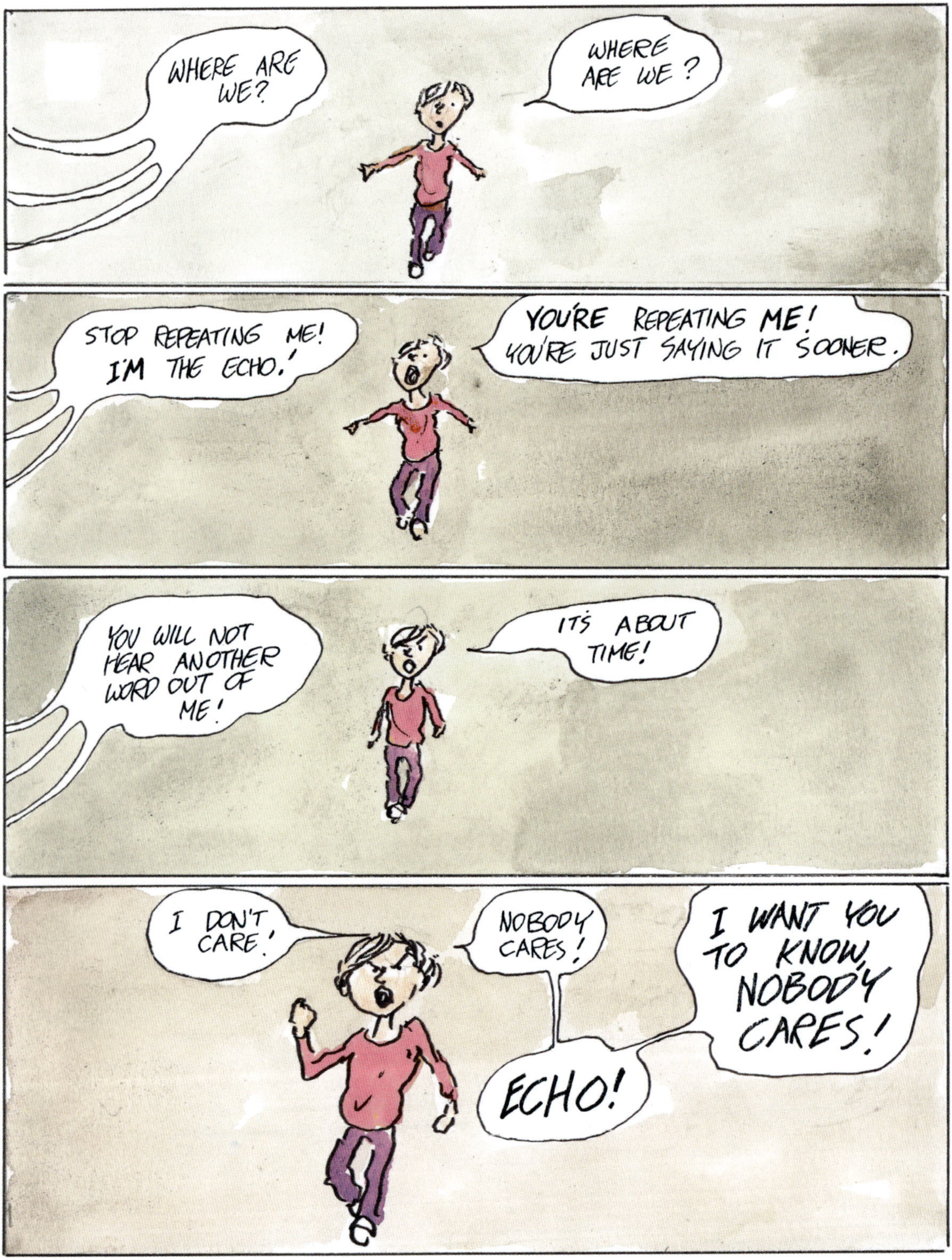
WHERE ARE WE?
WHERE ARE WE?
STOP REPEATING ME! I'M THE ECHO!
YOU'RE REPEATING ME! YOU'RE JUST SAYING IT SOONER.
YOU WILL NOT HEAR ANOTHER WORD OUT OF ME!
IT'S ABOUT TIME!
I DON'T CARE!
NOBODY CARES!
I WANT YOU TO KNOW, NOBODY CARES!
ECHO!

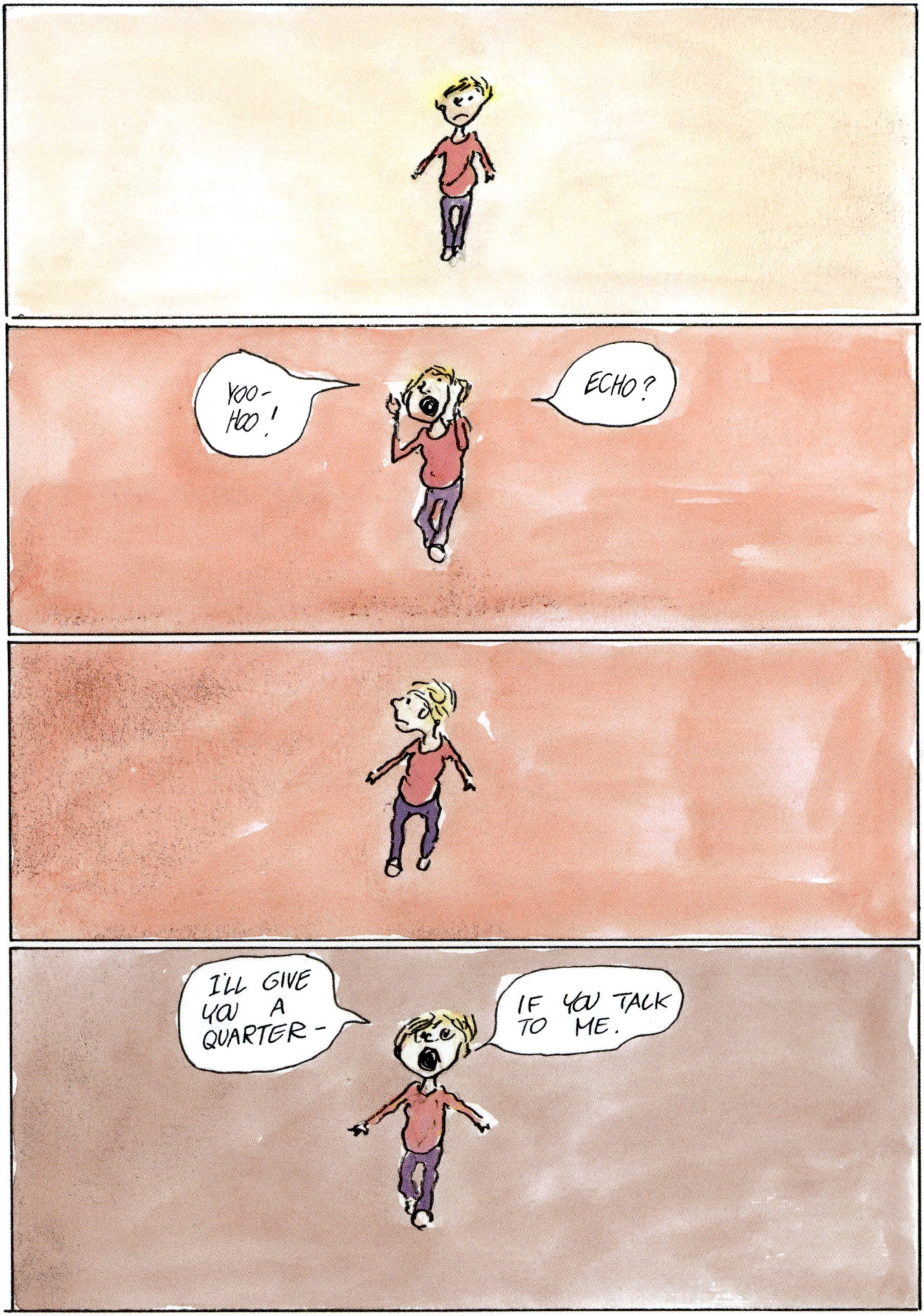
YOO-HOO!
ECHO?
I'LL GIVE YOU A QUARTER-
IF YOU TALK TO ME.

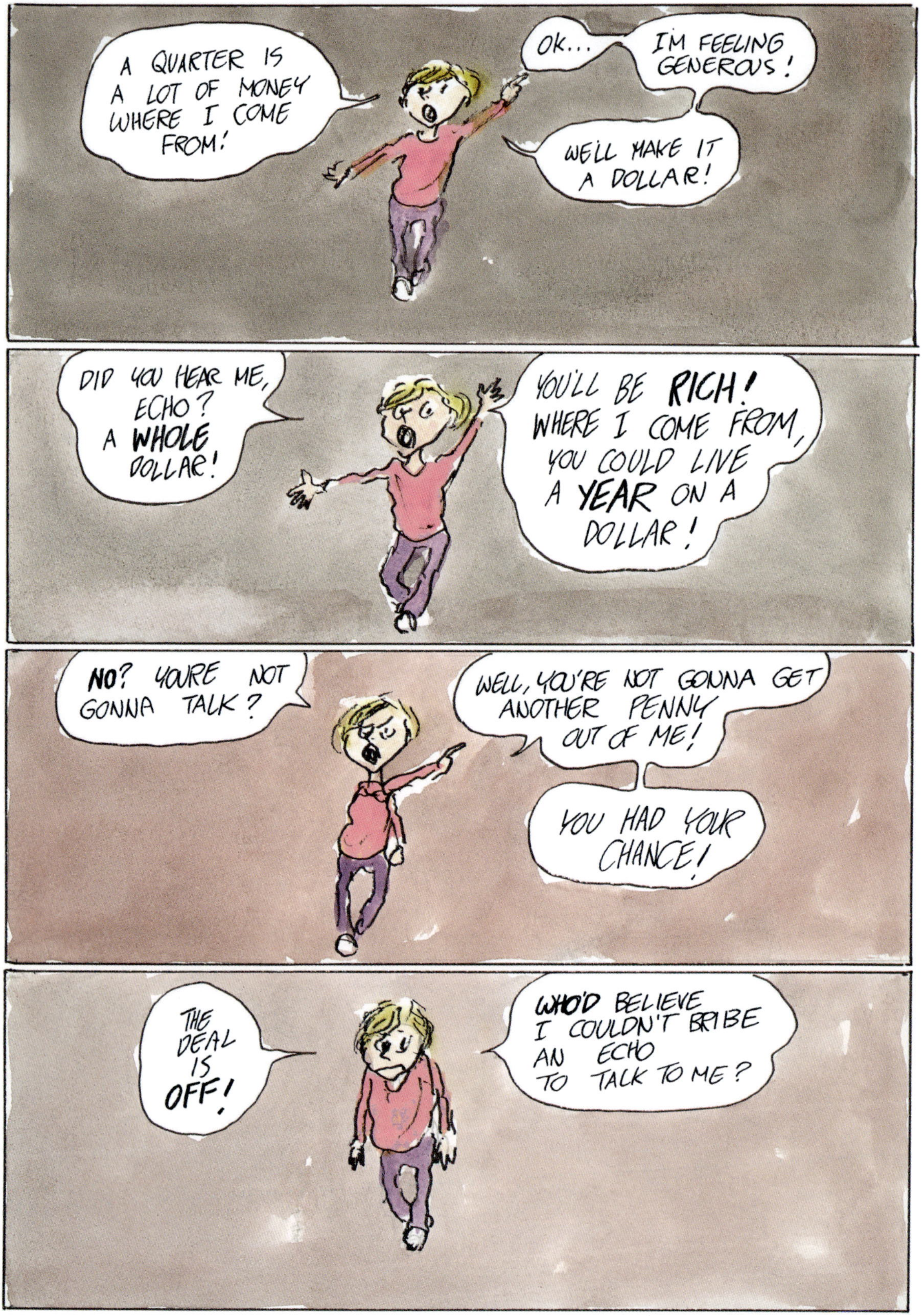
A QUARTER IS A LOT OF MONEY WHERE I COME FROM!
OK...
I'M FEELING GENEROUS!
WE'LL MAKE IT A DOLLAR!
DID YOU HEAR ME, ECHO? A **WHOLE** DOLLAR!
YOU'LL BE **RICH!** WHERE I COME FROM, YOU COULD LIVE A **YEAR** ON A DOLLAR!
NO? YOU'RE NOT GONNA TALK?
WELL, YOU'RE NOT GONNA GET ANOTHER PENNY OUT OF ME!
YOU HAD YOUR CHANCE!
THE DEAL IS **OFF!**
WHO'D BELIEVE I COULDN'T BRIBE AN ECHO TO TALK TO ME?

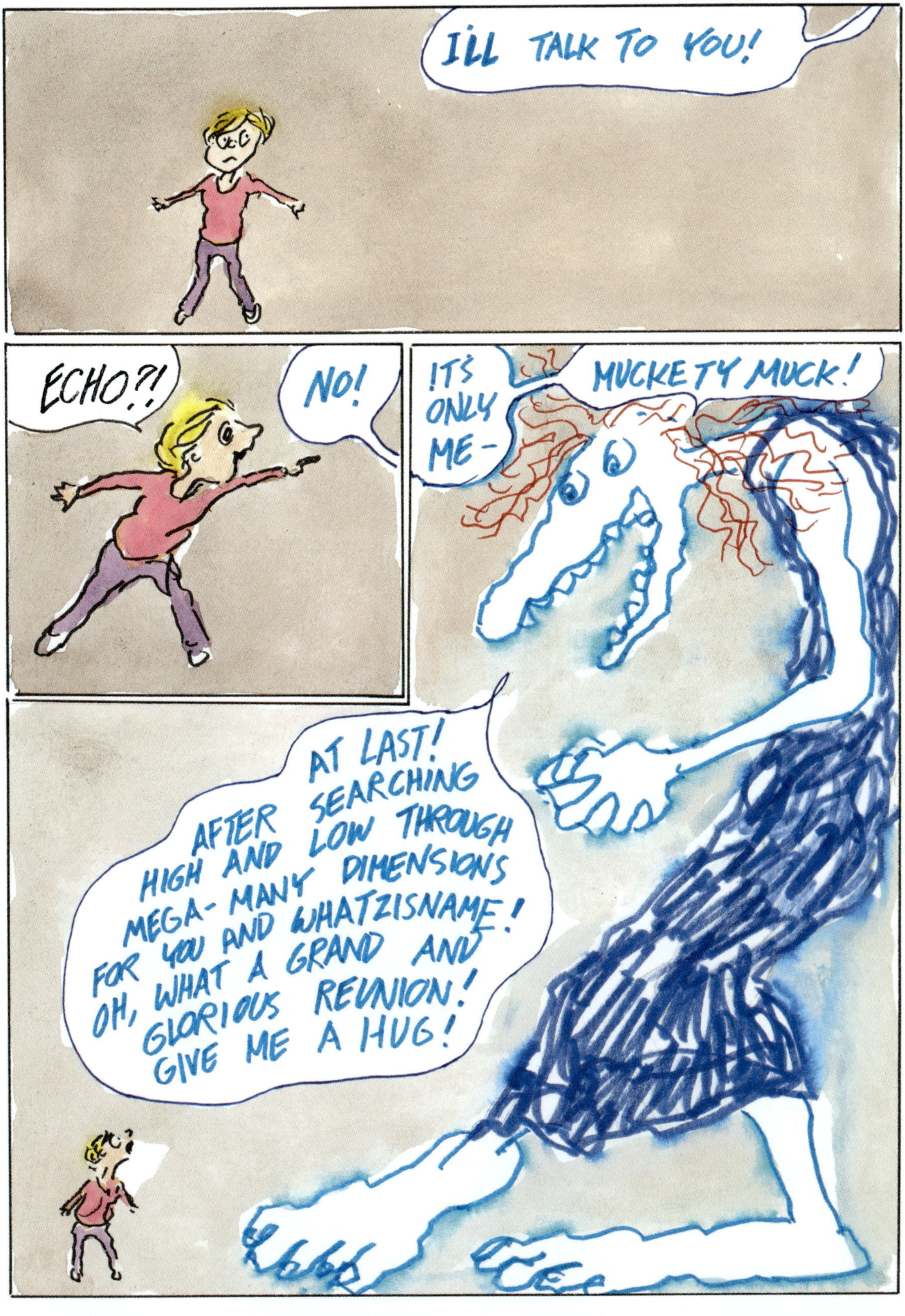
I'LL TALK TO YOU!
ECHO?!
NO!
IT'S ONLY ME-
MUCKETY MUCK!
AT LAST! AFTER SEARCHING HIGH AND LOW THROUGH MEGA-MANY DIMENSIONS FOR YOU AND WHATZISNAME! OH, WHAT A GRAND AND GLORIOUS REUNION! GIVE ME A HUG!

CHAPTER 31 • UH-OH . . .

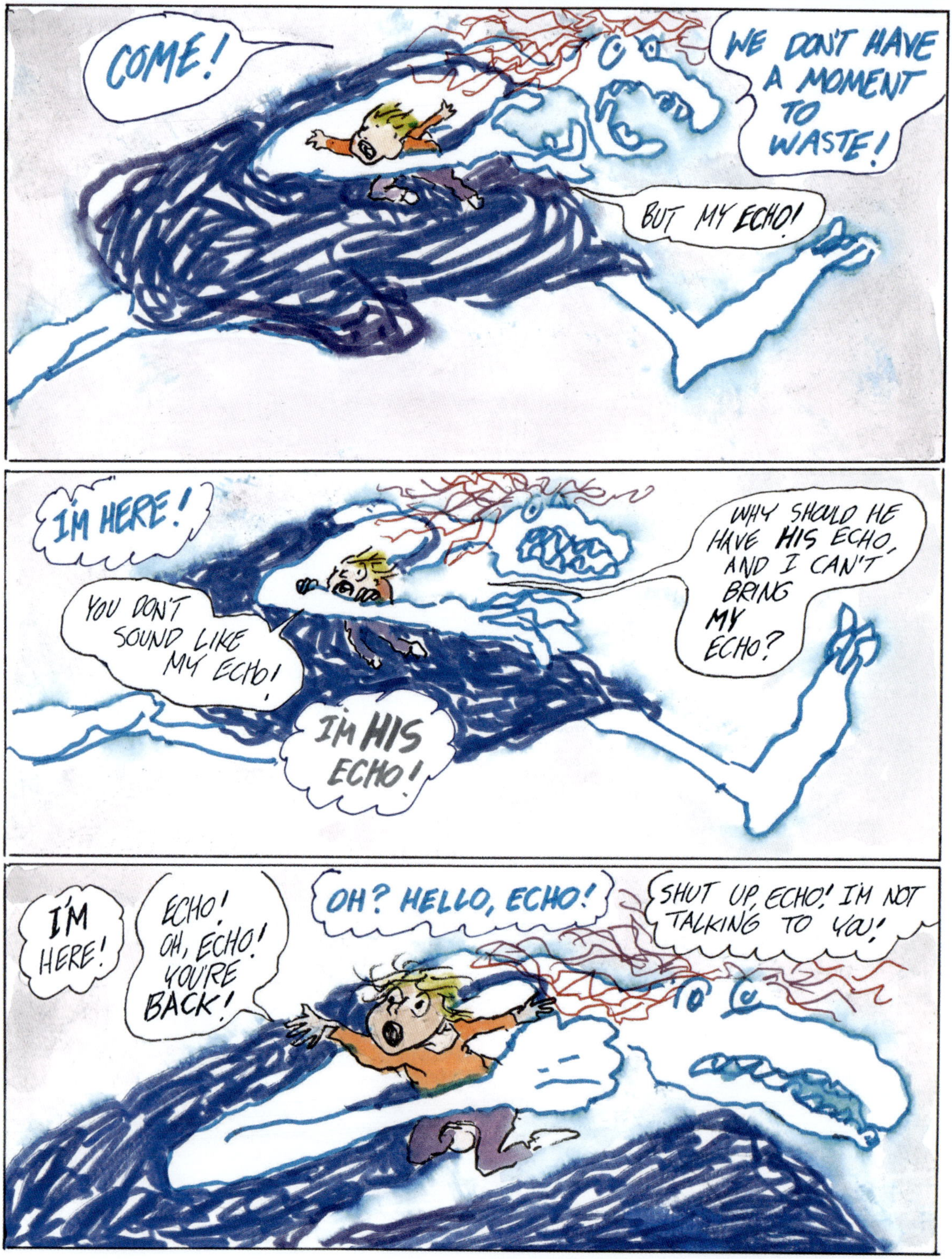
COME!
WE DON'T HAVE A MOMENT TO WASTE!
BUT MY ECHO!
I'M HERE!
YOU DON'T SOUND LIKE MY ECHO!
WHY SHOULD HE HAVE HIS ECHO, AND I CAN'T BRING MY ECHO?
I'M HIS ECHO!
I'M HERE!
ECHO! OH, ECHO! YOU'RE BACK!
OH? HELLO, ECHO!
SHUT UP, ECHO! I'M NOT TALKING TO YOU!

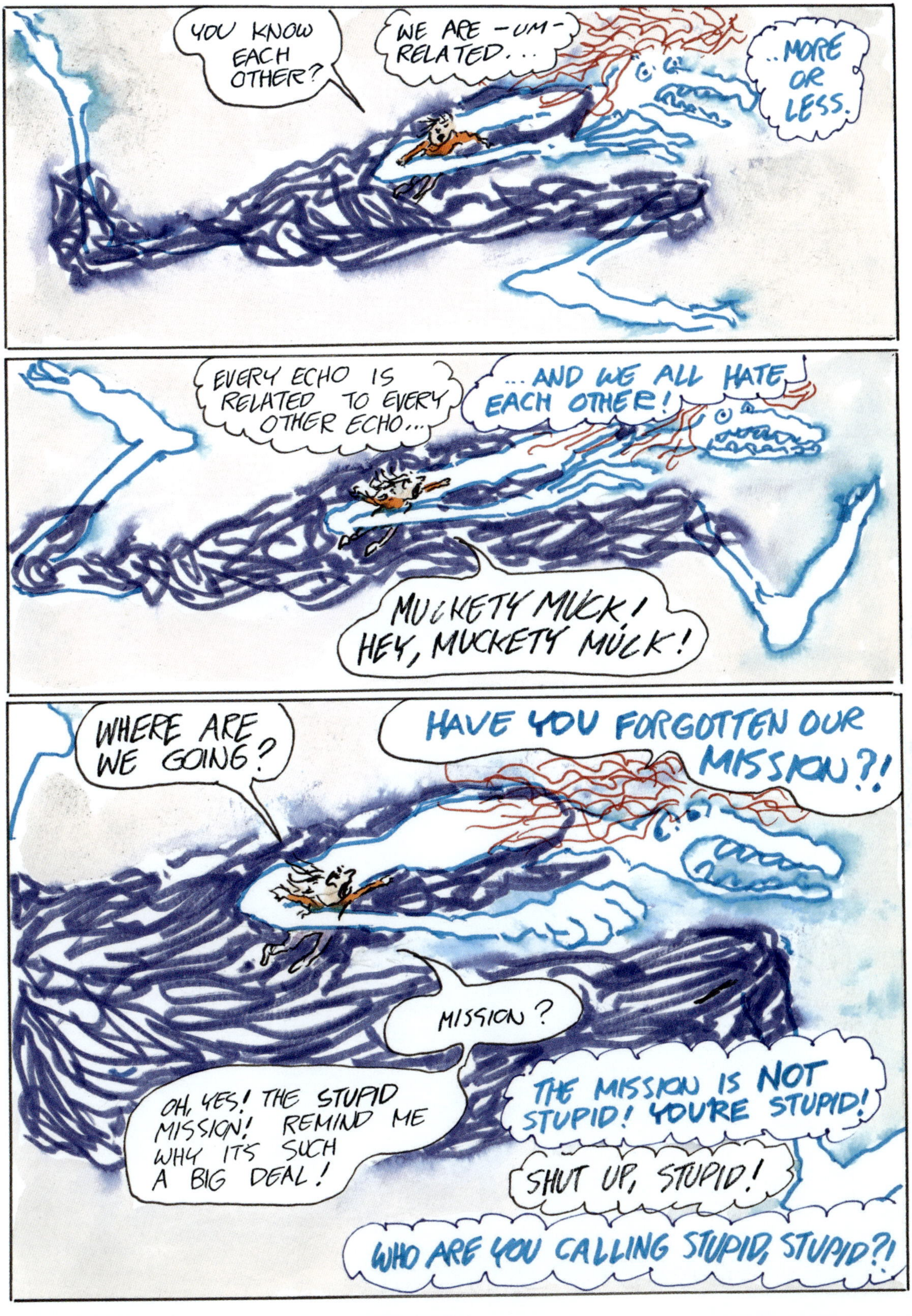
YOU KNOW EACH OTHER?
WE ARE —UM— RELATED...
...MORE OR LESS.
EVERY ECHO IS RELATED TO EVERY OTHER ECHO...
...AND WE ALL HATE EACH OTHER!
MUCKETY MUCK! HEY, MUCKETY MUCK!
WHERE ARE WE GOING?
HAVE YOU FORGOTTEN OUR MISSION?!
MISSION?
OH, YES! THE STUPID MISSION! REMIND ME WHY ITS SUCH A BIG DEAL!
THE MISSION IS NOT STUPID! YOU'RE STUPID!
SHUT UP, STUPID!
WHO ARE YOU CALLING STUPID, STUPID?!

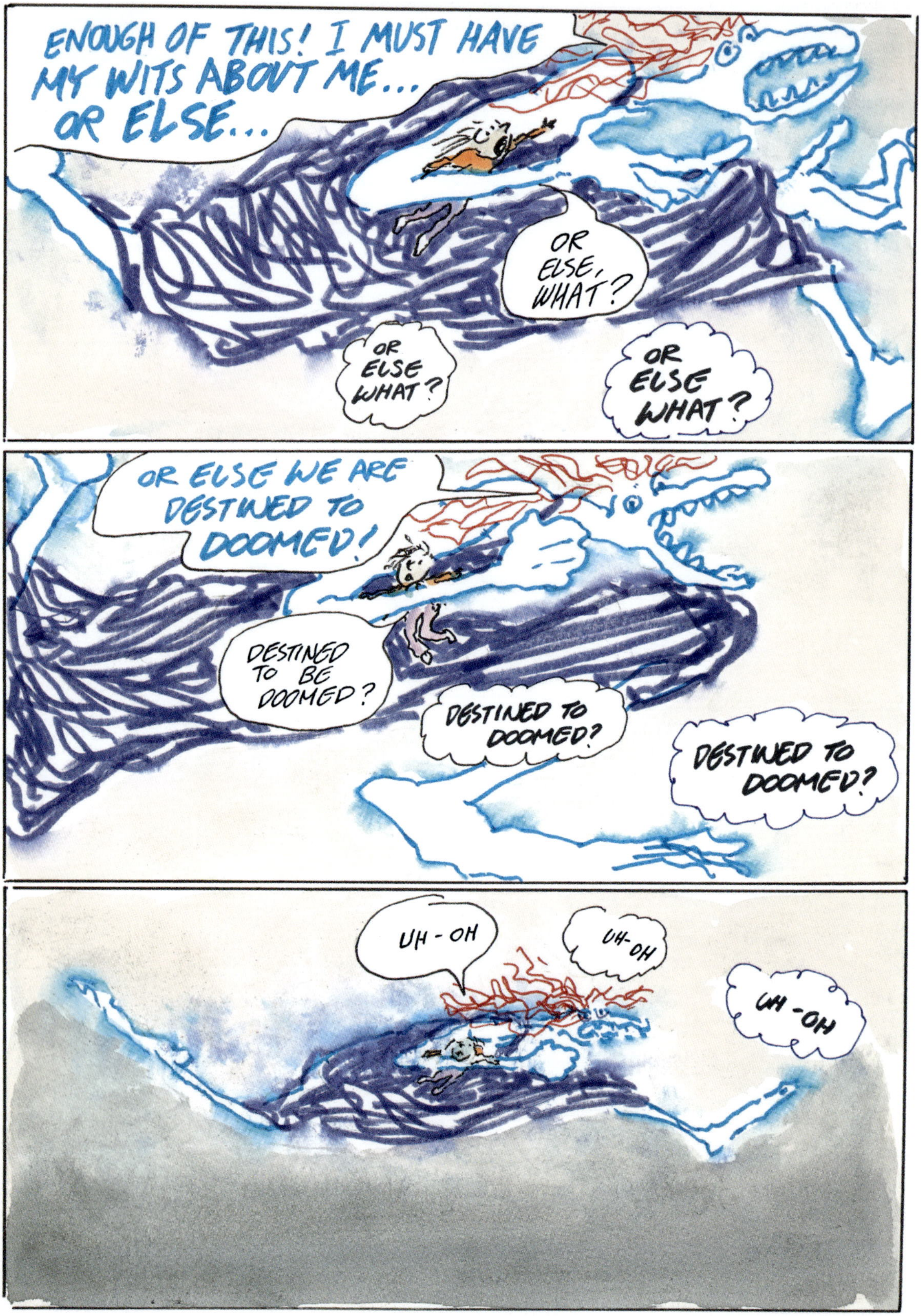
ENOUGH OF THIS! I MUST HAVE MY WITS ABOUT ME... OR ELSE...
OR ELSE, WHAT?
OR ELSE WHAT?
OR ELSE WHAT?
OR ELSE WE ARE DESTINED TO DOOMED!
DESTINED TO BE DOOMED?
DESTINED TO DOOMED?
DESTINED TO DOOMED?
UH-OH
UH-OH
UH-OH

CHAPTER 32 • THE LOST HEAD

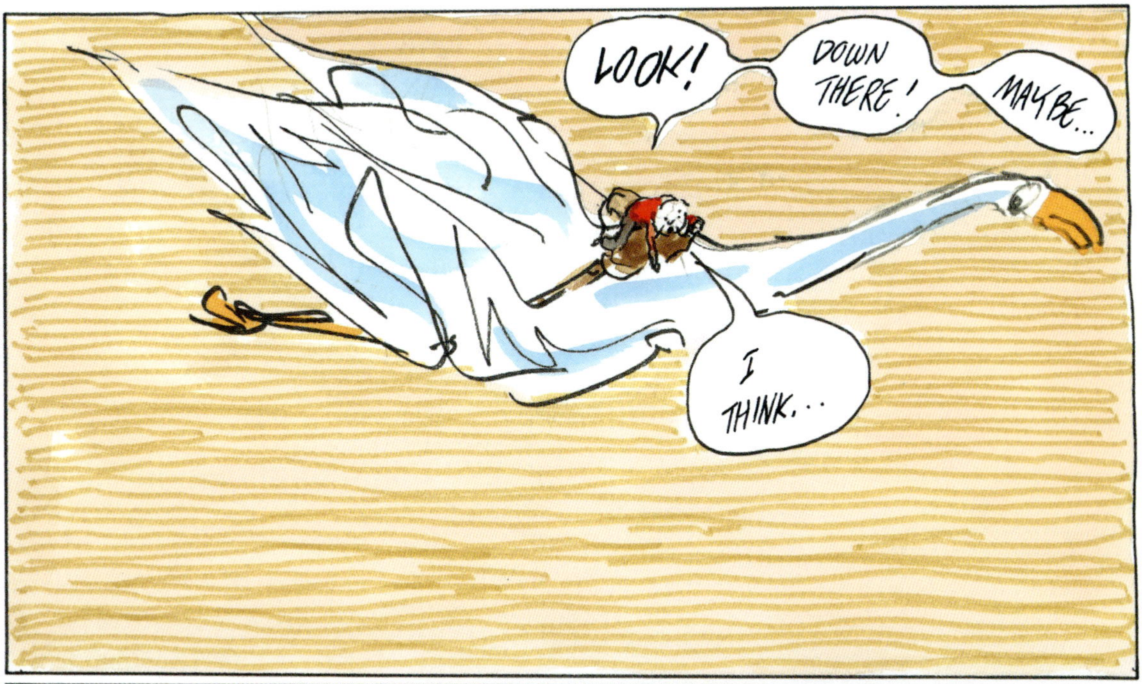
LOOK!
DOWN THERE!
MAYBE...
I THINK...

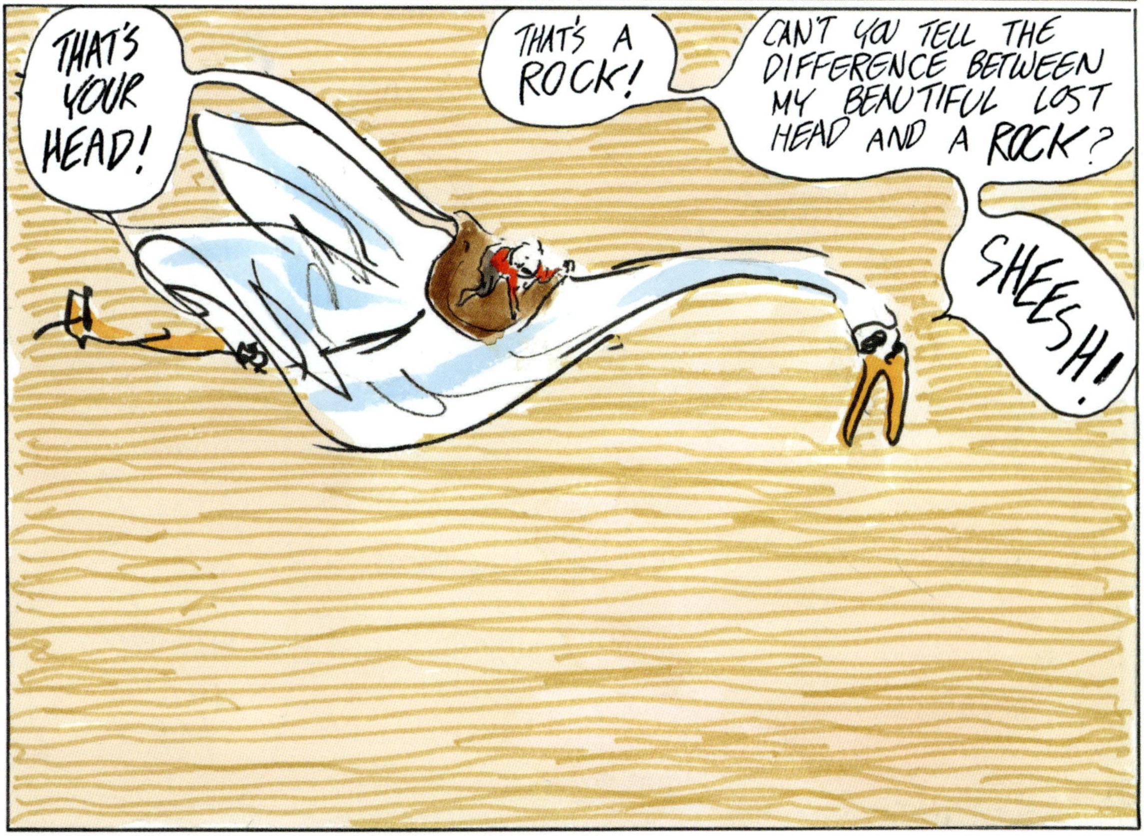
THAT'S YOUR HEAD!
THAT'S A ROCK!
CAN'T YOU TELL THE DIFFERENCE BETWEEN MY BEAUTIFUL LOST HEAD AND A ROCK?
SHEESH!

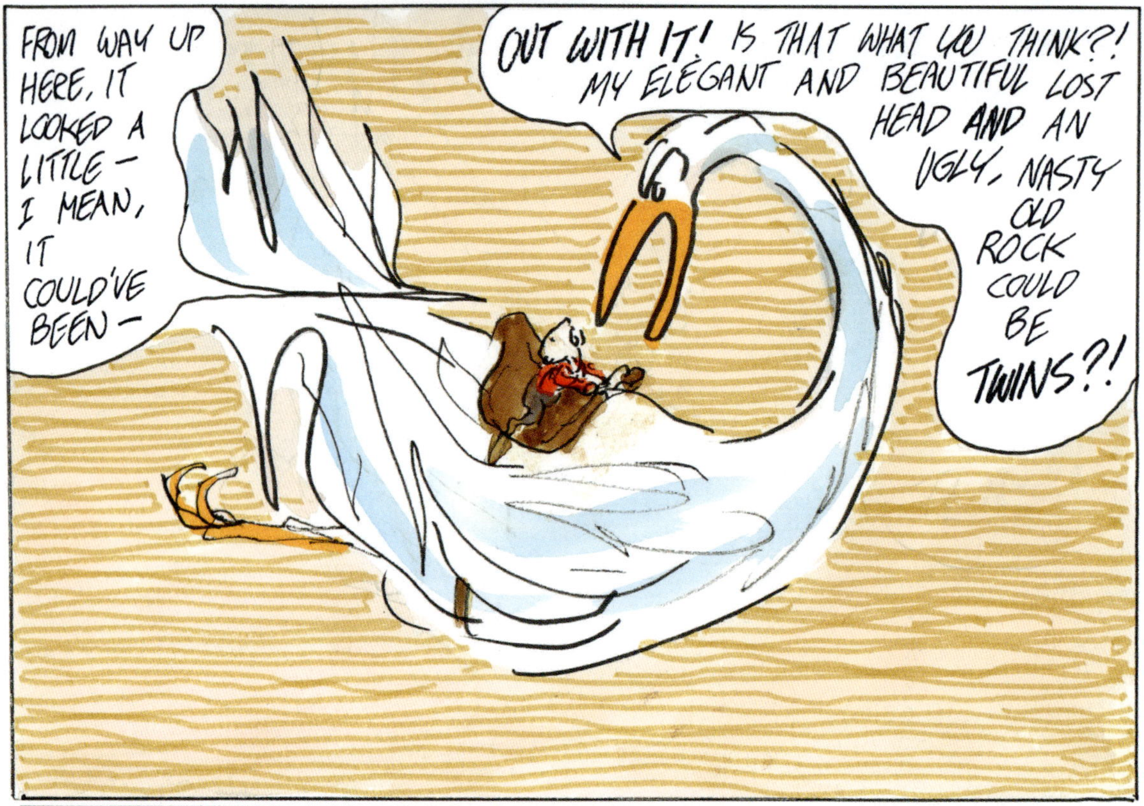
FROM WAY UP HERE, IT LOOKED A LITTLE— I MEAN, IT COULD'VE BEEN—
OUT WITH IT! IS THAT WHAT YOU THINK?! MY ELEGANT AND BEAUTIFUL LOST HEAD AND AN UGLY, NASTY OLD ROCK COULD BE TWINS?!

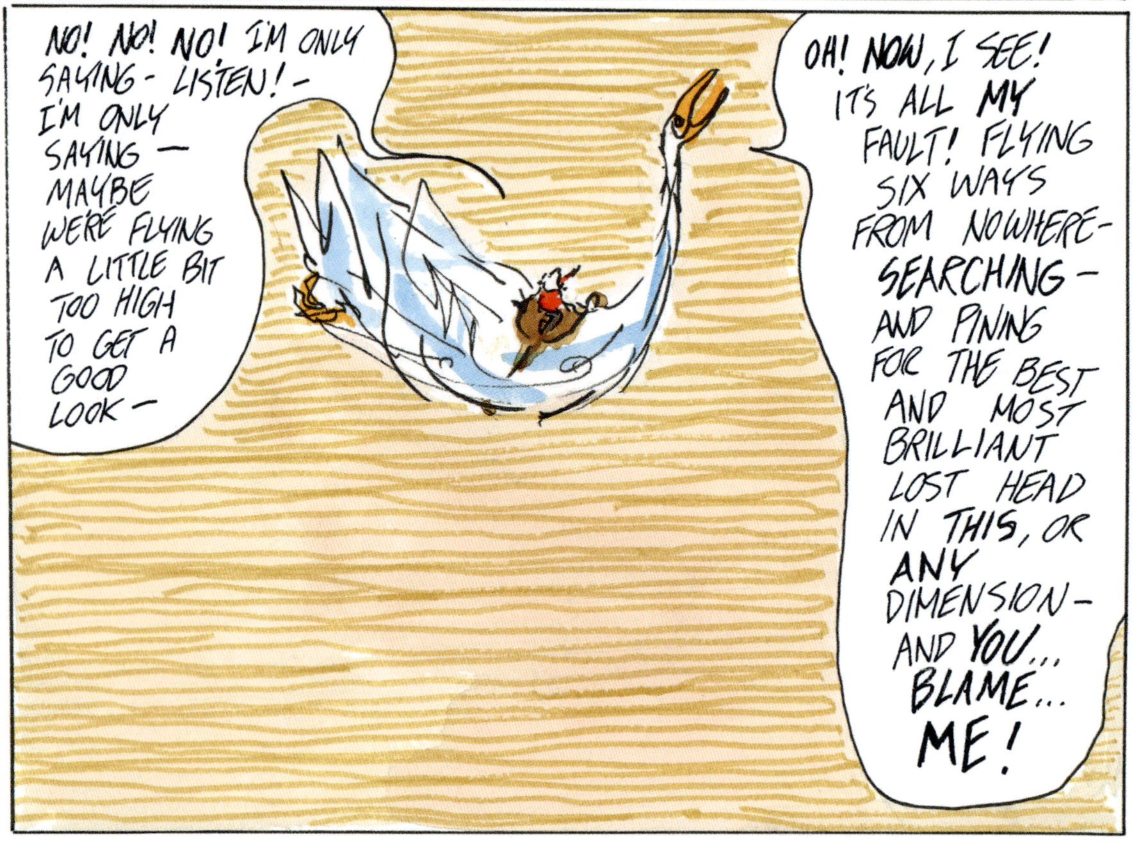
NO! NO! NO! I'M ONLY SAYING - LISTEN! - I'M ONLY SAYING — MAYBE WE'RE FLYING A LITTLE BIT TOO HIGH TO GET A GOOD LOOK—
OH! NOW, I SEE! IT'S ALL MY FAULT! FLYING SIX WAYS FROM NOWHERE- SEARCHING— AND PINING FOR THE BEST AND MOST BRILLIANT LOST HEAD IN THIS, OR ANY DIMENSION- AND YOU... BLAME... ME!

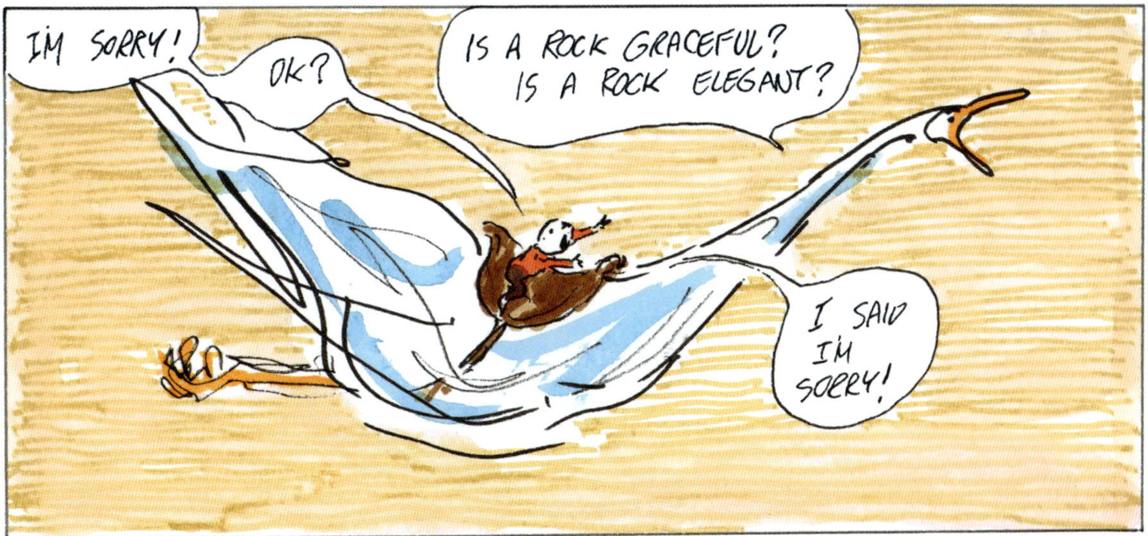

I'M SORRY!
OK?
IS A ROCK GRACEFUL? IS A ROCK ELEGANT?
I SAID I'M SORRY!

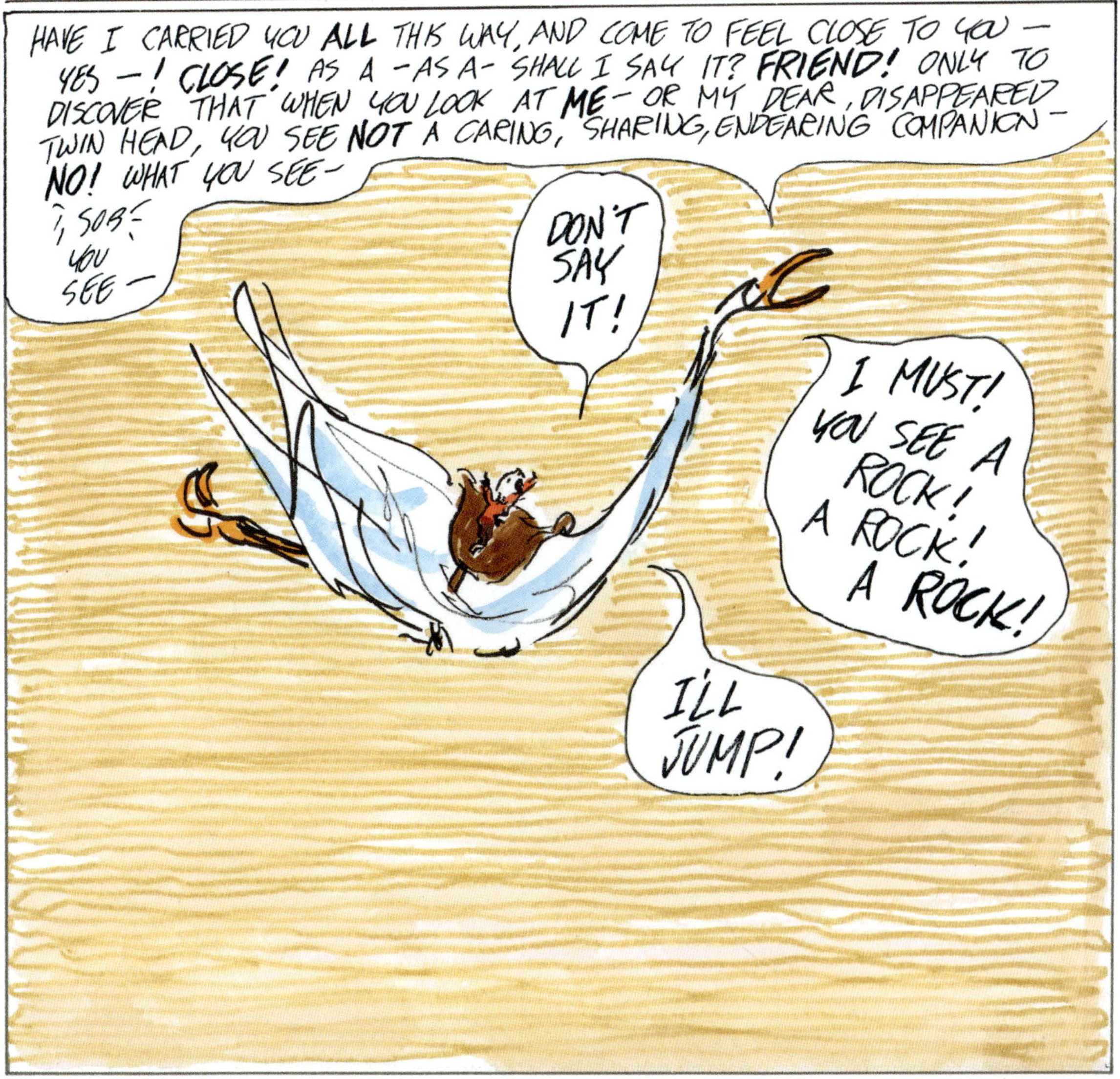

HAVE I CARRIED YOU **ALL** THIS WAY, AND COME TO FEEL CLOSE TO YOU — YES —! **CLOSE!** AS A — AS A — SHALL I SAY IT? **FRIEND!** ONLY TO DISCOVER THAT WHEN YOU LOOK AT **ME** — OR MY DEAR, DISAPPEARED TWIN HEAD, YOU SEE **NOT** A CARING, SHARING, ENDEARING COMPANION — **NO!** WHAT YOU SEE —
SOB
YOU SEE —
DON'T SAY IT!
I MUST! YOU SEE A ROCK! A ROCK! A **ROCK!**
I'LL JUMP!

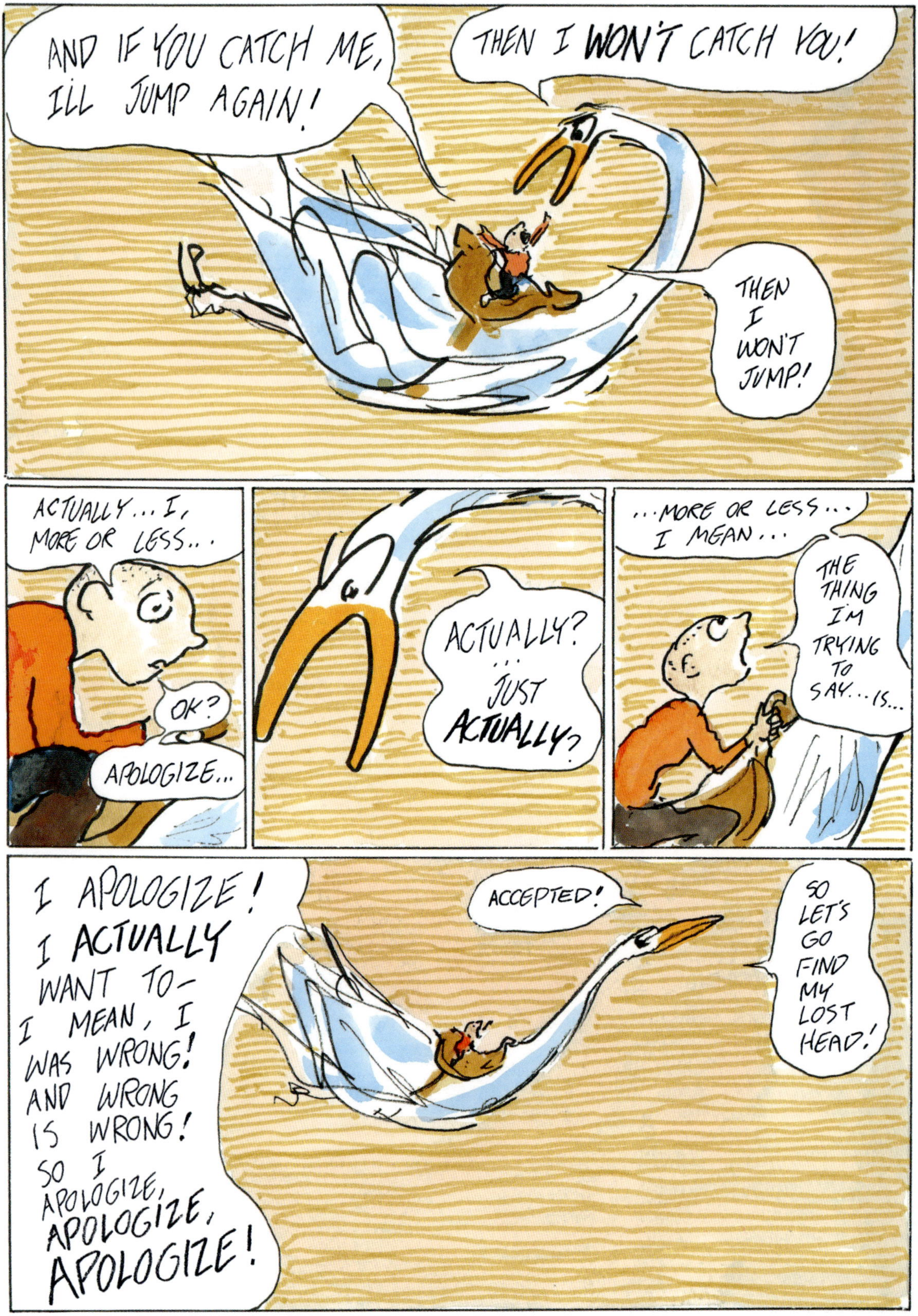
AND IF YOU CATCH ME, I'LL JUMP AGAIN!
THEN I WON'T CATCH YOU!
THEN I WON'T JUMP!
ACTUALLY... I, MORE OR LESS...
OK?
APOLOGIZE...
ACTUALLY? ... JUST ACTUALLY?
...MORE OR LESS... I MEAN...
THE THING I'M TRYING TO SAY... IS...
I APOLOGIZE! I ACTUALLY WANT TO- I MEAN, I WAS WRONG! AND WRONG IS WRONG! SO I APOLOGIZE, APOLOGIZE, APOLOGIZE!
ACCEPTED!
SO LET'S GO FIND MY LOST HEAD!

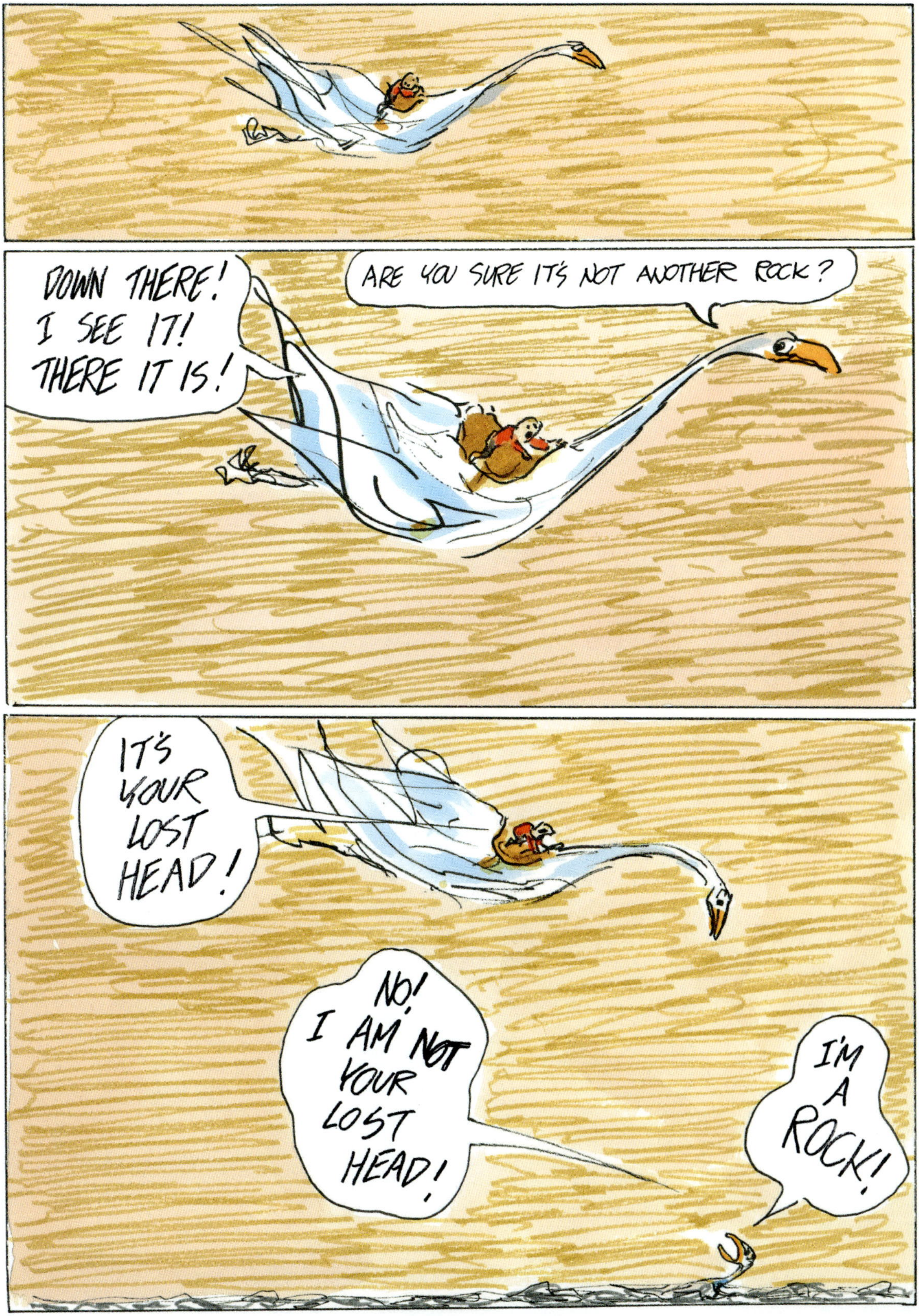
DOWN THERE! I SEE IT! THERE IT IS!
ARE YOU SURE IT'S NOT ANOTHER ROCK?
IT'S YOUR LOST HEAD!
NO! I AM NOT YOUR LOST HEAD!
I'M A ROCK!

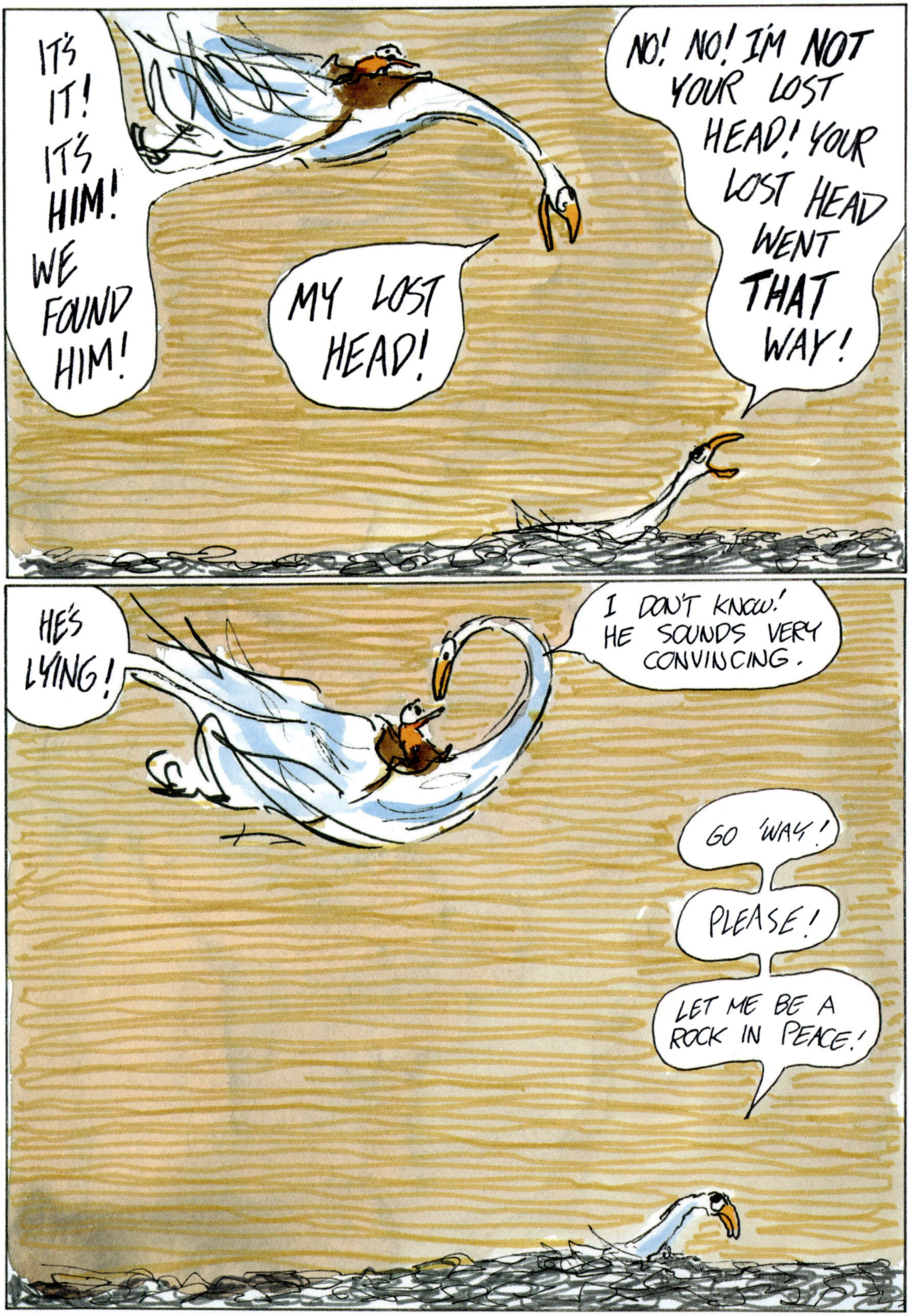
IT'S IT! IT'S HIM! WE FOUND HIM!
MY LOST HEAD!
NO! NO! I'M NOT YOUR LOST HEAD! YOUR LOST HEAD WENT THAT WAY!
HE'S LYING!
I DON'T KNOW! HE SOUNDS VERY CONVINCING.
GO 'WAY!
PLEASE!
LET ME BE A ROCK IN PEACE!

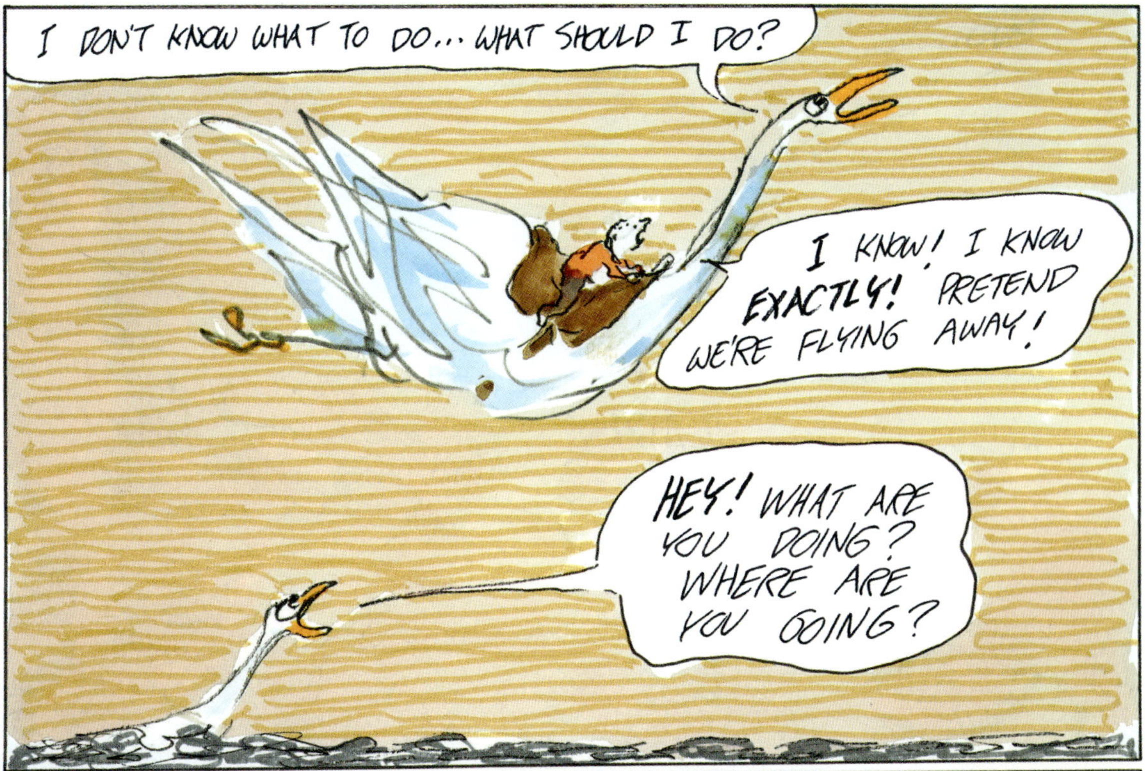
I DON'T KNOW WHAT TO DO... WHAT SHOULD I DO?
I KNOW! I KNOW EXACTLY! PRETEND WE'RE FLYING AWAY!
HEY! WHAT ARE YOU DOING? WHERE ARE YOU GOING?

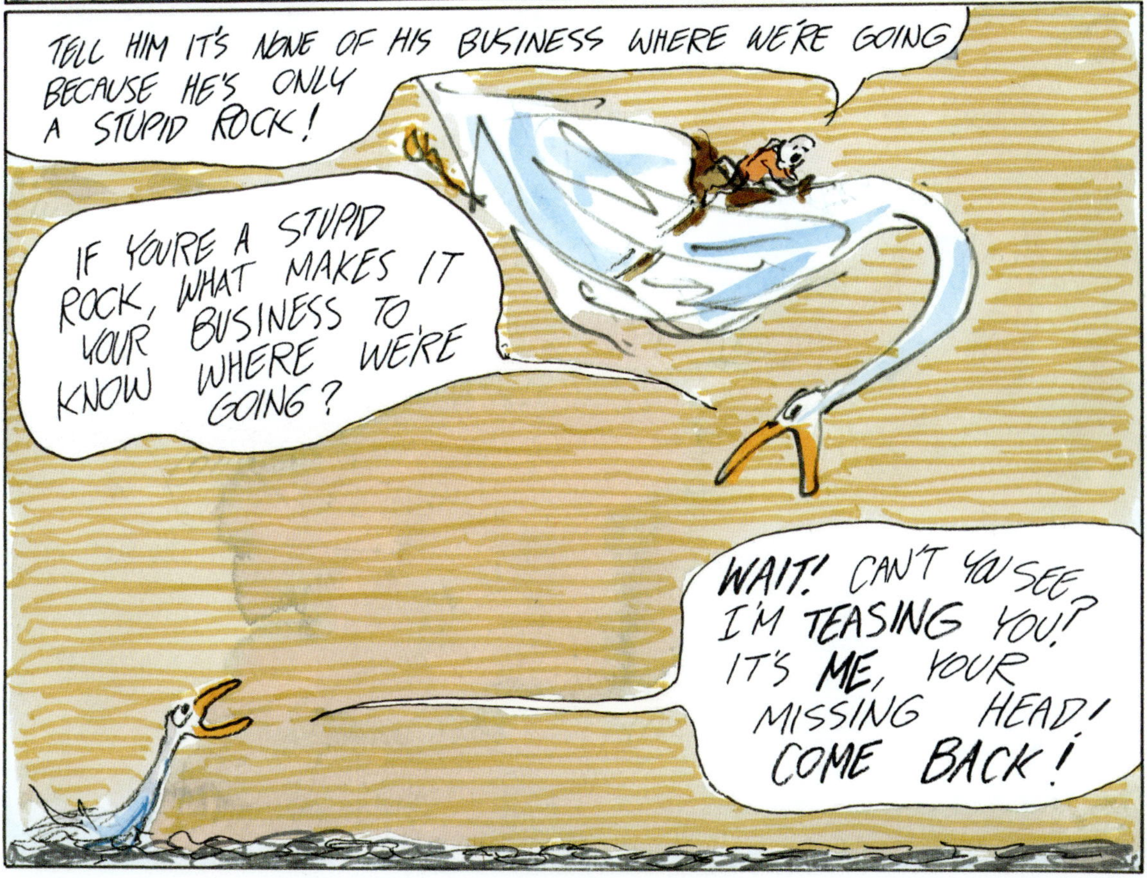
TELL HIM IT'S NONE OF HIS BUSINESS WHERE WE'RE GOING BECAUSE HE'S ONLY A STUPID ROCK!
IF YOU'RE A STUPID ROCK, WHAT MAKES IT YOUR BUSINESS TO KNOW WHERE WE'RE GOING?
WAIT! CAN'T YOU SEE I'M TEASING YOU? IT'S ME, YOUR MISSING HEAD! COME BACK!

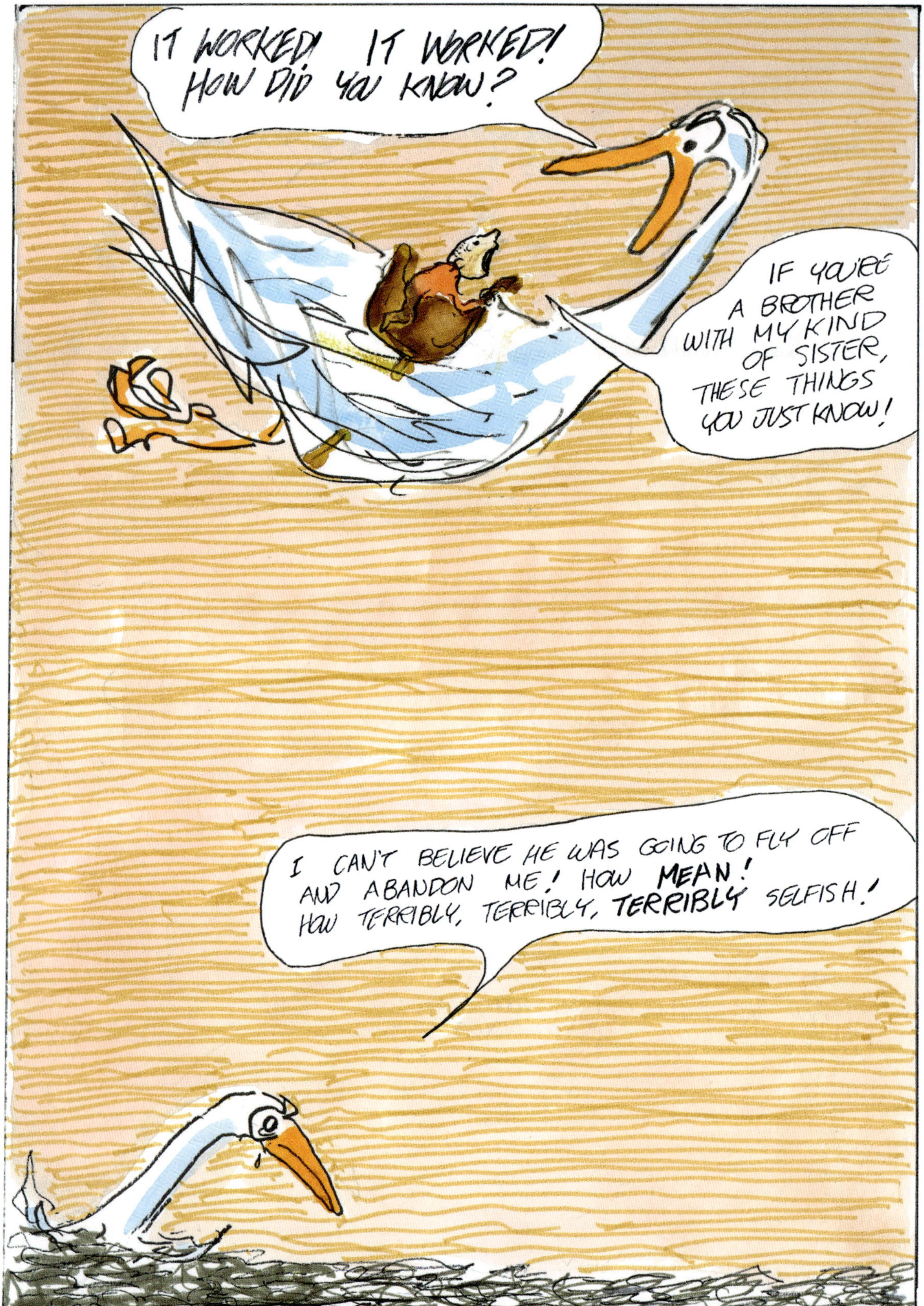
IT WORKED! IT WORKED! HOW DID YOU KNOW?
IF YOU'RE A BROTHER WITH MY KIND OF SISTER, THESE THINGS YOU JUST KNOW!
I CAN'T BELIEVE HE WAS GOING TO FLY OFF AND ABANDON ME! HOW MEAN! HOW TERRIBLY, TERRIBLY, TERRIBLY SELFISH!

CHAPTER 33 • MOMMY'S STORY

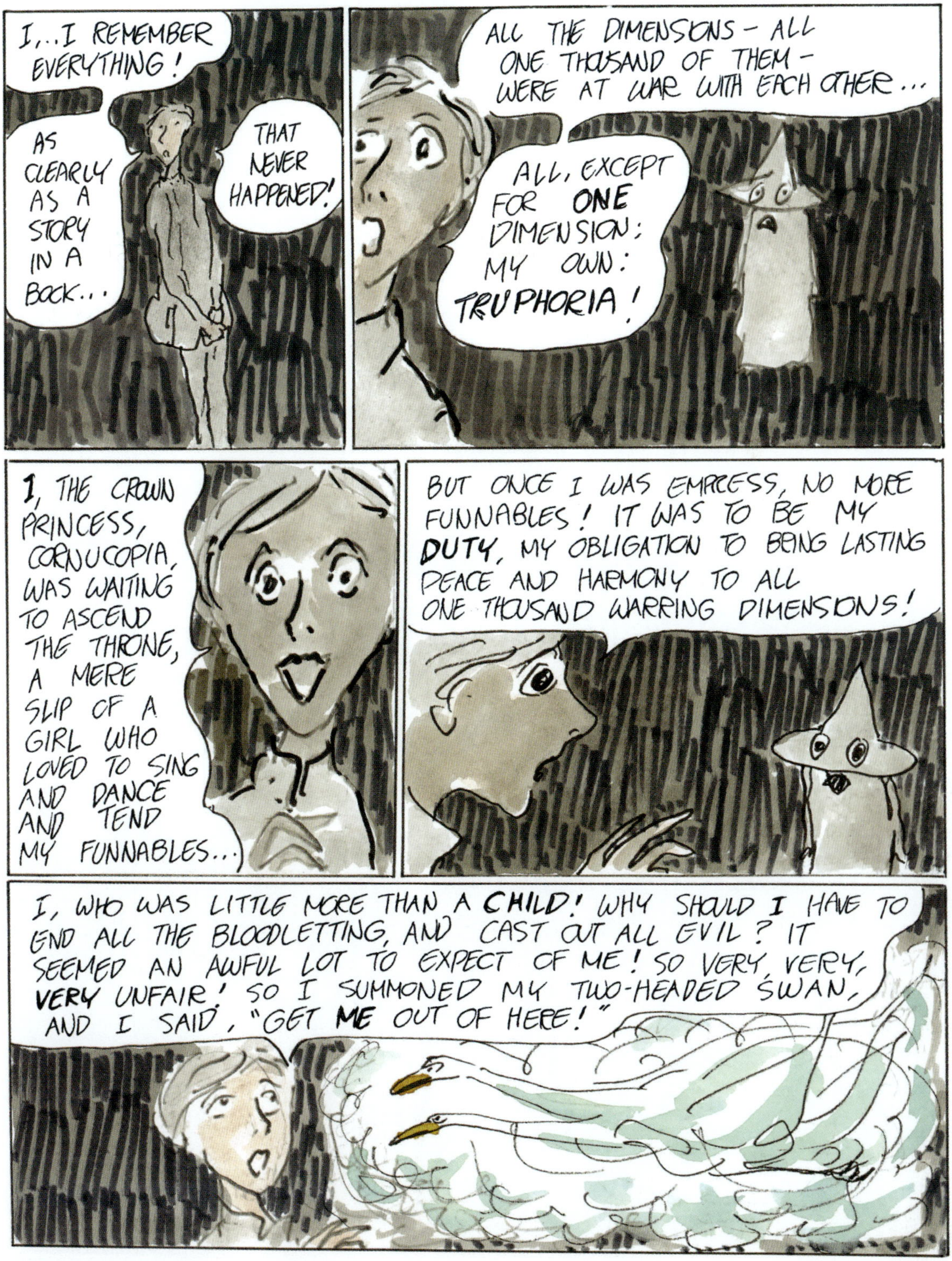

I,..I REMEMBER EVERYTHING!
AS CLEARLY AS A STORY IN A BOOK...
THAT NEVER HAPPENED!
ALL THE DIMENSIONS - ALL ONE THOUSAND OF THEM - WERE AT WAR WITH EACH OTHER...
ALL, EXCEPT FOR ONE DIMENSION; MY OWN: TRUPHORIA!
I, THE CROWN PRINCESS, CORNUCOPIA, WAS WAITING TO ASCEND THE THRONE, A MERE SLIP OF A GIRL WHO LOVED TO SING AND DANCE AND TEND MY FUNNABLES...
BUT ONCE I WAS EMPRESS, NO MORE FUNNABLES! IT WAS TO BE MY DUTY, MY OBLIGATION TO BEING LASTING PEACE AND HARMONY TO ALL ONE THOUSAND WARRING DIMENSIONS!
I, WHO WAS LITTLE MORE THAN A CHILD! WHY SHOULD I HAVE TO END ALL THE BLOODLETTING, AND CAST OUT ALL EVIL? IT SEEMED AN AWFUL LOT TO EXPECT OF ME! SO VERY, VERY, VERY UNFAIR! SO I SUMMONED MY TWO-HEADED SWAN, AND I SAID, "GET ME OUT OF HERE!"

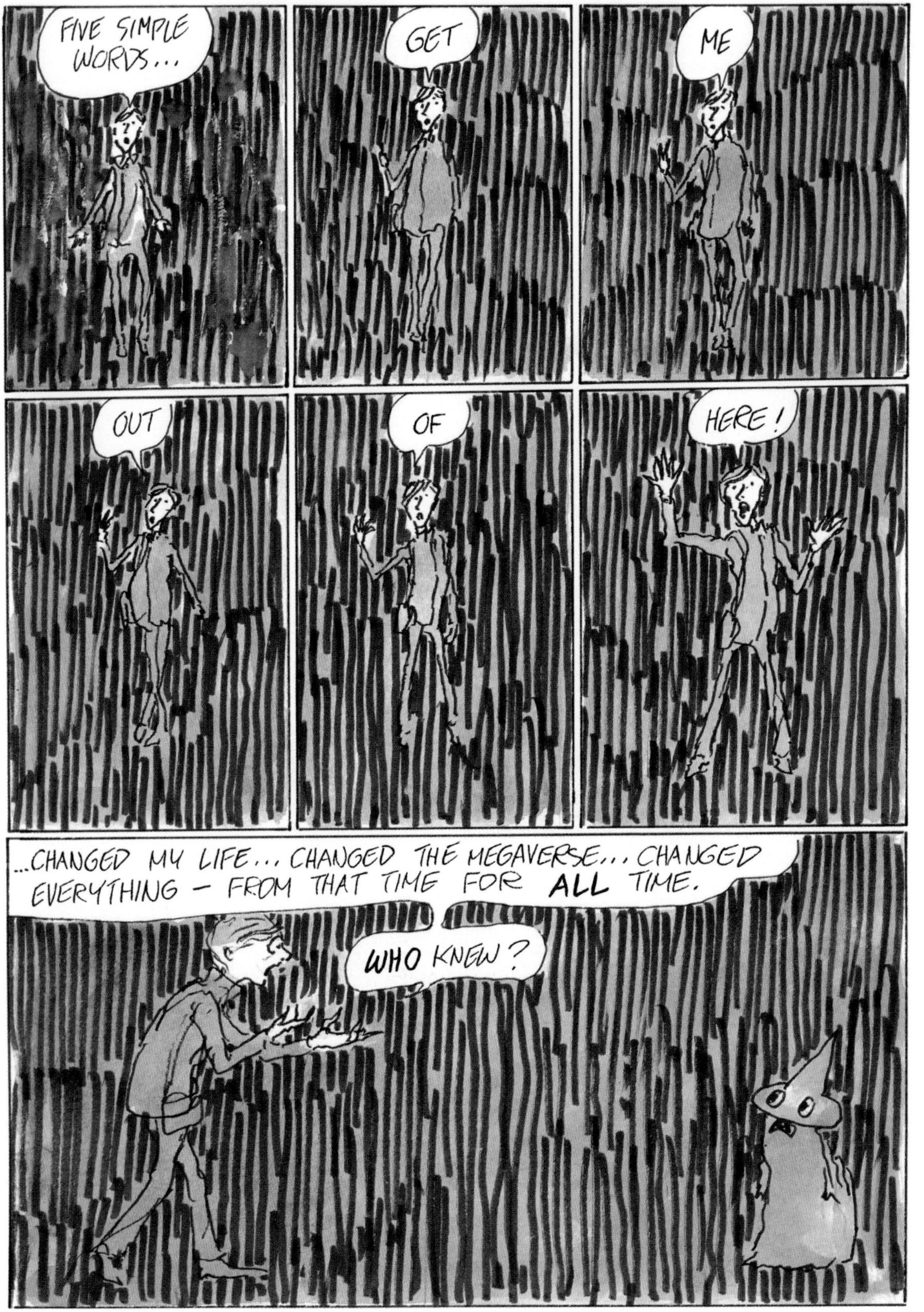
FIVE SIMPLE WORDS...
GET
ME
OUT
OF
HERE!
...CHANGED MY LIFE... CHANGED THE MEGAVERSE... CHANGED EVERYTHING - FROM THAT TIME FOR ALL TIME.
WHO KNEW?

CHAPTER 34 • CHOMP!

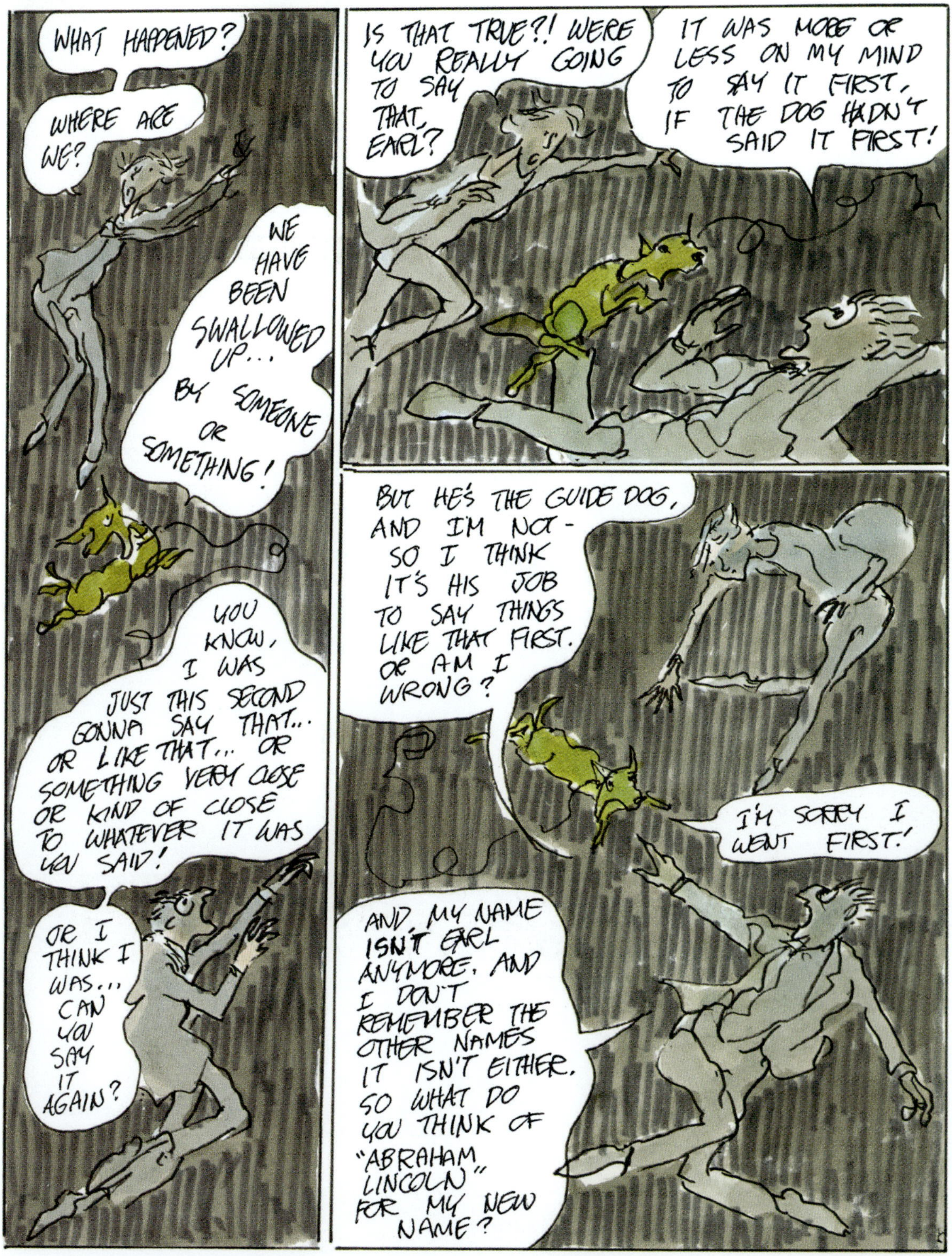
WHAT HAPPENED?
WHERE ARE WE?
WE HAVE BEEN SWALLOWED UP... BY SOMEONE OR SOMETHING!
YOU KNOW, I WAS JUST THIS SECOND GONNA SAY THAT... OR LIKE THAT... OR SOMETHING VERY CLOSE OR KIND OF CLOSE TO WHATEVER IT WAS YOU SAID!
OR I THINK I WAS... CAN YOU SAY IT AGAIN?
IS THAT TRUE?! WERE YOU REALLY GOING TO SAY THAT, EARL?
IT WAS MORE OR LESS ON MY MIND TO SAY IT FIRST, IF THE DOG HADN'T SAID IT FIRST!
BUT HE'S THE GUIDE DOG, AND I'M NOT- SO I THINK IT'S HIS JOB TO SAY THINGS LIKE THAT FIRST. OR AM I WRONG?
I'M SORRY I WENT FIRST!
AND MY NAME ISN'T EARL ANYMORE. AND I DON'T REMEMBER THE OTHER NAMES IT ISN'T EITHER. SO WHAT DO YOU THINK OF "ABRAHAM LINCOLN" FOR MY NEW NAME?

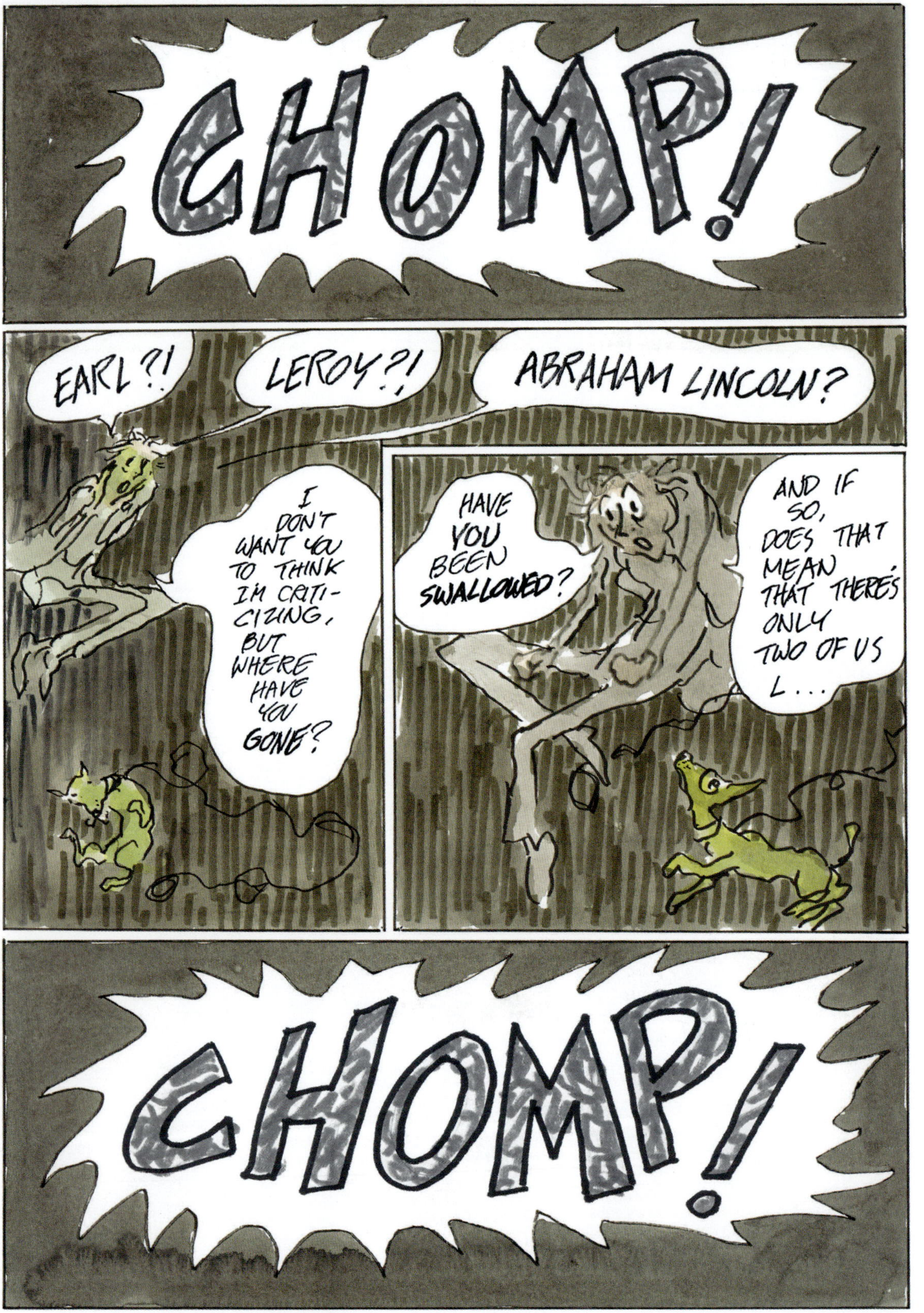
CHOMP!
EARL?!
LEROY?!
ABRAHAM LINCOLN?
I DON'T WANT YOU TO THINK I'M CRITICIZING, BUT WHERE HAVE YOU GONE?
HAVE YOU BEEN SWALLOWED?
AND IF SO, DOES THAT MEAN THAT THERE'S ONLY TWO OF US L...
CHOMP!

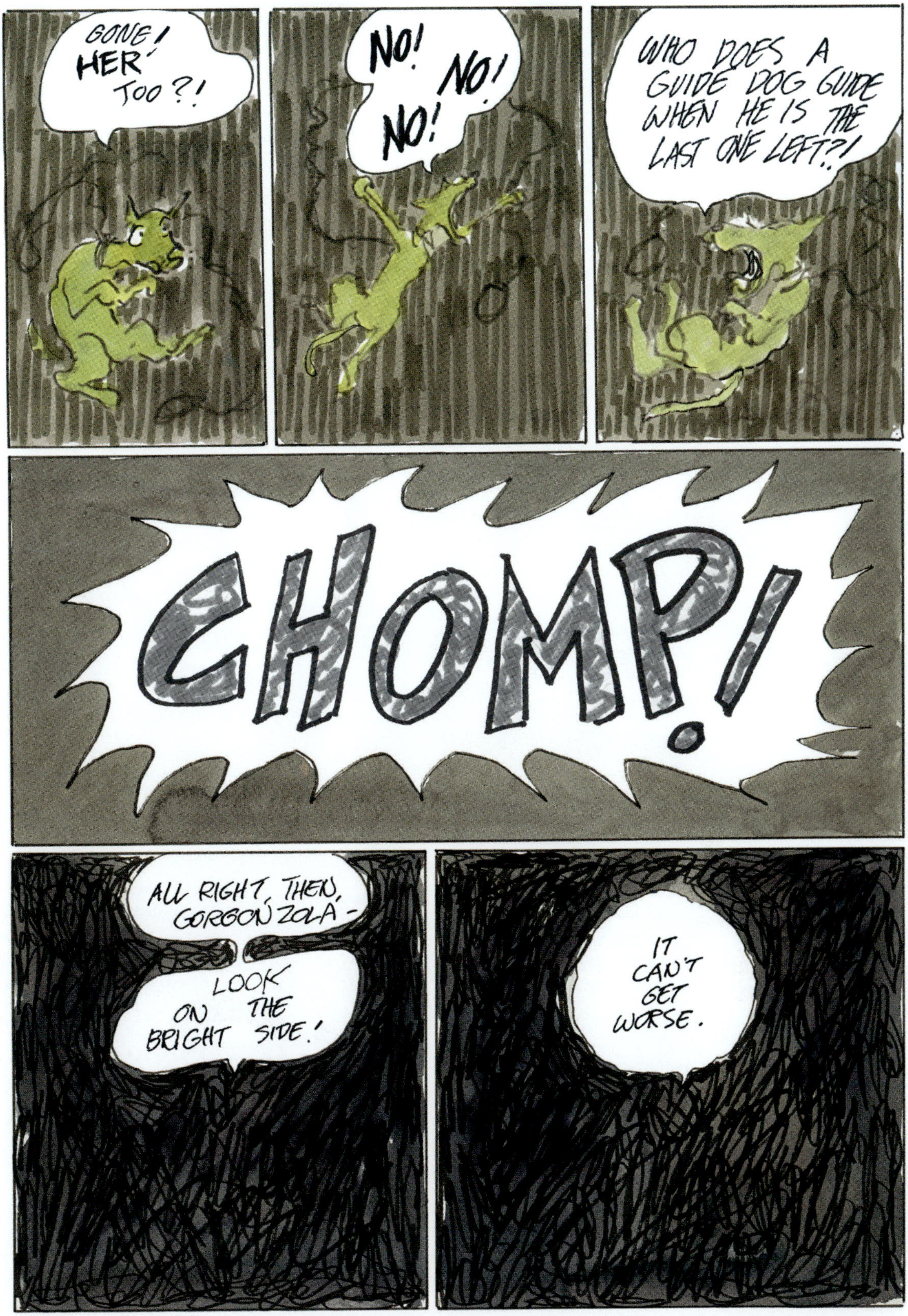
GONE! HER TOO?!
NO! NO! NO!
WHO DOES A GUIDE DOG GUIDE WHEN HE IS THE LAST ONE LEFT?!
CHOMP!
ALL RIGHT, THEN, GORGONZOLA -
LOOK ON THE BRIGHT SIDE!
IT CAN'T GET WORSE.

CHAPTER 35 • LONGING, BELONGING

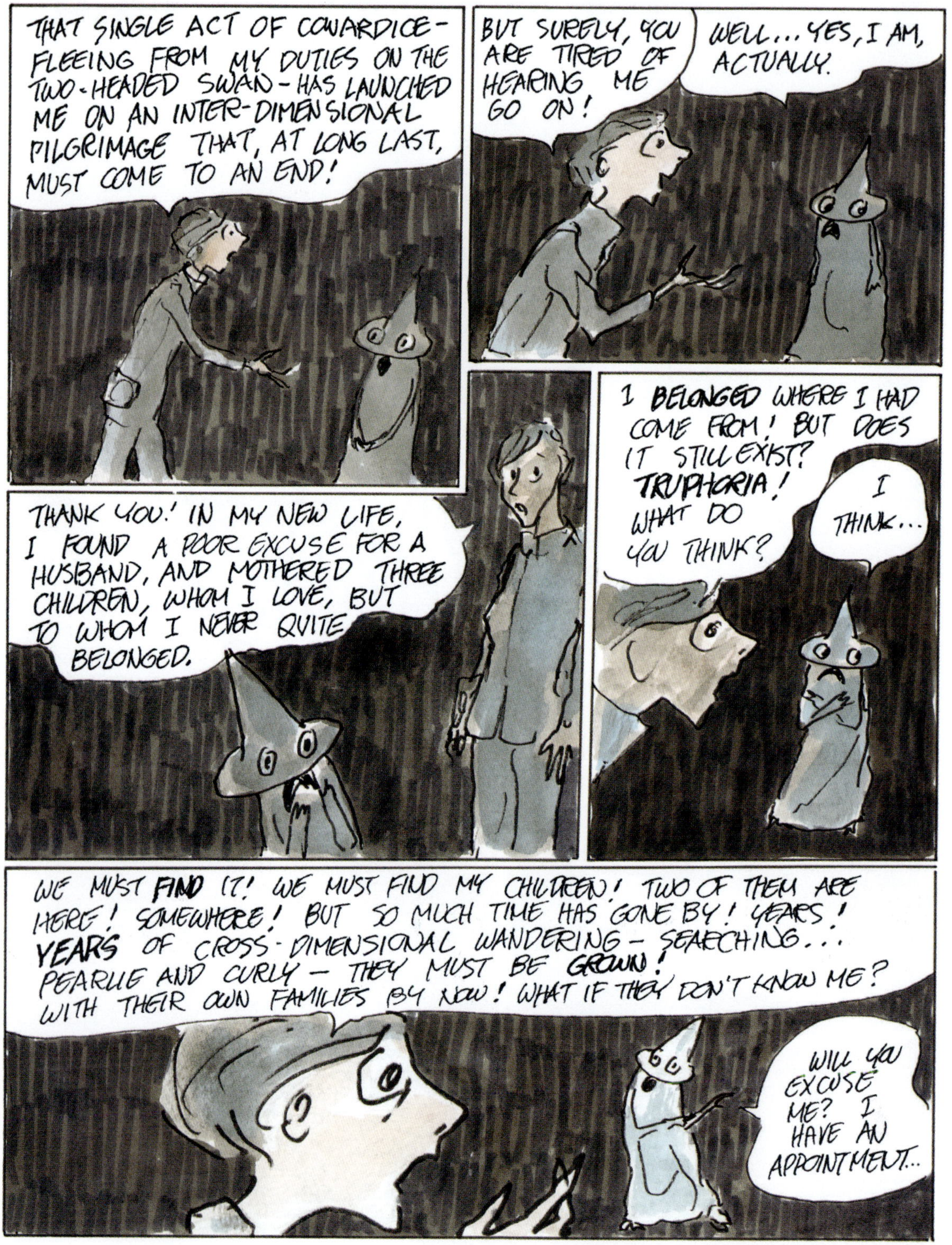
THAT SINGLE ACT OF COWARDICE—FLEEING FROM MY DUTIES ON THE TWO-HEADED SWAN—HAS LAUNCHED ME ON AN INTER-DIMENSIONAL PILGRIMAGE THAT, AT LONG LAST, MUST COME TO AN END!
BUT SURELY, YOU ARE TIRED OF HEARING ME GO ON!
WELL... YES, I AM, ACTUALLY.
THANK YOU! IN MY NEW LIFE, I FOUND A POOR EXCUSE FOR A HUSBAND, AND MOTHERED THREE CHILDREN, WHOM I LOVE, BUT TO WHOM I NEVER QUITE BELONGED.
I **BELONGED** WHERE I HAD COME FROM! BUT DOES IT STILL EXIST? **TRUPHORIA**! WHAT DO YOU THINK?
I THINK...
WE MUST **FIND** IT! WE MUST FIND MY CHILDREN! TWO OF THEM ARE HERE! SOMEWHERE! BUT SO MUCH TIME HAS GONE BY! YEARS! **YEARS** OF CROSS-DIMENSIONAL WANDERING—SEARCHING... PEARLIE AND CURLY—THEY MUST BE **GROWN**! WITH THEIR OWN FAMILIES BY NOW! WHAT IF THEY DON'T KNOW ME?
WILL YOU EXCUSE ME? I HAVE AN APPOINTMENT...

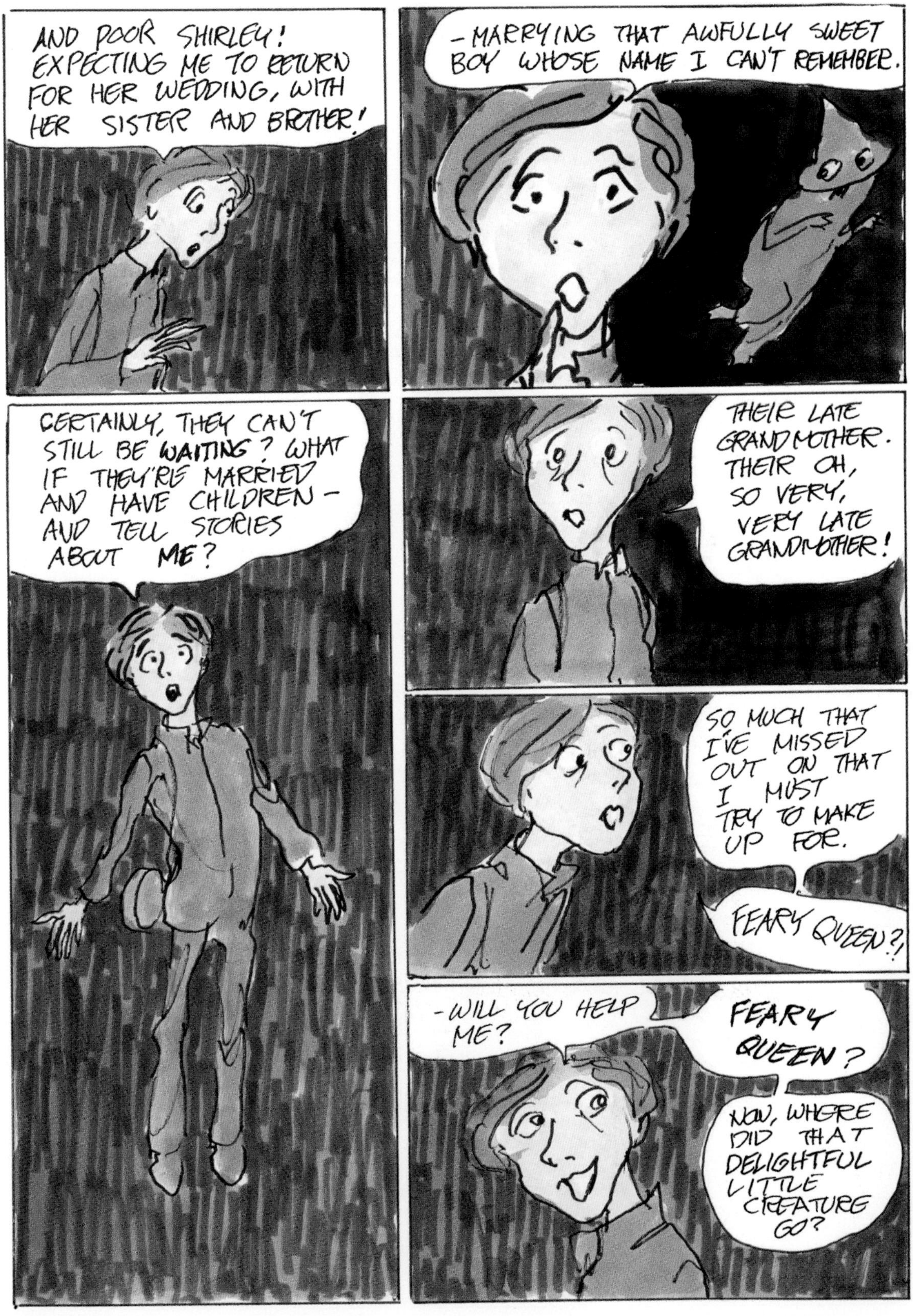
AND POOR SHIRLEY! EXPECTING ME TO RETURN FOR HER WEDDING, WITH HER SISTER AND BROTHER!
-MARRYING THAT AWFULLY SWEET BOY WHOSE NAME I CAN'T REMEMBER.
CERTAINLY, THEY CAN'T STILL BE **WAITING**? WHAT IF THEY'RE MARRIED AND HAVE CHILDREN - AND TELL STORIES ABOUT **ME**?
THEIR LATE GRANDMOTHER. THEIR OH, SO VERY, VERY LATE GRANDMOTHER!
SO MUCH THAT I'VE MISSED OUT ON THAT I MUST TRY TO MAKE UP FOR.
FEARY QUEEN?
-WILL YOU HELP ME?
FEARY QUEEN?
NOW, WHERE DID THAT DELIGHTFUL LITTLE CREATURE GO?

CHAPTER 36 • THE DOOMANIANS

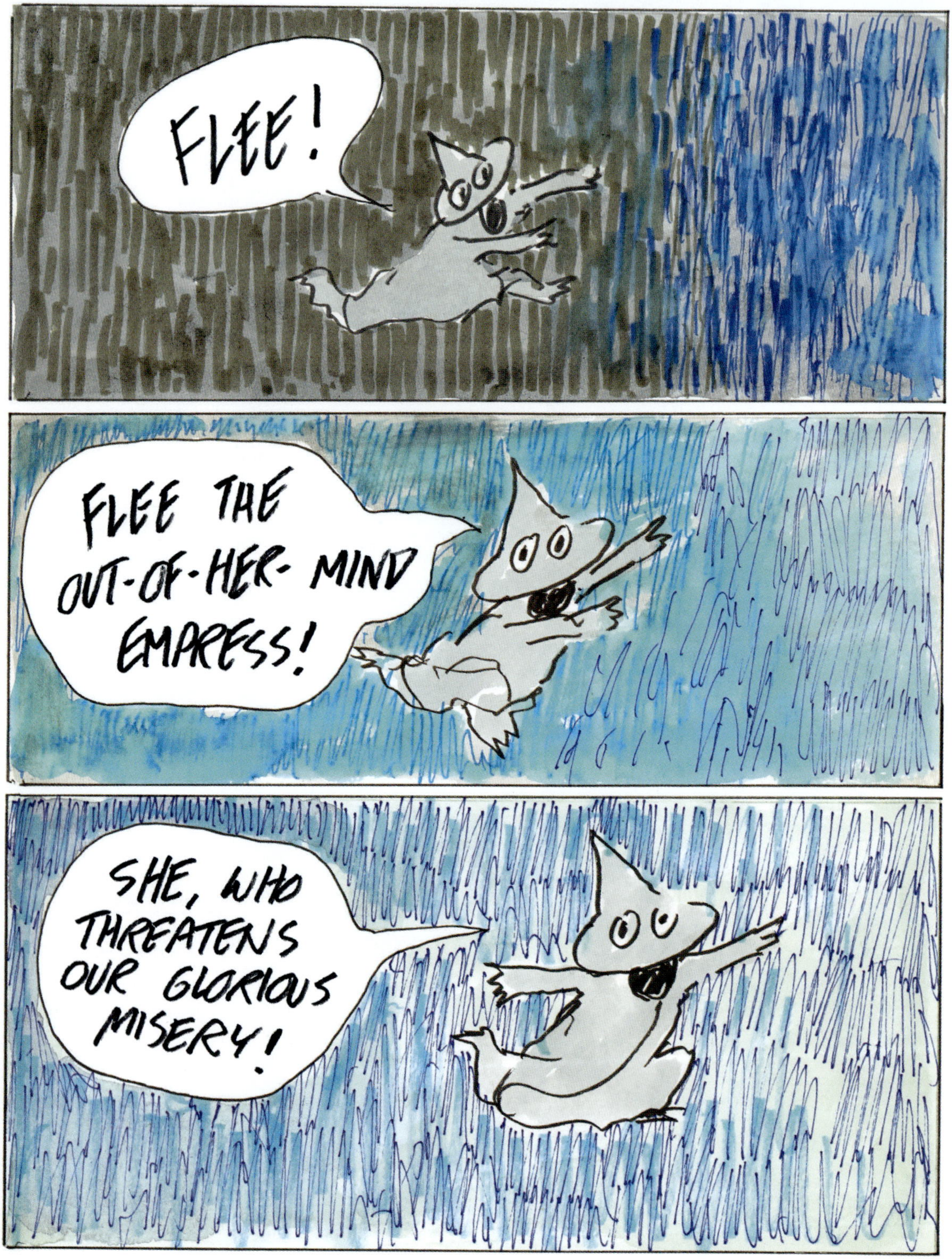
FLEE!
FLEE THE OUT-OF-HER-MIND EMPRESS!
SHE, WHO THREATENS OUR GLORIOUS MISERY!

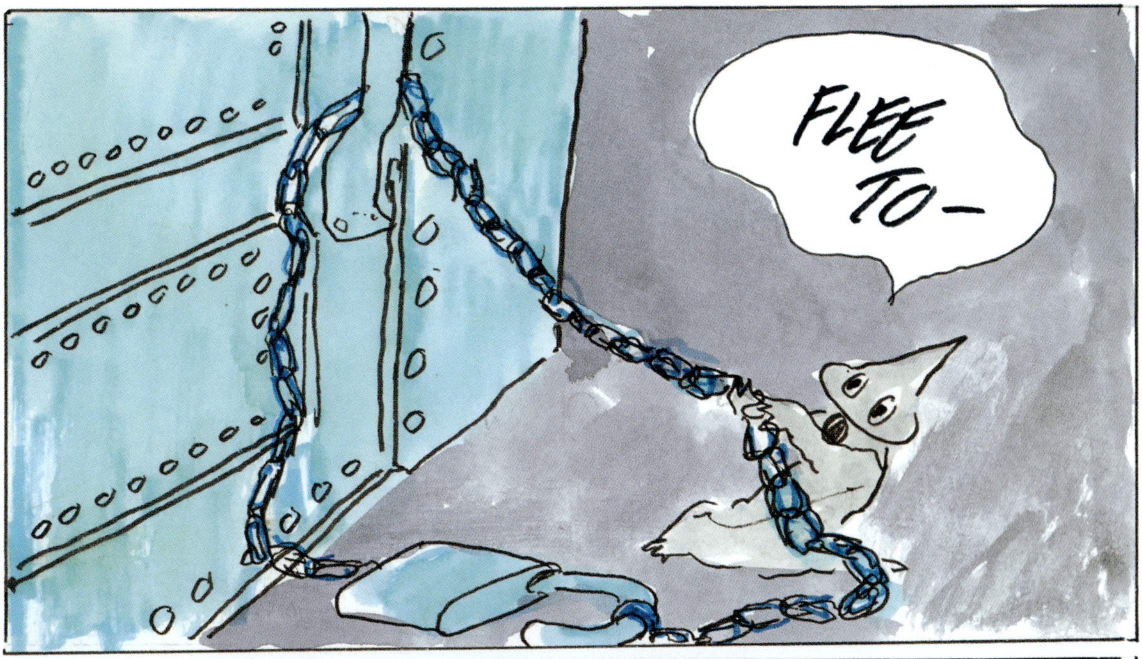
FLEE TO—

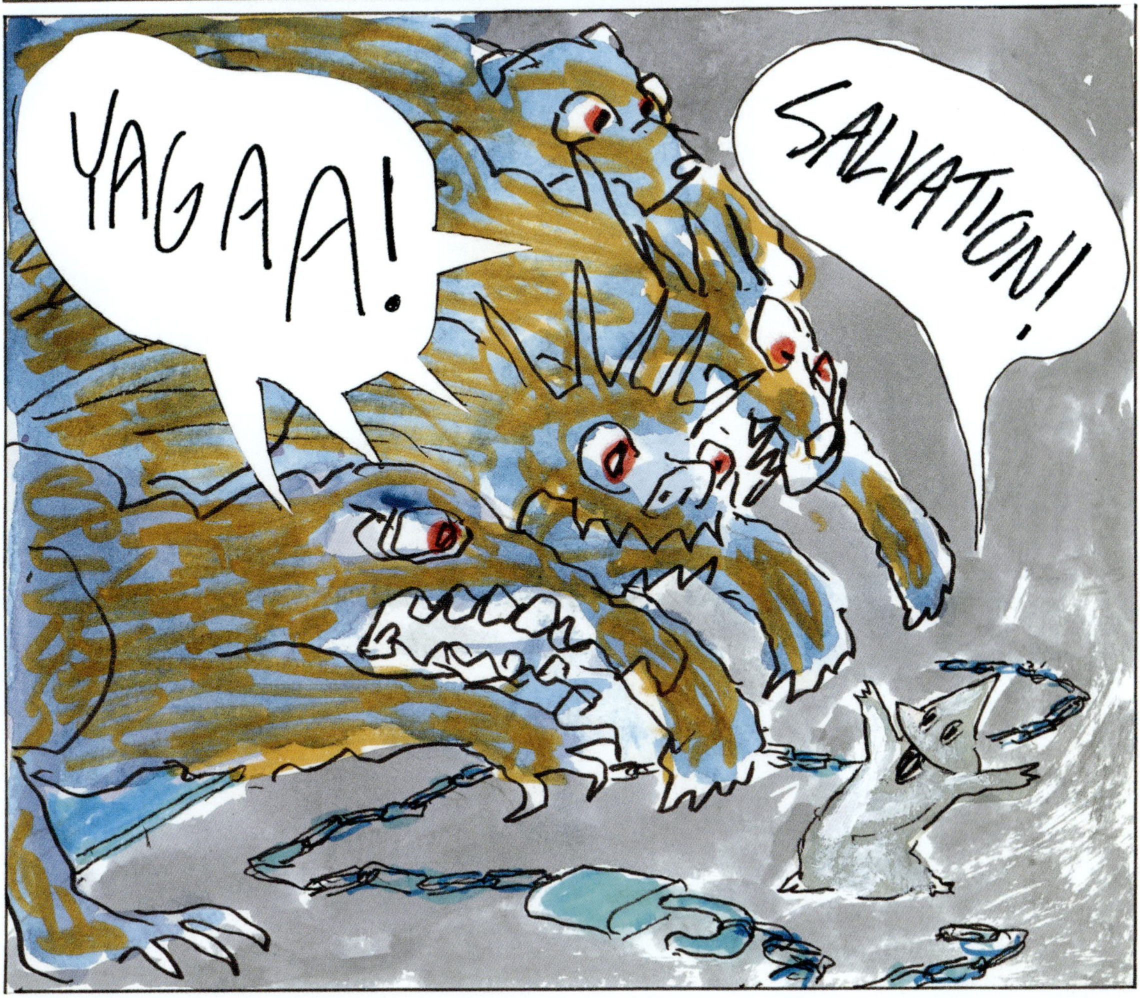
YAGAA!
SALVATION!

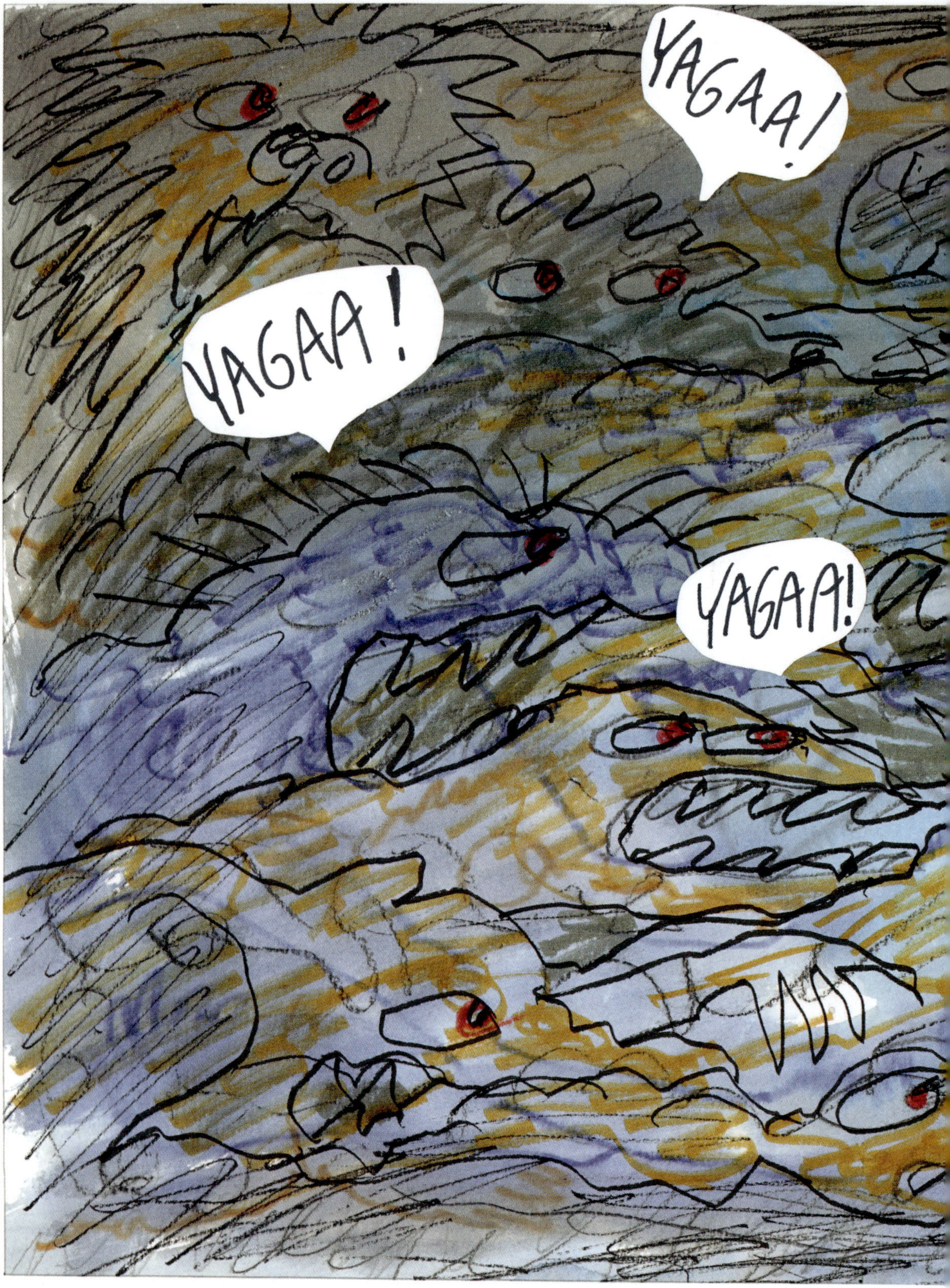
YAGAA!
YAGAA!
YAGAA!

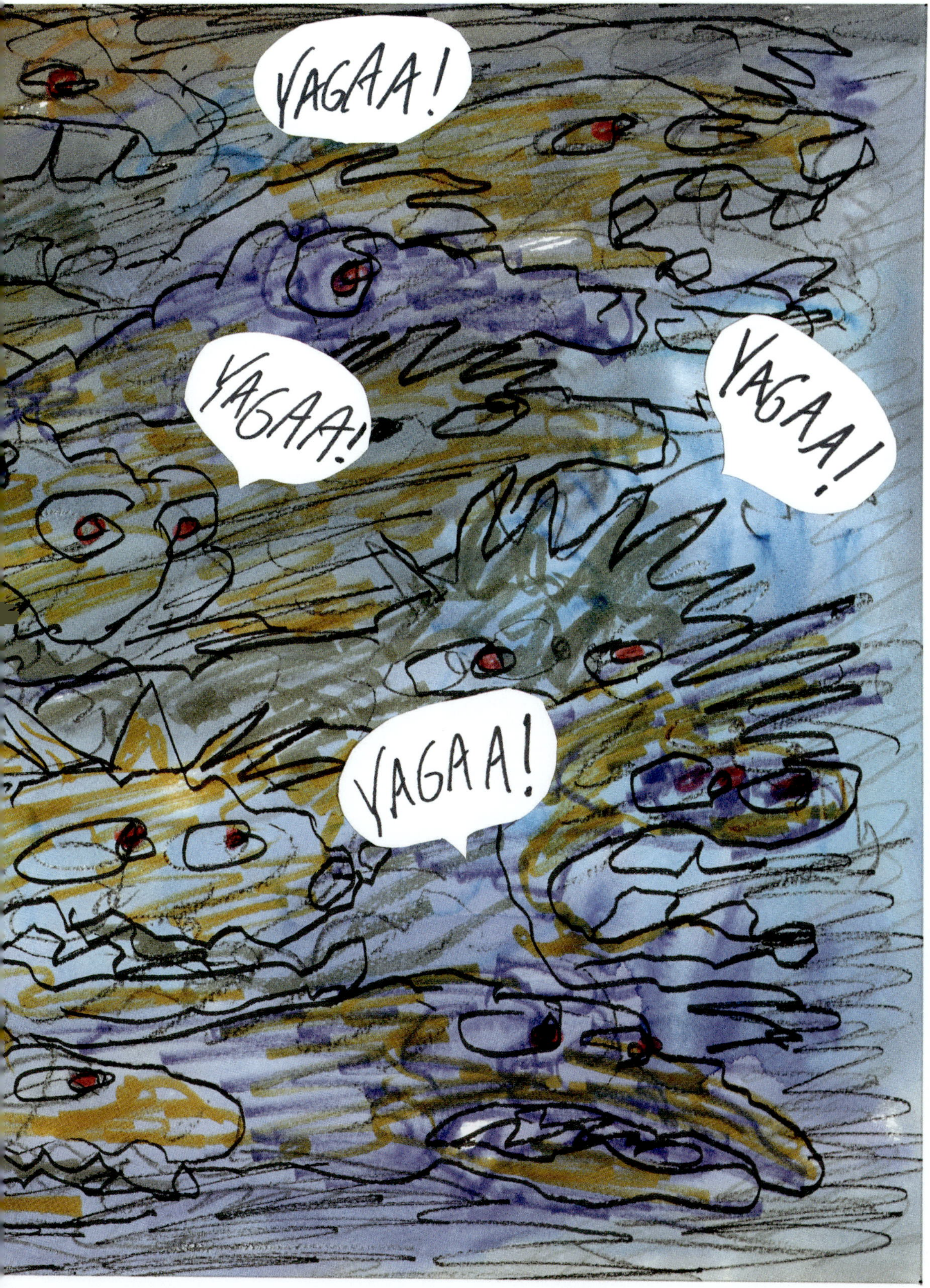
YAGAA!
YAGAA!
YAGAA!
YAGAA!

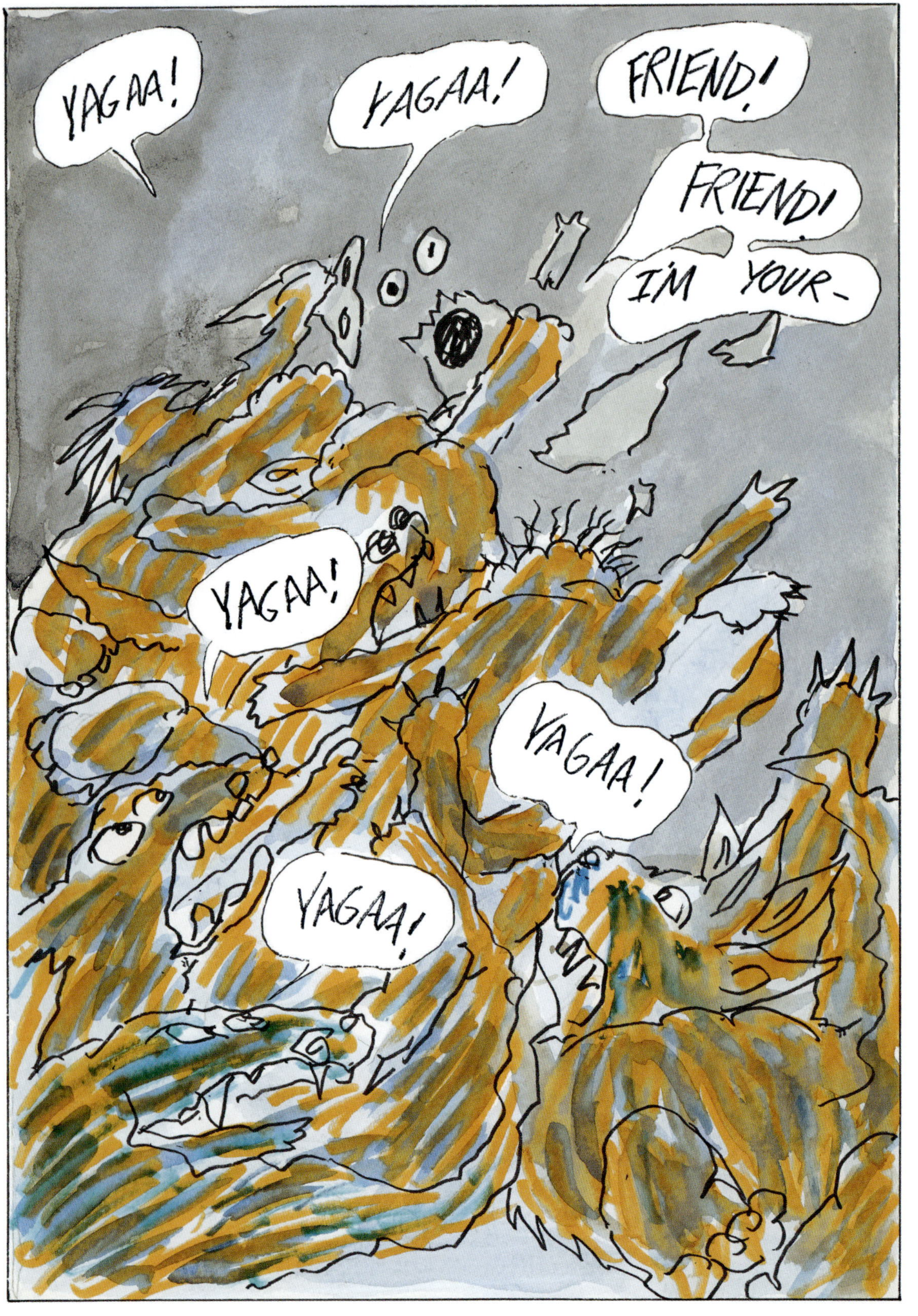
YAGAA!
YAGAA!
FRIEND!
FRIEND!
I'M YOUR-
YAGAA!
YAGAA!
YAGAA!

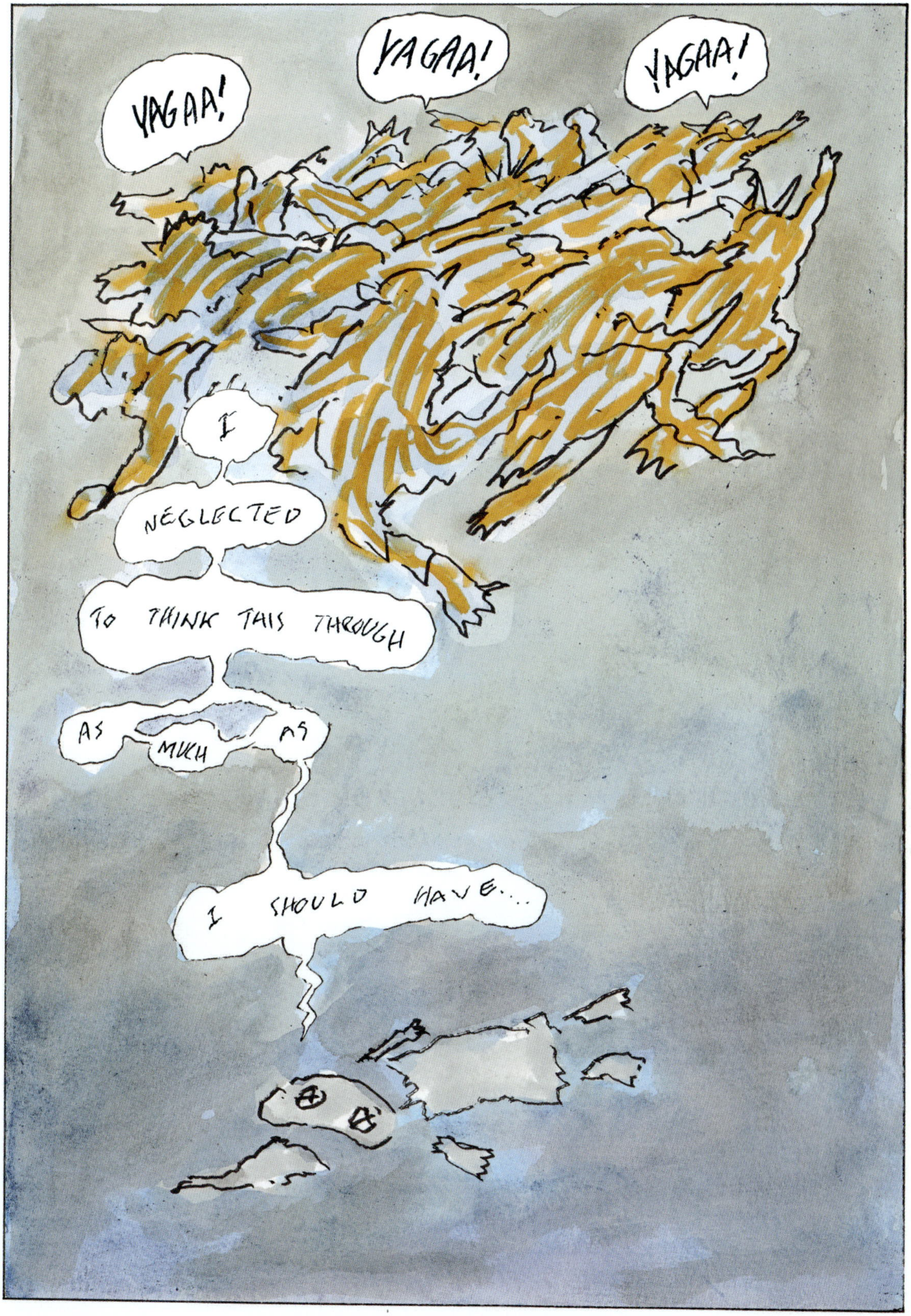
YAGAA!
YAGAA!
YAGAA!
I
NEGLECTED
TO THINK THIS THROUGH
AS MUCH AS
I SHOULD HAVE...

CHAPTER 37 • MAKING IT UP

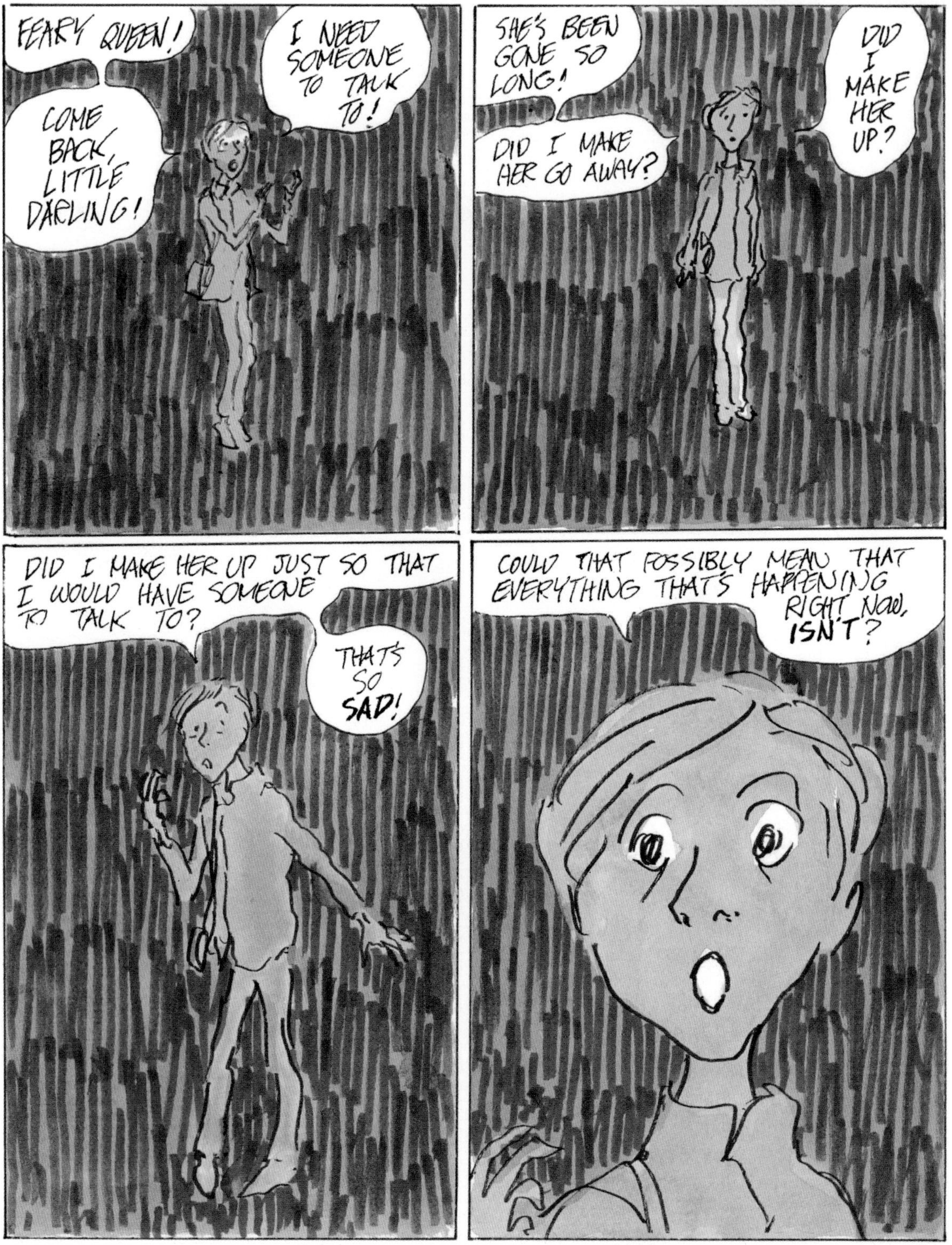
FEARY QUEEN!
COME BACK, LITTLE DARLING!
I NEED SOMEONE TO TALK TO!
SHE'S BEEN GONE, SO LONG!
DID I MAKE HER GO AWAY?
DID I MAKE HER UP?
DID I MAKE HER UP JUST SO THAT I WOULD HAVE SOMEONE TO TALK TO?
THAT'S SO **SAD!**
COULD THAT POSSIBLY MEAN THAT EVERYTHING THAT'S HAPPENING RIGHT NOW, **ISN'T?**

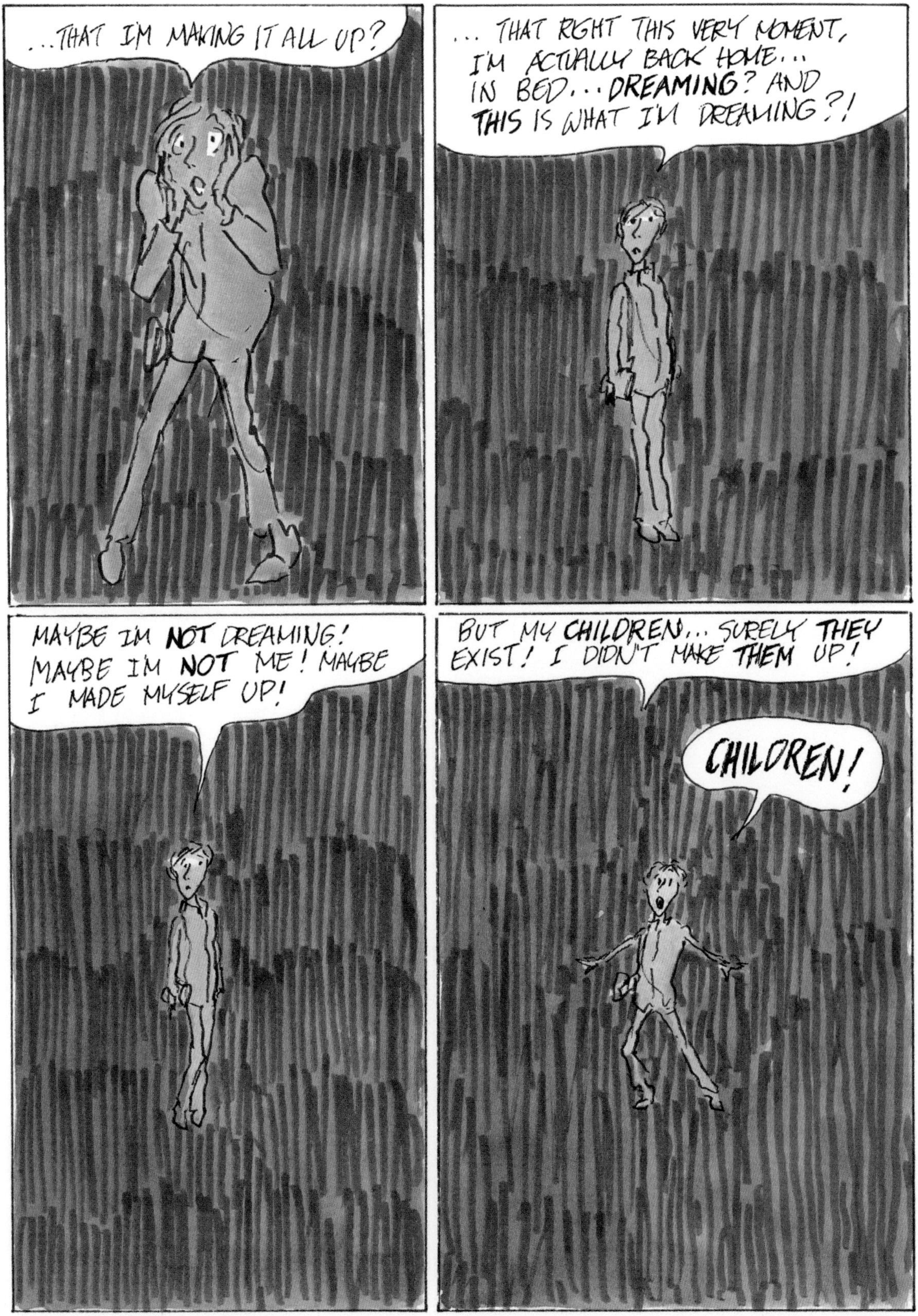
...THAT I'M MAKING IT ALL UP?
... THAT RIGHT THIS VERY MOMENT, I'M ACTUALLY BACK HOME... IN BED... DREAMING? AND THIS IS WHAT I'M DREAMING?!
MAYBE I'M NOT DREAMING! MAYBE I'M NOT ME! MAYBE I MADE MYSELF UP!
BUT MY CHILDREN... SURELY THEY EXIST! I DIDN'T MAKE THEM UP!
CHILDREN!

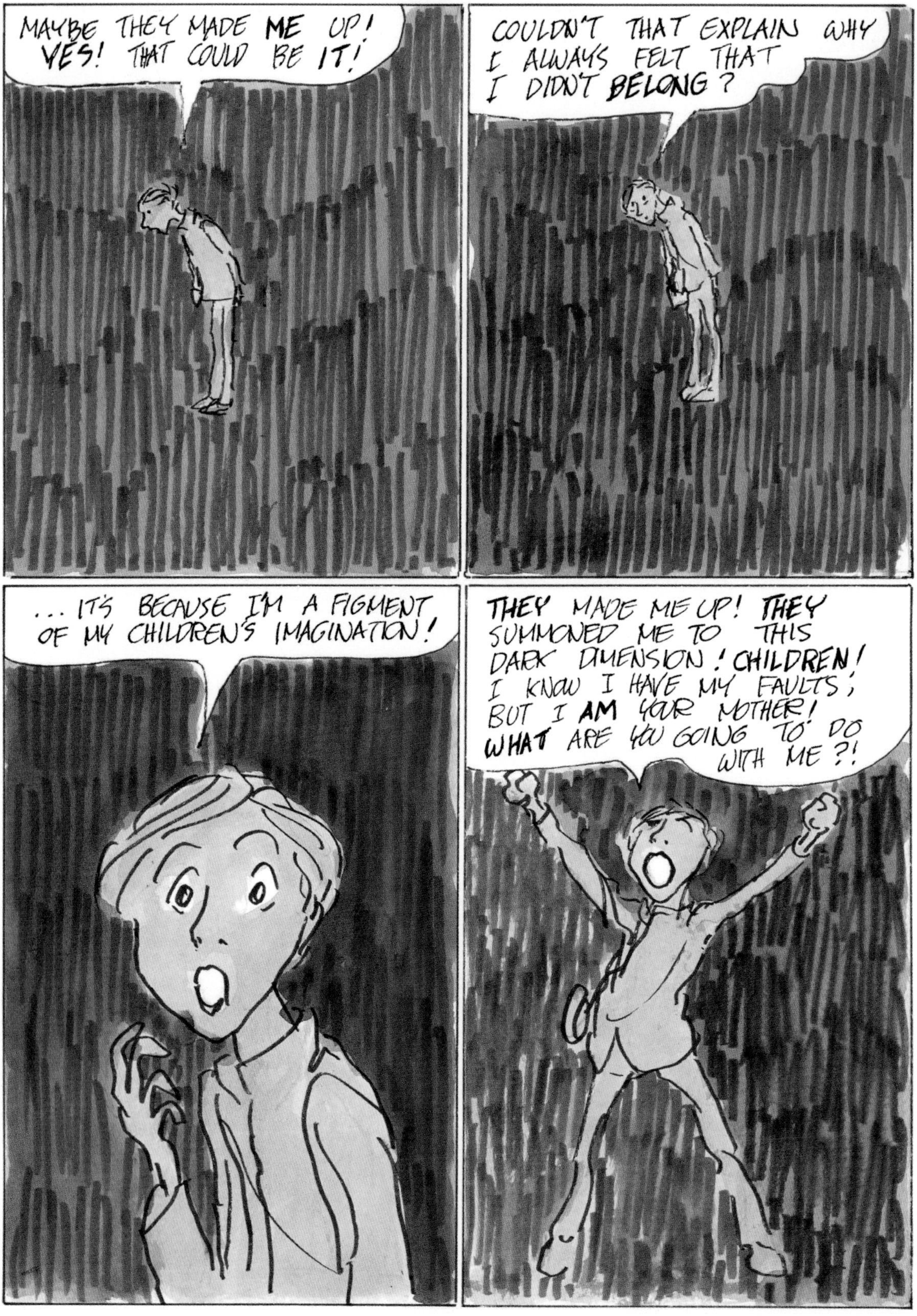
MAYBE THEY MADE ME UP! YES! THAT COULD BE IT!
COULDN'T THAT EXPLAIN WHY I ALWAYS FELT THAT I DIDN'T BELONG?
...IT'S BECAUSE I'M A FIGMENT OF MY CHILDREN'S IMAGINATION!
THEY MADE ME UP! THEY SUMMONED ME TO THIS DARK DIMENSION! CHILDREN! I KNOW I HAVE MY FAULTS, BUT I AM YOUR MOTHER! WHAT ARE YOU GOING TO DO WITH ME?!

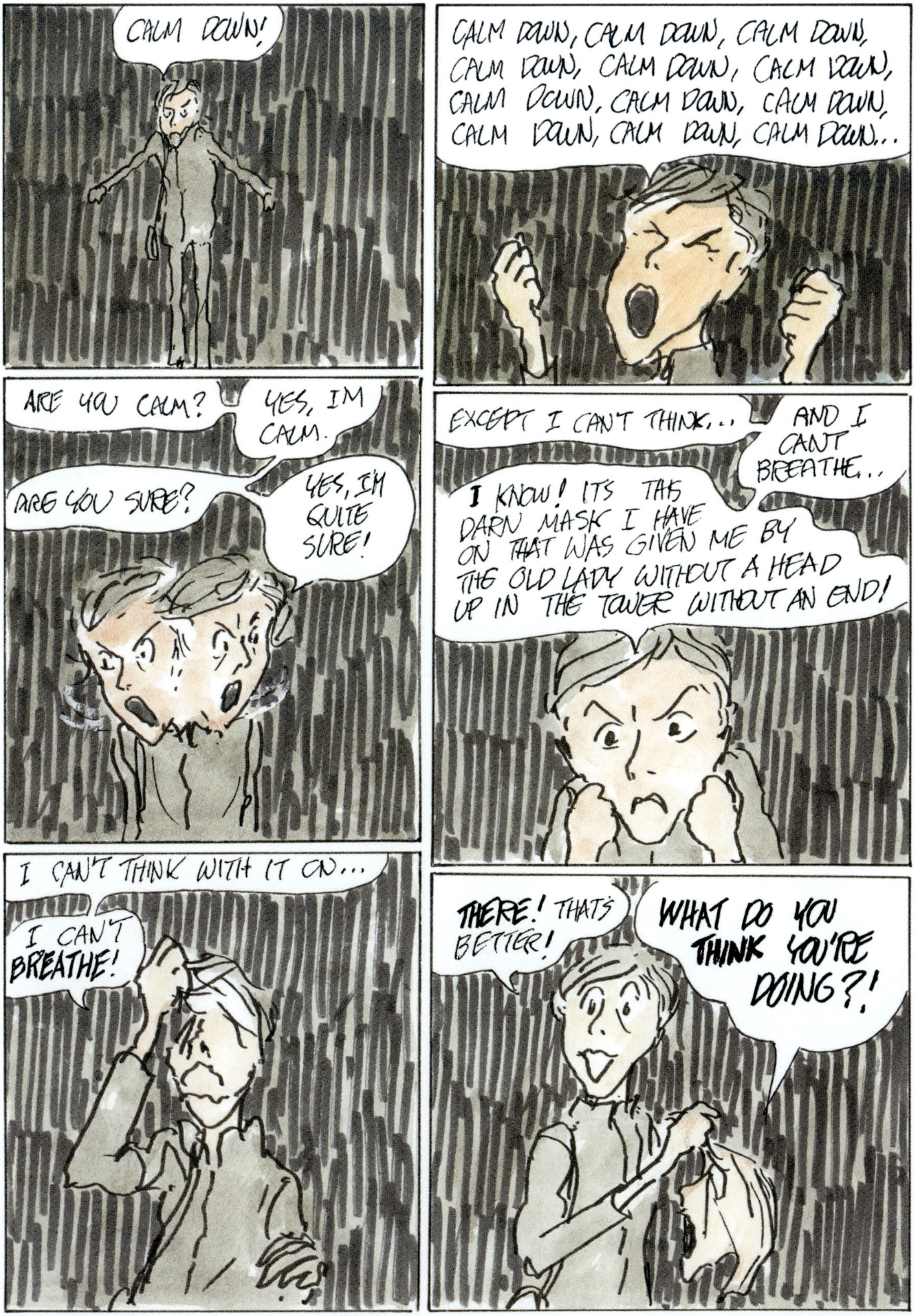
CALM DOWN!
CALM DOWN, CALM DOWN, CALM DOWN, CALM DOWN, CALM DOWN, CALM DOWN, CALM DOWN, CALM DOWN, CALM DOWN, CALM DOWN, CALM DOWN, CALM DOWN...
ARE YOU CALM?
YES, I'M CALM.
ARE YOU SURE?
YES, I'M QUITE SURE!
EXCEPT I CAN'T THINK...
AND I CANT BREATHE...
I KNOW! ITS THIS DARN MASK I HAVE ON THAT WAS GIVEN ME BY THE OLD LADY WITHOUT A HEAD UP IN THE TOWER WITHOUT AN END!
I CAN'T THINK WITH IT ON...
I CAN'T BREATHE!
THERE! THAT'S BETTER!
WHAT DO YOU THINK YOU'RE DOING?!

CHAPTER 38 • ATTACK!

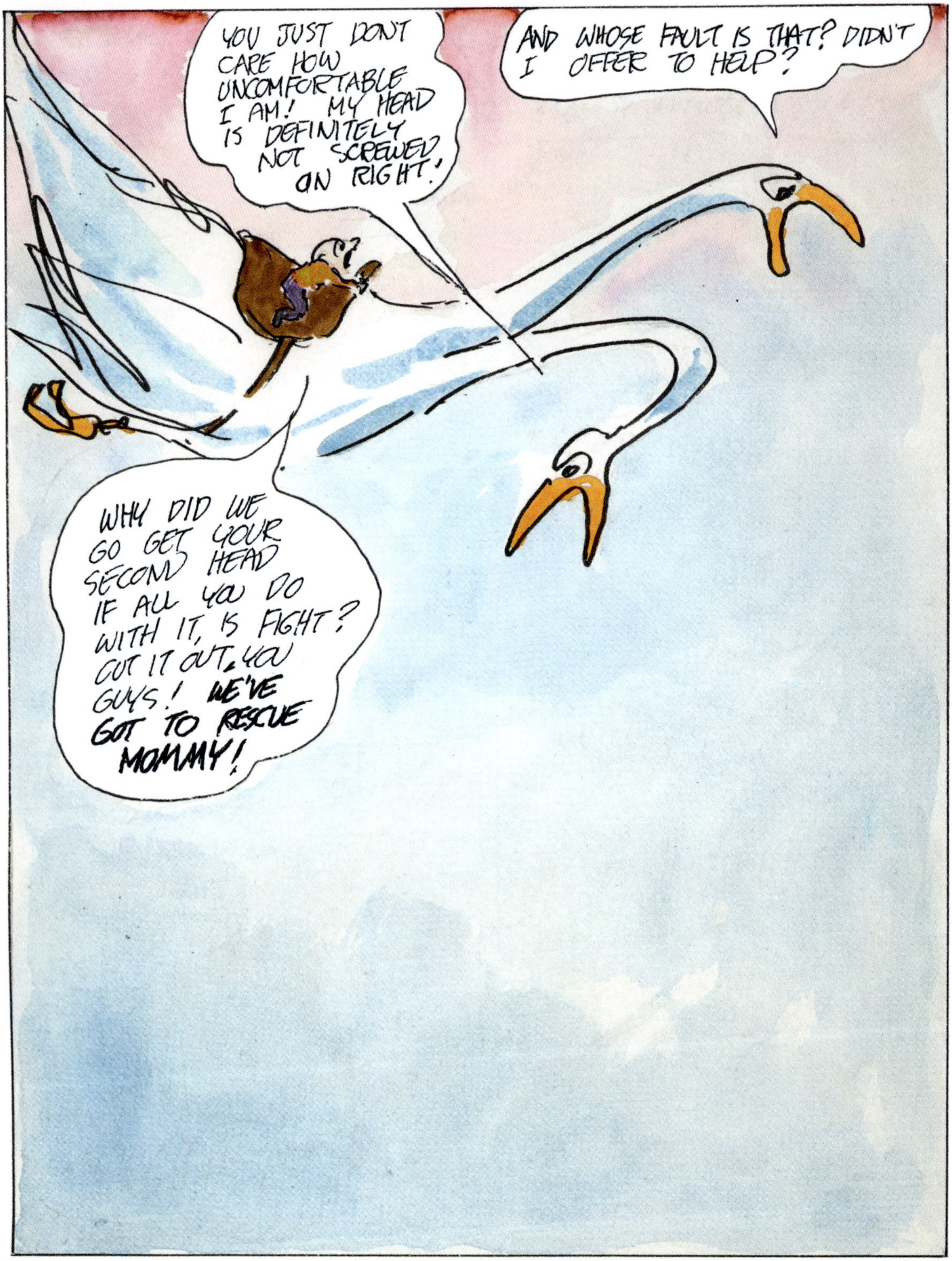

YOU JUST DON'T CARE HOW UNCOMFORTABLE I AM! MY HEAD IS DEFINITELY NOT SCREWED ON RIGHT!
AND WHOSE FAULT IS THAT? DIDN'T I OFFER TO HELP?
WHY DID WE GO GET YOUR SECOND HEAD IF ALL YOU DO WITH IT, IS FIGHT? CUT IT OUT, YOU GUYS! WE'VE GOT TO RESCUE MOMMY!

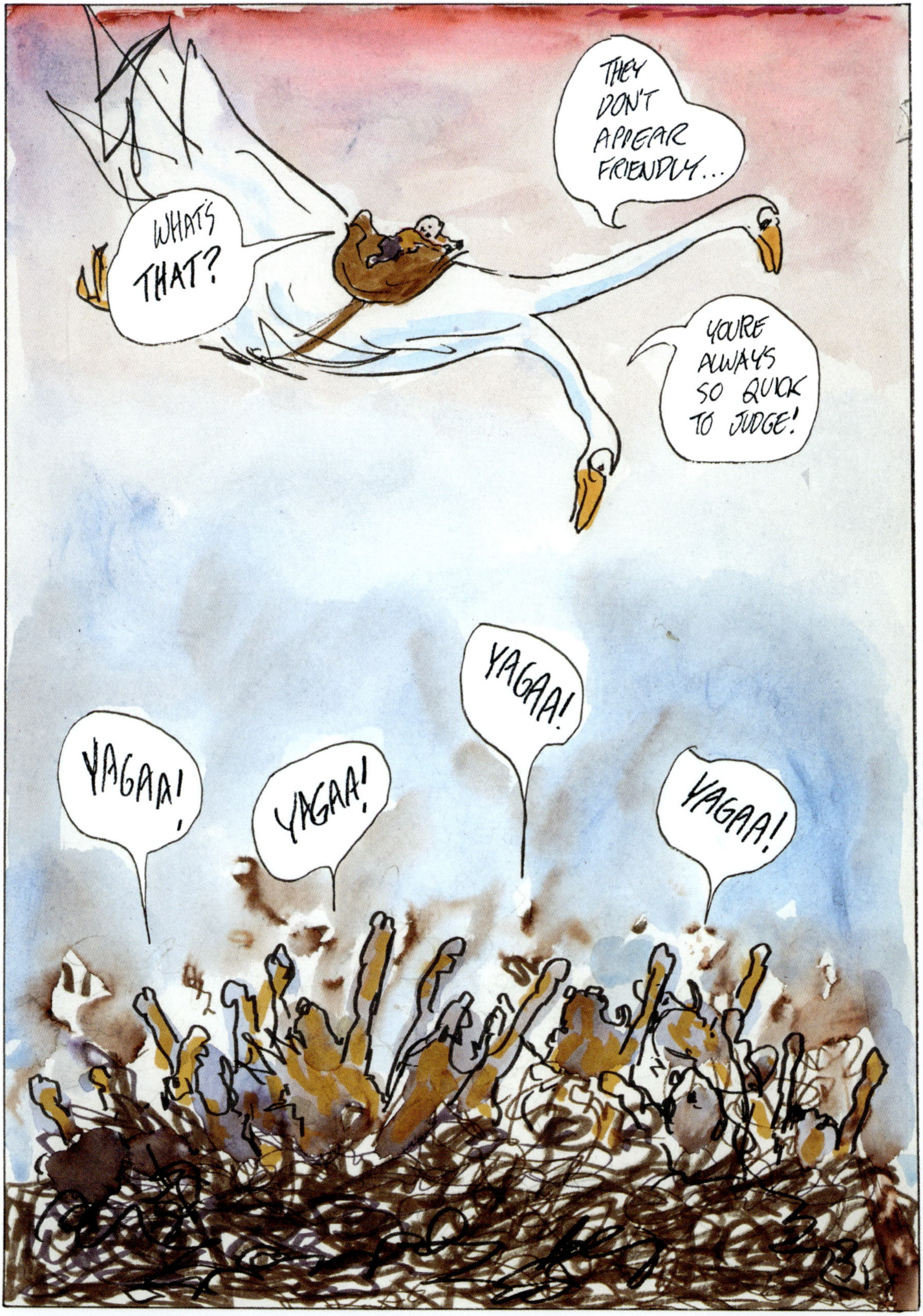
WHAT'S THAT?
THEY DON'T APPEAR FRIENDLY...
YOU'RE ALWAYS SO QUICK TO JUDGE!
YAGAA!
YAGAA!
YAGAA!
YAGAA!

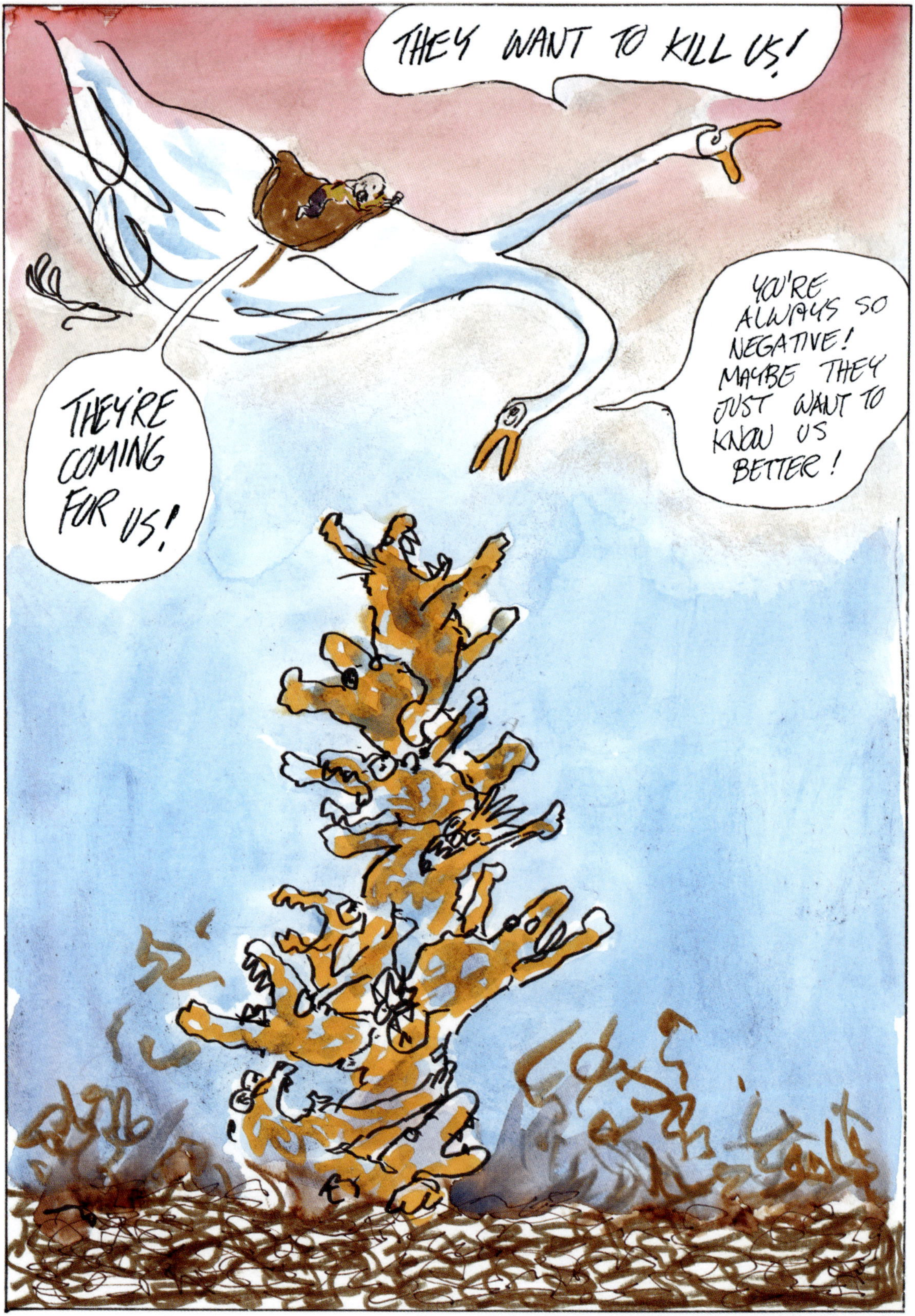
THEY WANT TO KILL US!
THEY'RE COMING FOR US!
YOU'RE ALWAYS SO NEGATIVE! MAYBE THEY JUST WANT TO KNOW US BETTER!

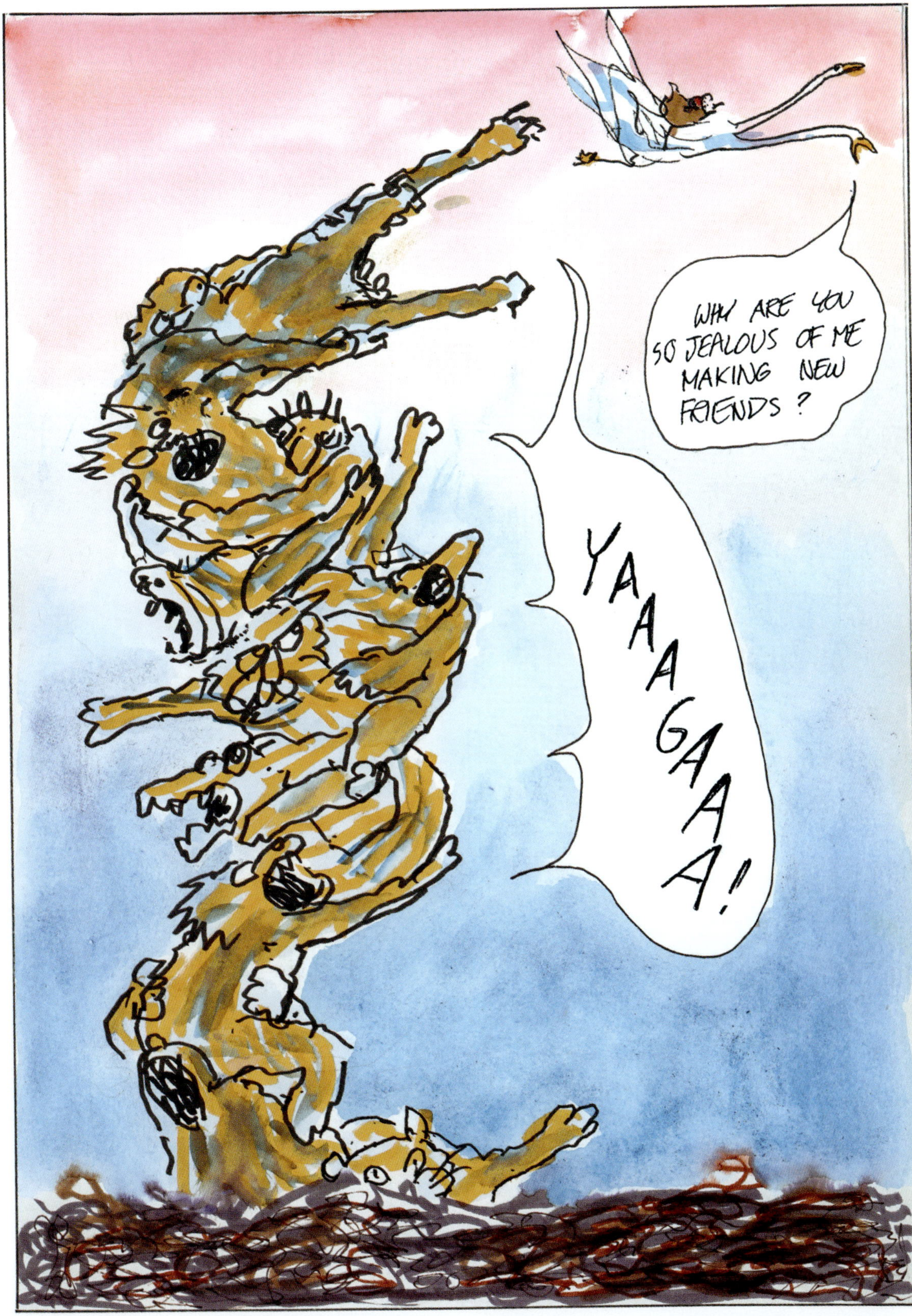
WHY ARE YOU SO JEALOUS OF ME MAKING NEW FRIENDS?
YAAAAGAAAA!

CHAPTER 39 • FACE-TO-FACE

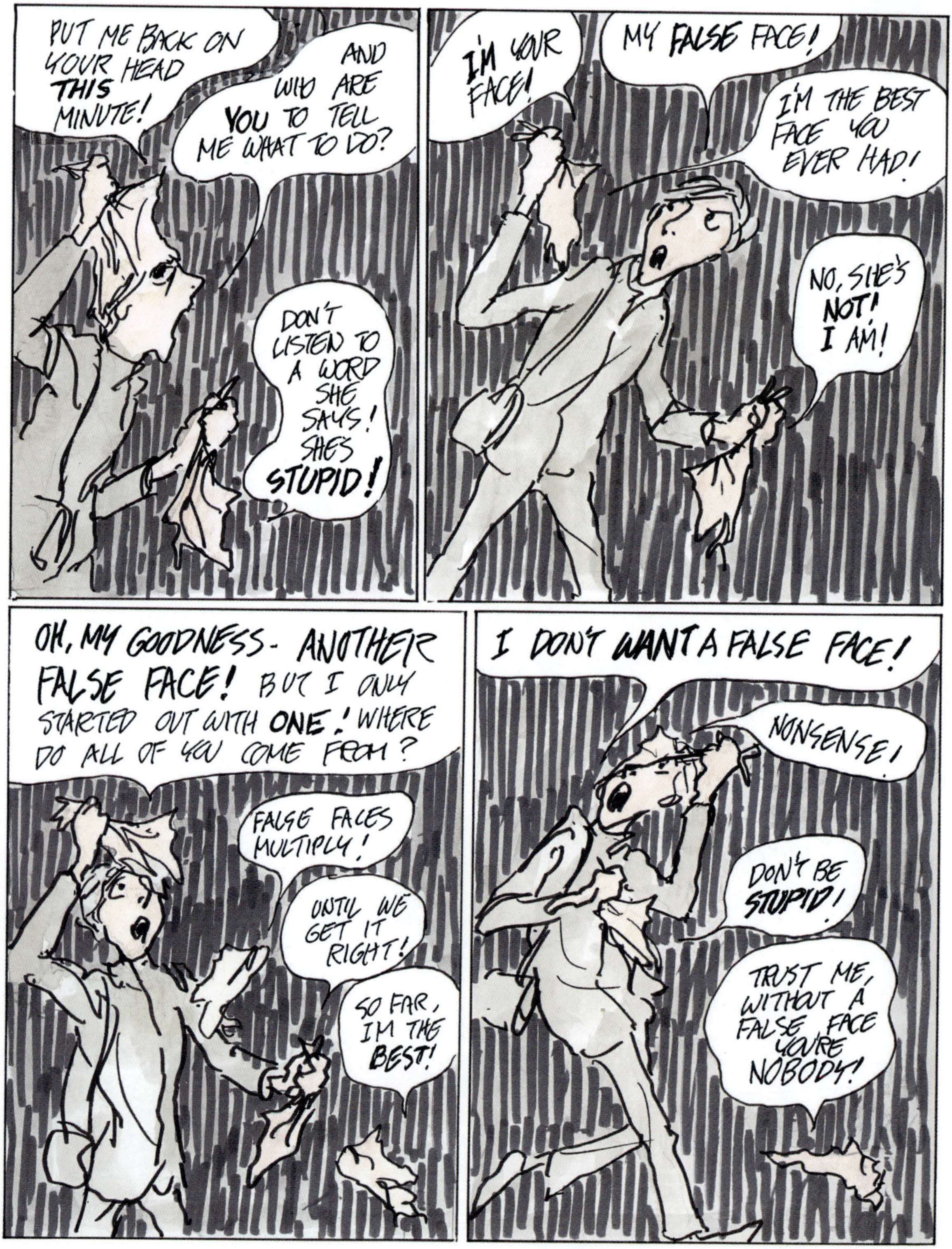

PUT ME BACK ON YOUR HEAD THIS MINUTE!
AND WHO ARE YOU TO TELL ME WHAT TO DO?
DON'T LISTEN TO A WORD SHE SAYS! SHE'S STUPID!
I'M YOUR FACE!
MY FALSE FACE!
I'M THE BEST FACE YOU EVER HAD!
NO, SHE'S NOT! I AM!
OH, MY GOODNESS- ANOTHER FALSE FACE! BUT I ONLY STARTED OUT WITH ONE! WHERE DO ALL OF YOU COME FROM?
FALSE FACES MULTIPLY!
UNTIL WE GET IT RIGHT!
SO FAR, I'M THE BEST!
I DON'T WANT A FALSE FACE!
NONSENSE!
DON'T BE STUPID!
TRUST ME, WITHOUT A FALSE FACE YOU'RE NOBODY!

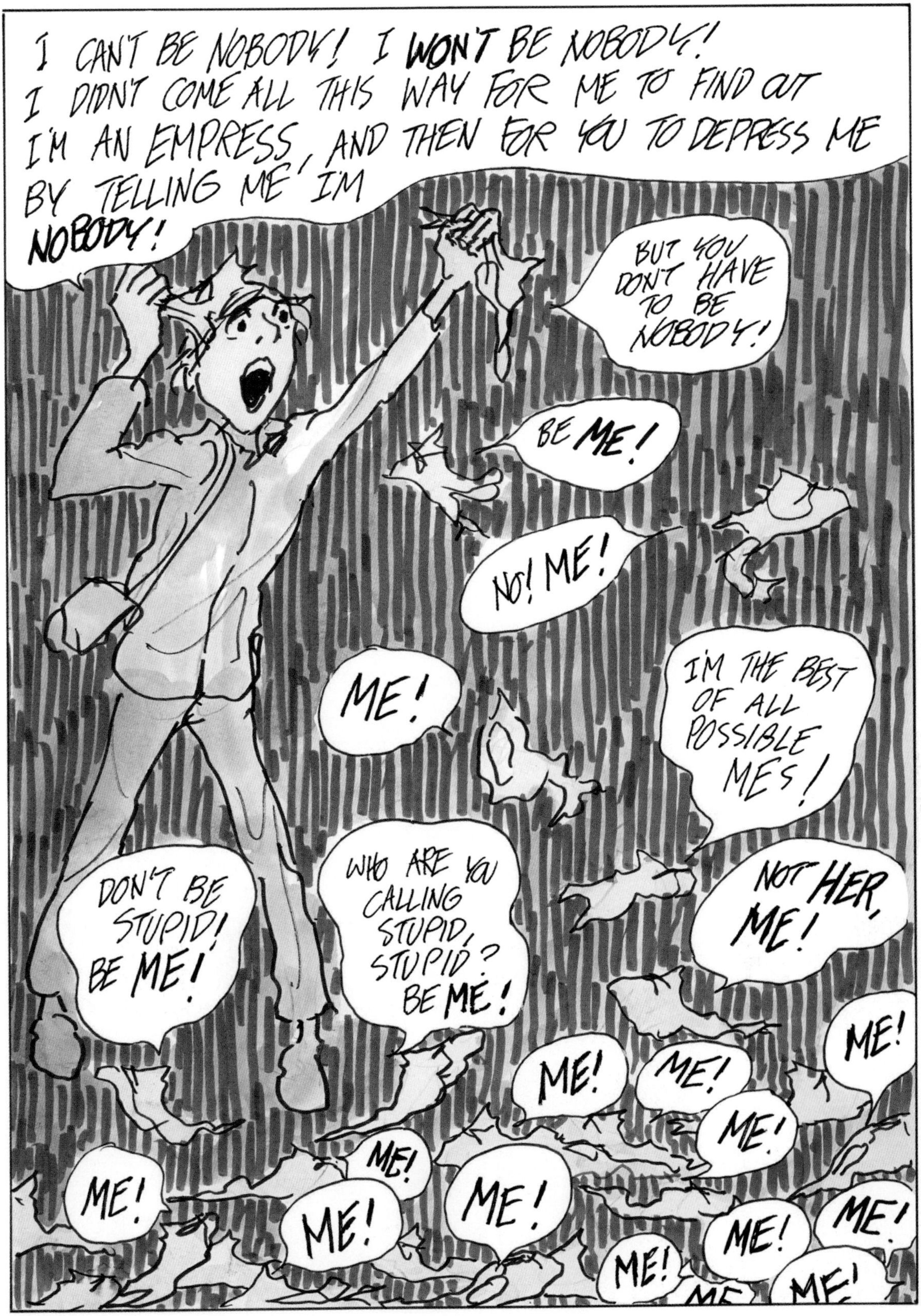
I CAN'T BE NOBODY! I WON'T BE NOBODY! I DIDN'T COME ALL THIS WAY FOR ME TO FIND OUT I'M AN EMPRESS, AND THEN FOR YOU TO DEPRESS ME BY TELLING ME I'M NOBODY!
BUT YOU DON'T HAVE TO BE NOBODY!
BE ME!
NO! ME!
ME!
I'M THE BEST OF ALL POSSIBLE ME'S!
DON'T BE STUPID! BE ME!
WHO ARE YOU CALLING STUPID, STUPID? BE ME!
NOT HER, ME!
ME!
ME!
ME!
ME!
ME!
ME!
ME!
ME!
ME!
ME!
ME!
ME!

CHAPTER 40 • WHERE'S HERE?

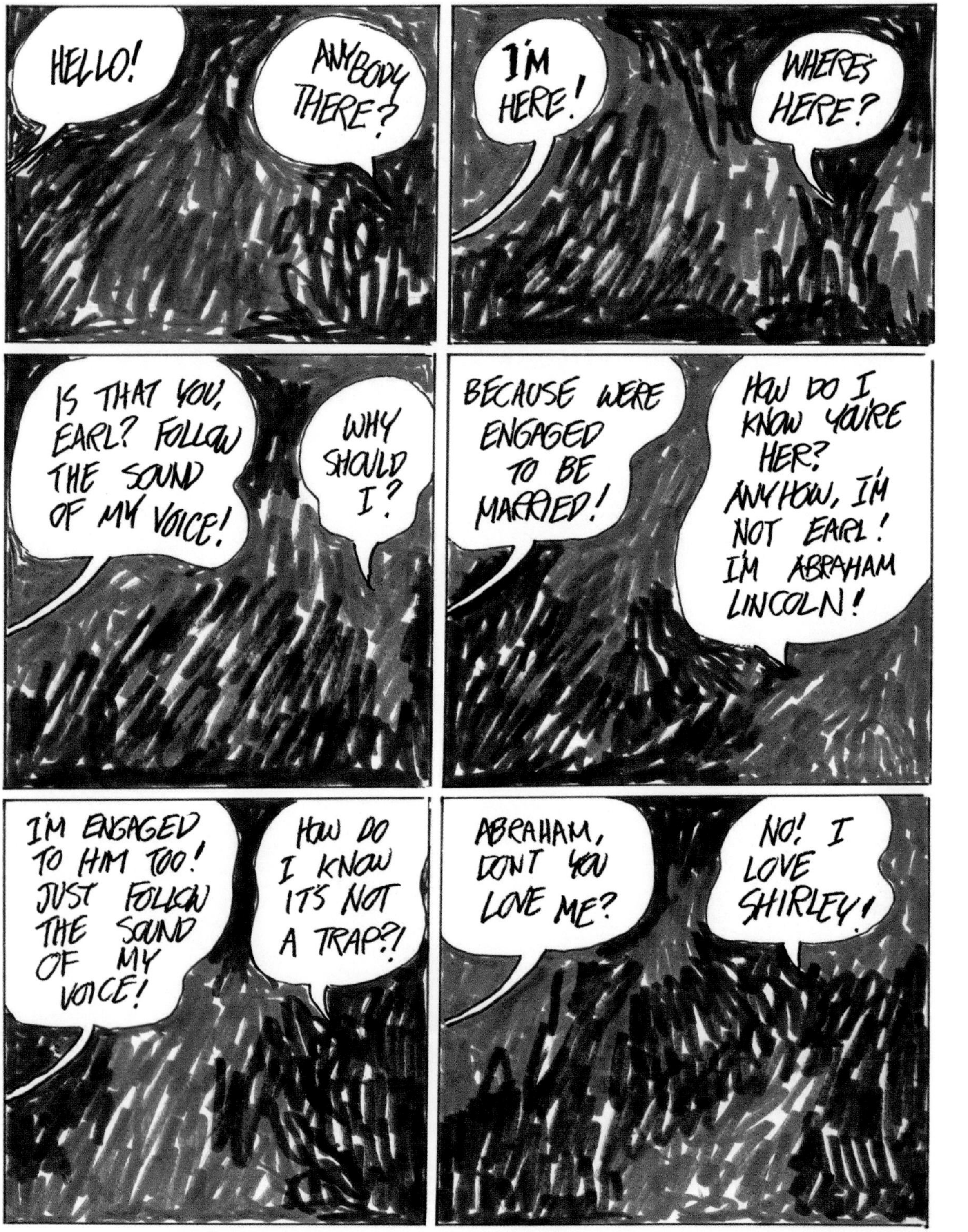

HELLO!
ANYBODY THERE?
I'M HERE!
WHERE'S HERE?
IS THAT YOU, EARL? FOLLOW THE SOUND OF MY VOICE!
WHY SHOULD I?
BECAUSE WERE ENGAGED TO BE MARRIED!
HOW DO I KNOW YOU'RE HER? ANYHOW, I'M NOT EARL! I'M ABRAHAM LINCOLN!
I'M ENGAGED TO HIM TOO! JUST FOLLOW THE SOUND OF MY VOICE!
HOW DO I KNOW IT'S NOT A TRAP?!
ABRAHAM, DONT YOU LOVE ME?
NO! I LOVE SHIRLEY!

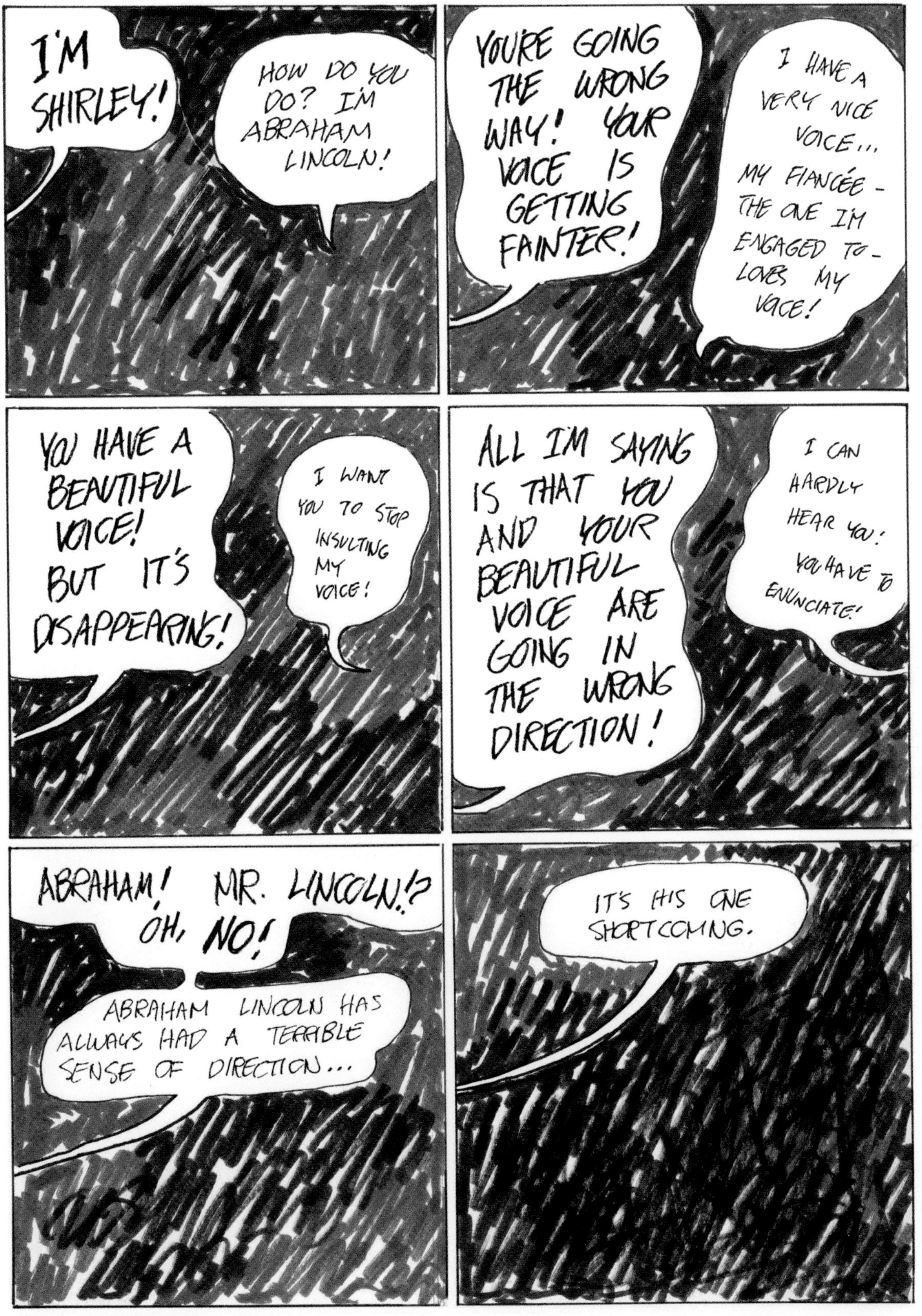
I'M SHIRLEY!
HOW DO YOU DO? I'M ABRAHAM LINCOLN!
YOU'RE GOING THE WRONG WAY! YOUR VOICE IS GETTING FAINTER!
I HAVE A VERY NICE VOICE... MY FIANCÉE - THE ONE I'M ENGAGED TO - LOVES MY VOICE!
YOU HAVE A BEAUTIFUL VOICE! BUT IT'S DISAPPEARING!
I WANT YOU TO STOP INSULTING MY VOICE!
ALL I'M SAYING IS THAT YOU AND YOUR BEAUTIFUL VOICE ARE GOING IN THE WRONG DIRECTION!
I CAN HARDLY HEAR YOU! YOU HAVE TO ENUNCIATE!
ABRAHAM! MR. LINCOLN!? OH, NO!
ABRAHAM LINCOLN HAS ALWAYS HAD A TERRIBLE SENSE OF DIRECTION...
IT'S HIS ONE SHORTCOMING.

CHAPTER 41 • NO WORRY

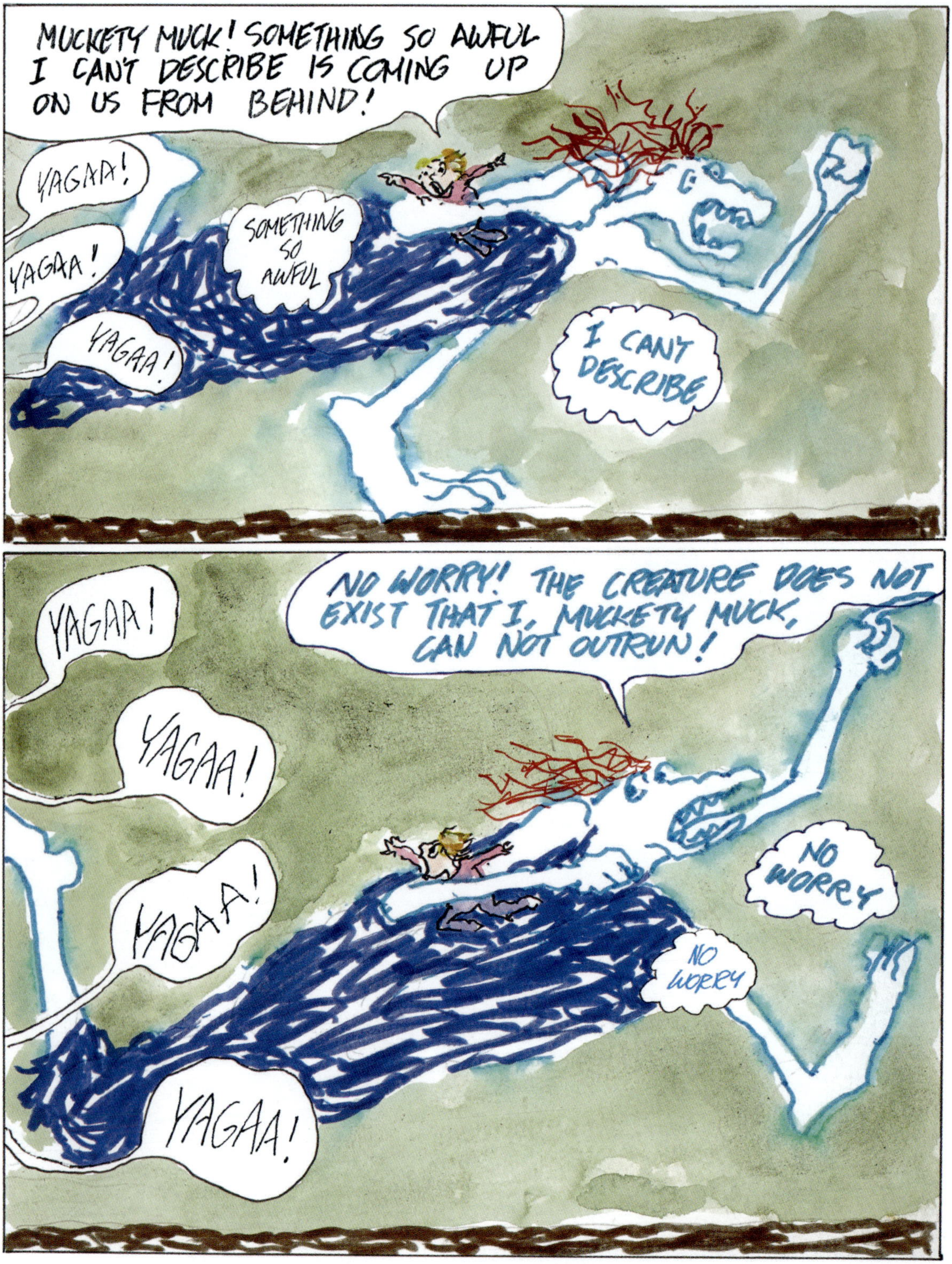

MUCKETY MUCK! SOMETHING SO AWFUL I CAN'T DESCRIBE IS COMING UP ON US FROM BEHIND!
YAGAA!
YAGAA!
YAGAA!
SOMETHING SO AWFUL
I CAN'T DESCRIBE
NO WORRY! THE CREATURE DOES NOT EXIST THAT I, MUCKETY MUCK, CAN NOT OUTRUN!
YAGAA!
YAGAA!
YAGAA!
YAGAA!
NO WORRY
NO WORRY

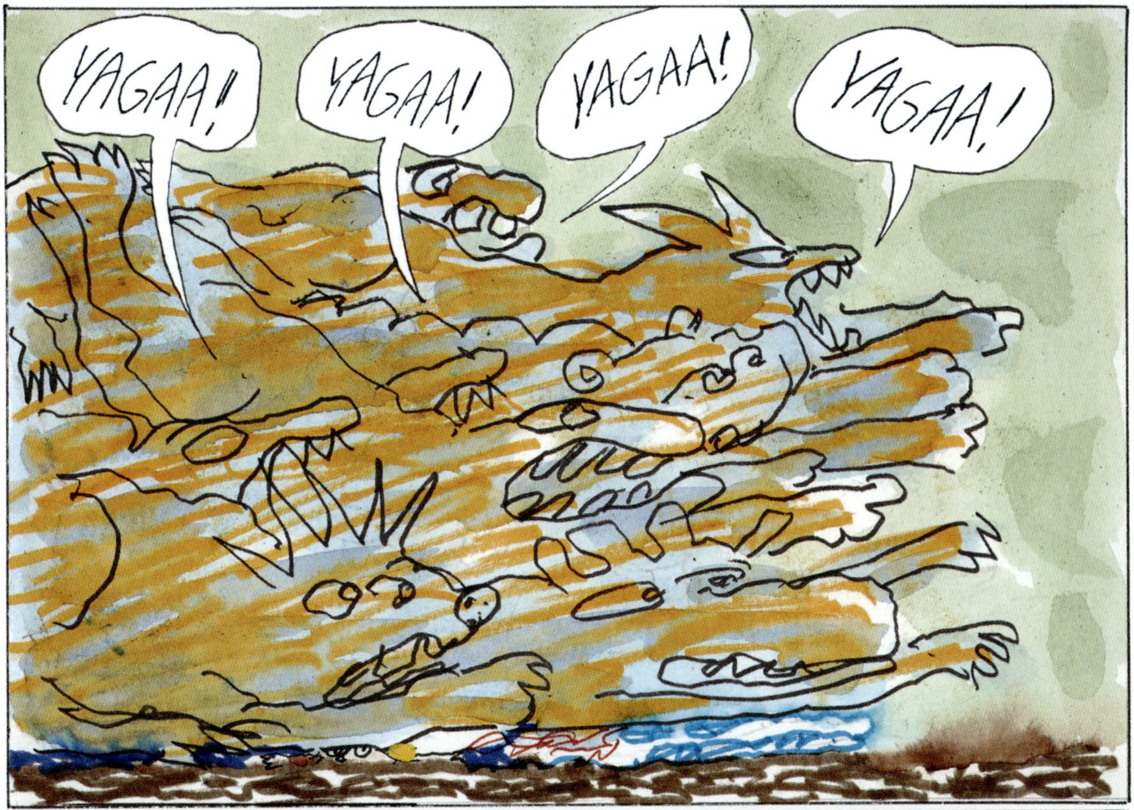
YAGAA!
YAGAA!
YAGAA!
YAGAA!

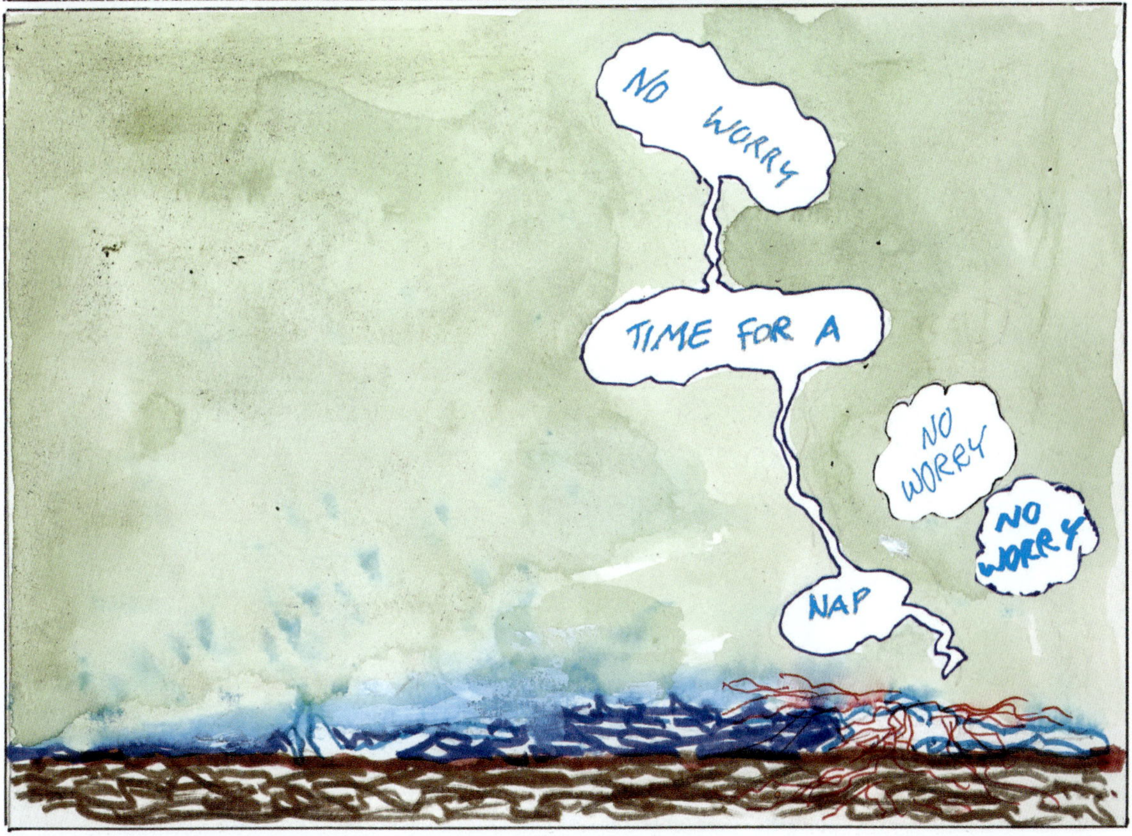
NO WORRY
TIME FOR A
NAP
NO WORRY
NO WORRY

CHAPTER 42 • ONE MORE DUMB THING

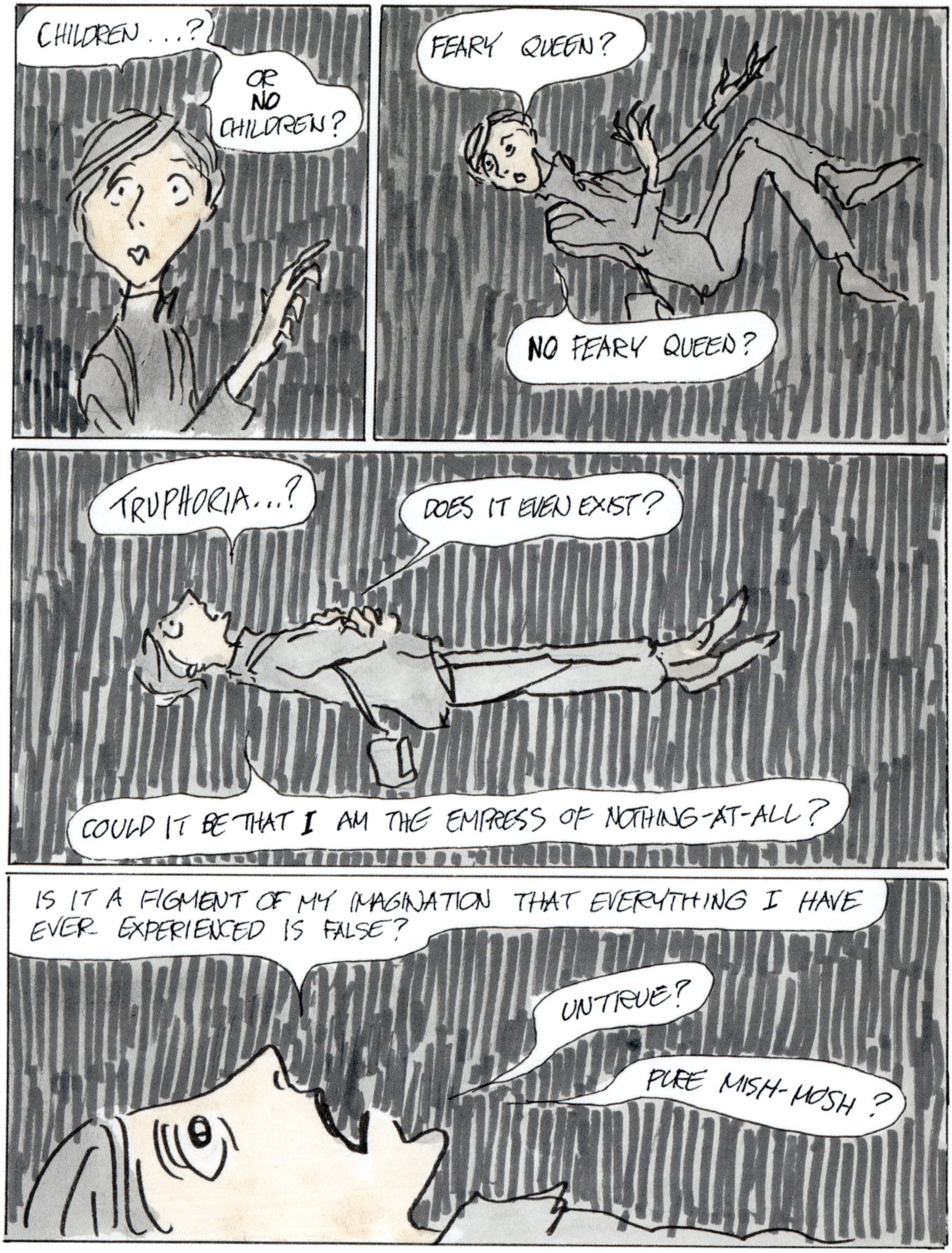
CHILDREN . . . ?
OR NO CHILDREN?
FEARY QUEEN?
NO FEARY QUEEN?
TRUPHORIA . . . ?
DOES IT EVEN EXIST?
COULD IT BE THAT I AM THE EMPRESS OF NOTHING-AT-ALL?
IS IT A FIGMENT OF MY IMAGINATION THAT EVERYTHING I HAVE EVER EXPERIENCED IS FALSE?
UNTRUE?
PURE MISH-MOSH?

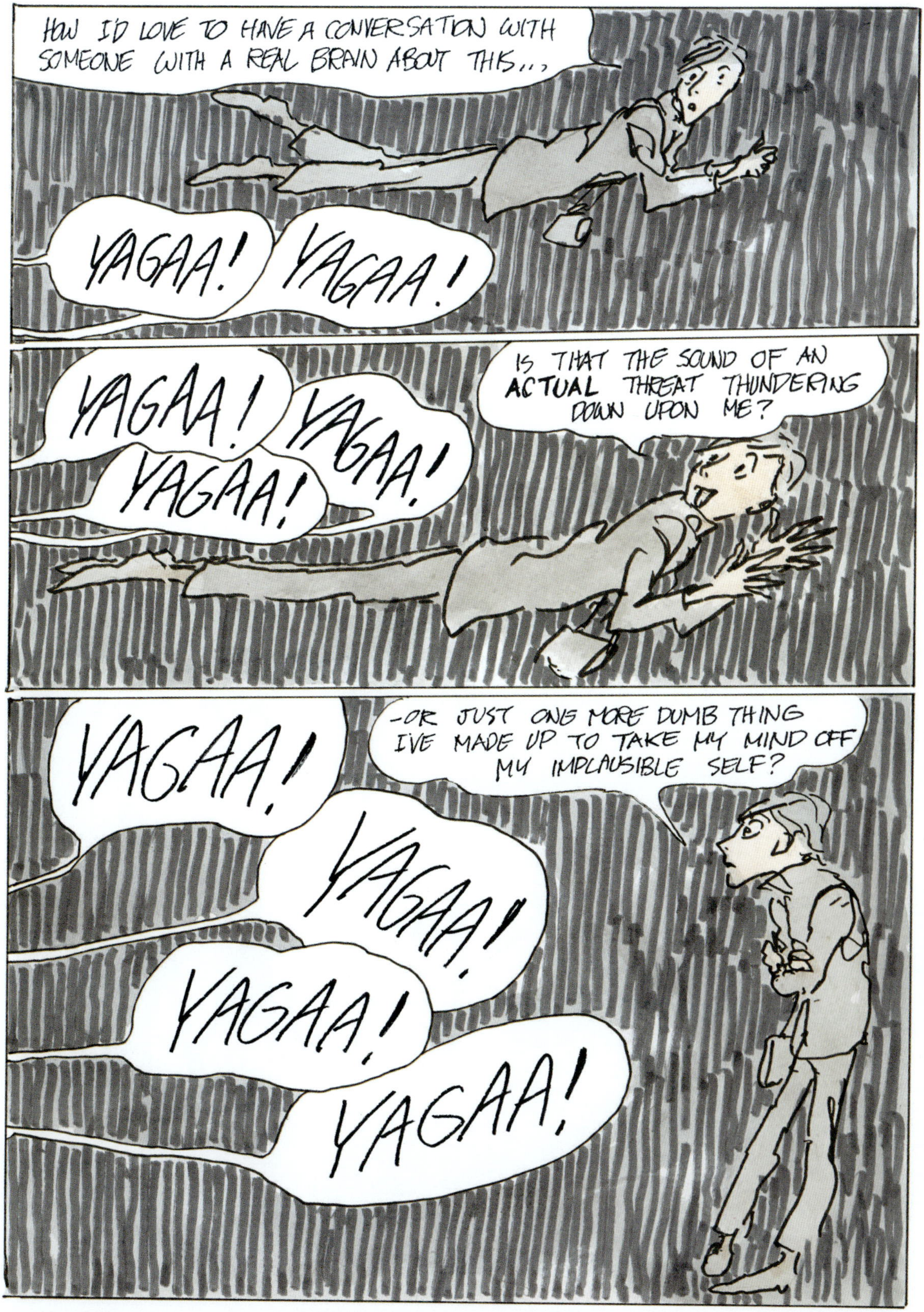
HOW I'D LOVE TO HAVE A CONVERSATION WITH SOMEONE WITH A REAL BRAIN ABOUT THIS...
YAGAA!
YAGAA!
YAGAA!
YAGAA!
YAGAA!
IS THAT THE SOUND OF AN ACTUAL THREAT THUNDERING DOWN UPON ME?
YAGAA!
-OR JUST ONE MORE DUMB THING I'VE MADE UP TO TAKE MY MIND OFF MY IMPLAUSIBLE SELF?
YAGAA!
YAGAA!
YAGAA!

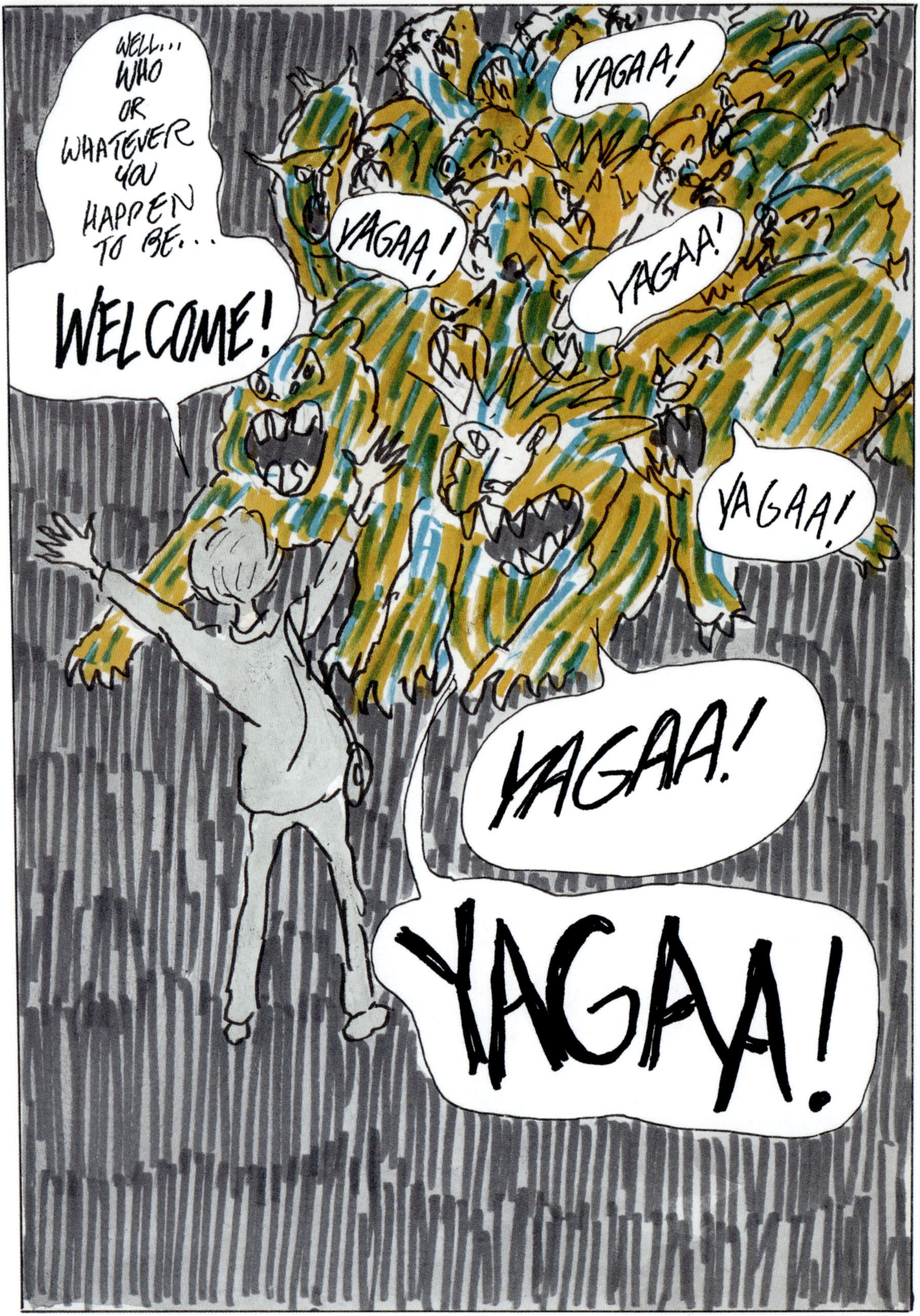
WELL... WHO OR WHATEVER YOU HAPPEN TO BE... WELCOME!
YAGAA!
YAGAA!
YAGAA!
YAGAA!
YAGAA!
YAGAA!

CHAPTER 43 • ARF/MEOW!

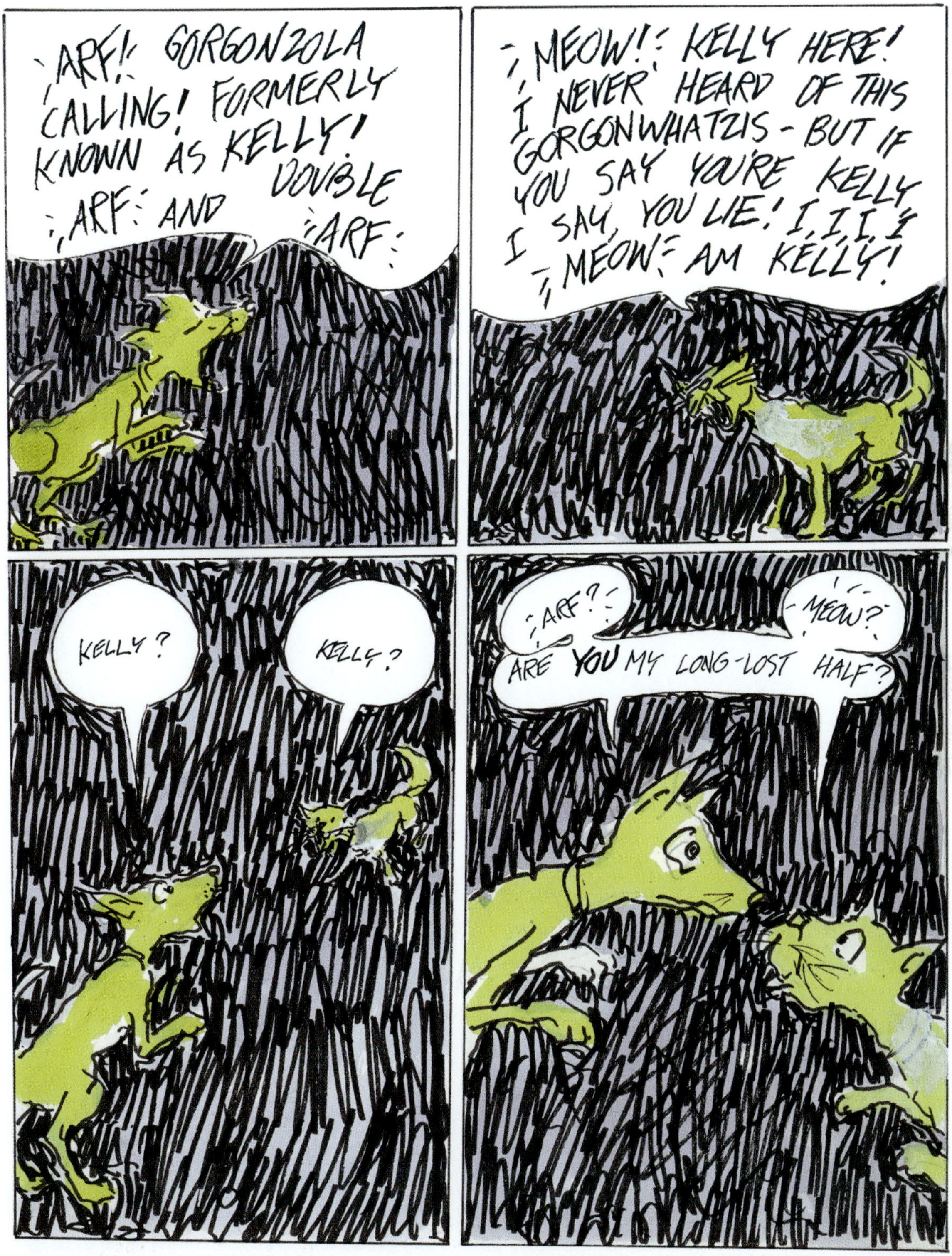
ARF! GORGONZOLA CALLING! FORMERLY KNOWN AS KELLY! ARF AND DOUBLE ARF
MEOW! KELLY HERE! I NEVER HEARD OF THIS GORGONWHATZIS - BUT IF YOU SAY YOU'RE KELLY I SAY, YOU LIE! I, I, I MEOW AM KELLY!
KELLY?
KELLY?
ARF?
MEOW?
ARE YOU MY LONG-LOST HALF?

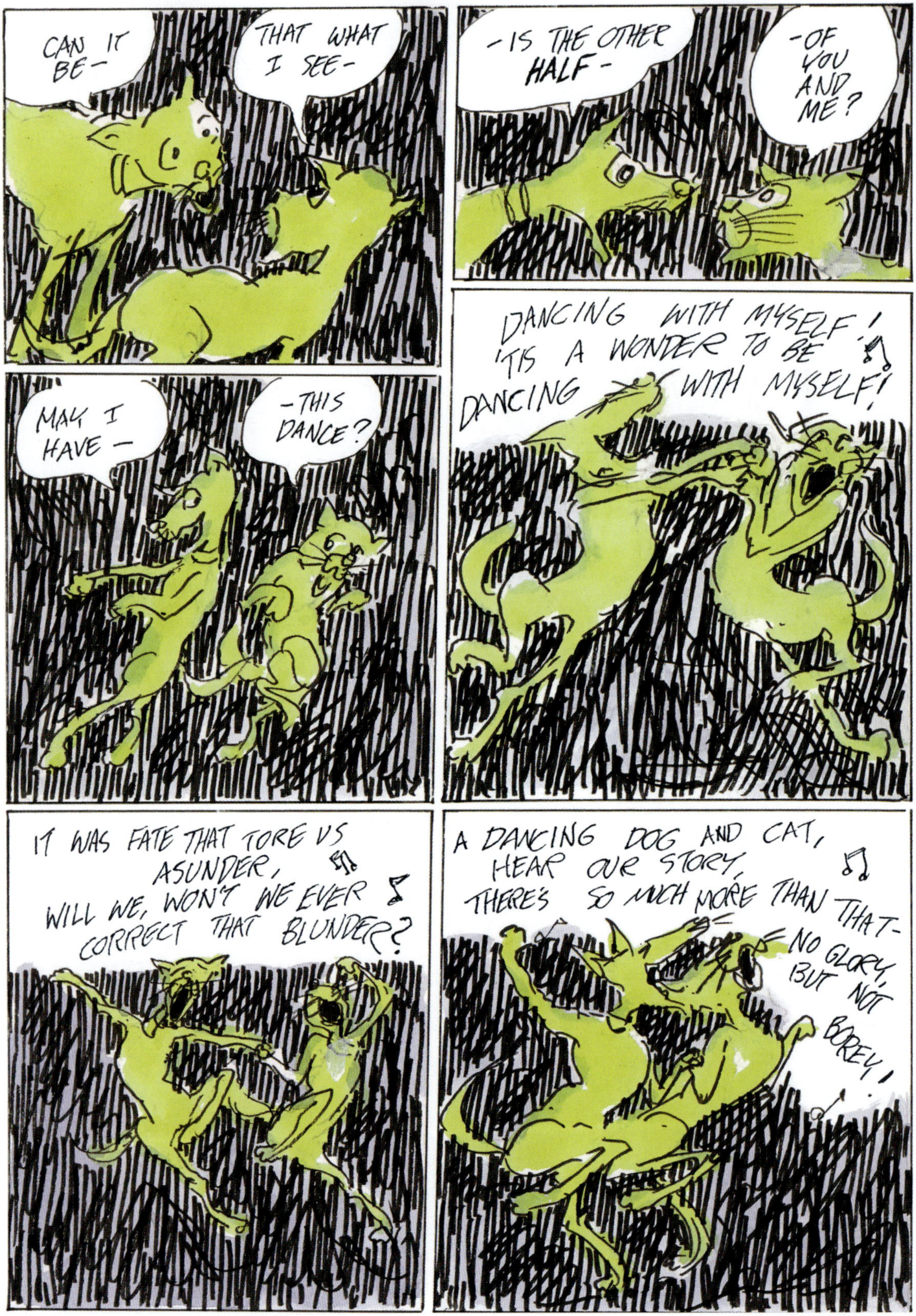

CAN IT BE-
THAT WHAT I SEE-
-IS THE OTHER HALF-
-OF YOU AND ME?
MAY I HAVE-
-THIS DANCE?
DANCING WITH MYSELF! 'TIS A WONDER TO BE DANCING WITH MYSELF!
IT WAS FATE THAT TORE US ASUNDER, WILL WE, WON'T WE EVER CORRECT THAT BLUNDER?
A DANCING DOG AND CAT, HEAR OUR STORY, THERE'S SO MUCH MORE THAN THAT-
-NO GLORY, BUT NOT BOREY!

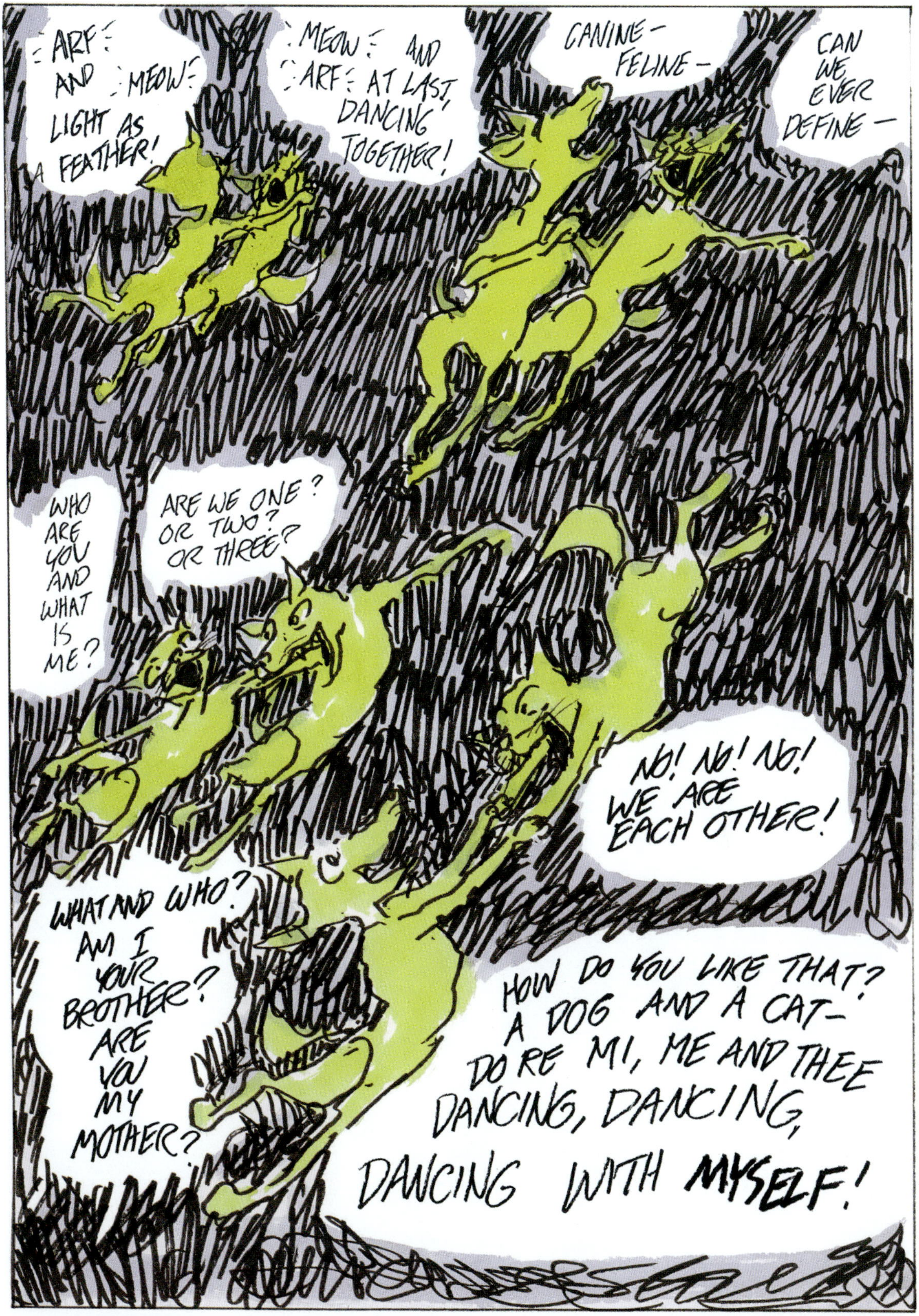
ARF AND MEOW LIGHT AS A FEATHER!
MEOW AND ARF AT LAST, DANCING TOGETHER!
CANINE-
FELINE-
CAN WE EVER DEFINE-
WHO ARE YOU AND WHAT IS ME?
ARE WE ONE? OR TWO? OR THREE?
NO! NO! NO! WE ARE EACH OTHER!
WHAT AND WHO? AM I YOUR BROTHER? ARE YOU MY MOTHER?
HOW DO YOU LIKE THAT? A DOG AND A CAT- DO RE MI, ME AND THEE DANCING, DANCING, DANCING WITH MYSELF!

CHAPTER 44 • NAUGHTY DOOMANIANS

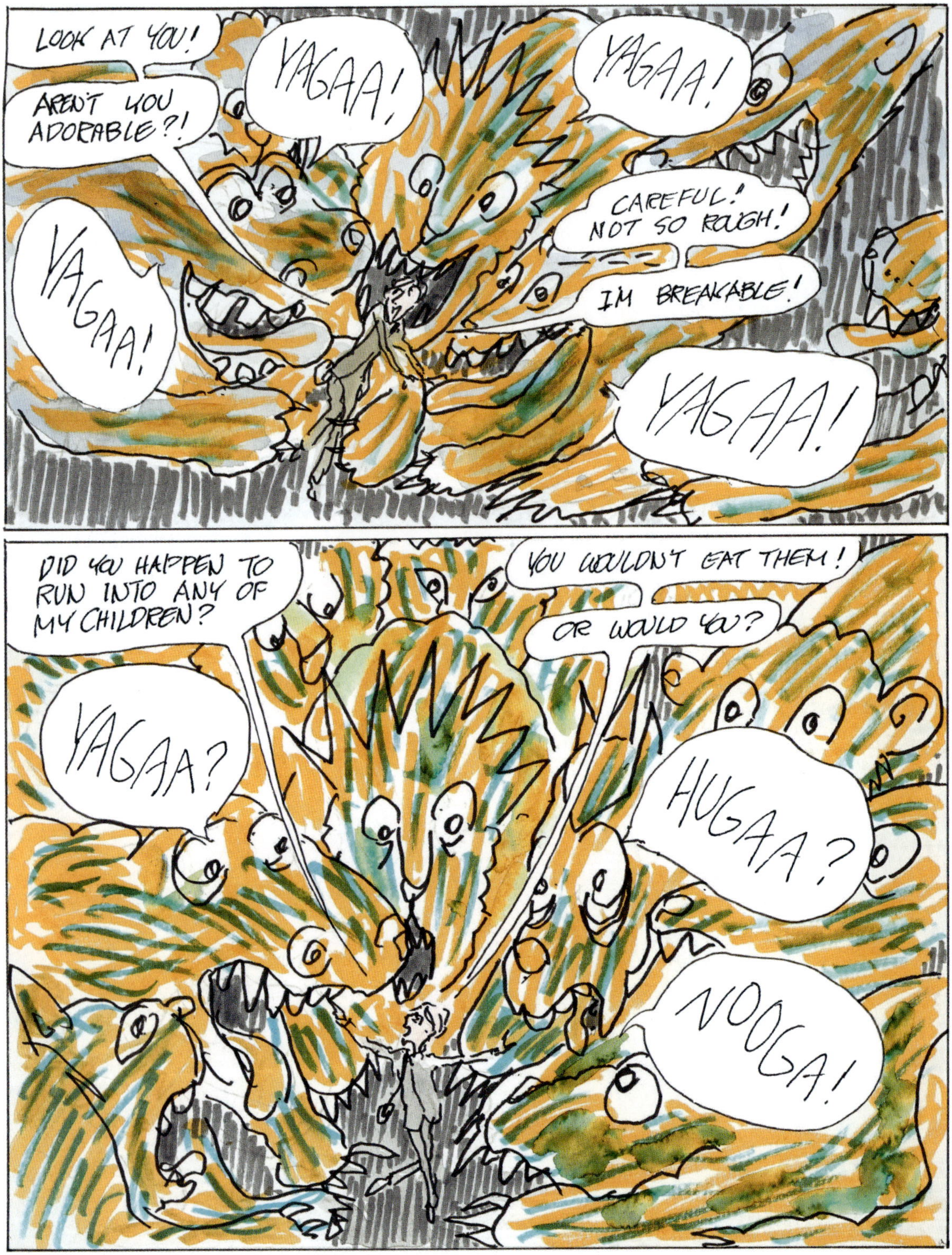
LOOK AT YOU!
AREN'T YOU ADORABLE?!
YAGAA!
YAGAA!
YAGAA!
CAREFUL! NOT SO ROUGH!
I'M BREAKABLE!
YAGAA!
DID YOU HAPPEN TO RUN INTO ANY OF MY CHILDREN?
YOU WOULDN'T EAT THEM!
OR WOULD YOU?
YAGAA?
HUGAA?
NOOGA!

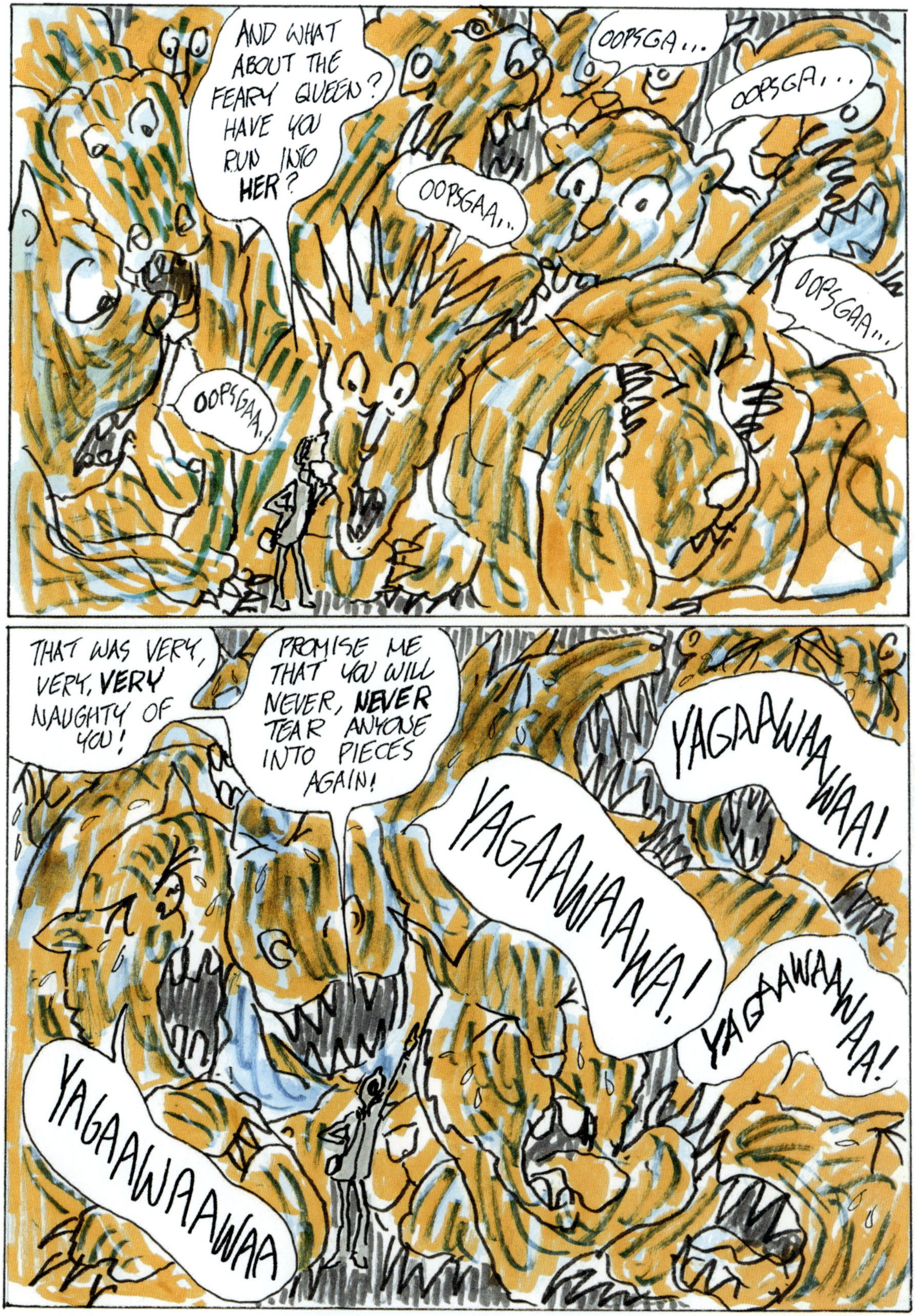
AND WHAT ABOUT THE FEARY QUEEN? HAVE YOU RUN INTO **HER**?
OOPSGA...
OOPSGA...
OOPSGAA...
OOPSGAA...
OOPSGAA.
THAT WAS VERY, VERY, **VERY** NAUGHTY OF YOU!
PROMISE ME THAT YOU WILL NEVER, **NEVER** TEAR ANYONE INTO PIECES AGAIN!
YAGAAWAAWAA!
YAGAAWAAWA!
YAGAAWAAWAA!
YAGAAWAAWAA

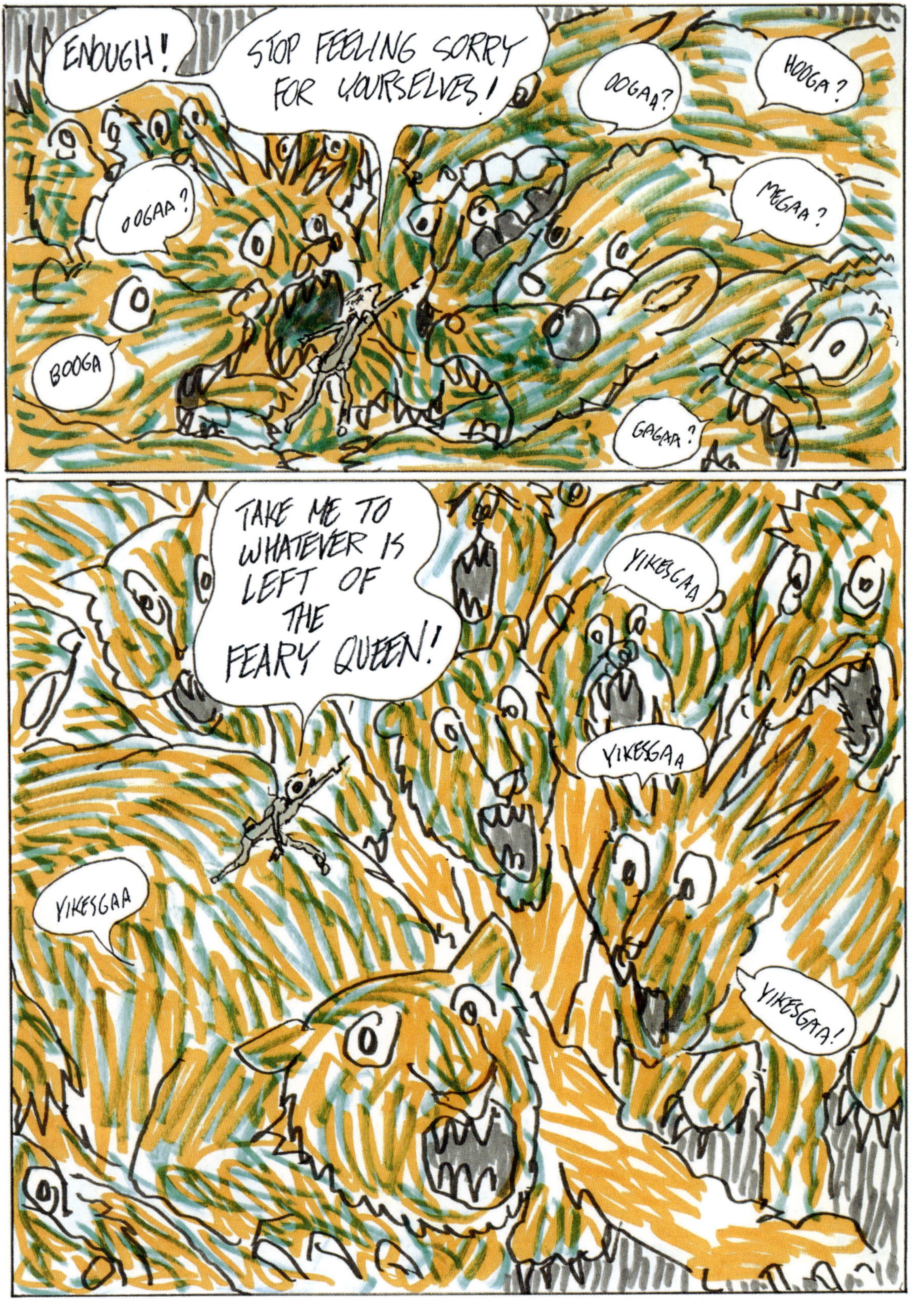
ENOUGH!
STOP FEELING SORRY FOR YOURSELVES!
OOGAA?
HOOGA?
OOGAA?
MEGAA?
BOOGA
GAGAA?
TAKE ME TO WHATEVER IS LEFT OF THE FEARY QUEEN!
YIKESGAA
YIKESGAA
YIKESGAA
YIKESGAA!

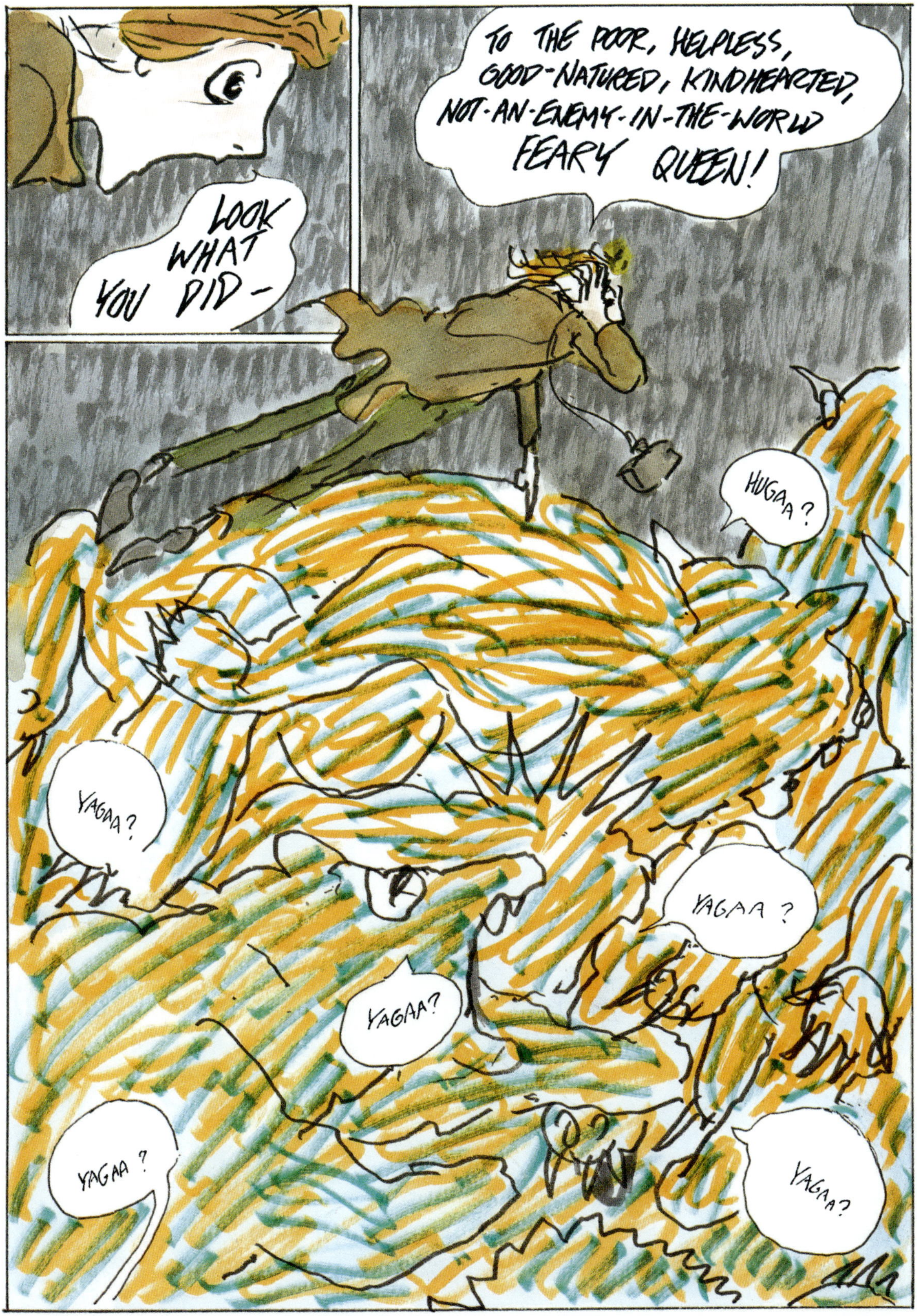
LOOK WHAT YOU DID -
TO THE POOR, HELPLESS, GOOD-NATURED, KINDHEARTED, NOT-AN-ENEMY-IN-THE-WORLD FEARY QUEEN!
HUGAA?
YAGAA?
YAGAA?
YAGAA?
YAGAA?
YAGAA?

CHAPTER 45 • DEAD, NOT DEAD

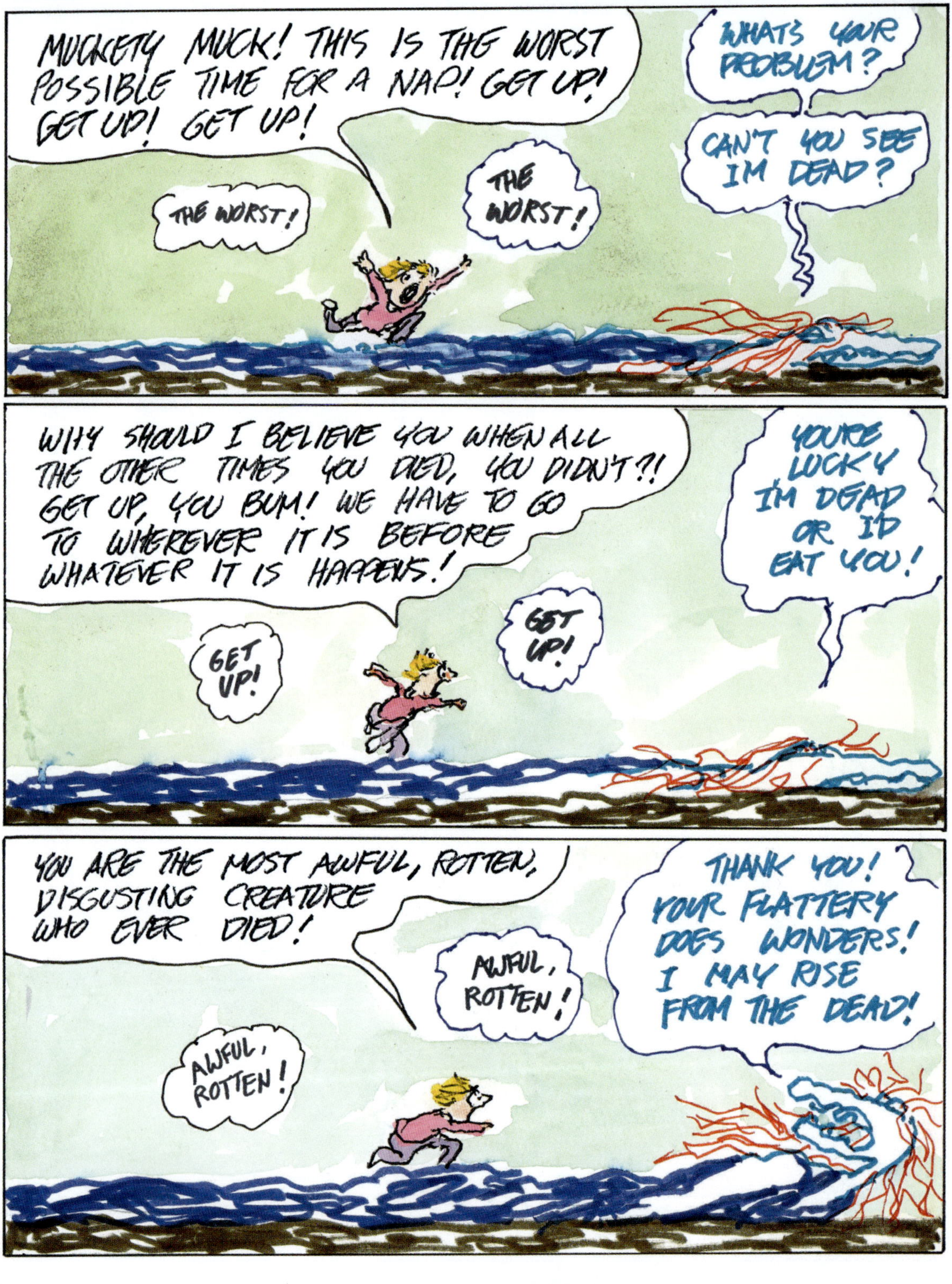
MUCKETY MUCK! THIS IS THE WORST POSSIBLE TIME FOR A NAP! GET UP! GET UP! GET UP!
THE WORST!
THE WORST!
WHAT'S YOUR PROBLEM?
CAN'T YOU SEE I'M DEAD?
WHY SHOULD I BELIEVE YOU WHEN ALL THE OTHER TIMES YOU DIED, YOU DIDN'T?! GET UP, YOU BUM! WE HAVE TO GO TO WHEREVER IT IS BEFORE WHATEVER IT IS HAPPENS!
GET UP!
GET UP!
YOU'RE LUCKY I'M DEAD OR I'D EAT YOU!
YOU ARE THE MOST AWFUL, ROTTEN, DISGUSTING CREATURE WHO EVER DIED!
AWFUL, ROTTEN!
AWFUL, ROTTEN!
THANK YOU! YOUR FLATTERY DOES WONDERS! I MAY RISE FROM THE DEAD!

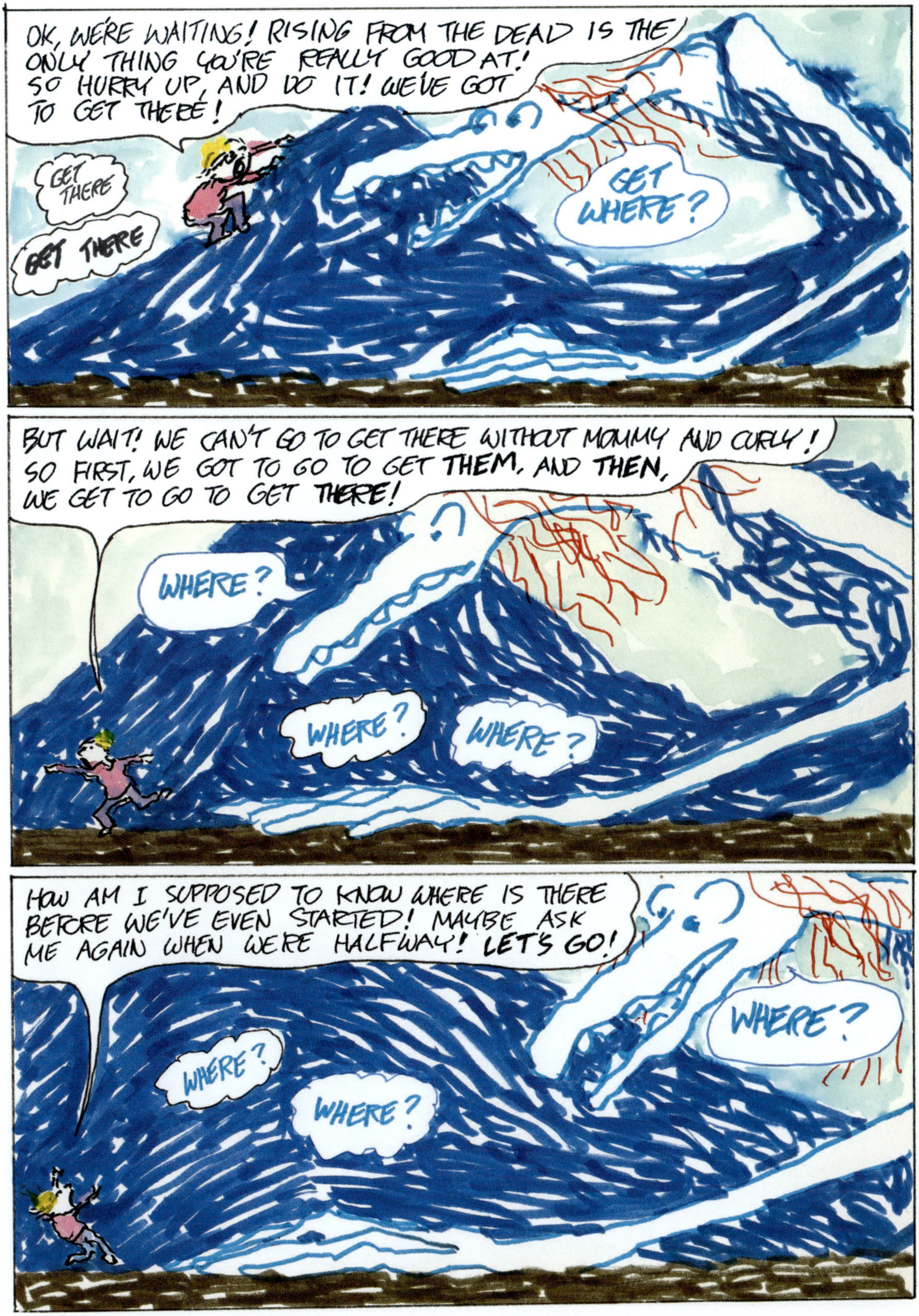
OK, WE'RE WAITING! RISING FROM THE DEAD IS THE ONLY THING YOU'RE REALLY GOOD AT! SO HURRY UP, AND DO IT! WE'VE GOT TO GET THERE!
GET THERE
GET THERE
GET WHERE?
BUT WAIT! WE CAN'T GO TO GET THERE WITHOUT MOMMY AND CURLY! SO FIRST, WE GOT TO GO TO GET **THEM**, AND **THEN**, WE GET TO GO TO GET **THERE**!
WHERE?
WHERE?
WHERE?
HOW AM I SUPPOSED TO KNOW WHERE IS THERE BEFORE WE'VE EVEN STARTED! MAYBE ASK ME AGAIN WHEN WE'RE HALFWAY! **LET'S GO!**
WHERE?
WHERE?
WHERE?

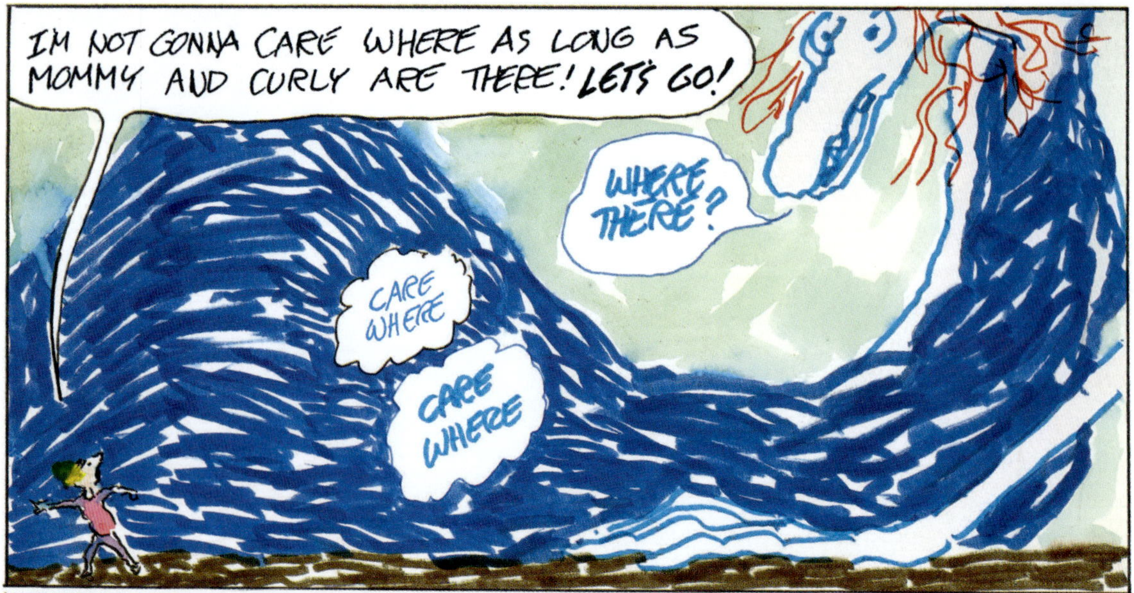
I'M NOT GONNA CARE WHERE AS LONG AS MOMMY AND CURLY ARE THERE! **LET'S GO!**
WHERE THERE?
CARE WHERE
CARE WHERE

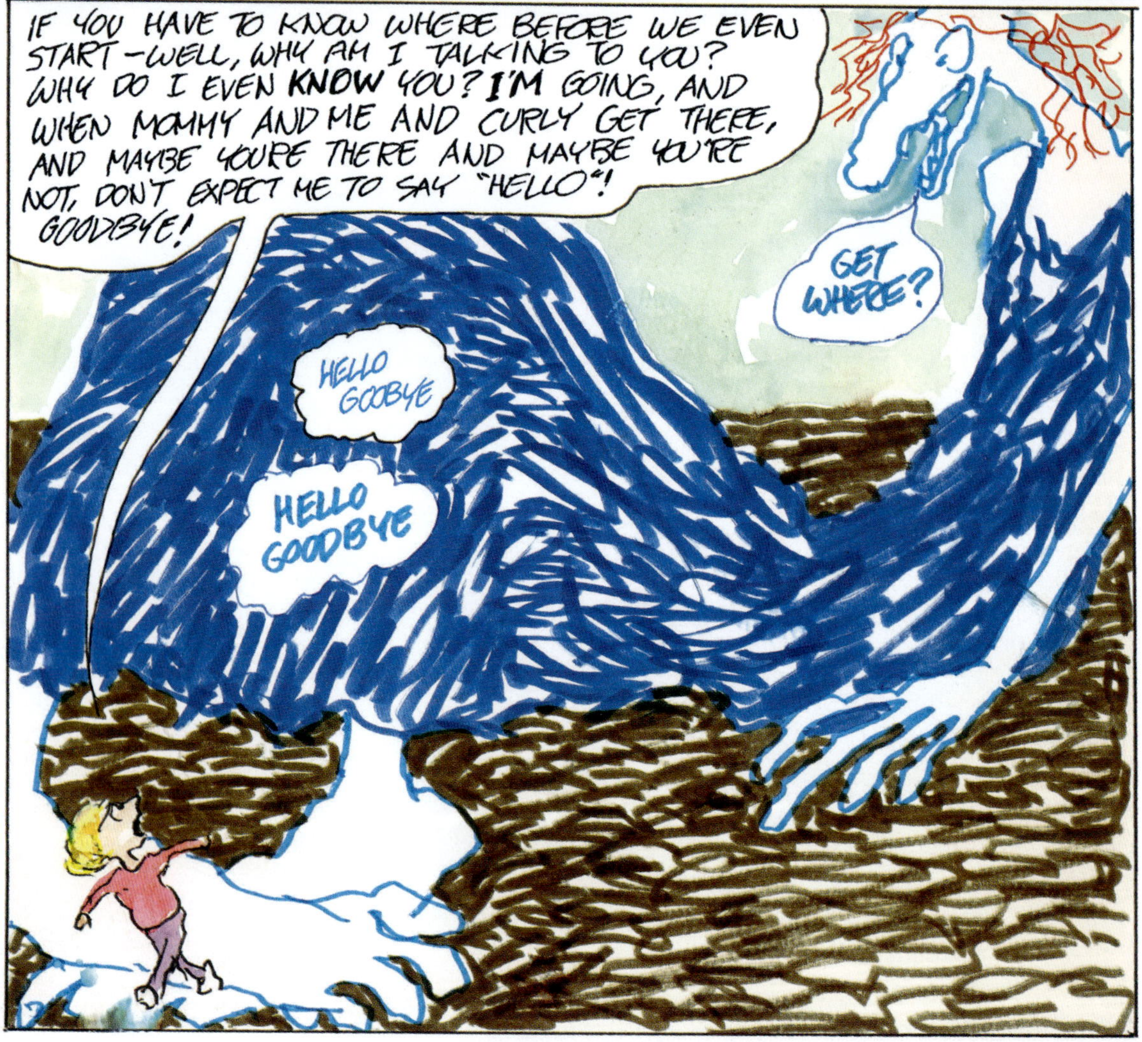
IF YOU HAVE TO KNOW WHERE BEFORE WE EVEN START—WELL, WHY AM I TALKING TO YOU? WHY DO I EVEN **KNOW** YOU? **I'M** GOING, AND WHEN MOMMY AND ME AND CURLY GET THERE, AND MAYBE YOU'RE THERE AND MAYBE YOU'RE NOT, DON'T EXPECT ME TO SAY "HELLO"! GOODBYE!
GET WHERE?
HELLO GOOBYE
HELLO GOODBYE

CHAPTER 46 • DARK LOVE

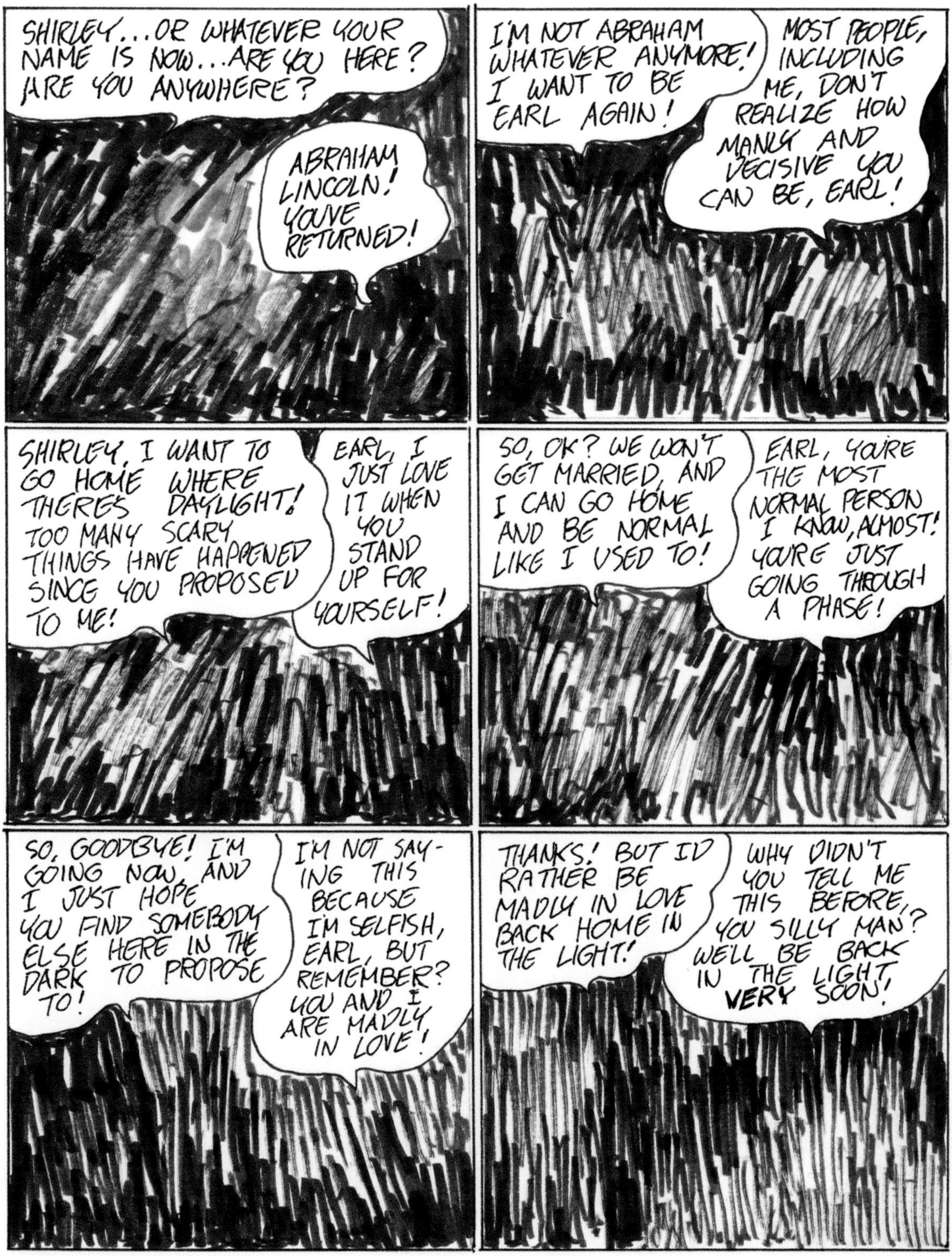

SHIRLEY...OR WHATEVER YOUR NAME IS NOW...ARE YOU HERE? ARE YOU ANYWHERE?
ABRAHAM LINCOLN! YOU'VE RETURNED!
I'M NOT ABRAHAM WHATEVER ANYMORE! I WANT TO BE EARL AGAIN!
MOST PEOPLE, INCLUDING ME, DON'T REALIZE HOW MANLY AND DECISIVE YOU CAN BE, EARL!
SHIRLEY, I WANT TO GO HOME WHERE THERE'S DAYLIGHT! TOO MANY SCARY THINGS HAVE HAPPENED SINCE YOU PROPOSED TO ME!
EARL, I JUST LOVE IT WHEN YOU STAND UP FOR YOURSELF!
SO, OK? WE WON'T GET MARRIED, AND I CAN GO HOME AND BE NORMAL LIKE I USED TO!
EARL, YOU'RE THE MOST NORMAL PERSON I KNOW, ALMOST! YOU'RE JUST GOING THROUGH A PHASE!
SO, GOODBYE! I'M GOING NOW, AND I JUST HOPE YOU FIND SOMEBODY ELSE HERE IN THE DARK TO PROPOSE TO!
I'M NOT SAY-ING THIS BECAUSE I'M SELFISH, EARL, BUT REMEMBER? YOU AND I ARE MADLY IN LOVE!
THANKS! BUT I'D RATHER BE MADLY IN LOVE BACK HOME IN THE LIGHT!
WHY DIDN'T YOU TELL ME THIS BEFORE, YOU SILLY MAN? WE'LL BE BACK IN THE LIGHT, VERY SOON!

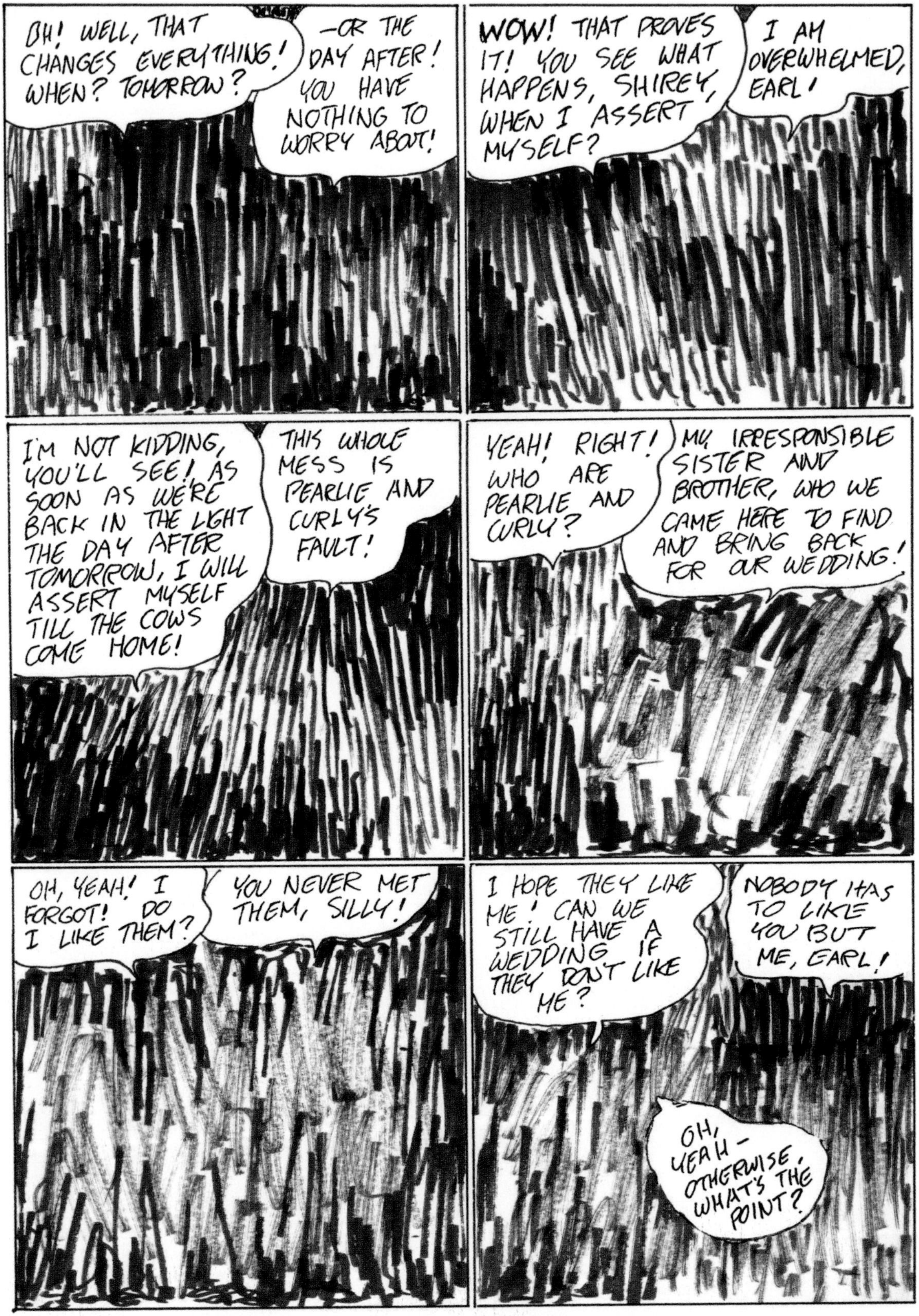

OH! WELL, THAT CHANGES EVERYTHING! WHEN? TOMORROW?
—OR THE DAY AFTER! YOU HAVE NOTHING TO WORRY ABOUT!
WOW! THAT PROVES IT! YOU SEE WHAT HAPPENS, SHIREY, WHEN I ASSERT MYSELF?
I AM OVERWHELMED, EARL!
I'M NOT KIDDING, YOU'LL SEE! AS SOON AS WE'RE BACK IN THE LIGHT THE DAY AFTER TOMORROW, I WILL ASSERT MYSELF TILL THE COWS COME HOME!
THIS WHOLE MESS IS PEARLIE AND CURLY'S FAULT!
YEAH! RIGHT! WHO ARE PEARLIE AND CURLY?
MY IRRESPONSIBLE SISTER AND BROTHER, WHO WE CAME HERE TO FIND AND BRING BACK FOR OUR WEDDING!
OH, YEAH! I FORGOT! DO I LIKE THEM?
YOU NEVER MET THEM, SILLY!
I HOPE THEY LIKE ME! CAN WE STILL HAVE A WEDDING IF THEY DON'T LIKE ME?
NOBODY HAS TO LIKE YOU BUT ME, EARL!
OH, YEAH — OTHERWISE, WHAT'S THE POINT?

CHAPTER 47 • DARK TRUTH

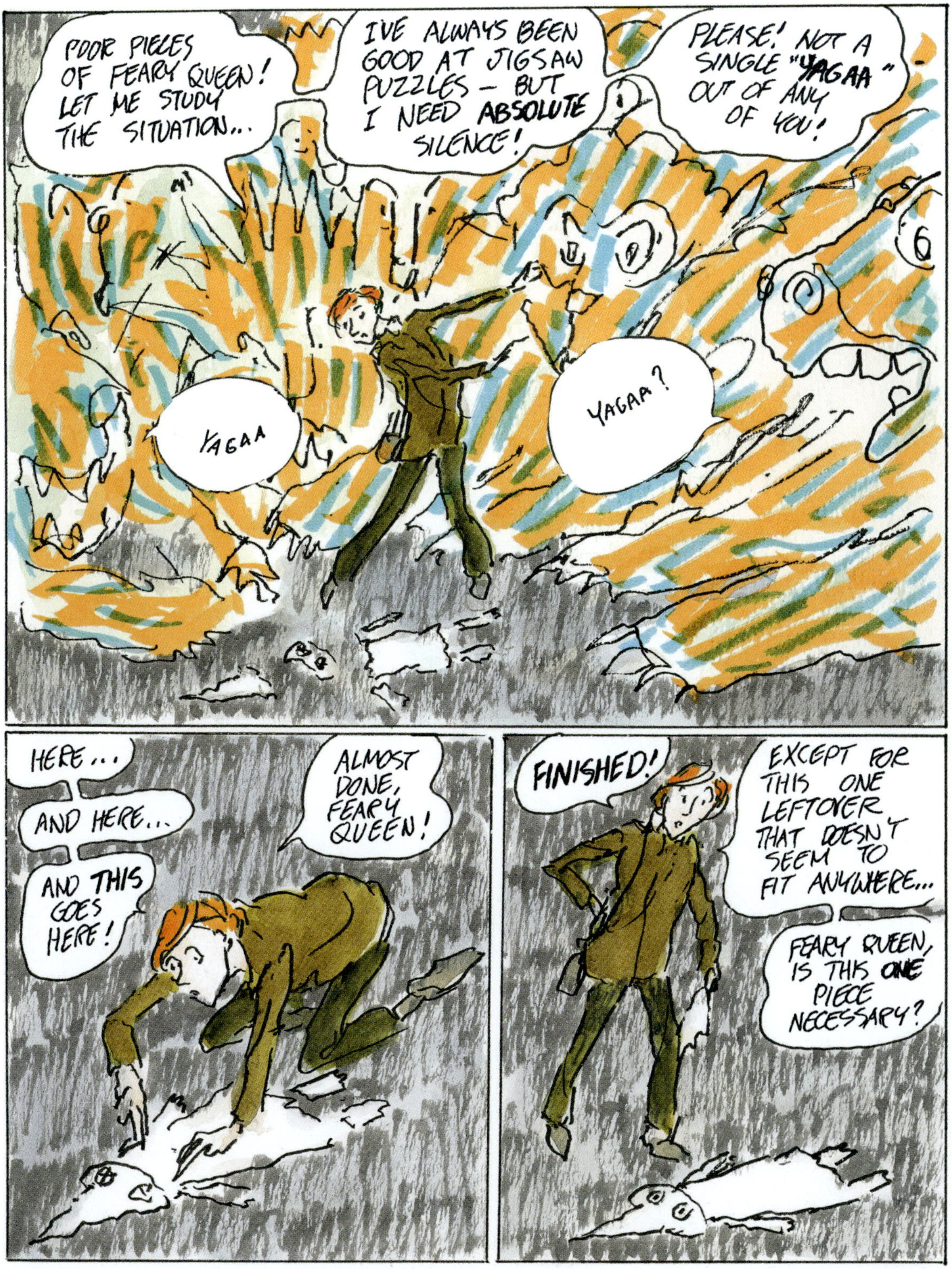
POOR PIECES OF FEARY QUEEN! LET ME STUDY THE SITUATION...
I'VE ALWAYS BEEN GOOD AT JIGSAW PUZZLES — BUT I NEED **ABSOLUTE** SILENCE!
PLEASE! NOT A SINGLE "**YAGAA**" OUT OF ANY OF YOU!
YAGAA
YAGAA?
HERE...
AND HERE...
AND **THIS** GOES HERE!
ALMOST DONE, FEARY QUEEN!
FINISHED!
EXCEPT FOR THIS ONE LEFTOVER THAT DOESN'T SEEM TO FIT ANYWHERE...
FEARY QUEEN, IS THIS **ONE** PIECE NECESSARY?

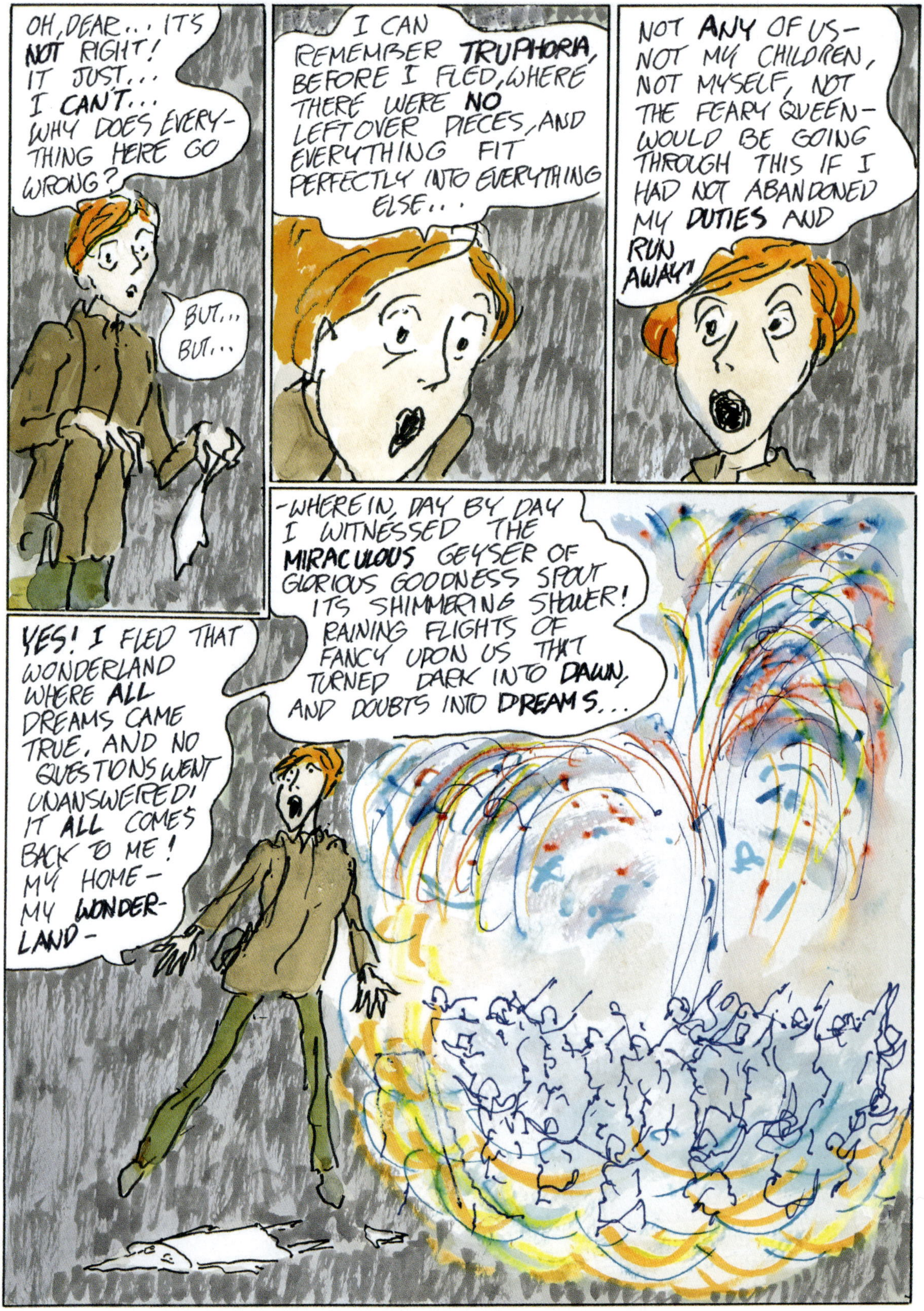
OH, DEAR... IT'S NOT RIGHT! IT JUST... I CAN'T... WHY DOES EVERYTHING HERE GO WRONG?
BUT... BUT...
I CAN REMEMBER TRUPHORIA, BEFORE I FLED, WHERE THERE WERE NO LEFTOVER PIECES, AND EVERYTHING FIT PERFECTLY INTO EVERYTHING ELSE...
NOT ANY OF US– NOT MY CHILDREN, NOT MYSELF, NOT THE FEARY QUEEN– WOULD BE GOING THROUGH THIS IF I HAD NOT ABANDONED MY DUTIES AND RUN AWAY!
YES! I FLED THAT WONDERLAND WHERE ALL DREAMS CAME TRUE, AND NO QUESTIONS WENT UNANSWERED! IT ALL COMES BACK TO ME! MY HOME– MY WONDERLAND–
–WHEREIN, DAY BY DAY I WITNESSED THE MIRACULOUS GEYSER OF GLORIOUS GOODNESS SPOUT ITS SHIMMERING SHOWER! RAINING FLIGHTS OF FANCY UPON US THAT TURNED DARK INTO DAWN, AND DOUBTS INTO DREAMS...

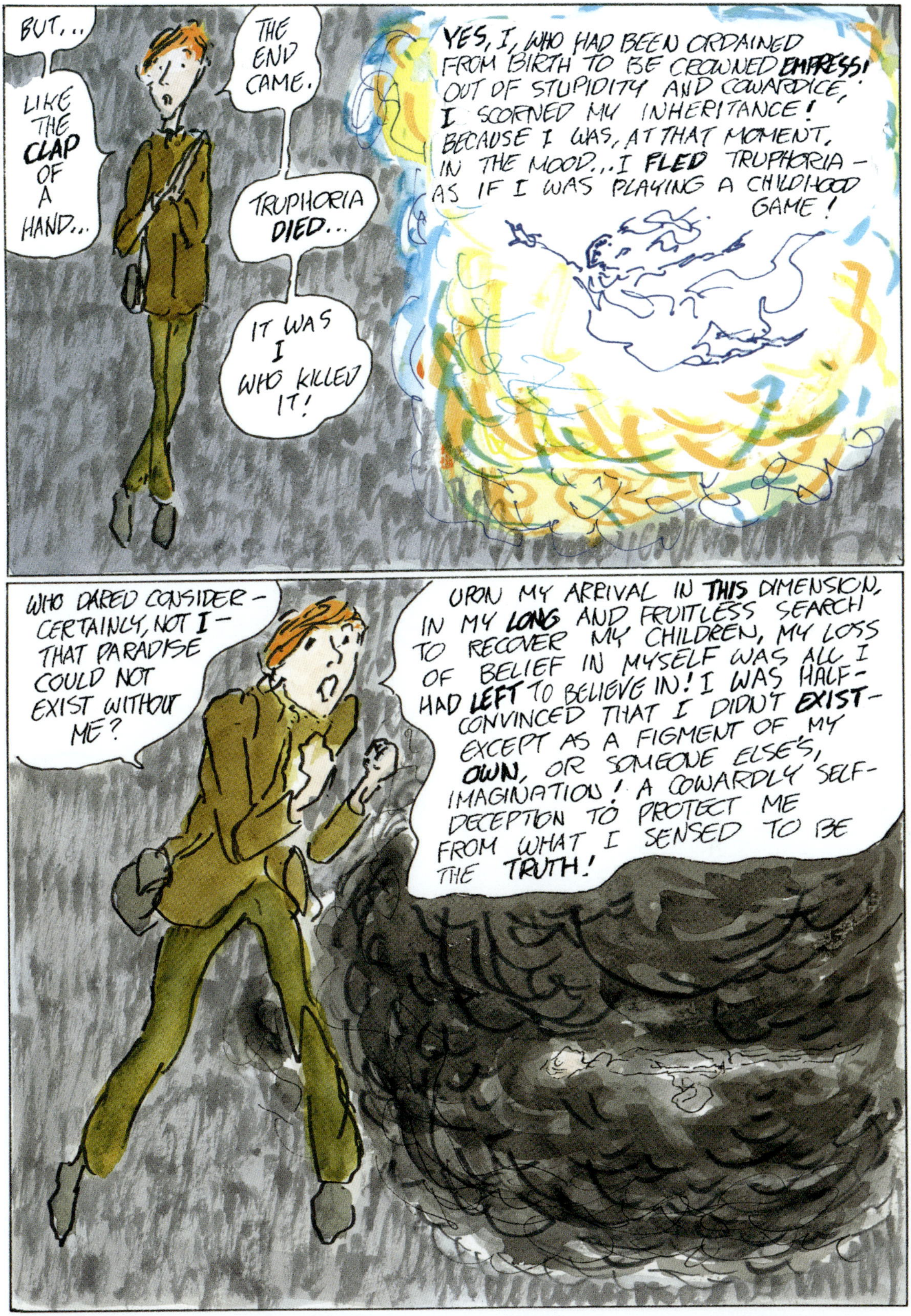
BUT, ..
LIKE THE CLAP OF A HAND...
THE END CAME.
TRUPHORIA DIED...
IT WAS I WHO KILLED IT!
YES, I, WHO HAD BEEN ORDAINED FROM BIRTH TO BE CROWNED EMPRESS! OUT OF STUPIDITY AND COWARDICE, I SCORNED MY INHERITANCE! BECAUSE I WAS, AT THAT MOMENT, IN THE MOOD... I FLED TRUPHORIA - AS IF I WAS PLAYING A CHILDHOOD GAME!
WHO DARED CONSIDER - CERTAINLY, NOT I - THAT PARADISE COULD NOT EXIST WITHOUT ME?
UPON MY ARRIVAL IN THIS DIMENSION, IN MY LONG AND FRUITLESS SEARCH TO RECOVER MY CHILDREN, MY LOSS OF BELIEF IN MYSELF WAS ALL I HAD LEFT TO BELIEVE IN! I WAS HALF-CONVINCED THAT I DIDN'T EXIST - EXCEPT AS A FIGMENT OF MY OWN, OR SOMEONE ELSE'S, IMAGINATION! A COWARDLY SELF-DECEPTION TO PROTECT ME FROM WHAT I SENSED TO BE THE TRUTH!

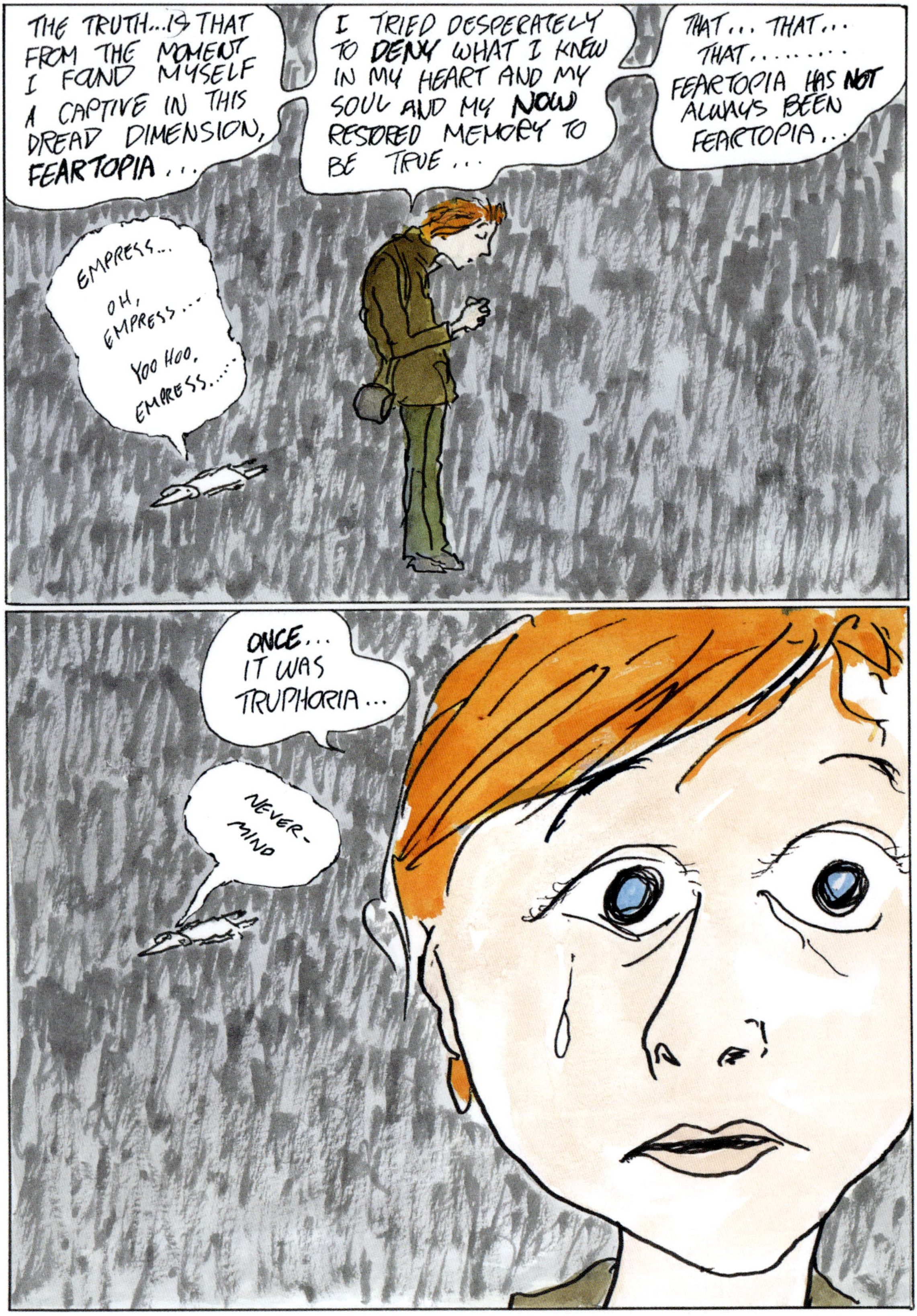
THE TRUTH... IS THAT FROM THE MOMENT I FOUND MYSELF A CAPTIVE IN THIS DREAD DIMENSION, **FEARTOPIA**...
I TRIED DESPERATELY TO **DENY** WHAT I KNEW IN MY HEART AND MY SOUL AND MY **NOW** RESTORED MEMORY TO BE TRUE...
THAT... THAT... THAT........ FEARTOPIA HAS **NOT** ALWAYS BEEN FEARTOPIA...
EMPRESS... OH, EMPRESS... YOO HOO, EMPRESS......
ONCE... IT WAS TRUPHORIA...
NEVER-MIND

CHAPTER 48 • IT'S REALLY ME

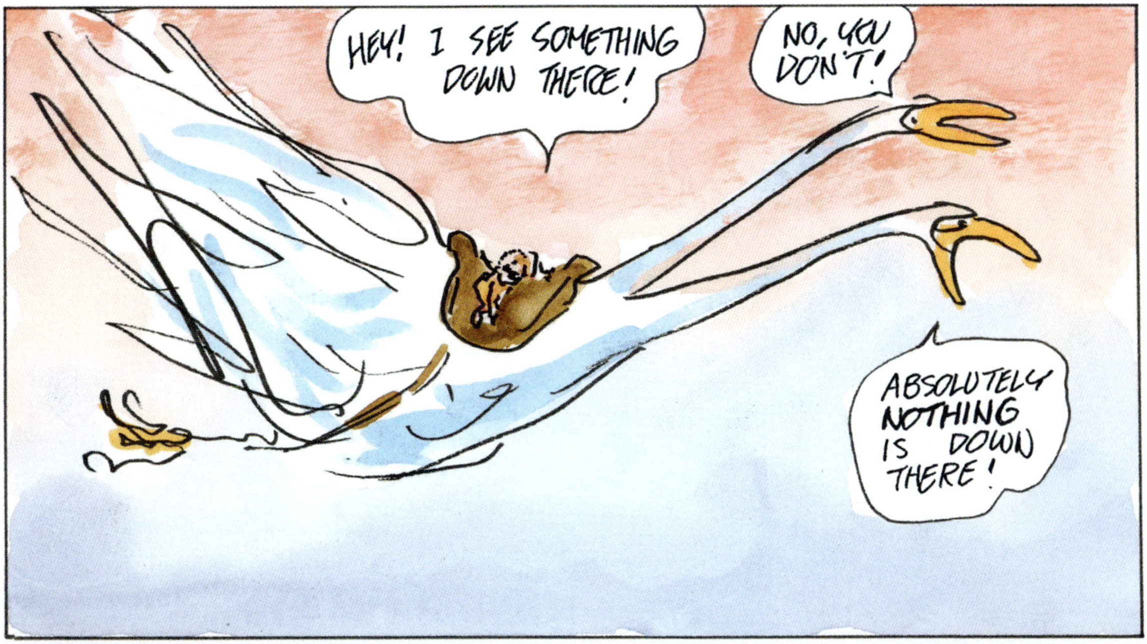
HEY! I SEE SOMETHING DOWN THERE!
NO, YOU DON'T!
ABSOLUTELY NOTHING IS DOWN THERE!

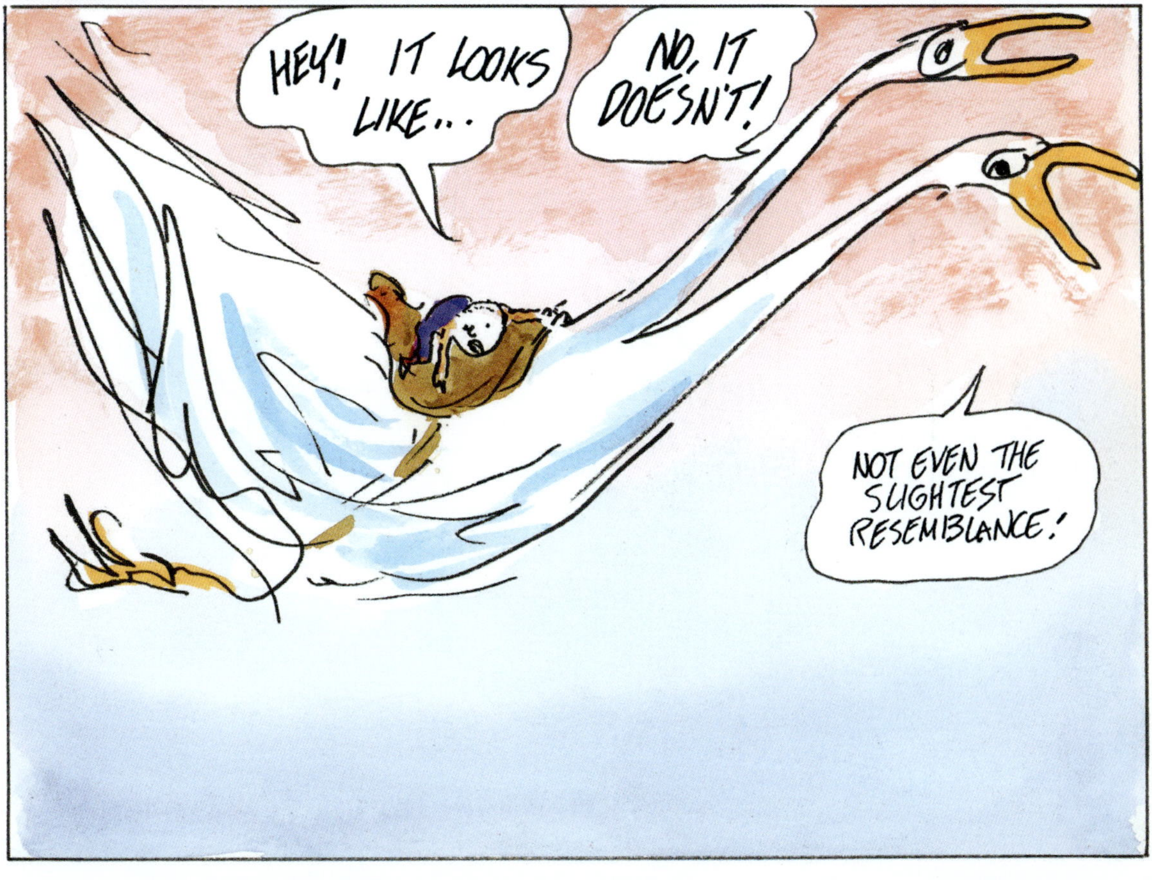
HEY! IT LOOKS LIKE...
NO, IT DOESN'T!
NOT EVEN THE SLIGHTEST RESEMBLANCE!

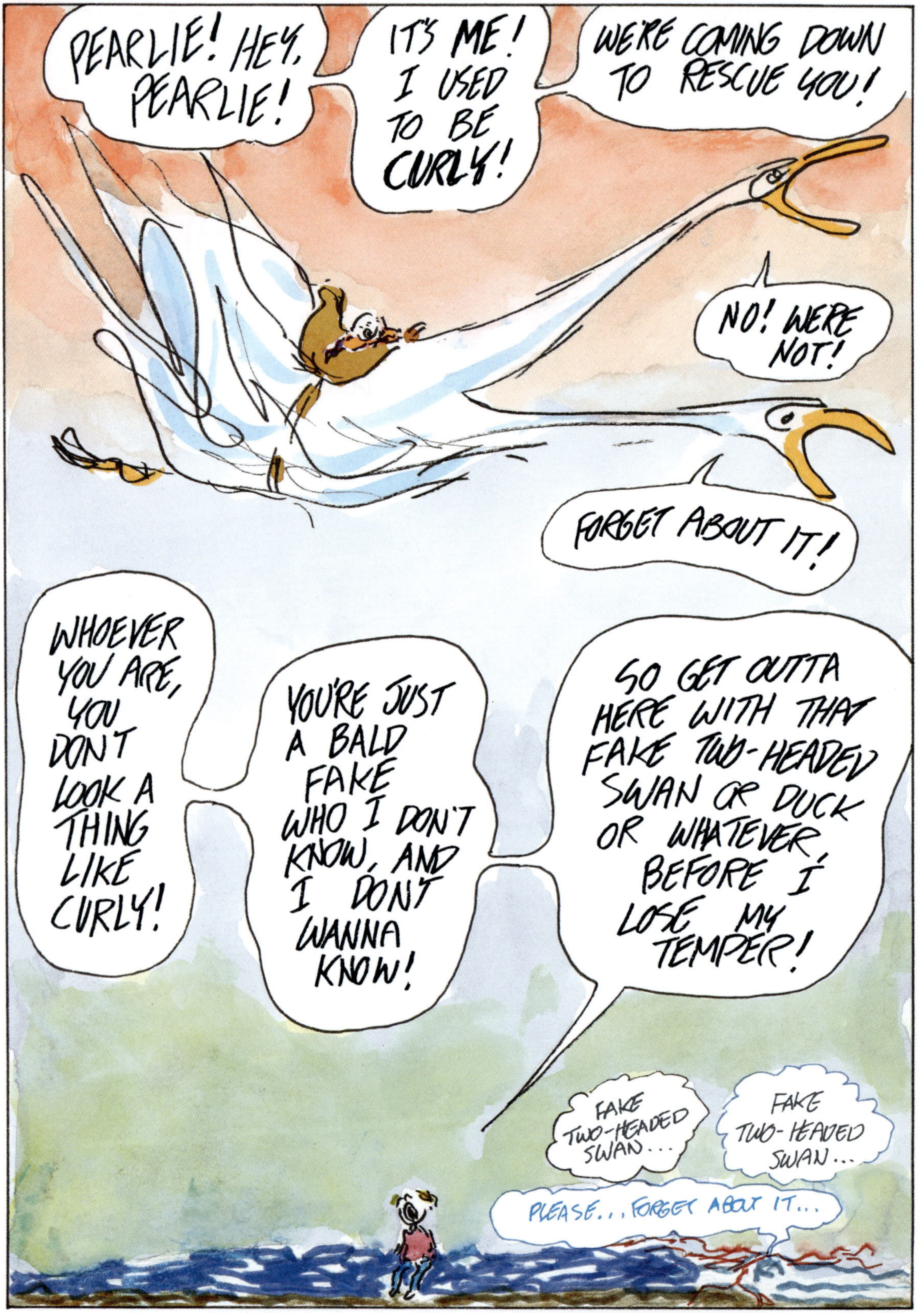
PEARLIE! HEY, PEARLIE!
IT'S ME! I USED TO BE CURLY!
WE'RE COMING DOWN TO RESCUE YOU!
NO! WE'RE NOT!
FORGET ABOUT IT!
WHOEVER YOU ARE, YOU DON'T LOOK A THING LIKE CURLY!
YOU'RE JUST A BALD FAKE WHO I DON'T KNOW, AND I DON'T WANNA KNOW!
SO GET OUTTA HERE WITH THAT FAKE TWO-HEADED SWAN OR DUCK OR WHATEVER, BEFORE I LOSE MY TEMPER!
FAKE TWO-HEADED SWAN...
FAKE TWO-HEADED SWAN...
PLEASE... FORGET ABOUT IT...

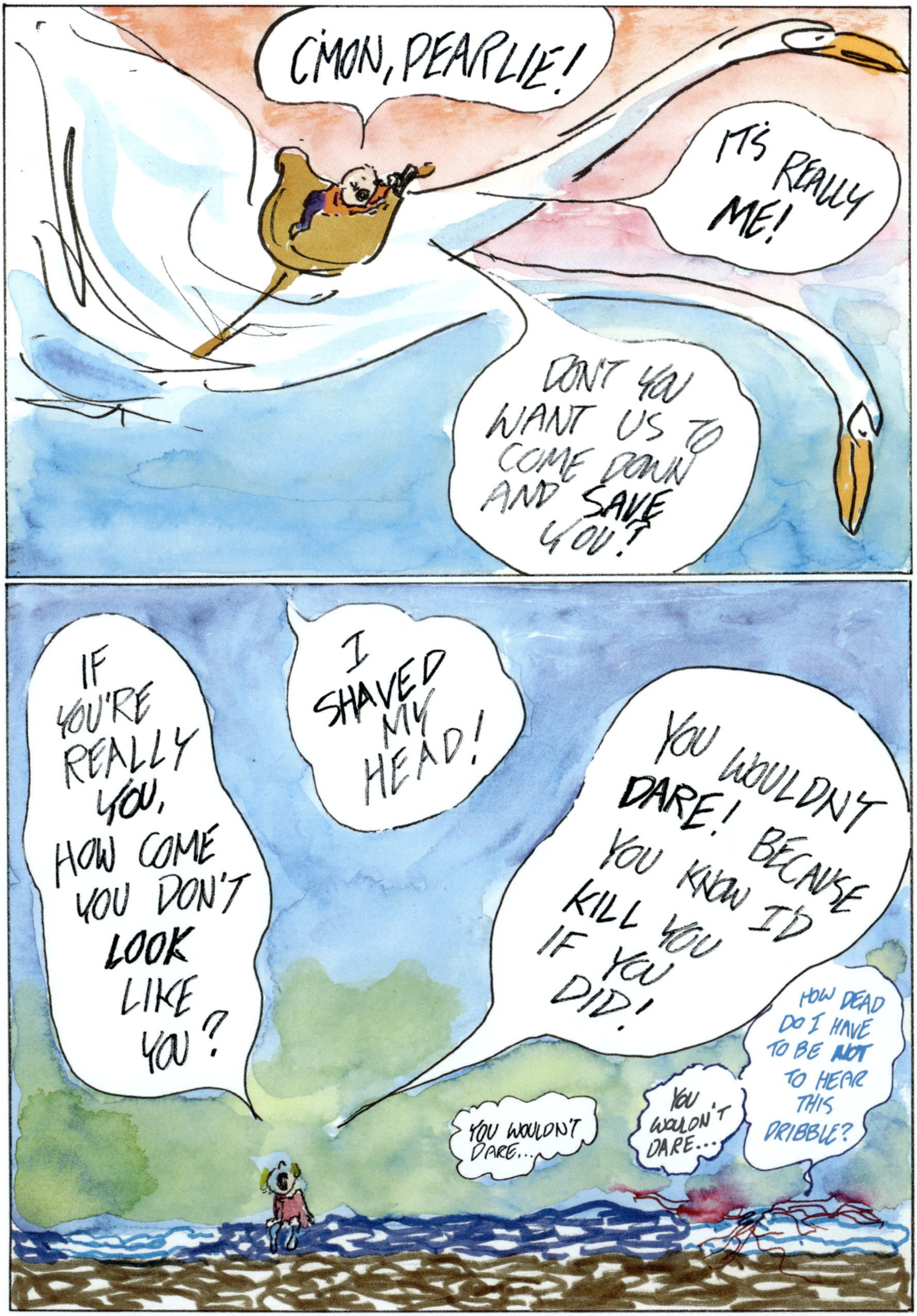
C'MON, PEARLIE!
IT'S REALLY ME!
DON'T YOU WANT US TO COME DOWN AND SAVE YOU?
IF YOU'RE REALLY YOU, HOW COME YOU DON'T LOOK LIKE YOU?
I SHAVED MY HEAD!
YOU WOULDN'T DARE! BECAUSE YOU KNOW I'D KILL YOU IF YOU DID!
YOU WOULDN'T DARE...
YOU WOULDN'T DARE...
HOW DEAD DO I HAVE TO BE NOT TO HEAR THIS DRIBBLE?

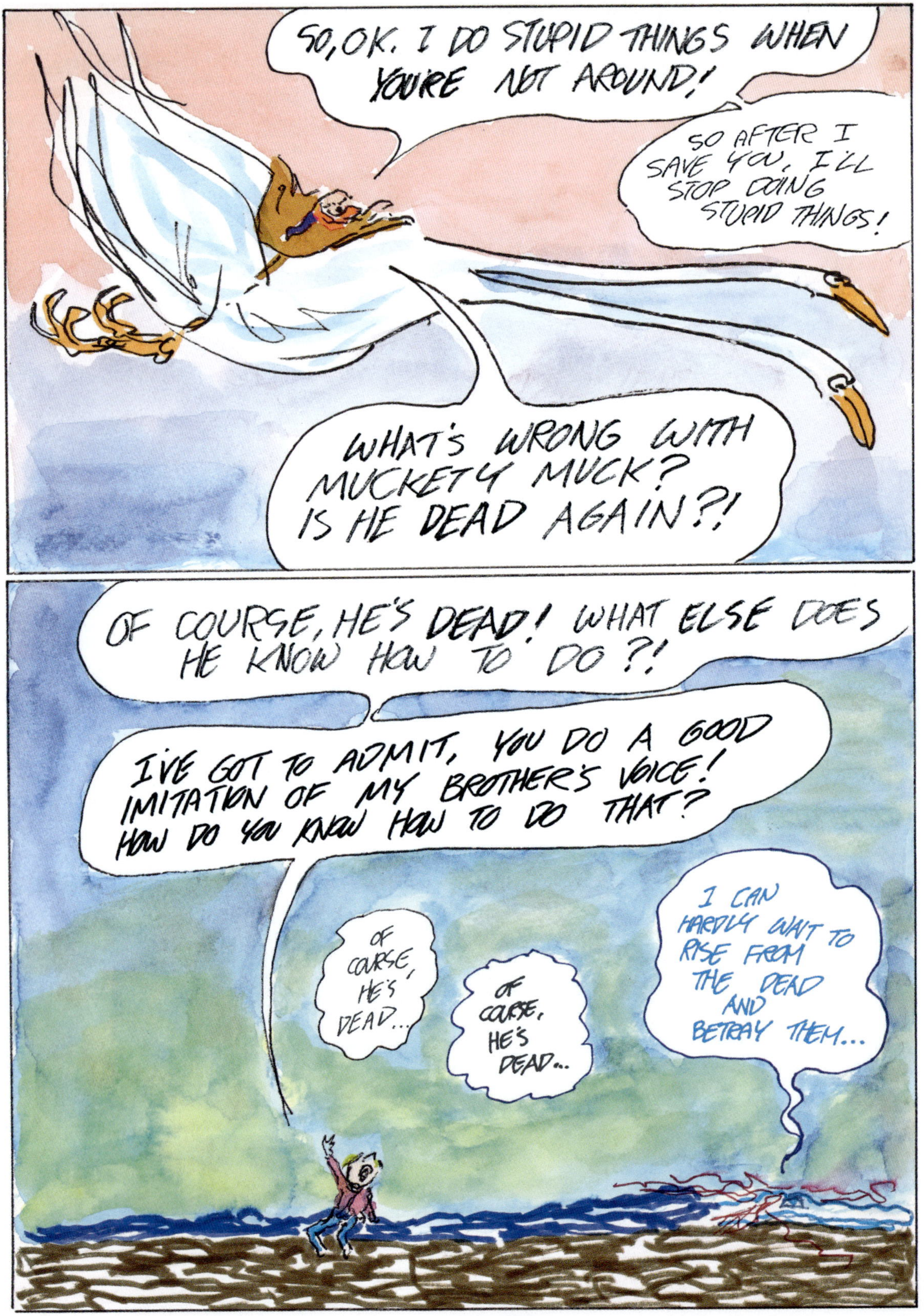
SO, OK. I DO STUPID THINGS WHEN YOU'RE NOT AROUND!
SO AFTER I SAVE YOU, I'LL STOP DOING STUPID THINGS!
WHAT'S WRONG WITH MUCKETY MUCK? IS HE DEAD AGAIN?!
OF COURSE, HE'S DEAD! WHAT ELSE DOES HE KNOW HOW TO DO?!
I'VE GOT TO ADMIT, YOU DO A GOOD IMITATION OF MY BROTHER'S VOICE! HOW DO YOU KNOW HOW TO DO THAT?
OF COURSE, HE'S DEAD...
OF COURSE, HE'S DEAD...
I CAN HARDLY WAIT TO RISE FROM THE DEAD AND BETRAY THEM...

CHAPTER 49 • SIX SEEDS

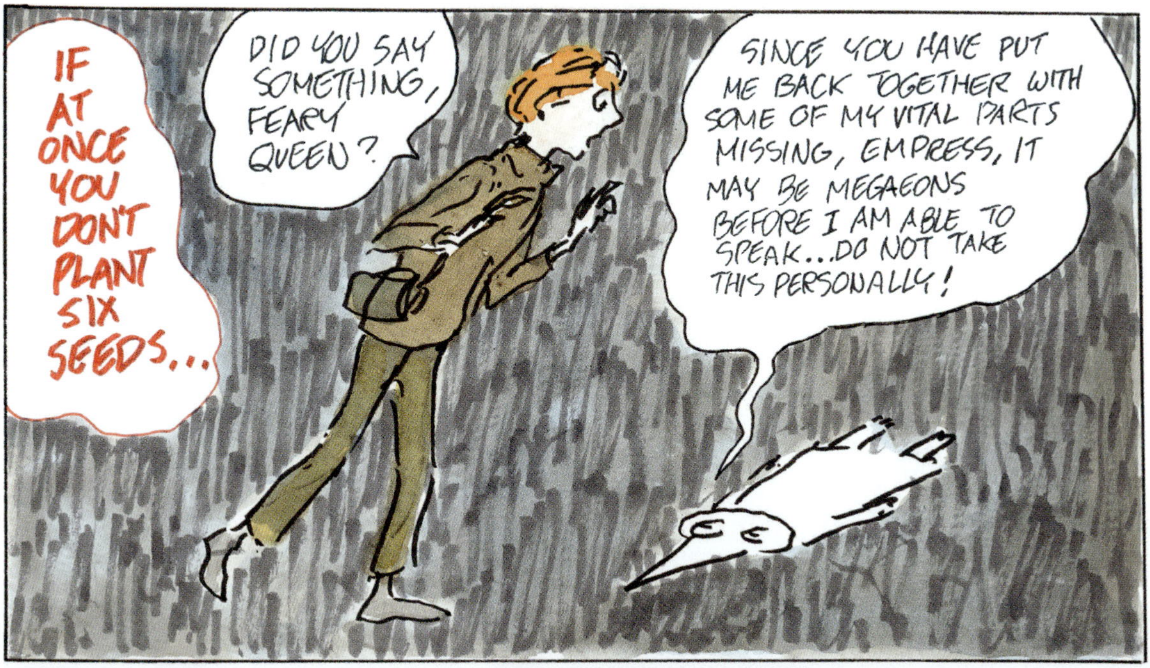
IF AT ONCE YOU DON'T PLANT SIX SEEDS...
DID YOU SAY SOMETHING, FEARY QUEEN?
SINCE YOU HAVE PUT ME BACK TOGETHER WITH SOME OF MY VITAL PARTS MISSING, EMPRESS, IT MAY BE MEGAEONS BEFORE I AM ABLE TO SPEAK...DO NOT TAKE THIS PERSONALLY!

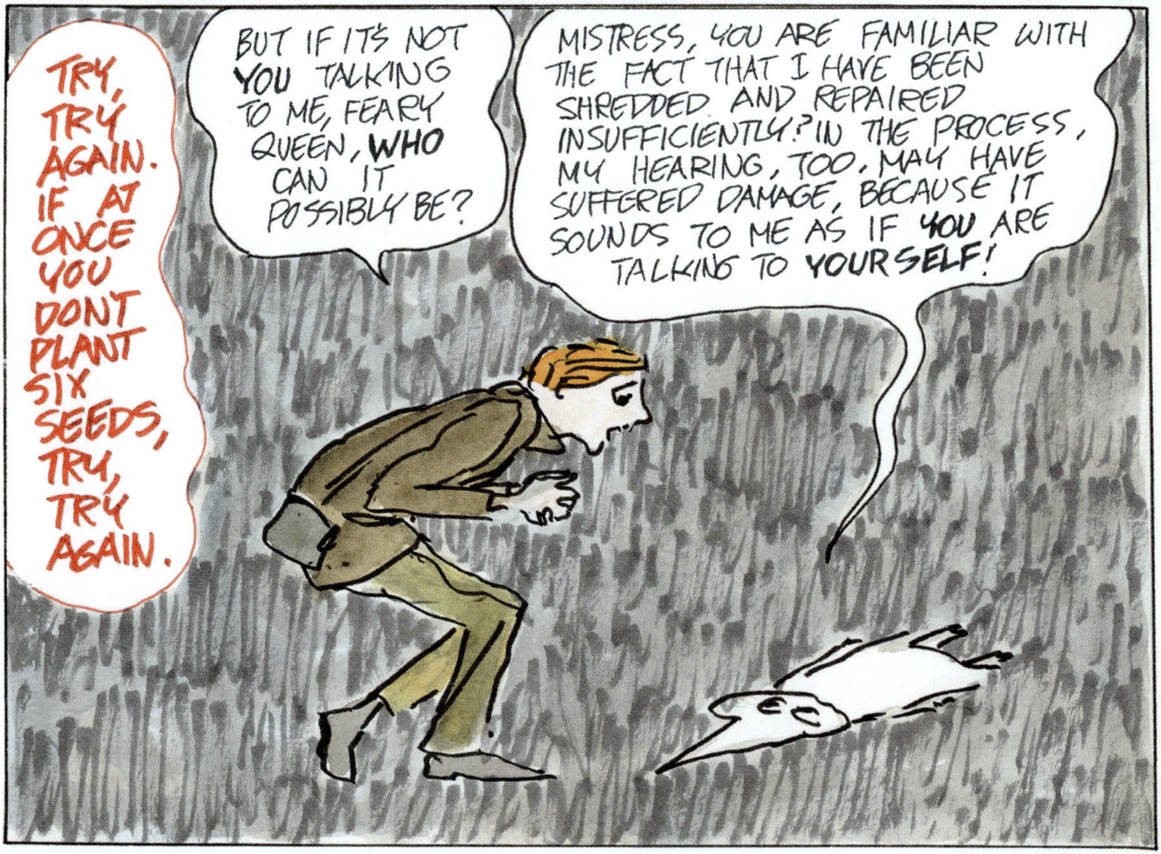
TRY, TRY AGAIN. IF AT ONCE YOU DONT PLANT SIX SEEDS, TRY, TRY AGAIN.
BUT IF IT'S NOT YOU TALKING TO ME, FEARY QUEEN, WHO CAN IT POSSIBLY BE?
MISTRESS, YOU ARE FAMILIAR WITH THE FACT THAT I HAVE BEEN SHREDDED AND REPAIRED INSUFFICIENTLY? IN THE PROCESS, MY HEARING, TOO, MAY HAVE SUFFERED DAMAGE, BECAUSE IT SOUNDS TO ME AS IF YOU ARE TALKING TO YOURSELF!

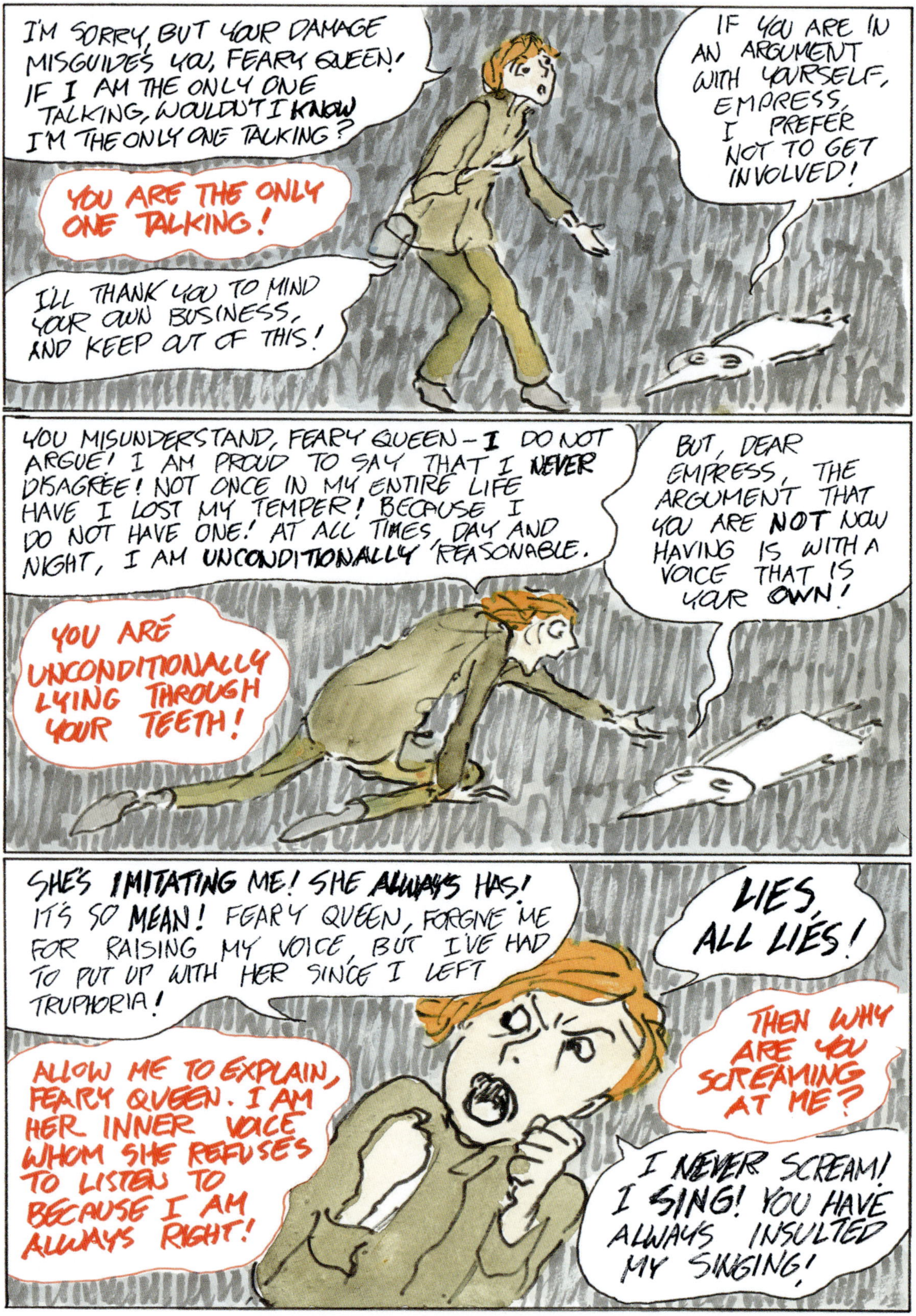
I'M SORRY, BUT YOUR DAMAGE MISGUIDES YOU, FEARY QUEEN! IF I AM THE ONLY ONE TALKING, WOULDN'T I KNOW I'M THE ONLY ONE TALKING?
IF YOU ARE IN AN ARGUMENT WITH YOURSELF, EMPRESS, I PREFER NOT TO GET INVOLVED!
YOU ARE THE ONLY ONE TALKING!
I'LL THANK YOU TO MIND YOUR OWN BUSINESS, AND KEEP OUT OF THIS!
YOU MISUNDERSTAND, FEARY QUEEN—I DO NOT ARGUE! I AM PROUD TO SAY THAT I NEVER DISAGREE! NOT ONCE IN MY ENTIRE LIFE HAVE I LOST MY TEMPER! BECAUSE I DO NOT HAVE ONE! AT ALL TIMES, DAY AND NIGHT, I AM UNCONDITIONALLY REASONABLE.
BUT, DEAR EMPRESS, THE ARGUMENT THAT YOU ARE NOT NOW HAVING IS WITH A VOICE THAT IS YOUR OWN!
YOU ARE UNCONDITIONALLY LYING THROUGH YOUR TEETH!
SHE'S IMITATING ME! SHE ALWAYS HAS! IT'S SO MEAN! FEARY QUEEN, FORGIVE ME FOR RAISING MY VOICE, BUT I'VE HAD TO PUT UP WITH HER SINCE I LEFT TRUPHORIA!
LIES, ALL LIES!
THEN WHY ARE YOU SCREAMING AT ME?
ALLOW ME TO EXPLAIN, FEARY QUEEN. I AM HER INNER VOICE WHOM SHE REFUSES TO LISTEN TO BECAUSE I AM ALWAYS RIGHT!
I NEVER SCREAM! I SING! YOU HAVE ALWAYS INSULTED MY SINGING!

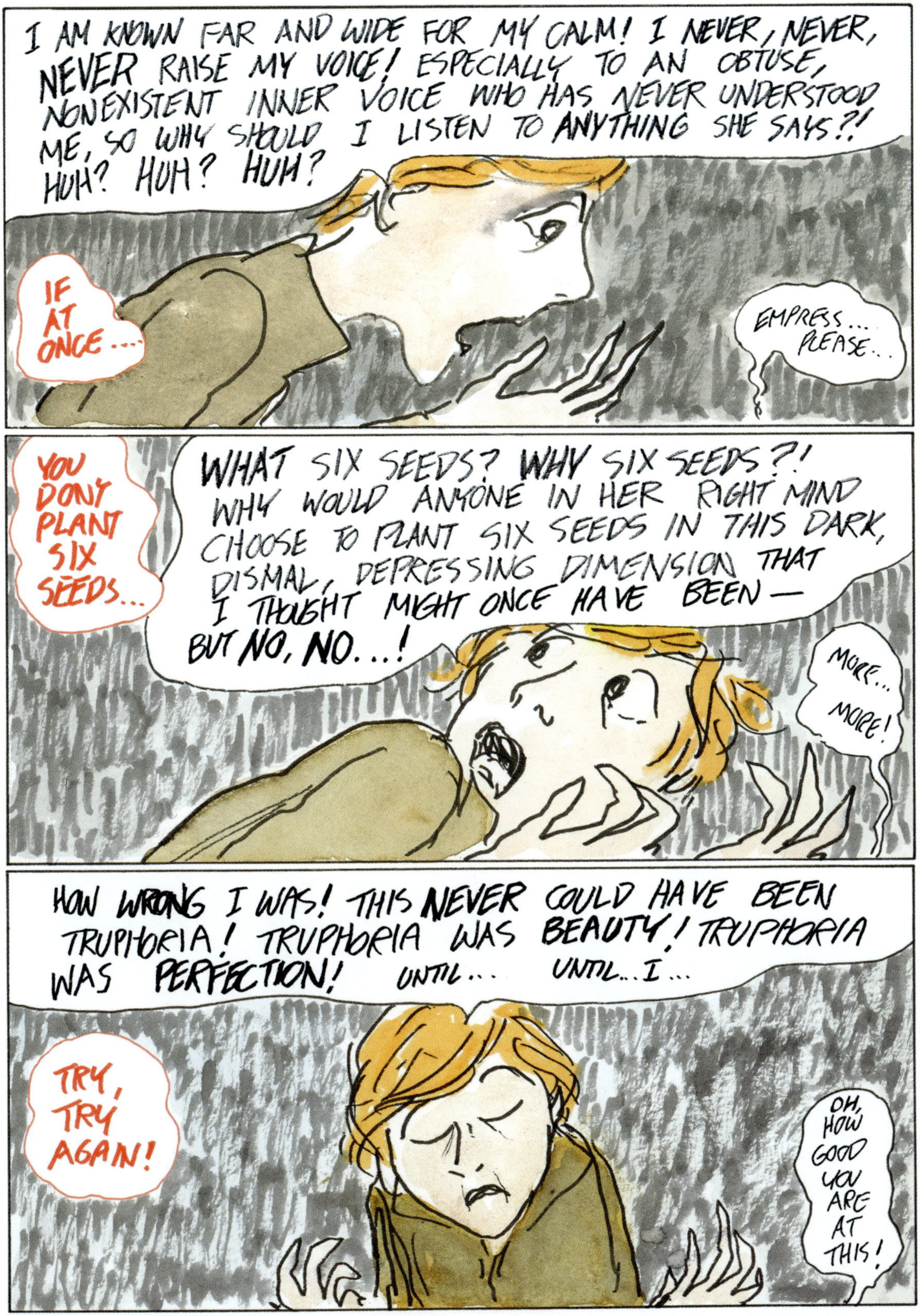
I AM KNOWN FAR AND WIDE FOR MY CALM! I NEVER, NEVER, NEVER RAISE MY VOICE! ESPECIALLY TO AN OBTUSE, NONEXISTENT INNER VOICE WHO HAS NEVER UNDERSTOOD ME, SO WHY SHOULD I LISTEN TO ANYTHING SHE SAYS?! HUH? HUH? HUH?
IF AT ONCE....
EMPRESS... PLEASE...
YOU DON'T PLANT SIX SEEDS...
WHAT SIX SEEDS? WHY SIX SEEDS?! WHY WOULD ANYONE IN HER RIGHT MIND CHOOSE TO PLANT SIX SEEDS IN THIS DARK, DISMAL, DEPRESSING DIMENSION THAT I THOUGHT MIGHT ONCE HAVE BEEN— BUT NO, NO...!
MORE... MORE!
HOW WRONG I WAS! THIS NEVER COULD HAVE BEEN TRUPHORIA! TRUPHORIA WAS BEAUTY! TRUPHORIA WAS PERFECTION! UNTIL... UNTIL... I...
TRY, TRY AGAIN!
OH, HOW GOOD YOU ARE AT THIS!

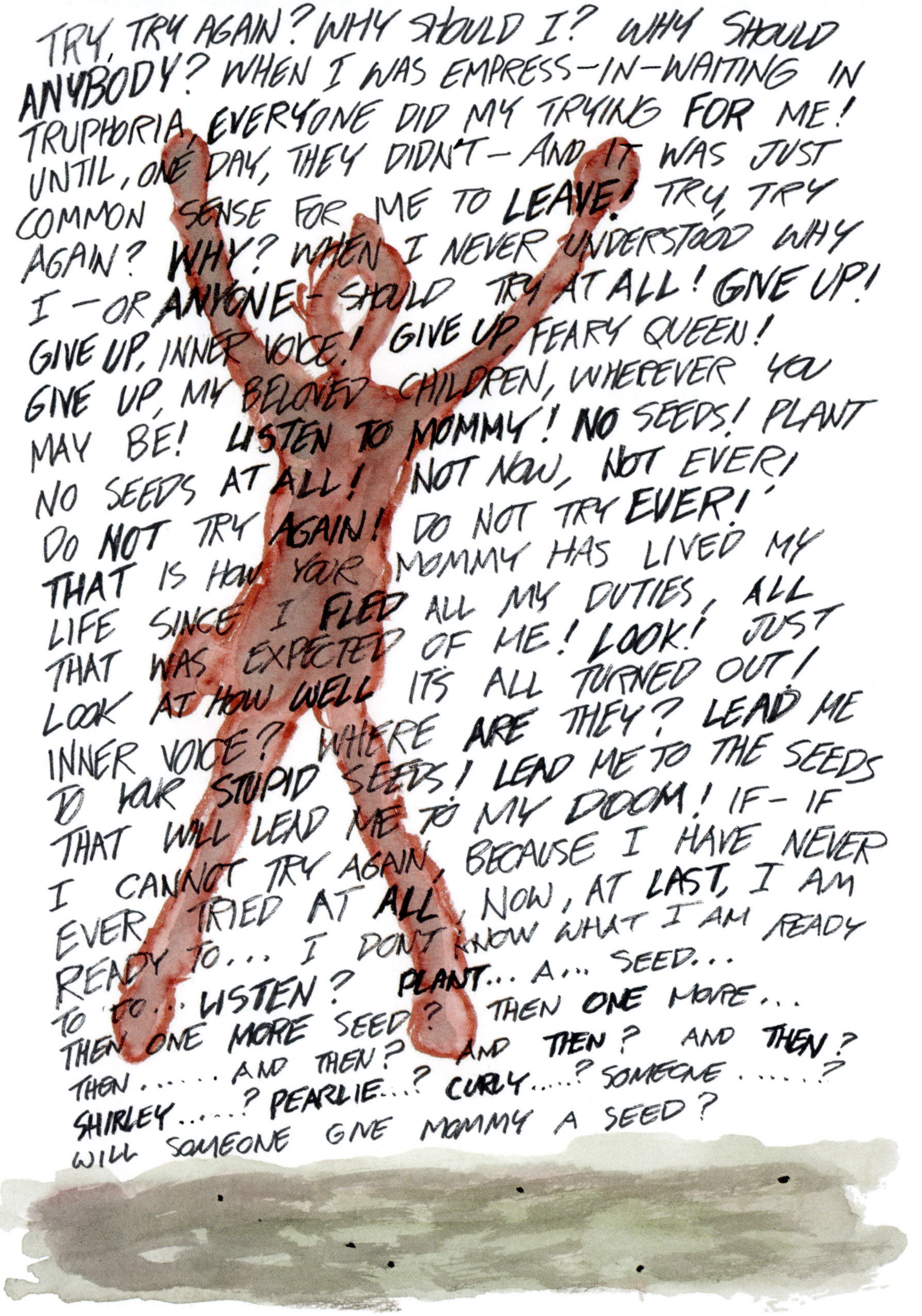
TRY, TRY AGAIN? WHY SHOULD I? WHY SHOULD
ANYBODY? WHEN I WAS EMPRESS-IN-WAITING IN
TRUPHORIA, EVERYONE DID MY TRYING FOR ME!
UNTIL, ONE DAY, THEY DIDN'T— AND IT WAS JUST
COMMON SENSE FOR ME TO LEAVE! TRY, TRY
AGAIN? WHY? WHEN I NEVER UNDERSTOOD WHY
I —OR ANYONE— SHOULD TRY AT ALL! GIVE UP!
GIVE UP, INNER VOICE! GIVE UP, FEARY QUEEN!
GIVE UP, MY BELOVED CHILDREN, WHEREVER YOU
MAY BE! LISTEN TO MOMMY! NO SEEDS! PLANT
NO SEEDS AT ALL! NOT NOW, NOT EVER!
DO NOT TRY AGAIN! DO NOT TRY EVER!
THAT IS HOW YOUR MOMMY HAS LIVED MY
LIFE SINCE I FLED ALL MY DUTIES, ALL
THAT WAS EXPECTED OF ME! LOOK! JUST
LOOK AT HOW WELL ITS ALL TURNED OUT!
INNER VOICE? WHERE ARE THEY? LEAD ME
TO YOUR STUPID SEEDS! LEAD ME TO THE SEEDS
THAT WILL LEAD ME TO MY DOOM! IF— IF
I CANNOT TRY AGAIN, BECAUSE I HAVE NEVER
EVER TRIED AT ALL, NOW, AT LAST, I AM
READY TO... I DON'T KNOW WHAT I AM READY
TO TO... LISTEN? PLANT... A... SEED...
THEN ONE MORE SEED? THEN ONE MORE...
THEN...... AND THEN? AND THEN? AND THEN?
SHIRLEY.....? PEARLIE...? CURLY.....? SOMEONE.....?
WILL SOMEONE GIVE MOMMY A SEED?

CHAPTER 50 • LOST AND FOUND

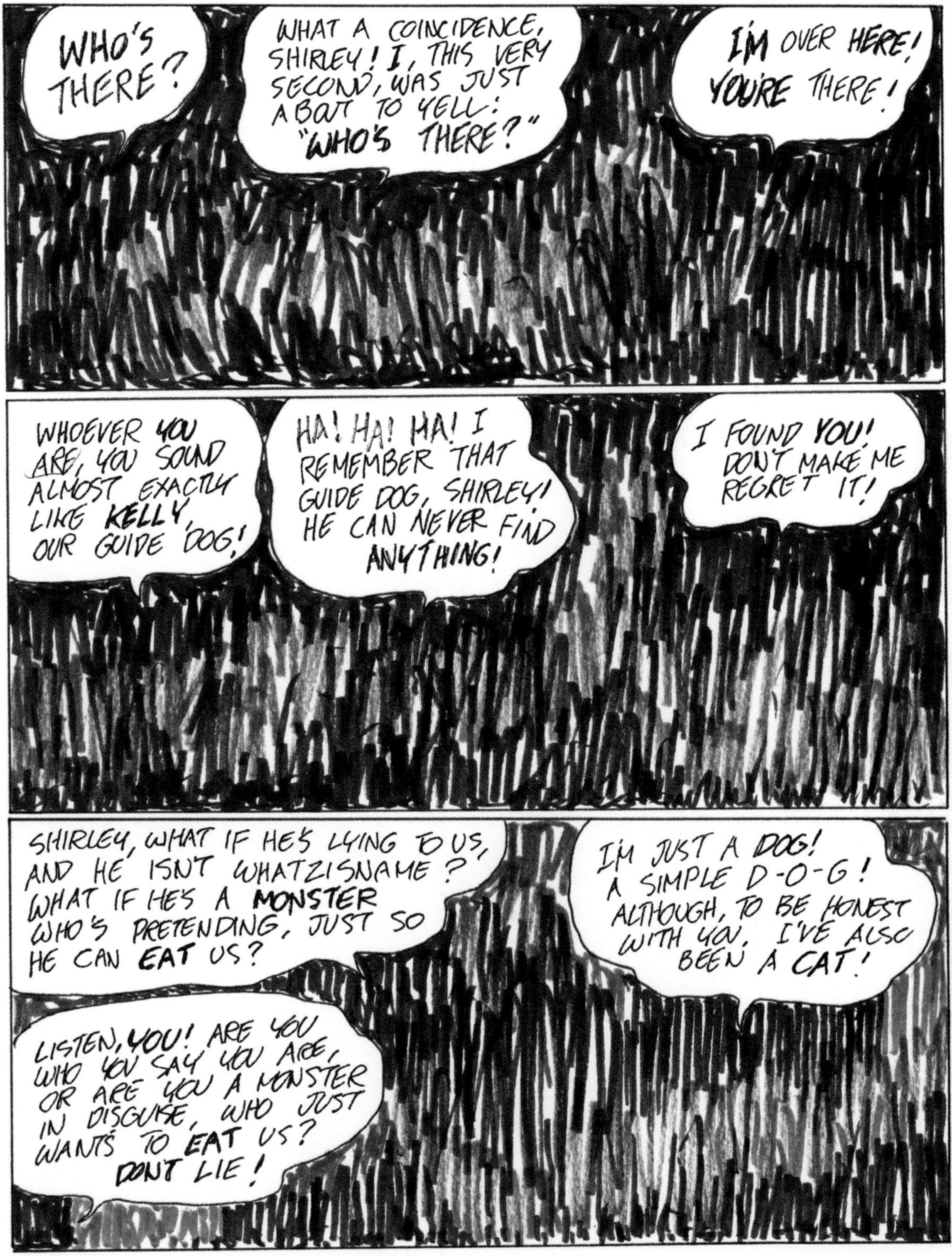
WHO'S THERE?
WHAT A COINCIDENCE, SHIRLEY! I, THIS VERY SECOND, WAS JUST ABOUT TO YELL: "WHO'S THERE?"
I'M OVER HERE! YOU'RE THERE!
WHOEVER YOU ARE, YOU SOUND ALMOST EXACTLY LIKE KELLY, OUR GUIDE DOG!
HA! HA! HA! I REMEMBER THAT GUIDE DOG, SHIRLEY! HE CAN NEVER FIND ANYTHING!
I FOUND YOU! DON'T MAKE ME REGRET IT!
SHIRLEY, WHAT IF HE'S LYING TO US, AND HE ISN'T WHATZISNAME? WHAT IF HE'S A MONSTER WHO'S PRETENDING, JUST SO HE CAN EAT US?
I'M JUST A DOG! A SIMPLE D-O-G! ALTHOUGH, TO BE HONEST WITH YOU, I'VE ALSO BEEN A CAT!
LISTEN, YOU! ARE YOU WHO YOU SAY YOU ARE, OR ARE YOU A MONSTER IN DISGUISE, WHO JUST WANTS TO EAT US? DON'T LIE!

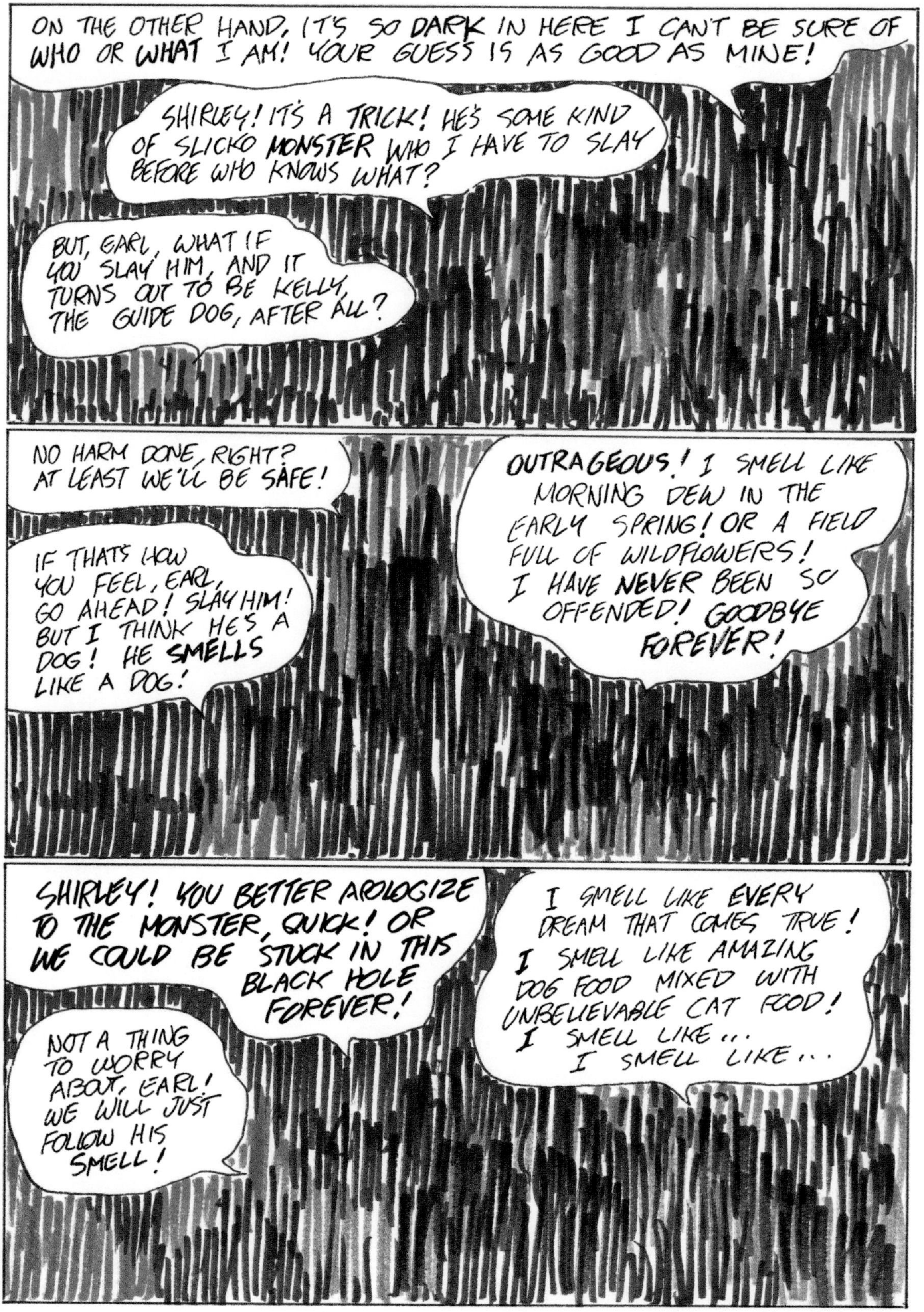
ON THE OTHER HAND, IT'S SO DARK IN HERE I CAN'T BE SURE OF WHO OR WHAT I AM! YOUR GUESS IS AS GOOD AS MINE!
SHIRLEY! IT'S A TRICK! HE'S SOME KIND OF SLICKO MONSTER WHO I HAVE TO SLAY BEFORE WHO KNOWS WHAT?
BUT, EARL, WHAT IF YOU SLAY HIM, AND IT TURNS OUT TO BE KELLY, THE GUIDE DOG, AFTER ALL?
NO HARM DONE, RIGHT? AT LEAST WE'LL BE SAFE!
IF THATS HOW YOU FEEL, EARL, GO AHEAD! SLAY HIM! BUT I THINK HE'S A DOG! HE SMELLS LIKE A DOG!
OUTRAGEOUS! I SMELL LIKE MORNING DEW IN THE EARLY SPRING! OR A FIELD FULL OF WILDFLOWERS! I HAVE NEVER BEEN SO OFFENDED! GOODBYE FOREVER!
SHIRLEY! YOU BETTER APOLOGIZE TO THE MONSTER, QUICK! OR WE COULD BE STUCK IN THIS BLACK HOLE FOREVER!
NOT A THING TO WORRY ABOUT, EARL! WE WILL JUST FOLLOW HIS SMELL!
I SMELL LIKE EVERY DREAM THAT COMES TRUE! I SMELL LIKE AMAZING DOG FOOD MIXED WITH UNBELIEVABLE CAT FOOD! I SMELL LIKE... I SMELL LIKE...

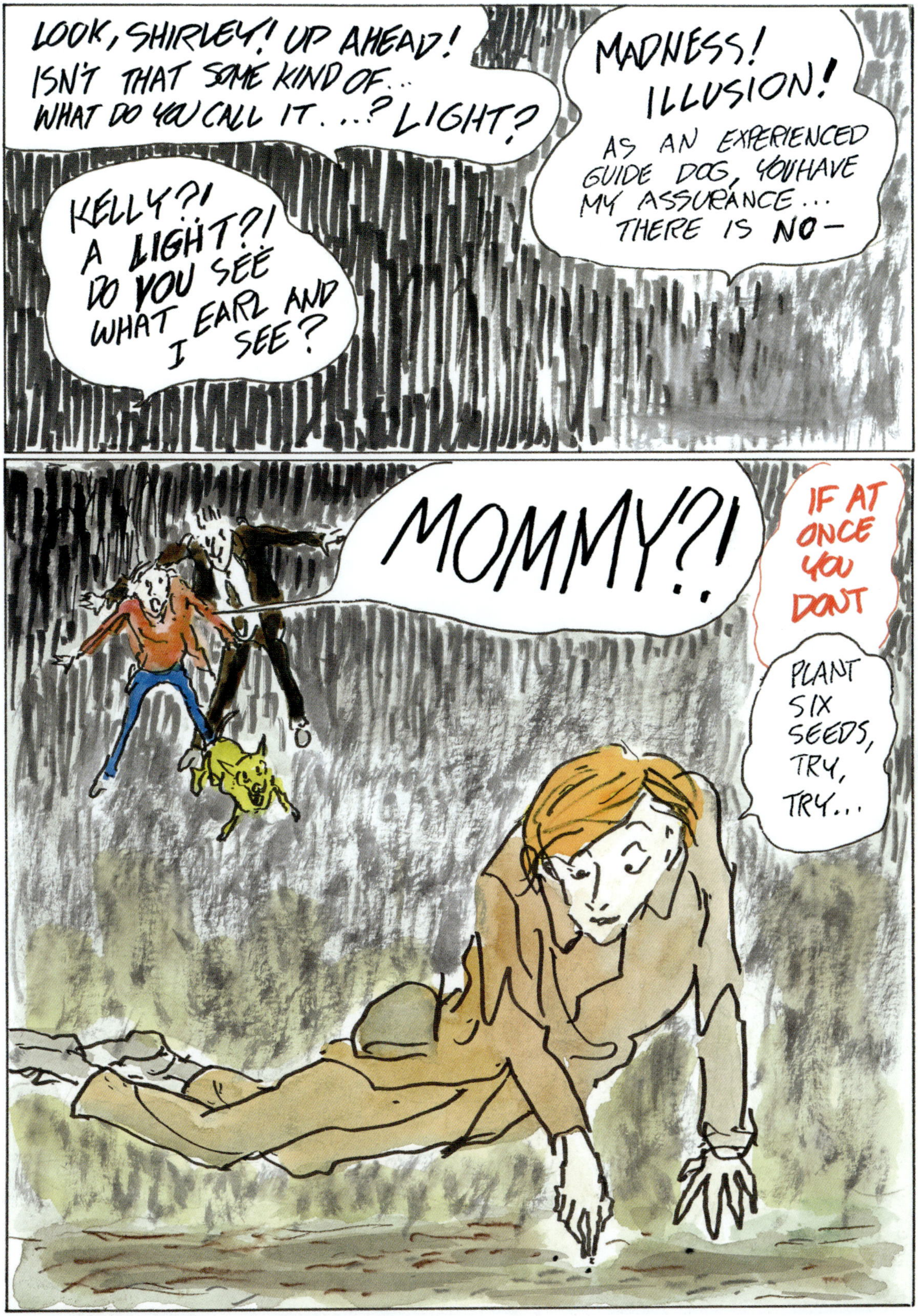
LOOK, SHIRLEY! UP AHEAD! ISN'T THAT SOME KIND OF... WHAT DO YOU CALL IT...? LIGHT?
MADNESS! ILLUSION! AS AN EXPERIENCED GUIDE DOG, YOU HAVE MY ASSURANCE... THERE IS NO-
KELLY?! A LIGHT?! DO YOU SEE WHAT EARL AND I SEE?
MOMMY?!
IF AT ONCE YOU DON'T
PLANT SIX SEEDS, TRY, TRY...

CHAPTER 51 • FAKE DEAD

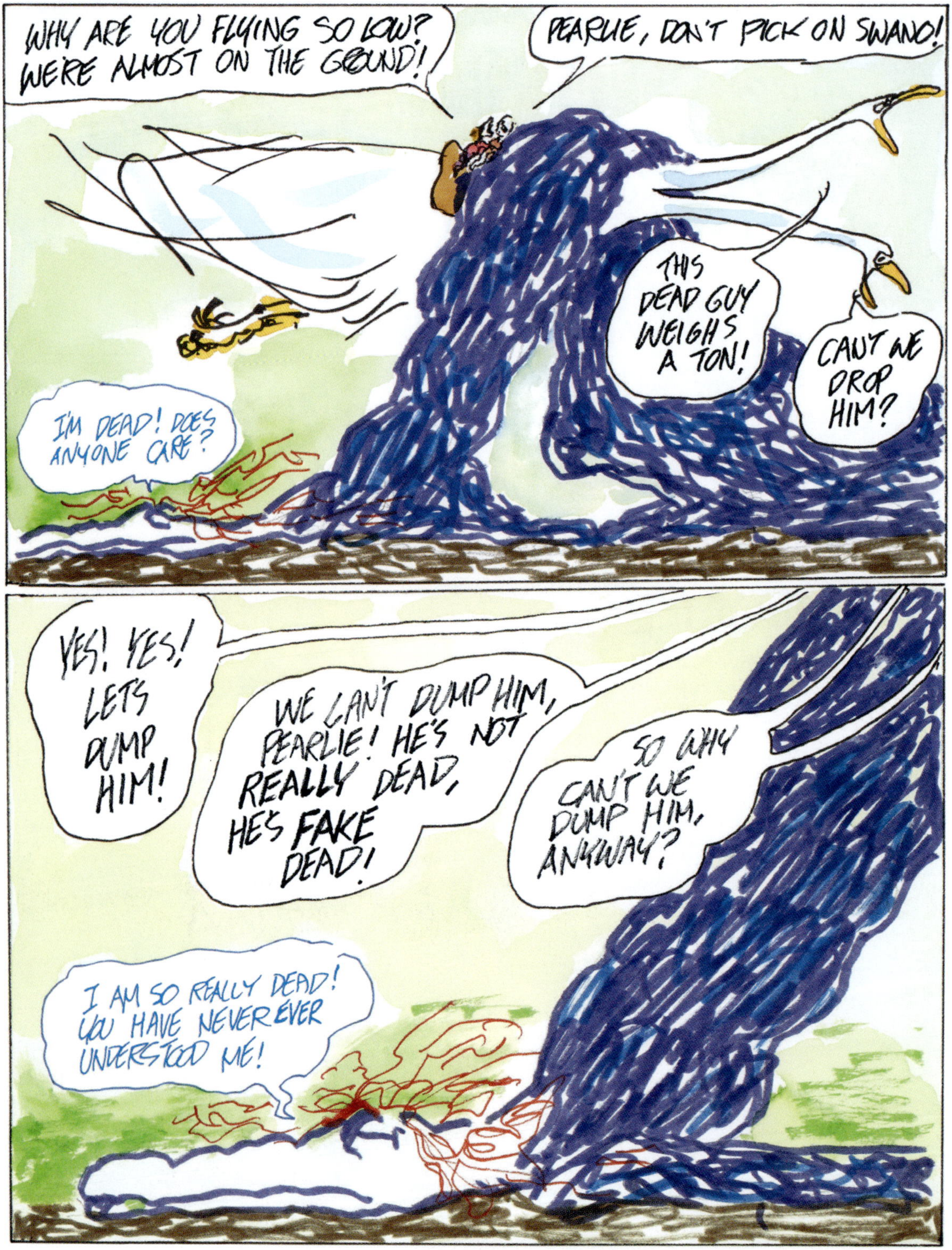
WHY ARE YOU FLYING SO LOW? WE'RE ALMOST ON THE GROUND!
PEARLIE, DON'T PICK ON SWANO!
THIS DEAD GUY WEIGHS A TON!
CAN'T WE DROP HIM?
I'M DEAD! DOES ANYONE CARE?
YES! YES! LET'S DUMP HIM!
WE CAN'T DUMP HIM, PEARLIE! HE'S NOT REALLY DEAD, HE'S FAKE DEAD!
SO WHY CAN'T WE DUMP HIM, ANYWAY?
I AM SO REALLY DEAD! YOU HAVE NEVER EVER UNDERSTOOD ME!

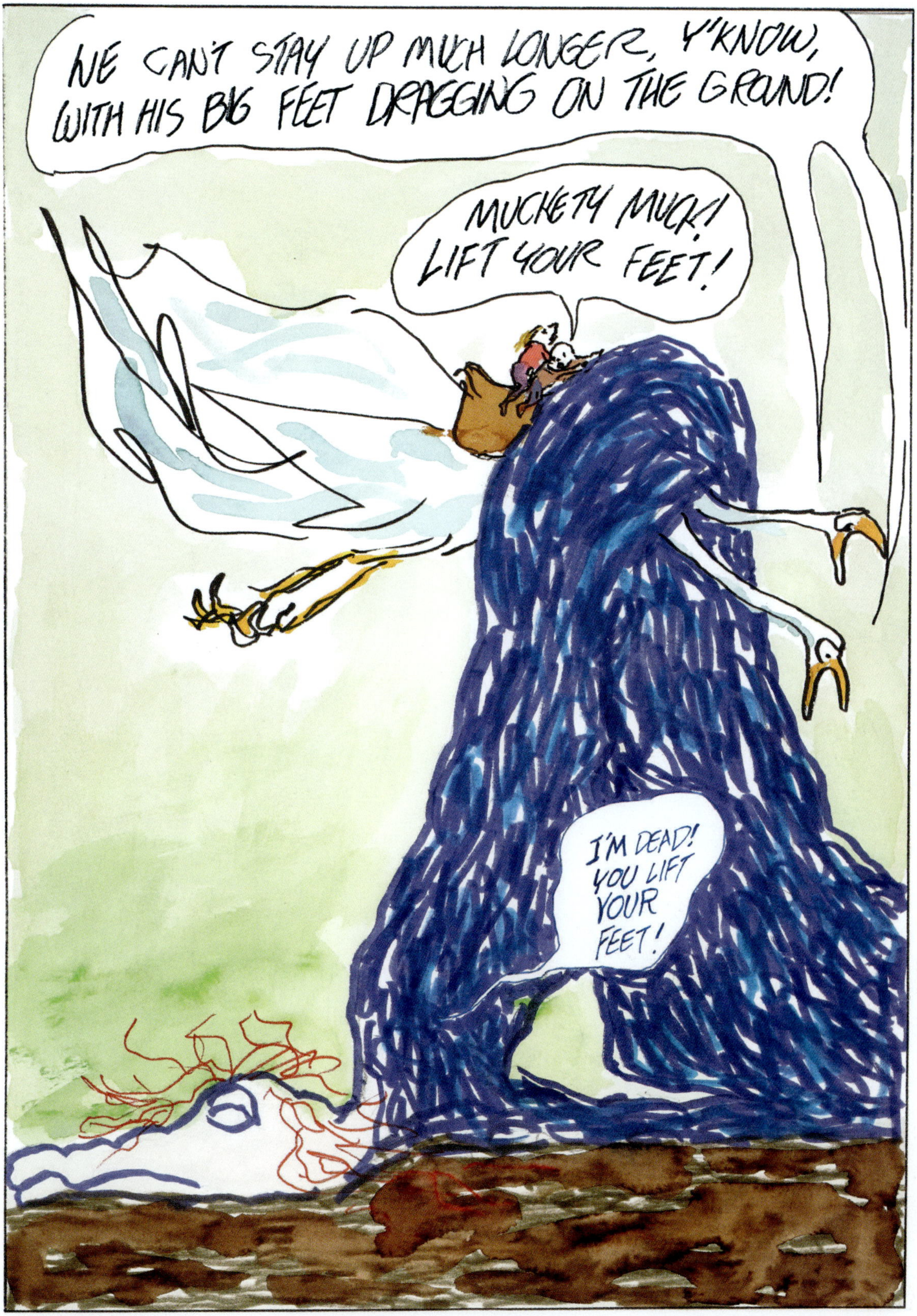
WE CAN'T STAY UP MUCH LONGER, Y'KNOW, WITH HIS BIG FEET DRAGGING ON THE GROUND!
MUCKETY MUCK! LIFT YOUR FEET!
I'M DEAD! YOU LIFT YOUR FEET!

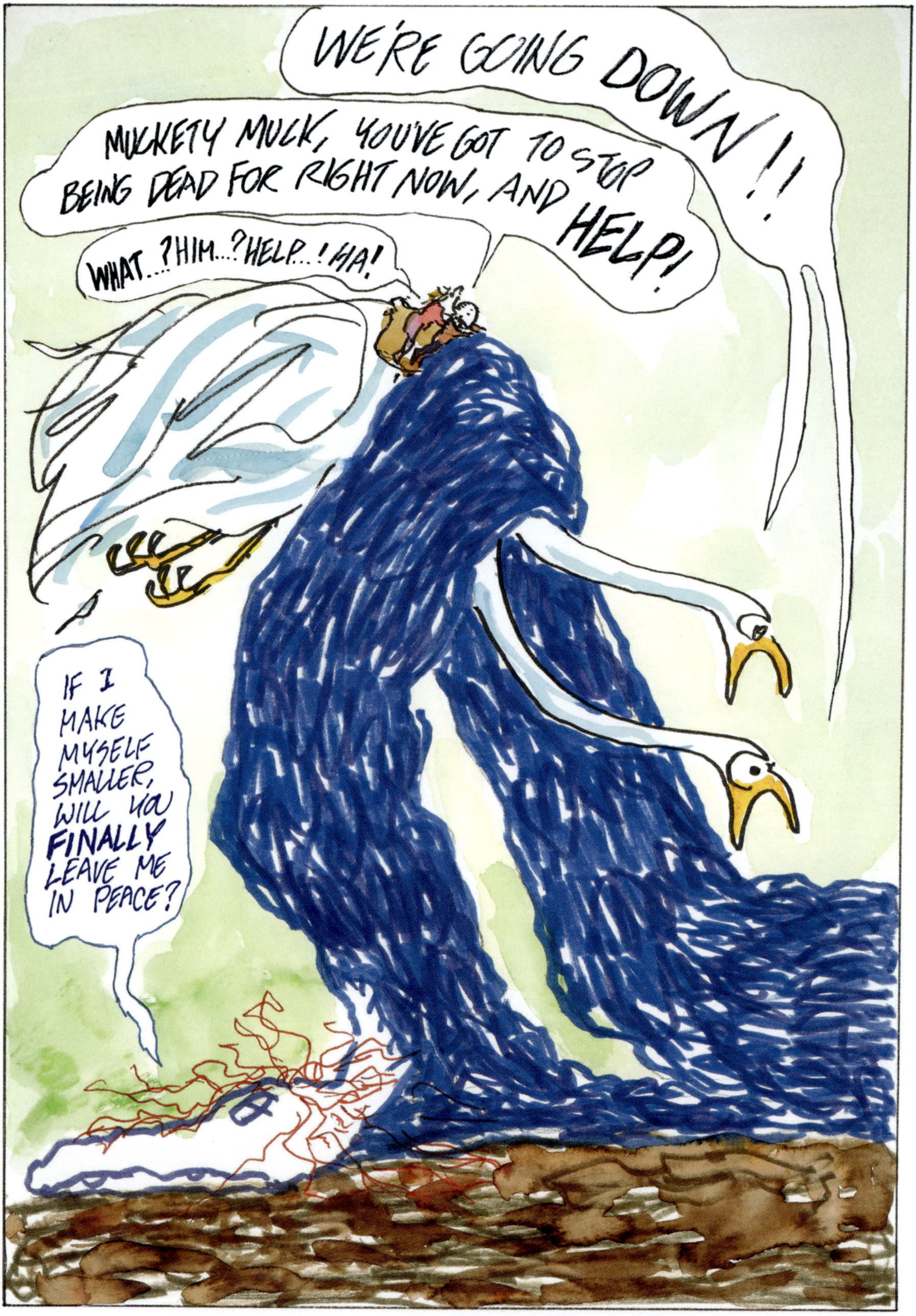
WE'RE GOING DOWN!!
MUCKETY MUCK, YOU'VE GOT TO STOP BEING DEAD FOR RIGHT NOW, AND HELP!
WHAT...?HIM...?HELP...!HA!
IF I MAKE MYSELF SMALLER, WILL YOU FINALLY LEAVE ME IN PEACE?

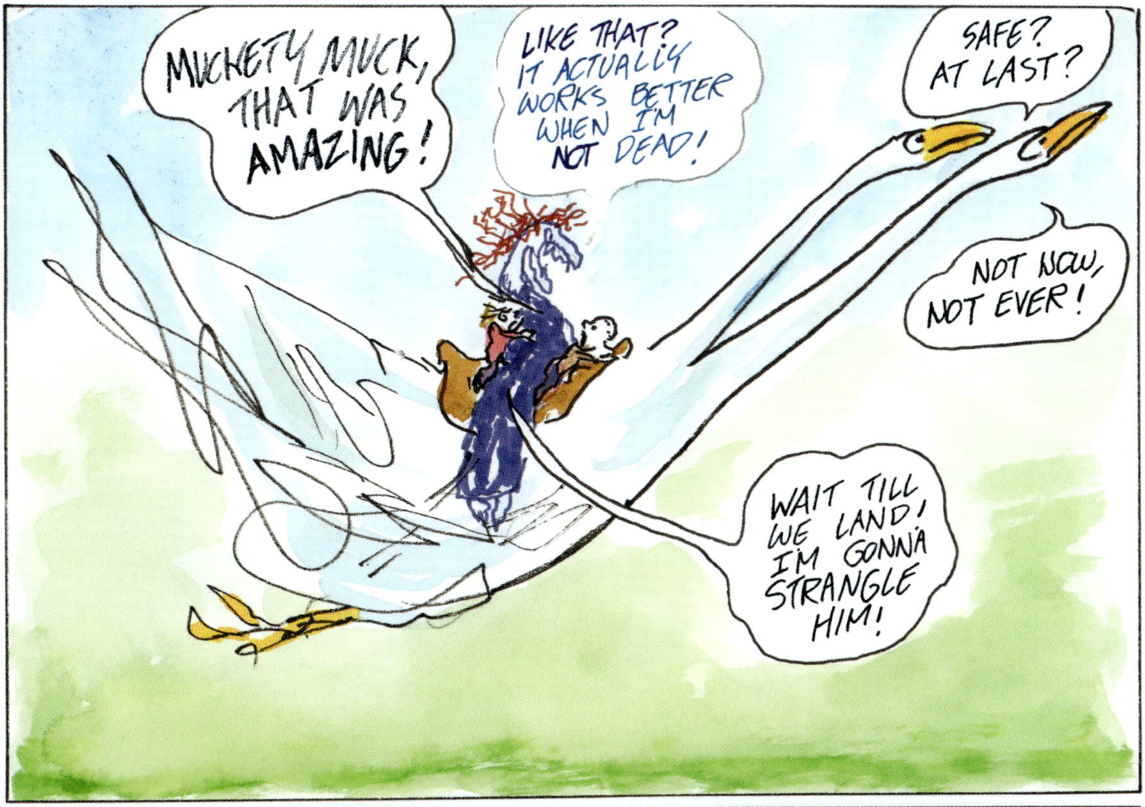
MUCKETY MUCK, THAT WAS AMAZING!
LIKE THAT? IT ACTUALLY WORKS BETTER WHEN I'M NOT DEAD!
SAFE? AT LAST?
NOT NOW, NOT EVER!
WAIT TILL WE LAND, I'M GONNA STRANGLE HIM!

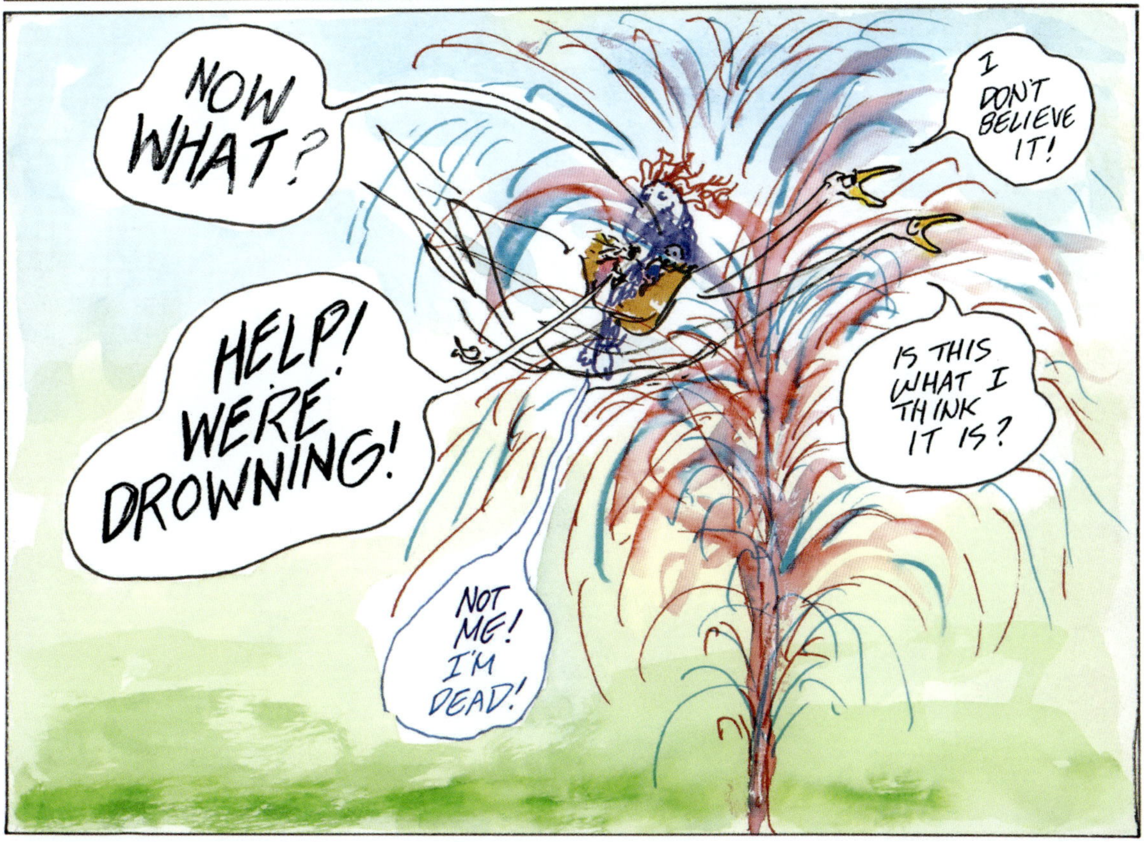
NOW WHAT?
I DON'T BELIEVE IT!
HELP! WE'RE DROWNING!
IS THIS WHAT I THINK IT IS?
NOT ME! I'M DEAD!

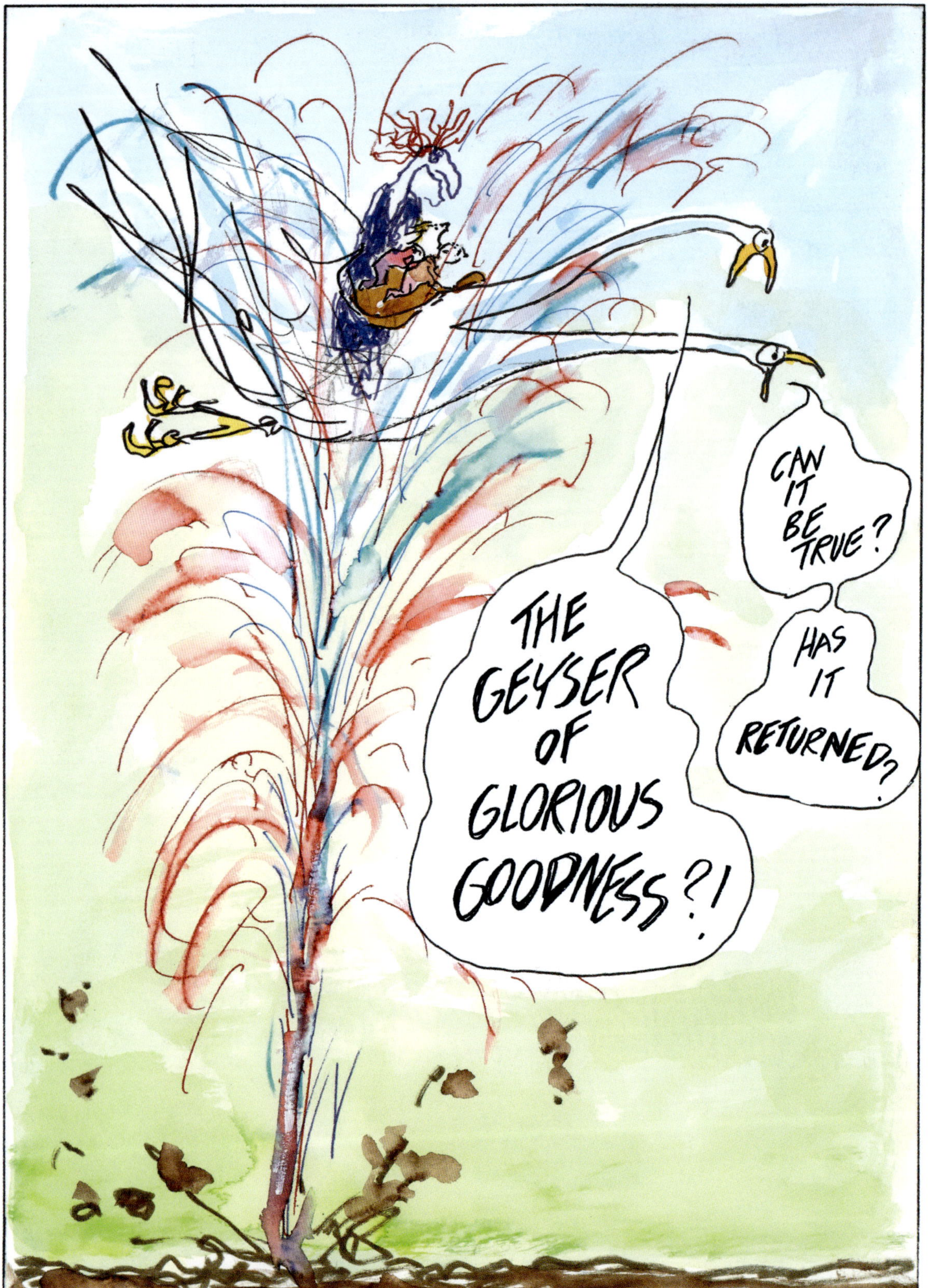
CAN IT BE TRUE?
HAS IT RETURNED?
THE GEYSER OF GLORIOUS GOODNESS?!

CHAPTER 52 • A GEYSER GALA!

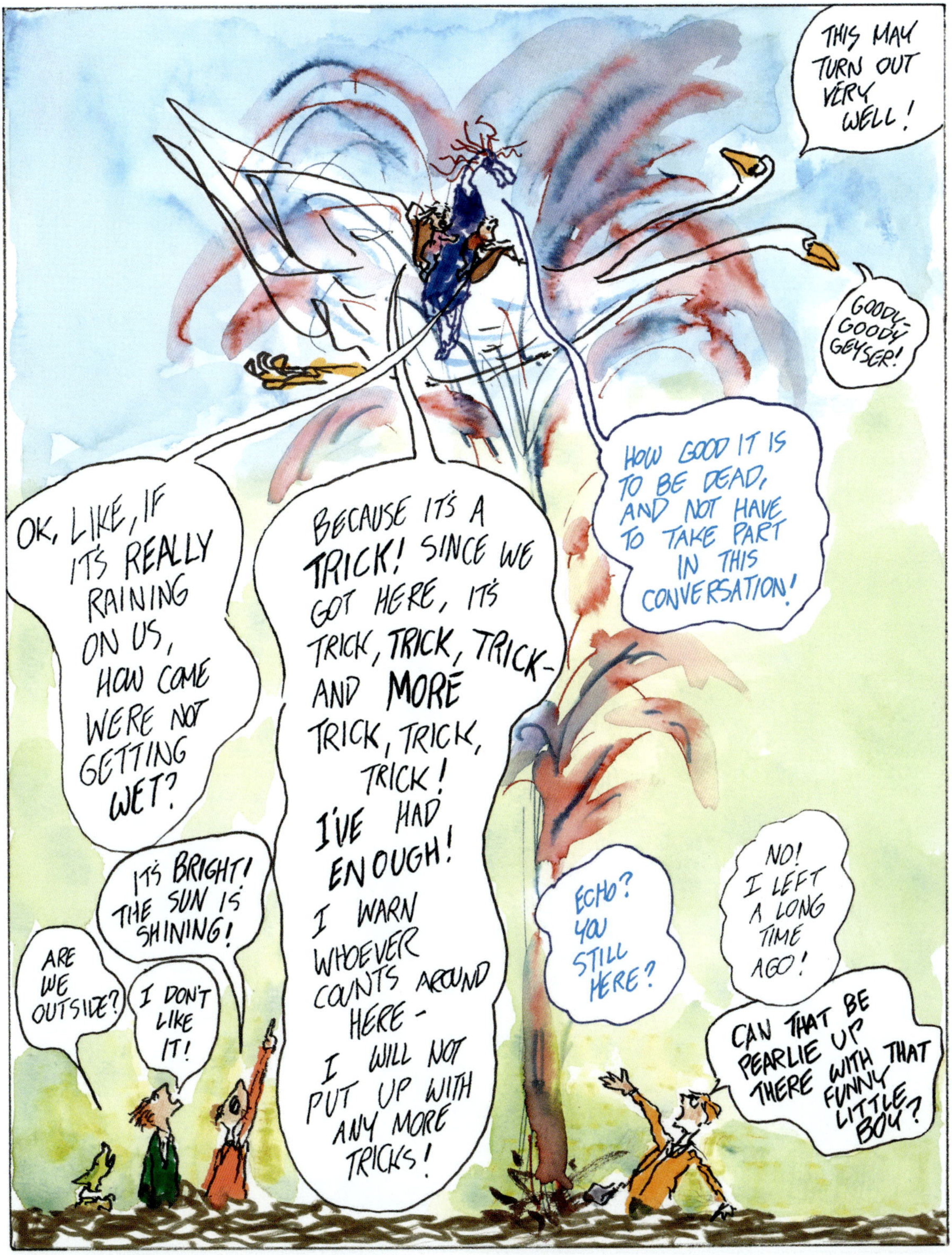
THIS MAY TURN OUT VERY WELL!
GOODY-GOODY GEYSER!
HOW GOOD IT IS TO BE DEAD, AND NOT HAVE TO TAKE PART IN THIS CONVERSATION!
OK, LIKE, IF IT'S REALLY RAINING ON US, HOW COME WE'RE NOT GETTING WET?
BECAUSE IT'S A TRICK! SINCE WE GOT HERE, IT'S TRICK, TRICK, TRICK- AND MORE TRICK, TRICK, TRICK! I'VE HAD ENOUGH! I WARN WHOEVER COUNTS AROUND HERE- I WILL NOT PUT UP WITH ANY MORE TRICKS!
IT'S BRIGHT! THE SUN IS SHINING!
ARE WE OUTSIDE?
I DON'T LIKE IT!
ECHO? YOU STILL HERE?
NO! I LEFT A LONG TIME AGO!
CAN THAT BE PEARLIE UP THERE WITH THAT FUNNY LITTLE BOY?

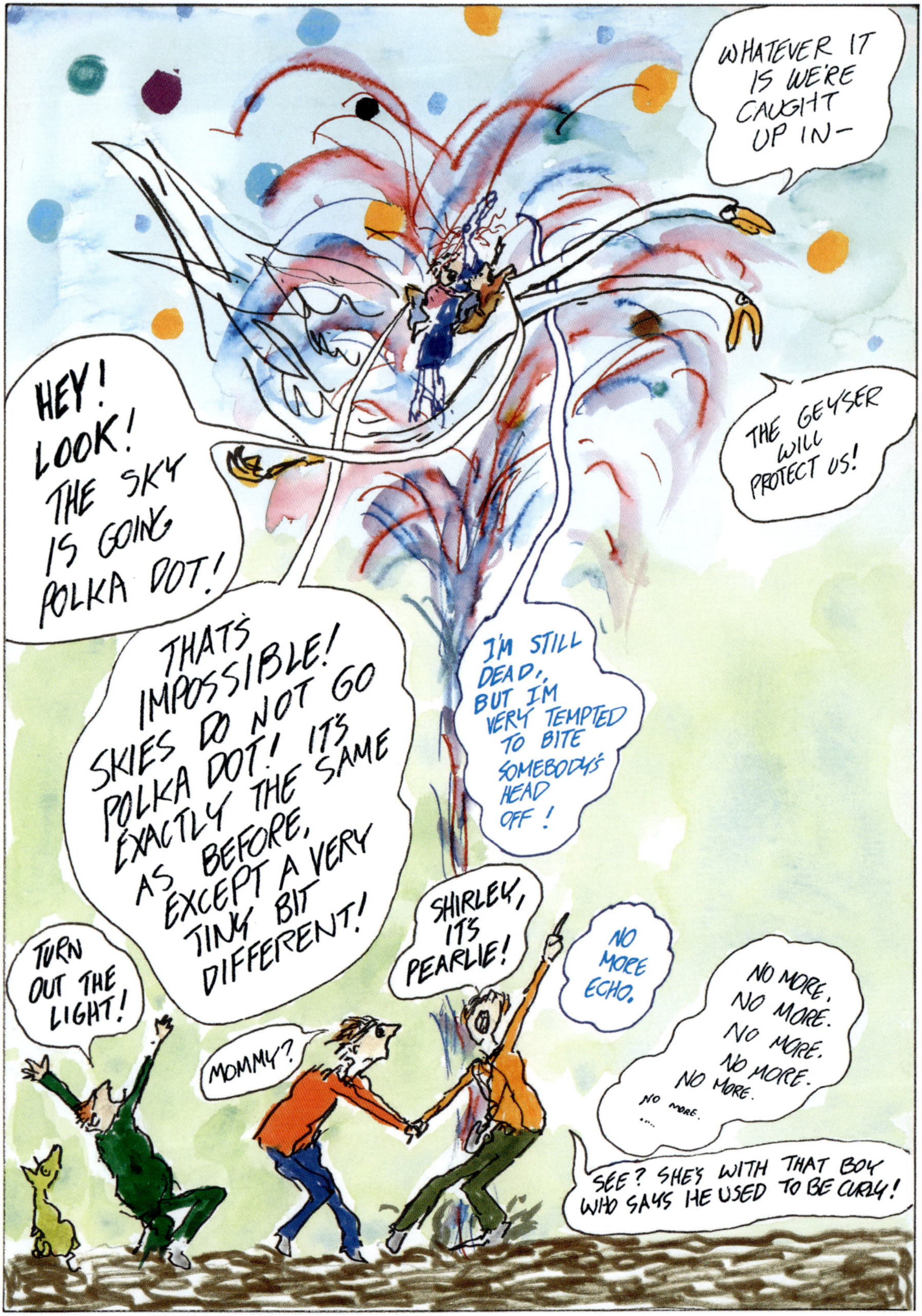

WHATEVER IT IS WE'RE CAUGHT UP IN—
HEY! LOOK! THE SKY IS GOING POLKA DOT!
THE GEYSER WILL PROTECT US!
THAT'S IMPOSSIBLE! SKIES DO NOT GO POLKA DOT! IT'S EXACTLY THE SAME AS BEFORE, EXCEPT A VERY TINY BIT DIFFERENT!
I'M STILL DEAD, BUT I'M VERY TEMPTED TO BITE SOMEBODY'S HEAD OFF!
TURN OUT THE LIGHT!
SHIRLEY, IT'S PEARLIE!
NO MORE ECHO.
NO MORE. NO MORE. NO MORE. NO MORE. NO MORE. NO MORE. ....
MOMMY?
SEE? SHE'S WITH THAT BOY WHO SAYS HE USED TO BE CURLY!

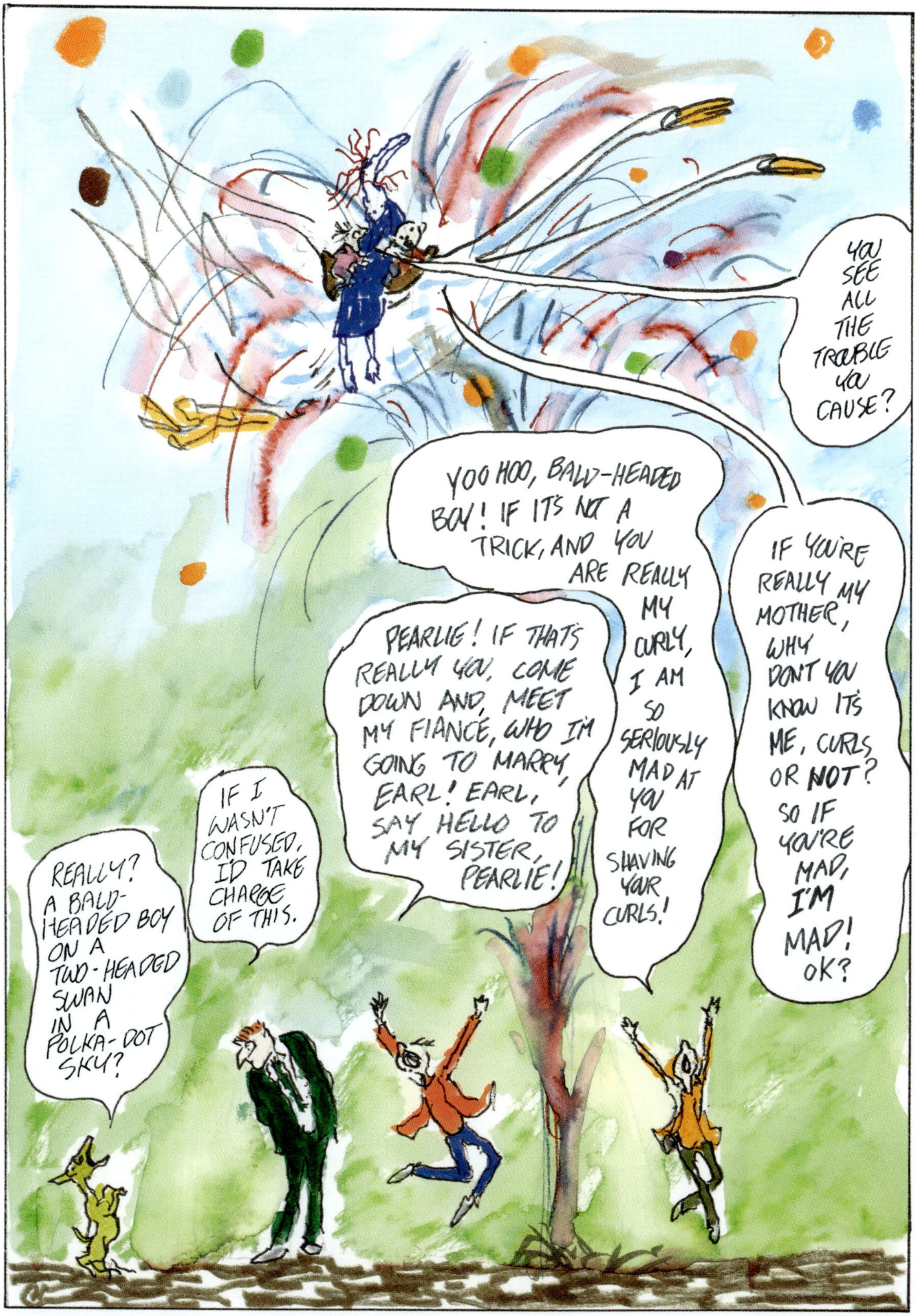
YOU SEE ALL THE TROUBLE YOU CAUSE?
YOO HOO, BALD-HEADED BOY! IF IT'S NOT A TRICK, AND YOU ARE REALLY MY CURLY, I AM SO SERIOUSLY MAD AT YOU FOR SHAVING YOUR CURLS!
IF YOU'RE REALLY MY MOTHER, WHY DON'T YOU KNOW IT'S ME, CURLS OR NOT? SO IF YOU'RE MAD, I'M MAD! OK?
PEARLIE! IF THAT'S REALLY YOU, COME DOWN AND, MEET MY FIANCE, WHO I'M GOING TO MARRY, EARL! EARL, SAY HELLO TO MY SISTER, PEARLIE!
IF I WASN'T CONFUSED, I'D TAKE CHARGE OF THIS.
REALLY? A BALD-HEADED BOY ON A TWO-HEADED SWAN IN A POLKA-DOT SKY?

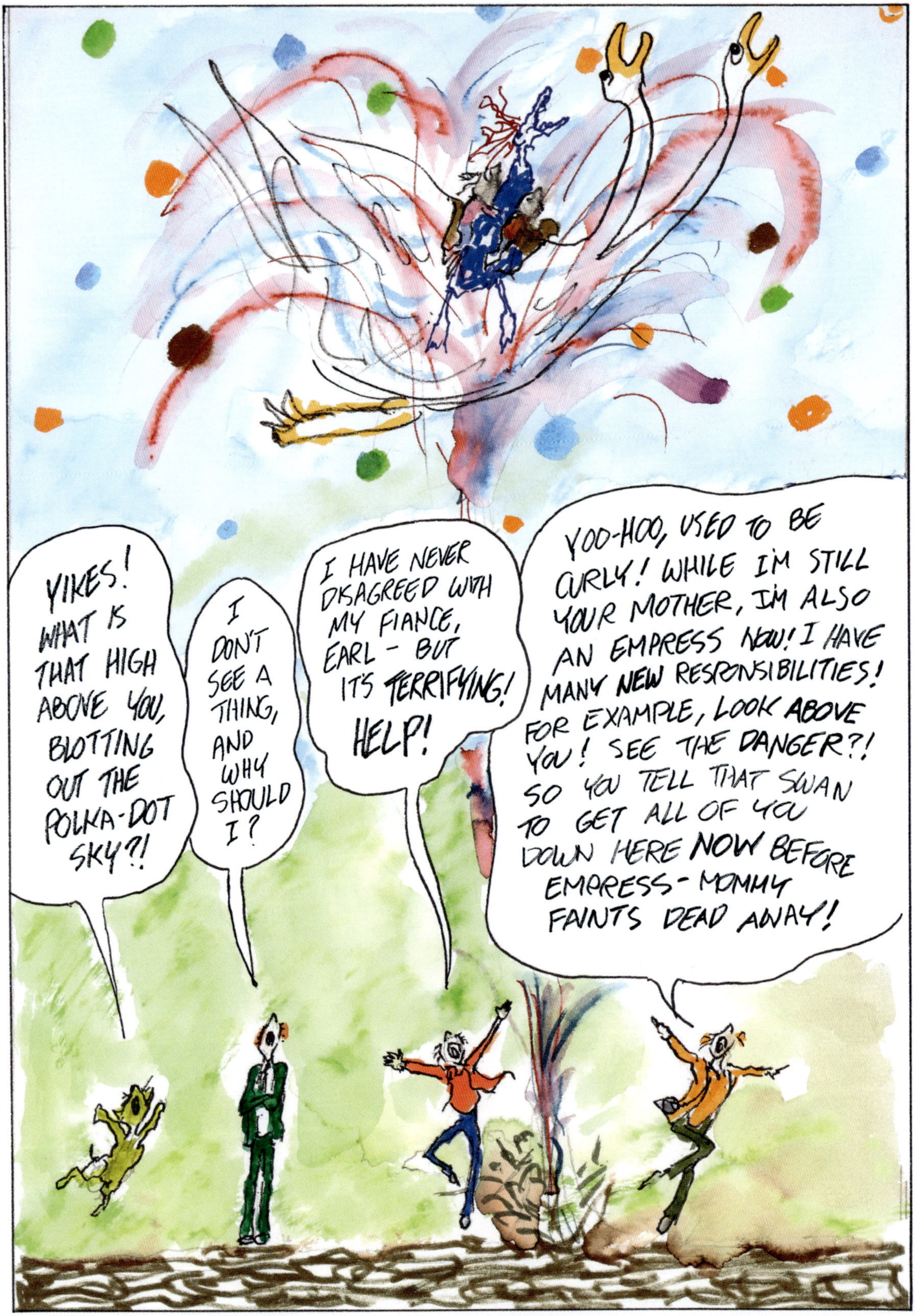
YIKES! WHAT IS THAT HIGH ABOVE YOU, BLOTTING OUT THE POLKA-DOT SKY?!
I DON'T SEE A THING, AND WHY SHOULD I?
I HAVE NEVER DISAGREED WITH MY FIANCE, EARL - BUT IT'S TERRIFYING! HELP!
YOO-HOO, USED TO BE CURLY! WHILE I'M STILL YOUR MOTHER, I'M ALSO AN EMPRESS NOW! I HAVE MANY NEW RESPONSIBILITIES! FOR EXAMPLE, LOOK ABOVE YOU! SEE THE DANGER?! SO YOU TELL THAT SWAN TO GET ALL OF YOU DOWN HERE NOW BEFORE EMPRESS-MOMMY FAINTS DEAD AWAY!

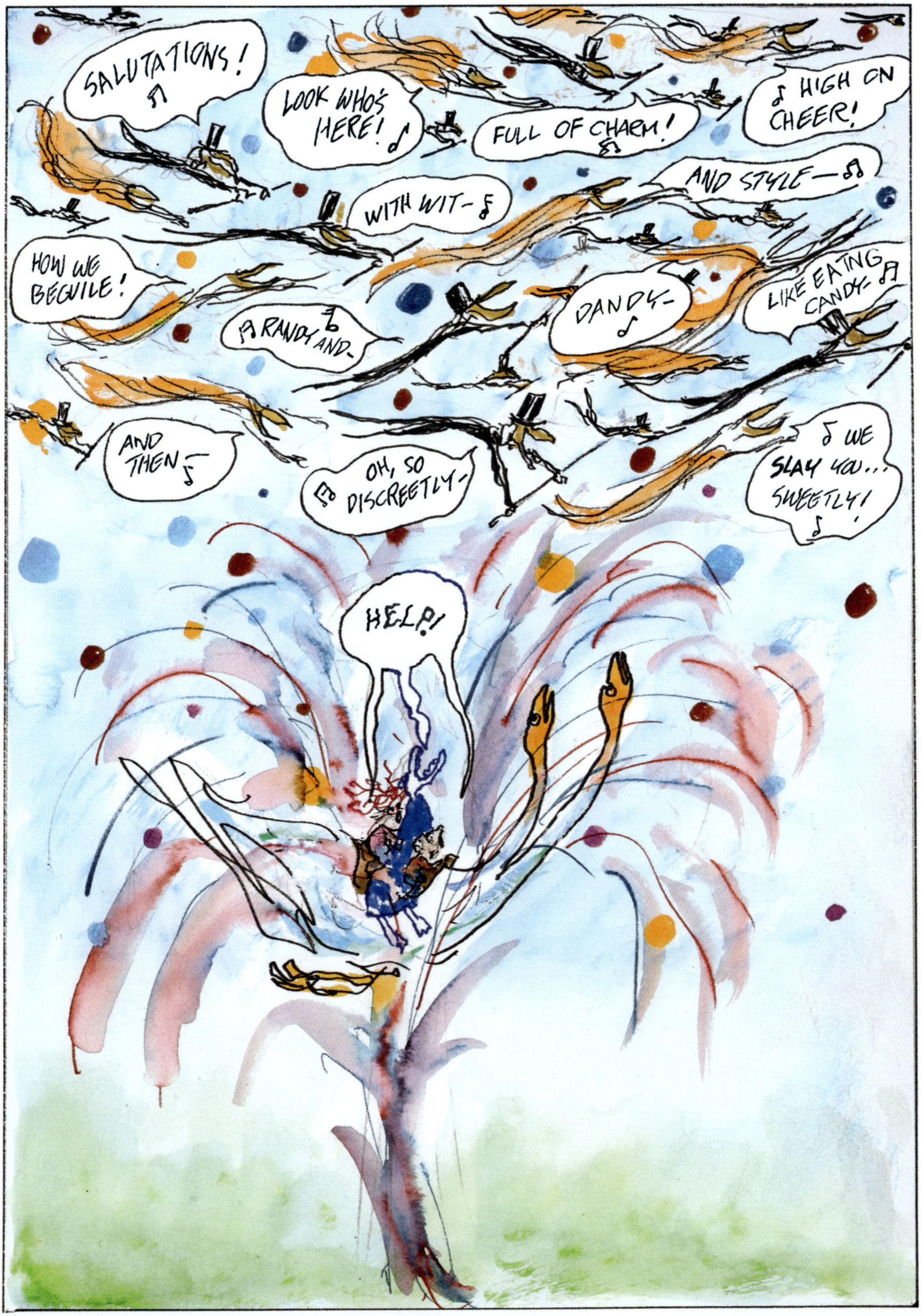
SALUTATIONS!
LOOK WHO'S HERE!
FULL OF CHARM!
HIGH ON CHEER!
AND STYLE—
WITH WIT—
HOW WE BEGUILE!
RANDY AND—
DANDY—
LIKE EATING CANDY—
AND THEN—
OH, SO DISCREETLY—
WE SLAY YOU... SWEETLY!
HELP!

CHAPTER 53 • THE ELEGANTICS

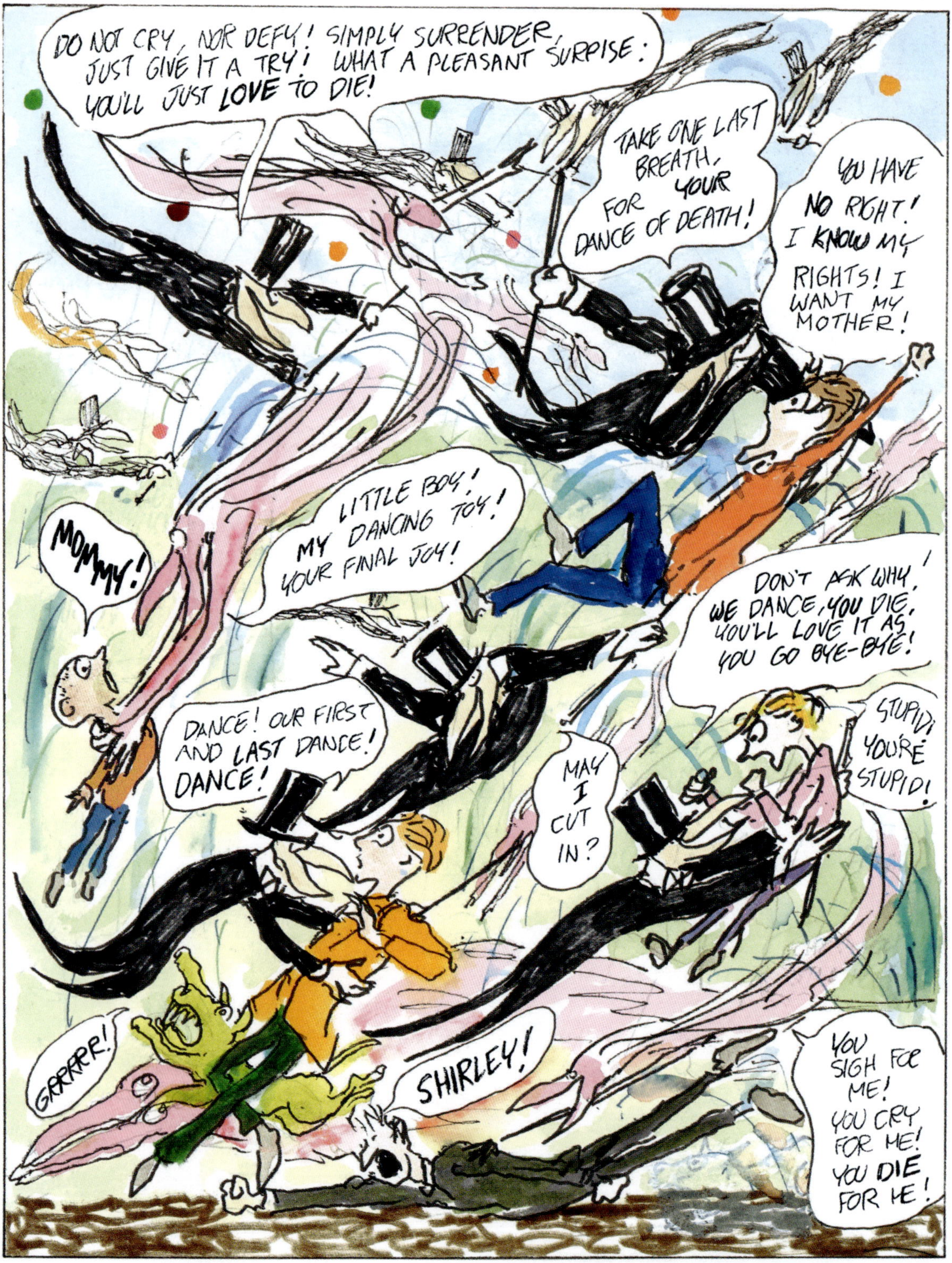
DO NOT CRY, NOR DEFY! SIMPLY SURRENDER, JUST GIVE IT A TRY! WHAT A PLEASANT SURPISE: YOU'LL JUST LOVE TO DIE!
TAKE ONE LAST BREATH, FOR YOUR DANCE OF DEATH!
YOU HAVE NO RIGHT! I KNOW MY RIGHTS! I WANT MY MOTHER!
MOMMY!
MY LITTLE BOY! MY DANCING TOY! YOUR FINAL JOY!
DON'T ASK WHY, WE DANCE, YOU DIE. YOU'LL LOVE IT AS YOU GO BYE-BYE!
DANCE! OUR FIRST AND LAST DANCE! DANCE!
MAY I CUT IN?
STUPID! YOU'RE STUPID!
GRRRRR!
SHIRLEY!
YOU SIGH FOR ME! YOU CRY FOR ME! YOU DIE FOR ME!

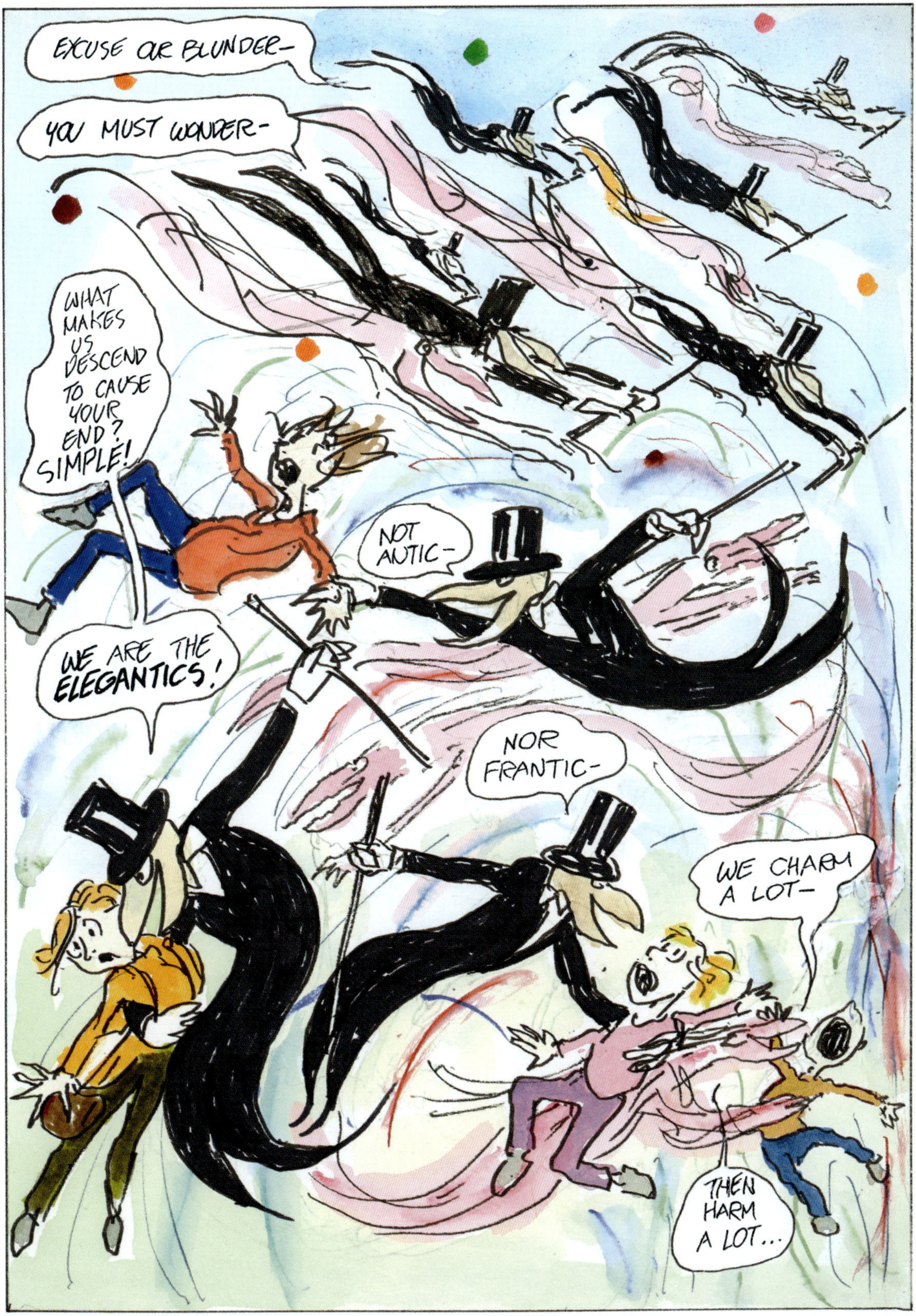
EXCUSE OUR BLUNDER-
YOU MUST WONDER-
WHAT MAKES US DESCEND TO CAUSE YOUR END? SIMPLE!
WE ARE THE ELEGANTICS!
NOT ANTIC-
NOR FRANTIC-
WE CHARM A LOT-
THEN HARM A LOT...

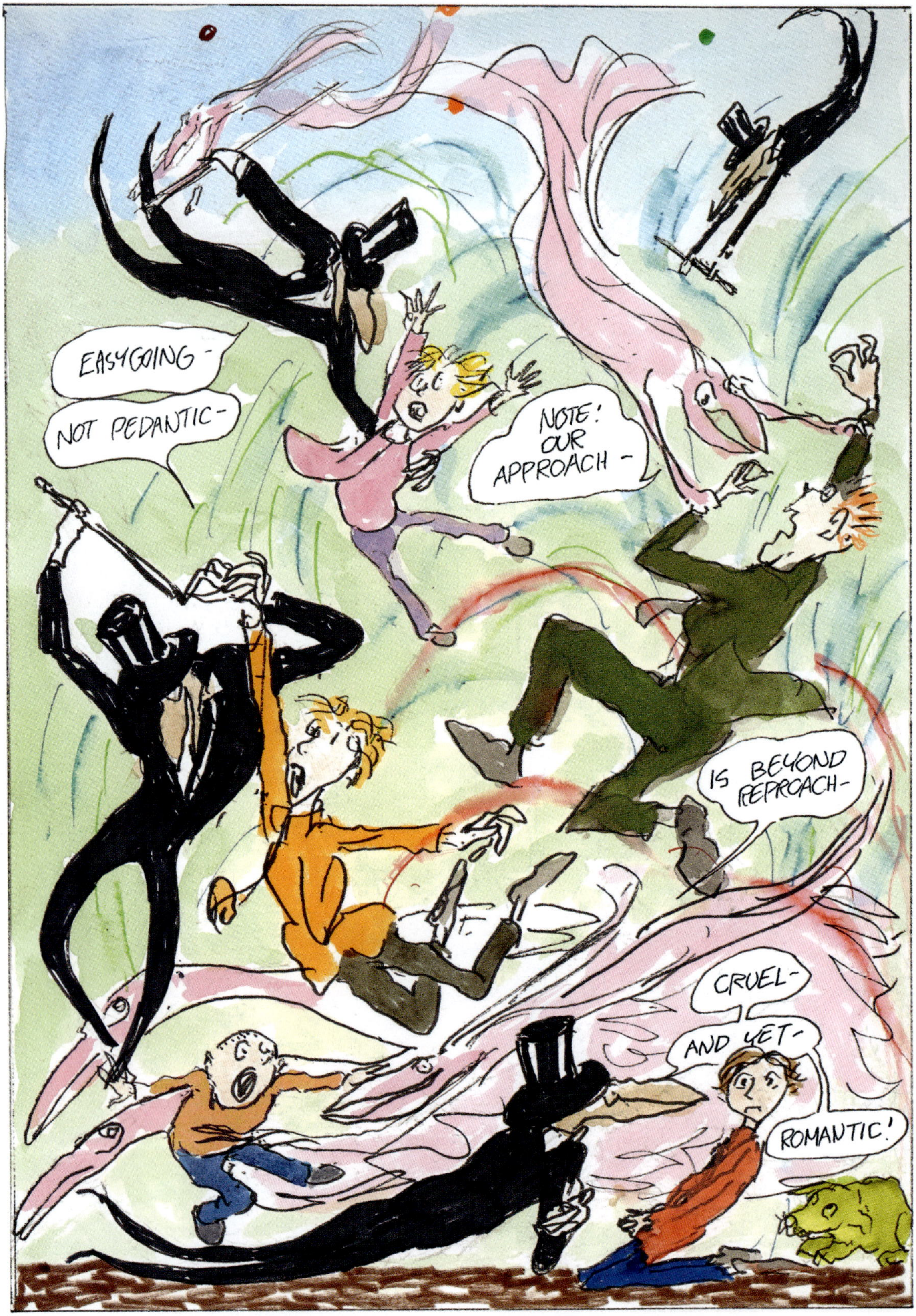
EASYGOING-
NOT PEDANTIC-
NOTE! OUR APPROACH -
IS BEYOND REPROACH-
CRUEL-
AND YET-
ROMANTIC!

CHAPTER 54 • THE ROMANCE OF DEATH

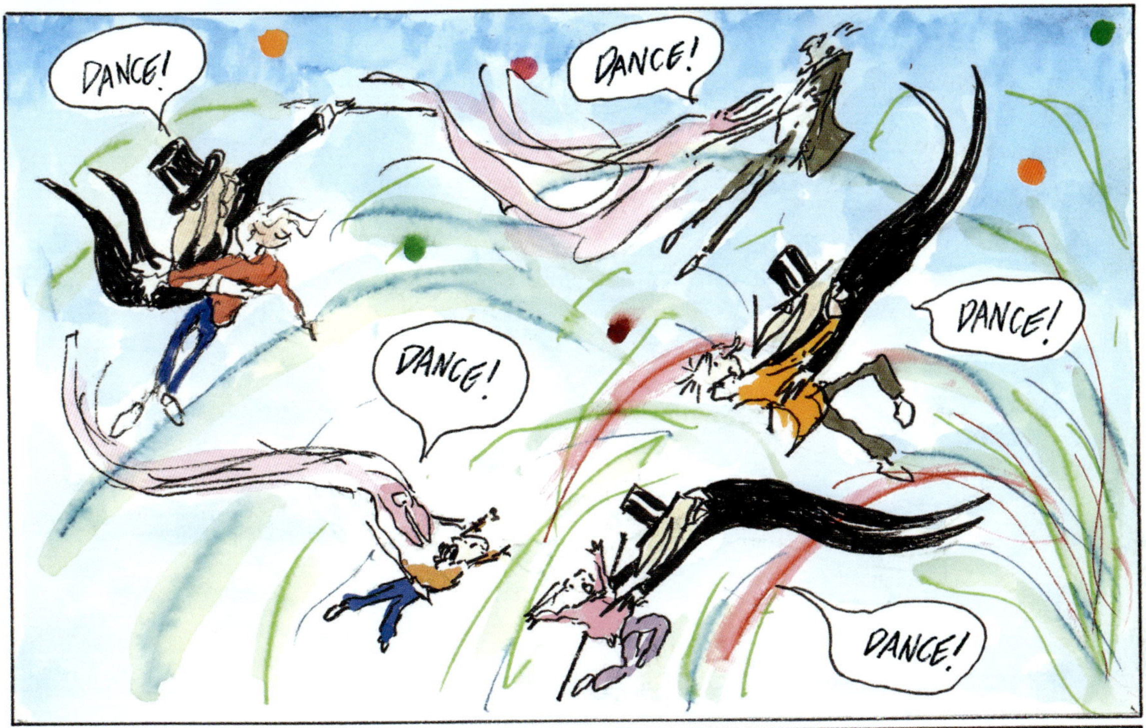
DANCE!
DANCE!
DANCE!
DANCE!
DANCE!

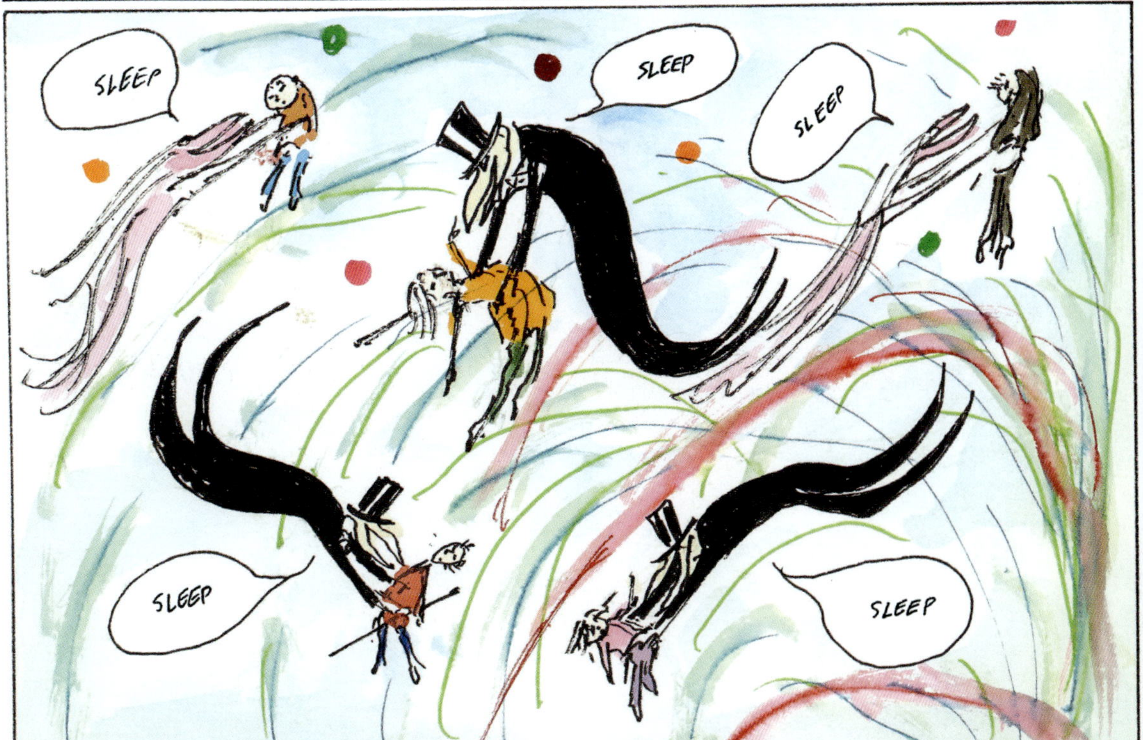
SLEEP
SLEEP
SLEEP
SLEEP
SLEEP

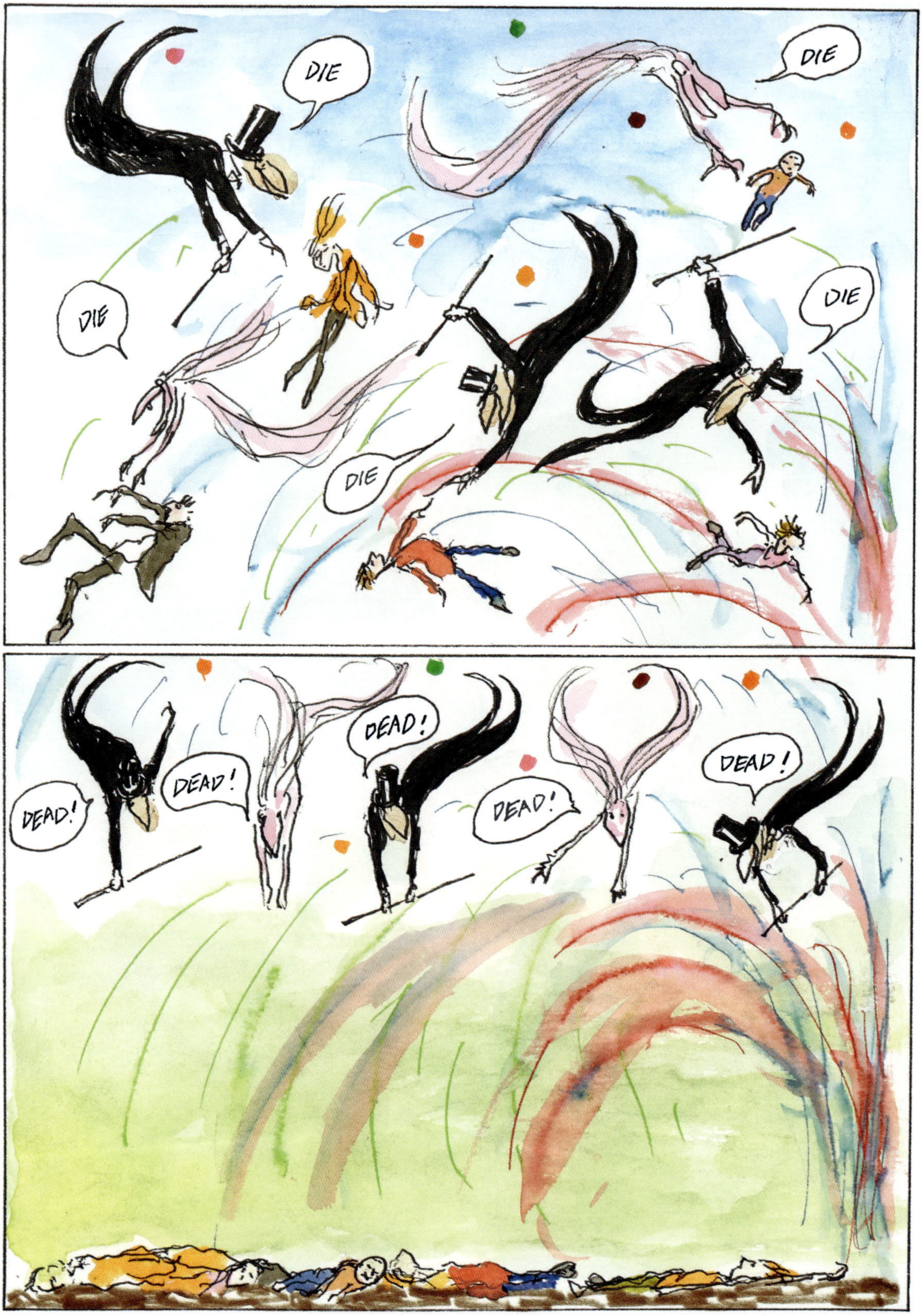
DIE
DIE
DIE
DIE
DIE
DEAD!
DEAD!
DEAD!
DEAD!
DEAD!

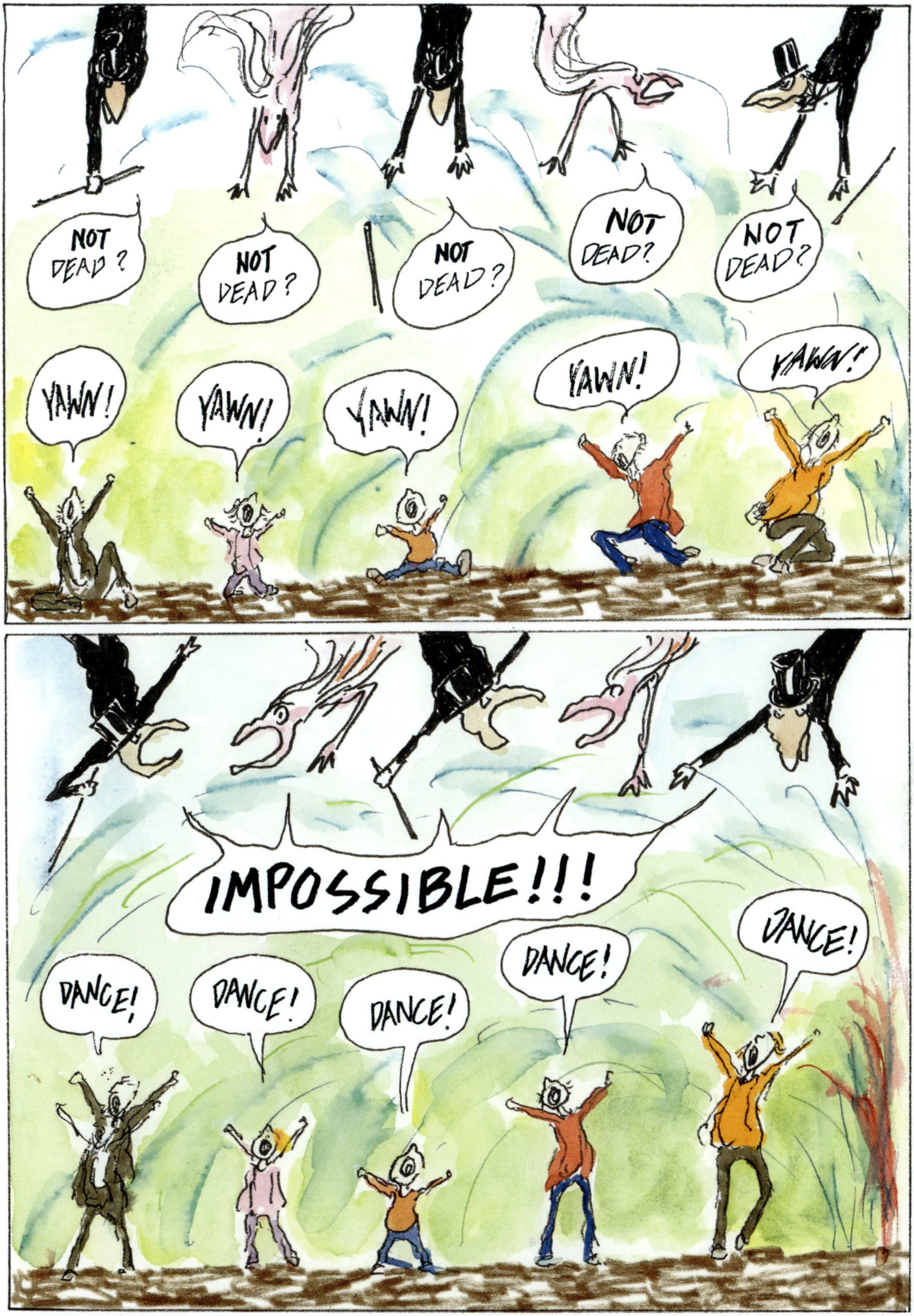
NOT DEAD ?
NOT DEAD ?
NOT DEAD ?
NOT DEAD?
NOT DEAD?
YAWN!
YAWN!
YAWN!
YAWN!
YAWN!
IMPOSSIBLE!!!
DANCE!
DANCE!
DANCE!
DANCE!
DANCE!

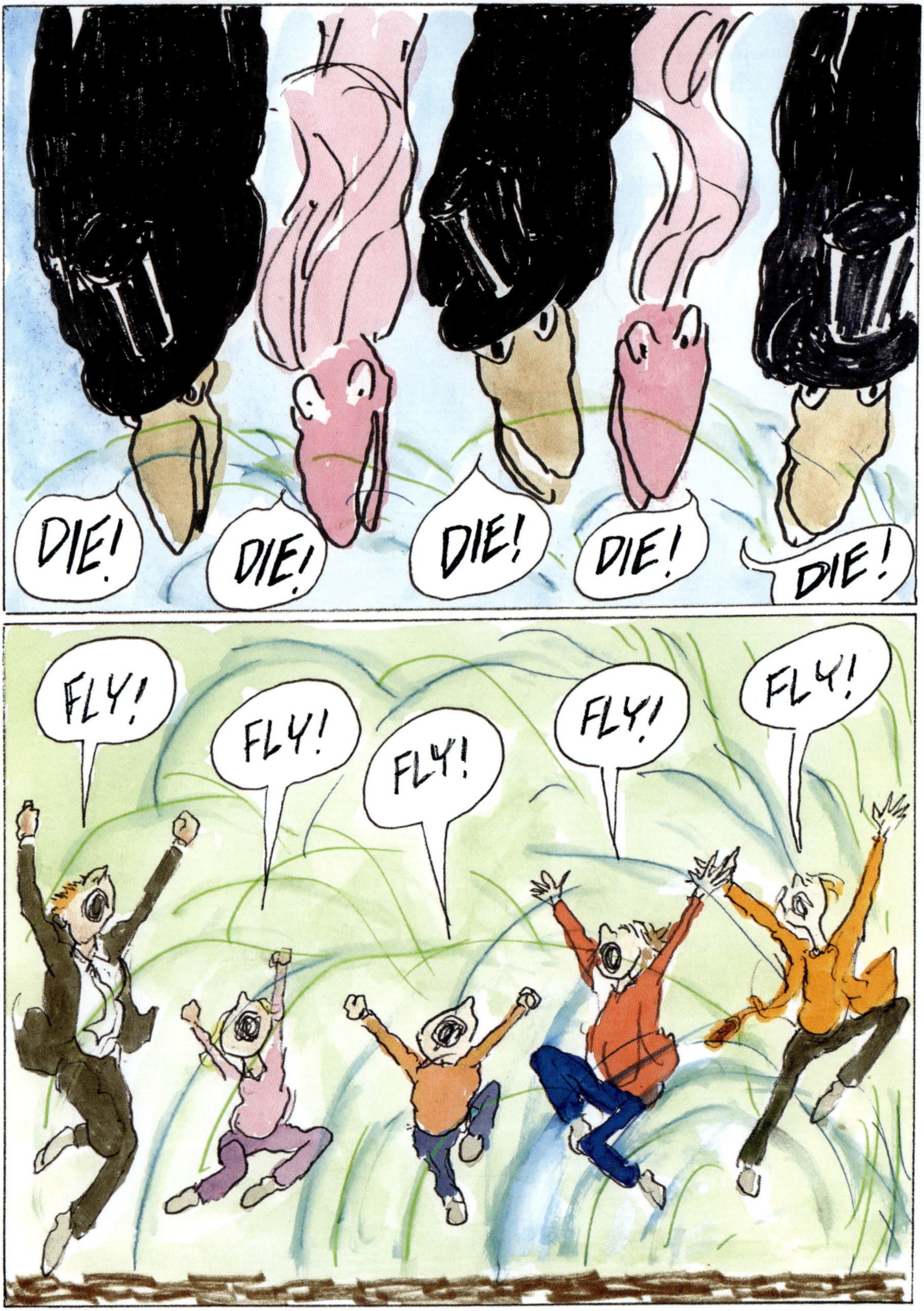
DIE!
DIE!
DIE!
DIE!
DIE!
FLY!
FLY!
FLY!
FLY!
FLY!

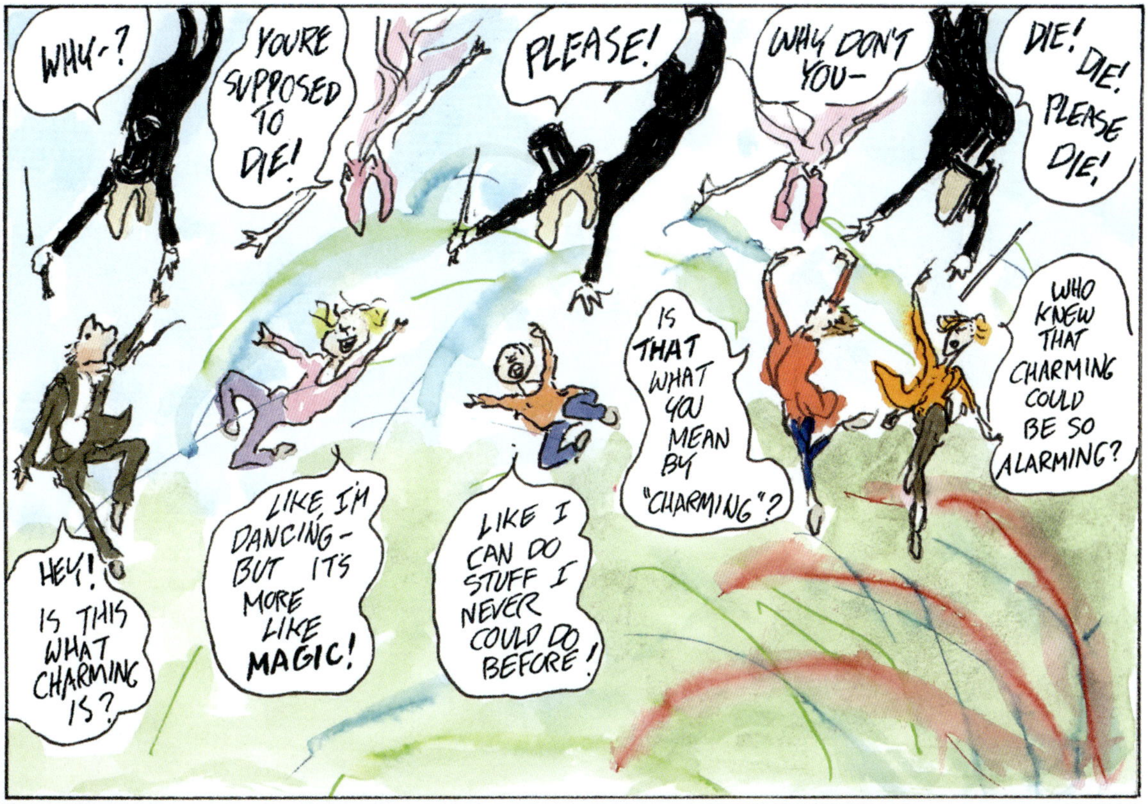
WHY-?
YOU'RE SUPPOSED TO DIE!
PLEASE!
WHY DON'T YOU-
DIE! DIE! PLEASE DIE!
HEY! IS THIS WHAT CHARMING IS?
LIKE I'M DANCING- BUT IT'S MORE LIKE MAGIC!
LIKE I CAN DO STUFF I NEVER COULD DO BEFORE!
IS THAT WHAT YOU MEAN BY "CHARMING"?
WHO KNEW THAT CHARMING COULD BE SO ALARMING?

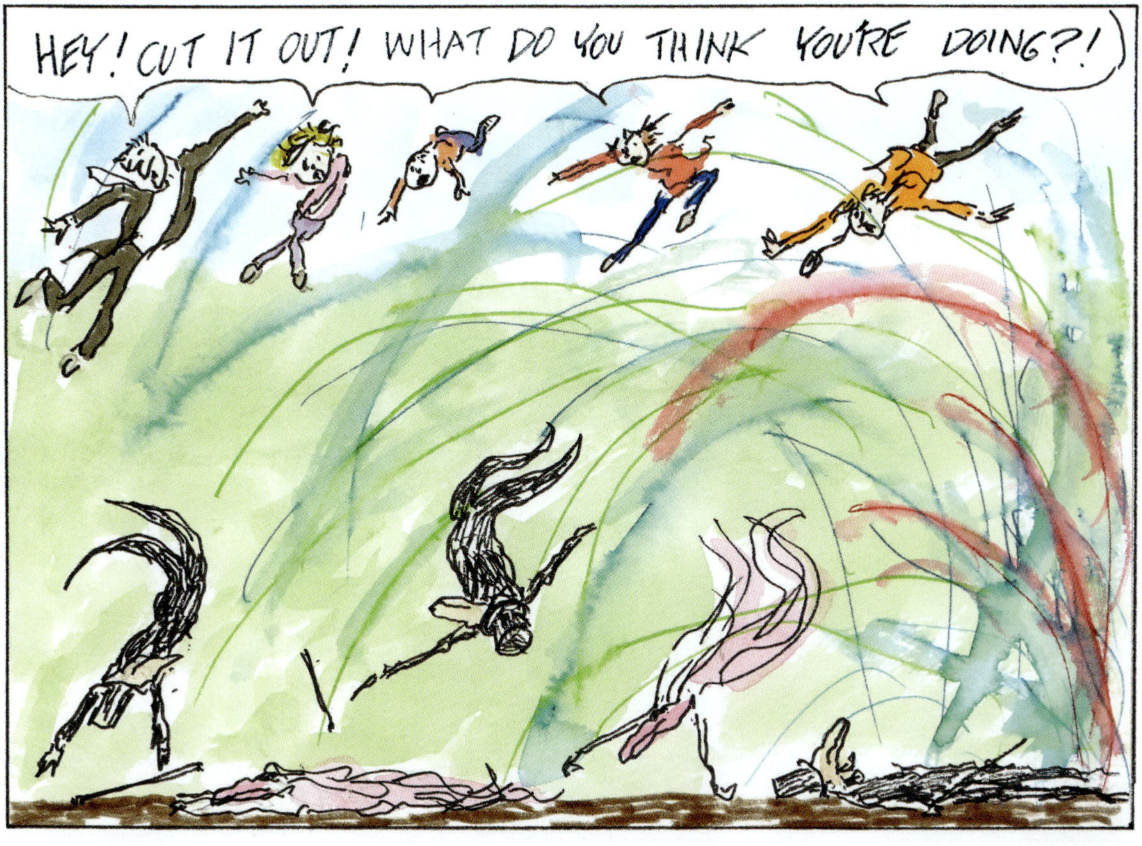
HEY! CUT IT OUT! WHAT DO YOU THINK YOU'RE DOING?!

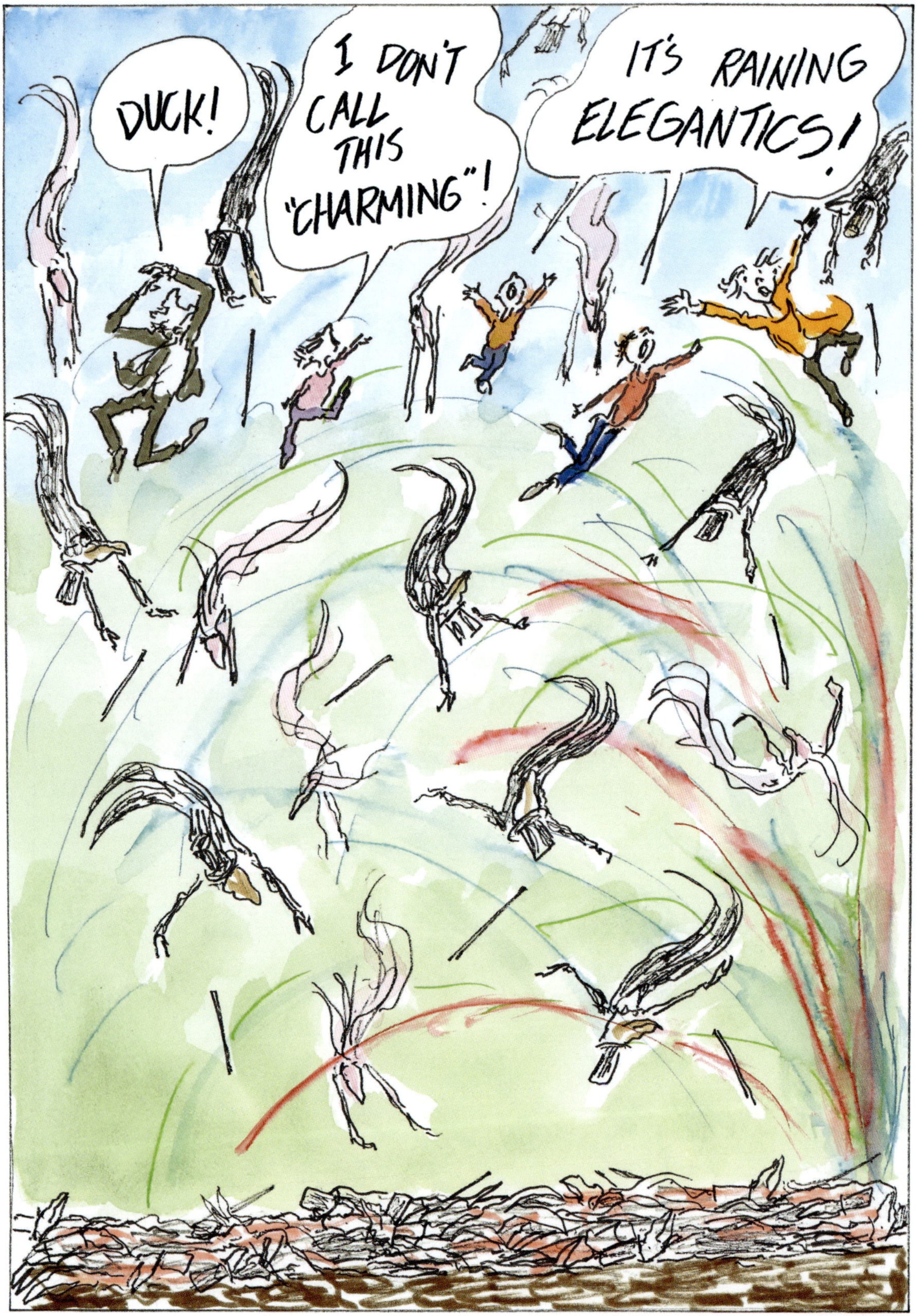
DUCK!
I DON'T CALL THIS "CHARMING"!
IT'S RAINING ELEGANTICS!

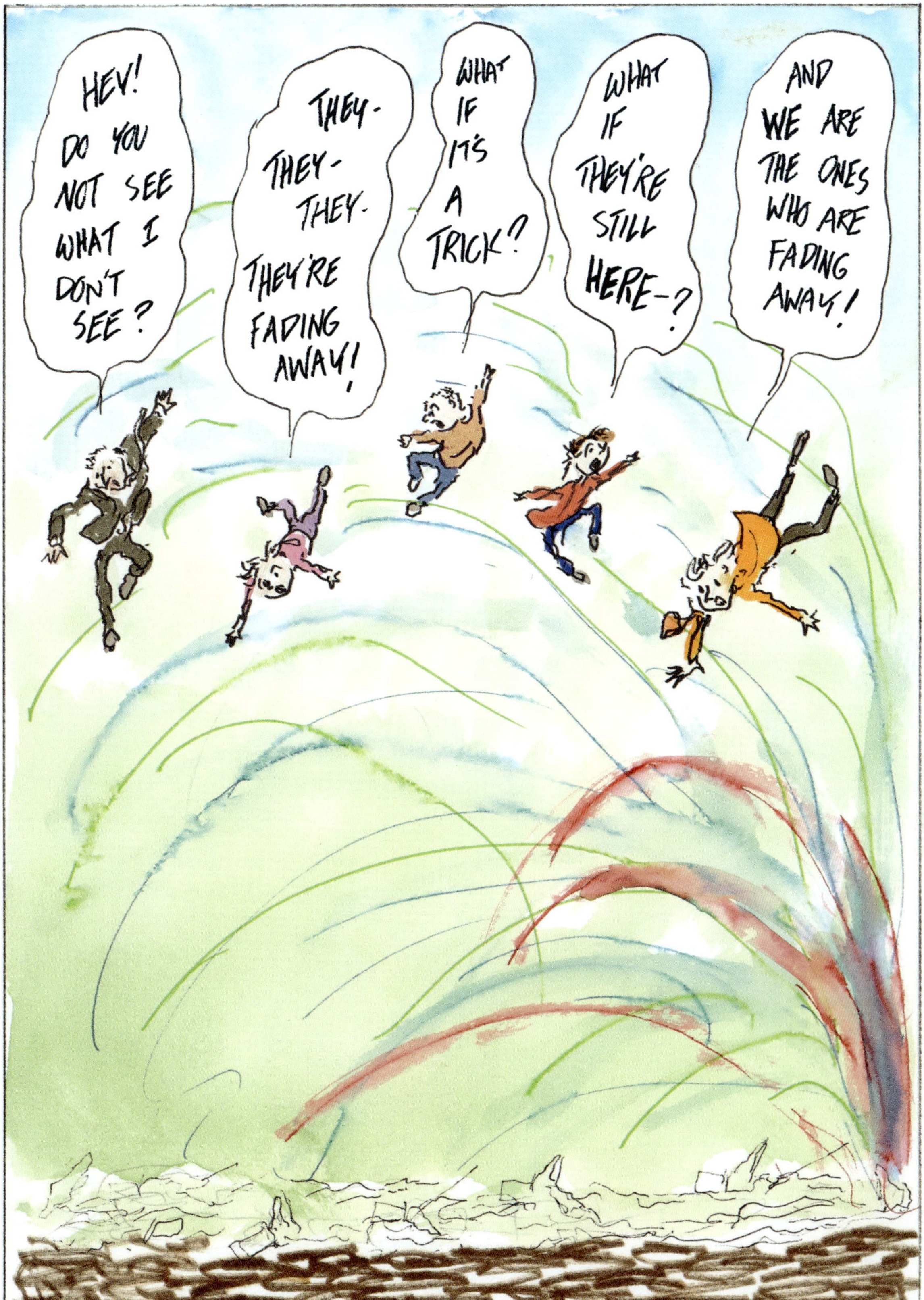
HEY! DO YOU NOT SEE WHAT I DON'T SEE?
THEY- THEY- THEY- THEY'RE FADING AWAY!
WHAT IF IT'S A TRICK?
WHAT IF THEY'RE STILL HERE-?
AND WE ARE THE ONES WHO ARE FADING AWAY!

CHAPTER 55 • UNFAIR MOMMY

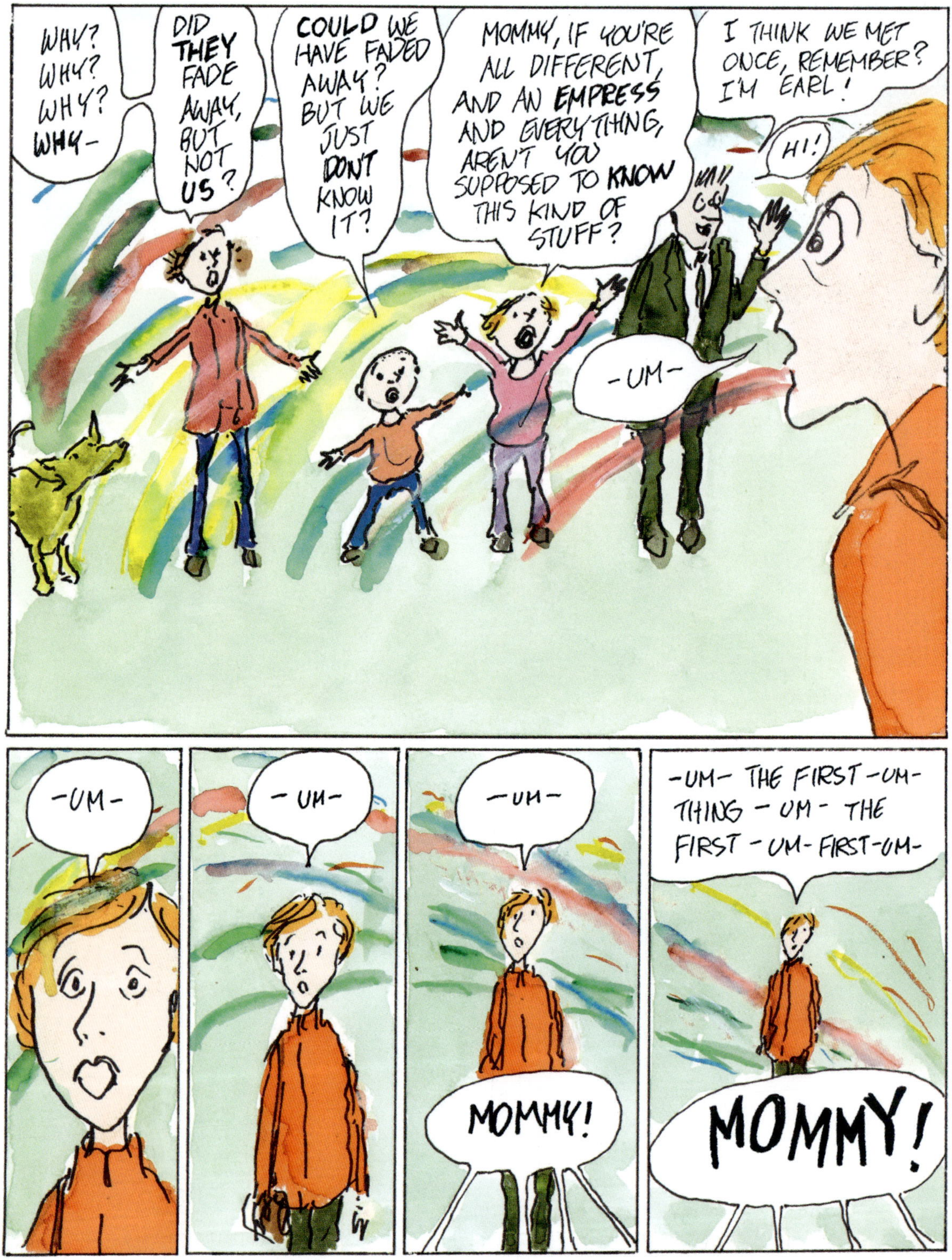
WHY? WHY? WHY? WHY-
DID THEY FADE AWAY, BUT NOT US?
COULD WE HAVE FADED AWAY? BUT WE JUST DON'T KNOW IT?
MOMMY, IF YOU'RE ALL DIFFERENT, AND AN EMPRESS AND EVERYTHING, AREN'T YOU SUPPOSED TO KNOW THIS KIND OF STUFF?
I THINK WE MET ONCE, REMEMBER? I'M EARL!
HI!
-UM-
-UM-
-UM-
-UM-
MOMMY!
-UM- THE FIRST -UM- THING -UM- THE FIRST -UM- FIRST -UM-
MOMMY!

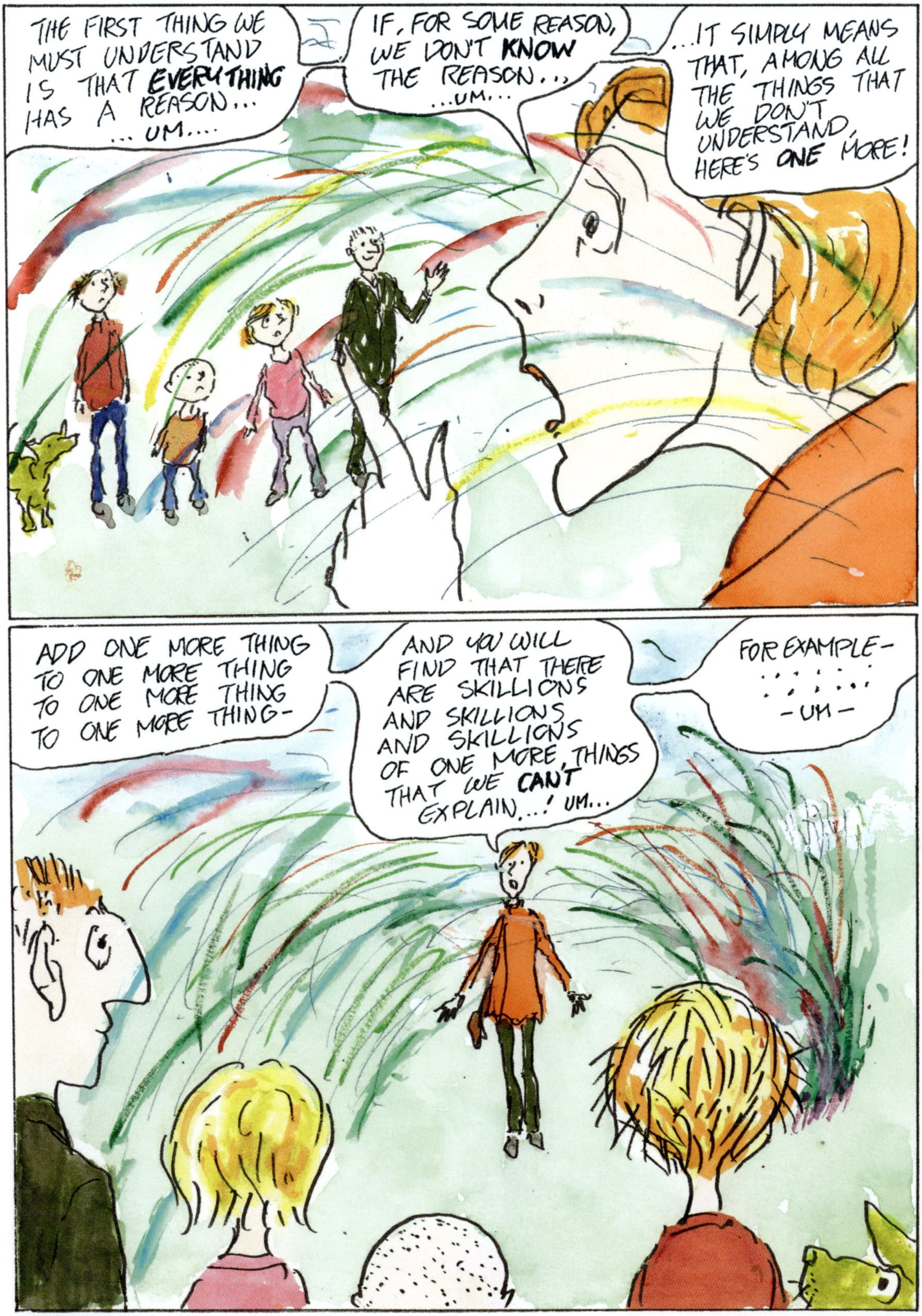
THE FIRST THING WE MUST UNDERSTAND IS THAT **EVERYTHING** HAS A REASON... ...UM....
IF, FOR SOME REASON, WE DON'T **KNOW** THE REASON... ...UM...
...IT SIMPLY MEANS THAT, AMONG ALL THE THINGS THAT WE DON'T UNDERSTAND, HERE'S **ONE** MORE!
ADD ONE MORE THING TO ONE MORE THING TO ONE MORE THING TO ONE MORE THING-
AND YOU WILL FIND THAT THERE ARE SKILLIONS AND SKILLIONS AND SKILLIONS OF ONE MORE, THINGS THAT WE **CAN'T** EXPLAIN...! UM...
FOR EXAMPLE- .... -UM-

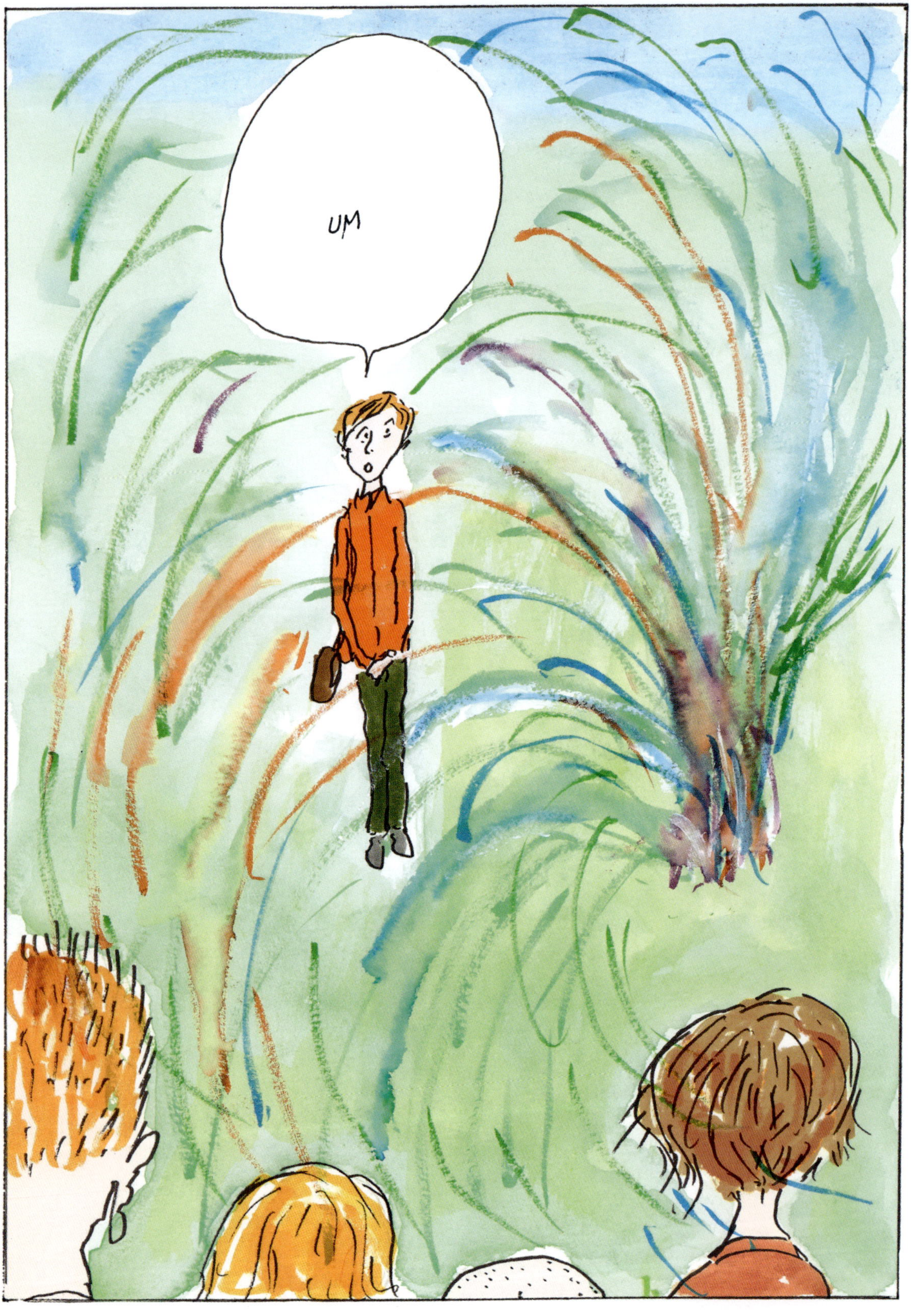
UM

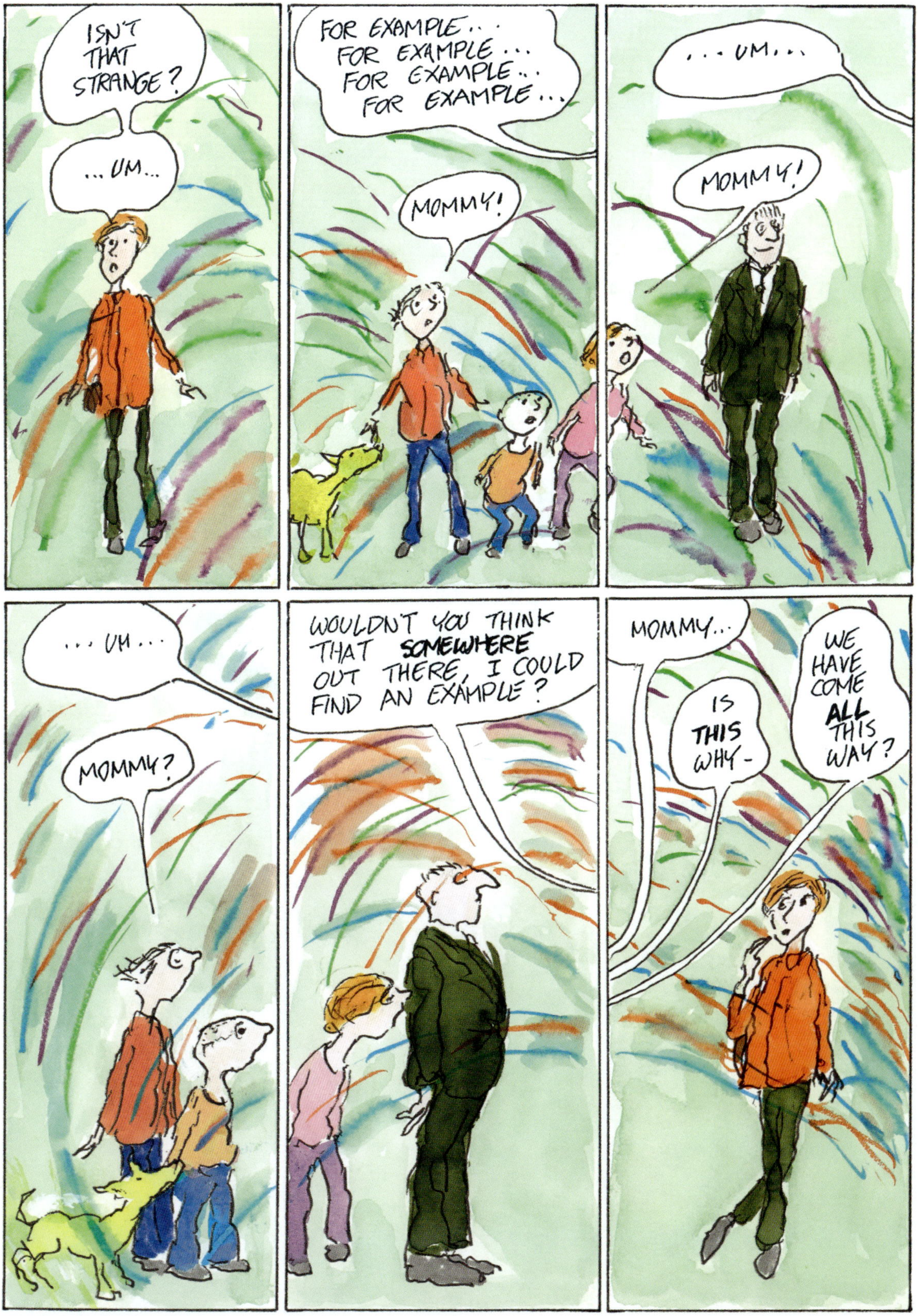
ISN'T THAT STRANGE?
...UM...
FOR EXAMPLE... FOR EXAMPLE... FOR EXAMPLE... FOR EXAMPLE...
MOMMY!
...UM...
MOMMY!
...UM...
MOMMY?
WOULDN'T YOU THINK THAT SOMEWHERE OUT THERE, I COULD FIND AN EXAMPLE?
MOMMY...
IS THIS WHY-
WE HAVE COME ALL THIS WAY?

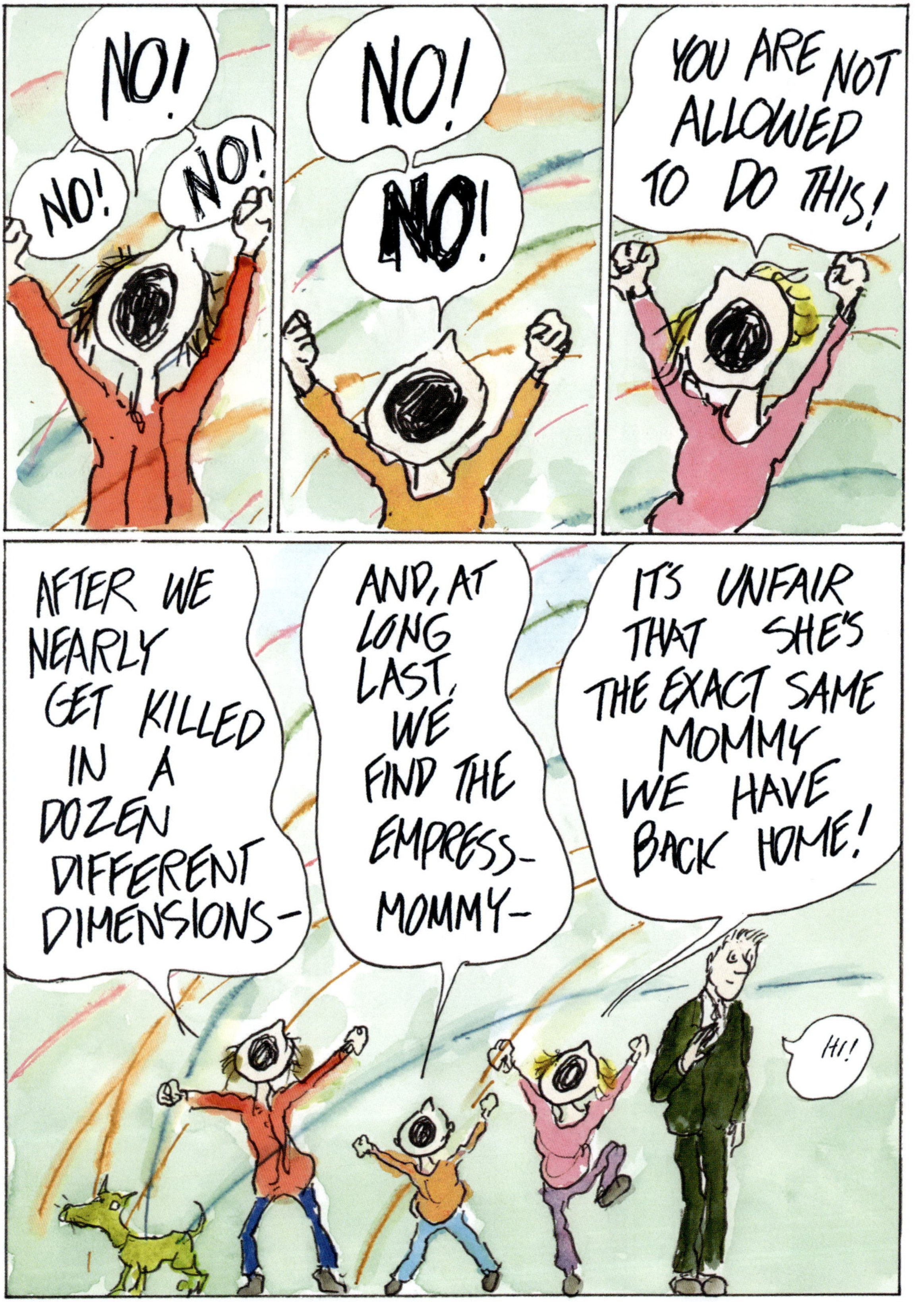
NO!
NO!
NO!
NO!
NO!
YOU ARE NOT ALLOWED TO DO THIS!
AFTER WE NEARLY GET KILLED IN A DOZEN DIFFERENT DIMENSIONS-
AND, AT LONG LAST, WE FIND THE EMPRESS-MOMMY-
IT'S UNFAIR THAT SHE'S THE EXACT SAME MOMMY WE HAVE BACK HOME!
HI!

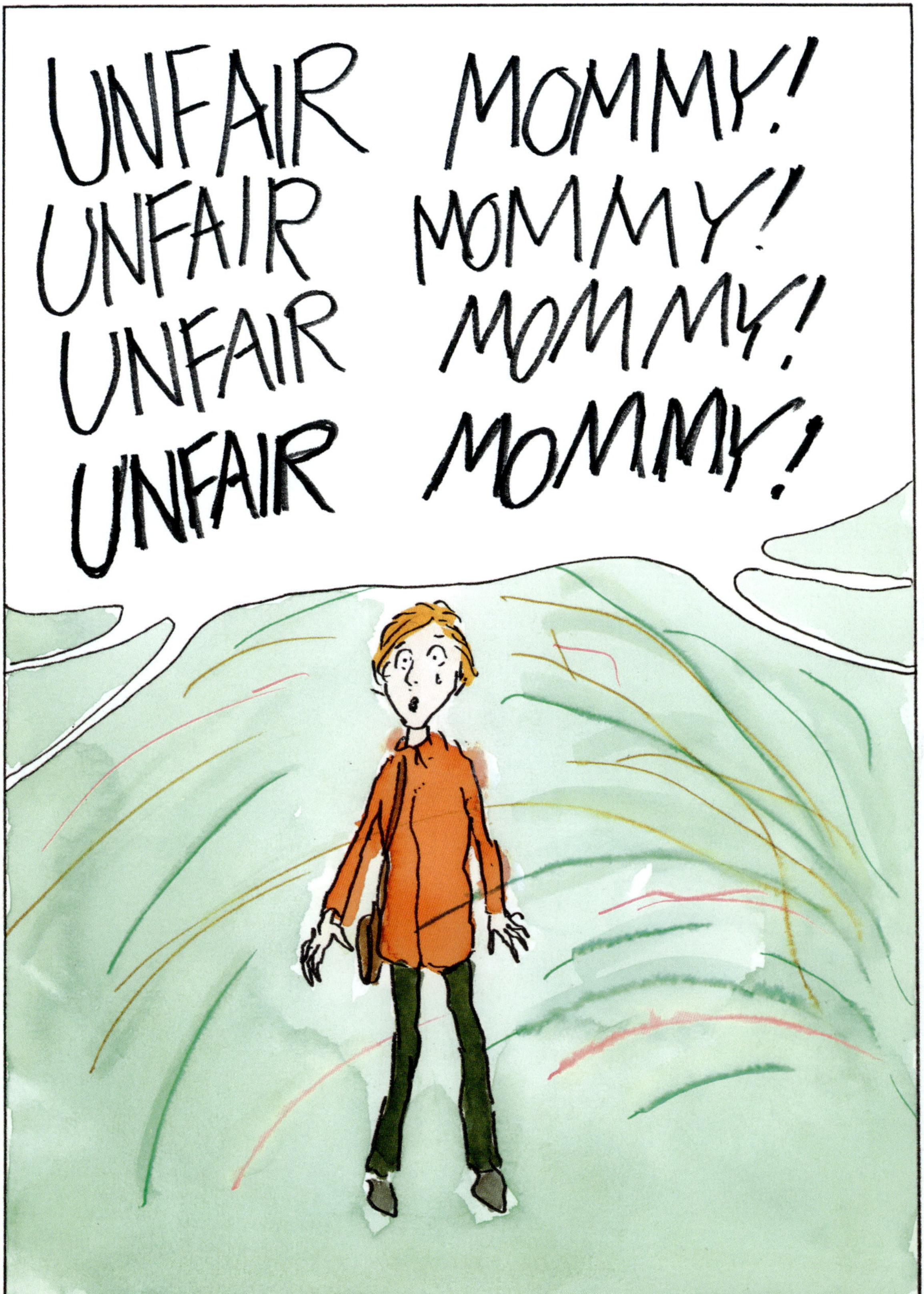
UNFAIR MOMMY!
UNFAIR MOMMY!
UNFAIR MOMMY!
UNFAIR MOMMY!

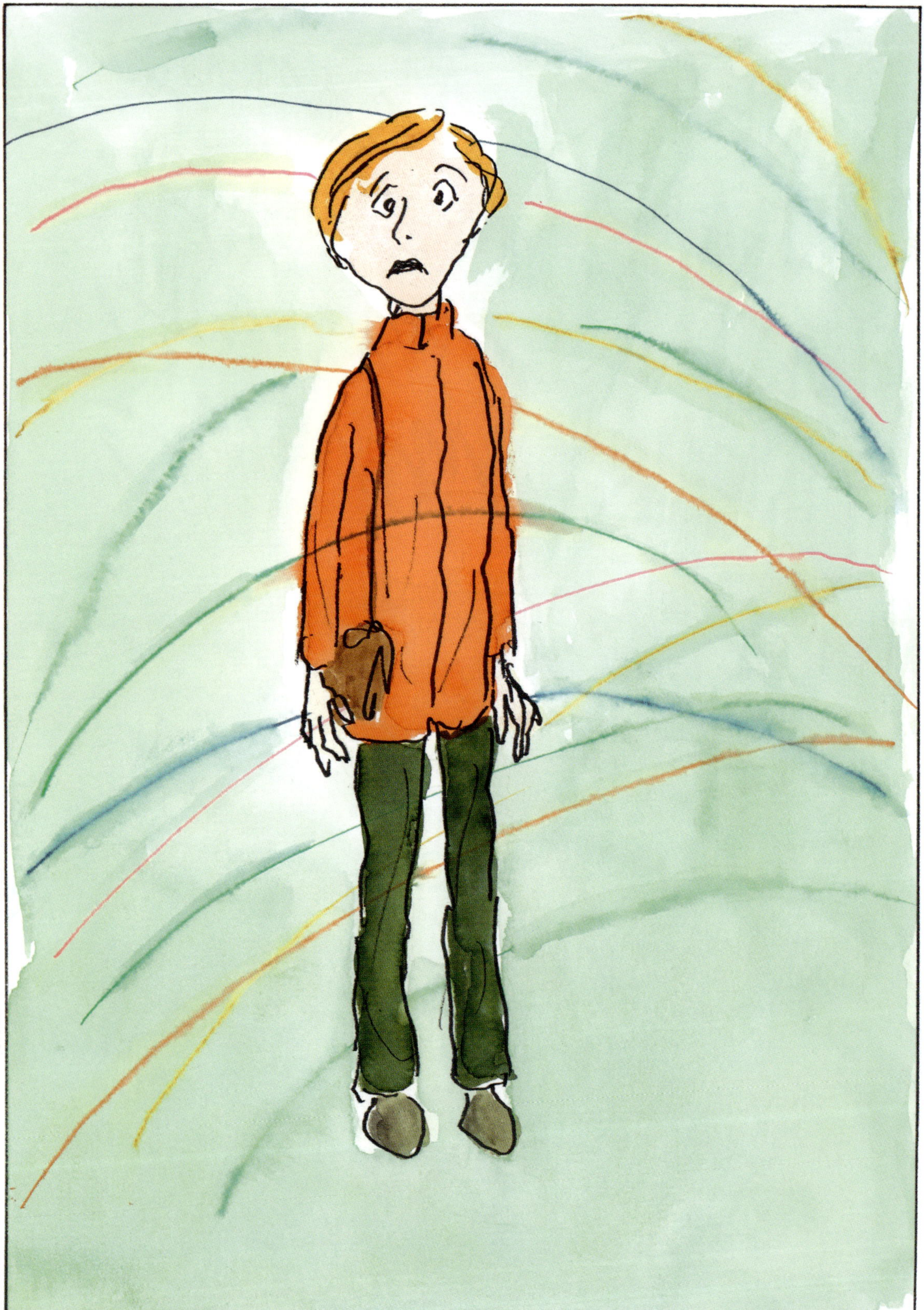

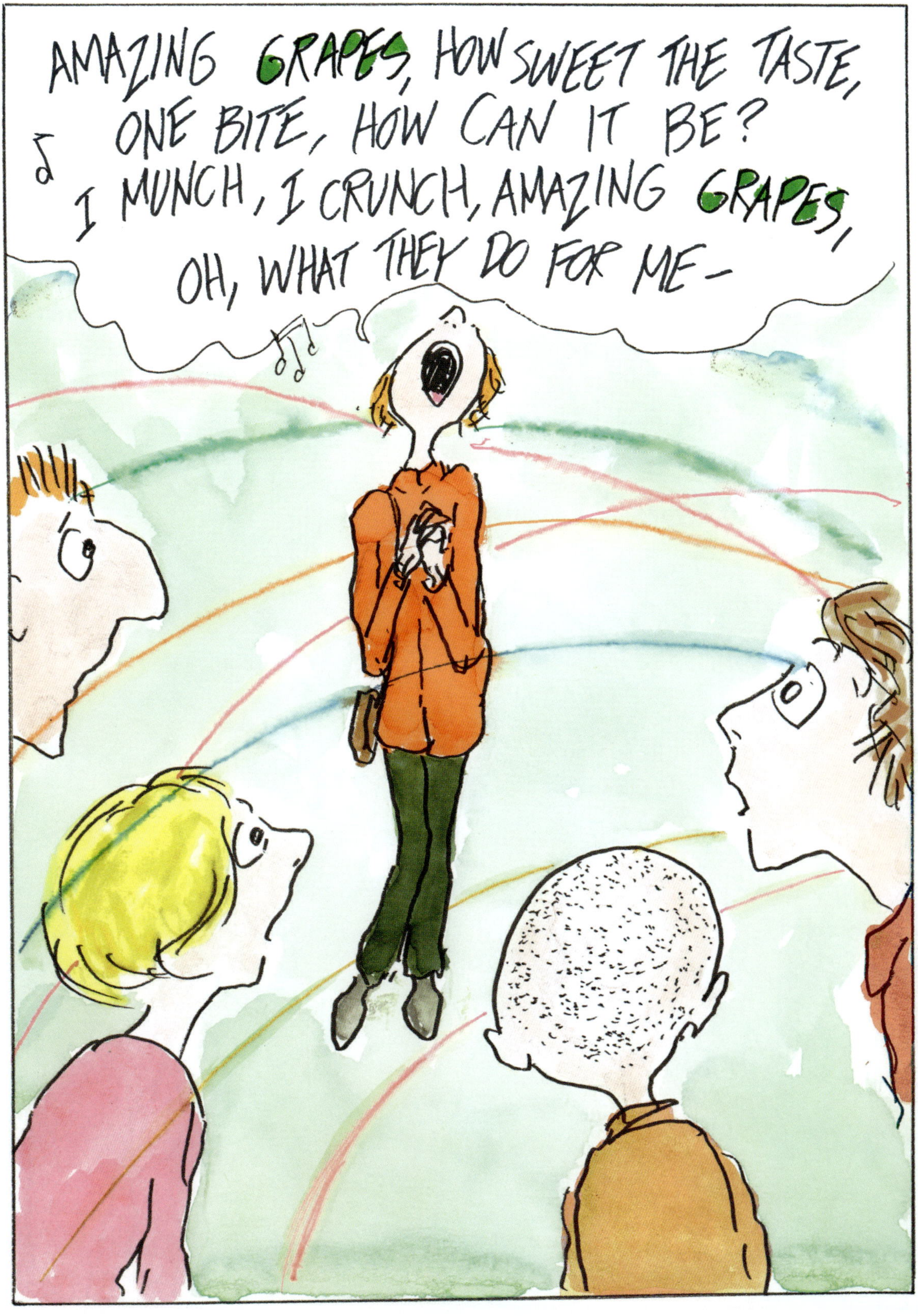
AMAZING GRAPES, HOW SWEET THE TASTE,
ONE BITE, HOW CAN IT BE?
I MUNCH, I CRUNCH, AMAZING GRAPES,
OH, WHAT THEY DO FOR ME–

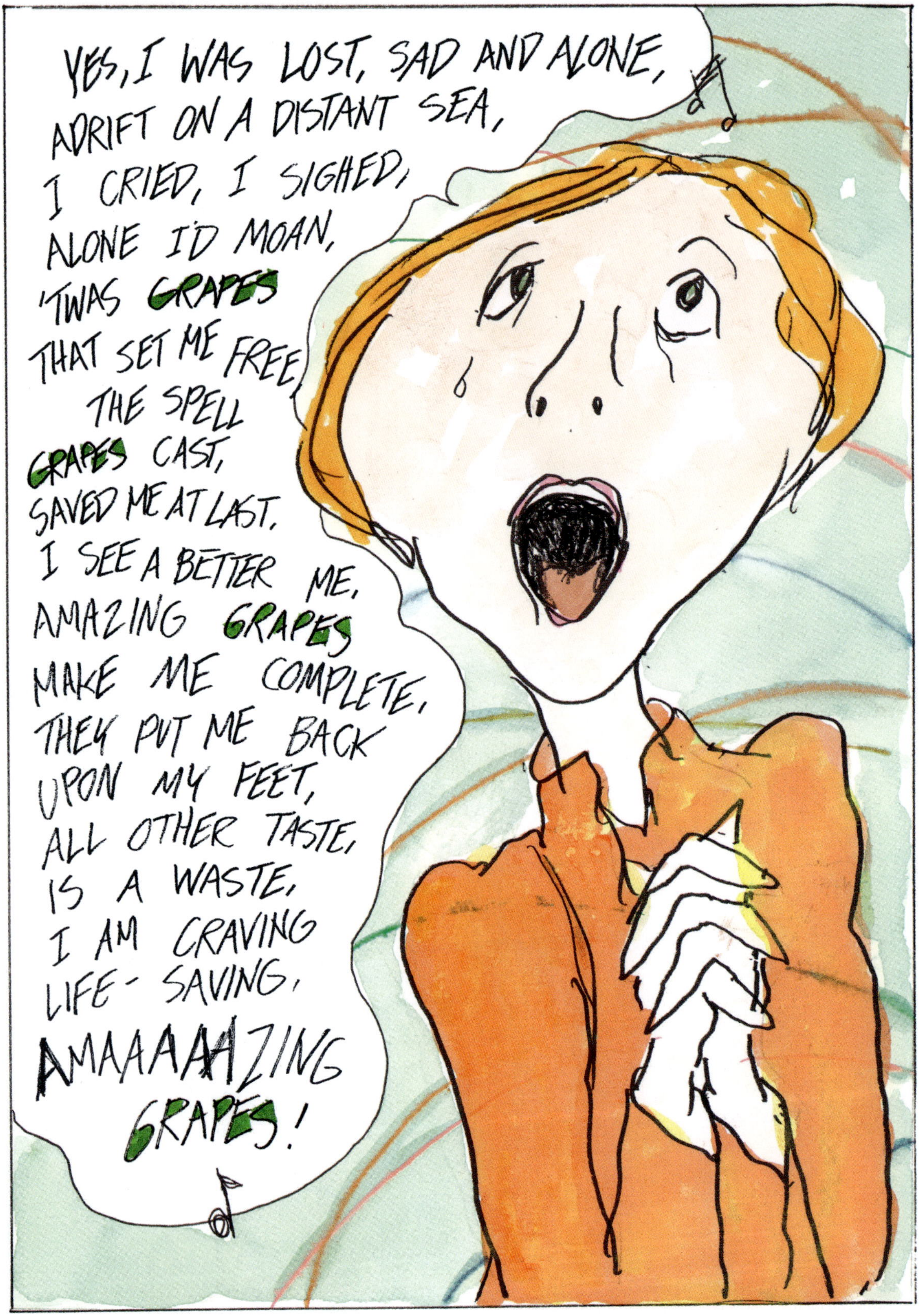
YES, I WAS LOST, SAD AND ALONE,
ADRIFT ON A DISTANT SEA,
I CRIED, I SIGHED,
ALONE I'D MOAN,
'TWAS GRAPES
THAT SET ME FREE,
THE SPELL
GRAPES CAST,
SAVED ME AT LAST.
I SEE A BETTER ME,
AMAZING GRAPES
MAKE ME COMPLETE,
THEY PUT ME BACK
UPON MY FEET,
ALL OTHER TASTE,
IS A WASTE,
I AM CRAVING
LIFE-SAVING,
AMAAAAAZING
GRAPES!

CHAPTER 56 • EMPRESS-MOMMY

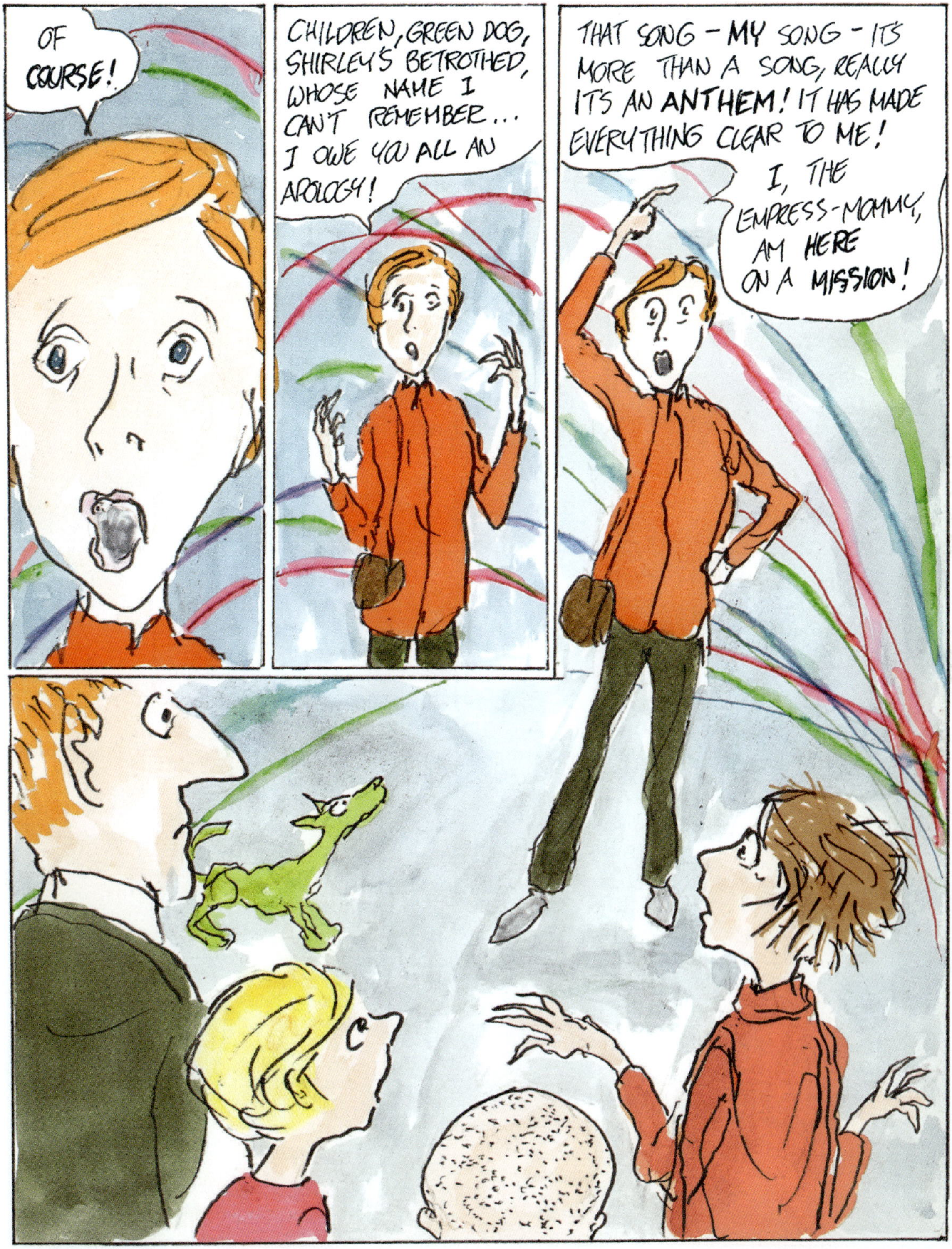

OF COURSE!
CHILDREN, GREEN DOG, SHIRLEY'S BETROTHED, WHOSE NAME I CAN'T REMEMBER... I OWE YOU ALL AN APOLOGY!
THAT SONG - MY SONG - IT'S MORE THAN A SONG, REALLY IT'S AN ANTHEM! IT HAS MADE EVERYTHING CLEAR TO ME!
I, THE EMPRESS-MOMMY, AM HERE ON A MISSION!

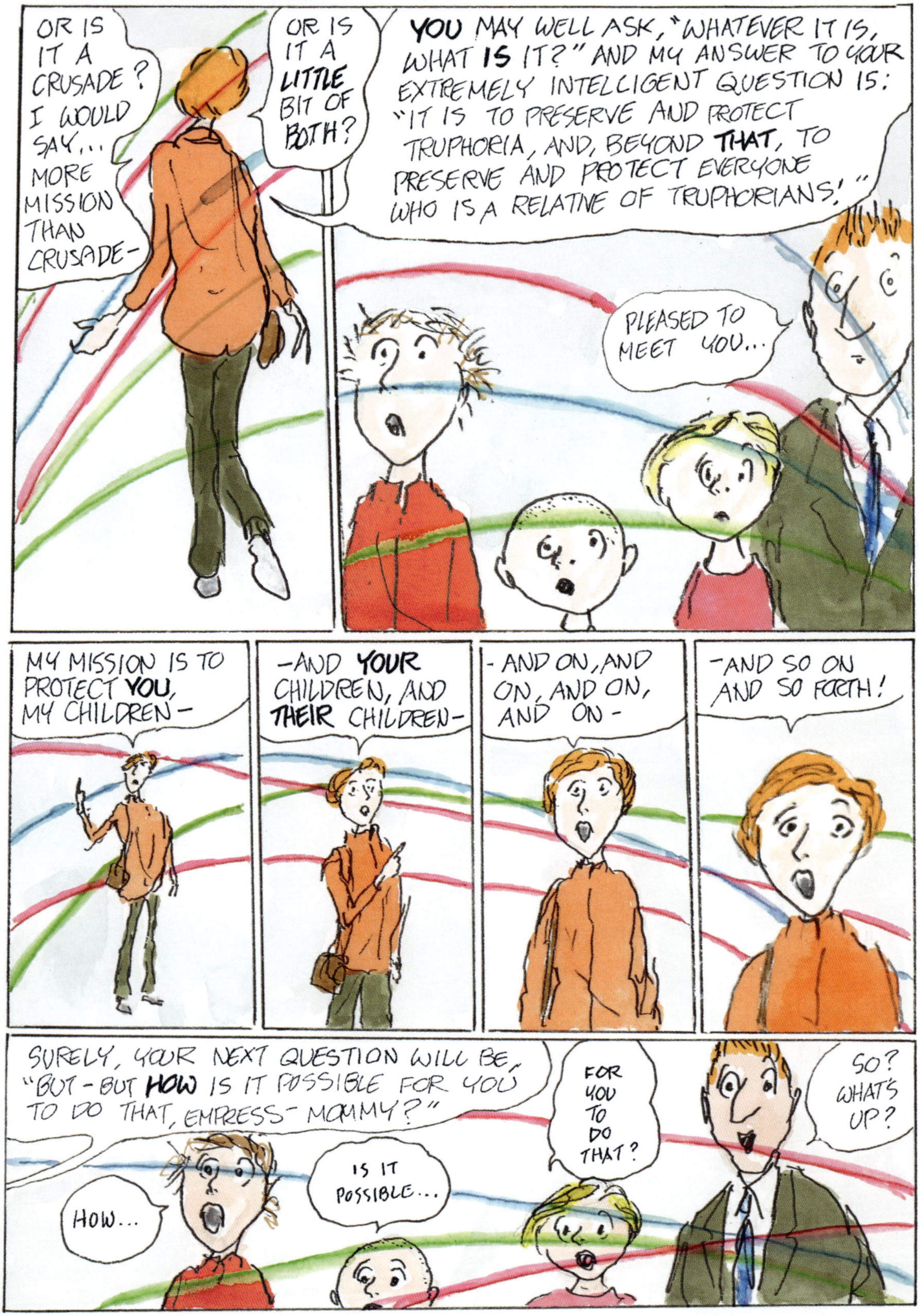
OR IS IT A CRUSADE? I WOULD SAY... MORE MISSION THAN CRUSADE-
OR IS IT A LITTLE BIT OF BOTH?
YOU MAY WELL ASK, "WHATEVER IT IS, WHAT IS IT?" AND MY ANSWER TO YOUR EXTREMELY INTELLIGENT QUESTION IS: "IT IS TO PRESERVE AND PROTECT TRUPHORIA, AND, BEYOND THAT, TO PRESERVE AND PROTECT EVERYONE WHO IS A RELATIVE OF TRUPHORIANS!"
PLEASED TO MEET YOU...
MY MISSION IS TO PROTECT YOU, MY CHILDREN-
-AND YOUR CHILDREN, AND THEIR CHILDREN-
-AND ON, AND ON, AND ON, AND ON-
-AND SO ON AND SO FORTH!
SURELY, YOUR NEXT QUESTION WILL BE, "BUT-BUT HOW IS IT POSSIBLE FOR YOU TO DO THAT, EMPRESS-MOMMY?"
HOW...
IS IT POSSIBLE...
FOR YOU TO DO THAT?
SO? WHAT'S UP?

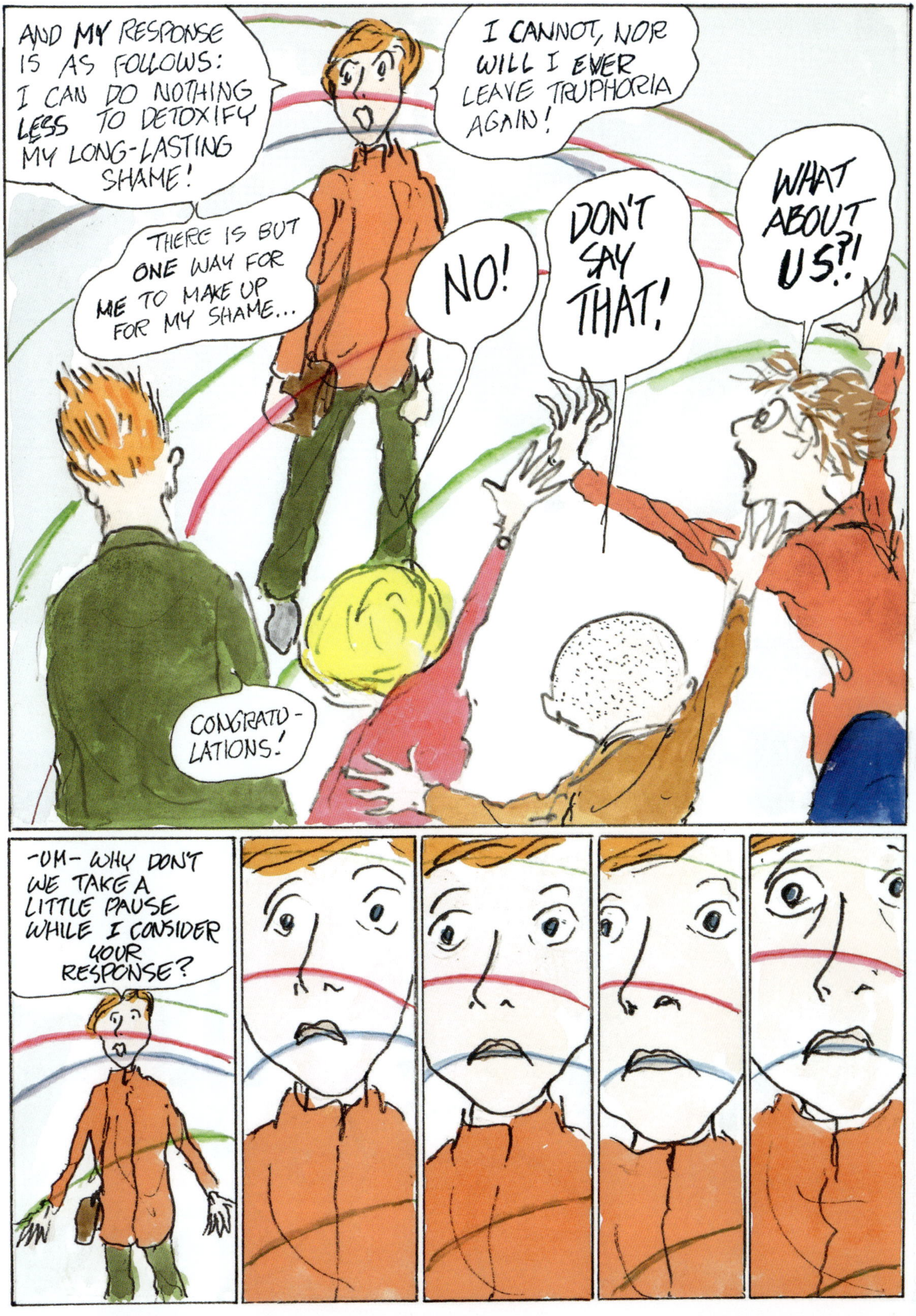
AND MY RESPONSE IS AS FOLLOWS: I CAN DO NOTHING LESS TO DETOXIFY MY LONG-LASTING SHAME!
I CANNOT, NOR WILL I EVER LEAVE TRUPHORIA AGAIN!
THERE IS BUT ONE WAY FOR ME TO MAKE UP FOR MY SHAME...
NO!
DON'T SAY THAT!
WHAT ABOUT US?!
CONGRATU-LATIONS!
-UM- WHY DON'T WE TAKE A LITTLE PAUSE WHILE I CONSIDER YOUR RESPONSE?

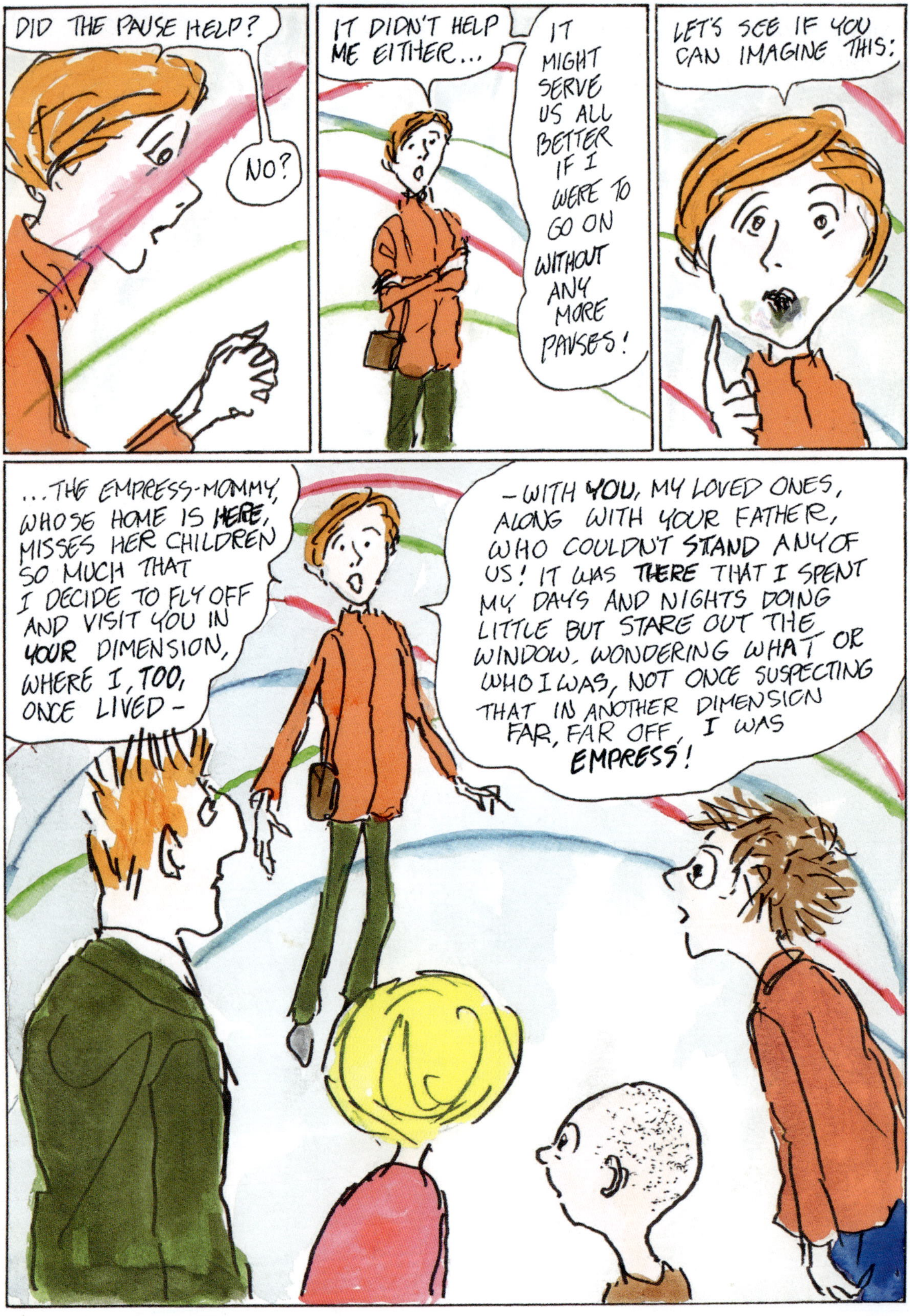
DID THE PAUSE HELP?
NO?
IT DIDN'T HELP ME EITHER...
IT MIGHT SERVE US ALL BETTER IF I WERE TO GO ON WITHOUT ANY MORE PAUSES!
LET'S SEE IF YOU CAN IMAGINE THIS:
...THE EMPRESS-MOMMY, WHOSE HOME IS HERE, MISSES HER CHILDREN SO MUCH THAT I DECIDE TO FLY OFF AND VISIT YOU IN YOUR DIMENSION, WHERE I, TOO, ONCE LIVED-
-WITH YOU, MY LOVED ONES, ALONG WITH YOUR FATHER, WHO COULDN'T STAND ANY OF US! IT WAS THERE THAT I SPENT MY DAYS AND NIGHTS DOING LITTLE BUT STARE OUT THE WINDOW, WONDERING WHAT OR WHO I WAS, NOT ONCE SUSPECTING THAT IN ANOTHER DIMENSION FAR, FAR OFF, I WAS EMPRESS!

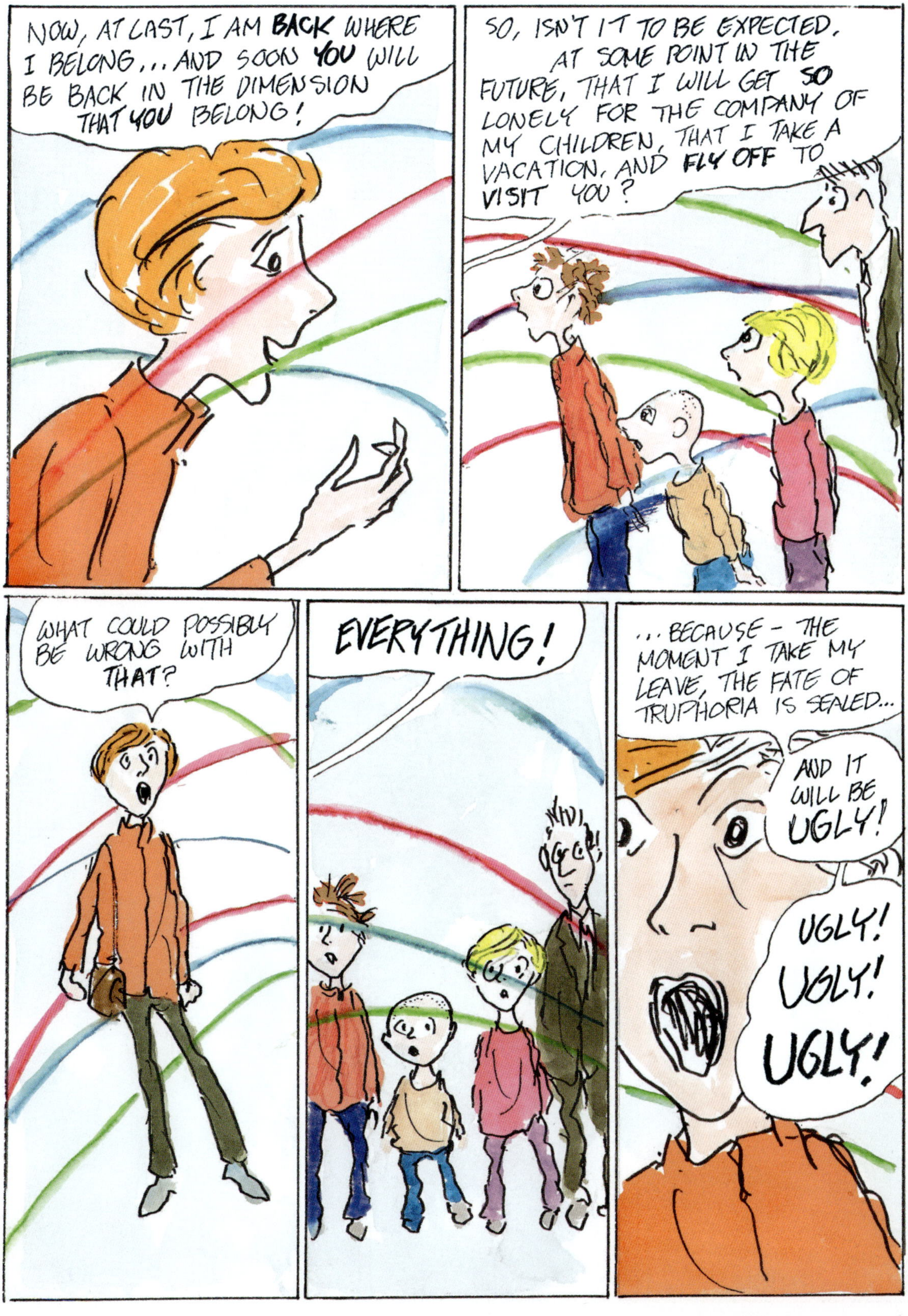
NOW, AT LAST, I AM BACK WHERE I BELONG... AND SOON YOU WILL BE BACK IN THE DIMENSION THAT YOU BELONG!
SO, ISN'T IT TO BE EXPECTED. AT SOME POINT IN THE FUTURE, THAT I WILL GET SO LONELY FOR THE COMPANY OF MY CHILDREN, THAT I TAKE A VACATION, AND FLY OFF TO VISIT YOU?
WHAT COULD POSSIBLY BE WRONG WITH THAT?
EVERYTHING!
...BECAUSE - THE MOMENT I TAKE MY LEAVE, THE FATE OF TRUPHORIA IS SEALED...
AND IT WILL BE UGLY!
UGLY! UGLY! UGLY!

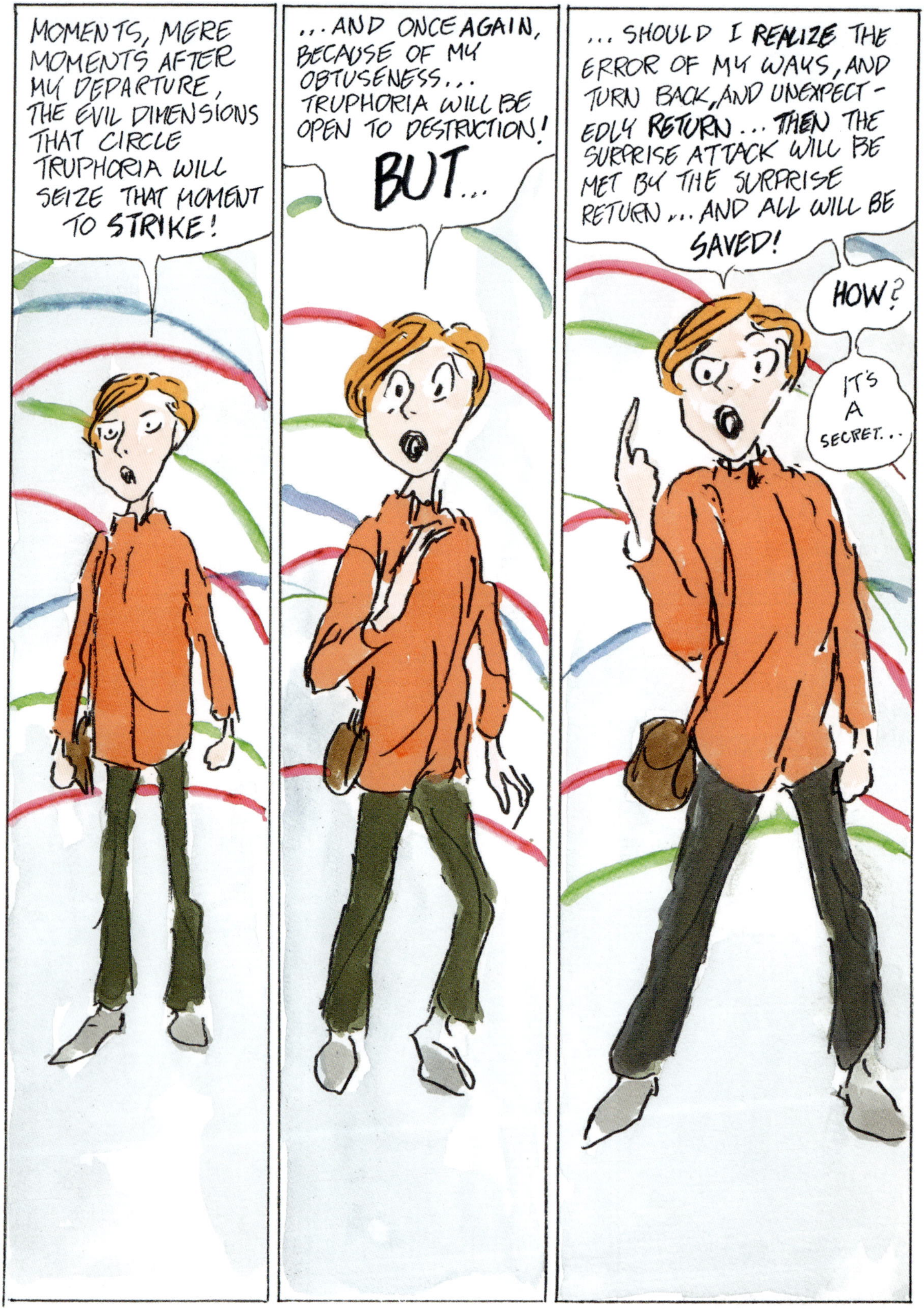
MOMENTS, MERE MOMENTS AFTER MY DEPARTURE, THE EVIL DIMENSIONS THAT CIRCLE TRUPHORIA WILL SEIZE THAT MOMENT TO STRIKE!
...AND ONCE AGAIN, BECAUSE OF MY OBTUSENESS... TRUPHORIA WILL BE OPEN TO DESTRUCTION! BUT...
...SHOULD I REALIZE THE ERROR OF MY WAYS, AND TURN BACK, AND UNEXPECTEDLY RETURN... THEN THE SURPRISE ATTACK WILL BE MET BY THE SURPRISE RETURN... AND ALL WILL BE SAVED!
HOW?
IT'S A SECRET...

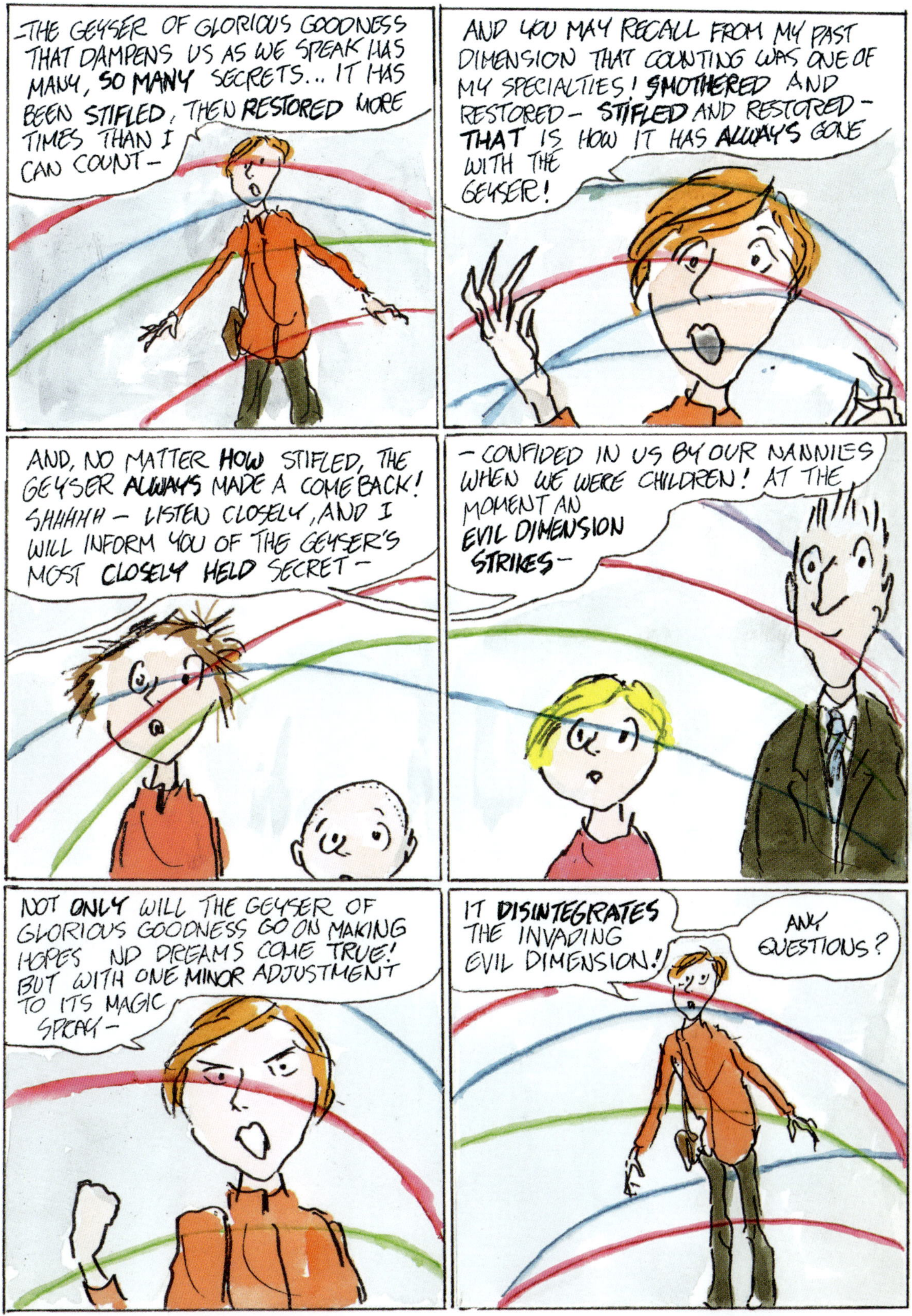
-THE GEYSER OF GLORIOUS GOODNESS THAT DAMPENS US AS WE SPEAK HAS MANY, SO MANY SECRETS... IT HAS BEEN STIFLED, THEN RESTORED MORE TIMES THAN I CAN COUNT-
AND YOU MAY RECALL FROM MY PAST DIMENSION THAT COUNTING WAS ONE OF MY SPECIALTIES! SMOTHERED AND RESTORED- STIFLED AND RESTORED- THAT IS HOW IT HAS ALWAYS GONE WITH THE GEYSER!
AND, NO MATTER HOW STIFLED, THE GEYSER ALWAYS MADE A COMEBACK! SHHHHH - LISTEN CLOSELY, AND I WILL INFORM YOU OF THE GEYSER'S MOST CLOSELY HELD SECRET-
-CONFIDED IN US BY OUR NANNIES WHEN WE WERE CHILDREN! AT THE MOMENT AN EVIL DIMENSION STRIKES-
NOT ONLY WILL THE GEYSER OF GLORIOUS GOODNESS GO ON MAKING HOPES ND DREAMS COME TRUE! BUT WITH ONE MINOR ADJUSTMENT TO ITS MAGIC SPRAY-
IT DISINTEGRATES THE INVADING EVIL DIMENSION!
ANY QUESTIONS?

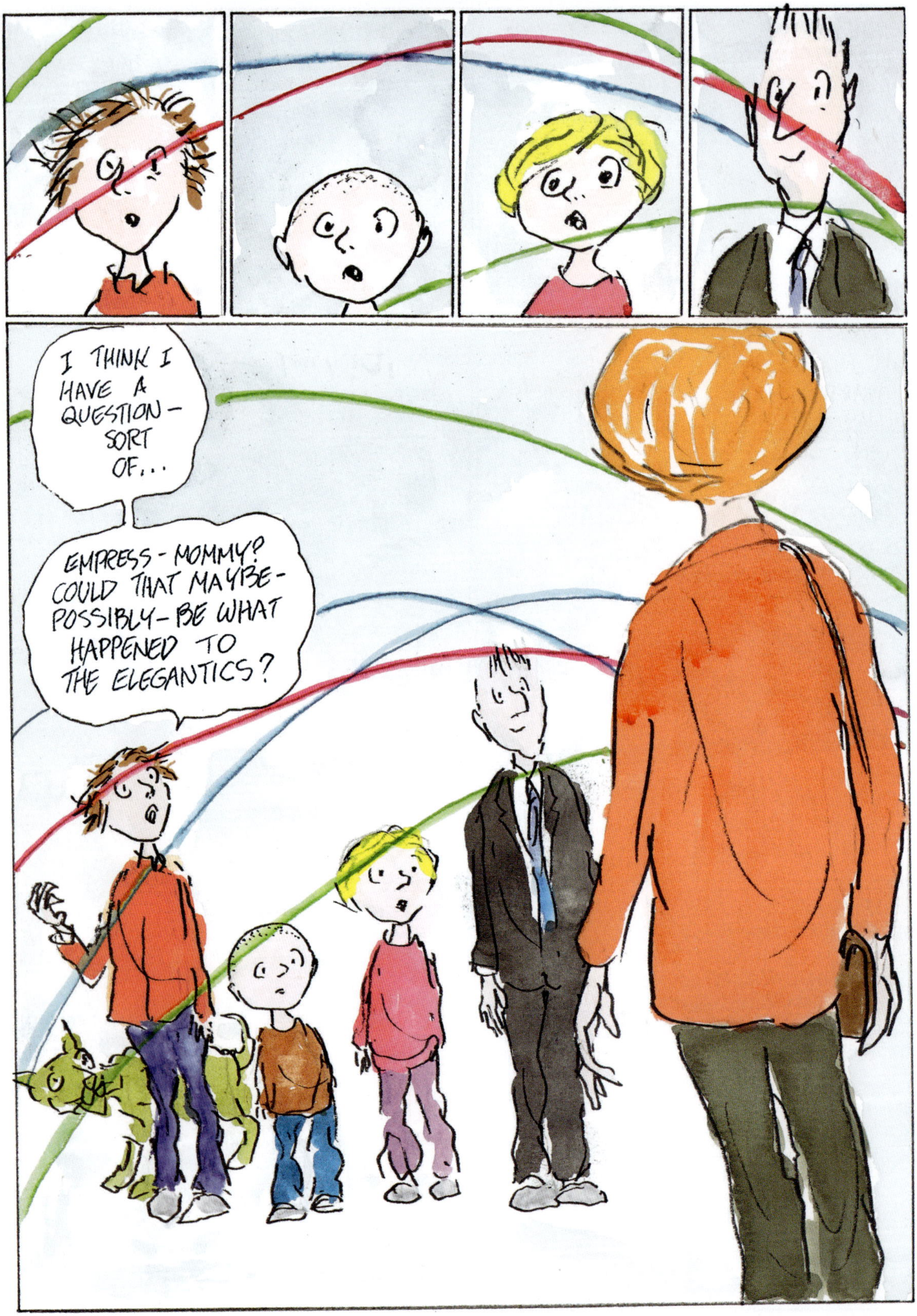
I THINK I HAVE A QUESTION—SORT OF...
EMPRESS-MOMMY? COULD THAT MAYBE—POSSIBLY—BE WHAT HAPPENED TO THE ELEGANTICS?

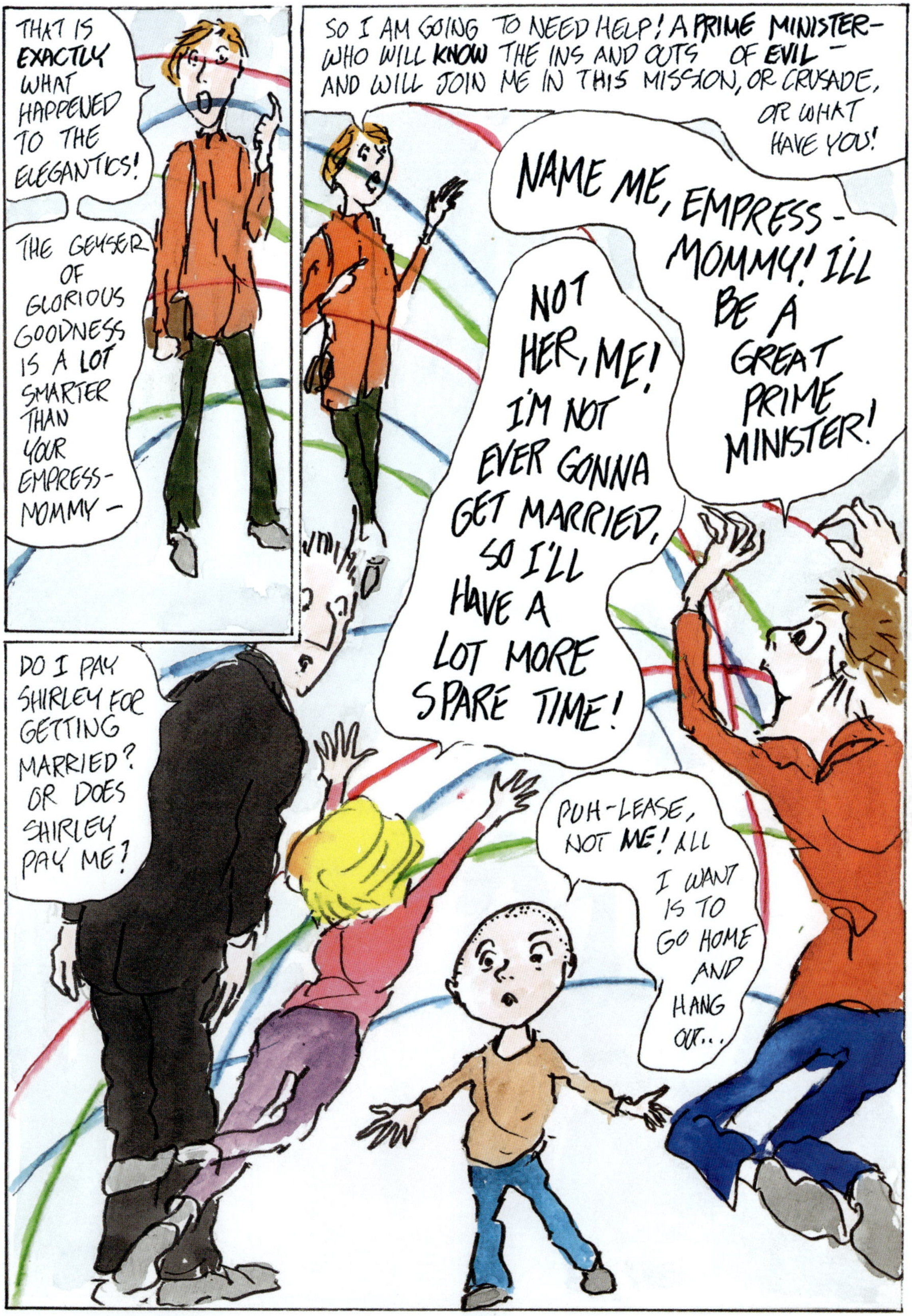
THAT IS **EXACTLY** WHAT HAPPENED TO THE ELEGANTICS!
THE GEYSER OF GLORIOUS GOODNESS IS A **LOT** SMARTER THAN YOUR EMPRESS-MOMMY—
SO I AM GOING TO NEED HELP! A **PRIME MINISTER**—WHO WILL **KNOW** THE INS AND OUTS OF **EVIL**—AND WILL JOIN ME IN THIS MISSION, OR CRUSADE, OR WHAT HAVE YOU!
NAME ME, EMPRESS-MOMMY! I'LL BE A GREAT PRIME MINISTER!
NOT HER, ME! I'M NOT EVER GONNA GET MARRIED, SO I'LL HAVE A LOT MORE SPARE TIME!
DO I PAY SHIRLEY FOR GETTING MARRIED? OR DOES SHIRLEY PAY ME?
PUH-LEASE, NOT **ME**! ALL I WANT IS TO GO HOME AND HANG OUT...

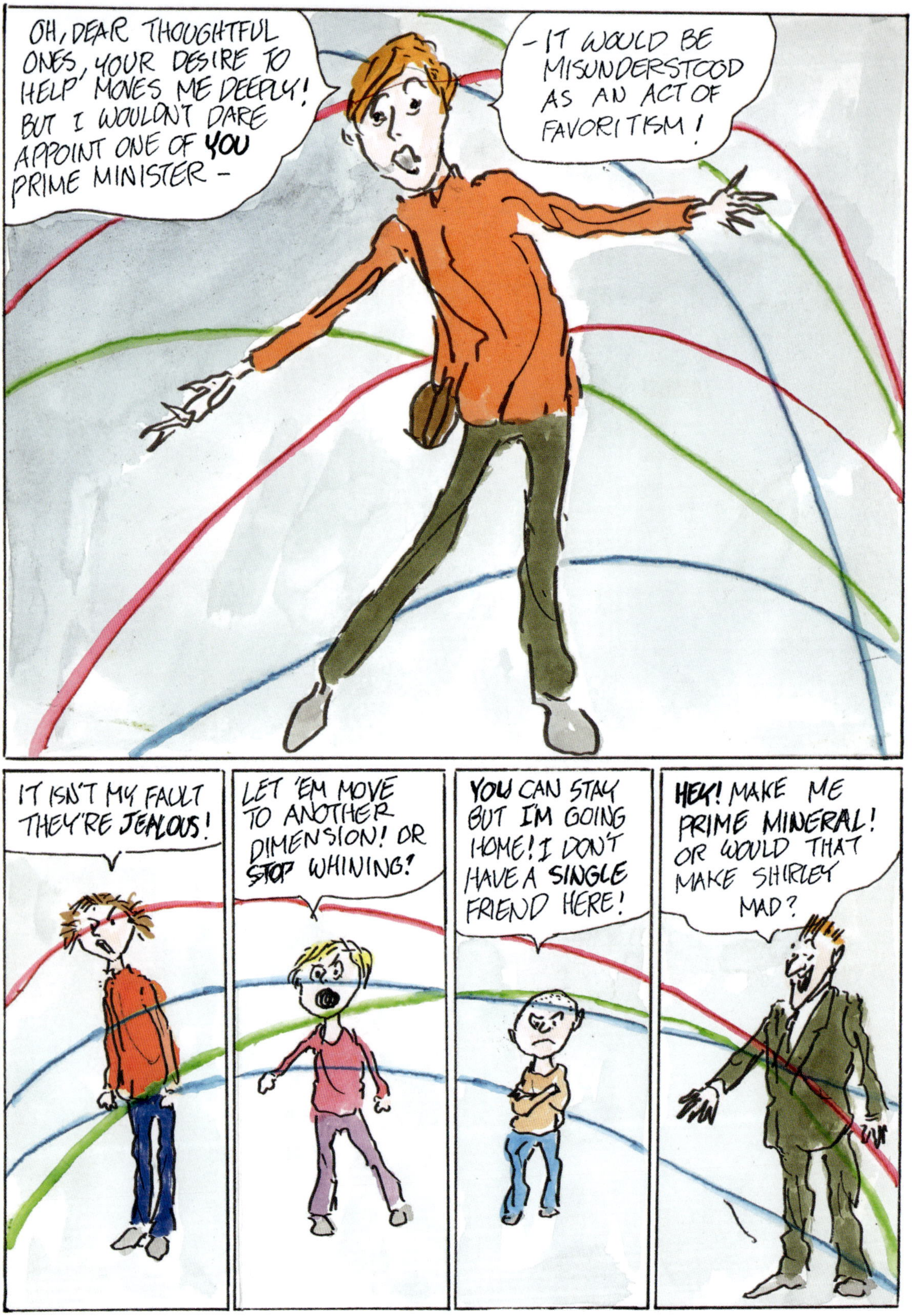
OH, DEAR THOUGHTFUL ONES, YOUR DESIRE TO HELP MOVES ME DEEPLY! BUT I WOULDN'T DARE APPOINT ONE OF **YOU** PRIME MINISTER –
– IT WOULD BE MISUNDERSTOOD AS AN ACT OF FAVORITISM!
IT ISN'T MY FAULT THEY'RE **JEALOUS**!
LET 'EM MOVE TO ANOTHER DIMENSION! OR **STOP** WHINING!
YOU CAN STAY BUT **I'M** GOING HOME! I DON'T HAVE A **SINGLE** FRIEND HERE!
HEK! MAKE ME **PRIME MINERAL**! OR WOULD THAT MAKE SHIRLEY MAD?

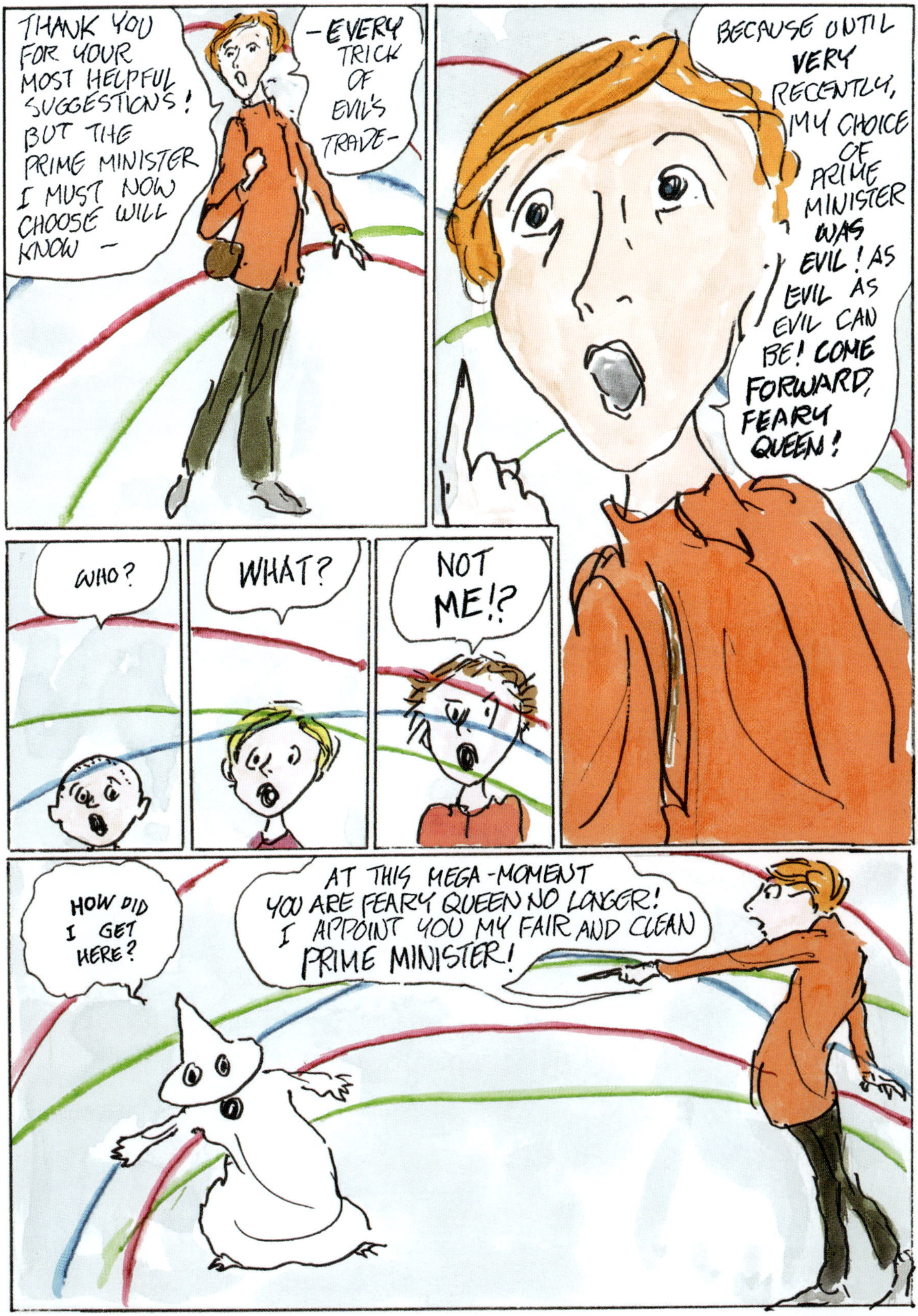
THANK YOU FOR YOUR MOST HELPFUL SUGGESTIONS! BUT THE PRIME MINISTER I MUST NOW CHOOSE WILL KNOW -
-EVERY TRICK OF EVIL'S TRADE-
BECAUSE UNTIL VERY RECENTLY, MY CHOICE OF PRIME MINISTER WAS EVIL! AS EVIL AS EVIL CAN BE! COME FORWARD, FEARY QUEEN!
WHO?
WHAT?
NOT ME!?
HOW DID I GET HERE?
AT THIS MEGA-MOMENT YOU ARE FEARY QUEEN NO LONGER! I APPOINT YOU MY FAIR AND CLEAN PRIME MINISTER!

CHAPTER 57 • FAREWELL, FEARY QUEEN

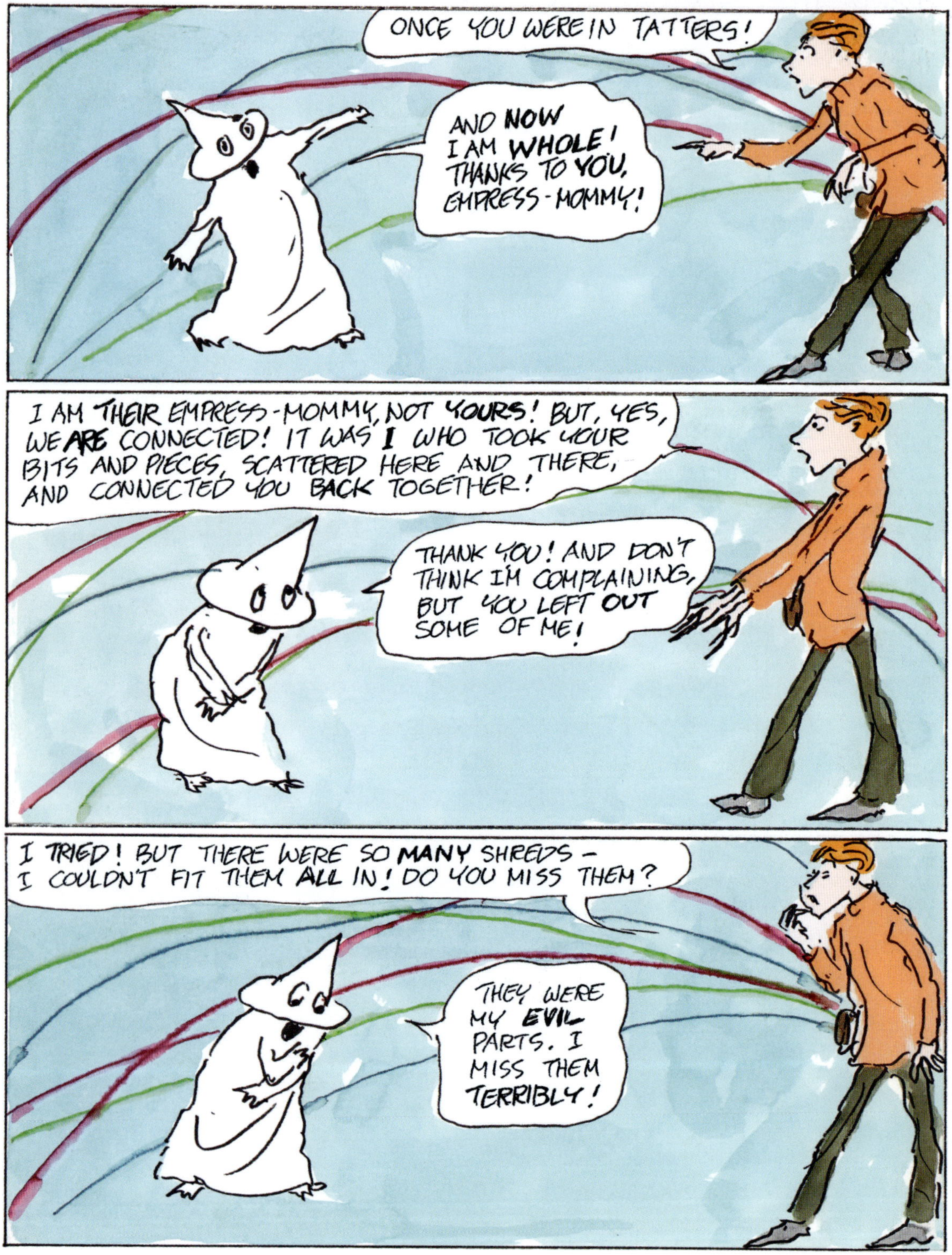
ONCE YOU WERE IN TATTERS!
AND **NOW** I AM **WHOLE**! THANKS TO **YOU**, EMPRESS-MOMMY!
I AM **THEIR** EMPRESS-MOMMY, NOT **YOURS**! BUT, YES, WE **ARE** CONNECTED! IT WAS **I** WHO TOOK YOUR BITS AND PIECES, SCATTERED HERE AND THERE, AND CONNECTED YOU **BACK** TOGETHER!
THANK YOU! AND DON'T THINK I'M COMPLAINING, BUT YOU LEFT **OUT** SOME OF ME!
I **TRIED**! BUT THERE WERE SO **MANY** SHREDS — I COULDN'T FIT THEM **ALL** IN! DO YOU MISS THEM?
THEY WERE MY **EVIL** PARTS. I MISS THEM **TERRIBLY**!

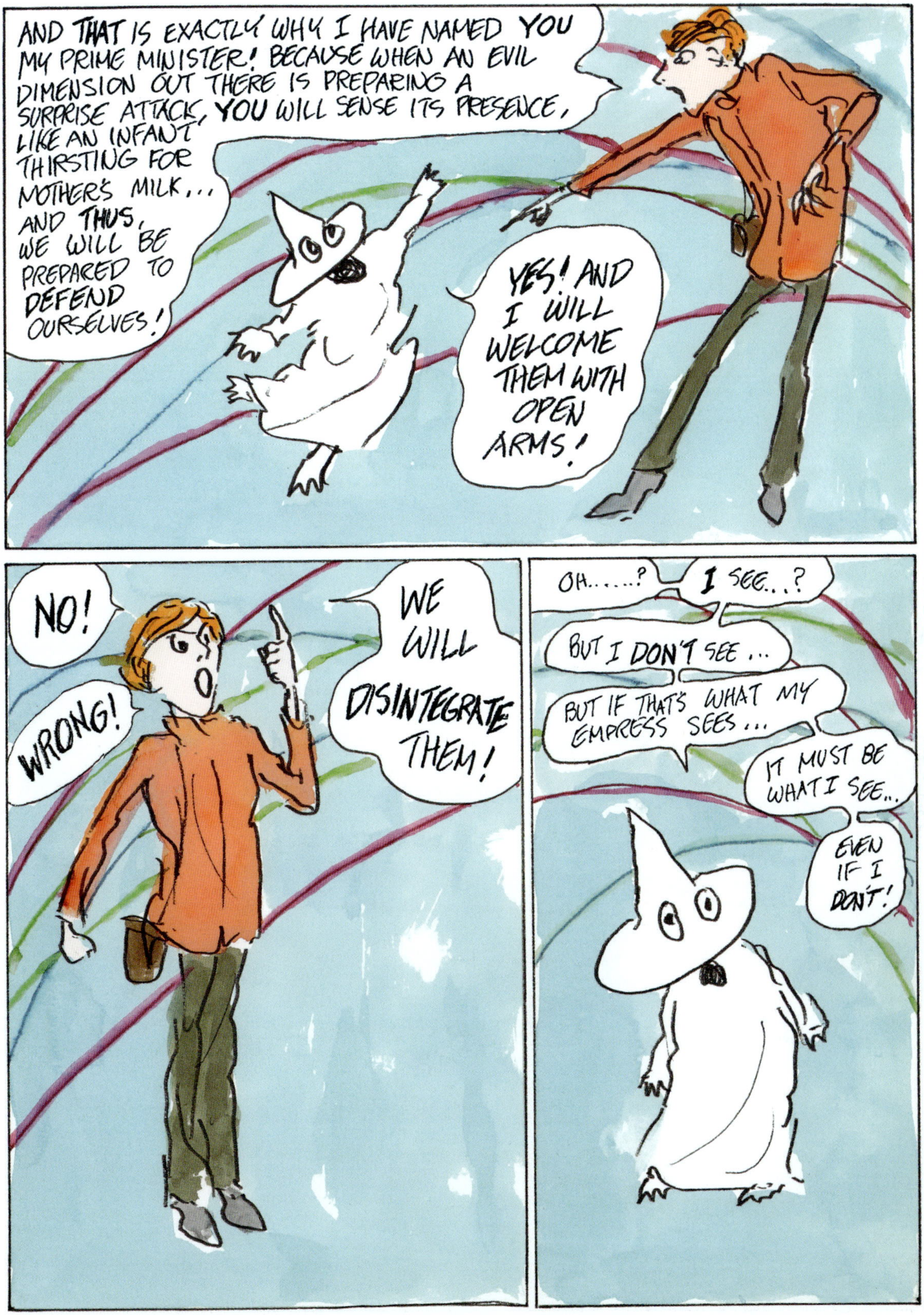
AND THAT IS EXACTLY WHY I HAVE NAMED YOU MY PRIME MINISTER! BECAUSE WHEN AN EVIL DIMENSION OUT THERE IS PREPARING A SURPRISE ATTACK, YOU WILL SENSE ITS PRESENCE, LIKE AN INFANT THIRSTING FOR MOTHER'S MILK... AND THUS, WE WILL BE PREPARED TO DEFEND OURSELVES!
YES! AND I WILL WELCOME THEM WITH OPEN ARMS!
NO!
WRONG!
WE WILL DISINTEGRATE THEM!
OH......?
I SEE...?
BUT I DON'T SEE...
BUT IF THAT'S WHAT MY EMPRESS SEES...
IT MUST BE WHAT I SEE...
EVEN IF I DON'T!

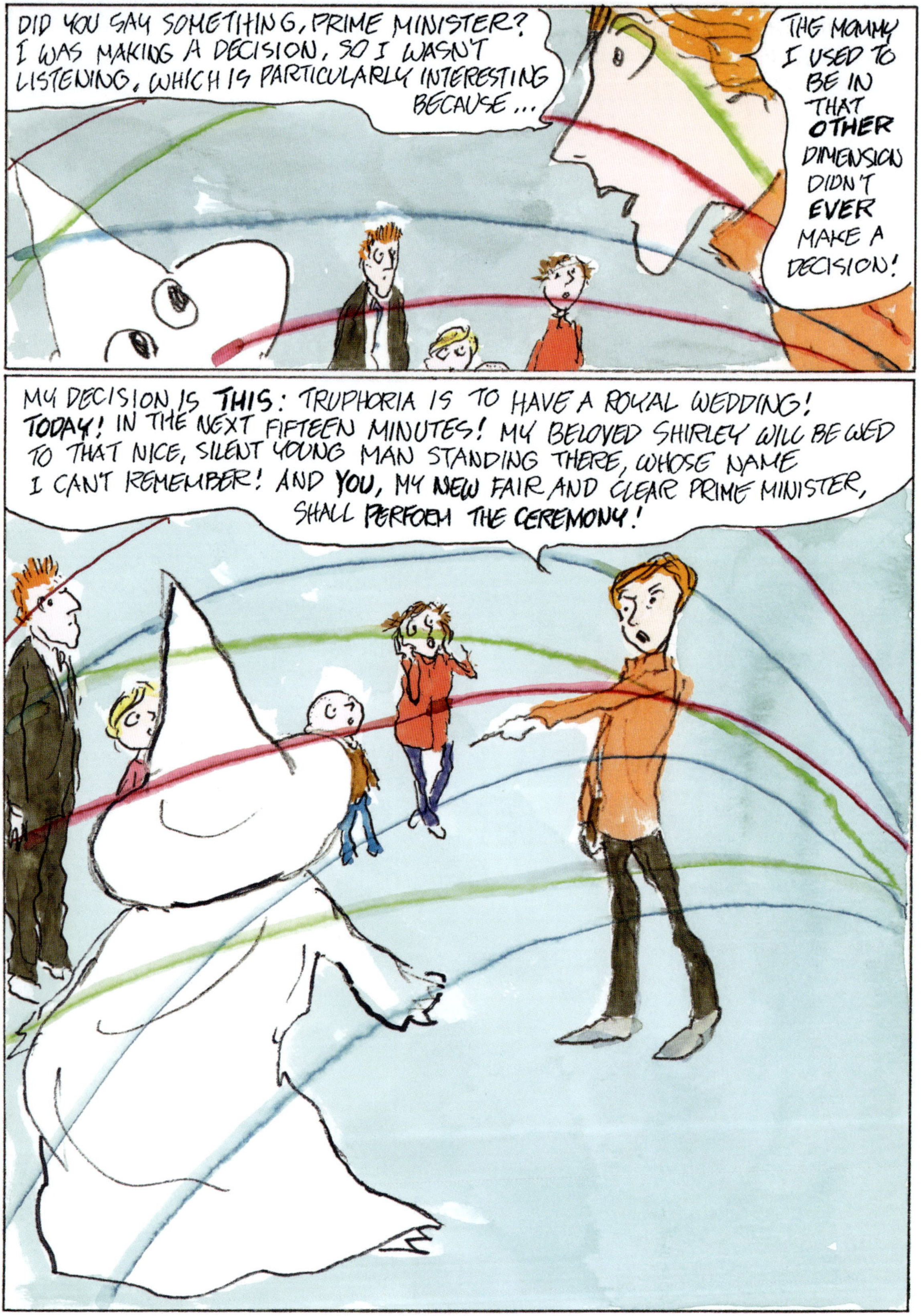
DID YOU SAY SOMETHING, PRIME MINISTER? I WAS MAKING A DECISION, SO I WASN'T LISTENING, WHICH IS PARTICULARLY INTERESTING BECAUSE ...
THE MOMMY I USED TO BE IN THAT OTHER DIMENSION DIDN'T EVER MAKE A DECISION!
MY DECISION IS THIS: TRUPHORIA IS TO HAVE A ROYAL WEDDING! TODAY! IN THE NEXT FIFTEEN MINUTES! MY BELOVED SHIRLEY WILL BE WED TO THAT NICE, SILENT YOUNG MAN STANDING THERE, WHOSE NAME I CAN'T REMEMBER! AND YOU, MY NEW FAIR AND CLEAR PRIME MINISTER, SHALL PERFORM THE CEREMONY!

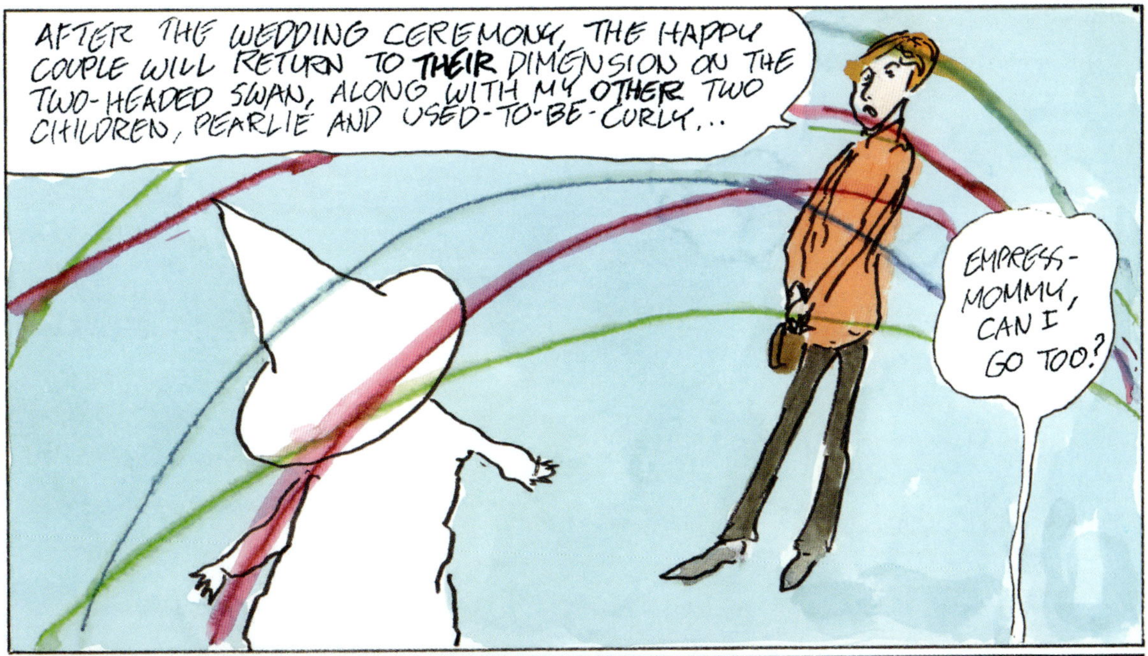
AFTER THE WEDDING CEREMONY, THE HAPPY COUPLE WILL RETURN TO **THEIR** DIMENSION ON THE TWO-HEADED SWAN, ALONG WITH MY **OTHER** TWO CHILDREN, PEARLIE AND USED-TO-BE-CURLY...
EMPRESS-MOMMY, CAN I GO TOO?

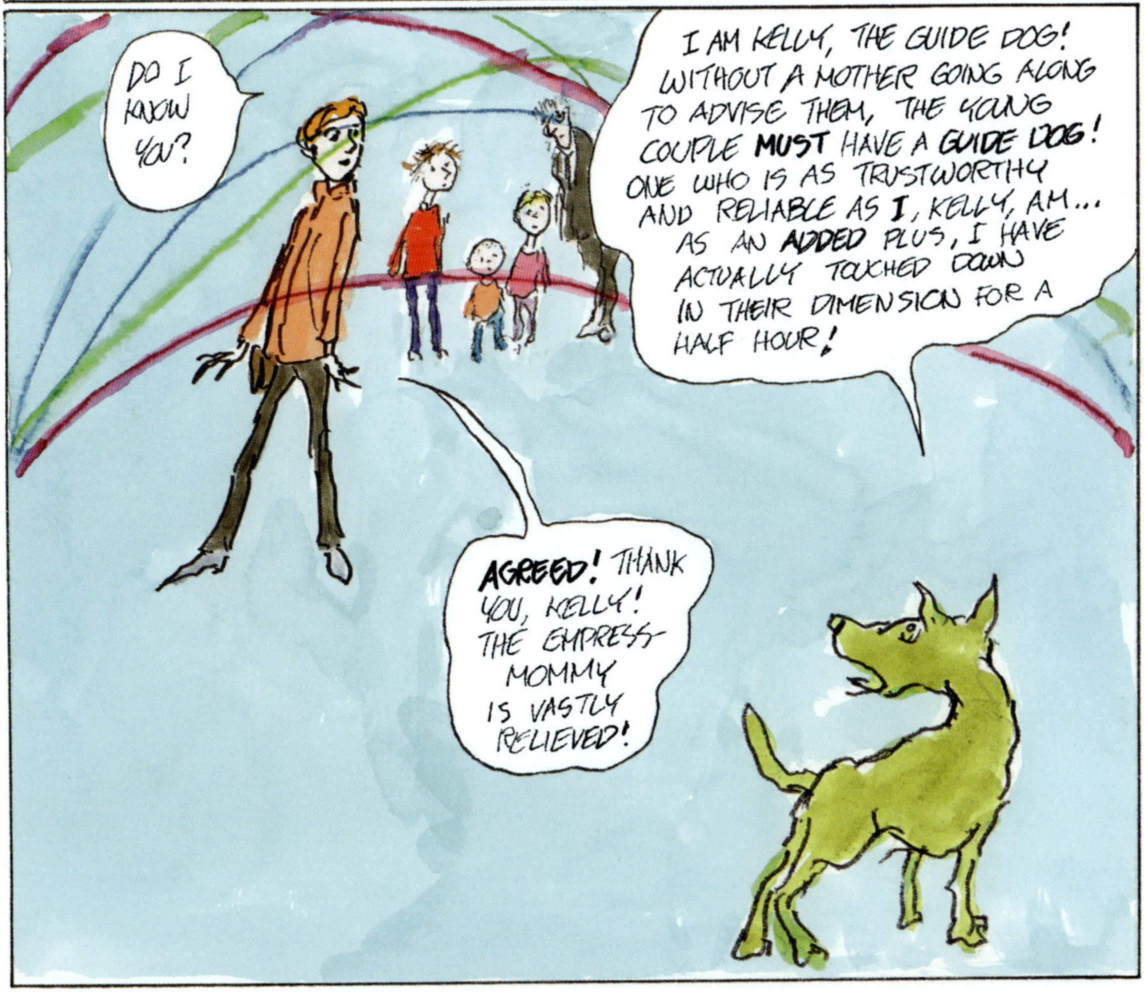
DO I KNOW YOU?
I AM KELLY, THE GUIDE DOG! WITHOUT A MOTHER GOING ALONG TO ADVISE THEM, THE YOUNG COUPLE **MUST** HAVE A **GUIDE DOG**! ONE WHO IS AS TRUSTWORTHY AND RELIABLE AS **I**, KELLY, AM... AS AN **ADDED** PLUS, I HAVE ACTUALLY TOUCHED DOWN IN THEIR DIMENSION FOR A HALF HOUR!
AGREED! THANK YOU, KELLY! THE EMPRESS-MOMMY IS VASTLY RELIEVED!

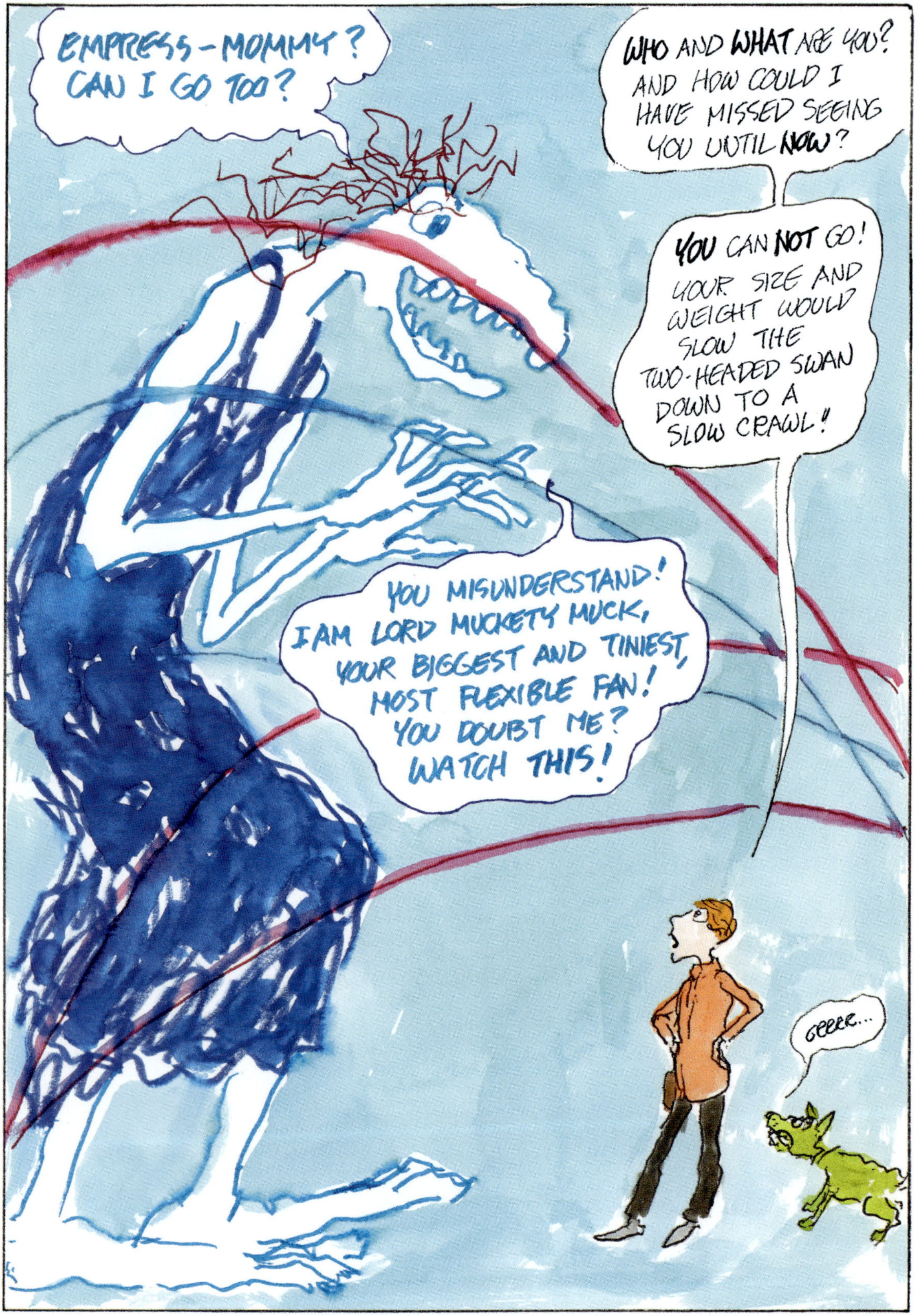
EMPRESS-MOMMY? CAN I GO TOO?
WHO AND WHAT ARE YOU? AND HOW COULD I HAVE MISSED SEEING YOU UNTIL NOW?
YOU CAN NOT GO! YOUR SIZE AND WEIGHT WOULD SLOW THE TWO-HEADED SWAN DOWN TO A SLOW CRAWL!
YOU MISUNDERSTAND! I AM LORD MUCKETY MUCK, YOUR BIGGEST AND TINIEST, MOST FLEXIBLE FAN! YOU DOUBT ME? WATCH THIS!
Grrrr...

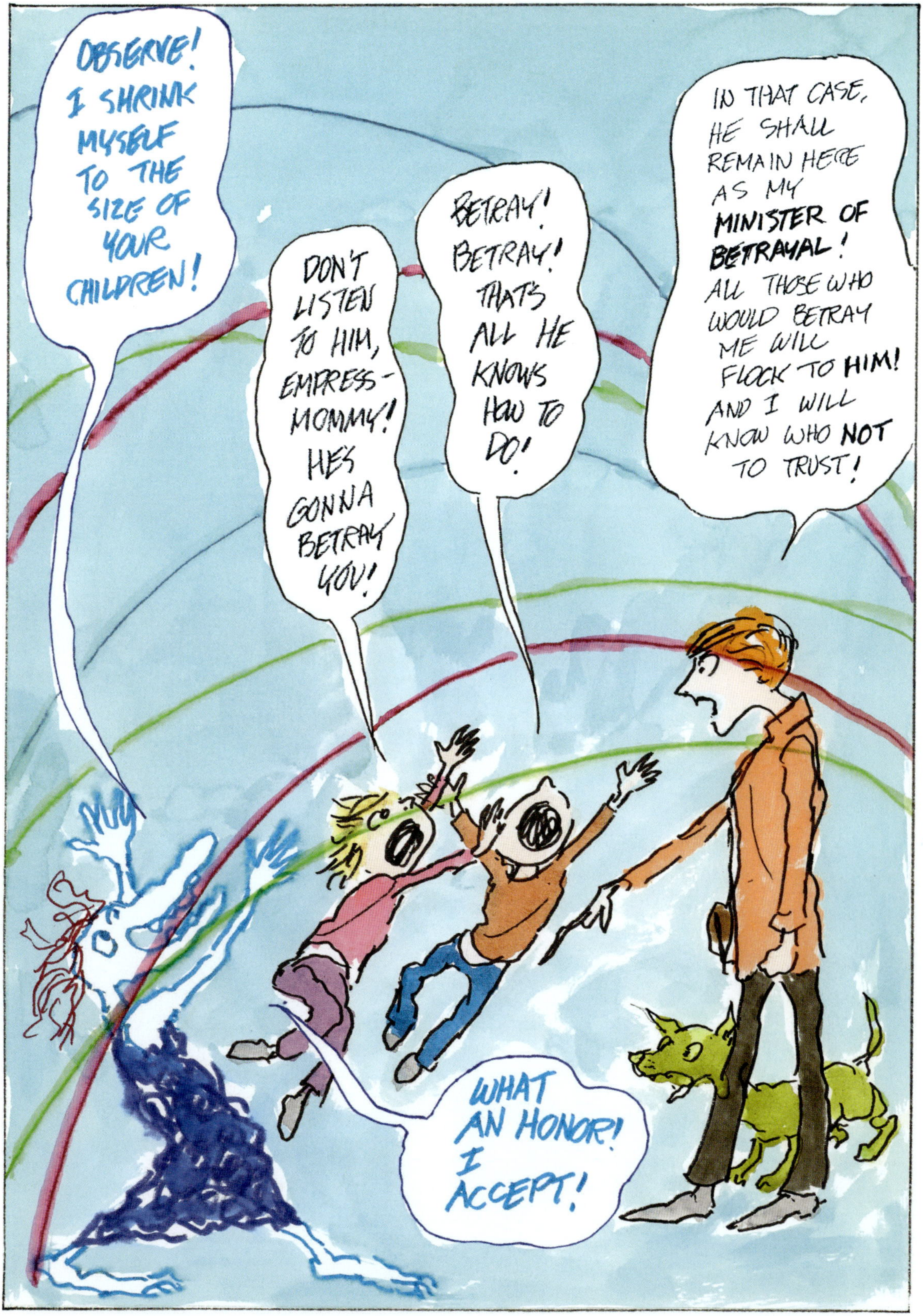
OBSERVE! I SHRINK MYSELF TO THE SIZE OF YOUR CHILDREN!
DON'T LISTEN TO HIM, EMPRESS-MOMMY! HE'S GONNA BETRAY YOU!
BETRAY! BETRAY! THAT'S ALL HE KNOWS HOW TO DO!
IN THAT CASE, HE SHALL REMAIN HERE AS MY **MINISTER OF BETRAYAL**! ALL THOSE WHO WOULD BETRAY ME WILL FLOCK TO **HIM**! AND I WILL KNOW WHO **NOT** TO TRUST!
WHAT AN HONOR! I ACCEPT!

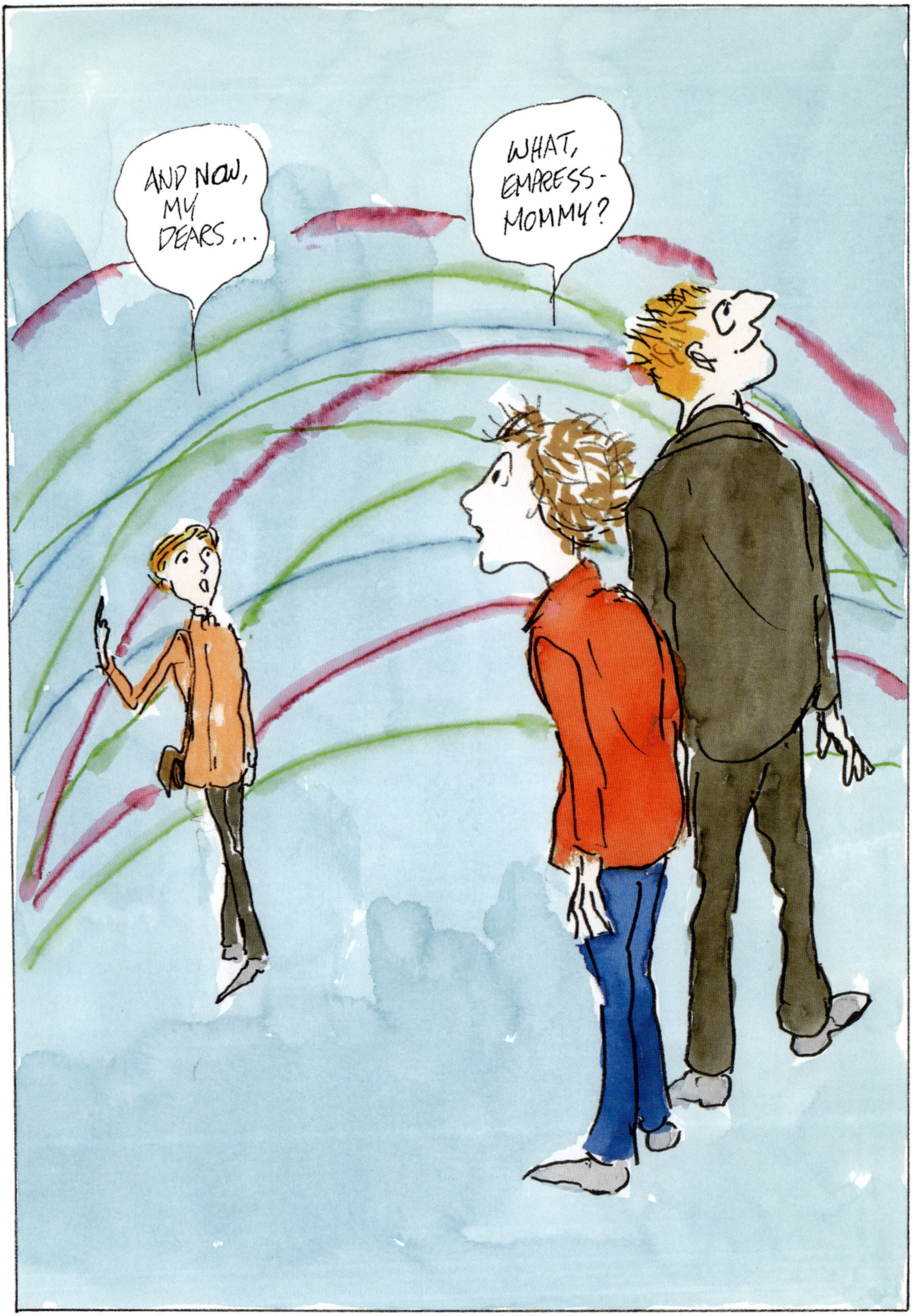
AND NOW, MY DEARS...
WHAT, EMPRESS-MOMMY?

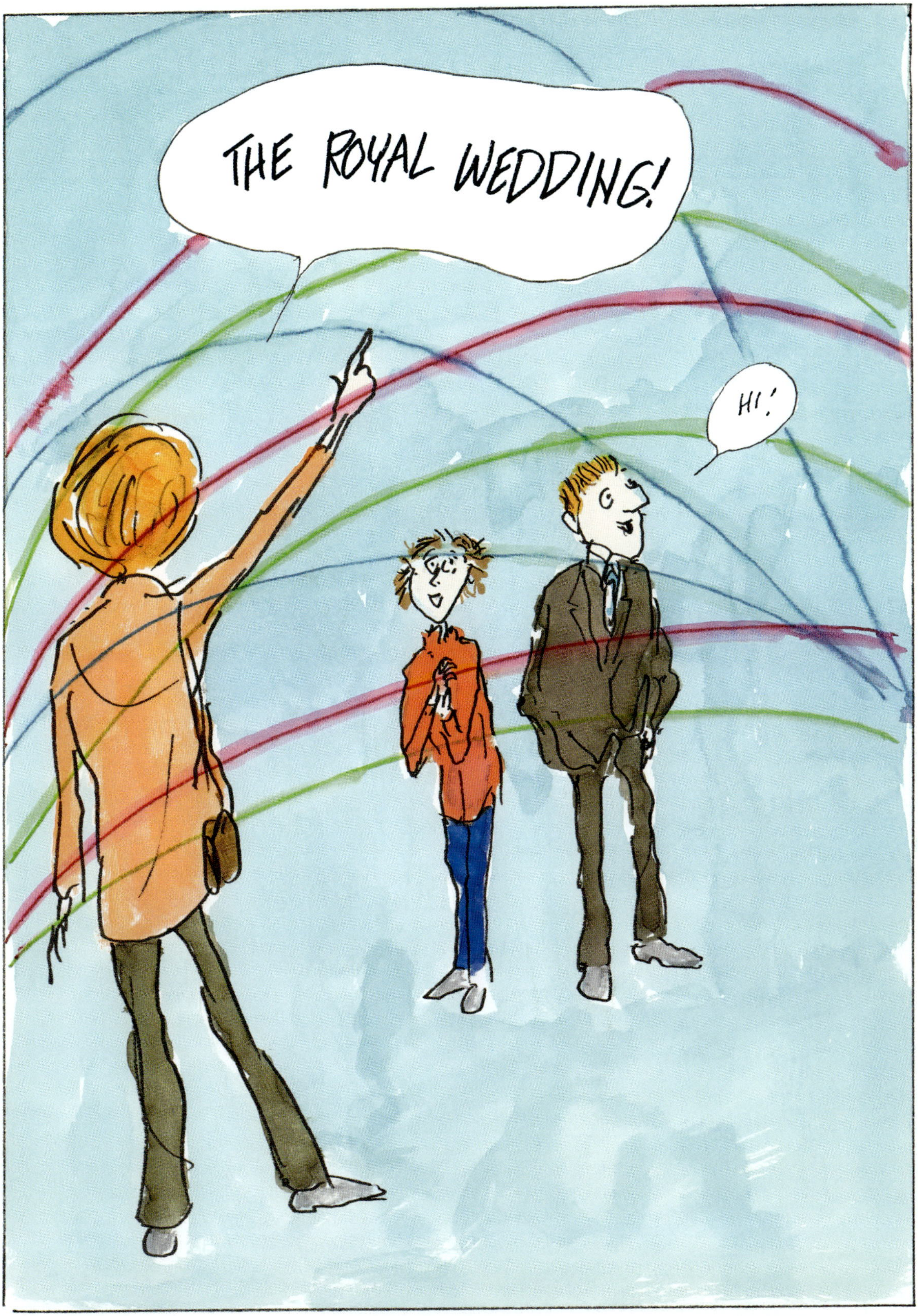
THE ROYAL WEDDING!
HI!

CHAPTER 58 • THE ROYAL WEDDING OF SHIRLEY TO WHATZISNAME

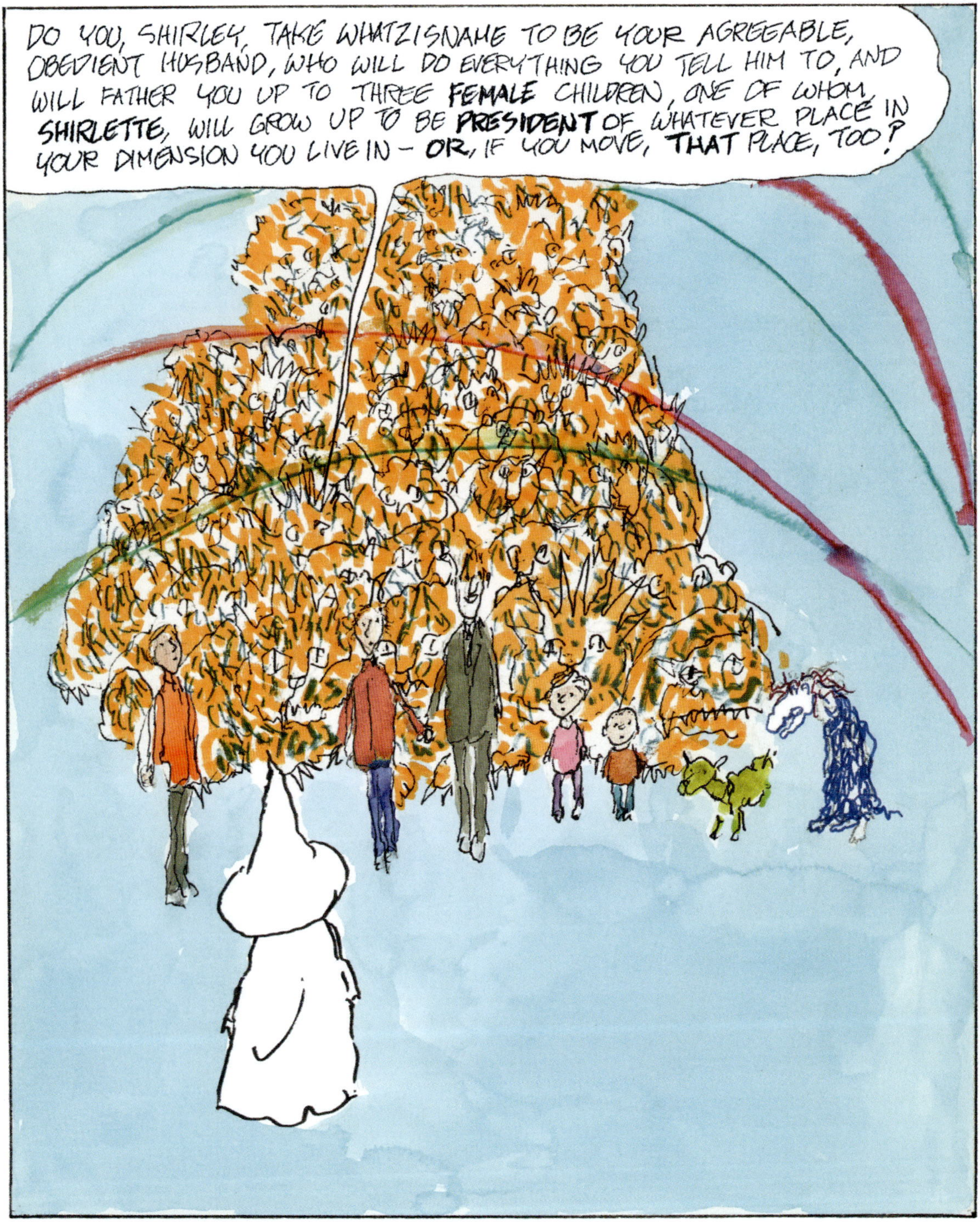
DO YOU, SHIRLEY, TAKE WHATZISNAME TO BE YOUR AGREEABLE, OBEDIENT HUSBAND, WHO WILL DO EVERYTHING YOU TELL HIM TO, AND WILL FATHER YOU UP TO THREE **FEMALE** CHILDREN, ONE OF WHOM, **SHIRLETTE**, WILL GROW UP TO BE **PRESIDENT** OF WHATEVER PLACE IN YOUR DIMENSION YOU LIVE IN – **OR**, IF YOU MOVE, **THAT** PLACE, TOO?

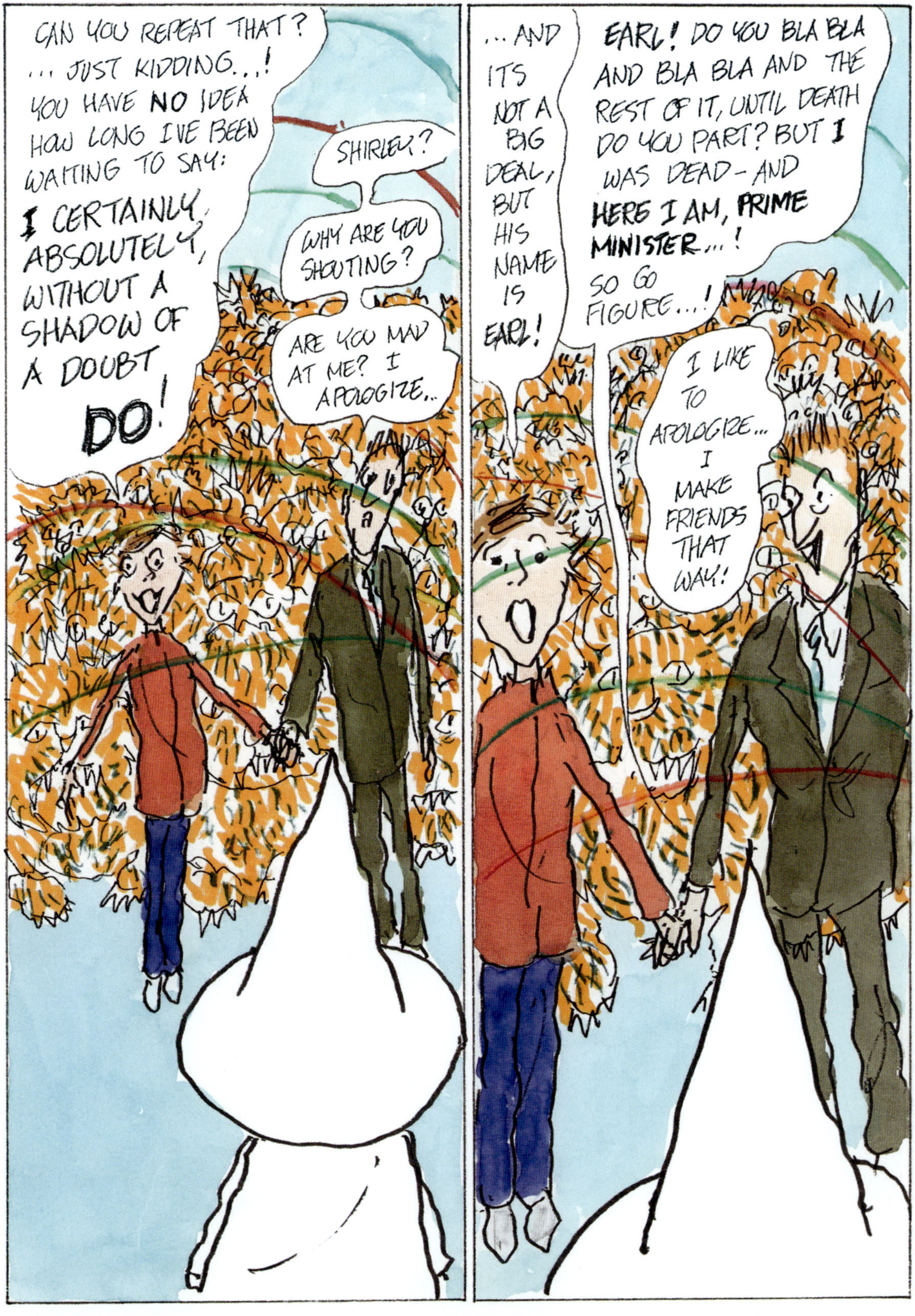

CAN YOU REPEAT THAT? ... JUST KIDDING...! YOU HAVE NO IDEA HOW LONG IVE BEEN WAITING TO SAY: I CERTAINLY, ABSOLUTELY, WITHOUT A SHADOW OF A DOUBT DO!
SHIRLEY?
WHY ARE YOU SHOUTING?
ARE YOU MAD AT ME? I APOLOGIZE...
...AND ITS NOT A BIG DEAL, BUT HIS NAME IS EARL!
EARL! DO YOU BLA BLA AND BLA BLA AND THE REST OF IT, UNTIL DEATH DO YOU PART? BUT I WAS DEAD - AND HERE I AM, PRIME MINISTER...! SO GO FIGURE...!
I LIKE TO APOLOGIZE... I MAKE FRIENDS THAT WAY!

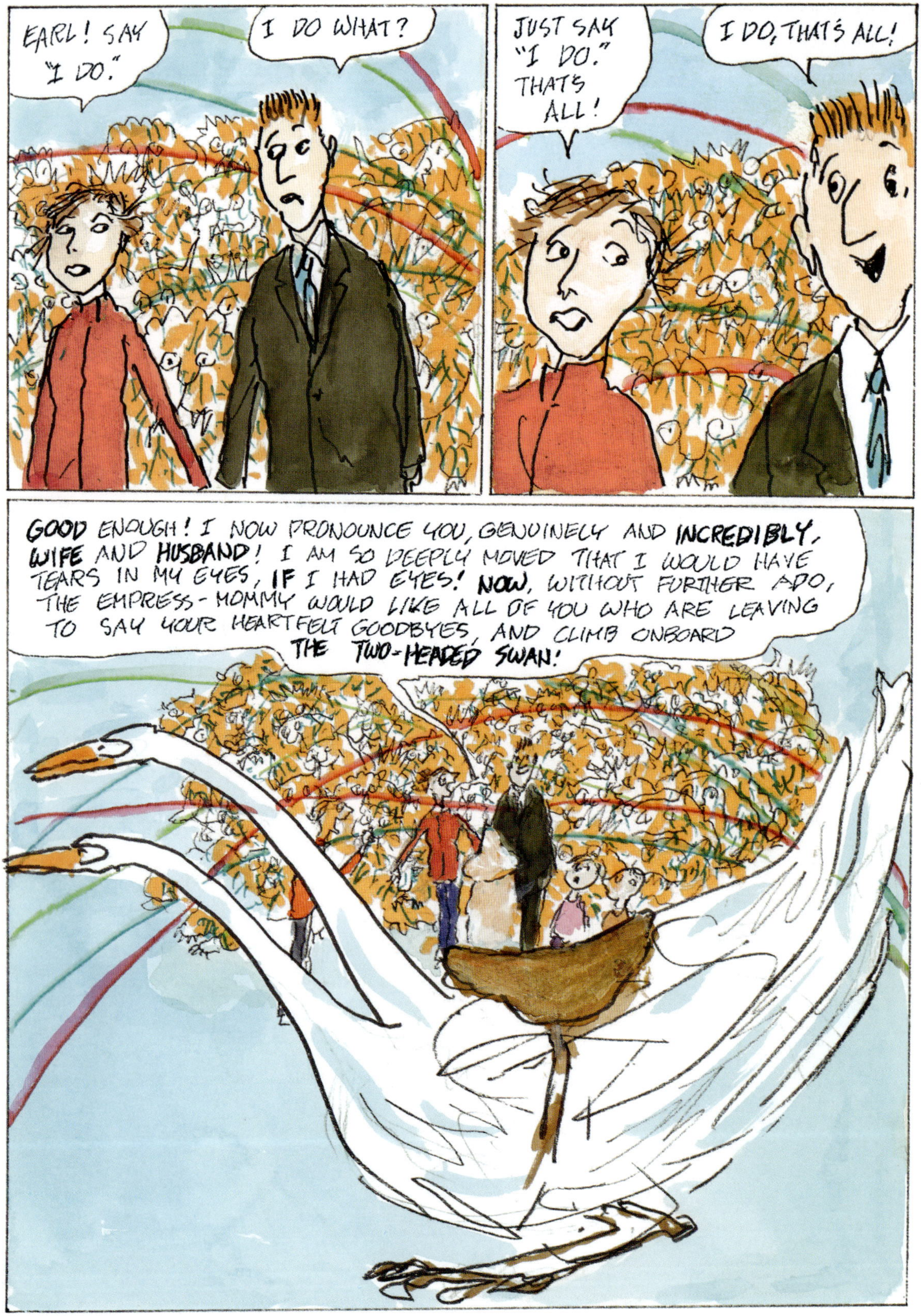
EARL! SAY "I DO."
I DO WHAT?
JUST SAY "I DO." THAT'S ALL!
I DO, THAT'S ALL!
GOOD ENOUGH! I NOW PRONOUNCE YOU, GENUINELY AND INCREDIBLY, WIFE AND HUSBAND! I AM SO DEEPLY MOVED THAT I WOULD HAVE TEARS IN MY EYES, IF I HAD EYES! NOW, WITHOUT FURTHER ADO, THE EMPRESS-MOMMY WOULD LIKE ALL OF YOU WHO ARE LEAVING TO SAY YOUR HEARTFELT GOODBYES, AND CLIMB ONBOARD THE TWO-HEADED SWAN!

AMAZING GRAPES, HOW SWEET THE TASTE,
ONE BITE, HOW CAN IT BE?
I MUNCH, I CRUNCH, AMAZING GRAPES,
OH, WHAT THEY DO FOR ME.

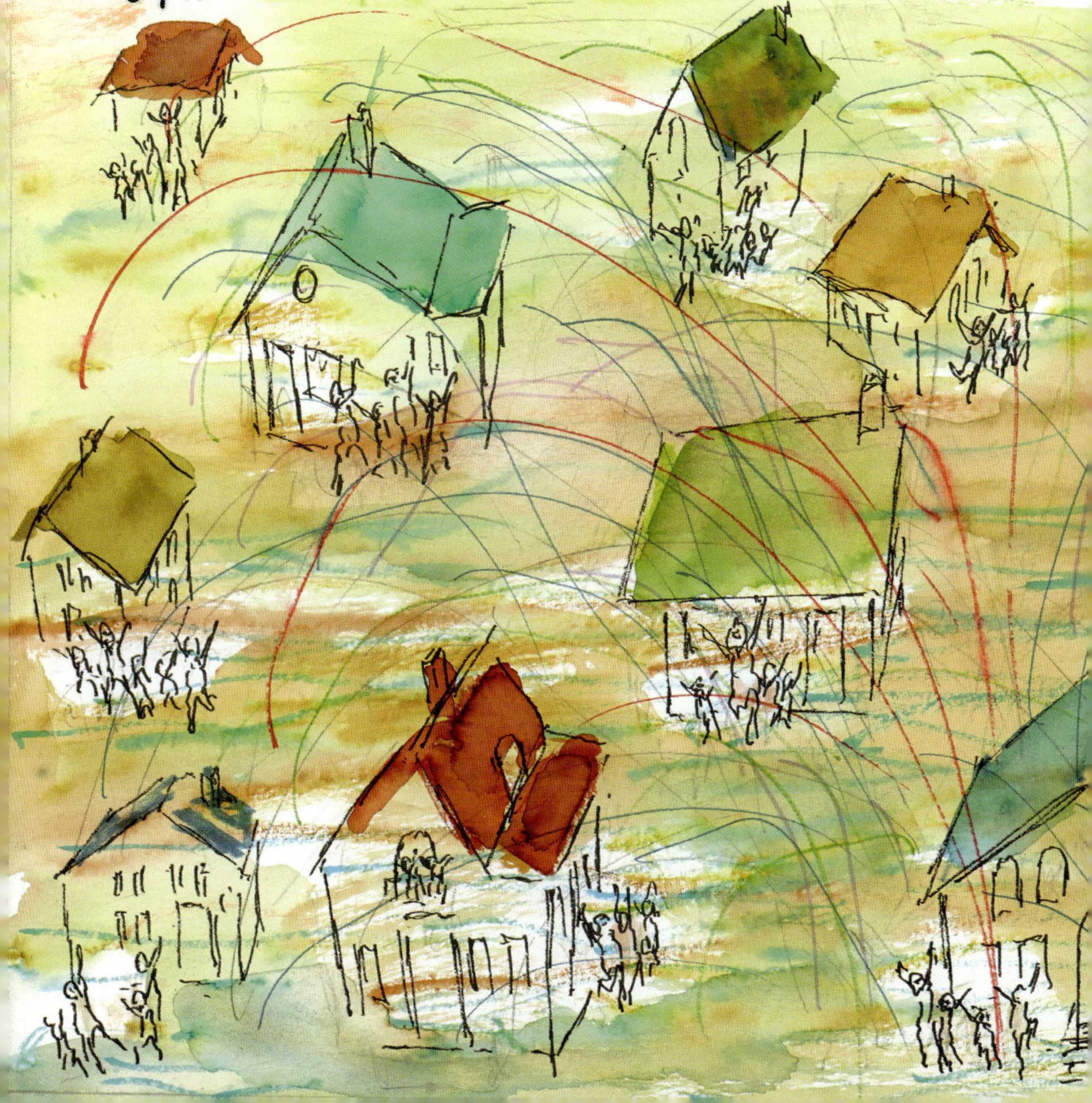

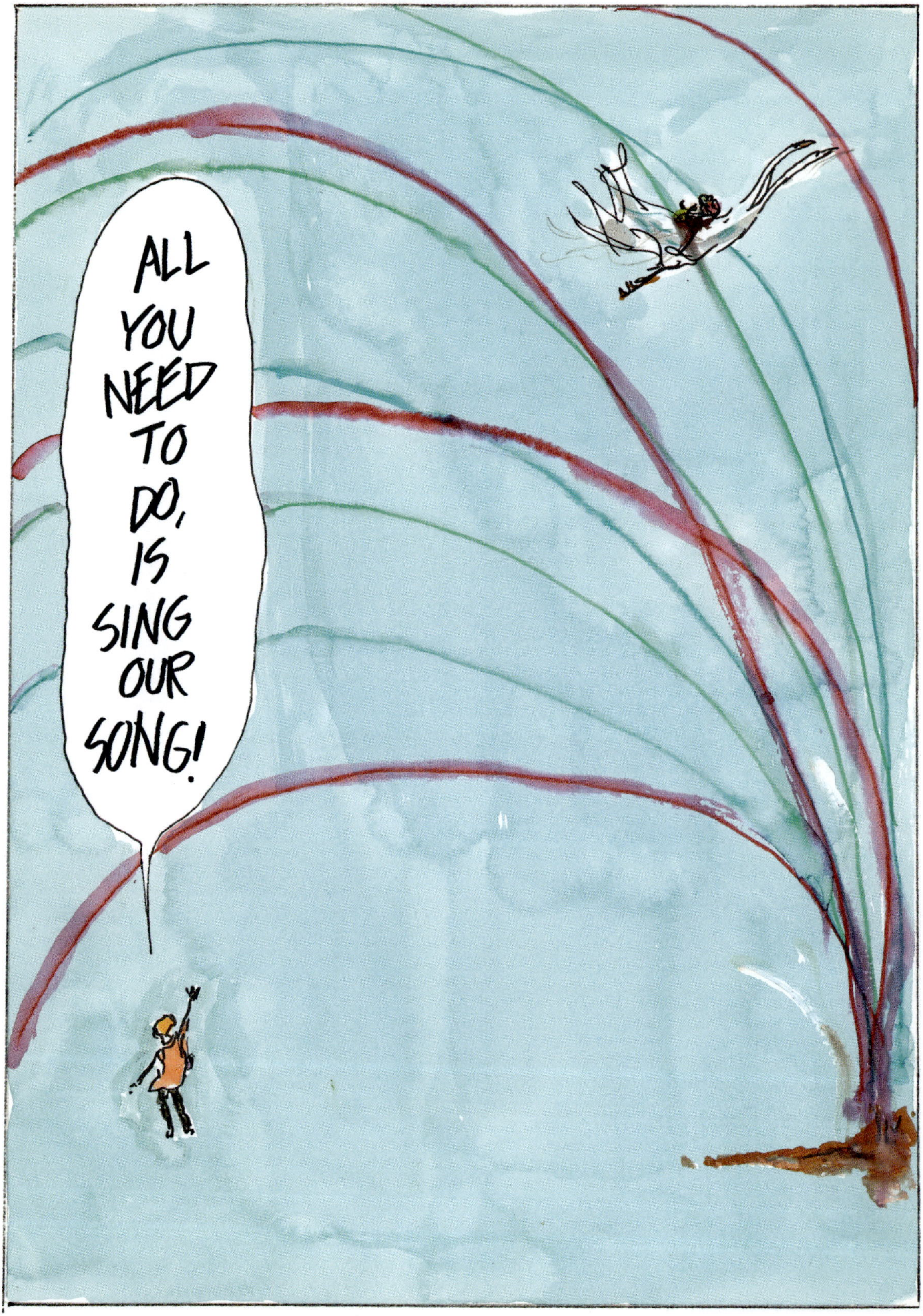
ALL YOU NEED TO DO, IS SING OUR SONG!

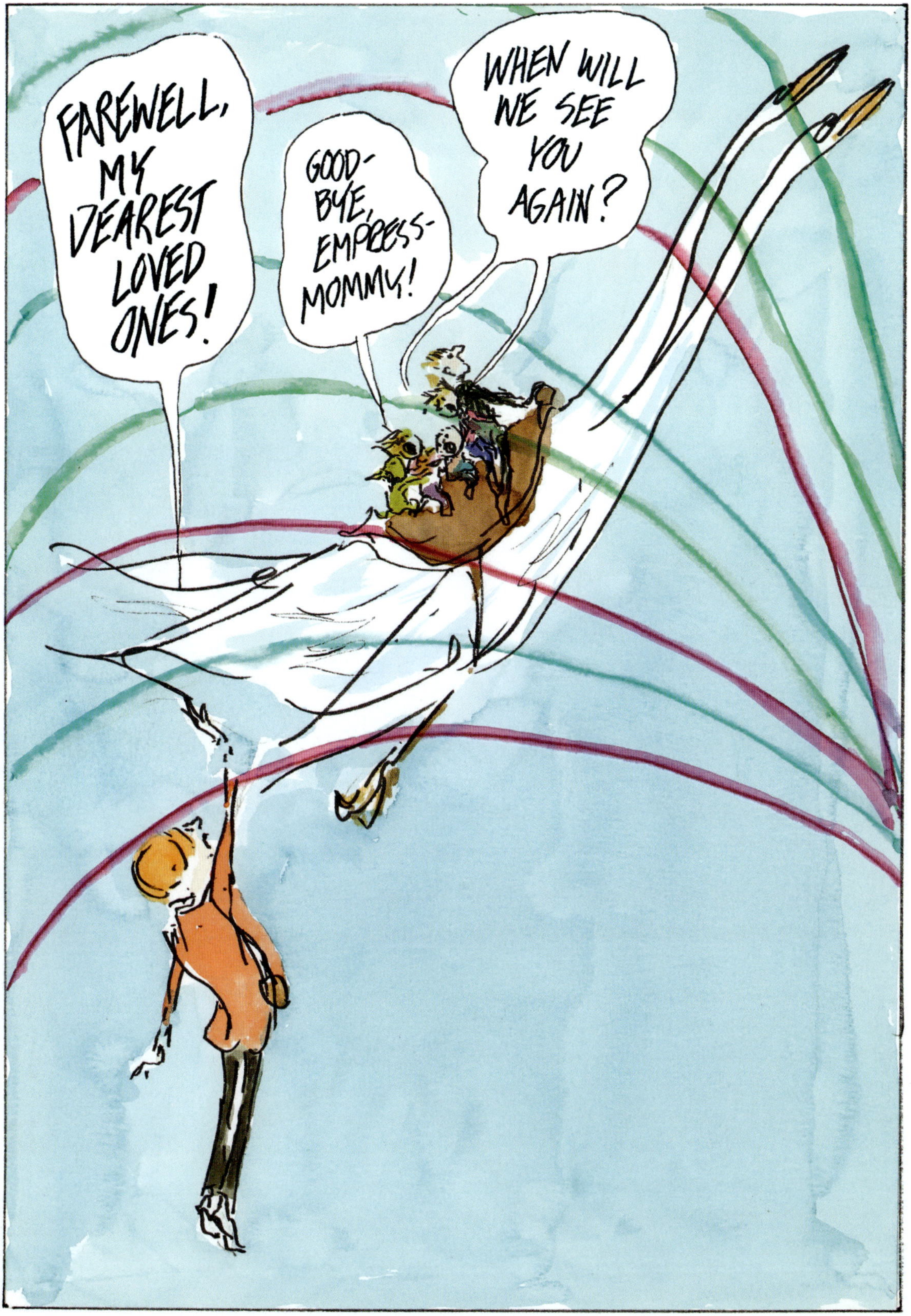
FAREWELL, MY DEAREST LOVED ONES!
GOOD-BYE, EMPRESS-MOMMY!
WHEN WILL WE SEE YOU AGAIN?

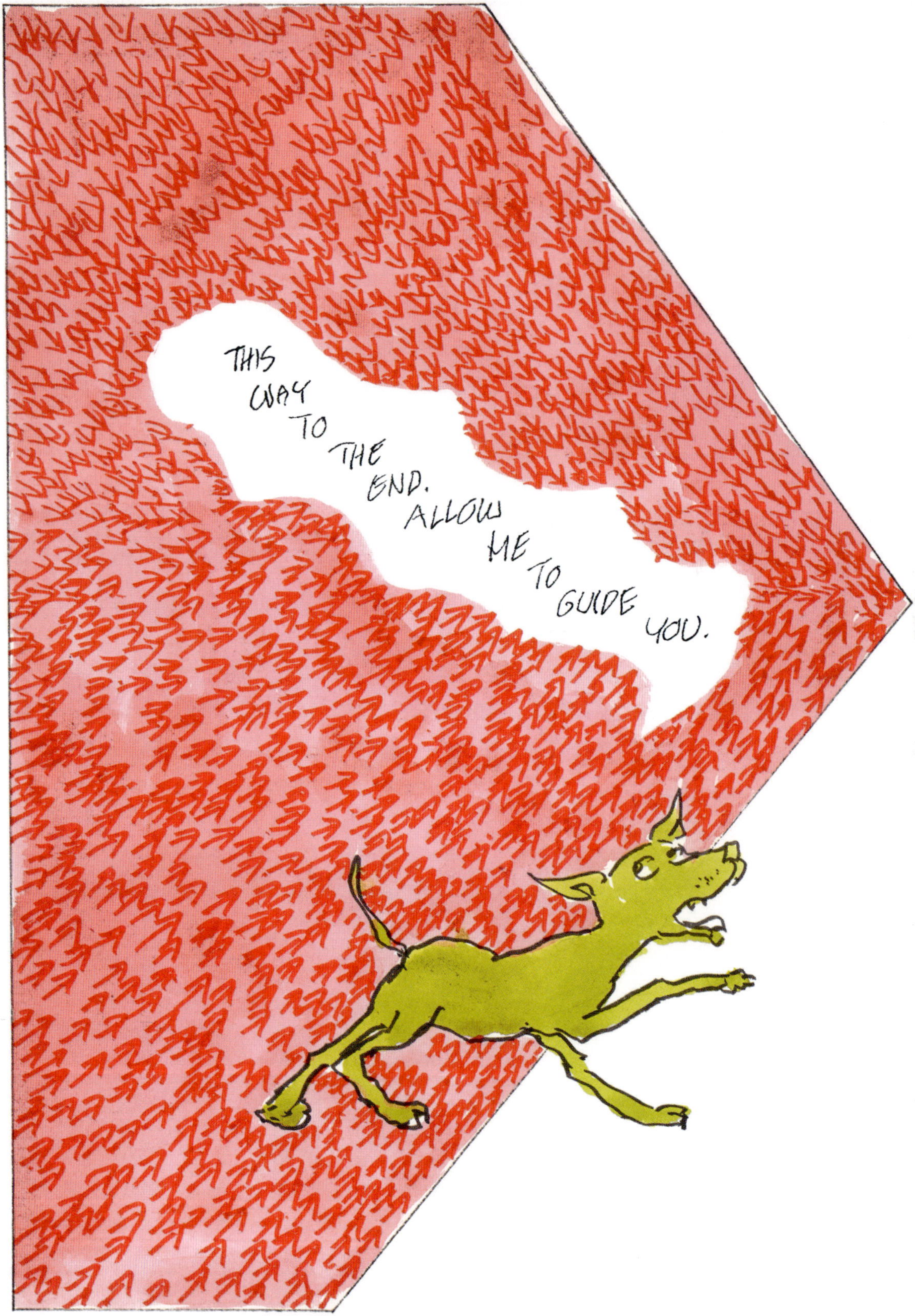
THIS WAY TO THE END. ALLOW ME TO GUIDE YOU.

YES, I WAS LOST, SAD AND ALONE,
ADRIFT ON A DISTANT SEA.
I CRIED, I SIGHED, ALONE I'D MOAN,
'TWAS GRAPES THAT SET ME FREE.

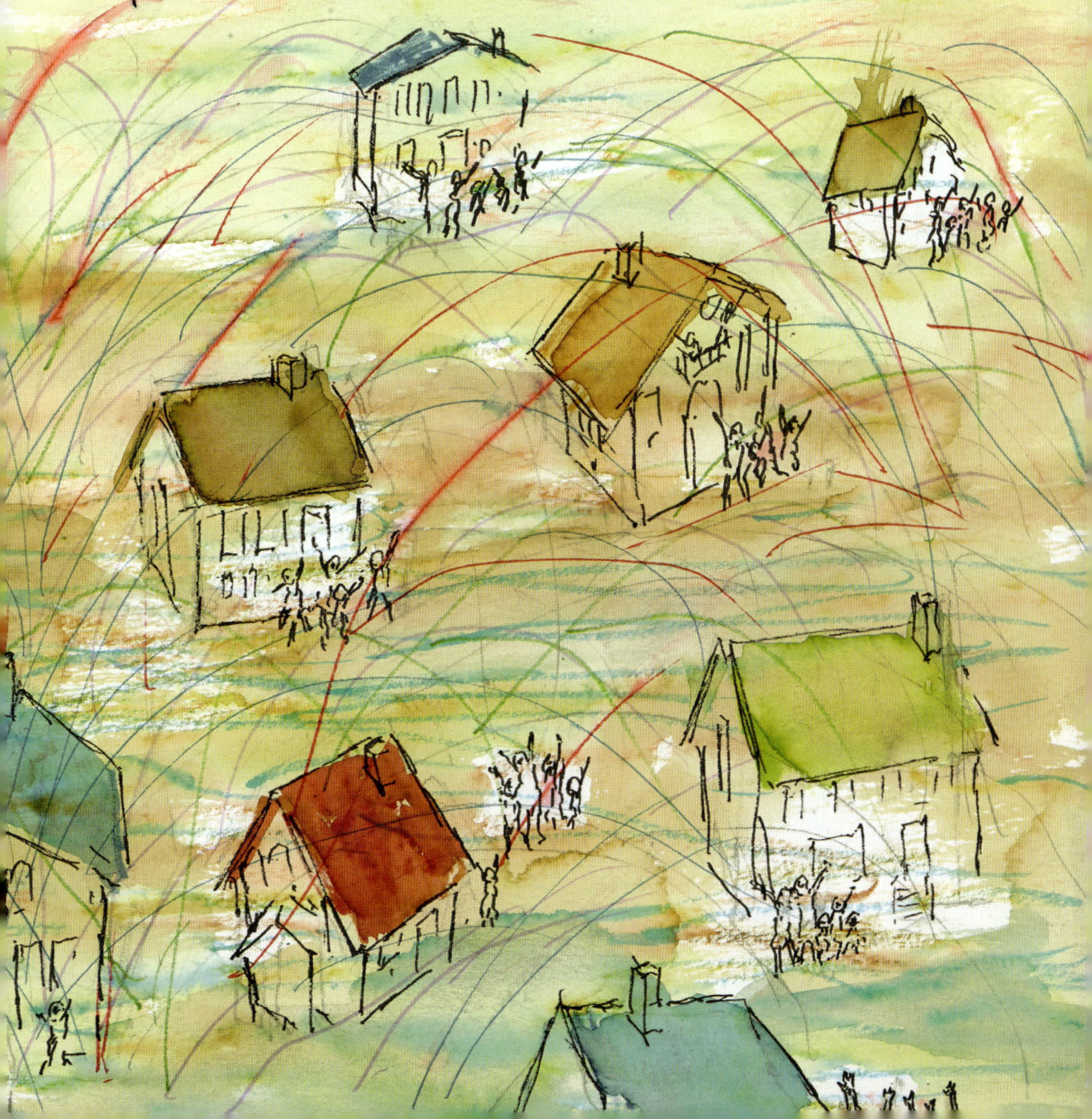

And also to MILT GROSS, one of our greatest cartoonists, who in 1930 published "He Done Her Wrong," a silent movie on paper, and possibly the first graphic novel — every bit as brilliant today as it was when I was a "Nize Baby." (Another Gross book)

Text and pictures copyright © 2024 by Jules Feiffer

Library of Congress control number: 2023944813

HarperCollins Publishers, New York, NY 10007

Printed and bound by Papercraft in Malaysia

Designed by Steve Scott

First edition, 2024

24 25 26 27 28 COS 6 5 4 3 2 1